THE
INFERNAL DEVICE
& OTHERS

Also by
Michael Kurland

The Professor Moriarty novels
The Infernal Device
Death by Gaslight
The Great Game

The Alexander Brass novels
Too Soon Dead
The Girls in the High–Heeled Shoes

THE
INFERNAL DEVICE
& OTHERS

A PROFESSOR MORIARTY OMNIBUS

Michael Kurland

ST. MARTIN'S MINOTAUR ❦ NEW YORK

www.minotaurbooks.com

ISBN 0-312-25273-0

First Edition: August 2001

10 9 8 7 6 5 4 3 2 1

CONTENTS

A BRIEF INTRODUCTION

The two books in this volume, The Infernal Device *and* Death by Gaslight, *are set in, let us call it, the "world" of Sherlock Holmes. The third book in the series,* The Great Game, *is due out in hardcover from St. Martin's Press momentarily. A fourth book, tentatively titled* The Empress of India, *should follow in the coming year.*

These books have Professor James Moriarty as a protagonist and Sherlock Holmes himself as a major character. They are set in the world Conan Doyle established for his brilliant detective, which centers on the London at the end of the nineteenth century; a world of hansom cabs and gas lamps, coal scuttles and gasogenes, clever disguises, secret societies, and a pea-soup fog that surrounds, envelops, and turns every passing footstep into a mystery and the sound of each passing four-wheeler into a romance. Conan Doyle's creation remains with all of us, as Vincent Starrett has said, "in a romantic chamber of the heart, a nostalgic corner of the mind, where it is always 1895."

And this is a fine place to be, and I am proud to set my novels there, and delighted that these first two books were as well received as they were by those who love this fantasy world as I do.

But although my stories are set in that world, and I try very hard to be faithful to its spirit, these are my stories and my agent is not Sir Arthur Conan Doyle. My books are neither parodies nor pastiches of the stories of Dr. Watson. I would not dream of trying to pastiche the Master; it would be a game I could not win. There would be shame in writing stories either better or worse than the Canon.

Besides, my point of view is different from that of Conan Doyle, my interests, and the interests of my audience, are other than those of Doyle or his readers, and during the eighty-five years that have passed since the last story of the Canon was penned, the world of Sherlock Holmes has changed from the world of Sir Arthur's youth, in the living memory of most of his readers, to a world of myth, of a better time when evil was nasty and bad, and good was pure and wonderful, and the two were never confused. And as the century passed the Canon has taken its place alongside the King James Bible, the plays of Shakespeare, the works of Dickens, as being part of the common heritage of all English-speaking people.

So, please, these books are not Apocrypha; they are, I insist, neither pastiche nor parody. They are historical novels based on new research.

Watson is Boswell, Holmes was lost without his Boswell—and I am, perhaps, Dumas, or Frazer, or Plutarch; at any rate a later source.

I hope you enjoy the books.

MICHAEL KURLAND
FEBRUARY 2001

A FEW WORDS OF ACKNOWLEDGMENT

I would like to thank Bernard Geis and Judy Shafran, who had faith in the idea, and Keith Kahla, who has shown infinite patience and support. And, of course, Sir Arthur Conan Doyle, the literary giant on whose shoulders I stand.

THE
INFERNAL DEVICE

PROLOGUE

He who has one enemy will meet him everywhere.

—ALI IBN-ABU-TALIB

The urchin proceeded cautiously through the thick London fog, with only an occasional half-skip betraying the solemnity with which he regarded this mission and, indeed, life itself. Occasionally he paused to peer at the brass numbers on a brick gatepost or puzzle over a street sign. He could have raced blindfolded through the streets near his home, but this was a long way from Whitechapel.

Stopping at a brick house fronted by a high wrought-iron fence, he carefully compared its address with that on the envelope he clutched in his grimy hand. Then he mounted the steps and attacked the door with his fist.

The door opened, and one of the largest men the lad had ever seen stared stolidly down at him. "There is a bell," the man said.

"Werry sorry," the lad said. " 'As I the 'onor of knocking up sixty-four Russell Square?"

"You have. It is."

"Is you Professor James Moriarty?"

"I am Mr. Maws, the professor's butler."

"Gawn!" the boy said. "Butlers ain't called 'Mr.' I knows that much."

"I am," Mr. Maws said.

The lad considered this for a moment as though wrestling with a difficult equation. Then he backed up a step and announced, "I 'as a envelope for Professor James Moriarty what I is supposed to 'and 'im personal."

"I'll take it," Mr. Maws said.

The lad backed up, ready to run. "I is supposed to 'and this 'ere envelope to Professor James Moriarty 'imself, and not to nobody else."

Mr. Maws squatted down to approximate the boy's height. "But I am the professor's butler," he said. "You know about butlers. I stand in the position of *loco habilitus* to Professor Moriarty under the common law. Giving me the envelope is the same as giving it to Professor Moriarty himself. That's my job, you see."

"Gor!" the urchin said, unconvinced.

"Here," Mr. Maws said, reaching into his waistcoat pocket and pulling out a shilling. He held it between his thumb and forefinger. "It's my job to pay for them, too."

"Coo-eee!" the lad said. "A bob!" He stared at the coin in fascination for a moment, then quickly exchanged it for the envelope and ran off down the street.

Mr. Maws took the envelope inside and carefully closed and bolted the door before further examining it. It was of stiff yellow paper. Written across the front, in what Mr. Maws took for a foreign hand, was *Professor Moriarty—Into His Hands* over *64 Russell Sqr.* On the back, across the flap, was *Personal and most urgent.* It was sealed with a blob of yellow wax bearing no imprint. Mr. Maws sniffed it, squeezed it, and held it before a strong gaslight before putting it on a salver and bringing it into the study.

"Letter," he said.

"I thought the first post had come," Professor Moriarty said, without looking up from the worktable where he was slowly heating a flask of dark-colored liquid over a spirit lamp.

"A young ragamuffin delivered this by hand a few moments ago," Mr. Maws explained. "He ran off before I could inquire where he had obtained it. Incidentally, sir, the gentleman with the prominent nose is still lurking across the way in Montague Place."

"Ah!" Moriarty said. "So we still interest Mr. Sherlock Holmes with our little comings and goings, do we? Good, good." He took the flask off the fire and set it aside. "Just raise the blinds, will you. Mr. Maws? Thank you." He pinched a pair of pince-nez glasses onto his nose and examined the envelope. "Of European manufacture, I should say. Eastern European, most likely. Meaningless of itself—so much is being imported these days. But the handwriting has a definite foreign flavor. Look at that 'F.' Best see what's inside, I suppose."

Moriarty slit the envelope open along the top with a penknife and removed the stiff sheet of paper folded within. The message was block-printed in the same hand as the envelope:

MUST AT ONCE MEET WITH YOU REGARDING TREPOFF MATTER. YOUR AID
URGENTLY SOLICITED. WILL CALL THIS EVENING. TAKE ALL CARE.

V.

"Curious," Moriarty said. "The writer assumes that I know what he's talking about. Anything about a Trepoff in the popular press, Mr. Maws?"

Mr. Maws, an avid reader of the sensational dailies, shook his head. "No, sir," he declared. "It *is* a puzzler, sir."

"It does present a few interesting features," Moriarty admitted. "Hand me down my extra-ordinary file for the letter 'T,' will you?"

Mr. Maws went to the shelf and removed the appropriate volume from the set of clipping-books in which Professor Moriarty kept note of those items and events that, although seemingly commonplace, his keen intellect had perceived were actually out of the ordinary. He handed the thick book to the professor.

"Hm," Moriarty said. "It looks as though 'T' were ready for a subdivision. Let me see." He flipped through the volume. "Tessla. Theodora the ant-woman. The Thanatopsis Club. Tropical poisons. Trantor. The Truthseekers Society. Nothing under Trepoff. As I thought." He put the volume down. "Well, there is nothing to be gained in speculation when we shall soon have the facts."

The doorbell rang, and Mr. Maws went to answer it, while Moriarty took the letter over to his worktable and contemplated the shelf of stoppered reagents.

"A package, sir," Mr. Maws said, returning to the room with a small, carefully wrapped box. "Likely from the same person."

Moriarty glanced at the carefully printed address. "Similar," he said, "but not the same. Now why—of course!" He turned to his butler. "Who delivered this?"

"A small, very fair-looking gentleman, sir."

"What did he do? That is, did he just hand it to you?"

"He inquired if this was the right residence, sir. And then he unwrapped a carrying-string and handed me the package. Oh, yes; he did ask me particular if it would be delivered to you right away."

"I'm sure he did," Moriarty exclaimed. Grabbing the package from Mr. Maw's hands, he pitched it through the closed front window, knocking out several panes of glass.

The box exploded before it hit the ground, taking out the rest of the window and sending glass shards and fragments of wood and brick flying back into the room.

Moriarty's hand went numb. He looked down to discover that a sliver of glass had ripped through the sleeve of his smoking jacket and sliced into his upper forearm. Bright red blood pulsed through the wound, soaking the sleeve and dripping onto the hardwood floor.

"Interesting," Moriarty said, pulling the handkerchief from his breast pocket to staunch the flow of blood. "Very interesting!"

ONE
STAMBOUL

What is Fate that we should seek it?
—HAFIZ

Constantinople, the city of a hundred races and a thousand vices, was split in half by that thumb of the Bosporus known throughout recorded history as the Golden Horn. On one side, Stamboul, outpost of Asia; on the other Galata and Pera, terminus of Europe. A floating bridge connected Galata and Stamboul. The Galata side was European and nineteenth century. The men wore top hats and gaiters, and the ladies favored French bonnets and French perfumes; the hotels had gaslight and indoor plumbing.

Stamboul was Roman and Byzantine and Turk and Arab; ancient and timeless. It smelled of Levant. The men wore turbans and fezzes and the women were veiled. Caravan drivers from Baghdad spread their goods in the Covered Bazaar, and one ate only with one's right hand.

An early morning fog covered the Golden Horn, with here and there the mast of a caique poking through, and the great dome of St. Sofia looming out on the Stamboul side. From the breakfast veranda of the Hotel Ibrahim in Pera, Benjamin Barnett peered out over the mist boiling below and tried to pick out landmarks that matched the sketches in his guidebook. Finally, closing the book in disgust and putting it back in his pocket, he returned to his shirred eggs. "Nothing looks right," he complained to his table companion. "I mean, it's beautiful, but I can't line it up with the book. And I sure can't read the street signs. I guess I'd better hire a guide."

"If you are determined to go," Lieutenant Sefton said, folding his two-day-old *Times* carefully and putting it to the right of his plate, "I suppose I'd better come along. Show you the ropes and all that. Keep you from harm, if you see what I mean."

7

"Thanks a lot for the offer," Barnett said, attacking the last bit of egg on his plate, "but I think I can take care of myself."

"No doubt," Lieutenant Sefton said, eyeing the stocky, self-composed young American. "You Yanks seem to make a fetish of taking care of yourselves. Comes from living on the edge of the frontier, I shouldn't wonder. Outlaws and Red Indians and all that."

"Um," Barnett replied, trying to decide if he was having his leg pulled. He had first met Sefton four days before when he boarded the Simplon Express in Paris, and during the entire three-day trip the tall, angular officer of Her Most Britannic Majesty's Navy had not displayed anything resembling a sense of humor. They had spent a good part of the journey playing bid whist with two German engineers. Sefton was a cool, calculating player who never overbid his hand, which was as good a basis for a friendship as any Barnett could think of, and better than most.

Barnett's employers, the *New York World*, had sent a coded telegram to him in Paris. Royce's Complete Telegraphers' Phrase Code made for stilted communications, but it saved money. And a twopenny newspaper saved all the money it could.

> Gybut Constantinople uhwoz nonke ukhox tydyc fowic adgud world

Barnett had dug out his leather-bound Royce and written the message out in pencil in his notebook:

> *Go to Constantinople. Telegraph report on Ottoman testing new submersible. Expenses paid. Accreditation waiting. International Editor, the* New York World.

The *New York World* was very proud of its coverage of military and naval news. Many of its readers followed the power politics of Europe, as unfolded in its pages, as eagerly as others followed the sports pages.

During these last decades of the nineteenth century Constantinople was a focus of European intrigue. Four wars had been fought in twenty years for pieces of the crumbling Ottoman Empire, and no one dared guess when the next one would start, or which of the great powers would be involved. England, France, Russia, Austria, and

Prussia had all lost troops in sight of the clear blue waters of the Sea of Marmara.

Sultan Abd-ul Hamid, the second of that name, and the twenty-ninth Osmanli sultan to rule from the Seraglio in Stamboul since Mehemmed el Fatih—the Conqueror—took Byzantium in 1453, would not give up his European possessions easily. He armed his Mamelukes with Maxim machine-pistols, and his Janizaries with Nordenfeldt field pieces. He had Portsmouth Naval Yards build him a battleship, had Krupp Germania Aktiongesellschaft fabricate three gunboats, and now had had the Garrett-Harris submersible boat shipped over from Hartford, Connecticut, for sea trials.

And—to encourage his friends and discourage his enemies—he invited the world to watch.

And the *World* wanted Barnett to watch. So he'd packed two suitcases, sent a note of apology to the young lady of the *Folies* who was to have dined with him, notified his *concierge* to watch his *logement* while he was gone, and made it to the Gare de l'Est with forty seconds to spare.

Now, four days later, Barnett and Lieutenant Sefton were break-fasting together on the glassed-in veranda of the Hotel Ibrahim. The Simplon Express had arrived in Constantinople the afternoon before, and Barnett had gone right to the American Embassy in Pera. A native clerk informed him that the ambassador was out, the assistant ambassador was out, and the secretary was out. The clerk was the only one there, and he was leaving shortly. And he had never heard of either Benjamin Barnett or the *New York World*.

Barnett waved his telegram at the clerk. "I'm supposed to have papers to watch the submersible trials. It's all arranged."

The clerk examined the telegram and then smiled politely. He had a gold incisor. "English?" he asked, making it sound like a disease.

"It's in the Royce Telegraphers' Code," Barnett explained. "Look, I've got a translation here in this notebook."

"Return Monday, *effendim*," the clerk said, straightening his tie and adjusting his fez. "The ambassador will be here then. I must close the office."

"But the sea trials start Saturday!"

The clerk shrugged and closed the window.

Barnett now had no choice but to go to the Sublime Porte in Stamboul, the seat of the Osmanli government, where the necessary permissions could be obtained. Such was Lieutenant Sefton's advice, at any rate, and Barnett had no one else to ask.

Sefton pushed back his chair and stood up. "Take my word for it, Barnett," he said in his clipped, inflectionless voice. "If I don't come along with you, you're fated to spend the rest of the week warming one of the marble benches in the courtyard." He took his gold-tipped walking stick and tucked it under his arm. "I offer you the use of my years of acquaintanceship with the convolutions of Osmanli bureaucracy. I must go to the Sublime Porte at any rate, to see about my own accreditation."

Barnett nodded his acquiescence. "I'm convinced," he said. "I just didn't want to put you to any trouble, but as you're going at any rate, I'd be glad of your assistance." Was it his imagination, or did Lieutenant Sefton seem overly anxious to accompany him?

They left the hotel together and walked down the hill to Galata and the floating bridge. The fog was almost burned off now, and the clear March air smelled of some unidentifiable spice. Lieutenant Sefton pointed out the sights as they walked and told anecdotes of the timeless city. "I've been away for two years," he said, "but nothing changes. Across the bridge in Stamboul twenty years or two hundred could pass, and still nothing would change."

"Were you here long?" Barnett asked.

"Long enough," Sefton said. "I was junior naval attaché to our embassy. Then I was naval attaché. Finally, they decided that I'd gone native and shipped me home." He laughed, but the memory was clearly a bitter one.

"And now you're back."

"Yes."

"Excuse me if I ask too many questions," Barnett said. "It's a habit that you get into if you're a journalist."

"Quite all right," Sefton said. "Actually, I'm here on the same business you are: the sea trials of the Garrett-Harris submersible. I seem to have become the Royal Navy's submarine expert."

"Ah!"

Sefton bounced his walking stick against the sidewalk. "The Royal Navy, you understand, has no interest in submarines."

"No interest?" Barnett asked.

Lieutenant Sefton nodded. He evidently got a great deal of perverse pleasure from telling this story. "The Holland submersible was tested in New Haven, Connecticut, last year, and I observed. My report was favorable. I strongly suggested purchasing one and beginning our own testing program for the craft.

"The report went all the way up to the First Lord of the Admiralty. He scribbled one line across the cover and sent it back, and that was the end of that."

"One line?"

"Yes. It was: 'Of what use is a boat which sinks?' "

The street they were following ended in a steep flight of stairs, below which the blue waters of the Golden Horn danced and shimmered in the late morning sun. The sails and masts of a myriad of boats of all shapes and sizes bobbed and nodded in front of them. There were galleys and galleons, caiques and scows, ships of every age and race of Man. Directly ahead of them, like a great humpback watersnake, was the floating bridge. Over a quarter mile long, it had a line of shops and coffeehouses along one side of a roadway that was wide enough for two four-wheelers to pass abreast. The bridge floated on pontoons, and a draw section in the middle could be raised to let the water traffic through.

Off in the distance two great buildings rose out of the haze on the Stamboul side. The dome of the Mosque of the Sultana Validé shimmered directly in front of them, and off to their left, gleaming white across the water, the *suleimanieh*, the gigantic and ancient mosque of Soliman, straddled a tall hill and frowned out over both the Golden Horn and the Sea of Marmara.

They descended the stairs and each paid his penny to the white-robed toll collector. The bridge was as crowded, Barnett thought, as the Bowery on a Saturday afternoon. And such people as were never seen on the streets of New York: Persians in flaring red robes and tall, conical hats; Circassians with curled blond beards, wearing long, black caftans and bearskin caps. . . . Four black Turks trotted by with an ebony and ivory sedan chair on their shoulders. A veiled harem girl stared soulfully through the gauze curtains at Barnett, and then giggled as the chair passed.

"I'm getting a peculiar feeling as we cross this bridge," Barnett told Sefton. "It's hard to explain, but it's as though we were going, step by step, backward in time."

"The nineteenth century has yet to reach Stamboul," Sefton agreed, "for all that it's almost over. For us, it's 1885. For them"—he pointed with his stick at three women in front of them wrapped in layer after layer of concealing linen—"who is to say what year—

what age—it is. As they reckon time, it is the year 1302 of the Hegira. These young ladies are *halaiks*—slave girls—belonging to the harem of some emir, and the two tall Negro gentlemen escorting them are eunuchs from his court."

They reached the Stamboul side of the bridge, and Barnett stepped thoughtfully into an alien world. "Well!" he said, *"there's* an article for my paper. We're still a mite sensitive on the subject of slavery in the United States, having eliminated it from our own shores a bare twenty years ago. And you might say we did it the hard way, too. Is slavery an accepted institution here?"

Lieutenant Sefton nodded, the trace of a hard smile on his face. "Slavery, bigamy, harems, eunuchs, exotics, exquisites—and a hundred things we've never heard of, and another hundred for which English has no words."

"Goddamn!" Barnett said. "You'll have to tell me all about it. This might make the Sunday Supplement! Course, I'm not exactly sure how to explain to our readers what a eunuch is, but I'll give it a stab and let the rewrite desk worry about it."

The Sublime Porte, a connected maze of palaces and gardens surrounded by a high wall, contained the palace of the sultan's chief minister, the grand vizier, along with the ministries of foreign affairs and war. Lieutenant Sefton led the way into the palace and took Barnett through a series of offices and waiting rooms. In each he spoke to someone, a few lire notes changed hands, and they were forwarded to the next. Although the official language of the Ottoman government was French, Sefton spoke in Turkish, and Barnett merely stood by and tried to look intelligent.

Finally, they were taken to a richly appointed room on an inner courtyard of the palace. "We have arrived," Sefton said, sinking into a gold-brocade overstuffed armchair. "The Captain Pasha himself is going to see us."

"The Captain Pasha?"

"The Osmanli equivalent of the First Lord of the Admiralty," Sefton explained, darting his eyes around the room like some great hawk.

"Was it really necessary to bribe all those people to get here?" Barnett asked.

Lieutenant Sefton focused his gaze on Barnett and studied him as he would a whist hand. "You *are* serious," he decided. "My dear man, those weren't bribes. You're in the Levant. Simple gratuities, incentives. Thus we arrived in this office in slightly over an hour instead of two weeks. This despite the fact that the Captain Pasha actually wants to see us."

"I wasn't making a moral judgment," Barnett assured him. "This sort of thing exists in the States. It's just the openness of it here that surprises me. A Tammany politico would take you in the back room with the lights turned down low. And he'd have four relatives and a judge all ready to swear that he was somewhere else at the time."

"Our Western ways are slow to take hold here," Lieutenant Sefton said, "no matter how hard we try to show them the superiority of our methods."

A very short, very wide man waddled through a door at the far end of the room. He wore a fur-trimmed green robe, under which yellow boots peeked out as he walked. His face was creased in a permanent smile. "Ah, my dear, dear Captain Sefton," he said, with a pronounced British accent, crossing the room with his arms outstretched. "My heart leaps with pleasure that you have been able to return to Constantinople."

"Your Excellency," said Sefton, jumping to his feet and pulling Barnett with him. "It is good to see you again. I am pleased that my government has once more sent me here to watch and learn from the master."

The Captain Pasha waved a pudgy hand of disclaimer at the praise and turned to Barnett. "And you must be the American correspondent, Mr. Benjamin Barnett." He took Barnett's hand and pumped it with the enthusiasm of one who is unaccustomed to the ritual of handshaking and still finds it faintly amusing. "We are honored at your presence here, sir. A representative of the press of your great democracy is always welcome."

"The honor is mine, Your Excellency," Barnett said, keeping to the spirit of the exchange. "It gives me an occasion to acquaint myself with your remarkable city."

"Ah, yes," the Captain Pasha said. "Constantinople, the jewel of cities. You are lucky to have Captain Sefton as your guide. He knows the city as few Europeans do."

"Lieutenant," Lieutenant Sefton said pointedly.

The Captain Pasha turned around, his hands in the air, his fingers waggling in horror. "No!" he said. "It cannot be! A man of your talent and intelligence still only a lieutenant? I will not permit it! Come, I offer you an immediate commission in the naval service of Sultan Abd-ul Hamid. You shall come in as a full commander.

Captain next year. In five years you shall be *oula*, in ten, *bala*. Guaranteed. My word."

Sefton gave a polite half-bow. "Every man knows the worth of your word, Excellency. I am disconsolate that I cannot accept your offer."

"And why not?" asked the Captain Pasha. He flipped his hand at the outside world. "They do not appreciate you. I do. You will have a career of honor and reward in a navy that values your ability. And remember that Sultan Abd-ul Hamid is an ally of your Queen Victoria. There can be no dishonor in fighting in the cause of an ally. I give you my most solemn word," he said seriously, "that if we ever declare war upon Great Britain I shall release you from your service."

"I shall consider your words, Excellency," Lieutenant Sefton said, "and I thank you for them. Even though I am afraid that it can never be."

"Never be?" the Captain Pasha chuckled. "You should not use such terms. Is it not written that no man's eye can pierce the veil that hides the face of tomorrow?" He turned to Barnett. "My secretary will bring you the documents you need. I shall arrange for you both to have places on board His Supreme Highness's steam yacht *Osmanieh*, from which to observe the trials. May Allah, in His Infinite wisdom, assure that we meet again soon."

The Captain Pasha left as abruptly as he had entered. A moment later his secretary came in and handed them each a thick gray envelope sealed in red wax bearing the device of the star and crescent. Then a tiny page boy in an ornate red-and-gold uniform escorted them through the maze of hallways to the outside world.

Lieutenant Sefton glanced up at the sun, then checked its position against his pocket watch. "It is still early," he said, "although we do seem to have missed our lunch hour. Would you like to see the Covered Bazaar? It's quite fascinating, really. We can have a bite to eat on the way, if you like." He headed off down a cobblestone street, tapping a marching beat on the stones with the ferrule of his stick.

"Was the Captain Pasha serious?" Barnett asked, falling into step beside him.

"About what?"

"Taking you on as a captain in the Turkish navy?"

"Oh, yes," Sefton assured him. "It's quite commonly done, actually. One way for a second-rate service to upgrade their officer corps. The Royal Navy always has more officers than it needs. Some chaps have done quite well in the service of foreign governments."

"Are you going to take him up on it?"

"My dear man," Sefton said, raising one eyebrow quizzically. "After all, I haven't gone quite *that* native."

Lieutenant Sefton led the way through a complex of narrow, twisting streets and alleyways. Barnett followed, looking this way and that at the exotically unfamiliar city he was passing through. He concentrated on observing the details of costume and architecture and taking an occasional note in the small black notebook he always kept in the inner pocket of his jacket. He would be expected to file several reports on "local color" so the readers of the *New York World* could vicariously experience the thrills of wandering through old Stamboul. The reports would take over a month to reach New York by ship's mail, but the *World* would never pay cable rates for background or filler material.

Barnett asked Lieutenant Sefton to stop for a moment at a small square with a cracked, dry water fountain in the middle. "I want to get the feel of this," he said, going over to inspect the inscription, which told, in a language he could not read, about a battle that had long since been forgotten.

"All very scenic, no doubt," Lieutenant Sefton said, leaning on his stick.

The mellifluous chanting of the *Mu'adhdhin* sounded from the towering minarets all over Stamboul, calling the Faithful to afternoon prayer, and within a few seconds the streets were virtually empty as the locals went inside to perform the prescribed ritual.

Then, over the chanting, came the sound of many running feet. A tall European turned the corner a block away and headed toward the square at a dead run, coattails flying. A second later a gang of Arabs boiled around the corner behind him, waving a variety of weapons, intent on catching up.

"I say," Lieutenant Sefton said, "an Englishman seems to be in trouble. We'd better come to his aid."

Barnett put his notebook away and took off his jacket. "He might be French," he said.

"Nonsense, man—look at the cut of those trousers!"

Folding his jacket carefully, Barnett put it on the rim of the fountain. Long experience at barroom brawling had taught him that bruises heal, but ripped jackets must be replaced.

Lieutenant Sefton twisted the handle of his stick and slid out an eighteen-inch blade. "The Marquis of Queensberry wouldn't approve," he said, "but those chaps aren't gentlemen."

"I don't suppose you have another of those pigstickers concealed about your person, do you?" Barnett asked, eyeing the approaching mob and the assortment of curved knives they were waving. "If it's to be that sort of a party . . ." He picked up his jacket again and wrapped it around his arm. The custom governing barroom disputes on the Bowery limited the engagement to fisticuffs and an occasional chair or bottle, but—other places, other habits.

"Here," Sefton said, tossing him the body of the stick. "It's rolled steel under the veneer. Feel free to bash away with it."

"Thanks," Barnett said, hefting the thin steel tube. The tall stranger had almost reached them, and the mob was close behind. Holding the truncated stick like a baseball bat, Barnett advanced to the attack.

MORIARTY

He is a genius, a philosopher, an abstract thinker.
—SHERLOCK HOLMES

He was conspicuously tall, and thin to the point of emaciation. He carried himself with the habitual stoop of one who must traverse doorways constructed for a lesser race, and this stoop, taken with his high, domed forehead and penetrating gaze, gave him the look of some great predatory bird. His mind was quick and incisive, and his actions were ruled by logic. His passions—were his alone, and few of his associates were privy to them.

He ran down the Street of the Two Towers, closely pursued by six silent men in dirty brown burnooses. One of them had been following him since he left his hotel, and the six together had attacked him as he left the shop of a dealer in ancient brass instruments a few blocks away. He was deciding among the four most logical means of escape when two men in European dress, waving menacing weapons, raced to his aid. At first he thought they might be trying to cut him off, but they were clearly aiming for his pursuers and not for him. This altered the situation.

In an instant, he had stopped running and turned around to face his attackers, his feet firmly planted and his arms together and extended in the *baritsu* defense posture.

The Arab nearest him leaped, curved blade high in the air, and brought it down in an overhand arc aimed straight at his temple. With a deceptively easy-looking twist of his body he moved aside, grasped his assailant's knife-arm as he passed, and pinned it behind. The Arab made the mistake of trying to twist free, and he screamed with shock and pain as his shoulder joint pulled out of its socket.

Then Barnett and Sefton reached the scene. The lieutenant, using his swordstick like an épée, took two of the Arabs on in classical Italian style, his left hand raised languidly behind him. Barnett, swinging his stick freely in both hands, rushed at the others.

One of the attackers yelled out a few words in a guttural language, and his comrades broke off the fighting and raced away in as close to five different directions as they could manage in the narrow street. Lieutenant Sefton, who had downed one of the men with the first thrust of his blade, raced after another, yelling at him to stop and fight.

"Pah!" the tall man spat, straightening up and glaring after the retreating figures. "Amateurs! I am insulted."

"Excuse me?" Barnett said, trying to catch his breath.

Moriarty dusted himself off. "Thank you for your assistance," he said. "I seem to have lost my hat."

Lieutenant Sefton chased the retreating Arab to the corner before giving up. "Too big a head start," he lamented, returning to the square. He took the body of his swordstick back from Barnett and returned the blade to its scabbard. "Are you all right, sir?"

"Yes," Moriarty said. "Except for a slight rent in the jacket sleeve and the loss of my stick and my hat. I owe you gentlemen a great debt. Your assistance alleviated a troublesome situation."

"Glad to help," Barnett said briefly. He personally thought it might have been a bit more than "troublesome," but he held his tongue. Traditional British understatement, he decided.

"Couldn't allow a fellow Englishman to be molested by cut-throat Arabs without doing something," Lieutenant Sefton said. "My pleasure, I assure you. I am Lieutenant Auric Sefton, Royal Navy. My companion is Mr. Benjamin Barnett, an American."

Moriarty shook hands with both of them. "From the great city of New York, I perceive," he told Barnett. "Although most recently from Paris. And a journalist, if I am not mistaken."

"Why, that's quite right," Barnett said, looking with amazement at the tall man.

"Of course it is. I am Professor James Moriarty. I think we could all use a chance to catch our breath. Come, there's a small coffeeshop a few blocks from here. If you would care to accompany me, it would be my pleasure to offer you a cup of that thick brew which the Turk, in his wisdom, calls coffee."

"Why did those chaps attack you?" Sefton asked.

"I have no idea," Moriarty said. "Let us go to the coffeeshop, where I can sit down. I think I lead too sedentary an existence. My

wind isn't what it should be. I promise I'll answer your questions
there. Oh—one last thing . . ." Moriarty bent over the body of the
downed attacker and gave it a perfunctory examination. "All right,"
he said, straightening up. "It is as I thought. Let us go."

The tables at the coffeeshop were arranged outside on the sidewalk,
under a wide awning. Barnett and Sefton instinctively picked a table
with a bench against the wall, where they could sit facing the street.
Moriarty calmly sat facing them across the postage-stamp-sized table.
"My usual preference is also the seat with the, ah, view," Moriarty
told them, smiling grimly. "But with you two stalwart gentlemen
guarding my rear, I feel confident that there will be no surprises. Is
it to be *shekerli* or *sade*, gentlemen?"

"What's that?" Barnett asked.

"Sweet or bitter," Sefton explained. "The coffee."

"Oh," Barnett said. "Sweet. Very sweet."

The waiter was a short, wide man, sporting a great handlebar
mustache and swathed in a white apron. He approached his European customers and performed an impressive dumb show to indicate
that whatever language they spoke, he didn't. Moriarty spoke to him
in Turkish, interrupting him in mid-gesture, and his face lit up. A
minute later he was back at the table, making the coffee in the cus-
tomary small brass pot over a charcoal burner.

"Your knowledge of the language is excellent," Lieutenant Sefton complimented Moriarty. "I have lived here for some time, and I
don't speak it nearly so well. Have you been in Constantinople
long?"

"On the contrary," said Moriarty. "I have been here for but
three days. I leave tomorrow."

Lieutenant Sefton leaned forward. "And you haven't been here
before?"

"Never."

"Then where did you learn Turkish?"

"I have developed a system for learning languages," Moriarty
said. "I now speak nine. I confess that Turkish was something of a
challenge for the system; I never expected to have to use it. When I
learned that I had to go to Odessa on business, I couldn't resist
arranging to spend a few days here in Constantinople, both to see
the city and to practice my Turkish."

"Then you are a professor of languages?" Barnett asked.

Moriarty shook his head. "Using my system, the learning of languages is no great task for one of superior intellect," he said. "My degree is in mathematics. When I was younger I held the Chair of Mathematics at a small provincial university, but I am no longer so employed."

"You don't know who attacked you?" Lieutenant Sefton asked, getting back to the matter at hand. "We should probably report the ruffians to the authorities."

"I have no idea," Professor Moriarty said. "I came out of a shop and two of them attempted to propel me into an alley, where the others waited. I broke away. Aside from the fact that they were amateur assassins, and definitely not Arabs, I know nothing whatever about them."

"Why do you say they were not Arabs?" Lieutenant Sefton asked. "They looked like Arabs to me."

"Such was their intent, but there were a few small details they missed," Moriarty said. "One of them called to the others, and he did not speak Arabic. And the characteristic butternut color of their skin—was greasepaint."

"Greasepaint?"

"Yes." He pulled out his pocket handkerchief and displayed a dark brown stain across one corner. "The gentleman you left *hors de combat* was wearing this. I suspected it, so I ran the handkerchief across his chin."

Lieutenant Sefton took the handkerchief and examined the stain. "Curiouser and curiouser," he said. "So it was more than just an attempted robbery. It did seem to be quite a pack to be hounding one retired professor of mathematics."

"Yes," Moriarty said dryly. "I thought so myself."

"Tell me, Professor," Barnett said. "I don't want to seem to pry into your affairs, but you're not here, by any chance, to watch the sea trials, are you?"

"Sea trials?" Moriarty asked, sounding puzzled.

"The Garrett-Harris submersible boat," Barnett explained. "Day after tomorrow."

"No, gentlemen, I have nothing to do with the trials. I would find it fascinating to watch them, but I cannot stay. My business in Odessa calls me away tomorrow."

"Then you are not with Her Majesty's Government in any way?" Lieutenant Sefton asked.

The idea seemed to amuse Professor Moriarty greatly. "You have my word," he assured Sefton.

"Say!" Barnett said. "I meant to ask: how did you know I'm a journalist, and from New York?"

"And Paris," Lieutenant Sefton added.

Moriarty touched his finger to his ear. "If you could hear yourself," he said, "you wouldn't have to ask the second part of that question. As to the first: the notebook in your inner pocket, the sharpened pencils in your breast pocket, the writing callus on your right forefinger—all point in a certain direction. And to verify my deduction, I had only to look at the signet on your ring. The New York Press Club sigil is not unfamiliar to me."

"I see," Barnett said, fingering the ring Moriarty had mentioned and nodding his head slowly. "And Paris? How did you know I had come from Paris?"

"Your shoes, sir," Moriarty said. "Unmistakable."

"Is that all?" Lieutenant Sefton asked. "How simple!"

Moriarty laughed—a dry, humorless sound. "For a moment you thought I'd done something clever, is that it?" He leaned forward and fixed Sefton with his gray eyes.

"Well, yes, I—"

"My little feats of deductive and inductive reasoning are only clever until they are explained. I must learn, like magicians, never to divulge my methods. Conjurers never explain their illusions. Neither do the other sort."

"What other sort?" Lieutenant Sefton asked.

"Mentalists, mystics, mediums: all practitioners of the occult. The gentlemen who blow bugles from inside cabinets and start stopped pocket watches. The ladies who hold long conversations with your poor deceased Aunt Tillie and Lord Nelson. And the only thing Lord Nelson can find to say is, 'It's very beautiful up here and we're all very happy.' And death seems to have given a certain cockney lilt to his speech that it never had in life."

"You seem quite conversant with the subject, sir," Barnett said.

"Conjuring has been a fascination of mine," Moriarty told him. "And I have made a special study of human gullibility. The number of patent idiocies that otherwise intelligent people believe, or profess to believe, never cease to amaze me."

"For example?" Barnett said, finding himself intrigued with this ex-professor of mathematics.

"The examples are endless. People have fought wars in the ridiculous belief that one religion is somehow superior to another or that one man is inherently better than another."

"That is a bit strong, sir," Barnett said.

"Do you profess to believe, sir," Sefton asked, "that all men are exactly equal?"

"Certainly not. I, for example, am superior. But this superiority is due to clearly establishable intellectual capacity, not to the lightness of my skin, the blondness of my hair, or the blind chance of my being born in England rather than in Abyssinia." This statement was delivered with such bland assurance that it was clearly neither conceit nor arrogance from Professor Moriarty's point of view, but a simple assertion of fact.

The waiter brought over a small plate of candies. "Try one," Lieutenant Sefton said, shoving it over to Barnett. "*Rahat loukoum.* Call them 'Turkish delights' in England. Go with the coffee."

"I've heard of them," Barnett said, sampling one of the small squares. It was a sweet gel of assorted fruits, which did indeed go well with the thick Turkish coffee.

Professor Moriarty took a small leather case from his pocket. "Allow me to give you gentlemen my card," he said. "I expect you both to look me up at your earliest opportunity."

Barnett took the proffered pasteboard and looked at it:

JAMES C. MORIARTY, Ph.D. 64 RUSSELL SQUARE *CONSULTING*

"Consulting?" he asked.

Moriarty stared at him with a curious intensity. Barnett had the odd feeling that the professor could see through his skin to the soul beneath. And, further, that he wasn't being judged but merely examined and classified by this strange, intense man. "Consulting," Moriarty affirmed.

Lieutenant Sefton examined the card at arm's length. "I say," he said. "At what do you consult? Who consults you?"

"I answer questions," Professor Moriarty explained patiently. "I solve problems. Very occasionally I perform services. My rates vary with the difficulty of the task."

"Is there much demand for such a service?" Barnett asked.

"I am never at a loss for commissions and my rates are quite high. Of course, I am paid only for success."

"You mean you guarantee success?" Lieutenant Sefton asked, incredulously.

"No man can guarantee success at any task. What I do is minimize the chance of failure."

"It sounds fascinating," Barnett said. "I shall surely look you up after this assignment, when I next visit London. I might do an article about you and your business for my newspaper, the *New York World*, if you don't mind."

"I mind!" Moriarty said sharply. "Further, I absolutely forbid it. I have neither the need nor the desire for notoriety."

"Well," Barnett said, standing up and putting his cup down. "I'm sorry."

Moriarty waved Barnett back into his seat. "No need to take offense," he said, signaling the waiter for another pot of coffee. "I am aware that many people like to read about themselves. I do not happen to be one of those people. If I am ever to be known to the world, it must be for my scientific endeavors. If I am remembered at all by history, it will be for the research I am doing rather than for the occupation, however novel, which supports this research."

"What sort of scientific work are you engaged in?" Barnett asked, sitting back down.

"I am doing theoretical studies in the realm of astronomical physics," Professor Moriarty said. "There are certain anomalies in the behavior of light—but I don't want to bore you."

"Not at all, not at all," Lieutenant Sefton said politely. "You really must go into it in detail sometime; I'm sure it will be fascinating."

"How nice of you to say so," Moriarty murmured.

They had one last cup of coffee together before separating. Barnett and Lieutenant Sefton offered to walk the professor back to his hotel, but he refused. "I do not anticipate any further trouble," he said.

"I hope you're right," Lieutenant Sefton said. They shook hands, and the professor strode off.

"Queer cove, that," Sefton commented thoughtfully as he and Barnett started back to the Hotel Ibrahim. "Do you suppose he's anywhere near as intelligent as he thinks he is?"

Barnett thought about it for a minute. "I reckon he is, Lieutenant," he said. "You know, I just reckon he is."

DEATH

He who commands the sea commands everything.
—THEMISTOCLES

It was cold, damp, foggy, and uncomfortable—altogether as one would expect on a small caique in the Bosporus just after dawn in mid-March. "They can't find the yacht," Lieutenant Sefton announced after the boss *caiquejee* yelled to him in Turkish.

"What?" Barnett asked in disbelief.

"They can't—"

"I know. I heard."

"Then why did you say 'what?' " Sefton asked irritably.

"Why can't they find the yacht?"

"Because it isn't in sight." Lieutenant Sefton waved his hand at the fog. "There doesn't seem to be too much of anything in sight."

The boss *caiquejee*, a small, swarthy man with immense biceps and a mustache that seemed to curl around his ears, started an earnest, profound discussion with Lieutenant Sefton that involved much pounding on the oarlock and gesticulating. The assistant *caiquejee* shipped his oar, and he and Barnett stared silently at each other while the discussion went on. After a few minutes of this, Barnett found that he was getting increasingly nervous. "What's happening?" he asked Sefton at the first pause in the discussion.

"There are two problems," Lieutenant Sefton said. "The first is that, although Turkish is our only common language, my friend here speaks it worse than I do. It seems to be a tradition in the Stamboul docks that all the *caiquejeem*—oarsmen—are recruited from somewhere in Eastern Europe. The second problem is that they want to return to the dock now. I'm trying to convince him that they were hired to take us to the *Osmanieh* and that their job isn't done until they find it, wherever it is."

The boss *caiquejee* said something slowly and distinctly to Barnett, then wiped his mustache carefully with his sleeve and spat into the sea. His companion nodded and spat out the other side of the boat. They both glared at Barnett.

"What's happening now?" Barnett demanded.

"They are not afraid of you," Sefton explained. "They just want you to know that."

"Why," Barnett asked with a sinking feeling in his stomach, "should they be afraid of me?"

"When my friend here suggested that we could swim out to the *Osmanieh* if we wanted to find it so badly, I told him of your reputation."

The two *caiquejeem* spat again, almost in unison.

"My reputation?" Barnett asked.

"Yes. I told them that you were reputed to have a long knife and a short temper. I told them you were a cowboy from America. They know about cowboys."

"Wonderful," Barnett said. "What's that noise?"

"Noise?" Sefton asked.

The boss *caiquejee* clapped his hands together. "*Mujika!*" he yelled, slapping his assistant on the back. He turned to Barnett with a wide, black-toothed grin. "*Mujika!*" he insisted, holding his fists clenched with the thumbs sticking straight up and wobbling them in front of him.

"Bells," Sefton said. "Ship's bells. It must be the yacht."

The *caiquejeem* bent to their task with renewed vigor, and soon the sharp lines of the steam-yacht *Osmanieh* materialized before their eyes through the fog. Two smartly uniformed seamen aboard the yacht lowered a boarding ladder as the caique pulled alongside.

"Aha!" The boss *caiquejee* said, as Barnett stepped past him to grab the ladder. "Bang, bang!"

Barnett started. "What the hell?" he said.

"Bang, bang!" the *caiquejee* repeated, shooting his finger at Barnett. "Buffalo Beel. Beely de Keed. Whil'Beel Hitkook. Bang, bang!" He grinned and slapped Barnett on the back. "Cowboy!"

"Yes, yes," Barnett said, smiling back weakly. "That's right."

With this encouragement, the *caiquejee* broke into an expansive statement, accompanied with chest-thumping and a lot of wiggling of fingers.

"Well," Lieutenant Sefton said, staring back down at them from halfway up the ladder. "I wrought better than I knew. It appears that you have a friend for life, Barnett."

"What's he saying?" Barnett demanded.

"He says that he has a brother in Chicago, so he knows all about cowboys. His brother writes once a month. He, himself, hopes to move to America where all men are soon rich and they wear six-shooters."

"Well, I guess we're all brothers under the skin," Barnett said vaguely, as he climbed up the ladder.

"Bang, bang!" the *caiquejee* cried. "Steekemoop!"

The officer at the head of the ladder checked their papers and passed them on to a midshipman, who took them aft to the main cabin.

There were about twenty other guests in the cabin, mostly from the press and diplomatic corps of European countries. Red-robed servants wearing long, curved-toe slippers walked silently about, passing out cups of coffee and small breakfast cakes. Some minutes later, when the last of the invited guests found their way through the fog, the yacht got underway and the Captain Pasha came down to talk to the group. He spoke of the Osmanli naval tradition, and of Sultan Abd-ul Hamid's desire to live in peace with all his neighbors. He spoke of world trade and water routes, and of the strategic position of the Bosporus. He urged them to eat more of the little cakes, and assured them that they would be impressed with the day's display.

"Awfully confident, don't you think?" Lieutenant Sefton murmured to Barnett. "From my past experience with submersibles, they'll be lucky to get the thing running at all on the first trial. Either it won't start, or it won't sink, or it will sink only bow-first or upside down. Balky little beasts, these things are."

"I thought you were pro-submarine," Barnett said.

"Pro-submarine? Is that an Americanism, or merely journalese? Yes, I am impressed by the potential of the craft. When the designers get all the mechanical problems solved and the beasts become a bit more dependable, they'll be invaluable to the navy."

"How will they be used in warfare?" Barnett asked.

"They will primarily be used for scouting and messenger service, as well as for guarding harbors and fleets at anchor and such duty."

"What about attacking other ships?" Barnett asked. "I kind of picture them sneaking up on battleships and sinking them."

Sefton shook his head. "That's a common misconception—fostered, if I may say so, by the sensational press. You must take into account the limitations inherent in the device. First of all, they can never be used in the open ocean; they are too fragile and their range is too limited. Secondly, a submersible could never go against a modern capital ship. It would have to get too close to launch its torpedo. It would be vulnerable to the ship's gun battery. One shell from even a six-inch gun would sink any submersible, whereas it would take a dozen Whitehead torpedos to do any significant damage to a ship of the line."

"You disappoint me," Barnett said. "I thought the submersible was the weapon of the future. Now I don't know what to tell the readers of the *New York World*.

"Oh, it is the weapon of the future," Sefton said. "Properly employed by an imaginative commander, submersibles would have a decisive effect on the outcome of any naval battle. They will eventually change the complexion of naval warfare."

"What do you know of the Garrett-Harris?" Barnett asked. "Is it any good?"

"Excellent," Lieutenant Sefton said. "There are said to be some clever innovations on the craft. If what I've heard is true, they have developed a valving mechanism that I would most especially like to get a look at."

"I doubt if you'll get the chance," Barnett said.

"Well, they're certainly not going to trot it out for inspection," Lieutenant Sefton agreed. "We've been invited to watch the boat perform, not to examine its innards. I fear one would have to pay for that privilege."

The fog was clearing now, and the foreign observers were called on deck by a Turkish officer. There, a hundred yards off the port beam, rode the Garrett-Harris submersible boat. It looked like a giant steel cigar, and rode so low on the water that the deck was awash and only the small conning tower was clear of the waves. The craft rocked and rolled alarmingly with every swell that washed over it, but there was something very businesslike in the look of the riveted steel-clad deck, and an ominously efficient look to the streamlined, cigar-shaped hull.

Sultan Abd-ul Hamid came onto the flying bridge of the *Osmanieh*, causing an instant swell of whispering and murmuring among his foreign guests. It had not been known that he would be present, and the diplomats aboard were trying to decide what his

27

presence signified, so that they could send portentous reports to their governments.

The sultan waved his hand at the two men perched on the wet deck of the submersible, and they popped open a hatch and scrambled below.

"The test commences," announced the Turkish officer.

A spray of foam churned up from the rear of the Garrett-Harris as the four-bladed screw turned over, and the ship moved foward cleanly through the sea.

Barnett took out his notebook and a pencil and stared pensively at the retreating craft. *The ironclad cigar cut through the water with nary a ripple on either side to mark her passage,* he wrote. *Slowly she sank beneath the waves until but one slim tube connected her with the surface, and then that, too, disappeared. Now only the slight phosphorescence of her wake marked her passage beneath the surface of the Bosporus.*

"You will excuse me," Lieutenant Sefton murmured in Barnett's ear. "I have some business to transact."

"Of course," Barnett said, hardly noticing as Sefton moved away. His attention was held by the spectacle before him. There, a couple of hundred yards away, a sloop sailing confidently up the deep channel was being stalked by a craft riding under the calm surface of the Bosporus.

The Turkish officer rang a small bell to get their attention. "You are about to witness a major happening in naval warfare," he announced solemnly. "When, during the American Civil War, the Confederate States' submersible *Hunley* sank the Union *Housatonic* it used a torpedo affixed to a long lance. But the Garrett-Harris boat has solved the problem of launching mobile projectiles from under the water. It is equipped with a device to enable it to fire one of the new design sixteen-inch Whitehead torpedoes without coming to the surface. The torpedo will then unfailingly propel itself to the target. Please observe!"

Barnett took up his pencil: *Now the slim vision tube returns to the surface, almost invisible in the slight swell. The Garrett-Harris moves into position to line up on its unsuspecting target. There is a pause while the target sloop sails into the perfect spot for the launching of the Whitehead torpedo, which carries a dummy warhead but in wartime would be filled with eighty pounds of high explosive. Now, with the sloop perfectly lined up—with twenty-five members of the international press and diplomatic corps watching from along the rail of the royal yacht* Osmanieh, *and Abd-ul Hamid II, Sultan of the Osmanli Empire, himself watching from the bridge—*

A giant plume of water shot up from the hidden submersible. As the sound of a tremendous explosion reached the yacht, the little undersea boat threw itself out of the water bow first and then fell back, breaking in half as it hit. For a second the two halves floated separately, and Barnett thought he saw someone inside the forward half scrambling to get out; then a wave closed over the halves and they disappeared from view.

The underwater shockwave hit the yacht, which bobbed and tossed violently for a few seconds, knocking several people down. Water from the explosion plume fell back, soaking those on deck and adding to the general confusion. Barnett saw some activity at the rear of the yacht, where sailors were trying to heave a line to someone who had been washed overboard by the wave. Finally the man grabbed it, and they hauled him back up.

Nothing was to be seen of the Garrett-Harris submersible or its two operators.

A motor launch took the assembled foreigners back to the quay on the Stamboul side of the Golden Horn. They were assured by an expressionless captain of marine that a statement would be issued later by the proper authority.

Barnett and Lieutenant Sefton walked back to their hotel. "What do you suppose happened?" Barnett asked.

"It blew up," Sefton said.

"That much is clear," Barnett agreed, trying not to look annoyed, "but how?"

"It could be faulty venting of the gasses from the electrical accumulators," Sefton said, "but personally I doubt it."

"What, then?"

"A deliberate act of subversion by foreign agents."

Barnett took out his notebook. "I was hoping you'd say that. Pray, continue."

"I'm sorry, but I can't possibly be quoted on this," Lieutenant Sefton said. "You'll have to get some Turkish authority to say it. But that shouldn't be too difficult." Sefton seemed nervous and distracted. "Excuse me, old chap," he said as they reached the Hotel Ibrahim. "I must dash off now. See you at dinner, what?"

"Very good," said Barnett, himself a little distracted by the need for sending an immediate cable to the *World* outlining what had happened. He settled himself at one of the small desks in the writing room to compose a message. The idea was to be as brief as possible. A long cablegram would follow, night rate, detailing the story, but this would serve to put the editors on guard for it and give them time to decide how much space it deserved. They could get the engraver working on the illustration. Perhaps they could even get a two-line "newsbreak" squib on the front page of an earlier edition. Barnett poised his pencil over the paper.

> Garrettharris Submersible destroyed by explosion
> during Trial Espionage suspected more follows
> BARNETT

That was too long. He tried again:

> Submersible spy exploded testing more
> BARNETT

There. That was the sort of economy of expression—and of the paper's money—of which the *World* cable editor approved. It was even briefer than he could do with the Royce Telegraphers' Code. He got a cable blank from the front desk and wrote it up, then called for a page boy to deliver it to the cable office. Then he wandered into the hotel bar to have a small glass of sherry before dinner. He would work on the story after dinner, probably long into the night, and get it into the cable office before the rate change at eight the next morning.

Lieutenant Sefton returned in time to join Barnett for dinner, but his thoughts were clearly elsewhere. Barnett was getting to know him well enough to read his expression now, and he thought that Sefton looked both worried and pleased—as a reporter would when he has an exclusive on a big story and is waiting for it to come off.

"Do you want to tell me about it?" Barnett asked finally, over the pudding.

"About what?"

Barnett described his interpretation of the lieutenant's expression to him. Sefton thought it over. Then he said, "Yes, I think I do want to tell you about it. I wish to enlist your aid."

Barnett pulled in his chair and looked expectant.

"Can you be discreet?" Sefton asked.

"Half a newsman's job is *not* telling what he knows," Barnett said. "Otherwise his news sources will dry up."

"Will you swear to keep this a secret until I tell you otherwise and only reveal as much as I say you can?"

Barnett thought it over. "Unless I get it from another source," he said.

"Fair enough," Sefton agreed. With an elaborately casual gesture, he glanced around the room. Then he leaned back on his elbows and stared intently at Barnett. He smiled. It was the first time Barnett had ever seen him smile. "I am a spy," he said.

Barnett was conscious that Sefton was watching his reaction, so he did his best not to react. "How interesting," he said. "Why are you telling me?"

"As I said, to enlist your aid."

"I thought you people never asked outsiders to assist."

"There are no hard and fast rules. Perhaps some day there may be a rulebook for espionage, but not yet. I worship at the altar of expediency, and right now I desperately need your help. So I ask."

"I don't know the litany," Barnett said.

"What? Oh, I see. Unfortunate image, that."

"You didn't have anything to do with the submersible blowing up this afternoon?"

"No. On my honor. I would have done my best to prevent it, had I known. The Turks are our allies for the moment. We don't do things like that for practice, you know."

"What sort of help do you need—and why should you ask me?"

"A man is to deliver some information to me later tonight. I do not altogether trust him. I would like you along to, as you might say, watch my back. As to why I asked you—well, we're in the same sort of business, really. We collect information. You merely disseminate it more broadly than I do. And, in this case, there should be a good story in it for you."

"One I can use?"

"Oh, yes. But I shall ask you to suppress some small points, such as my involvement."

"You fascinate me," Barnett said. "I assume it involves the Garrett-Harris."

"Correct."

"Excuse me for harping on this, but why can't you get help from one of your own people?"

"There is no one else within a thousand miles."

"Your embassy?"

"They know nothing of this. They would disapprove. The Foreign Office, under Mr. Gladstone, does not approve of gentlemen reading other people's mail."

"Who do you work for?"

"The Naval Intelligence Service."

"Sounds impressive."

"It's quite small and understaffed."

"Nobody," Barnett said, "has ever accused me of being a gentleman. I'm your man."

"Good." Sefton nodded his satisfaction. "I must go now. There is some other business I have to transact this evening. Can you meet me in my room at twelve o'clock?"

"Midnight it is," Barnett said cheerfully.

He spent the three hours until midnight writing the first draft of his story. There was no point in doing the rewrite until after the midnight meeting—when he might have a new end to the story.

It was five minutes to twelve by Barnett's pocket Ingersol when he closed his writing portfolio. He splashed some water on his face, put a fresh collar on, and slipped into his jacket. After a moment's consideration he picked up his stick and tucked it under his arm. It had no blade concealed in the shaft, but it was stout ash and would serve to turn a knife.

He walked down the hall to Lieutenant Sefton's room and tapped softly on the door. There was a brief scuffling sound from inside the room, and then silence. Barnett tapped again. The door swung open at his touch this time. The room was dark except for a reading lamp by the bed. In the yellow glow of the lamp Barnett saw Lieutenant Sefton lying supine across the coverlet. His head was off the side of the bed and blood from an open wound at the temple was spurting onto the polished wood floor.

For a moment Barnett was frozen with shock as the scene registered on his brain. Then the meaning of the still-flowing blood came through: Sefton must still be alive! Barnett pushed the door open wide and looked around. The window in the far wall was open and the blinds were swinging gently back and forth. The assailant must have made good his escape by this path, and it must have been within the past minutes, perhaps even as Barnett knocked. But it was more important now to save Sefton's life than to pursue his assailant.

Barnett rushed over to the bed and pulled Lieutenant Sefton's head gently back onto the sheet. He ripped off one of the pillowcases to make a bandage.

There was a faint scraping noise behind him. He turned. . . .

FOUR

ODESSA

Politics is a way of life.
—PLUTARCH

The room was large. Sunlight from the two floor-length casement windows fell into a tessellated parallelogram across the marble floor, intersecting the great oak desk in the room's center, but leaving the corners in perpetual dusk. The desk and two chairs were the only furniture in the room. The polished top of the desk was bare except for an ornate baroque inkstand and a plain, leather-framed blotter. Fifteen feet off the floor, a narrow balcony ran around three of the walls. The ceiling was lost in gloom.

Moriarty sat in an absurdly short chair in front of the desk and waited. Two burly men in identical brown suits had escorted him into the room, seated him in the squat, low-backed chair, then turned on their heels and marched out, their footsteps echoing across the marble. He was left alone.

There came occasional faint scraping sounds from above, as though someone on the balcony were observing him, but he displayed no interest in the sounds and did not look up. Shortly they ceased.

When the sunlight had moved from the inkwell to the edge of the blotter a man entered through a small door in the far wall. The door was instantly closed behind him. *"Sdravsoitye, Gospodine Moriarty,"* he said, taking his place behind the great desk. *"Kak vye pojyevoitye?"* He was a slender man who looked quite young, but his face was lined with his years and what he had seen and what he had done. He wore a thin mustache which looked alien to his face, as though he had put it on for the occasion.

"Nye panyemi Po-Russkie?" the man said. "You do not speak Russian? I am sorry. My name is Zyverbine. I am in charge of the

Foreign Branch of the *Okhrannoye Otdelenie*, the Imperial Department of State Protection. You come to us highly recommended. Would you tell me something about yourself?"

"No," Moriarty said.

There was a long pause. "No?" Zyverbine repeated.

"You already know everything you need to know about me."

Zyverbine suppressed a smile. He touched a concealed stud on the desk and the top drawer slid open. He removed a folder from the drawer. "Moriarty," he said, reading from the folder, "James Clovis. Born in 1842 in Bradford-on-Avon, Wiltshire, of Thomas Moriarty, headmaster of the Bradford School, and his wife, née Anne DeFauve, a woman of French extraction. Has an older brother, James Francis, a booking agent for the Great Central Railway, and a younger brother, James Louis, a major in the Royal Gloucestershire Foote, a regiment which has the traditional privilege of remaining covered when in the Queen's presence.

"James Moriarty—James *Clovis* Moriarty, that is—enrolled at the University of Aberdeen at the age of fourteen, living with an uncle in that city."

"Named?" Moriarty interrupted.

Zyverbine flipped the page and looked up, his pale blue eyes now expressionless. "Paul DeFauve," he said. "Your mother's brother. Teaches music and tunes pianos. Now living in Bath."

Moriarty laughed, which seemed to displease Zyverbine. "That is not accurate?" he demanded.

"Quite accurate," Moriarty admitted. "You have impressed me with your ability to cull the public record and make files. Now, could we get on with this?"

Zyverbine closed the file and replaced it in the drawer. "I am not altogether sure that you are the man for this job," he said.

Moriarty shrugged. "That is your affair. You paid my passage to come out here and listen. I came out here. I am prepared to listen. I am neither impressed with nor intimidated by your stage setting, but neither am I offended by it. I suppose it serves some purpose in dealing with the children that usually face you across this desk."

"Stage setting?" Zyverbine put his hands on the desk, the slender white fingers pressed into the polished wood. "What are you talking of?"

"This room," Moriarty said, waving his hand about. "The artful gloom. The vast empty space. Leaving me here alone. The noises overhead. The sawed-off legs of this chair to make me lower than you. It is all stage setting. Reading me the file to intimidate me with your wealth of sterile facts. I'm sorry, but I'm not impressed. If you have a job for me, tell me what it is, and let's get on with it."

Zyverbine moved his foot, and the door in the far wall popped open. "Bring another chair," he directed the brown-suited man who appeared in the doorway. "You're right," he told Moriarty. "We of the Okhrana spend much of our time trying to intimidate everyone we deal with, including one another. It is all ridiculousness, is it not?"

Moriarty sat himself in the new chair, which was of normal height. He fixed his gaze on Zyverbine and remained silent until they were once again alone in the room. Then he said, "What do you want me to do?"

"Bear with me for another moment," Zyverbine replied, lacing his fingers together under his chin. "I have a few questions for you. We have, as you say, paid your way here for this interview. Surely we have the right to ask a few questions."

A scraping sound came from the balcony. Moriarty did not look up. "Proceed," he said.

Zyverbine nodded. "What do you know of explosives?" he asked.

Moriarty considered. "Of the chemistry," he said, "I know what is known. Of the history, I know very little. Of the utilization, I have a complete knowledge in some specialized areas."

"Such as?"

"I can blow open a safe without harming its contents," Moriarty said. "But I could not, without further research, destroy a building or a bridge. I am more familiar with the use of nitroglycerine than nitrocellulose or picric acid."

"What do you know of submersible boats?"

"I presume you mean warships, rather than diving bells or similar apparatus?"

"That is correct."

"The Turks are testing one."

"Yes."

"It is of American design."

"Yes."

"I know little further."

"Are you familiar with the scientific principles of operation?"

"Certainly."

"Ah!"

"*Zyverbine!*" a harsh voice called from the balcony above Moriarty. "*Sprosy yevo ob anarkhistakh!*"

"What do you know of politics?" Zyverbine asked, without looking up or acknowledging the voice.

"As little as possible," Moriarty said. "The subject does not interest me."

"Do you not feel that any one form of government is superior to another?"

"I have never seen it demonstrated to be so," Moriarty said.

"Do you believe that sovereigns rule by the will of God or the sufferance of the people?" Zyverbine asked.

Moriarty thought about this for a moment. "We are of different religions," he said finally.

"I am not asking about the fine points of dogma," Zyverbine replied. "Whether you are Orthodox, Roman, or a Protester is of no importance for the subject of this conversation."

"I am an atheist," Moriarty said.

This remark was greeted by an extended silence from Zyverbine and the unseen one above.

"*Ateyst!*" the unseen one said finally, "*Bezbozhnik!*"

Zyverbine looked up. He and the unseen one had a brief, intense conversation. Then there was the sound of a door slamming on the balcony.

Zyverbine transferred his gaze to Moriarty. "That is not in my file," he said.

"That is not my concern."

"A man is about to enter this room," Zyverbine said, leaning forward. "Stand up when he comes in. Bow when I introduce you."

Moriarty shrugged. "As you say."

"I wish I had phrased that question differently," Zyverbine said, "although I commend your honesty. You understand it does not make one whit of difference to me whether you believe in one god or twelve. You would seem to be the best man to handle this job, and your private beliefs are not my concern. But the Grand Duke is certain to feel differently."

"A grand duke," Moriarty said. "Of the royal line?"

"Yes. Of course. You will respect his incognito."

"Naturally. And I can appreciate his concern for religion. One who claims to rule by the will of God must dislike even the thought of atheists."

* * *

The man who entered the room was fully as tall as Moriarty but with massive shoulders and a barrel chest beneath his severely cut gray sack coat. His hair was gray, but his square-cut beard was pitch black and his eyes were light blue.

Zyverbine jumped to his feet. "Professor Moriarty, may I present Count Brekinsky," he said.

Moriarty stood and gave a bow that managed not to look too much like a parody. "Your Grace," he said.

"Yes, yes," Brekinsky said. "Sit down. Professor Moriarty, I am a blunt man. I have a question for you."

Moriarty remained standing. "Ask," he said.

"Why do you do what you do?"

"For money."

The man calling himself Count Brekinsky held out his left hand toward Zyverbine. "The file!"

Zyverbine pulled Moriarty's file from the drawer and handed it across the desk.

Brekinsky studied it. "Our information is that you control the greatest criminal organization in Great Britain."

"Not so," Moriarty said.

Brekinsky looked up from the file and fixed Moriarty with his gaze. "Our information is wrong?"

"There is no such organization," Moriarty said. "I have some men in my employ. The number varies, never more than ten or fifteen. Occasionally the acts they perform in the course of their duties are contrary to the laws of the land. The other, ah, criminals that your informant would have me controlling merely consult me from time to time. If my advice is useful, they pay me for it. I in no way control their actions or give them orders. That is not my concern."

"But they pay you for this advice?" Count Brekinsky asked.

Moriarty nodded. "That is my concern," he acknowledged. "I sometimes describe myself as the world's first consulting criminal." There was a hint of a smile on his face.

"You think of yourself as a criminal?" Brekinsky asked. "Does not this bother you?"

Moriarty shrugged. "Labels," he said, "do not bother me. The fact that I am, on occasion, in conflict with the laws of my country does bother me, but it is the laws that must give way. I live by my own ethical and moral code, which I do not break."

"You have a right to live beyond the law?" Zyverbine asked.

"If I do not get caught."

"And yet you consider yourself—trustworthy?" Brekinsky asked.

"When I give my word," Moriarty said, "it is never broken."

Brekinsky tapped the file. "Our records indicate that you are trustworthy," he said, clearly doubtful.

"One does not have to believe in the God of Abraham and Moses to keep his word," Moriarty said.

"Ah," Brekinsky said, grabbing at the phrase. "Then you do believe in some sort of deity?"

"I am willing to admit of the concept that there is a guiding force in the universe," Moriarty said, choosing his words carefully.

"I will interpret that as a belief in God," Brekinsky said. "I could not return to Moscow and tell the Tsar, my brother, that we have employed someone in this matter who does not believe in God."

"He is acceptable?" Zyverbine asked.

"Yes," Brekinsky said. "He is acceptable. I pray God he is acceptable! You may tell him."

"Very well, your Grace."

Brekinsky stuck out his hand, and Moriarty took it. "You are shaking the hand of a Romanoff," Brekinsky said. "We have long memories for good and evil." He turned and left the room.

Moriarty sat down. "Well?" he said to Zyverbine.

"Russia and Great Britain have been to war three times this century," Zyverbine said, "but each time it has been a minor conflict, of marginal concern to the real interests of either country."

"Yes," Moriarty said. "So?"

"A war between the two countries, with both sides fully committed, would be a horrible thing. The world's greatest land power against the world's greatest sea power. It would go on for years. Millions of people would die. It could turn into a global conflict, pulling the other nations of the world irresistibly into its vortex."

"Yes."

"It is possible that one man, in England now, could cause this tragedy. He is a madman. You must stop him. He calls himself Trepoff."

"Trepoff!" Moriarty said. "I have seen the name."

"Indeed?" Zyverbine said.

"Yes. I received a communication from someone wishing to speak to me concerning one 'Trepoff,' who said he would call in the evening. It seemed to assume some prior knowledge of the matter that I did not have. Shortly after the note, I received a bomb. The man never called."

"So!" Zyverbine said, clasping his hands together. "Was the note signed? If so, with what name?"

"The letter 'V' was affixed to the bottom."

"Vassily!" Zyverbine exclaimed, nodding his head almost imperceptibly up and down. "Vassily!"

"Vassily?" Moriarty asked.

"Yes. We did not know that he had tried to seek your aid, although it was from him that we first got your name. He was our best agent in England. He is dead."

"Dead."

"Some weeks after warning us of Trepoff's presence in England, and of his intentions, Vassily Vladimirovitch Gabin, known in London as Ned Bunting, the street artist, died of drinking poisoned soup."

"I'm sorry," Moriarty said.

"His widow received the Imperial Order of Merit, Second Class, and a pension of thirty roubles a month," Zyverbine said.

"Very thoughtful," Moriarty said.

"I understand Vassily was a very good street artist. They paint directly on the pavement, do they not? Street artists?"

"They draw on the pavement," Moriarty told him, "with colored chalks. A very transitory art form."

Zyverbine sighed. "Transitory," he said. "Impermanent. The epitaph of a spy."

"Tell me about this Trepoff," Moriarty said. "The man has evidently already tried to kill me once, and was undoubtedly responsible for Bunting's death as well. I'd better at least know what he looks like."

"I wish I could help you," Zyverbine said. "There is no man who knows what Trepoff looks like. He has at times disguised himself as an old man, a youth, and even a woman, and gone undetected each time."

"I see," Moriarty said. "Can you tell me anything about him? How is he going to bring about a war between Russia and Great Britain?"

"I don't know," Zyverbine said.

"I somehow suspected that you were going to say that," Moriarty said.

"It is, perhaps, not as stupid as it sounds," Zyverbine said. "Permit me to explain."

"I encourage you to explain," Moriarty told him.

"Yes," Zyverbine said. "Tell me, Professor, how much do you know of Russian history?"

"What any educated Englishman would be expected to know," Moriarty said, "which is to say, practically nothing."

"The history of my country over the past thirty years," Zyverbine said soberly, "has been written in blood. When Tsar Alexander II ascended the throne in 1855 and liberalized the policies of his father, Nicholas, he was rewarded by increasingly frequent assassination attempts. He dissolved the hated Special Corps of Gendarmerie, and in 1866 the nihilist Karakozoff shot at him in St. Petersburg. He reduced the power of the Secret Third Section, and in 1867 the Polish anarchist Berezowski attempted to assassinate him in Paris. He later abolished the Third Section, and the nihilist Solovioff attempted to murder him on April 14, 1879.

"The Okhrana attempted to infiltrate these nihilist groups and to protect the life of the Tsar, but although we had fair success, it was too late. On March 13, 1881, as he was passing a cheese factory on Malaya Sadova Street, on the way to visit his former mistress, the Princess Catherine, a white handkerchief was waved by the nihilist Sophya Perovskaya and two bombs went off by his sledge."

"I remember reading of the assassination," Moriarty said, "although not in such detail. The bombs did the job, then?"

"The first bomb killed two of the Tsar's Cossack guards. Alexander dismounted to go to their aid, and the second bomb killed him."

"That was four years ago," Moriarty said.

Zyverbine stood up. "Four years ago, Alexander III became Tsar of all Russians," he said, crossing himself, "and we of the Okhrana took a blood vow to protect him and his family against anarchists, nihilists, and revolutionaries. We intend to keep that vow."

"Very commendable, I'm sure," Moriarty said. "Trepoff is, then, a nihilist?"

"On the contrary, Professor Moriarty," Zyverbine said. "Trepoff is the leader of the *Belye Krystall*—the White Crystal, a group of right-wing fanatics within the External Agency of the Okhrana."

"You mean that this Trepoff, who murdered your best agent in England—and who, incidentally, tried to kill me—is himself an agent of the Okhrana?"

"Unfortunately," Zyverbine said, sitting back down and staring across the great desk, "that is exactly what I mean." He held his hands out, palms up. "You must understand, the Okhrana is unlike any organization you are familiar with. For one thing, the Okhrana consists of tens of thousands of people—a population larger than that of many small countries. Most of them work for the Internal Agency."

"Russians spying on other Russians."

"That is right," Zyverbine said. "Indeed, even the External Agency is mostly comprised of Russians spying on other Russians. Over the past twenty years many thousands of Russians have left their homeland. Among them were many anarchist intellectuals fleeing the Okhrana and taking their plots with them. Many of them—indeed most of them—have settled in London. There are a few in Paris and one small group in Berlin and some old men in Vienna; but most of the younger, more active anarchists are gathered in the East End of London."

"I know of them," Moriarty said. "In fact, it would be hard not to. They are said to create all sorts of problems for the police. They have established their own private clubs, which are the gathering places for Eastern European revolutionaries, nihilists, socialists, and other political activist types that the police believe to be troublemakers."

"Indeed," Zyverbine said. "Tell me, in your country, what is the prevailing opinion of these émigrés?"

"I would say it is mixed," Moriarty replied, thoughtfully. "Most Englishmen would approve of their ideals, as they conceive them to be: freedom, social justice—high moral goals. And yet they go around shooting grand dukes and bombing trains, and that sort of thing is frowned upon. There is also a strong belief among both the police and the criminal classes that the anarchists support both themselves and their movement by robbing banks, also frowned upon."

Zyverbine nodded and looked satisfied. "Just so," he said, "just so!"

"This pleases you?" Moriarty asked.

"Of course," Zyverbine told him. "We work very hard to create this image. Not, you understand, that it isn't true. We just emphasize here, expose there"—he touched the air with his forefinger at different imaginary points—"and show these people up for what they are."

Zyverbine paused before he went on. "Trepoff, of course, is

more difficult to deal with, and the damage he could do to our relations with your great nation is grave indeed. Which is why we have called for you. Will you take the job, and what are your terms?"

"I don't believe," Moriarty said, "that you have, as yet, defined the job."

"You are correct, of course," Zyverbine said. "We have been talking around it. Well—to the point: we have discovered that Trepoff is determined to so discredit the Russian émigré community in London that your country will be forced to deport them all. He plans to commit some act that is so heinous, so atrocious, that your English citizens will rise up and force your government into taking such action."

"Why?" Moriarty asked.

"The anarchist heads in London wag the tails in Moscow and St. Petersburg," Zyverbine said. "When the next attempt is made on the life of Alexander III, it will almost certainly come on orders and plans from London."

"If they are ejected from London," Moriarty said, "they will merely settle elsewhere."

"Our goal is to keep them in motion," Zyverbine said. "This makes it harder for them to plan or to raise money, and easier for us to infiltrate their organizations."

"I see," Moriarty said.

"But what Trepoff and the Belye Krystall are planning . . ." Zyverbine shook his head. "A major outrage is not wise. It is too dangerous, too full of pitfalls. Who can tell what will happen if the plan backfires?"

"If he is caught," Moriarty said, "or if the Okhrana itself is otherwise implicated . . ."

"At the least, a terrible revulsion of feeling in Great Britain against Russia," Zyverbine said. "At the most—war!"

Zyverbine sat motionless for almost a minute, his head resting in the palm of his hand. Moriarty made no effort to prompt him. At last Zyverbine spoke. "Who is to say what this madman Trepoff is planning? The destruction of a British battleship, the murder of a member of the Royal Family, blowing up Parliament, mass murder in the streets of London . . . All are equally possible. And if he is apprehended and traced to the Okhrana—"

"I understand," Moriarty said.

"You must also understand that the Tsar, my master, is a great friend of Great Britain and your Queen."

"Three wars in the past sixty years," Moriarty reminded Zyverbine.

"His father." Zyverbine shrugged. "Besides, they were mere differences of opinion. But they have created a climate where England distrusts Russia. One little mistake—"

"The mistaken blowing up of one battleship," Moriarty suggested.

"Exactly! And so Trepoff must be stopped."

"Can't you recall him?" Moriarty asked.

"The Belye Krystall is a secret organization within a secret organization," Zyverbine said. "They are fanatical in their beliefs and actions. Even the Tsar himself could not order Trepoff to stop. He believes that he acts for the greater good of the state and expects no reward beyond the successful completion of his task. In fact, he would gladly sacrifice his life to accomplish his objective. Such men are infinitely dangerous."

"Have you considered informing Scotland Yard or the British Secret Service?"

"And tell them what?" Zyverbine demanded. "That a representative of the Russian Secret Police is planning to commit a violent crime against an unknown objective and we'd be obliged if they stopped him? First of all, it would make us look like fools; and second of all if they didn't catch him, they would always suspect that we had planned it that way. No. This way, if he isn't stopped, there is always the chance that he'll get away with it—and we'll have to settle for that."

Moriarty rubbed his slender hands together. "I must confess that I find the problem an intriguing one," he said. "You want me to discover one man, whom you cannot describe, out of the population of Great Britain, before he commits an unknown crime of magnificent proportions." He thought for a minute. "I suppose he speaks fluent English?"

"Like a native."

"Good, good," Moriarty said. "An intriguing problem, indeed. You must tell me what is known of this man and his methods. I assume *something* is known."

"We have an extensive dossier on Trepoff and the Belye Krystall," Zyverbine said. "Of course, much of it is guesswork, rumor, unconfirmed reports, gross exaggeration, and deliberately misleading facts planted by sympathizers."

"Better and better," Moriarty said. "This case will give free rein to the processes of logic—the one touchstone by which one can infallibly separate truth from fiction. I think I can promise you that, given sufficient time before he attempts this outrage—and I do not need much time—Trepoff will be apprehended."

"Then you will work for us?" Zyverbine asked.

"I shall."

"You see a way to proceed?"

"I see five," Moriarty said. "Two of them look especially promising."

"I will get you the dossier," Zyverbine said, rising from his desk.

Moriarty held up his hand. "First," he said, "there is the matter of my fee."

F I V E

A BARGAIN

Have the courage to live. Anyone can die.
— ROBERT CODY

The mud-faced warder peered in through the small, barred window in the cell door. "Is here," he announced, positively.

Barnett sat up and rubbed his eyes. "What?"

"Is here! You see?"

"Who's here?" Barnett asked, squinting into the bright square of light framing the warder's face. "The American minister? Did the *World*'s lawyer show up?"

"Is here," the warder repeated. Then he stomped away down the corridor.

It seemed hours before he returned, followed by a tall man in a black frock-coat. The warder worked the heavy bolt on the door and pulled it outward on its ancient hinges. "Go in," he said. "I wait."

Barnett's eyes took a moment to adjust to the light from the gas lamps in the corridor that now flooded into his unlit cell. "Professor Moriarty!" he exclaimed, recognizing his tall visitor. "What are you doing here?"

"I might well ask the same question of you. However, to be specific, I have come to talk with you." He looked about. "There is no chair?"

"Here," Barnett said, moving to the far end of his wooden cot. "Sit here, please."

"Very well," Moriarty said, sitting on the cot next to Barnett.

"How did you get here?" Barnett demanded.

"I bribed the governor of the prison," Moriarty said. "It seems to be the way they do things here."

"Yes, but I mean why?" Barnett asked. "That is, I'm delighted to see you. If you've come to help me, I'm overwhelmed." He passed his hand over the stubble on his face. "You will forgive my appearance. For some reason, they won't allow me to shave."

"It's almost impossible to notice your appearance in this murk. I would say that I've come to help you. Whether you agree or not will depend upon what, exactly, you think your situation is."

"What do you mean?" Barnett asked. He gestured around him. "This dank, tiny, stone cell is my situation." There was a tremor in his voice which he did his best to suppress.

"Describe for me," Moriarty said, "the events of the past two weeks as they seem to you."

"That—that—" Barnett paused, swallowed what may have been an involuntary sob, and took a deep breath. "You must excuse me," he said. "It's the damp."

Barnett thought back over all that had happened to him in the past few weeks. Two weeks and three days ago he had been a respected, well-paid correspondent for the *New York World*, and now he was reduced to the state of a wretch, chained to the wall of a cell in the great stone prison of Mustafa II.

"This all began," he said at last, "when the Garrett-Harris submersible blew up in the water. Have you heard about that?"

"Pay no mind to what I have heard, or what I may know," Moriarty said. "Tell me what happened to *you*. Tell it in your own way, relating what facts you think are relevant."

"But why are you concerned?" Barnett asked. "You know that I am sentenced to death?"

"We will discuss what I know and why I am here at the proper time," Moriarty said patiently. "Bear with me, please." He shifted his position on the cot, and put his hand down where he had been sitting. "The straw is damp," he said. "Intolerable!"

"I wish that were all I had to tolerate," Barnett told him. "You know they think I'm a spy? They question me hour after hour some days, and then days go by when I see no one at all."

"The fact that the Osmanli authorities believe you to be a spy is probably the only thing that is keeping you alive," Moriarty said. "The tradition here is to execute with the bowstring within three days after sentencing."

"The bowstring?" Barnett touched his hand to his throat. "I thought they cut off your head."

"Not in cases of espionage or treason. The sentence is to be garrotted by a fine bowstring. If you happened to be of royal blood, a silken bowstring is specified. You are not, I presume, of royal blood?"

Barnett jumped to his feet. "What do I care what sort of bowstring they choke me with?" he demanded angrily. "I did nothing! Nothing! Why won't anybody believe me?"

"I, for one, believe you. Tell me what happened. And please try to remain calm." He gestured toward the warder standing outside, who was becoming concerned at Barnett's activity. "He may decide that visitors overexcite you and request me to leave."

Barnett sat down. "I'm sorry," he said. "My story—let me tell you my story. I only hope to God that you can help.

"Lieutenant Sefton—the gentleman who came to your aid with me—was murdered in his room the evening after the submersible was destroyed. You've surely heard about the murder?" Moriarty opened his mouth to speak, but Barnett interrupted him, "Yes, yes; again I apologize. I shall pay no attention to what you may or may not know. I'll just tell you my story as it happened.

"Lieutenant Sefton was a British agent—a spy. He evidently had some information about the destruction of the Garrett-Harris. He asked me to aid him and I agreed. I was to meet him in his room at midnight, and we would proceed to some undisclosed destination. I had the impression that it would be wise if I came prepared for trouble, so I brought my walking stick.

"When I arrived at the door to Sefton's room, it must have been almost midnight. I heard a scuffling sound from within. The door opened when I pushed at it, and I entered. Lieutenant Sefton was lying across the bed with a great wound in his skull. The window was wide open. There was nobody else in the room—or so I thought at the time.

"I rushed to the bed to aid Lieutenant Sefton, who was still alive, but barely. Suddenly someone struck me from behind, and I fell, unconscious, to the floor."

"You saw no one?"

"I neither saw nor heard anyone. Were it not for the evidence of the bump on the back of my head, I'd have no reason to believe that there was anyone else in that room."

"And then?"

"When I came around—it couldn't have been more than a few minutes later—the room was full of men. The night manager, the floor man, and several guests were all milling about, waiting for the police to arrive. It was the night manager, as a matter of fact, who brought me around by pouring the pitcher of water from the bureau over my head.

"I immediately tried to go to Lieutenant Sefton's aid. He was so far gone now that I couldn't tell whether he was still breathing, but nothing had been done to staunch the flow of blood from his head wound." Barnett lowered his head into his palm and began sobbing softly, this one dreadful memory overcoming his already fragile composure.

"Yes," Moriarty prompted. "And?"

"And they wouldn't let me!" Barnett said without looking up. "Those moronic—those incredible idiots wouldn't let me touch him. They thought that I'd struck him, you see. So they held me back when I attempted to go to him, and by the time a doctor arrived, he had bled to death!"

"How do you know Lieutenant Sefton was a spy?" Moriarty asked.

Barnett looked up. "What?"

"Lieutenant Sefton," Moriarty said. "You stated he was a spy. How do you know?"

"He told me so."

"Ah. Continue."

"When the police arrived they searched me. They found my walking stick on the floor, with blood on the ferrule, and they found several papers in my jacket pocket that appeared to be sections of the plans for the valving mechanism of the Garrett-Harris submersible."

"You, of course, have no idea how they got there."

"They weren't there when I left my room," Barnett insisted. "Whoever struck me on the head must have shoved the papers into my pocket; although why anyone would want to do such a thing is beyond me."

"The motives of men," Moriarty said, "are often quite beyond rational explanation. Although, in this case, the reason seems quite clear."

"Clear to you, maybe," Barnett said. "I've been beating my brains trying to figure it out for these past weeks."

" 'Beating your brains,' although a fascinating idiom, hardly seems a way to induce profitable ratiocination," Moriarty commented. "However, continue. You were accused of this crime?"

"This crime?" Barnett laughed hoarsely. "What you mean, Professor, is those crimes! I was accused of the crime of murdering Lieutenant Sefton and of the crime of being a spy. For good measure, what they'd also like to believe is that I blew up their precious submersible. That's what they've been trying to get me to admit when they question me, hour after hour, until I think I'm going mad."

"There you are," Moriarty said, shaking his head. "If you are not beating your own brain, you are having someone else do it for you."

"Look—" Barnett said.

"Now, now," Moriarty said, putting his hand on Barnett's shoulder. "I assure you I do take this seriously—very seriously, indeed. I am willing to help you—if you believe and understand that no one else can."

"What do you mean?" Barnett asked, staring at the professor.

"There was a trial?" Moriarty asked.

"You could call it that," Barnett said. "I wanted to wait until I could get legal help, but they weren't buying that. Three days after the murder I stood before a magistrate. I asked for the American minister to aid in my defense. An American counsel came as a spectator; the minister was otherwise engaged. I asked the *World*—my paper—to get me a lawyer. He hasn't shown up yet. Meanwhile, I was tried and convicted in something like three hours, and I've been here ever since."

"The trouble is, you see, that they also believe you to be guilty."

"You mean the American minister and my paper? How can they?"

"Why not? You were found alone in the room with Sefton. There were signs of a struggle. Obviously you fought over the plans, you struck him with your stick, and then he knocked you unconscious before falling back in a swoon on the bed. After all, the plans were in your pocket."

"But the open window?"

"It was inspected by the police. Nobody leaped to the ground— or at least, there were no marks."

"But what would I want with the plans?"

Moriarty shruggéd. "What do spies ever want with the plans, or the papers, or the treaties, or whatever they steal? In any case, that's of no concern to the police."

"So you think my people are not going to help me?" Barnett asked.

"Your people are going to forget about you as rapidly as is decently possible."

"But you believe me innocent?" Barnett asked. "And you are willing to help me?" He shook his head and stared at the wall. "How can you help me? How can *anyone* help me?"

"I know you to be innocent, as it happens," Moriarty said. "And I *can* help you."

"How?" Barnett asked.

"First you must realize that I am your last hope," Moriarty said. "And then you must agree to my terms."

"Terms?"

"Correct."

"What is it that you want? No—first tell me how you know me to be innocent."

"As you may remember, when you saw me last I told you I was going to Odessa."

"Yes."

"While there I had access to some secret files of the Russian government—never mind how. What I read in the files, combined with some knowledge of my own, led me to the conclusion that you were not guilty of the murder of Lieutenant Sefton, the theft of the plans, or the destruction of the Garrett-Harris submersible."

"But then—you heard of all this in Odessa?"

"No, I heard of it quite by accident when I arrived back in Constantinople. But the chain was immediately clear to me."

"I see," Barnett said. "Well, then, couldn't you take this information to the proper authorities and convince them of my innocence? Or is that what you are proposing 'terms' for? You want to extract some promise from me in return for getting me released from this foul prison? Of course I'll agree to anything—but what assurance have you that I will fulfill the terms of our bargain once I get out? A promise issued under these conditions is not considered binding in any court of law west of the Suez."

"You misunderstand," Moriarty said. "I cannot get your conviction overturned by appealing to any authority. My conclusion is based on an assortment of random facts, connected only by my inference. No authority, east or west of Suez, is going to release a convicted felon because of a chain of inference concocted by a defrocked professor of mathematics. Besides, you must understand that the Osmanli authorities have a strong vested interest in seeing that you remain guilty of these crimes: they have already so informed

Sultan Abd-ul Hamid, and one does not easily confess an error to the Shah of Shahs."

"Well then," Barnett said, "for my own piece of mind, tell me: What is your evidence?"

Moriarty took a large handkerchief from an inner pocket and fastidiously wiped his hands. "Before I left London," he said, "someone tried to kill me. Then again, when I arrived here in Constantinople, as you know, an attempt was made."

Barnett nodded. "I thought you didn't know why you were attacked," he said.

"I did not at the time," Moriarty said. "But when I arrived in Odessa I discovered that the Russian principal I had come to see wished to hire me to apprehend a dangerous man who is fanatically devoted to the Russian cause."

"The Russians want to hire you to catch someone devoted to their own cause?" Barnett asked.

"I will explain at some future time—if ever," Moriarty said. "For the moment, accept the fact."

"Go on," Barnett said.

"The Russian agent was aware that an attempt had been made to solicit my aid before I left London," Moriarty said. "It clearly was he who tried to kill me, both in London and here."

"Okay," Barnett said.

"Therefore, he followed me here. He did not follow me to Odessa, since I was taken aboard an Imperial steam-frigate for the trip there and back. Therefore, he was in Constantinople when the submersible exploded. Therefore, he was in Constantinople when Lieutenant Sefton was murdered and you were blamed."

"You have seen him?" Barnett asked.

"I have no idea who he is or what he looks like. It may not have been the subject himself, but one of his henchmen. I am assured that he has henchmen."

"But why would this mysterious man have done this thing to me?" Barnett demanded.

"Ah, but you see, he did not do this to you," Moriarty said. "He did this to the Ottoman Empire, the traditional enemy of Russia for these past hundred years. You merely happened along at the opportune moment."

"To be charged with murder."

"Yes."

"You mean that, with no preparation, on the spur of the moment, he was able to arrange for the destruction of the Garrett-Harris submersible and the theft of the plans?"

"Why not? I could have done the same." Moriarty refolded his handkerchief and replaced it in his pocket. "I must assume that Lieutenant Sefton somehow became aware of this agent's activities, and that is why Sefton was killed. I assure you that the casual murder of one man means no more to our Russian friend than the swatting of a fly.

"The sections of the plans were thrust into your pocket to give the authorities a convenient scapegoat, so they would look no further for the culprit. And this was successful. I imagine he took those plans he thought would be useful and left you only with those he didn't need." Moriarty smacked his hands together. "All this executed, as you say, on the spur of the moment. The man is capable, courageous, and cunning. Truly a fit antagonist."

"I'm convinced," Barnett said. "So how do you plan to get me out of here, and what do you want from me in return?"

"I plan to arrange for your escape," Moriarty said, "and quickly, before the authorities tire of attempting to obtain from you information which you do not possess. For on that day you will die."

Barnett shuddered. "Cheerful," he said.

"What I want from you," Moriarty told him, "is two years of your life. I would like to employ you. I shall endeavor to remove you from this place, and in return you will work for me for two years."

"Why?"

"You are good at your profession, and I have use for you."

"And after the two years?"

"After that, your destiny is once again your own."

"I accept!"

"Good!" Moriarty stood up and looked around the cell. "Bear up and be patient! You shall not be here much longer." He shook hands with Barnett and then strode out of the cell.

The stocky warder slammed the door behind him, and Barnett heard the heavy bolt sliding into place.

NARY A MONK

Gawd knows, an' 'E won't split on a pal.
—KIPLING

It was scant minutes after dawn, and the sun was still pushing its way up out of the Black Sea as the *Mu'adhdhin* was preparing to call the faithful to Friday morning prayer. Five brown-clad monks came down the Street of Venyami the Good and presented themselves at the East Gate of the ancient Prison of Mustafa II. "We have come to shrive such of the prisoners as are of the Christian faith," the spokesman for the monks told the gate guard in heavily Greek-accented Turkish. "It is Shrove Friday."

The guard smiled, a wide smile that showed both his teeth. "I would be glad to be of assistance," he said, giving a palms-up shrug, "but I have not the authority."

One of the monks produced a thick parchment, folded and creased many times, and handed it to the spokesman, who passed it through the bars to the guard. "Within here is the authority," he said.

The guard unfolded the parchment, holding it open with both hands, and examined the cursive writing within, first with one eye and then with the other. "I'll have to show this to the Captain of the Guard," he decided finally. "I cannot make heads nor tails from it."

"But certainly," the talkative monk agreed.

The guard thrust the parchment out through the bars. "Come back at eight," he said. "The captain makes his rounds at eight."

"Too bad," the monk said, shaking his head slowly.

"Too bad?"

"We cannot wait. Tradition demands that we begin now, so we shall have to go to another prison."

"Too bad, indeed," the guard agreed, smiling his tooth-exhibiting smile.

"We shall have to pay to someone else the traditional gate-keeper's fee." The monk took a small ornate purse from his robes and shook it so the coins within jingled.

"The gatekeeper's fee?"

"The traditional gatekeeper's fee," the monk agreed. "Legend has it that Simon, our patron saint, knocked three times and was not admitted, and then he paid the gatekeeper and he was admitted. This was the gatekeeper's fee."

"How much is this fee—this traditional gatekeeper's fee?"

"Two gold medjidié."

"Two?"

"That is so."

"Gold medjidié?"

"Yes."

"Hold on! Wait right here. Perhaps I can . . . The captain might be . . . You just wait right here. I won't be long. Don't go away." The guard closed the wooden door behind the ancient iron bars and disappeared within.

The talkative monk turned to his four silent, brown-cowled friends. "Ah," he said, "the power of the almighty medjidié." Three of them nodded under their deep cowls, the fourth remained still and silent.

It was no more than a minute before the guard returned, bringing with him a short, surly man with a wide, bristling mustache who was busily buttoning the last few buttons on his gold-striped dark blue trousers. "Now, now," the short man said, adjusting his wide gold sash, "who are you people? What's the story I hear? Where is this document? Where are these supposed gold medjidié? You're not trying to bribe an officer in the performance of his duty, now, are you?"

"You are the Official of the prison?" the monk asked, respect-fully.

"I am the Captain of the Guard," the captain said.

"We are monks of the Simonite order," the monk told him. "We celebrate a sixteen-hundred-year-old ceremony: the Shriving of the Prisoners. Every year on Shrove Friday we go to a different prison and shrive those prisoners who are Christian, or those of other faiths who wish to be shriven. We ask three times to be admitted, and then pay the traditional gatekeeper's fee. We enter and shrive the prisoners. Then we pay the Official of the Prison one of the gold medjidié for each prisoner we have shriven. Please, who is the Official of the Prison?"

The Captain of the Guard stroked his mustache. "I am," he announced finally. "You say you have an authority?"

The monk handed the parchment to the captain, who spread it open and studied it. "This is an authority to visit prisons in the service of your religious practice?" the captain asked.

"That is correct."

"It is signed by Sultan Bayezid II?"

"Correct."

"Four hundred years ago?"

"Just a trifle more than that."

"This is still good?"

"It has never been rescinded."

"You have, perhaps, something more recent?" the captain pleaded, seeing the promised gold dissolving before he had even a chance to taste it. "I cannot permit you to enter the Prison of Mustafa II on a four-hundred-year-old authority."

"Well, then," the monk said, reaching doubtfully into his robes, "there is this." He handed through the bars an official-looking document with etched red borders, stamped, sealed, notarized, embossed, impressed, and triply signed.

"Why, this is signed by the Grand Vizier, the Commander of Prisoners, and the Djerrah Pasha!" the Captain of the Guard said. "There'll be no trouble about your shriving the prisoners."

"Ah, well," the monk said, "if you prefer these recent signatures to that of a four-hundred-year-old sultan, so be it."

The captain shook his head. "You religious people," he said tolerantly. "Wait, I will get four guards to accompany you. We cannot afford any trouble. Some of these men are desperate."

"Very good of you," the monk said.

The captain called forth four guards and then opened the gate. "Enter," he said.

"May we be admitted?" the monk asked.

"Didn't I just tell you to enter?" the captain said.

"May we be admitted?" the monk asked.

"What's the matter, don't you understand Turkish?" the captain said. "Now, look—"

"May we be admitted?" the monk asked again.

A great light dawned on the gate guard. "Only if you pay the fee," he said, winking at the captain.

"Here you are," the monk said; "two gold medjidié."

"Enter," the gate guard said.

"Ah!" the captain said.

The five monks entered the prison in a close group, with two guards in front of them and two behind. The captain led the group across the courtyard and into the corridors which housed the prisoners. Then he fell behind and watched as the group went from cell door to cell door calling in Turkish and Greek, "Are you Christian? Do you wish to be cleansed of your sins?" Occasionally the call was made in French and English, and if the captain thought that strange he said nothing. Every time a prisoner responded and the cell door was opened, he mentally added one more gold medjidié to the growing count.

Because the prisoners were bored and any activity was a welcome novelty, many of them conceived a sudden desire to be cleansed of their sins. The monks slowly worked their way down the corridor, stopping at door after door, shriving the damned. Devout Musselmen and Zoroastrians did not admit them, neither did the paranoid nor the catatonic, but most of the prisoners welcomed the monks and the diversion they represented.

Two or three of the monks would enter the cell when bidden by the prisoner and close the door behind them. The other monks would kneel outside the cell door and pray for the prisoner's soul. The monks spent between three and ten minutes inside each cell they entered.

For the first hour the guards kept a close watch on the monks, one of them going into each cell along with the shrivers; but as time passed and nothing remarkable happened, they relaxed their vigilance and grew bored, squatting together to talk when the monks entered a cell.

It was well along in the third hour before the Simonites reached Benjamin Barnett's cell. "Do you want to be cleansed of your sins?" came the call from the corridor.

Barnett, who had been dozing, woke with a start as the ghostly voice boomed through the cell: "Do you want to be cleansed of your sins?" this time in French. He looked around wildly before realizing that the voice came from someone with his mouth close up against the cell door.

"What do you want?" Barnett called.

There was a rattling and thumping, and the cell door opened to admit three men in brown robes who seemed to glide into the room joined at the shoulders. Barnett had a glimpse of another two kneeling in front of the cell before the door swung closed.

"Quick!" the nearest monk whispered in French. "Remove your garments!"

"What?"

"The Professor Moriarty sent us. Remove quickly your garments. We are to exit you from this place."

Without further discussion Barnett stripped off the few gray rags that the prison authorities had given him. "What are you going to do?" he asked. "I am chained to the wall."

"We have prepared ourselves for that eventuality," the monk told him. "However, we must hasten ourselves."

The three monks separated from each other, and an amazing thing happened; the monk in the middle silently folded up and collapsed until there was nothing left of him except a bundle of brown clothes on the floor.

Barnett gasped and took an involuntary step backward. He didn't know what he had expected to happen, but it surely wasn't this.

"Hush!" the monk on his left whispered sharply, putting his forefinger to his lips.

"*Mon Dieu!* but I am sorry," the other monk said. "I should have paused to realize how startling that would appear if unwarned."

"What happened to him?" Barnett demanded, pointing to the empty robes.

"Ah, but you see there was no 'him,' " the monk said. "He was merely simulated by wires in the robes artfully manipulated by my comrade here and myself. Now he and you are about to merge."

"No time for talk," the left-hand monk said, whipping a pocket razor out from his robes and twisting it open. "To work!"

The other monk took two small phials from inside his robes and handed one of them to Barnett. "This is a vegetable oil," he said. "Apply it to all parts of your beard and rub it in. This will facilitate the shaving of your face."

Barnett carefully and thoroughly anointed his three weeks of stubble with the oil while the monk stropped the razor on a small piece of leather sewn to his sleeve. Then he tested the blade on the back of his hand, nodded approval, and approached Barnett. "Move not your face," he warned.

Barnett held his face motionless while the monk artfully applied the razor. The other monk crouched on the floor and unstoppered his second phial. "Hold still your feet," he said.

"What are you doing?" Barnett demanded, trying to peer down his nose without moving his face.

"Applying oil of vitriol to the link connecting your foot to this chain," the monk told him. "It will take a few minutes. Hold still!"

Barnett kept completely still, from face to feet, and let the two monks work on him. When the one had finished shaving him he took a rag and spread grease over Barnett's face. "Darken your skin," he said. "Remove prison whiteness."

Two minutes later, Barnett, in brown robes, his face deeply concealed by the cowl, his feet in worn monk's sandals thoughtfully provided by his escorts, walked out of his cell. For another ten minutes, the group continued through the prison, chanting and praying and shriving. Then, the circle completed, they arrived back at the East Gate and paid the head tax to the Captain of the Guard, carefully counting out each gold medjidié into the palm of his hand.

"In Simon's name we bless you," the speaking-monk said.

"Come back soon," the guard captain replied, transferring the gold to a leather purse.

"Next Shrove Friday," the monk said. "You have my word."

64 RUSSELL SQUARE

To trust is good; not to trust is better.
— VERDI

Barnett arrived at 64 Russell Square rolled inside a 600-year-old Kharvan rug. He was unrolled in the butler's pantry by the two men who had brought him, working under the direction of a tall woman in a severe black dress. "Very good," she told the men as Barnett unfolded from the rug. "Now take it into the front parlor. Mr. Maws will tell you what to do with it."

Barnett stood up and did a couple of knee-bends to get the blood circulating in his legs again. "Hello," he said.

The woman extended a slender hand. "I am Mrs. H," she said. "Professor Moriarty's housekeeper. You are Mr. Benjamin Barnett."

"That's right," Barnett said, taking the hand.

"You'll be wanting a bath. Come with me." She led him up two flights of stairs. "This will be your room," she said, opening a door in the hall to the left of the landing. "The bath is across the way. Fresh linens on the bed and towels on the washstand. There's hot water. I'll have a bath drawn for you while you get out of those garments. Leave them outside the door and I'll see that they're disposed of."

Barnett looked down at the filthy laborer's garb the monks had supplied him with before he left Constantinople. It had not gained anything in cleanliness in the weeks he had been crossing Europe. "But Mrs. H," he said, "I have nothing else to wear."

"Your clothing," she told him, "is in that wardrobe and in this chest of drawers."

Barnett pulled open the top drawer of the chest. Inside were a row of starched white shirts. A brief inspection convinced him that they were his own, from his Paris flat. "How did these get here?" he demanded.

"Express," she said. "I'll see to your bath." And with a satisfied nod, she turned and left.

Barnett closed the door and happily stripped off the rags he was wearing. His red velvet dressing-gown was on a hook in the wardrobe, and he gratefully enveloped himself in it. This Professor Moriarty, he reflected, seemed to be a gentleman not only of extraordinary capabilities but of immense attention to detail. Barnett only now noticed that there, on the dressing table, across from the bureau, was the silver comb and brush set that had been his sole inheritance from his father. By the door rested the three sticks and two umbrellas that had been in his umbrella stand. The framed portrait of his mother that had been on his writing-desk now sat on the night table by the solid four-poster bed. There was an envelope on the dressing table next to the brushes with BARNETT printed on it in block letters. Inside was a second envelope—which he recognized. The tape marks still crossed it where it had been fastened to the underside of the third drawer down in the armoire of his Paris flat. And inside that were still the five hundred-franc notes that served as his emergency money supply.

Barnett dropped the envelope back on the dressing table and thoughtfully crossed the hall to the bathroom. A maid—a black-haired girl who couldn't have been over sixteen—was pouring the last of a pail of hot water into the large scoopback porcelain tub. She tittered when she saw Barnett and backed out of the small room. Barnett stared after her. Are red velvet dressing-gowns a bit too advanced for staid old London, he wondered, or is she one of those girls who titters at everything? He'd have to find out. It wouldn't do to have an outrageous dressing-gown. Shutting and bolting the door, the force of a habit from long years of living in rooming houses, he hung up the offending garment and eased himself slowly into the steaming hot water.

An hour later, scrubbed, clean-shaven, and immaculately dressed for the first time in over a month, Barnett was taken by Mrs. H to see Professor Moriarty. "He's in his basement laboratory," she told him, leading the way. "We do not disturb him there unless it is important, but I have instructions concerning you."

"What sort of instructions, Mrs. H?" he asked.

"As soon as you're presentable," Mrs. H told him, "I'm to bring you in."

"You know," Barnett said, following behind her as she opened the door to a narrow staircase on the main floor, "it feels very awkward calling you 'Mrs. H.' I feel as though I'm taking undue familiarity."

"It's what I'm called," she said.

"What sort of a name is that—just the initial?" Barnett asked.

"Short," she replied.

After two turns in the narrow stairs they crossed a door that led onto a landing overlooking a large, cement-floored basement room which had been turned into a modern laboratory. Low wooden tables were spread in a circle about the room, leaving the central area bare. On one table, a series of retorts and gathering-tubes were clamped in place over small Bunsen lamps. On another, a complex arrangement of lenses and mirrors was fastened to a revolvable wooden stand ready to twist into motion at the turn of a crank. The cabinets along the walls were furnished with every conceivable sort of chemical and physical apparatus that Barnett was familiar with, and many that he was not.

"Do not distract him," Mrs. H instructed Barnett in a whisper, nodding at the tall figure of Professor Moriarty sitting stooped over a large journal at a writing table in the corner. "Wait here until he speaks to you. He dislikes having his train of thought interrupted, particularly when he is in the laboratory." Nodding again, she went back upstairs, leaving Barnett on the landing.

After a while Moriarty looked up from his writing. Then he stoppered the inkwell and put down the pen. "You look a good deal better than the last time I saw you," he told Barnett. "Welcome to London. Welcome to my household. I trust you had an acceptable trip."

"Not very," Barnett said, going down the last few steps and crossing the room to Moriarty's desk. "I was smuggled across the Bohemian border in a caravan of wagons loaded with fresh-clipped wool being taken to be combed and washed. The smell was indescribable."

"It kept away the border guards," Moriarty said.

"I was carted across Rumelia with four other people in a pox-wagon," Barnett said.

"Nobody tried to stop you," Moriarty commented.

"From Bosnia through Austria we became a traveling team of acrobats. I couldn't tumble, so I caught the others and held them up. My shoulders and my legs still ache."

"Nobody ever looks at the low man," Moriarty said.

"In Italy we finally caught the train," Barnett said. "It was a fourth-class local. Have you ever traveled fourth class from Trieste to Milan?"

"You would have attracted attention in first class with your clothing," Moriarty said. "And you would have attracted more attention trying to buy other clothing."

"In Milan we became part of a circus and spent a couple of weeks reaching Paris. I cleaned the animal cages in the menagerie."

"It sounds like an enriching experience," Moriarty said.

"And they wouldn't let me go to my apartment in Paris."

"Does it strike you as brilliant for an escaped felon, wanted for murder, to stroll over to his apartment to collect his clothes?" Moriarty took a small notebook from his pocket and consulted its pages. "In Rumelia you picked a fight with the wagon driver," he said, "a fact that I find incomprehensible, since you had no language in common. On the train outside of Milan a farm woman accused you of stealing a chicken, and you argued with her until the conductor was called."

"I didn't steal her chicken," Barnett said. "It squeezed through the wicker cage and flapped its way out of the carriage. It's a wonder she didn't lose the other six."

"And as I pointed out, in Paris you had to be restrained from going to your apartment to get a change of clothes."

"You should have told me that you were having all my things brought here," Barnett said. "How did you manage to get by the concierge?"

"I had a letter from you," Moriarty said dryly, "authorizing my agent to remove your belongings. You paid her an extra month's rent in lieu of notice."

"I did?" Barnett said. "I see." He looked around for a chair. "May I sit?"

"Of course," Moriarty said. "There is a stool under that table. Pull it over."

Barnett retrieved the long-legged work stool which was lying on its side, set it up, and straddled it a few feet from Moriarty's desk. "You were having me watched as I crossed Europe," he said.

"The three who accompanied you are in my employ, as you should have surmised," Moriarty said. "They conceived it to be part of their function to send me a report on your behavior. Actually, there are many favorable points in the report. I would like to have seen the way you smiled and mumbled inanely at that Austrian border guard until he gave up and let you through. And you acquitted yourself quite well in dealing with the conductor on that Italian train, although you should have arranged things so that he was never called."

"That woman called me a thief," Barnett protested.

"There is no magic in epithets," Moriarty said. "You don't have to ward off their effects by disputing them."

"I suppose you're right," Barnett said, grudgingly. "Still, it grates."

Moriarty returned the notebook to his pocket. "I am satisfied that, if induced to exercise discretion, you would be a competent and useful assistant to me. Are you ready to discuss the terms of your employment?"

"I'd like to know what the job is," Barnett said. "I have gathered over the past few weeks that you are no ordinary professor. What is this consulting business of yours?"

"First we must have an understanding. All else is open to discussion, save this one thing only: you must never divulge anything that you learn while in my employ—not about me, my associates, my activities, my comings and goings, my possessions, my household, nor indeed anything at all related to your employment. This ban does not terminate when and if your employment terminates, but is to continue throughout the remainder of your life. And beyond."

"Beyond?"

"Words outlive people. You must not keep a diary or write an autobiography or memoir that in any way touches upon the time you spend with my organization."

"That's quite a ban," Barnett said.

"Can you keep it?"

"I reckon so."

"Regardless of whether you agree or disagree with any of my activities, whether you find them in opposition to your religion or ethics or even morally repugnant to you?"

Barnett gave a low whistle. "That *is* quite a ban!" he said.

"Can you keep it? Can you give me your unqualified word?"

"What if I say no?"

"I dislike indulging in idle supposition, Mr. Barnett. Say either yes or no, and we shall continue the discussion on that basis."

"Well, about these, ah, morally repugnant acts—if I find any of your activities to be offensive to me, am I obliged to engage in them myself?"

"Certainly not, by no means. It would not be to my interest to employ a man for a job he finds offensive."

"Well, with that understanding I guess I can keep my mouth shut about your doings. And I confess that with this preamble you've got me mighty curious as to just what these doings might be."

Professor Moriarty slipped a pair of pince-nez glasses onto his nose and peered through them at Barnett. "You swear to keep your silence?" he asked.

"Cross my heart, Professor," Barnett said, with a wide smile.

"There is less humor in this than you think," Moriarty said, "for I shall hold you to that oath. So think on it seriously and give me a serious answer."

Barnett raised his hand. "You have my word, Professor Moriarty, that I shall never speak of your affairs to anyone. I swear this on the memory of my mother, which I hold sacred. And if that's not good enough for you, I can't offer anything better."

"That completely satisfies me. As you become privy to my affairs, you will see why I require such an affirmation from all my associates. And you will also see how seriously I regard it." He took a pocket-watch from his waistcoat pocket and snapped it open. "We shall regard your employment as commencing now," he said. "It is five past two in the afternoon of Tuesday, May fifth, 1885."

"Is it?" Barnett asked. "I had quite lost track of the days."

"On the hour of two P.M. on May fourth, 1887—which will be, I believe, a Wednesday—you are quits with me. Until then you are in my employ at an annual salary of—let me see—how much were your New York City employers paying you?"

"Ten dollars a week," Barnett said. "They discourage anyone from thinking of his employment on an annual basis."

"I shall make it five pounds a week," Moriarty said, "if that is satisfactory."

"Satisfactory?" Barnett laughed. "Why, that's well over twice as much. I'll say it's satisfactory!"

"And then, of course, there's your room," Moriarty said. "Since it is at my request that you'll be living in this house, I can't very well charge you rent. So you may consider your room and such meals as you eat here as complimentary. And incidentally, I think you'll find Mrs. Randall a more than adequate cook."

"Then you want me to keep that room?"

"Is it satisfactory?" Moriarty inquired. "If so, I would have you keep it."

"Exactly what is my position to be in your organization?" Barnett asked. "And exactly what sort of organization do you have?"

"I solve problems," Moriarty told him. "I am a consultant, taking on my clients' problems for a fee. Some of them are purely cerebral, and I solve those by sitting in my study, or working in my laboratory, or taking a long walk through London; I find walking very stimulating to the mental processes. But other problems require deductive or inductive reasoning from facts, from evidence; and that evidence must be assembled. And each glittering fact must be tested, like a gold sovereign, to see if it rings true."

"I see," Barnett said.

Moriarty smiled, "By which you mean you do not see. But you soon will, you soon will." He removed his pince-nez glasses, cleaned them with a piece of flannel from his desk, and then replaced them firmly on his nose. "Your hours are to be those required to accomplish your assignment, when you have one," he continued. "In recompense, when you have no assignment you are free to do as you like whatever the time of day. We have not allowed the concept of 'office hours' to infiltrate our little domain."

"That's agreeable," Barnett said. "I much prefer that scheme, as a matter of fact. Do you have anything for me now?"

"Anything for you . . ." Moriarty rubbed his chin with his left hand. "I think you'd better use the first few days to get acquainted with my household and my organization. If you need anything, ask Mrs. H, the housekeeper, or Mr. Maws, the butler. I shall arrange to have someone show you around the rest of the organization and introduce you to those whom you should know or who should know you."

"Very good, Professor. And I haven't as yet had a chance to thank you for rescuing me from that Turkish jail. I have no doubt that you saved my life."

"I think we shall both benefit from your, ah, timely release," Moriarty said. He offered Barnett his hand, which was firmly taken. "Welcome to my employ, Mr. Barnett," he said.

"I trust you don't have to go quite so far afield for all your employees, Professor."

"If you mean Constantinople," Moriarty said, "that is unique. If you mean prison, you would be surprised at the number of people working for me in one capacity or another who were found in prison. There is one characteristic you do not share with the others. You were innocent."

With that, Moriarty dismissed Barnett and returned to his scientific note-taking.

Barnett returned to the ground floor and hunted up Mrs. H, who was in a small room off the pantry. "You're in my office, Mr. Barnett," she told him as he looked curiously around the room. "What may I do for you?"

"I was wondering if it was too late to get some lunch," he asked her. "I spent the morning wrapped up in a rug."

"Go into the dining room, Mr. Barnett," she said. "I shall see that you are served."

"Thank you, Mrs. H," he told her. "I appreciate it."

"Humpf," she said.

Barnett retreated to the dining room, where he was shortly served a large omelette with jam, by a somber-looking maid-of-all-work who curtsied before scurrying out of the room. He found the omelette excellent, and as he sat eating in comfort for the first time in over a month, he fell to musing over his recent past and his probable future.

As much as it might smack of involuntary servitude, working for Professor Moriarty for the next two years promised to be quite interesting. Barnett still didn't have any clear idea of what Moriarty did, or what he would be expected to do for Moriarty, but he had formed the notion that it wasn't quite proper and might be quite exciting. And Barnett, who had just passed his twenty-eighth birthday, was of the opinion that a bit of impropriety and a dash of adventure were the salt and leavening that made the load of life worth eating. Barnett was one of those souls who often felt oppressed by the straitlaced notions of the times he had been born into, and although he would not—at least he was firmly convinced he would not—condone outright immorality, there was something about the touch of impropriety that appealed to him.

When Barnett had finished his omelette and was beginning to wonder what to do next, the hall door opened and a small, almost tiny man wearing a natty fawn-colored suit and yellow spats and carrying a spotless brown bowler tucked under his left arm glided into the room. "Afternoon, afternoon," he said. "Permit me to introduce myself. The name is Tolliver; 'Mummer' Tolliver, they calls me, or just 'the Mummer.' "

"I'm Benjamin Barnett," Barnett said.

" 'Course you are," Tolliver said. "And welcome to our little ménage, I says. The professor, he asked me to show you around, seeing as how you're to be a fellow resident."

"Oh," Barnett said. "You live here, then?"

" 'Course I do. Up in the attic. I've got my little room up there. Closer to the sky, you know." He pulled out one of the chairs and reversed it, then jumped up on it, straddling the seat and leaning his chin on the top bar of the straight back. "First off, I should tell you who else shares this impressive abode with us. There's the professor himself, of course; and Mr. Maws, the butler; and Mrs. H, the house-keeper; and Mrs. Randall, the cook; and Old Potts."

"Old Potts?"

"Right. He has a room in the basement, he has. Spends his days blowing glass and suchlike for the professor's scientifical experi-ments."

"He's really into this science stuff, then?" Barnett asked.

" 'Course he is. He's a genius, the professor is. A scien-bleeding-tifical genius. He's always writing things and figuring things, you know. And he studies little things that you can only see under a microscope, and great tremendous things like the distance from here to the Moon or the Sun. A couple of years ago, when we was out at his cottage on Crimpton Moor, he had a couple of us measure off five miles professional-like with instruments so he could set up some sort of apparatus and determine the proper distance of the Moon and Mars and some stars what he thought might be closer than the others.

"And then sometimes he gets to talking about his work and the way them other professors don't understand him and laugh at his theories 'cause they're too blind to see what's right under their very noses, and he's going to get the last laugh when someone else smart enough to understand his theories comes along, even if it takes a hundred years. And then he gets into the technical stuff, all about waving lights, even though there isn't any e-ther, and nobody alive has any idea of what he's talking about, but it for certain does make you feel important just to listen to him."

"But he doesn't do that all the time," Barnett said. "I mean, this other business takes up most of his time, and the science is just a hobby. Is that right?"

"I'd say it was the other way 'round," the Mummer said. " 'Course he does spend most of his time on these here activities what make the money and employ the services of the likes of you and me. But this is the hobby. The science stuff and his experiments is really his life. He's told me many a time that if he's ever to be remembered for his time on this earth, it will be for his scientifical theories."

"What about the rest of the household?"

"I'll bite," the Mummer said. "What about it?"

"Mrs. H, the housekeeper, for example. What's her real name?"

"You'd best ask her that."

"I have."

"You're a braver man than me, then. I never have."

"What about Mr. Maws?" Barnett said. "Why is he called 'Mr.'? I've always understood that butlers were called simply by their last name."

"That is correct, so they are. "Except, 'course, below stairs, so to speak. The other servants in a household always call the butler 'Mr.'—at least, to his face."

"But everyone seems to call Mr. Maws 'Mr. Maws.' "

" 'Course they do," the Mummer said. "He was called Mr. Maws by all when he were in the fancy, back around fifteen years ago."

"The fancy?"

"Prizefighting, Mr. Barnett. Gentleman Jimmy Maws went twenty-three rounds to a decision for the bare-knuckle heavyweight championship of England. Unofficial, of course, since it were illegal at the time. That was back in 1872, I believe. Mr. Maws won the championship and six months' penal servitude for engaging in an illegal prizefight contest."

"I'm impressed," Barnett said.

The Mummer jumped from his chair. "Come," he said. "Let me show you about the house."

EIGHT
SHERLOCK HOLMES

He appears to know every detail of every horror
perpetrated in the century.
— JOHN H. WATSON, M.D.

The next afternoon at about half past two Mr. Maws showed Sherlock Holmes, a private inquiry agent who lived in Baker Street, into Moriarty's study. Moriarty stood by his desk, his shoulders stooped, his hands behind his back, and glared out at Holmes, his gray eyes piercingly clear under his thick black eyebrows. "I won't say it's a pleasure to see you," Moriarty said, "because that would spoil your day. I will say that I expected you, but not quite so soon. What do you want?"

Holmes dropped into the black leather armchair and crossed his legs. "I don't like to let too many weeks go by without looking in on my old mentor and professor," he said, tapping the sole of his shoe with the spiked ferrule of his stick. "I grow curious as to what sort of deviltry you're up to now, and rather than spend the next few weeks hanging about at your window in a variety of puerile disguises, I thought I'd come in and inquire."

"Counting on my elephantine conceit, you assume that I'll be unable to resist telling you," Moriarty said. "This time, I fancy, I shall resist. But you do your disguises an injustice. They are consummate works of art. When I see you mincing down the street as an unemployed curate or hobbling along as an old bookseller, it's all I can do to stop myself from clapping you on the back and congratulating you on your performance."

"Those disguises are not meant to fool you, Professor. They would fool nine-tenths of humanity, they would pass the scrutiny of any of Scotland Yard's current crop of inspectors, they would befuddle my colleague, Dr. Watson; but they are not meant to fool you. I would have to take much greater care and more profound subtlety to fool you."

"I have no doubt that you could if you put your mind to it," Moriarty said. "I have no doubts about your ability; indeed, I admire it. It's your damned single-minded persistence I object to. I am no Jean Valjean to have you dogging my footsteps for the remainder of my life."

"Come, Professor Moriarty," Holmes said, smiling a satisfied smile, "a man who chooses to live outside the social, moral, and legal confines of our society must not be surprised when that society chooses to keep a close eye on him. You are that man. And I am that eye."

"A touching bit of metaphor," Moriarty said.

"I followed you to Odessa."

Moriarty shook his head. "That's good, Holmes," he said, "that's very good. I should have guessed. How did you manage from Stamboul?"

"I saw you board the Russian frigate," Holmes said. "I was actually on the dock near you at the time. I hired a steam launch when you boarded the frigate, and I beat you to Odessa by four hours."

"You're good, Holmes, I'll give you that," Moriarty said, staring his unblinking stare. "But why do you hound me? Go apprehend a bank robber. Use your talents to lay your hands on a forger, arrest a poisoner, clap the cuffs on a resurrectionist; perform some useful deeds with this avocation of yours, but leave me be!"

"Avocation?" Holmes stood up. "My dear Moriarty, I would be vastly surprised if you were not guilty yourself of each of the crimes you have enumerated. I have often said in private that you are the most dangerous man in London, if not in Europe. If I were to utter such a statement in public you could collect damages for slander; that's how clever you are. But scheming with the Russians against your own country—Professor Moriarty, even for you this is too much!"

"Stop dogging my footsteps, Holmes," Moriarty said, cold fury evident in his voice. "Both my morals and my methods are beyond you. You make me your life's work, while to me you are but a minor annoyance."

"I am quite your equal in this game we are playing, Professor," Holmes said calmly. "I am merely more constrained by the rules than you are." He thumped his cane on the floor. "And I only have to make you my life's work until you are safely and securely behind bars, after which I'll be free to concentrate on the lesser criminals, the pilot fish that always swim in the wake of a shark."

"There can be no truce between us?"

"Never!" Holmes replied.

Moriarty nodded and took a deep breath. Slowly the fury disappeared from his eyes. "So be it. I shall endeavor to keep out of your clutches. But I warn you, Holmes, you are playing in a deeper game than you know. Do not open any unexpected packages, do not walk under parapets, avoid mysterious meetings with strangers, never take the first cab in the rank."

"Am I to understand that you are threatening me, Professor?"

"Not at all," Moriarty said. "Merely alerting you. It is circumstances that are threatening you if you are going to get involved in my affairs at this time. There have been three attempts to kill me in the past ten days; twice by bombing and once by dropping a chimney on me as I passed a building being demolished. It makes life quite interesting, I find."

"The same people who sent you a bomb before you left for Odessa?"

"Presumably," Moriarty said. "What do you know about that?"

"I was across the street when the bundle came hurtling out your front window—that very window, I believe—and exploded."

"Ah, yes," Moriarty said, "I had forgotten."

"Who are these people who are taking such interest in doing a service for humanity?" Holmes asked.

"I cannot tell you any more about them," Moriarty said. "But if you follow me too closely, they are liable to take an interest in you."

"I'll be careful."

"Please," Moriarty said. "I'd hate anything to happen to you before you had achieved your life's ambition. Good day, Mr. Holmes." Moriarty rang for the butler.

"Don't bother," Holmes said, "I'll find my own way out."

"No bother, Mr. Holmes. Drop in again soon for another little chat."

"You have my word," Holmes said.

LONDON

Hell is a city much like London.
—SHELLEY

Mummer Tolliver devoted the next few days to showing Barnett around Professor James Moriarty's London and introducing him to the people he would be dealing with in Moriarty's service. Although very few people were in his constant employ, the professor had associates all over the city. There were those in every social class, in every profession, and in almost every institution, guild, club, and business who were ready to do Moriarty a service or repay a favor.

In a cellar below a warehouse in Godolphin Street, almost in the shadow of the great tower of the Houses of Parliament, Barnett met Twist, London's most deformed beggar and the head of the Mendicants' Guild—an organization with rules as strict and as strictly enforced as those of the British Medical Association or the Queen's Dragoon Guards. It was Twist and his corps of wretches who enabled Moriarty to make good his boast that he had eyes on every street corner in London.

Twist looked Barnett up and down with his one good eye—the right one had a great patch over it—and then shook his head doubtfully at the Mummer. " 'E's fly?" he demanded.

"He's fly," the Mummer insisted. "The professor sprung him from quod in Araby. He's to be the professor's principal. 'Course he's fly. Who says he ain't?"

Twist took the patch from his right eye and stared up at Barnett with it, as though seeking confirmation for what his left eye had shown him. The right eye had a milky-white disc covering most of the cornea, and Barnett found it very disconcerting to have it staring at him. He was having trouble following the conversation, but he didn't want to ask for an explanation for fear it would make Twist think him a complete outsider.

Twist replaced the patch, stared thoughtfully for a minute at Barnett's shoes, and then nodded. "If the professor says you're fly," he told Barnett, "that's jonnick with me. 'As the Mummer 'ere given you the office?"

" 'Course I hasn't," the Mummer interjected. "I leaves that to you, as always. It's not my place."

" 'E's right," Twist said to Barnett. "It's my place and it's my privilege." He hobbled over to a table in one corner of the large cellar, which was filled with low wooden tables and lower wooden benches. "We'll do it by the book," he said. "And 'ere it is." He opened a large, ancient ledger and turned the pages slowly and carefully until he reached the last one with writing on it. "They are those," he said, "as think I'm the oldest thing around 'ere, but this book is far older than any living man. It's the Maund Book and all as 'ave ever been members of the London Maund, which we now call by the appellation of the Mendicants' Guild, are signed by they name, or they mark, and sealed with they thumb into this book. This book was opened in 1728, in the second year o' the reign of George the Second."

Barnett went over and, with Twist's permission, examined the book, turning a few pages and peering at the ancient leather binding and the lists of signatures and strange hieroglyphics. He noticed a squiggle with a straight line over it and two X's at each end, and "the Connersty Barker, his mark," written after. Each signature had a strange brown blob at the end, which Barnett decided was the thumbseal Twist had mentioned. "Absolutely fascinating," Barnett said. "You have a piece of history here."

"Ain't it the truth!" Twist said, pleased at the observation. "And they's nobody what gets to see it without I say so." He produced an inkstone and poured a few drops on it from a bottle under the table. "Gin," he explained, pulling a goose feather from a cubbyhole. With a couple of quick swipes of his pocketknife he created a passable point, which he rubbed into the gin-moistened ink. "What moniker?" he asked.

"How's that?" Barnett said.

"What moniker?" Twist repeated. "You can't use your own, you see."

"Oh!" Barnett said, as the light dawned. "Moniker! Nickname!"

"Right enough," Twist agreed.

"I've never used one," Barnett said.

"Why'nt you jolly him one?" the Mummer suggested.

Twist considered. "Got it," he said. "We'll moniker 'im after 'is quod. You go in the Maund Book as 'Araby,' if that's jonnick with you."

"Sounds fine," Barnett said, wondering what all this was leading up to.

Twist carefully and painstakingly wrote the date at the start of the line, twisting his head around so that his left eye could watch what his right hand was doing. Then he handed the quill to Barnett. "Write your moniker or make your mark," he instructed.

Barnett wrote "Araby" neatly after the date and then, staring at it and feeling it looked naked by itself, added "Ben" after it. "Araby Ben," he said. "How's that?"

"Good," Twist said, taking back his quill. He took Barnett's right thumb with his left hand and, with a sudden gesture, jabbed a long brass pin into the ball of the thumb.

"Hey!" Barnett yelped, jerking his hand back.

"Squeezed out a couple of drops of blood," Twist said, sticking the pin back into the lining of the filthy waistcoat he was wearing. "Then press your thumb after your moniker."

Barnett dutifully squeezed his thumb until two drops of his blood pooled on top. "You should be careful with that needle," he said. "You could give someone blood poisoning."

"I've pledged 'alf an 'undred men with this selfsame needle," Twist said, "and ain't none of 'em dead yet, barring a couple who've swung."

Barnett made his thumbprint in the book, and Twist closed it. "Yer a member now," he said.

"Give him the office," the Mummer said.

Twist struck a pose. "You see what I'm doing?" he asked Barnett.

"No," Barnett said, seeing nothing unusual in Twist's appearance beyond what was dictated by his deformity.

"Right enough," Twist said. "But any o' your fellow members of the guild would see right off that you was passing them the office." He held up his left hand. "Left 'and," he said, "with the thumb protruding, as it were, from between the first and second fingers. Not a natural pose, but not queer enough to be noted."

"I see," Barnett said.

"If you 'ave a message what you want delivered, but you're un-der the eye of some busy, or somefing of the kind, just give the office when you pass a street beggar. If 'e returns it, give 'em the message or drop it somewhere in 'is sight."

"Twist here will have it within the hour," the Mummer said with as much pride as if he'd invented the system himself. "And the pro-fessor in another."

Barnett nodded. Although he couldn't imagine what possible use such an elaborate signaling and message-carrying system could be to Moriarty, he was impressed. "You certainly have evolved an efficient system," he said.

" 'Course it is," the Mummer said. "E-bloody-ficient."

"Don't forget your moniker, now," Twist said. "That's the name I knows you as. Good meeting you, Araby Ben. Good luck to you."

The tour of London continued. Mummer Tolliver introduced Barnett to a motley assortment of characters that would have kept the feature editor of the *New York World* ecstatic for a year if Barnett had sent him character sketches.

"MacReady's the name," announced the red-faced man in the shop in Belgravia. "Eddie MacReady at your service, whatever that service may be. Service for two or service for two hundred, it's all the same to me." The sign over his door said: "Edward MacReady— Superior Catering Service," and below it in smaller print was the legend: "Fine meals for fine people; catered, served, cleared by liv-eried waiters. 2 to 200 on a day's notice."

"Any friend of the professor's is a friend of mine," Eddie de-clared, pumping Barnett's hand. "And some strange friends he's got, too. But I'm no one to talk; not after what he did for me. He set me up in this business, I don't mind telling you. He had faith in me when nobody else did."

Here MacReady paused for Barnett's response. "He's a remark-able man," Barnett said, feeling on safe ground with that statement.

"That he is," MacReady agreed solemnly.

" 'Course he is," Mummer Tolliver said, looking around pug-naciously for someone to disagree. "Who says he ain't?"

And they moved on to Old Brompton Road, where Barnett was introduced to Isaac Benlevi, artificer and toolmaker. The old gentle-man in a floor-length leather apron was just putting the finishing touches on an escapement mechanism designed for the equatorial mounting of Moriarty's telescope, a twelve-inch reflector housed at his private observatory on Crimpton Moor.

Barnett examined the beautifully tooled device with pleasure; he had always had a fondness for machines and contrivances. But the Mummer waved it off with disgust. "Haven't you got nothing what could interest a chap in my line, Mr. Benlevi?" he asked with a broad wink "You've always got such loverly toys, ain't you got nothing today?"

"Ah, Mr. Tolliver, my little friend," Benlevi said, patting him on the shoulder. "The problems of your trade have always intrigued me. I am constantly thinking of simple contrivances to make your life easier. As a matter of fact, there is something I'd like you to look at. It isn't perfect yet. I'd like your opinion. It's in the back, I'll bring it out."

"What trade is that?" Barnett asked the Mummer, as Benlevi disappeared into the back room.

The Mummer brushed the dust off his yellow spats and flicked a piece of lint from his fawn-colored suit. "Not ashamed to say it," he told Barnett, "though there's some as would beat around the bush. I was in the swell. Out of it now, course. Still keep my hand in, though, and I won't say that I don't."

"A swell?" Barnett asked.

"*In* the swell," the Mummer said. "I was a sneak thief with the swell mob, blokes what dressed and acted like swells so's we could mingle amongst them at the race-course and the opera and suchlike places."

"You gave it up when you went to work for the professor, did you?"

"Let us say I became a specialist," the Mummer said. "Now, Mr. Benlevi, what have you got to show?"

"Here's my latest toy for your trade, Mummer," Isaac Benlevi said, holding up a shiny black leather Gladstone bag. "Take a look."

The Mummer took the bag and examined it from every angle. "It's a Gladstone, right enough. From the outside anyway."

"Open it," Benlevi said. "Go on!"

The Mummer pushed the catch and the bag popped open. It was divided into two sections and lined with thick black velveteen. The Mummer peered inside and then poked his hand in and felt around. "Empty," he said. "What's the wheeze?"

"A very old wheeze, indeed, Mummer," Benlevi said. "All done up in new cloth. Watch!" He rummaged the shelf behind him for a minute and finally produced a small precision chronometer and put it on the counter. Then he snapped the Gladstone bag closed and set it down over the chronometer. When he lifted the bag again, the instrument was gone. "Neat and clean and all in a flash," he said.

The Mummer grabbed the bag out of his hand and opened it. He looked inside, then he stuck in his hand and repeated his earlier motions, prodding the sides, top, and bottom of the velveteen lining. Then he turned the Gladstone bag upside down and shook it. "Mr. Benlevi, you're a bloody genius, that's what you are," he declared solemnly, putting the bag down. "I have witnessed a miracle."

"A miracle of craftsmanship," Benlevi agreed. He lifted the bag and touched a concealed spring in the handle. Immediately the bottom flopped open and the chronometer dropped to the counter. "It must be reset for each grab," he said. "It will take anything up to six inches square and two or three inches high. Perfect for jewelry trays. A clockwork mechanism grabs the item and holds it securely in a hidden chamber beneath the cloth."

"What's your price?" the Mummer asked.

Benlevi shook his head. "It is not yet perfected," he said. "When I can swear to its proper operation, I'll sell it—but not before. I'll let you know."

The Mummer shook his head sadly as they left Benlevi's shop. "I hunger sometimes for the old days, Mr. Barnett," he said. "Humorous times we had in the old days."

"Stealing wallets?"

"Right enough. And skins and dummies and sneezers and props—"

"Sneezers? Props?"

"Sorry," the Mummer said. "Sneezers is snuffboxes—some very rare snuffboxes the gentry walk around with. And props is what's pinned or fastened to the outer garment, such as pins and brooches and suchlike. Skins and dummies is handbags and pocketbooks."

"I see," Barnett said.

They walked to the corner, where the Mummer hailed a passing hansom cab. "One last stop, Guv," he said, giving the cabby an address in the East End.

"I may be mistaken, since I'm not too familiar with London,"

Barnett said as the hansom moved out to enter the stream of traffic, "but we seem to have gone back and forth across London today in a great zigzag. Aren't we going back now in the direction we came from only a couple of hours ago?"

"Traveling roundabout London is the best way to get to know the city," the Mummer told him.

So Barnett leaned back in the cab and watched as the streets of London passed under the two wheels of the hansom and district gave way to district with the bewildering changes of character that were commonplace in this amalgam of towns which had grown into the world's greatest city. Up they went past Victoria Station, sooty monument to the queen who had lent her name to the age. Then around Westminster Abbey and toward Trafalgar Square, passing the prime minister's residence, the Admiralty, and the spot where Charles I was beheaded. All the while, Mummer Tolliver kept up a running commentary on the history of the buildings and monuments they passed which was so rich and so personal that Barnett had a sudden image of Tolliver, with spade in hand and that irrepressible cockney grin lighting his face, busily laying the cornerstone of every public building in London since the eleventh century.

In less than half an hour, their hansom pulled into Upper Swandam Lane, which despite its name was not much more than an alley sitting behind the wharves lining the north side of the Thames to the east of London Bridge. "See that slop shop, cabby?" the Mummer called to the driver perched over their heads. "Right to the other side of that, if you please."

The cabby pulled past "Abner's Nautical Outfitters, Uniforms for all Principal Lines" and stopped before the unmarked door on the far side. The Mummer tossed him a shilling and hopped down. "Here we are," he told Barnett. "Come along."

Barnett climbed out of the cab and stepped gingerly through the muddy street to the sidewalk. In the late afternoon light the building he faced seemed to have a strange and exotic character. Three stories high, it was constructed from ruddy bricks that might have seen service in some ancient Celtic fortress and then lain buried for two thousand years before being resurrected for their present use in this Upper Swandam Lane facade. There were no windows on the ground floor, and those on the second and third were fitted with great iron shutters, crusted with layers of maroon paint. The front door, large enough to pass a four-wheeled carriage when opened, was similarly of iron, and featureless except for six iron bands bolted to it in a crisscross pattern and a small window at eye level, not more than four inches square.

"What is this place?" Barnett asked.

"What would you say it was?" the Mummer responded.

"The treasure house of some Indian maharaja," Barnett said, staring up at the building, "who's in London buying modern plumbing supplies for his palace."

The Mummer cocked his head to one side and stared up at Barnett's face, as though half afraid he might have said something funny. And then, reassured, he went and stood in front of the great iron door.

Inside of half a minute the peephole in the door opened and someone within examined them carefully. *That's peculiar*, Barnett mused. *How did he know we were out here?*

A small door, which had been artfully concealed by the pattern of iron bands in the large door, sprang inward, and a Chinese boy in his mid-teens, wearing a frock coat and a bowler hat, nodded and smiled at them from inside. "Mr. Mummer," he said, "and, as I trust, Mr. Barnett. Please enter."

The Mummer nodded Barnett through the door and then stepped in after him. "Afternoon, Low," he said. "Where's your dad?"

The youth had closed the small door and slid two heavy bolts silently into place. "Come," he said. They were in a large room filled with orderly rows of packing cases stacked one atop the other. Two gas mantles affixed to stone pillars near the door were lit, but out of their circle of harsh light the area quickly receded into gloom and then into utter black. It was impossible to judge the size of the room, but Barnett instinctively felt that it was immense.

The Chinese youth picked up a lantern and led them down the aisle to an iron staircase and then preceded them up to the next floor.

At the top of the stairs they passed through an anteroom into a medium-sized room that was fitted out like an antique store or a curio shop. The iron shutters were thrown back on the two windows and the late afternoon sun shone directly in, illuminating some of the finest Oriental furniture and pottery that Barnett had ever seen. A teak cabinet and several brass-fitted teak traveling chests were along the wall. In the middle of the room a large walnut table inlaid with ivory dragons at the four corners attracted Barnett's attention. He had a slight knowledge of Chinese furniture, which was in vogue in Paris at the moment, and he had never seen anything so fine. And the dragons were representations of the Imperial dragon—forbidden to anyone not of Manchu blood.

"I never thought I'd say this about a piece of furniture," Barnett said, "but this is the most beautiful thing I've ever seen."

The boy nodded and smiled. "My father's," he said. "Come." He led the way past rows of delicate vases with the traditional patterns of long-defunct dynasties to another staircase, and they followed him up to the third floor. (*Second floor,* Barnett reminded himself. *Here it's ground floor, first floor, second floor. When in London . . ."*)

This floor was again one long room, but a row of windows and a mosaic of skylights in the ceiling flooded it with what was left of the daylight. The room was divided into sections: one held several large tables and drafting boards; another had a small furnace or forge resting on a stone slab; across the room was a complex of interconnected chemical apparatus on a scale several times larger than that in Professor Moriarty's basement laboratory. The whole center area had been cleared out and the floorboards scrubbed clean, and long bolts of white silk were laid out on it in a complex pattern that meant nothing to Barnett. Several men in white smocks and felt slippers were crouched on different parts of the pattern industriously sewing one section of white silk to another section of white silk. It looked to Barnett like makework in a madhouse.

It was then that Barnett noticed the tall, stoop-shouldered figure of Professor Moriarty hovering about one of the drawing boards. He held a pencil in one hand and a large gutta percha eraser in the other, and he alternately attacked a paper pinned to the board with one and then the other. Standing at his right shoulder, peering intently at the drawing growing under Moriarty's hand, was a tall, thin, elderly Chinese in a sea-green silk robe. Every time Moriarty drew in a line or wrote down a figure, the Chinese gentleman ran the fingers of his left hand along a small ivory abacus he held in his right and then murmured a few words into Moriarty's left ear.

With the Mummer tagging close behind him, Barnett strode across the room to join Moriarty.

"Ah, Barnett," Moriarty said, glancing up from his work, "Tolliver. Just on time, I see."

" 'Course," the Mummer said.

"Mr. Benjamin Barnett," Moriarty said, "allow me to introduce Prince Tseng Li-chang, a former minister from the court of the son of Heaven to various Western nations, and quite possibly the finest mathematical mind of the nineteenth century. Mr. Barnett, as I mentioned, is a journalist."

Prince Tseng bowed. "Professor Moriarty has told me something of your travail, Mr. Barnett," he said in a deep, precise voice. "I trust you shall find your period of association with Professor Moriarty to be a stimulating and rewarding experience. He has an incisive mind, quick as a crossbow dart; it is only his occasional companionship that makes my years of exile tolerable."

Barnett's journalist's ear perked up. "Exile?" he repeated.

Prince Tseng nodded sadly. "My step-cousin-in-law, the Empress Dowager Tz'u-hsi, who rules China through her adopted son, the Emperor Kuang-hsü, has no use for Western ways. She chooses to believe that if you ignore the barbarians at the gates and insult their envoys, they will go quietly away. I advised her otherwise and she did not wish to listen. Soon she no longer wanted to see me or tolerate my presence. I was allowed to request the privilege of residing elsewhere."

"And so the Empress Dowager has lost a valuable advisor," Moriarty said. "And I have gained a trusted friend."

"Say," Barnett said, "if you don't mind my asking, what is all this?" He swept his hand around to indicate all the diverse activities that filled the room.

"This is my factory," Professor Moriarty said. "On the floor below, Prince Tseng manufactures antiques, while up here I create dreams."

"Two conundrums," Barnett said.

"Not at all, not at all," Prince Tseng said. "Here, look!" He went to a ring set into the floor and pulled it up, opening a three-foot-square trapdoor which led down to the floor below. Squatting by the opening, he gestured down. "There you see my workshop. There are my skilled artisans engaged in re-creating the T'ang, the Sung, the Yüan, and the Ming dynasties through representations of their art. Very precise representations."

Barnett gingerly approached the square hole in the floor. Directly below, a row of young women with kerchiefs tied around their heads sat before a long table. Each of them was painting patterns on a piece of unfired pottery with a fine Chinese brush.

"There is a great demand for the antiquities of my country, Mr. Barnett," Prince Tseng said. "It is a vogue—a fad. Unfortunately, very few of these objects have left my country. But the demand must be filled, must it not?" He dropped the trapdoor back into place and stood up.

"That's very interesting," Barnett said, for want of anything better to say. He was in the curious position of not knowing what reaction to have. Here was a prince of the royal family of China—if he was to be believed—presently in exile for unpopular political opinions, who supported himself by manufacturing fake Chinese antiques.

"Not all that interesting, Mr. Barnett," Prince Tseng said. "It's very mundane, really. It's what I must do to finance my work."

"You mean all this?" Barnett asked, gesturing around the room.

"No, sir. My work takes place in my homeland."

"All this," Professor Moriarty interrupted, "is mine. My responsibility entirely. Prince Tseng is good enough to aid me with the calculations and with his scientific insight, but the project is mine."

Barnett looked around the room again. The workers seemed to have tacitly agreed that it was time to quit for the day; they had gathered at a row of wooden lockers and were exchanging their smocks and slippers for street clothes. "I hope this doesn't appear a naive question," Barnett said, "but just what is going on in here?"

"You see before you," Moriarty said, indicating the neat mounds of white silk with a wave of his hand, "the beginnings of what is to become the world's first aerostat observatory."

"Aerostat—"

"An aerostat is a balloon that is filled with some gaseous substance which makes it lighter than air," Prince Tseng said.

"Yes," Barnett said. "Of course. My Uncle Ben was a balloonist in McClellan's army during the Rebellion. After the war he used to give exhibition balloon rides at county fairs. I helped him for a summer, and he taught me a bit about ballooning. It's the juxtaposition of the two words that puzzled me. Does an aerostat observatory observe aerostats or observe from an aerostat?"

"Ah!" Moriarty said. "Our journalistic friend possesses both a practical knowledge of ballooning and a rudimentary sense of humor. A valuable assistant, indeed. I don't trust a man without a sense of humor. For your enlightenment, Barnett"—Moriarty swiveled one of the large, wheeled chalkboards around, revealing a drawing pinned to the reverse side—"this is what the apparatus will look like. It is designed to rise up into the comparatively tranquil air that prevails four or five miles above the earth. It will carry an astronomical telescope of special design and a crew of five: two to work the aerostat and three to perform the experiments and observations."

The drawing, a carefully lined rendering, showed a cluster of balloon gasbags surrounding a central core that must have been the telescope. An elongated, closed gondola was suspended below, and various pieces of equipment, the purpose of which Barnett could not even guess at, were shown affixed to the sides of the gondola.

"Trapped as we are beneath a vast ocean of air that randomly refracts, reflects, and otherwise distorts the rays of light which pass through it," Moriarty said, "we cannot hope to observe properly, much less understand, the universe which we are immersed in and are a part of. And until we manage to understand properly at least the elemental laws by which the universe is run, we cannot hope to begin to understand ourselves: our design, our function, and our purpose, if any."

"Surely," Barnett said, "you can't hope to loft a telescope of any appreciable size with a bunch of balloons."

"True," Moriarty said, returning the chalk board to its original position, "but my calculations indicate that once above nine-tenths of the Earth's atmosphere, a five-inch refractor should achieve a clarity of vision that not even a twenty-inch one achieves on the ground. The twenty-inch has more gathering power, it is true, but in many cases that merely serves to make the blur brighter. Every astronomer has had the experience of having his field of vision become crystal-clear for just one instant, so the nebulosity he is staring at is as sharp as if etched on glass. But before he can put pencil to paper, the atmosphere has again transformed the image to a wavering, flickering blur too indistinct to understand correctly."

"What do you hope to accomplish with your aerostat telescope?" Barnett asked.

Moriarty shook his head. "I may discover the innermost secrets of the universe," he said. "Or then again, I may discover that through some hidden flaw I failed to anticipate, I get no usable information at all from the apparatus. As a very old friend of mine once told me, 'There is no shame in playing the cards that have been dealt to you as long as you play them to the best of your ability.' It was, of course, in another context." Moriarty looked around him. "Well, we seem to have done everything we can for today, gentlemen," he said. "Let us return to Russell Square and see what Mrs. Randall has prepared for us in the way of a supper. I think I could fancy a bit of mutton tonight, and I seem to remember Mrs. H saying something about mutton before I left the house. May I invite you to dine with us this evening, Prince Tseng?"

Tseng Li-chang bowed. "I think not, Professor," he said. "Many thanks for inviting me, but I think my son and I had best stay in this evening and partake of our own poor repast. He has lessons to do, and I could profitably use the time."

"Just as you say," Moriarty said. "I shall see you, then, within the week. Tolliver—go over to the cabstand on Commercial Road and see if you can pick us up a growler. We'll be downstairs."

"Have it here in half a minute, Professor," the Mummer said, and the little man darted back down the stairs, his jacket flapping.

TEN

THE FOUR-WHEELER

A man must make his opportunity,
as oft as find it.
—FRANCIS BACON

As the four-wheeler headed placidly toward Russell Square, Moriarty crossed his arms, lowered his chin onto his clavicle, and sank into a deep reverie. His eyes were open, but it was clear that his thoughts were elsewhere. Mummer Tolliver settled in one corner of the gently swaying growler and whistled to himself with a peculiar tuneless syncopation while rolling a half-crown back and forth along the backs of his fingers. He obviously was prepared to continue this occupation indefinitely.

Barnett stared out the window at the passing London scene. He had several disquieting notions to consider.

"You're right," Moriarty said suddenly, interrupting his thoughts. "I am a criminal. Does this distress you?"

"I'm not sure," Barnett said. "I haven't really . . ." He looked up in astonishment. "How the devil did you know what I was thinking."

Moriarty chuckled dryly. "My attention returned from the abstruse world of mathematics to the interior of this growler," he said, "to find you staring out the window. Then you glanced surreptitiously at Tolliver several times and back out the window. As we were passing Newgate Prison at the time, it was not hard to surmise your thoughts—at least in their general outline. The process of association is almost unavoidable, I have found. Tolliver has recently told you of his criminal background, and the sight of Newgate reminded you of this."

"I recall something like that going through my head," Barnett admitted.

"Then you looked from Tolliver to me, glanced back out the window, stared at your feet, and shuddered slightly. You were considering the possibility of your new association putting you back behind stone walls. I confess that for a second I thought it might be merely a memory of Stamboul, but the shudder was too prolonged for that—so you were clearly viewing a return to the life of a felon. Therefore, you are afraid that your new employment might meet with disfavor in the eyes of the authorities. You have decided, or perhaps deduced, that I am engaged in illegal activities—that I am a criminal."

Barnett leaned back in the leather seat and stared at Moriarty. "What a weak chain of inference!" he said.

"It's hard, almost impossible, properly to verbalize the complicated and complex chain of interrelated data that allows a genius to arrive at the correct inductive answer," Moriarty said. "Especially in human relationships. The tilt of a head, the twist of a knee, the inclination of the elbows, and a thousand other factors are analyzed by the unconscious brain without ever coming fully to conscious attention. The attempt to describe it is doomed to suffer from excessive simplification and generalization. The test, therefore, is in the accuracy of the observation. Did I pass that test?"

Barnett nodded. "Yes, sir," he said. "I will admit it; that is what I was thinking. Although you will excuse me if I continue to consider it as mostly a lucky guess."

Moriarty smiled. "In science," he said, "the test of validity is reproduceability. Keep that in mind, Barnett, as we march into the future together."

The occupants of the four-wheeler remained silent for several minutes. Then Moriarty said, "Now about my, ah, criminal activities. Do you regret accepting employment with a criminal?"

"I don't know, Professor. There are crimes, and then there are crimes."

"A brilliant observation," Moriarty commented. "Am I to understand by this that there are some crimes you would condone and others you would find opprobrious?"

"I think that's true of everyone," Barnett said.

"Not so!" Moriarty said. "Most individuals in our enlightened society would neither commit nor condone any crime. They would cheerfully allow a child of twelve to starve to death working twelve hours a day over a shuttle-loom for a shilling a week; but then that is not a crime." He raised his hand. "But just let—Wait a second! What's that?"

"What?" Barnett asked, peering around.

"Do you hear that?"

"I hear nothing wrong," Barnett said, listening intently. "As a matter of fact, I can't hear anything over the horse's hooves."

"Indeed!" Moriarty said. "And the horse has just gone over wooden planking, such as is installed in the street to cover a temporary excavation for sewer lines and the like." He tried the door handle. "And, as there is no such excavation on the direct route to Russell Square, I deduce we have taken the wrong turning. We are now on Grey's Inn Road, I believe."

"Perhaps the jarvey knows a shortcut," the Mummer suggested, from his corner of the four-wheeler.

"And perhaps he's fixed the door handles so we won't fall out and hurt ourselves," Moriarty said.

"How's that?" the Mummer said. He tried the handle on his side and found it immoveable. "Why, that bloody barsted," he said, his voice raised in indignation. "What's the name of 'is game anyway?"

"Now, now, Mummer," Moriarty said, "don't lose your aitches; it's taken you long enough to acquire them."

"What's happening?" Barnett asked. "Won't the doors open?"

"They won't. And what's happening is that we're being abducted," Moriarty said, "like in one of the popular novels. Although I don't believe your virtue is in any danger." He wiggled a finger at Tolliver. "I thought I warned you about taking the first cab in the rank."

"Wasn't any rank," the Mummer said. "The growler was proceeding down the bloody street and I hailed him."

"Indeed," Moriarty said. "How convenient." He rapped on the roof of the four-wheeler with his stick. "Cabby!" he called. There was no response. Barnett wondered whether he had expected one.

Moriarty leaned forward in his seat, resting his chin on his hands, which were laced over the ivory handle of his stick. "This seems inane," he said. "They surely can't expect us to just sit here until the carriage arrives at some secret destination. My first inclination is to do just that, to learn who we are dealing with. But our mysterious adversaries will surely try to do away with us, growler and all, at the first opportunity. I'd suggest we exit from this clarence cab lockbox as expeditiously as possible. Mummer, remove that window and try the outside knob."

"It don't roll down, Professor," the Mummer said.

"I didn't suppose it would," the professor said. "Break the glass!"

The Mummer took a cosh from his belt and broke the glass out of the window on his side of the four-wheeler, while Moriarty used his stick to do the same on the other side.

"It don't open from the outside neither," the Mummer called.

"Remove the rest of the glass," Moriarty said, "and get out the window. Fast!"

There were a couple of thumping noises from overhead, and Barnett saw the cabby swing off his seat and drop to the street, where he fell, quickly regained his feet, and disappeared from view as the four-wheeler continued to move on at an accelerated pace.

"Whatever's going to happen is going to happen now," Barnett cried. "The jarvey's just left us."

The cab jounced and clattered down the street, lurching madly from side to side as the tempo of the horse's gait changed from a placid trot to a frenetic gallop.

"I rather think the jarvey did something to annoy our steed as a parting gesture," Moriarty said, knocking the remaining shards of glass out of the window on his side. "Thus enhancing an already interesting experience. Mr. Barnett, if you would make your way to the street through this window . . ."

Barnett looked out at the pavement, which was passing under the wheels of the cab at a dizzying speed. Then he glanced across the cab at Tolliver, who was already most of the way out of the window on his side. He shrugged. "This will ruin my suit," he said. Grabbing the leather strap above the door, he swung his legs out the window, twisted through, and dropped.

The cab swerved just as he let go, and he fell heavily on his side and slid across the cobblestones. A second later, Moriarty followed him out the window, hitting the ground feet-first, and then rolling forward in the *baritsu* manner to absorb the impact before coming neatly to his feet again.

The cab, now bouncing and clattering wildly behind an increasingly frenzied horse, barely missed a carter's wagon to its left and then careened into a lamppost on the right. Bouncing off the lamppost, it twisted over until it was riding on just two wheels. The traces gave way under the twisting force, and the horse, suddenly freed, raced off down the street. The four-wheeler righted itself again, now heading directly toward a bank on the corner. As it reached the curb, it exploded in a cloud of black smoke, sending wood and iron fragments hurtling through the air to clatter against the walls and breaking windows up and down the block. Barnett instinctively covered his face with his arms, but miraculously none of the fragments touched him.

When most of the debris had come to rest, Barnett got up and dusted himself off. His leg burned where he had scraped it, and his good French frock coat and trousers were now suitable only for the dustbin, but there seemed to be no other damage done. He looked around and saw Moriarty crossing the road to where Mummer Tolliver was lying. The Mummer's tiny body, one leg twisted at an unnatural angle, lay quite still. Somehow, despite the explosion debris and dust all around him, Tolliver's checkered suit and yellow spats were still neat and spotlessly clean, but his face was covered with blood.

Moriarty knelt by the Mummer and cleaned his face off with his pocket handkerchief. Cautiously he straightened the twisted leg and then undid the Mummer's tight high collar and loosened his cravat. "He's breathing," he told Barnett. "Let us get him home."

"Shouldn't we take him to the nearest hospital?" Barnett asked.

"St. Bartholomew's is probably the closest hospital," Moriarty said. "And my house is quite a bit closer, a good bit cleaner, and has most of the facilities." Lifting Tolliver as gently as he would a small child, Moriarty rose. "Flag down that cab," he directed Barnett. "We'll stop at the house first, and then you go on to Cavendish Square and bring back a physician named Breckstone. He's the only man in London I'd trust to treat anything more complicated than a head cold."

Barnett hailed the growler, which was busy trying to turn around and avoid the blocked far end of the street. A uniformed policeman came around the corner at a dead run as they boarded the cab. "Here, here," he yelled, continuing past them toward the wreckage. "What's all this?"

ELEVEN

THE SCENT

When you have eliminated the impossible, whatever remains, however improbable, must be the truth.
— SIR ARTHUR CONAN DOYLE

I have been remiss," Moriarty said. "I have allowed my own interests, my own desires, to distract me from an assignment which I accepted in all good faith, just because there is no one here to prod me into activity. While I have been concerning myself with anomalies in the orbit of an asteriod, Trepoff has been planting his infernal devices about me with the assiduity of a British gardener setting roses."

"It would seem so," Barnett said. It was the morning after the exploding four-wheeler, and Moriarty had called Barnett into his study after the latter had finished his breakfast.

"As a result of my stupidity, Tolliver nearly lost his life. Had he indeed died, I would never have forgiven myself," Moriarty said, pacing back and forth in the small area between his desk and the bookcase upon which rested his clipping books. "It is one thing for me to blithely ignore these threats and sidestep these attacks while pursuing my own affairs. It is quite another for me to subject my associates to these dangers without at least giving them a chance to engage themselves in the Trepoff affair."

"How is the Mummer?" Barnett asked, in part to find out and in part to get Moriarty off a line of self-abasement that Barnett found uncomfortable.

"Doctor Breckstone was here again this morning, before you descended," Moriarty said, with just possibly a hint of reproach in his voice. "The haematoma over the right parietal has somewhat subsided and it looks as though there is no underlying fracture. Aside from a severe headache, which Doctor Breckstone feels should subside in a day or so, and some minor abrasions, Tolliver is none the worse for his experience. You might go up and see him."

"I shall," Barnett said.

"Good. He refuses opiates for his headache, so he remains quite querulous. I don't like him snapping at the maids, and Mrs. H is far too busy. Go and let him snap at you for a while so he won't take it out on the domestic help."

"I'm glad to discover that I have some useful function in this establishment," Barnett said, smiling ruefully. "And here I was beginning to think that you had nothing for me to do."

"On the contrary, I have a great deal for you to do," Moriarty said. He gave up pacing and sat down in the large leather chair behind his desk. "I have been giving some thought to the Trepoff problem, and you figure prominently in my plans."

"Say, Professor," Barnett said, "just exactly who, or what, is this Trepoff you keep talking about?"

"Trepoff is the man who blew up our clarence cab last evening. He is the man who committed the crime you were accused and convicted of in Constantinople."

Barnett thought about this for a minute. "Trepoff is the fellow the Russians want you to catch," he said.

"That's correct."

"Who is he?"

"Nobody knows," Moriarty said. "Let me explain." And inside of ten minutes he had told Barnett all that he knew of Trepoff and the Belye Krystall, withholding nothing. It was Moriarty's usual practice to burden his associates with no more information than they needed to perform their tasks, but on the Trepoff matter, there was, so far, not sufficient information to be selective about it.

While Moriarty spoke, Barnett longed to take out his small pocket notebook and jot down the facts in his private journalistic shorthand, but he fought the impulse. In his new position he was going to have to learn to rely more on his memory and less on his pencil. "It's a fascinating problem," he said when Moriarty had finished. "I don't see how to get a handle on it: finding a man you've never seen and can't identify in the midst of the world's largest city in time to prevent him from committing an unknown atrocity."

"It is a challenge," Moriarty admitted. "Although it is only the time constraint that makes it interesting. Any population can be sifted through for one individual member, given sufficient time. I have already begun several lines of inquiry. I confess I should have done more."

"I'll say," Barnett said.

Moriarty stared steadily at Barnett. "Perhaps your keener intellect has grasped some fact that has eluded me," he said. "You have some suggestion as to what course of action I should initiate?"

"I'm sorry, Professor," Barnett said. "I didn't mean it that way. It's just that—well—clearly, something has to be done."

"Quite right," Moriarty said. "And if it were your decision, what would you do? I did not mean to sound disparaging of your intellect; it is for that and for your extensive journalistic experience that I am employing you. So, as a journalist, if you were assigned to track down Trepoff for a story, how would you go about it?"

"Don't humor me, Professor," Barnett said. "If I spoke out of turn, I'm sorry."

"No, no," Moriarty said. "I have around me entirely too many men who are afraid to speak out of turn. Conversational interplay is a great aid to focusing one's thoughts on the subject at hand. Please do not ever allow my unfortunate tendency toward the sarcastic rejoinder to deter you from questioning, suggesting, or amplifying as you see fit. And I was quite serious in my question: How would you go about locating the elusive Trepoff?"

"Well," Barnett considered. "There are areas in London where Russian émigrés are known to congregate. That's probably the place to start."

"Quite right," Moriarty said. "And that is, indeed, where I began. There are nine revolutionary clubs run by expatriate Russians in the East End, of which the Bohemian Club seems to be the most popular. The center for intrigue, however, is a smaller establishment called the Balalaika. Behind and above the public rooms at the Balalaika are a complex of private rooms, in which all manner of scheming and plotting against every government in Europe would seem to go on. The owner, a Mr. Petruchian, has agreed to aid us, and one of my agents is now stationed behind the bar."

Barnett whistled softly. "You got the owner of an anarchist bar to help you? What do you have on him?"

"Petruchian is not himself an anarchist, you understand—merely the proprietor of a club. And while he might not be averse to an occasional bombing in St. Petersburg or Vienna, he is a loyal citizen of Britain. When I explained to him—after I had established my *bona fides*—that an atrocity was planned against his adopted homeland, he was eager to help."

Barnett would have been fascinated to find out how Professor Moriarty had established his *"bona fides,"* but he knew better than to inquire. Instead, he asked, "Have you found anything?"

"Precisely nothing."

"Do you know what you're looking for?"

"It would be enough to discover someone who is whispering of plots against some target here in Britain. Trepoff is probably recruiting his men from among the ranks of the genuine anarchists, but if so, he is being too subtle for me."

"Well, he certainly knows where you are," Barnett said.

"A fact that I have been hoping to put to good use," Moriarty said. "I have managed to trace three of the men who attempted to kill me, including last night's jehu. But they've all been hirelings, who know nothing of their employer." He slapped his hand down on the desk vehemently. "It is time to go on the offensive," he said, "before the man manages to kill one of us by sheer luck."

"You said you have something for me to do," Barnett said. "What is it? I confess I can't think of anything helpful."

"Ah, yes," Moriarty said. He leaned forward across the desk. "I want you to go to Fleet Street," he said, "and reacquaint yourself with your profession. I want you to become familiar with all the important dailies. Get to know the journalists who work for them."

"Sounds easy enough," Barnett said, "except for one thing— what do I tell them I'm doing there, and who do I say I am?"

"Your name is Benjamin Barnett," Moriarty said, "and you are going to open a news bureau. An American news bureau, I rather think. Rent an office in the area and hire a competent secretary; you'll need one for my plan in any case. Put a sign on the door. Something on the order of: 'Barnett's Anglo-American Telegraphic News Service.' I leave the exact wording to you."

"What happens when some random Turkish newsman or government official happens on the name 'Benjamin Barnett'?" Barnett asked.

"Ah, yes," Moriarty said. "That's the other thing I wished to see you about. I have good news for you: you are dead."

"What?"

"As far as the Ottoman government is concerned, you are dead. Shot while trying to escape, or something very like that. So the Gurra-Pasha reported to the Sultan, and so it shall be."

"Why would he do that?" Barnett asked.

"Better not look a gift Pasha in the mouth," Moriarty said. "I would assume he was trying to cover up the escape to protect his reputation. He waited a couple of weeks to make sure you were really gone and then officially notified Abd-ul Hamid Khan the Second, Sultan of Sultans, King of Kings, Shadow of God upon Earth, that you were killed while escaping. Thus he managed to please himself, Abd-ul Hamid, and you all at once, and hurt nobody. Would that all human intercourse were that simple."

Barnett nodded. "Such a short life," he said, "but lived to the full. I shall have to get the copy of the *New York World* that has my obituary and see what they have to say about me."

"A unique opportunity," Moriarty agreed. "I trust you will not be disappointed."

"At any rate that is certainly good news—and I wonder how many people would say that after being informed of their own deaths."

"Anyone of whom the report was in error, I fancy, would at least be amused. For the others I will not venture to speak."

"There's no chance that someone seeing my name or encountering me will report it to the Ottoman government?"

"There's every chance it will be reported. And no chance the report will be anything but studiously ignored. Would you like to be the one who informs the King of Kings that you had made a slight mistake in regard to the death of a prisoner?"

"I see what you mean," Barnett said. "Now, back to Fleet Street. I am to open a news service. What sort of news?"

"Anything out of the ordinary," Moriarty said. "I feel sure that there are many stories that come into a newspaper every day that are not used because they prove to be insufficiently interesting or questionably factual."

"That's so," Barnett said. "I'd say less than half of the stories that come over a city desk ever see print."

"And one class of these unused stories would be the unique event that looks as though it would be newsworthy if more information could be developed, but that additional information never comes to light—is that so?"

"Right," Barnett agreed. "That happens all the time. Someone comes up with one fascinating fact that looks as though there is a great story behind it, and you investigate it and get nowhere. And you never know for sure if there was anything there or not. And, of course, you can't use the story because you have insufficient information."

"These are the stories," Moriarty said, "in which I wish you to be most interested. This is where the spoor of Trepoff is to be found. You must look for the merest hints and traces, for this man will most assuredly cover his tracks with the cunning of a jungle beast."

"But what am I to look for?" Barnett asked. "How can I tell when one of these stories relates to Trepoff?"

"You must first eliminate those incidents which cursory investigation will show do not relate to Trepoff or the Belye Krystall. What is left you will write up and put into a notebook. I shall periodically go through the notebook and tell you which items warrant further consideration. Investigate bizarre crimes, seemingly senseless cruelties, and insane acts; look for the unique masquerading as the commonplace."

Barnett shook his head. "I'm sorry if I appear dense, Professor, but I'm still not clear on what sort of thing it would be most profitable to look at. Perhaps if you could give me some example . . ."

Moriarty stared at his laced fingers and thought for a moment. "Rather than an example," he said, "let me give you an analogy. Trepoff is like a general in some field army preparing for a battle. He will have his scouts out surveying the land; he will have training exercises for his troops; he will be preparing his logistics and supply; his spies will be probing for the enemy's weak points; his armorer may be preparing and testing weapons; and so on. I'm sure you can extend the analogy yourself well into the ridiculous. And each of these activities will leave a trace for the observer who knows what he is looking for—and looking at.

"Our problem is that we don't know precisely what we are looking for, so we shall have to examine a mass of inconsequentia to establish the relevance of what we are looking at. Can you follow this rather stretched-out line of metaphor?"

"I think so," Barnett said. "I hope so." He stood up. "I'll get to it."

"Good!" Moriarty said. "Other members of my organization will be out searching for data, each in his own specialized way, but I am very hopeful of the journalistic approach." He looked up at Barnett through narrowed eyelids. "Be careful!" he said. "Remember that in this game murder is an acceptable move."

"I'll keep it in mind," Barnett said.

TREPOFF

There are a thousand doors to let out life.
—PHILIP MASSINGER

In another quarter of London, in a small interior room lit only by a single candle, a man sat behind a screen. In front of the screen three men stood silently at attention.

"You are agreed?" the man behind the screen asked in a harsh whisper, beginning the litany.

"We are agreed," the three replied.

"You know there is no turning back?"

"There is no turning back," they repeated.

"You are completely dedicated to our sacred cause?"

"With our hands," they replied in unison, "with our heads, and with our hearts!"

"So do you each, separately, swear?"

"I do," each of the three answered, separately.

"On your life?"

"On my life."

"And on the lives of your parents and those you hold most dear?"

And then the three swore this solemn oath, although they did it perhaps a bit more slowly.

"Good," the man behind the screen said. "You are now members of the organization which has no name so that it cannot be betrayed. You will know only each other. You will make no attempt to find out my identity or the identity of anyone else who may communicate with you on behalf of the organization which has no name. You will obey orders willingly and without hesitation, no matter what the order might be. You will do this so that your children will be free.

"The penalty for disobeying orders is death.

"The penalty for betrayal is death.

"The penalty for failure is death.

"Are there any questions?"

The three shuffled nervously and looked at each other. "These orders," one of them finally asked; "how may we know that they come from you?"

"You are Gregory?" the man behind the screen asked.

Gregory nodded, then, realizing that the man behind the screen couldn't see him, said, "Yes."

"Good. You will be the leader of this cell. You will be taught a simple cipher and a series of code words. Orders will then be given to you to be passed on to the others."

Gregory nodded again. "That is good," he said.

"Go now," the man behind the screen said.

The three left, and the man behind the screen went to a small concealed panel in the wall and opened it and stared pensively through. When he had satisfied himself that the three had indeed left the building, and not merely the room, he closed the panel and used the candle to light the two gas fixtures on the wall. A few seconds later another man—tall, thin, ascetic-looking, dressed like a clergyman—entered the room through the door behind the screen. "Well?" he said.

"We'll see."

"They'll do," the tall man said.

"Anyone will do! Men are just tools. Handled properly, they will do the job you put them to; handled wrong, they will botch it."

"For some jobs," the tall man murmured, "you need the right tools."

The other considered this. "True," he said. "I mustn't commit the error of believing that all my—tools—are interchangeable. There is one job that has eluded success several times now."

"Moriarty."

"Yes. The professor of mathematics. Hirelings have not proved capable of handling him. I have avoided using our own people for fear that if they fail, they would lead him inevitably back here. We must assume that he is as cunning as we have been told, although I have seen no remarkable signs of it. He seems to escape our—arrangements—mostly by blind luck."

"Perhaps he is prescient," the tall man suggested. "Like that gentleman at the Music Hall who reads minds."

"I thought he was for a moment," the other said, "when I found that he had followed me to Constantinople. But it was pure chance. Pure chance."

The tall man sat down at a table by the far wall. "I have had a reply from St. Petersburg," he said.

"Ah, yes," the other said. He lit a small cigar and then blew out the candle. "And it said what?"

"The skilled men you require have been located. Transportation is being arranged."

"Excellent!"

"They do not speak English."

"No matter. It would be best if they did not speak at all, but that is too much to be hoped. How long?"

"Before they arrive, you mean? I don't know. It didn't say. Soon enough, I imagine."

"It cannot be soon enough. Training should have begun already. We cannot leave anything to chance. My plans are complete, and we commence the operation at once."

"What of Moriarty?"

"He is one of the only two men in London—in England—that could stand in our way. The police—bah! They are ill-trained incompetents. The infamous British Secret Service is otherwise occupied at present. But Professor James Moriarty, whom our brothers have seen fit to employ against us, and that notorious busybody, Mr. Sherlock Holmes, are very real threats. At the least they threaten to expose us, and discovery is tantamount to failure."

"Sherlock Holmes, the consulting detective?"

"Yes."

"He is aware of us?"

"Mr. Holmes has stumbled across one or two of our activities without realizing what they were. Curiously enough, he insists upon attributing them to Professor Moriarty. They seem to dislike each other. But Mr. Holmes is an astute observer, usually with an uncanny ability to draw the correct inference from a mass of seemingly unrelated data. He is sure to be called in to investigate certain aspects, certain outward manifestations, of our great plot as it progresses toward fruition. If so, it is possible that he will ascertain the truth. And if he fails, then we shall still have the professor of mathematics dogging our heels."

The tall man nodded thoughtfully. "It is clear that these two threats must be removed," he said.

"A successful commander," the other said, "uses his enemy's strengths against him. These two men represent our enemy's greatest strength; and I think I have devised a way to use them against each other. It requires but minor revisions in the great plan."

"Perhaps we should just have them removed," the tall man said. "Dead men cannot cause trouble."

"Dead men also cannot help," the other replied. "In my new plan the professor of mathematics and the consulting detective will unwittingly aid us. And *then* they will die. It will be humorous, no?"

"Show me!" the tall man demanded.

The other took out a small notebook. "Follow the scheme," he said. "See how the pieces fit together and one follows naturally from the one before. All culminating in the Supreme Act. It is elegant."

"Trace the steps," the tall man said.

"Listen!" the other commanded.

And he talked long into the night.

THIRTEEN

FLEET STREET

The moving finger writes . . .
—OMAR KHAYYÁM

London wears her history on her streets: the buildings, the facades, the monuments, the heroic statuary, the ornamental ironwork, the street signs, and even the paving stones. But especially the street signs. In any given mile, an average London street has only twelve blocks, but it can change names three times. As Oxford Street, for example, heads east, it becomes in turn New Oxford Street, Holborn, High Holborn, Holborn Viaduct, Newgate Street, Cheapside, and Poultry. And all of this in under two miles.

Benjamin Barnett, used to the grid-pattern uniformity of New York or the great boulevards of Paris, found the zigzag maze of London streets a constant delight. Each street, sometimes each block, had its own character, its own air, its own voice. Barnett walked the streets as much as he could over the next few weeks, trying to attain that distinctive intimacy with the city that would make him a good reporter. To know London intimately, of course, would take years, and even then he would really know only that part of the city which had become his "beat."

But if he was going to do his job, to help the professor in his search for the abnormal, he was going to have to learn what was normal in this, the largest city in the world and the center of the world's greatest empire.

Learning what was accepted was not difficult: the standards were pretty much the same over the civilized world these last decades of the nineteenth century. But the uncivilized world did not begin in Asia or darkest Africa; it peered around the corner in Lambeth, it waited in alleys in the East End, it skulked along the wharves and docks fronting the Thames. So Barnett had to go beyond what was accepted; he had to know what was condoned, condemned, controlled, misunderstood, overlooked, winked at, persecuted, prosecuted, and ignored. In these places lies the job of a reporter. It is in the interconnection of these elements that news is created.

Barnett found office space on the top floor of a small building on Whitefriars Street, just south of Fleet Street. He equipped it with a desk, a Grandall typewriter, a box of pencils, two reams of yellow paper, and a wastepaper basket, and felt at home. After much thought he found a sign painter and had him inscribe AMERICAN NEWS SERVICE across the door with *B. Barnett* in much smaller letters under it.

The next step, before he saw any of the British working press, was to establish his *bona fides*. There was no point in faking something that could just as easily be legitimate. He made up a list of New York and Boston newspapers that might take filler material from him—he'd worry about the rest of the country later. To start with, he sent a cable to his last employer, the *New York World*:

> Now working for American News Service comma
> London stop will you take news at space rates plus
> cable charges questionmark we pay for query
> comma you specify inches
>
> BENJAMIN BARNETT

Within four hours, the fastest turnaround time Barnett had ever seen on the transatlantic cable, he had his reply from the *World*, signed by Hardesty Gores, the managing editor himself:

> Why arent you in prison
>
> GORES

Barnett read the cable and scribbled a short reply for the boy to take back.

> I died
>
> BARNETT

The next morning, when Barnett arrived at the office to supervise the hanging of curtains and a few other necessary amenities, another cable from the *World* awaited him:

Want exclusive your personal story stop will take
to one hundred inches space rates

GORES

So there was his first account. And an interesting challenge it
would be, too, to write the story of his incarceration and escape
without violating the terms of his agreement with the professor. He'd
have to work on that one.

Barnett sent cables to the other papers on his list and turned his
attention to getting to know the editors and journalists of Fleet
Street. He started with the morning papers, which traditionally have
the better local reporting staff. A morning paper usually has the late-
breaking news and has to whip it into shape and dish it out for its
readers' breakfast enjoyment. An evening paper has time to reflect
and specializes in perspective and analysis of the news it gets from
the morning papers. Or so it was in New York, and so Barnett assumed it would be in London.

Within the next two days, Barnett had consulted with the city
editors of the *Daily Telegraph*, the *Daily News*, the *Standard*, and
the *Times*. Under the pretext of doing a series of articles for the
American market on crime in metropolitan London, he arranged to
have access to the newspapers' clipping files and to be apprised of
current happenings by messenger once a day. Newspapers tend to be
very responsive to the requests of outside journalists who are not
direct competitors. It was a cheap and effective sort of bread-casting.

Within a week, Barnett had replies from eleven East Coast dailies
to the effect that they were willing to see his queries and buy from
him at space rates if he had anything that interested them. "I have,"
he told Professor Moriarty over dinner, "quite inadvertently established myself in a business. I'm going to have to go out and hire that
secretary you suggested just to keep up with the legitimate stories,
not counting the research I'm doing for you. I didn't think it would
be so easy."

"You must be considered a good journalist by your American
peers," Moriarty suggested.

"I don't think that's it," Barnett said. "Not that I'm not a good
journalist, you understand. I'm the best. But I think what these papers see is the notoriety value of my byline. Something like this: 'Mr.
Barnett, our London correspondent, is the man who recently conducted a daring escape from a Turkish prison—no, make that a
Turkish dungeon—after being tried and convicted for the murder of

a British naval officer. A murder he assures us he did not commit. Full details in our Sunday edition.' "

"Fascinating. Clearly shows the advantages of compulsory literacy even in the most primitive cultures."

"Remember," Barnett told him, "that where I come from a woman who killed her lover with a nickel-plated revolver last year was acquitted of the crime when she told the jury that he had lied to her. And then she went on a vaudeville singing tour that took her to twenty-seven cities. Despite a voice like a bullfrog, she packed the house at every stop."

Moriarty put down his fork and stared at Barnett. "If I followed that properly," he said, "the moral of it would have to be, 'When in America keep nickel-plated revolvers out of the hands of women who can't sing.' " Then he chuckled and returned his attention to his pudding.

Barnett put an advertisement in the next morning's *Daily Telegraph* for a "secretary for a small news-office, conversant with the operation of typewriting machines. Reply to Box 252, Telegraph." He arranged for a messenger to deliver the replies to his office. By that afternoon's post he had sixteen replies, and by the following morning when he arrived at the office, eighty-seven.

He piled them all up on top of his new desk and settled down to go through them, with no clear idea of how to go about culling them down to manageable size. He found that a good many of the applicants eliminated themselves through unacceptable vagaries of grammar, syntax, or spelling. He counted the letters remaining: fifty-two. He had no interest in interviewing fifty-two people, and felt that he'd be even more helpless in deciding when actually faced with them than he was when merely faced with their letters of application. There were seventeen nearly identical letters in the pile. They each began, "I read with interest your advertisement in today's *Daily Telegraph . . .*" and continued, with little variation except for the name of the applicant, to precisely one inch from the bottom of the page. Barnett pulled them all out. Obviously copied from some popular letter-writing guide, he decided. Well, if he arbitrarily eliminated these as lacking in imagination, that still left thirty-five.

There was a knock at the door. Barnett looked up. More applications, no doubt. He put his pencil down. "Come in."

The office door opened, and a young lady entered. Barnett

watched her come in, then stood up politely. And then he fell in love. This was not unusual, although it was the first time since he had reached London. Barnett had fallen in love every other day in Paris, and at least once a week in New York. But each time it was a new and unique emotion, and not at all to be compared with any of the times before. Still, it had happened enough that he was able to control the emotion and not allow it to interfere with his conduct. If his heart was beating a little faster than a moment before, if he was breathing a little deeper, well, it was a hot day.

"Excuse me," she said, "are you Mr. Barnett?"

"Indeed I am, Madam," he said. "How may I assist you?" It wasn't what he wanted to say, he told himself, wishing for poetic words and romantic images to come springing to his lips. But none sprang, and even if one had, there were conventions that would prevent him from uttering, one-tenth-part of one syllable. So he merely smiled foolishly at the young lady and waited for her to speak.

"I have brought your mail," she said, holding forth a packet of letters in her daintily gloved hand, "from the *Daily Telegraph*."

"Oh," Barnett said. He took the letters and dropped them on top of the others. "Thank you."

The girl set herself firmly before the desk, took a deep breath, and said, "I should like to apply for the position myself. Of secretary. In this office."

"Oh," Barnett said. "I mean, ah, I see. Here, take a seat, why don't you? How interesting. Ah . . ." He plopped back down into his chair as she sat herself in the straightback wooden chair by the side of the desk. "I'm sorry if I seem surprised," he said, "but I'm not really prepared to interview anyone yet. I mean, I hadn't expected to see anyone until tomorrow. At the earliest. How did you get here, by the way? And what is your name?"

"I am sorry if I surprised you," the girl said. "My name is Perrine, Miss Cecily Perrine. I was quite determined, when I saw your advertisement, to apply for the position before anyone else had a chance to. To get the jump on them, as they say. So I took the liberty of ascertaining who had placed the advertisement. And then I came here under the pretext of bringing you your mail."

Barnett looked at the girl, trying to pierce the depths of the clear blue eyes that met his gaze without coyness or shyness. Her oval face was framed with light-brown curls under her straw bonnet. And she seemed totally without artifice. Which, Barnett reflected, was probably the highest form of artifice of all.

"Why?" he asked.

"Why did I come? Why do I want the position?"

"That's right, Miss Perrine," he said. "Why are you here?"

"I want to be a journalist," she said. "I want to work for a newspaper. But none of them will take me seriously. So when I saw the advertisement for a position in a small news-office, I decided to try for it. I thought that if I could get a start—even as a secretary—I might get a chance . . . I might be able to make a chance . . . I suppose it was silly . . ." Her voice trailed off and she looked away. Barnett could see that her hands were clenched and white, although her face was flushed. She was in the grip of some strong emotion, and she was not acting.

"There are lady journalists," Barnett said.

She looked back up at him, the scorn evident in the glare in her eyes and the set of her jaw. "Journalists!" she scoffed. "There are ladies, sir, who write dainty little pieces about social teas, and soirées, and whether the Dowager Duchess of Titipu wore mauve or lavender to the last garden party at Balmoral. That, sir, is not journalism, and you know it!" Then she put her gloved hand to her mouth and looked suddenly stricken. "Oh," she said. "I'm sorry. I *am* sorry. I can't help it. But none of the daily papers will hire a woman even as a secretary. If you knew how many times I've heard that a news-room is no place for a lady."

"You will have to learn to control your emotions," Barnett said gently.

"You're right, of course," Miss Perrine said, taking a deep breath and standing up. "Thank you for your time."

"I have three more questions for you, Miss Perrine, if you don't mind," Barnett said.

It was a second before she realized what he had said and then she sat slowly back down. "Yes?"

"Why do you want to be a reporter?"

She thought about it for a moment. "I don't exactly know," she said. "No one's ever asked me that before. Not in years. When I was twelve—I think it was twelve—I told my father I wanted to be a journalist and he laughed and asked me why. And I said something like, 'Because they find out the truth and then they tell people.' I had just read one of Mr. Dickens's novels, I don't even remember which one, and one of the characters was a journalist and I was impressed. It was a man, of course, but at the time that barrier didn't seem insurmountable."

"That's as good a reason as I've heard," Barnett said. "The only one better was advanced by a man named McSorley who covered the police beat for the New York *Daily American*."

"And what did Mr. McSorley say?" the girl asked.

"He said they were paying him twelve dollars a week," Barnett told her, "and that was more than he could make shoveling coal."

Miss Perrine thought about that for a minute, possibly trying to decide whether or not Barnett was making fun of her. "This man McSorley," she said, "didn't have to fight for his job."

Barnett smiled.

"What is your second question?" Miss Perrine asked.

"How did you manage to get here to apply for the position. The address, after all, is a box number, and the *Telegraph* is not supposed to give out the name or address of the box holder."

"I suppose technically it was wrong, Mr. Barnett," she said. "I've tried to explain to you why—"

"Not why, Miss Perrine," Barnett said. "How. Tell me how."

"It was simple enough," she told him. "I went to the window and told the clerk I was picking up the mail for Box Two-Three-Two. He said he understood it was to be sent on. I told him that that was the problem. I said we had expected far more replies than we had received and I wanted to make sure they were going to the right address. So he pulled the card and read me the name and address printed thereon. I assured him that it was right, took the few letters that had come since the last messenger, and here I am."

"I see," Barnett said. "Very effective. And my third question is: Can you spell?"

"Quite precisely," she said.

"Very good. Now tell me, do you still want the job?"

"Well," Miss Perrine looked around the office. "Quite frankly, Mr. Barnett, this is not how I pictured my introduction to journalism. This office, at the moment, seems quite innocent of any connection with any newspaper. Would you mind telling me, Mr. Barnett, exactly what the American News Service does, and what my duties would be?"

"We are a brand new company, Miss Perrine," Barnett said. "So new, in fact, that I use the editorial 'we,' as I am, at present, the sole proprietor and only employee of the American News Service. But from such humble beginnings, Miss Perrine, may come a great news organization.

"We gather news for our clients, which are American newspapers. Therefore, we try to anticipate what sort of news would appeal to the American reader. Once a day we will cable a query sheet with a *précis* of each story to our clients. They then specify which stories they are willing to pay for, and we send them."

"It sounds interesting," Miss Perrine said. "Although I'm afraid to imagine what sort of stories the American newspapers are interested in. Where do you get your stories, Mr. Barnett? You don't just cull the London dailies, do you?"

"I'm developing connections with the city editors of several of the larger papers," Barnett replied. "They will supply the basic facts—for a fee, of course. If the story seems to warrant it, there are several free-lance reporters I can hire to develop additional facts. I also do reporting work myself, but at present I have a private client who will take up much of my time away from the office."

"A private client, Mr. Barnett?"

The incredulous question made Barnett realize how strange the idea of a news bureau having a private client sounded to anyone with even a rudimentary notion of how such a business worked. "I am engaged in, ah, research, Miss Perrine, among the indigent and criminal classes in London. A private charitable foundation is supplying the financing."

"How fascinating!" Miss Perrine said. "You will have to tell me all about it!"

"I certainly shall," Barnett agreed. "Now as to your duties. At first they will be mainly secretarial, but as the service expands there will be an increasing amount of in-house journalistic writing to be done. If you can handle the work, it's yours."

"There's the matter of remuneration, Mr. Barnett," Miss Perrine reminded him.

"True," Barnett said. "I have no idea . . . What is the standard rate for secretarial help around here?"

"I believe that a capable secretary would command fifteen to twenty pounds a quarter. That is, a woman would. A man, of course, would get more. Say twenty-five or thirty pounds."

"Well, why don't we flout custom, Miss Perrine, and start you at twenty-five pounds a quarter. I have a feeling that your initiative and intelligence will prove invaluable to this organization. Perhaps even more than if you had been a man."

Miss Perrine gave Barnett a searching look, but his answering gaze was innocence itself. "Very well," she said, "when do you want me to begin?"

"You do use a typewriter, don't you?" Barnett asked.

Miss Perrine looked disapprovingly at his machine. "The Grandall is a good typewriter," she said, "but I prefer the Remington."

"As I shall need my own machine at any rate, I was planning to get a second. It shall be a Remington, as you say."

"Thank you, Mr. Barnett."

"As for starting, right now would seem a suitable time."

"Very good. What would you have me do?"

Barnett indicated the pile of letters on his desk. "Answer these," he said.

FOURTEEN

PASSING STRANGE

The City is of Night, perchance of Death
But Certainly of Night.
— JAMES THOMSON

Cecily Perrine proved to be more than Barnett could have hoped for. He had advertised for a secretary and he had found a wonder. She handled the business side of American News Service so well that it almost immediately ceased being merely a front for Barnett's other activity and became a profitable enterprise in its own right. Very quickly she became adept at providing what American newspapers would pay for, from crime news to war news, feature articles to in-depth studies of European affairs. Barnett suppressed his infatuation with her as best he could, and replaced it with admiration for her ability.

In the meantime, he was busy with his own task: searching through the crime news, the society pages, the letters to the editors (published and un-), and even the agony columns for that hint of the bizarre which might indicate the presence of Trepoff or the Belye Krystall.

The bizarre was not hard to find in London, but identifying the elusive hand of Trepoff was another matter. The head of a small child was found in a hatbox in the parcel room of Kensington station. Was Trepoff involved? A man in Walling left his house in the morning, was seen going back for his umbrella, and then disappeared from the face of the Earth. A strange explosion destroyed the house of a Paddington chalk-merchant, who was then found in the cellar, dead of the bite of a giant tropical spider. Was Trepoff the agent, and if so, to what end?

The great safe deposit vaults of the London & Midlands Bank were opened one Monday morning and discovered to be completely empty, with no discernible trace of how the event had happened. The police professed themselves to be baffled in one sentence, and in the next promised an "early arrest."

"It really is quite puzzling," Barnett told Moriarty that evening, "although I see no sign that our mysterious Trepoff is involved in it. The only set of keys, without which I am assured no man could have opened the vault doors unless he employed sufficient explosive to bring the building down around him, was in the hands of the branch manager continuously from the time he left the bank on Friday until he returned on Monday morning. The time clock on the vault was set by the assistant manager, in the manager's presence, as is their custom, and, indeed, did not release the mechanism until eight o'clock Monday morning. The electric alarm system, which connects with the local police station, was not set off. And the guard, who is locked in for the weekend, saw nothing unusual. Nevertheless, two large vaults have been completely emptied of their contents."

"It does not concern us," Moriarty told Barnett. "Trepoff was not involved."

"How can you be sure?"

Moriarty was bent over the small worktable in his study, titrating a clear reagent into a test tube half-full of brown liquid. For a time he did not answer, but continued to critically observe the liquid. All at once the brown color faded and the test tube was clear. Moriarty made a note in his notebook and kept watching as the reagent mixed with the now-clear liquid drop by drop. Within a minute there was another change, this one more gradual, until the liquid had turned a deep blue. Moriarty put the test tube aside and wrote a couple of quick lines in the notebook. Then he turned to Barnett.

"The bank manager keeps the keys to his branch—the entire set, mind you—on his dresser while he sleeps. Does this strike you as being a safe procedure?"

"I, ah, don't know," Barnett said. "I suppose not."

"Further, he does not share a bedroom with his wife, but sleeps alone. And he is a heavy sleeper. It would be no trick for a clever man to obtain impressions of the keys."

"I see," Barnett said, and by now he thought he was beginning to.

"The Briggs-Murcheson time clock is a fascinating device," Moriarty said, going over to his desk and sitting down. "Mr. Murcheson—Mr. Briggs is deceased—Mr. Murcheson would no doubt be quite surprised to discover that if a powerful electromagnet is placed in the proximity of the escapement mechanism and the current applied to it is reversed fifty times a second, the clock is speeded up to approximately twice its normal speed. Which means that if the clock were set for, let us say, the sixty-one hours between Friday at seven P.M. and Monday at eight A.M., and someone were to apply such an electromagnet in the appropriate place shortly after midnight Friday, he might expect the timing mechanism to be released at about four-thirty Sunday morning. It could, of course, be reset after someone had gained access to the interior of the vault."

"This is all just a theory, of course," Barnett said. "What of the guard?"

"Theoretically," Moriarty said, smiling, "we may assume that the gentleman, as is common with many of his sort, is fond of the bottle. A little laudanum mixed into the flask that he takes to work would effectively render him *non compos mentis* for the required period. And he could hardly be expected to mention it afterward, as it would cost him his job."

"And the electrical alarm?"

"Ah, yes," Moriarty said. "Which goes under the streets to the police station. A workman at the appropriate manhole, several blocks away from the bank, could easily render it inoperative for the required time."

"I see," Barnett repeated. And he was now sure he did.

"An aggregate of defenses, when taken together, may sound formidable," Moriarty said, "although when individually examined, they may be nothing of the sort." He laced his fingers together on the desk. "But let us leave off this theoretical discussion, however fascinating, and get on to more urgent matters. I have some word of Trepoff."

"You do?" Barnett said. "What have you found out? And how did you go about it?"

"I have spent every evening for the last few weeks playing chess at the Bohemian Club and at the Balalaika. The Russians have a passion for chess equaled only by their passion for intrigue. If I may say so, they are on the average better at chess."

"Weren't you afraid of being recognized? This Trepoff is trying to kill you, after all."

"He seems to have given up that notion—at least for the time being," Moriarty said. "And I took precautions against being recognized. Indeed, I passed you once as you rounded the corner of

Montague Place, and you failed to recognize me. I added thirty years to my age and took six inches off my height. You have no idea how tiring it is to appear six inches shorter for hours at a time."

"Have you made any contacts among the anarchists?" Barnett asked.

Moriarty nodded. "They trust me. I am an old gentleman who beats them at chess and refuses to allow them to discuss their politics around him because it's all a stupid game and will accomplish nothing. I rant at them about how stupid they are, so they trust me."

"You speak Russian?" Barnett asked.

"Well enough," Moriarty said. "I mostly listen."

"What sort of people are they?"

Moriarty shook his head. "They are as ineffectual as children. They talk and they talk, they plan, and they argue. Hour after hour they argue. They may kill a few people—it is easy to kill—but they cannot form a successful committee. So how can they ever hope to form a government?"

"What did you find out?"

"Trepoff, calling himself Ivan Zorta, has been recruiting from the anarchist community. He has formed a secret group, which does not appear to have a name, made up of three-man cells. He has extorted strong oaths of allegiance from those he has subverted, promising them something big, something earthshaking. And soon."

"Did you see him?"

"No. Nobody has ever seen him, or so they say over the chess table. That is why I believe Zorta to be Trepoff. That and the promise of something big that he is holding out to his recruits. Also, it is all, except for Zorta himself, a little too visible. Despite all the horrible oaths and vows of secrecy, everyone in the community knows of the organization with no name. Whatever it does will surely be blamed on the anarchists, which is just what Trepoff is trying to accomplish. Now, let's look at your reports for the day."

Moriarty skimmed over the four sheets of paper Barnett had brought home filled with the day's unusual events. Apart from the mysterious bank robbery, into which Barnett decided not to delve any deeper, Barnett didn't think there was anything of particular interest.

Moriarty evidently agreed with him, as he didn't pause at any of the items until he reached the last. This he read through twice, and then he put the paper down and tapped it with his finger. "Tell me about this," he said.

"Not much to tell," Barnett said. "It looked to be a fascinating story for a while, but turned out to be nothing in the end. Luckily, all the papers picked up the correction before it got into print.

"The story got out that the Duke of Ipswich's seventeen-year-old daughter was missing under mysterious circumstances My agent, a reporter for the *Standard*, went out to Baddeley, the Ipswich ancestral manor in Kensington, to check on it. The butler answered the door and would not permit a reporter on the premises, but he assured my man that he was mistaken and that there was nothing wrong. My agent went to the local police station and discovered that they had indeed been called some hours before—this was early morning, so make it late last night—and were informed that Lady Catherine, the daughter, was missing. She had been entertaining a small group of friends and they had been playing a game—fish, I believe it is called—that involved much scurrying about and concealment.

"Lady Catherine went out to conceal herself, apparently, and could not be found. After an hour, her friends got worried and went around the house calling for her to come out, but she didn't. So they and the servants organized a systematic search of the mansion, from top to bottom. When they didn't find her—and by now over two hours had passed—they called in the police."

"A wise move," Moriarty noted.

"The butler informed the constable that the house had been locked for the night before Lady Catherine's disappearance. There is a patent burglar alarm on all the doors and windows, and it had been turned on. This had not been set off. So far, a first-class mystery and a first-class story, I'm sure you'll agree."

"I do," Moriarty said. "What is the denouement?"

"Well, just before my agent and the several other reporters who had appeared went racing back to their city rooms, His Grace the Duke of Ipswich arrived back at Baddeley Hall in the ducal carriage and demanded to know what was going on. When he was told that his daughter was missing, he said that on the contrary, he had taken her away himself only two hours before. The duchess, Lady Catherine's mother, is ill and in confinement at *her* mother's, and the duke and Lady Catherine had driven off to visit. It was a spur-of-the-moment decision of the duke's to take his daughter, and she apparently didn't bother to mention it to anyone in the house. She stayed with her mother while the duke returned home."

"And the burglar alarms?"

"He has a key."

"Of course. He would have."

Barnett shrugged. "So a first-class mystery becomes an ordinary series of misunderstandings. Luckily, the truth came out before the story was published."

"The truth," Moriarty said, "has yet to come out."

"What do you mean?"

"Life does not normally attain the qualities of a bad Restoration comedy. When you look at it from the far side of the mirror—that is, as a past event, the implausibility is less evident. But examine the story point by point, as it is supposed to have happened, and see what evolves. The Duke of Ipswich decides to visit his sick wife, who has chosen to be ill at her mother's house. On his way out he sees his daughter, who happens to be hiding from everyone else in the house, and invites her along. They leave, without seeing anyone else, whether friend, guest, or servant. Which has the duke opening and closing his own doors and turning off and resetting his own alarms. Did the duke give any reason for this extraordinary behavior?"

"No," Barnett said. "Not that I know of. Is it really that extraordinary?"

"For a duke to open his own front door? I should think so. That's the sort of naiveté that occurs in children's fairy tales. There's a knock on the castle door, and the king goes to answer it. Dukes do not open their own front doors. And if any servant had let them out, he would have mentioned it when the search for Lady Catherine began."

"So you conclude?"

"That the girl is, indeed, missing. That the Duke was notified of her absence, probably by the abductors, and was rushing back to Baddeley Hall to see if it was true. That he immediately denied her absence because he had been warned by the abductors to do so."

"Isn't that a slender thread upon which to hang such a weighty conclusion?" Barnett asked.

"It will bear the weight," Moriarty said. "I'll go further: there's at least a sporting chance that this is Trepoff's opening gambit."

"Why do you say that? What signs of Trepoff do you see?"

"None," Moriarty admitted. "But yet I see nothing to indicate that it isn't Trepoff. And my nose detects the slight odor of the bizarre that makes this one of the few events you've brought to my attention that might involve Trepoff, and therefore it warrants further investigation."

"Do you want me to get one of my free-lance men out there?"

"He would see nothing," Moriarty said. "And if you will forgive the remark, you would not see much more. Therefore, we must go together." He reached for the bell-pull on the wall behind him.

"You mean now?" Barnett asked. "By the time we get there it will be after ten."

"If I'm correct," Moriarty said, "and if the duke's daughter has indeed been abducted, then I assure you he will be awake."

Mr. Maws appeared at the door, and Moriarty told him to go out and procure a four-wheeler. "See if Clarence or Dermot are at their stand," he suggested. "After our recent experience, I am partial to the jarvey I know. At any rate, have one back here in five minutes if you can. We'll be ready to leave then."

"Very good, Professor," Mr. Maws said.

As the four-wheeler, with Clarence atop, proceeded toward Kensington, Moriarty sat stooped like a great hawk, his prominent chin resting on his folded hands above the ivory handle of his stick, his eyes narrowed in thought. Barnett, across from him, kept silent out of respect for the professor's thought processes and amused himself by trying to decide what was occupying Moriarty's mind as they sped across London. Was it thoughts of the unfortunate duke and his missing daughter? Speculations as to the current state of the mysterious Trepoff's plans against Britain in general and Moriarty in particular? Satisfied musing about the current whereabouts of the goods that until recently had occupied the vaults of the London & Midlands Bank? Reflections, perhaps, on his latest monograph, bound copies of which had just been delivered from the printers, entitled, *Some Considerations on the Spectral Composition of Certain Interstellar Nebulosities*?

Professor Moriarty, Barnett thought, was certainly the most complex and contradictory man he had ever known. On the surface, the tall, thin, stoop-shouldered, introspective professor appeared no more interesting and no more sophisticated than any provincial schoolteacher who might combine a proficiency in mathematics with a better than average understanding of people. Yet Moriarty combined a true brilliance in mathematics, and indeed in all the physical sciences, with an unsurpassed intuitive insight into people. From a superficial examination of the man who sat opposite him in a railroad carriage, Moriarty could state the man's profession, marital status, interests, and possibly even add a few intimate details of his private life. When pressed to explain his methods, Moriarty drew an inductive path leading from his observations to his conclusions that made you feel foolish for not having seen it yourself. And he was usually, if not invariably, correct.

And yet this understanding of the actions and motives of other people did not seem to extend to any sort of empathy with or sympathy for his fellow human beings. Moriarty respected facts and admired the analytical and deductive facilities of the human animal. He had small use for any human emotion and no use at all for those people who, in his view, refused to use their brains.

He considered himself bound by no laws, yet would never break his oath or go back on his word. And for all that he professed a distaste for his fellow human beings, nothing could bring him more quickly to anger or provoke more of his biting scorn than an account of one person callously mistreating another.

Moriarty affixed his pince-nez to the bridge of his nose and turned his gaze to Barnett. "You have been staring at me for the past ten minutes," he said. "Have I suddenly developed a keratosis?"

"No," Barnett said. "No, sir. I apologize. But, to tell you the truth, I was thinking about you. About your attitudes."

"My attitudes?"

"Yes. Toward people."

"You refer, I assume," Moriarty said calmly, "to my characteristic revulsion toward my fellow man."

"I wouldn't have put it that strongly," Barnett said.

Moriarty snorted. "My fellow man is a fool," he said, "incapable of acting twice consecutively in his own interest, for the very good reason that he has only the sketchiest idea of what his interest is, or where it lies. He allows his emotions to override his puny intellect and blindly follows whichever of his fellows brays the loudest in his direction. He firmly believes in the existence of an almighty God, whom he pictures, somehow, as looking a lot like himself, and further believes that it matters to this Creator of the Universe whether He is prayed to in a kneeling or sitting position. He rejects Isaac Newton and Charles Darwin in favor of Bishop Ussher and the Davenport Brothers. He supposes that a planet a hundred times as massive as the earth, and a thousand million miles distant, was placed there solely to predict the outcome of his business affairs or his romantic dalliances. He believes in ghosts, poltergeists, mesmerism, spiritualism, clairvoyance, astrology, numerology, and a hundred other foolishnesses, but isn't sure about evolution or the germ theory of disease."

"Come, Professor," Barnett said, "is not that a bit broad? Surely there are exceptions."

"Indeed," Professor Moriarty said, nodding. "And it is the exceptions who make life interesting." He took a large handkerchief from his jacket pocket and, removing the pince-nez from his nose, polished the glasses carefully. "I am not a complete misanthrope, Mr. Barnett," he said, "and you must not imagine that I am. Indeed, it must be that on some unconscious level of my brain I am quite concerned about this hypothetical fellow man, or I wouldn't get so angry over his foibles."

"I thought, perhaps, it was just annoyance at recalling that you, yourself, are one of the creatures," Barnett said.

Moriarty considered this for a minute. "So I am," he said finally. "I had quite forgotten."

The four-wheeler turned left off Holland Park Avenue, and Moriarty pulled out his pocket-watch. "We're almost there," he said. "Strike a match, will you?"

Barnett obliged from the small packet of waterproofs he carried to light his occasional cigars.

"Ah!" Moriarty said. "It is still a quarter till the hour of ten. A bit late for calling, but I have no doubt that His Grace will see us."

A few minutes later they had turned past the ancient gateposts and were heading up the drive toward Baddeley Hall. As recently as fifty years before, this great three-story Tudor mansion had been the main house to the great estate of Baddeley, surrounded by hundreds of acres of well-managed land. But now Greater London had grown past Baddeley, and most of the managing was done by estate agents who collected the quarterly rents on street after street of semidetached cottages. It had ruined the duke's shooting—but had enormously increased his income.

Moriarty looked out of the carriage window and chuckled with satisfaction as they pulled around to the great oak doors that were Baddeley Hall's main entrance. "I was right," he said. "The trip was not in vain."

"What do you mean?" Barnett asked.

"See for yourself," Moriarty said. "Every lamp in the house must be lighted."

"A party?" Barnett suggested, feeling contrary.

"Nonsense!" Moriarty replied. "Where are the rows of waiting carriages? No, there are but two vehicles waiting in the drive: a closed landau bearing a crest I cannot make out from here and a hansom. Family friends and advisors, no doubt, come to aid the duke in his time of travail. Their drivers, I see, are warming themselves within the mansion while waiting for their passengers. However, I'm afraid that poor Clarence will have to wait out in the cold."

Clarence pulled up to the front steps and they dismounted. "I don't know how long we'll be," Moriarty told Clarence. "I think it wiser if you stay with your vehicle. I don't expect any trouble here now, but there's no point in taking unnecessary risks."

"That's quite all right, Professor," Clarence replied cheerily, taking off his bowler and scratching his bald head. "It ain't all that cold and it ain't raining. I have a flask of tea here, and there's enough light from these here gas fixtures to read the 'Pink 'un' by, so I'm content." He waved his hat at the horse. "Maud here gets nervous when I leave her alone at night, anyway."

"Very good, then," Moriarty said. He and Barnett mounted the steps together, and Barnett pulled the lion's-head bellpull by the door. Moriarty took out one of his calling cards and wrote "Ivan Zorta" in ink on the back.

The door opened, and a tall man in the Ipswich livery stared out impassively at them. "Yes?"

"I must see your master on a matter of the utmost importance." Moriarty said. "Show him this card."

The man placed the card on a tray. "Come in," he said, taking their hats and Moriarty's stick. "You may wait in there."

They crossed the entrance hall under the footman's watchful eye and entered a small reception room. Within a very few minutes a second, shorter but more regal-looking man—Barnett correctly surmised that this was the butler—came to fetch them. "His Grace will see you now," he said. "Please follow me."

Barnett followed Moriarty down the hall, staring with frank curiosity at his surroundings. This was the first time he had ever been in a duke's residence, and might well be the last, so he wanted to take it all in. The walls were rich, dark oak and hung with ancient family portraits interspersed with occasional pastoral scenes. There was a great, wide staircase that a troop of men could have marched down eight abreast. At its foot, by the intricately carved oak baluster, was a full suit of armor that looked, at least to Barnett's uneducated eye, as though it had once been worn in battle.

"In here, please, gentlemen," the butler said, showing them into the duke's private study. They entered, and the butler closed the doors behind them.

The duke was a man of medium height and middle age, very stocky, with muttonchop whiskers and a conservatively trimmed mustache. At the moment he was obviously in a fit of passion, which he was suppressing with difficulty and without much success. His face was beet-red, and he was striding back and forth on the edge of his rug with short, stiff-legged steps and flexing a heavy riding crop between his hands.

"Well," he said glaring at them, "what is it you want with me?"

"I am sorry to hear about Your Grace's loss," Moriarty said. "I know this must be very trying for you, so I shall be brief. To put it as simply as possible, I think I can be of assistance to you."

"Assistance, is it?" the Duke of Ipswich said, the short whip twisting spasmodically in his hands. "Very well, then, state your terms."

Moriarty looked a little surprised at this reception, but he continued. "I need some information first," he said. "I need to know how your daughter was abducted, as exactly as possible. I would like to see the scene. I must know whether the abductors have been in touch with you as yet, and if so, what are their terms. I assume they have, since the name I wrote on my card commended it to your attention."

"Name?" the Duke blinked. He walked over to his desk, picked up Moriarty's card and turned it over. "Ivan Zorta? This name means nothing to me."

"I see," Moriarty said, looking genuinely puzzled. "Then why—perhaps Your Grace has heard of me in some other context?"

"Must we continue this farce?" the duke demanded. "State your terms for returning my daughter and they will be met. I know your name."

Moriarty was silent for a moment, while the duke went back to pacing the floor, his knuckles white around the riding crop. A small sound escaped from the duke's mouth, but whether it was a cry of rage, pain, or anguish, Barnett could not tell. Barnett was horrified at this confusion, and angry that the duke would dare think them capable of such a crime.

"There is a serious misunderstanding, Your Grace," Moriarty said. "I assure you—"

"Enough!" the duke cried. "I have heard enough, I will suffer no more of this. It is with the utmost effort of will that I resist leaping at you, sir, and striking you and your companion down. I was told that it was almost certain that you were the agent of my daughter's disappearance, that anything this dastardly and clever had your mark on it. And now—and now, here you are, sir. Where is my daughter? If you have harmed her, I assure you that there is no place on this earth where I will not hunt you down and destroy you. Mark that, sir!"

"You were told?" Moriarty was astonished. "Who could have told you such a thing and for what purpose?" He suddenly jabbed an accusing finger at no one in particular. "Holmes!" he cried, his voice tight with anger. "You have employed Sherlock Holmes! And he is attempting to earn his undoubtedly impressive fee by convincing you that *I* am involved in this repulsive crime."

The door behind the desk opened, and the tall, ascetic figure of Sherlock Holmes stalked in. "Good evening, Professor," he said in his expressionless, carefully modulated voice. "I had, of course, recognized your hand in this crime, but I hardly expected to see you here yourself. Setting an example for your minions, perhaps?"

Moriarty swung around. "This is outrageous, Holmes! Are you going to give up any semblance of deduction from now on, and merely blame me for every crime in London?"

"In London, Moriarty?" Holmes said. "Why so limiting? Say rather, in the world, Professor. In the world!" He carefully walked back to the door and closed it. "But only among friends, you understand, would I say such a thing. And only the best sort of crimes: the clever, evil ones that require a master brain and an utter disregard for common sensibilities or morality."

"You have already said too much before two witnesses," Moriarty said, "and one of them noble. I could have you for slander, Holmes."

The Duke of Ipswich, who had been growing increasingly agitated as he listened to this exchange, suddenly threw down the riding crop. "Confound you, you bastard!" he cried, leaping forward. "What have you done with my daughter?" And as he slammed into Moriarty, his hands reached for the professor's neck.

Moriarty went down before the surprise blow, and the duke was on top of him, his hands around Moriarty's neck and his face apoplectic.

Moriarty took the nobleman's wrists and, with surprising ease, pulled them apart. Then, before either Barnett or Holmes could reach them, he had rolled over and come to his knees. His hands still held the duke's wrists in an iron grip. "I will release you, Your Grace, when you have calmed down," he said, his voice even.

The duke took several deep breaths, and then went limp. "I can't fight you," he said. "You have my daughter."

Moriarty released the duke and stood up, dusting himself off. He reached a hand out for the duke, who ignored it and pushed himself to his feet. "Your rug is really quite dusty," Moriarty said, slapping at his trousers. "You should speak to your staff."

The duke stood where he had risen, speechless and trembling. Holmes went over and helped him to a chair. "You have the upper hand this time, Moriarty," he said. "Make your demands."

Moriarty shook his head sadly. "For the last time," he said. "I know nothing of this crime aside from the bare fact that it occurred. The gentleman with me is Benjamin Barnett, an American journalist, and it is he who informed me that Lady Catherine was missing. I am possessed of some facts—unrelated to the event—that enabled me to develop a theory of the crime. I came here for the sole purpose of ascertaining whether that theory could be correct. If so, I am prepared to share these facts with you and aid you to the best of my ability in apprehending the criminal."

"Purely for the most altruistic motives, eh, Professor?" Holmes demanded with a sneer.

"Not at all," Moriarty said. "It would further my interests."

"I have no doubt of that," Holmes said. He turned to the duke. "It may interest Your Grace to know that the professor's friend here, Benjamin Barnett, is an escaped criminal, convicted of murder by a Constantinople court. There is, unfortunately, nothing the British authorities can do to send him back."

The duke held his hands out. "Just tell me how she is," he implored, his face now ashen and his eyes staring. "For mercy's sake! Tell me how she is."

"Your Grace," Moriarty said, "I give you my word of honor

that I know neither how your daughter is nor where she is. I had nothing to do with her abduction. Nothing. However, I can see that in the present state of affairs I can be of no help to you and you of none to me. If I hear of anything, I shall notify you. Please do not assault my messenger. In the meantime, put your trust in Sherlock Holmes; you cannot do any better. He is, under normal circumstances, an excellent consulting detective. However, in this case, he will not accomplish anything until he rids himself of this ridiculous fixation that I am at the root of every crime that is not immediately transparent to his gaze."

Moriarty walked to the door and opened it. "Mr. Barnett," he said. "I think we can find our own way out." Then he turned back to the duke, who was looking at him with a puzzled expression on his face. "My advice is not to call in Scotland Yard," he said. "This case is beyond them, and they will only bungle it. I hope your daughter is returned to you safely. Good night, Your Grace. Good night, Mr. Holmes."

He closed the door gently behind him, and he and Barnett walked silently down the long hall. The footman was waiting at the front door for them, with stick and hats.

INTERSTICES

As someday it may happen that a victim must be found,
I've got a little list—I've got a little list.

—W. S. GILBERT

For the next few weeks, having no instructions to the contrary, Barnett busied himself with the affairs of the American News Service, which steadily expanded. On Wednesday, June 25th, he promoted Miss Perrine—they agreed upon the title of "Cable Editor" as being the most appropriate—and instructed her to hire an assistant and a messenger boy. Then he purchased two more desks and yet another typewriter. "If this keeps up," he told Miss Perrine, as they received confirmation of their forty-third American newspaper account, the *San Francisco Call,* "we're going to have to search for larger quarters before the end of the month."

"The offices next door are vacant," Miss Perrine told him, "and the rental agent confirms that we can have them as of the first of July." She put her wide, red-trimmed hat on and adjusted it very carefully to the proper rakish angle before pinning it in place. She seemed unaware of Barnett's admiring gaze. "And, by the way," she said, "you are taking me to lunch."

"You've arranged for the offices?" Barnett asked.

She nodded.

"Without consulting me?"

"Yes."

Barnett shook his head. "And quite right, too," he said. "Where am I taking you?"

"Sweetings', I think," she said.

And so he did. And after the waiter had taken their order and gone away, he leaned forward across the table and regarded her steadily through unblinking eyes until she shifted her head nervously and looked away. "You're staring at me," she said.

"I am," he admitted. "But then, you're well worth staring at."

"Please!"

"And I was beginning to think you were quite without shame," he said. Seeing her shocked expression, he laughed. "You must admit that you've gained tremendously in self-assurance in the past—what is it?—three weeks."

"That is not the same thing," she said severely, "as being without shame."

"I take it back," Barnett said. "It was an ignorant, boorish comment, and I withdraw it."

"Indeed!" she said. "As for what you call my increase in self-assurance, that, I suppose, is true. It comes of discovering that I can do the job and that I can do it quite adequately."

"Quite excellently," Barnett amended. "But you told me that when I hired you."

"Yes," she said, "but I had never actually done it. Thinking you can do something, even to the point of moral certainty, is not the same as proving you can do it."

"Well, you've proven it," Barnett said. "You're a born writer and editor. You have an innate word sense, and you write good clean prose."

"Tell me something, Mr. Barnett," Miss Perrine said, "and tell me true. You don't have the phrase 'for a woman' left unsaid at the end of any of those sentences, do you? You're not saying I write well for a woman, or I have good word sense for a woman?"

"Cecily," Barnett said, "a piece of paper with typewritten words on it is entirely without gender. When we cable a story to one of our client newspapers, I don't append a statement, 'done in a feminine hand.' You are a good writer."

"Thank you," she said. "And thank you for calling me 'Cecily.' "

"Well," he said. "It just slipped out. I was afraid you'd think it forward of me."

"I do," she said.

The waiter brought their lunch, and Barnett busied himself with his salmon mousseline for a few minutes before looking up. "Say," he said, "there was something I meant to tell you. We have a new writer."

"Who?"

"Fellow named Wilde. Someone at the *Pall Mall Gazette* introduced him to me, and I talked him into doing a series of articles on understanding Britain for the Americans. Actually, I suppose, he'll write about whatever he chooses. These article writers always do. He's very good. We should have no trouble selling the series."

She put down her fork. "Oscar Wilde?" she asked.

"That's right."

"He's brilliant," she said. "But he tends to be very eccentric and he seems to love to shock. We'll have to watch his copy."

"I leave that to your immense good judgment," he said. "He's not doing it under his own name; maybe that will calm him down."

"What byline is he using?"

"Josephus."

"Why does he choose to disguise his name?"

"I asked him that," Barnett said. "And he told me—let me get it straight now—he said: 'Writing for Americans is like performing as the rear end of a music-hall horse—one does it only for the money and one would prefer to remain anonymous.'"

"That sounds like him," she said.

"He said it loud and clear and without pause when I asked him," Barnett said. "He's either a natural genius at the epigram, or he spends large amounts of time in front of a mirror at home, rehearsing."

They finished lunch and walked back to the office, chatting amiably about this and that. As they reached the entrance to the building, Cecily clutched his arm. "There's a gentleman to my left," she said without looking around. "Can you see him? Don't make a point of it; don't let him see you looking."

Barnett examined the fellow lounging by the door out of the corner of his eye. "I wouldn't exactly call him a gentleman," he whispered back, noting the man's ragged slop-chest apparel and the unkempt beard that fringed his chin from ear to ear. "He looks like an unemployed bargee."

"I don't know his profession," Cecily said, "but he was hanging about here all day yesterday. And I'm not sure, but I think he followed me home."

"Oh, he did, did he?" Barnett said slowly.

"Now, be careful!" Cecily exclaimed, as he stalked past her toward the sinister-looking man.

"Here, you!" Barnett said, a harsh note in his voice. He grabbed the man by his filthy collar and pulled him upright out of his slouching posture. "What do you mean, hanging around here? Do you want me to have the law on you?"

"I didn't mean no 'arm, Guv'nor," the man said, holding his

crumpled hand up in front of his face as if to ward off a blow. "S'welp me I didn't. Lummy! What you want to go about pickin' on the likes of me for?" He cringed and contrived to hide even more of his filthy face behind a protecting arm.

"Say!" Cecily Perrine said, taking a step toward them, her face showing puzzlement. "Where are you from, fellow?"

"What's 'at, miss?"

"Where were you raised?"

"Whitechapel, miss. Off Commercial Road, you know, miss."

"No, you weren't!" she said positively.

" 'Ow's 'at, miss?"

"Your accent is wrong," she said flatly. "It's close, but it's wrong."

Barnett looked from one to the other. "What's that?" he said.

"He is affecting that speech," Cecily said positively. "Doing it quite well, too. But he isn't from anywhere near Whitechapel. I'd say he was brought up in the North. Yorkshire, perhaps. He has spent some time in France, and was schooled at Cambridge."

Barnett released his hold on the man, who sank back down on the steps. "You're joking," Barnett said.

"Not at all," she assured him. "Whoever this gentleman is, he is not what he seems."

"Well?" Barnett said, glaring down at the man.

The man shook his head, a disgusted look on his face, and stood up. Without slouching over, he proved to be half a head taller than Barnett. "I should like to congratulate you, young woman," he said dryly, in quite a different accent than the one he had been assuming. "That is a remarkable talent you have."

Barnett started. "I know that voice!" he said.

"Indeed?" the man said.

"Yes. You're that detective—Sherlock Holmes."

"Indeed."

"What are you doing skulking about here, following this young lady home?"

Sherlock Holmes stretched and turned his head gingerly from side to side. "Accomplishing little beyond getting a stiff neck, it would seem," he said.

"That's not good enough, sir!" Barnett said. "Explain yourself!"

Holmes regarded Barnett steadily. "Surely it should not surprise you," he said, "that I am interested in the comings and goings of the minions of Professor James Moriarty. I must admit that I usually do not take quite so close an interest, but this American News Service has me intrigued. What nefarious function it serves in Moriarty's schemes, I confess I cannot fathom. At the moment. But, as you may discover, I am quite persistent."

"And I dislike being spied on," Barnett said. "This really must cease. And you must not annoy Miss Perrine anymore, or I'll report you to the police."

Holmes chuckled. "And you'd be well within your rights to do so," he admitted: "An interesting turnabout. But I am really quite determined to discover the function of this American News Service. At first I thought of coded messages. . . ."

Cecily gasped. "You're the one!" she said.

Barnett turned to her. "What now?"

"The manager of the District Telegraph office spoke to me the other day—Tuesday, I believe—when I brought in the day's traffic. He wished to know whether we were having any more trouble with garbled transmissions. I asked him what he was referring to. He said that a gentleman had come in the evening before, saying that he was from our office, and requested copies of everything that had been handed in that day. He had given the excuse that an American client had complained of garbled messages, and he wanted to check whether the fault lay with the typist in our office or the telegraph. I asked him if it was Mr. Barnett, and he said no, another gentleman. I meant to tell you about it. I thought perhaps it was someone from Reuters checking up on their new competition."

Barnett turned to Holmes. He felt quite calm, but a vein in his neck was throbbing. "I believe that's illegal," he said. "For someone so keen on preventing crime, you seem to indulge in a fair amount of it yourself."

Holmes smiled. *"Touché,"* he said. "Professor Moriarty picks his henchmen well."

"Just who is this Professor Moriarty?" Cecily demanded.

"An eminent scientist," Barnett told her, his voice hard. "A mathematician and astronomer. I am proud to have him as a friend."

"Professor James Clovis Moriarty," Holmes said, his words coming out precise and clipped, "is a scoundrel, a rogue, and a villain. He is also a genius."

Cecily Perrine crossed her arms and her right foot tapped impatiently on the step. "He must be quite a man indeed," she said, "if he causes you to dress like a tramp and follow innocent working girls all over London."

"I take my hat off to you, young lady," Holmes said, doffing the filthy cap he was wearing. "And I give you my word never to cause you the slightest annoyance again. If you don't mind my asking, how did you catch me up on my dialect? What did I do wrong?"

"You did nothing wrong," she said. "It was quite good. But you see, my father is Professor Henry Perrine, the world-famous phoneticist, the developer of the Perrine Simplified Phonetical Alphabet. He began to teach it to me when I was three. When I was seven I started going around to different neighborhoods and copying down what people said. Father used me in his lectures to prove the accuracy of his system. By the time I was ten I could tell to within two blocks where anyone in London grew up."

"What a useful skill!" Holmes cried. "Would it take me long to learn?"

"It takes no more than a week or two to master the Perrine Alphabet," Cecily said. "After that, it is but a matter of practice. Your ear quickly becomes aware of the different dialectal sounds after you have been taught the technique of how to transcribe them."

"Come, I must have it," Holmes said. "Does your father give lessons?"

"Why not ask him yourself," Cecily asked, "the next time you follow me home?"

Holmes laughed. "I shall go over there right now," he said. "Although I suppose I'd better make myself presentable first."

"My father won't notice the way you're dressed," Cecily told him. "With Father, speech is all. If a talking gorilla came to see him he would know within a block where the gorilla was from, and never notice that it was a gorilla."

"Thank you, Miss Perrine," Holmes said. "Nonetheless, I shall change before intruding myself upon your father. And you may rest assured that I shall not bother you again. However, I do ask you to reassess your relationship with Professor Moriarty. If you—or you, Mister Barnett—ever require my aid, you will find me at 221-B Baker Street. Good afternoon." And, with a slight bow, he pulled his cap back over his head and sauntered off down the street.

Cecily watched Holmes until he rounded the corner, and then turned to Barnett. "Who is this Professor Moriarty?" she asked him again. "Is he really a scoundrel and a rogue and all that?"

"Professor Moriarty saved my life once," Barnett told her. "And, even aside from that, I have more respect for him than for any man I have ever met. I think that Sherlock Holmes, for some reason, has what the French call an *idée fixe* on the subject of Professor Moriarty."

"Then he is not a villain?"

Barnett shrugged. "Who," he asked, "can look into the heart of any man?"

SIXTEEN

WORD FROM THE TSAR

*They brought me bitter news to hear
and bitter tears to shed.*
— WILLIAM JOHNSON CORY

Professor Moriarty, wrapped in a blue silk dressing gown with a large red-embroidered dragon of menacing aspect curled over its right shoulder, was stretched out on his bed, propped up by a mound of pillows. The bed curtains were tied off, and the bed was surrounded by chairs and footstools piled high with books. That part of the bed not occupied by Moriarty himself was equally laden.

With an air of annoyance, the professor looked up from the book he was reading as Barnett knocked, then walked in. "Well?" he snapped.

"I've brought today's reports from the agency," Barnett said.

"Anything of interest?"

"I don't think so."

"Leave them on the table."

"Okay," Barnett said, laying the two sheets of paper on the table by the window. Then he turned to Moriarty and seemed to hesitate, as though not sure what to say.

"Anything else?" Moriarty demanded.

"No."

"Then why are you standing there? Either say something or get out."

"Is there anything the matter, Professor?" Barnett asked. "Is there any way I can help?"

"You? I wouldn't think so." Moriarty gestured to the pile of books surrounding him. "I have here the assembled knowledge of the Western world, and a bit of the Eastern, and I have found no help. It constantly amazes me how many idiots write books."

"You've been up here for a week," Barnett said.

"True. I've been reading. Can you suggest anything more useful for me to do?"

"What about Trepoff?" Barnett asked.

"What about him? It's his move, and I can do nothing until he makes it. Now leave me alone, and don't come back until you have something of interest to tell me."

"All right," Barnett said, shrugging. "Although it still seems to me—"

"Go!" Moriarty shouted. And Barnett left the room.

Mrs. H was standing in the corridor by the staircase. "Well?" she asked.

Barnett shook his head. "I can't get him to do anything."

"Stubborn man," Mrs. H said. "Every few months he does this." She seemed to take it as a personal affront. "One time he stayed in that bedroom for upward of six weeks, and me running back and forth from the British Museum with armloads of books for him."

"What sort of books, Mrs. H?" Barnett asked.

She started downstairs and Barnett followed. "No particular sort," she said. "One day from the King's Library, one day from the Grenville Library. He has a special arrangement with the curator to get the books out. But he had to promise to stop writing in the margins."

"In the margins?"

"That's what. When he became particularly annoyed by some comment in some book, he'd scribble a reply in the margin. The curator made him promise to stop if he was to continue getting books. Now he writes the comments on scraps of foolscap, which he inserts at the page. Doctor Wycliffe, the curator, merely removes the foolscap scraps before returning the books to the shelves."

"A strange system," Barnett commented.

"It keeps them both happy," Mrs. H said. "Doctor Wycliffe is keeping a file of the professor's annotations. He says he's going to publish them someday, anonymously, as The Ravings of a Rational Mind. The professor was quite amused."

They entered the kitchen together, and Barnett perched on one of the little wooden stools that surrounded the heavy cutting table. "I can't figure Professor Moriarty out," he said. "He is undoubtedly the strangest human I have ever run across."

"Here now," Mrs. H said, her voice rising in sudden anger, "what do you mean by that?"

"Don't take me wrong, Mrs. H," Barnett said. "I don't mean that there's anything wrong with him. I mean, well, he's probably the smartest man I've ever known—"

"Or ever like to," Mrs. H interposed.

"There's no doubt about that," Barnett agreed. "But there are so many sides to him, if you see what I mean, that it's hard to really understand what sort of a person he is."

"He's a fine man," Mrs. H stated positively.

"Yes, of course he is. But what I mean is there are so many aspects to Professor Moriarty's character, he appears in so many guises to so many people, that it's hard to know which is the real Professor Moriarty. And then he's usually so active that two men and a small boy couldn't keep up with him, but now he withdraws to his bedroom and stays there for days at a time."

"He'll come out when there's a reason."

"And then there's Sherlock Holmes," Barnett said. "I've checked on him, and he's highly regarded. And he seems to think that the professor is the greatest villain unhanged. While all those who work for Professor Moriarty would willingly and gladly cut off their right arms if he asked it of them. How can you reconcile that?"

"Mr. Sherlock Holmes!" Mrs. H paused and sniffed. "Mr. Holmes is an ungrateful young man. He was looking for a saint and he discovered that the professor was only a human being. He never has been able to forgive him that."

"They knew each other?"

"Oh, yes. Years ago."

"What happened?"

Mrs. H sniffed again. "Tea's ready," she said.

Barnett made a few more attempts to draw her out, but Mrs. H had evidently decided that she had said quite enough, and she refused to be drawn. He had to settle for tea and scones.

It was after dark when a carriage pulled up to the door of 64 Russell Square and a tall man swathed in a light opera cape descended and rang the front door bell.

Mr. Maws answered the door promptly. "Yes?" he said, surveying the gentleman expressionlessly.

"I would speak with the Professor Moriarty."

"Who should I say is calling?"

"I am Count Boris Gobolski, accredited representative of His

Imperial Majesty Alexander the Third, Tsar of all the Russias, to the court of St. James."

Mr. Maws nodded almost imperceptibly. "Have you an appointment?" he asked.

"Your master will wish to see me," Count Boris Gobolski said. "Immediately. It is of utmost importance."

"Come in," Mr. Maws said. "Please wait in the front room. I will inform the professor that you are here."

Mr. Maws climbed the stairs and announced Gobolski's presence to Moriarty, who petulantly slammed closed the book he was reading. "Probably wants a report," he said. "There was nothing in our agreement about reports. Tell him . . ." He sat up. "No, I had better go myself. I will give the gentleman to understand that there is nothing to be gained by incessantly pestering me."

"He has never been here before, sir," Mr. Maws felt obliged to state.

"That's no reason for him to start now," Moriarty said. "This must be nipped in the bud. I cannot work without a free hand."

"Yes, sir," Mr. Maws said. "Shall I tell the gentleman that you will be down directly?"

"Yes, tell him that," Moriarty said, pulling on his shoes. "I suppose I'd better dress first. It wouldn't do to greet an ambassador in a dressing-gown."

"Shall I lay out your clothes?"

"No, never mind that," Moriarty said. "That's not a butler's job, I keep telling you."

"The professor does not have a personal valet," Mr. Maws observed.

"When I made you my butler, Mr. Maws," Moriarty said, casting aside his dressing gown and selecting a shirt from his wardrobe, "I little dreamed that you'd take the title so seriously."

"I know, sir," Mr. Maws said. "I believe it appeals to some sense of order in my soul. I really enjoy the position, you understand, sir."

"It has become self-evident," Moriarty said. "Now go and knock up Barnett on your way downstairs. Tell him to join us in the study as soon as he's presentable."

"Very good, sir."

Moriarty was dressed in ten minutes, and found Barnett waiting for him on the landing. "Good to see you up," Barnett said cheerfully.

"Bah!" Moriarty replied. He wiped his pince-nez and placed it over his nose, eyeing Barnett critically through the lenses. "Our relationship," he said, "is somehow not what I expected." Then he trotted down the stairs ahead of Barnett.

Mr. Maws was in the front hall, keeping a suspicious eye on the door to the front room. "Show Count Gobolski into the study," Moriarty directed him. "Have you lit the lamps?"

"I didn't want to leave the hall, Professor," Mr. Maws said.

"Of course," Moriarty said. Taking a box of waterproof vespas from his pocket, he entered his study and performed the service himself, lighting the overhead gas pendant and the ornate brass gas lamp on his desk.

Count Gobolski entered the room, his opera cape still wrapped around him. "Professor James Moriarty?" he asked.

Moriarty stood behind his desk. "Count Boris Gobolski?"

Gobolski nodded nervously, and his gaze shifted to Barnett, who was standing by the small worktable across the room. "Who is he?" he demanded.

"My assistant," Moriarty said. "Benjamin Barnett."

"My pleasure, Count," Barnett said, bowing slightly and smiling.

"I do not like this," Gobolski said. His English was precise and perfect, and only a slight liquidity in the consonants marked him as a foreigner.

"Pray be seated, Your Excellency," Moriarty said, indicating the leather chair by his desk. "I would prefer Mr. Barnett to remain, but if you wish him to leave . . ."

"No, no," Gobolski said, waving his arm vaguely at Barnett and dropping into the indicated chair. "I did not mean—" He paused and looked around the room. "I believe I was followed," he said. "Coming here, I mean."

"Ah!" Moriarty said. He reached behind him and gave a slight tug on the bellpull. "And what leads you to suspect that?"

"One develops a feel for such things," Gobolski said.

Mr. Maws opened the door and stepped inside.

"Would you like a libation, Your Excellency?" Moriarty asked. "A brandy, perhaps? I have a fine Napoleon I can offer you. Mr. Maws, see to it, will you? And send Tolliver out the back way to see if anyone is taking an interest in this house."

Mr. Maws nodded and left, silently closing the door behind him.

"And now, Count Gobolski," Moriarty said, "what brings you calling at this late hour? And whom do you suspect of taking an interest in your affairs?"

"I am a diplomat," Gobolski said, "not a conspirator. But for a Russian today, that means little difference. One has to learn to live with being followed, threatened, terrorized. One lives in the shadow of assassination." He smoothed his mustache down with a nervous gesture. "I for one, have never become used to it. Did you know," he asked, leaning forward, "that there is a police guard in front of my house twenty-four hours of the day?"

"It must be wearing," Moriarty said.

"Nine of the members of my staff are nothing more or less than bodyguards," Gobolski said.

Mr. Maws returned with the brandy glasses on a tray and distributed them, putting the tray with the bottle on a corner of the desk. Gobolski sniffed his drink suspiciously for a second and then drained the glass. "Excellent," he said. Mr. Maws refilled the glass.

"All of this," Gobolski said, "is the normal procedure." He sipped at the second glass. "Then I received a message from St. Petersburg today. Doubly encoded, so that when the code clerk was finished with it I then had to decode it again myself."

"Yes?" Moriarty encouraged.

"There was a message in it—and instructions. The message was for Professor James Moriarty. The instructions were for me. I have never heard of you before, you understand."

"I would not have expected you to have."

"My instructions were to bring the message to you myself, personally, and not allow anyone else to see it. That is unusual."

"I'm sure."

"The instructions further directed me to be careful," Count Gobolski said. "Be careful! When I already have twenty-four-hour policemen and nine armed guards." He smoothed his mustache. "I trust that the message holds some relevancy or importance for you. I confess that it conveys nothing of interest to me."

"I haven't seen it yet," Moriarty said, patiently.

"I tell you Mr.—Professor—Moriarty, there is enough to keep me busy in the diplomatic sphere without branching out into espionage. The External Branch of the Okhrana is responsible for espionage. It is not my job. The relationships between your country and mine—I assume you are British—are quite delicate. They require all of my time. I don't see why a man in my position has to act as a courier for messages of doubtful importance."

"May I see the message?" Moriarty asked.

"What? Oh, yes. Of course." Count Gobolski patted the pockets of his formal attire, and finally produced a slip of buff paper which he passed over to the Professor.

Moriarty read it, and then reread it, looking puzzled. "This is all?" he demanded.

Count Gobolski looked slightly startled at the change in Moriarty's manner. "All?" he said. "Of course it is all. Then I was right—the matter is of no importance? I am missing Wagner for nothing?"

"On the contrary, my dear Count," Moriarty said, "it is of the gravest importance. But it is incomplete; the most significant facts are missing." He held the slip of paper out. "Barnett, what do you make of it?"

Barnett took the paper and stood under the gas pendant to read it. It was printed in a crabbed hand, presumably Count Gobolski's, and read in its entirety:

FOUR SAILORS FROM BLACK SEA FLEET HAVE LEFT SEVASTOPOL FOR EN-
GLAND. JOINING TREPOFF SURELY. TRAVELING AS GERMANS POSSIBLY.
EXPECTED JULY TENTH.

"Trepoff needs sailors," Barnett said, handing the note back.

"So it would seem," Moriarty said. "And the tenth is only six days off." He transferred his attention back to Gobolski. "What do you know of Trepoff?"

"I?" Gobolski started. "Nothing. I know nothing of Trepoff. I have heard rumors, of course. Who has not? But I know nothing of this madman. Nothing. I think it is a joke, or a myth used to scare small children. It is said that he kills without warning. And that, although an agent of the Tsar, even the Tsar is afraid of him. Of course, that is not true. I know nothing of him."

Moriarty leaned forward. "Trepoff is in London," he said, tapping the desk. "He is real. You were sent with that message because of your exalted rank and station, because you could be trusted and no one else could. I thank you for coming. This is of the utmost importance, you must believe that. As important as any of your other work."

"Trepoff is in London?" Count Gobolski shot a nervous glance around the room and wiped his mustache. "Has your man ascertained yet whether my carriage is under observation?"

"He will inform us before you leave," Moriarty said. "But this message must be amplified." He tapped the paper. "You must send a reply requesting more detail."

"Detail?"

"Yes, Your Excellency. I need to know the identity of the four men. I need to know their ranks and their specialties."

"What for?" Gobolski said, honestly puzzled. "They are only sailors. If they were officers it would have said as much."

"But even sailors have specialties," Moriarty said patiently. "They may be deckhands, or gunners, or ordnance specialists, or artificers, or engine crew, or stewards, or any one of a dozen other jobs. If I know what they do, then I will have some idea of why Trepoff wants them. I need this information, Your Excellency."

Count Gobolski nodded. "Very clever. The specialties of sailors. I will send the message."

"Thank you."

There was a tapping at the study door, and Mummer Tolliver burst through. "I've got 'em pegged right enough for you, Professor," he said, coming to a halt in front of the desk.

"Then there *is* someone watching the house?" Moriarty asked. He looked pleased.

" 'Course there is, sir," the Mummer said. "There's three of 'em, as a matter of fact."

"Tell me about it," Moriarty said, rubbing his hands together thoughtfully.

"Yes, sir. There's a chap bent over in the shrubbery in the square, behind the equestrian statue of Lord Hornblower. He's keeping a weather eye on the carriage what's parked outside the door."

"My carriage?" Count Gobolski demanded.

"Right enough," the Mummer agreed. "And on the back steps of the British Museum, on Montague Place, there's a beggar with a horrible twisted lip selling pencils. Only it's a peculiar time to be selling pencils, says me, and he ain't no beggar, further."

"That sounds like a certain consulting detective of my acquaintance," Moriarty said. "I do hope he isn't too comfortable."

"And then, around the corner of the next block, over on Gower Street, there's a hansom cab setting, waiting for something."

"A fare, perhaps?" Moriarty suggested.

"Funny time to be waiting for a fare on Gower Street," the Mummer said. "I went over to him myself and tried to engage him."

"And?"

"He told me he was otherwise engaged. When I persisted, he told me several interesting things about my parentage that my father hasn't seen fit to mention. He spoke with an accent."

"What sort?" Moriarty asked.

The Mummer shrugged. "French," he said.

"Could it have been Russian?" Moriarty suggested.

" 'Course it could," Tolliver agreed. "French, Russian—they all sound the same, you know."

"Yes, I suppose they do," Moriarty said. "Anything else?"

"It is my opinion," Tolliver said, "that the gent lurking behind the statue and the gent atop of the hansom are working together."

"Interesting," Moriarty said. "On what do you base this observation?"

"Their hats," Tolliver said.

Barnett looked at his small friend. "Hats?" he said.

"Yes. Caps, actually. They both have the same cap, and it's a queer one, it is. Long beak, coming to a point almost, in front. With a little strap in the back with a buckle. Never seen one like it before, and here's two in one evening. That's why I think they're related, those two."

"Very good work, Tolliver," Moriarty said. He turned to Count Gobolski. "If you don't mind my asking, Your Excellency, where are you going from here?"

"To the house of—a friend—south of Kensington Gardens," Gobolski said. "Why do you ask?"

"Please write down the address and give it to Tolliver here," Moriarty said. "They will follow you when you leave here, but they will be prepared for someone attempting to follow them. That is, if it is the group I suspect. However, if Tolliver picks them up when you arrive at your friend's house instead of following them directly, we may catch them off guard. In that case we may be able to trace them back to their lair. Perhaps back to Trepoff himself."

"You believe this is possible?" Gobolski asked.

"I think it is, yes."

"You think this little man can do such a job?"

"Tolliver?" Moriarty said, turning to the Mummer.

"I ain't perfect," Tolliver said, "but I'm good."

Count Gobolski shrugged, obviously far from convinced, and wrote an address down on the back of one of his cards. He handed the card to Tolliver.

"I wants to change clothes for this job," the Mummer said, indicating his checked suit and high collar. "This ain't a suitable disguise. Give me a moment."

"We'll give you twenty minutes," Moriarty said, "ten minutes to change and a ten-minute head start."

"Twenty minutes?" Count Gobolski pulled out his pocket watch and inspected its face. "It is now ten twenty-five. I am already late."

"Patience, Your Excellency," Moriarty said, waving the Mummer out of the room, "there is much at stake here. Perhaps I could interest you in a brief game of chess to pass the time?"

"Chess?" Count Gobolski looked interested. "You play chess?"

"Barnett, hand down that board on the shelf behind you, if you will." Moriarty said. "And the Persian pieces in the box next to it."

The game went on for forty minutes, with the two men engrossed in the board between them, and Barnett an interested, if not engrossed, spectator. Finally, Moriarty pushed a black pawn forward and straightened up. "Checkmate, I believe, Your Excellency," he said. "A good game."

Count Gobolski stared at the board. Then he took a small notebook from his pocket and jotted down the sequence of moves in a quick, nervous hand. "Brilliant!" he said. "So fast and so sure. And you an Englishman!"

"Thank you," Moriarty said, taking the delicate ivory pieces and replacing them carefully in their box.

"Well!" Gobolski said, rising and putting his notebook away. "Now I am incredibly late. I hope it is to the good." He shook hands with Moriarty. "I will send your list of questions to St. Petersburg tomorrow," he said. "Perhaps you would play chess with me again some time?"

Moriarty rose and bowed. "My pleasure," he said.

SEVENTEEN
THE PUZZLE

*Life must be lived forward, but can only
be understood backward.*
— KIERKEGAARD

The cripple, squatting on his little body cart, pulled himself through the London streets with surprising speed, aided by his two short India-rubber-tipped sticks. Early risers on this Sabbath morning saw him pass and felt a touch of pity, a twinge of undefinable guilt (emotions his whole garb had been carefully designed to evoke), and more than one hand reached toward a pocketbook as he passed. He did not stop for alms, however, but pressed determinedly on, scurrying through the streets of Bloomsbury until he passed the British Museum and then hopping his cart dextrously up the steps of 64 Russell Square.

Mr. Maws opened the door upon hearing a persistent knocking, and looked stolidly down on the mendicant on the stoop. "Yes?"

The cripple rubbed the side of his nose with his right forefinger.

Mr. Maws stepped aside. "Enter," he said. "You may wait in the front room. He will be down directly."

Ten minutes later Professor Moriarty strode into the front room and glared down at the mendicant. "Well?" he demanded.

The cripple once again rubbed the side of his nose with his right forefinger. Then he ponderously winked at Moriarty, his face screwed up in an awful expression, and waited.

"Yes, yes," Moriarty said impatiently. "I already know that. Well?"

The cripple looked unhappy. "The Kensington Wheeler, they calls me," he said finally.

"And well they should," Moriarty agreed. "Why are you here?"

"Twist, 'e tells me right enough to come see the professor—you the professor?—and bring 'im a message."

"I am the professor," Moriarty said, as patiently as he could manage. "What is the message?"

"Twist, 'e says as how you'll stand a quid for this 'ere message," the Kensington Wheeler said firmly.

"I'll make it a guinea," Moriarty said, reaching into his waistcoat pocket, "if you'll get on with it." He held some coins out, which were grabbed and disappeared in an undefinable manner into the mendicant's rags.

The Kensington Wheeler tucked his sticks under him and assumed a narrative stance. "I 'as a spot," he announced, "to the right 'and side o' the doors o' the Church o' St. Jude on the south side o' River Thames, over in Lambeth. Sundays, that is. Rest o' the week I wheels about Kensington."

Moriarty nodded. "I see."

"Well, sir," the Kensington Wheeler continued, "no sooner 'as I assumed my spot this 'ere morning when a growler pulls up to the corner and two gents gets out dragging a third gent between them."

"This third gentleman was unconscious?" Moriarty asked.

"No, sir. 'E were right lively. 'E didn't want to go with those other two gents no ways. But 'e were a little chap, and they was considerable bigger."

"I see."

"Well, sir, these two big gents they pays me no mind, like I was part o' the wall, which is a usual reaction what people 'as. But the little chap, 'e sees me; and right off 'e gives me the office. Which weren't easy, what with these other two 'olding 'is arms, but 'e manages. And 'e calls out to them—but really to me, dontcherknow—'what you want to bother the Mummer for? The Mummer never 'urt you'—so I'd know who 'e is, like."

"Ah!" Moriarty said.

"Well, sir, these other two gents, they gives me the once-over, but I makes like I'm part o' the wall, which is what they thought in the first place, so they leaves me alone. As soon as they is out of sight, I 'eads out for the guild-'all, even it being the start of the 'eaviest time o' the day for me, cause the little chap gave me the office. Twist tells me to bring the tale 'ere, and you'd make it worth my while."

"Very interesting," Moriarty said. "You did well. You should have taken a cab here, though. I would have reimbursed you."

"Ain't no cab going to stop for me, Professor, even if I waves the money at the jarvey. Which I 'as done."

"I see. Well, you shall leave here in a cab. I'll have one here to take you wherever you wish to go. Can you tell me which way they took the Mummer as they left you?"

"Better 'n that," the beggar said, "I can show you what building they took 'im into."

"Excellent!" Moriarty said. "And so you shall. Go into the kitchen and tell Mrs. H to feed you. I'll be along presently, and we'll take a trip together. We must be quick about it, though."

"I'll be quicker than quick, Professor," the Kensington Wheeler said. "I'm not much of a one for eating, but if I could 'ave a drop o' something before we leaves, it would restore my spirits like."

"Whatever you like," Moriarty said. "Tell Mrs. H." He crossed the hall to his study while the Kensington Wheeler propelled himself to the rear of the house. After ringing for Mr. Maws, Moriarty touched a concealed stud on the left side of the bookcase behind his desk, and it promptly slid forward. Moriarty swung the bookcase aside and opened the cabinet behind it.

"You rang?" Mr. Maws stood by the door.

"Yes. Have you seen Mr. Barnett this morning?"

"I believe that he has just come down to breakfast, sir," Mr. Maws volunteered.

"Good," Moriarty said. "I shall require him—and you, Mr. Maws, if you would be good enough to accompany me." He slid open a door in the cabinet and contemplated the row of revolvers contained therein.

"Is it about Mr. Tolliver, sir?" Mr. Maws inquired.

"Yes. The Mummer seems to have fallen into the hands of the opposition. I have no idea what they plan to do with him, but I rather fancy it would be a good idea not to give them the time to do too good a job of it."

"Very good, sir," Mr. Maws said. "If we are to go armed, sir, I would prefer one of the Webley-Fosbery .455-caliber revolvers."

Moriarty handed over the requested weapon and a box of shells. "Change clothes into something a bit less butler-like," he said. "And ask Barnett to step in here as you pass the dining room."

"Very good, sir," Mrs. Maws said.

A minute later Barnett came into the study. Moriarty quickly informed him of what was happening and handed him a Smith & Wesson hammerless revolver and ammunition. "This is for self-protection," he said, "and, if necessary, a show of force. I don't know what we'll be coming up against, but if Trepoff is any part of it we'd best be prepared. He is a violently dangerous man."

Barnett loaded the revolver and thrust it into his belt. "Won't your London police object to gunplay of a Sunday afternoon?"

"It may require a bit of explaining," Moriarty admitted. "We could always tell them we are rehearsing an amateur theatrical. On the whole, it would be best if we don't have to use these weapons. Besides, I would like to speak with Tolliver's captors in some detail, a task which will be rendered easier if they are still alive."

"And," Barnett added, "if we are."

"True," Moriarty replied, buttoning his jacket and selecting a walking stick from the rack. "Let us be on our way. Oh, there you are, Mr. Maws. See about capturing us a growler, if you will, while I retrieve the Kensington Wheeler from the kitchen."

It was just past noon when the four-wheeler turned into Little George Street and pulled up at the Church of St. Jude. "We'd best stop here," Moriarty said. "Mr. Maws, if you would help the Wheeler down, we'll make sure we have the right building."

"I'll point 'er out to you, Professor," the Kensington Wheeler said, "but I ain't going inside with you. That there is your affair."

"Good enough," Moriarty said. "Just point the house out to Mr. Maws and you'll have more than earned your money." He closed the door of the cab. "Wait around the corner," he told the driver. "I don't know how long we'll be."

The driver touched his whip to his hat, and the four-wheeler clattered off.

Mr. Maws walked off alongside the wheeler and was back in a minute. "Fifth house down on the right, just as the gentleman described it," he said. "Far as I can tell there's no one at the windows. The blinds are drawn. How are we going to get in?"

"I've been giving it some thought," Moriarty said. "I could impersonate a gas man, but even a Russian wouldn't believe that if he remembered it's Sunday. Also, there may or may not be some urgency, depending on what plans they have for Tolliver. All in all, I'm afraid, the direct approach is the best."

"Then let's go!" Barnett said.

"Remember," Moriarty said, "an absolute minimum of violence. We want prisoners."

With that, the three of them walked at a measured rate down

the street to the fifth house and mounted the stoop. Moriarty knocked gently on the door.

" 'Oo's there?" a voice came through the closed door after a minute.

"It's Father Banion," Moriarty said in a deep, melodious voice, his face pressed close to the door. "I understand there's a sick man in there who requested my presence."

The bolt was pulled and the latch lifted. "There's no one sick in here, Father," the man inside said, opening the door slightly to pass the word.

Mr. Maws hit the door solidly with his shoulder and sprung it open. In a flash Moriarty was inside and had grabbed the man and wrapped an arm around his mouth. "There'll be someone very sick if you try to make a sound," he whispered. "I'll break your neck!"

The man struggled for a moment and then was still. His reaction was not one of belligerence, but rather of great surprise.

"Who are you?" Moriarty asked softly. "Don't raise your voice!" He released his hold on the man's neck enough for him to catch his breath and reply.

"I'm the porter, sir," the man squeaked. "And who are you? Sir?"

"Scotland Yard," Moriarty said. "This house is surrounded."

The man's mouth fell open. "The p'lice!" he said. "It's them foreign-looking gentlemen, ain't it?"

"What do you know about them?" Moriarty demanded in an undertone. "Speak quickly!"

"Nuffin', sir. They been here about a fortnight, sir. I didn't do nuffin', sir, whatever *they* did. There's a whole bunch of them upstairs now."

"I see," Moriarty said, "And how many to a bunch, my man?"

"I didn't watch them come in, you know. They don't like it if they think I'm watching them." The porter sniffed and wiped the back of his hand across his nose. "I'd say maybe a dozen, maybe a few more'n that."

Moriarty released the porter and turned to his two companions. "We seem to have bitten off a hefty morsel," he said.

"We could rush them," Mr. Maws said, flexing his shoulders.

"We could, indeed," Moriarty agreed. "Which would put us somewhat in the position of the fox rushing the hounds. But it is an option." He turned to the porter. "I'm afraid there's going to be some excitement here for the next little while. Have you a room? Good. Go to it now, and don't come out of it for the next half-hour."

When the man had gone, Moriarty stepped to the foot of the stairs and listened. The sound of subdued conversation came from above. "It doesn't sound like an interrogation," Moriarty said. "They probably have Tolliver locked up in one of the upstairs rooms while they discuss other matters."

"Perhaps one of their number is heating the hot irons even now, while the rest of them talk," Barnett suggested.

Moriarty shook his head. "They've only had him here for a few hours," he said. "And this must be a regularly scheduled meeting. Or, rather, a specially scheduled meeting, since these people usually don't assemble in groups larger than three. But at any rate, it must have been set in advance of their capturing Tolliver."

"It must be important, then," Barnett said.

Moriarty nodded. "Assuming our conclusions are correct," he added, "and this doesn't turn out to be a gathering of the Lithuanian branch of the Young Men's Christian Association." He pulled his pince-nez glasses from one pocket and a cloth from another and began assiduously polishing the lenses. "I'd give quite a lot to listen in on that conversation," he added.

"I could sneak upstairs," Barnett offered. "Perhaps I could overhear something."

Moriarty shook his head. "The chances of your being apprehended," he said, "are much larger than the chances of their speaking English."

"I hadn't thought of that," Barnett admitted.

Moriarty put his pince-nez back into his pocket. "We could get reinforcements," he said, "but that would take longer than we can afford. They may decide to transfer Tolliver to a safer place, since this house is undoubtedly going to be abandoned after this meeting. Indeed, Tolliver may already have been taken away."

"Then what do we do?" Barnett asked.

"We rush them, as Mr. Maws has suggested," Moriarty said. "But in such a fashion as to create an air of moral, if not numerical, superiority. I see that this house is constructed with a back stairs. Ideal for our purposes."

"How's that?" Barnett asked.

"We have to leave them a way out," Moriarty said, "or they'll come out over us."

Mr. Maws pulled his revolver from under his jacket. "Shall we go then, sir?"

Moriarty nodded and pulled a police whistle from his trouser pocket. "When I blow this," he said.

Mr. Maws smiled. " 'Under the shadow of Death,' " he said firmly, " 'Under the stroke of the sword, Gain we our daily bread.' "

Barnett turned to him. "What's that?"

"Kipling," Mr. Maws explained. "Are we ready?"

"Don't use that weapon unless they fire first," Moriarty instructed. "What we're after is a maximum of noise and confusion, but preferably without gunfire." He thought for a second, and then continued. "Mr. Maws, you take the stairs. Barnett, start on this corridor, but keep away from the back stairs. We have once again become Scotland Yard," he said. "And there are at least fifty of us. But somehow we've forgotten to cover the back exits."

"How careless of us," Barnett said.

At that instant an upstairs door opened and footsteps sounded over their heads. The murmur of voices grew louder.

Moriarty put the whistle to his lips and blew a triple blast. "All right up there!" he yelled. "This is the police. All of you come down with your hands over your heads. Resistance is useless!"

There was a moment of shocked silence from upstairs and then the murmur turned into a babble and the sound of footsteps increased in number, volume, and tempo.

Barnett started opening and slamming doors and shouting official-sounding instructions. "Simmons," he yelled, "take your men around the back! Dwyer, check these rooms out!"

Mr. Maws stomped up the front stairs with the stolid tread of the invincible English policeman. "You are all under arrest," he bellowed in a deep voice. "It is my duty to inform each of you that anything you say will be taken down and may be used in evidence. Come along quietly, now!"

The milling footsteps upstairs broke into a panicked scurrying, as one of them found the back stairs and reported the fact to the others. A heavy sofa was pushed out into the upstairs hall facing the front staircase, and two men squatted behind it, pointing a brace of long-barreled revolvers at the advancing figure of Mr. Maws.

Mr. Maws dropped as someone's gun went off, and the bullet

crashed through a print of *Mercy Interceding for the Vanquished*, which hung on the wall behind him. Mr. Maws's answering shot smashed into the door frame above the sofa.

There was a hurried whispering from behind the couch, and then a sliding sound, and then all was silent from above. Professor Moriarty climbed the stairs to where Mr. Maws lay and peered amusedly at the couch barrier. "The birds have flown," he said. "And a good thing, too."

Mr. Maws got up and dusted himself off. "Disgraceful!" he said. "I shall have to speak to that porter. I don't believe they clean this stair carpeting at all."

Barnett came up to join them. "Gone?" he asked.

"We have the building to ourselves," Moriarty said. "Except for the porter, and, I hope, Tolliver. You two go look for him. I wish to examine that meeting room and see if our friends left anything of interest in their haste."

"I hope those shots don't bring the real police," Barnett said.

"They may," Moriarty acknowledged. "In which case we are injured innocents. British stoic heroism. Saved a man from kidnappers—if Tolliver is here—but want no reward. After all, *we* didn't run away." He went up to the landing and boosted himself over the sofa. "But I'd better get a look at that room before they arrive."

Mr. Maws searched the rooms on the floor they were on, while Barnett climbed the last flight to the top floor and checked those rooms out. It was Barnett who found Tolliver. The third door he pushed open led to a lumber room full of disused furniture, Tolliver was securely trussed up and tied to a bed frame which rested against the far wall. Barnett cut the ropes with his pocketknife and released the brave little man.

"I heard the commotion when you arrived," Tolliver said. "What happened? If I might ask." He sat on a trunk and rubbed his arms briskly. "My hands are coming all over pins and needles," he explained. "They tied me a bit tight."

"It's good to see you, Mummer," Barnett said. "But you're going to have to become a bit more proficient at the art of following people so we don't have to rescue you every time you go out of an evening."

"I like that!" Tolliver said. " 'Ere I am trying to bring a bit of excitement into the lad's life, and 'e's full of reproach. After all, it's not 'im what got trussed up like a capon."

Barnett laughed. "Come on downstairs," he said. "The professor will want to say hello."

Moriarty was on his knees examining the floor in the meeting room when Barnett brought the Mummer down. "Don't touch anything!" he snapped as they entered the room. "I'm not through in here yet."

"You might at least," Barnett said, annoyed at Moriarty's lack of compassion, "tell the Mummer that you're glad to see him."

"Nonsense," Moriarty said, getting up and dusting off the knees of his trousers. "We're here, aren't we?"

"Well, I'm glad you come," Tolliver said. "I was beginning to get a bit concerned as to my future."

Mr. Maws appeared in the doorway. "Afternoon, Tolliver," he said. "Professor, I thought you might be interested to hear that I just glanced out a front window and noticed several large men taking up positions about the house."

"Scotland Yard," the Mummer said.

"Let us hope so," Moriarty said. He sighed. "No doubt they will remember about the back door. Ah, well. There doesn't seem to be anything of interest in this room, unfortunately. And to think, we had a whole room full of them here, and now they're all gone."

"Leaving nothing behind?" Barnett asked.

"Nothing of consuming interest," Moriarty said. "There's that hat"—he pointed—"and that picture, and a few cigarette butts of rather common brand."

Barnett went over to examine the picture, which was tacked to the wall by the door. A full-color portrait of Queen Victoria looking stuffily regal, it had been carefully cut out of a recent edition of the *Illustrated London News*.

"Well, well," Barnett said. "A patriotic bunch of anarchists. What will they think of next?"

The sound of someone pounding violently on the front door came up from below. "Open up!" an authoritarian voice bellowed. "This is the police!"

"Go down and let them in, Mr. Maws," Moriarty directed. But before Mr. Maws had reached the staircase, they heard the front door opening and the heavy feet of policemen treading on the stairs. "The porter!" Moriarty said. "I had quite forgotten about the poor porter. What must he think!"

Heavy footsteps sounded on the stairs, and a uniformed policeman came into view. " 'Ere now, just you stand still there!" he commanded. "There's three of them—no, four—up here, sir," he called back down the stairs.

"Oh, officer," Moriarty said in the concerned voice of a nervous schoolmaster, "thank God you've come at last. We thought you'd never get here."

That set the policeman back. Confusion reddened his already ruddy ears. "What's all this, then? What's all this?" he said.

"My young friend here," Moriarty said, indicating Tolliver, "has been imprisoned by a bunch of foreigners. We had just contrived to effect his release when you arrived. Surely it was our summons that brought you?"

"I don't know nothing about that, sir," the policeman said. "You'd better wait here, sir."

"We'll just come downstairs," Moriarty said. "There may be more of them on the upper story. Tolliver, take your cap," he added, indicating the piece of headgear hanging from the back of a chair.

"My cap?" said Tolliver. "Oh, yes. Thank you, sir."

They went downstairs, edging past the policemen who were gathering for the assault on the upper story. On the ground floor officers were going from room to room, while the porter stood with three plainclothes Scotland Yard men and Mr. Sherlock Holmes in the front hall.

"Holmes!" Moriarty said. "Whatever brings you to Lambeth? And Inspector Lestrade, I believe."

"Acting on information received," Lestrade said stiffly, "I obtained a warrant to search these premises. I was informed that you might be here, Professor, although, quite frankly, I didn't believe it. I'll have to ask you to explain your presence here, sir."

Holmes pushed Lestrade aside and stepped forward, his fists clenched. "Enough of this, Moriarty!" he snapped. "We have you now. Where is she? The house is completely surrounded, you might as well give it up."

Moriarty shook his head. "Honestly, Holmes, I have no idea what you are talking about. You must have arranged this little raid, so I thank you. I was wondering why they gave up so easily. They must have looked out the window and seen you arriving. But I don't know what brought you."

Holmes laughed. "Really, Professor, you disappoint me," he said. "Who must have left? I came here expecting to find you, and I found you. Where is the girl?"

"What girl?"

"The Duke of Ipswich's daughter, Lady Catherine."

"That again." Moriarty took his pince-nez from his pocket and affixed them to the bridge of his nose. "Holmes, please believe me. I had nothing to do with her abduction, and I have no knowledge of her present whereabouts. Is that what this is about? You followed me here, and decided that this is where I must have hidden her? Quite a piece of ratiocination." He turned to the inspector. "And on Sherlock Holmes's unsupported word you applied for a warrant? Giles Lestrade, I'm ashamed of you."

Lestrade looked embarrassed. "The professor has been of some assistance to the Yard in the past," he told Holmes. "And I know of nothing against him except some unsupported rumor and your theories, Mr. Holmes. Not that you, yourself, haven't come to our aid on occasion."

"Then you are not going to place Moriarty under arrest?"

"Now, Mr. Holmes," Lestrade said, looking acutely uncomfortable, "you know the law. If we find the young lady, and she accuses, ah, mentions the professor when she relates what happened, why then that'll be a different story. But as things stand . . ."

Holmes glared at Moriarty. "Disgraceful!" he said. "The greatest rogue unhung, and I can't even get him charged."

Moriarty shook his head. "Really, Holmes. And in front of witnesses, too. Actionable slander, I'd say." He shook his finger in Holmes's face, which caused Holmes to take an abrupt step backward. "As I've told you before, you must use your brain at all times, and never rely on preconceived notions. In this case, for example, if you would use your quite adequate powers of deduction and examine the premises, you would discover quite easily that I am speaking the truth. A group of Russian anarchists had the rooms upstairs. They had abducted my associate, Tolliver, here. I and my friends arrived to effect his release, and you were one step behind me."

Holmes snorted. "Anarchists!"

Moriarty turned to the porter, who was standing on the edge of the group, looking confused. "Is that not so?" he demanded.

"Right enough," the porter assented.

"And you have never seen me before today?"

"No, sir. Can't say as I have."

"Very convincing," Holmes sneered. "I'm going upstairs to look around," he told Lestrade. "Hold them here until I return, if you don't mind. You can at least do that, can't you?"

"Now, Mr. Holmes—" Lestrade said.

Moriarty smiled. "I shall remain, willingly, until you return," he said. "I believe that the front room is empty. We shall wait in there until you are quite satisfied." And pushing the door open with his stick, he strode into the room and settled into an overstuffed chair.

"Say, Professor," Barnett said, sitting across from Moriarty and speaking in a low voice. "What does that fellow have against you, anyway?"

"He believes me to be a villain," Moriarty said, staring at the wall opposite.

"Yes, but there are a lot of villains in this world," Barnett said. "And Holmes sure has it in for you in particular."

Moriarty was silent for a moment, and then his eyes focused on Barnett. "We knew each other some years ago," he said. "I was his tutor for a period. We were, I might say, as close to being friends as a tutor and his student ever get. He was a brilliant student, if a bit disorganized."

Moriarty fell silent. "Yes?" Barnett prompted.

"I was rebuffed by society," Moriarty continued, "at least that segment of society that I deemed important. I chose to live outside their laws to accomplish my ends. It was a deliberate decision that I have never regretted. My researches are more important to the future of the human race than the mores of this particular time and place.

"Holmes, also, was rebuffed by society, albeit an entirely different and particularly limited segment of society. He chose to get his revenge by being better than those who had rebuffed him. Which he certainly is. This—improvement—necessitated a certain rigidity of outlook. Thus, I am on one side of a barrier Holmes created, and he on the other. It is quite a shame."

Barnett's reportorial soul was unsatisfied with the answer, which managed to seem specific while remaining quite vague, but he sensed that he was not going to get a better one at the moment. He resolved to solve this mystery when the current excitement had died down enough to allow him to devote the time to it.

The door opened a minute later and Holmes stalked in with Lestrade at his heels. "The girl has not been in this house," he announced.

Moriarty nodded.

"There were other people here," Holmes conceded. "Fifteen or sixteen of them. Russians, for the most part, although several of them have been in England for some time. Tolliver would seem to have been their prisoner for a matter of hours. They arrived at different times over a period of about one day. They were discussing plans of some sort, certainly illegal. Whatever they have planned is going to take place in the near future; at least a week off, but no more than a month. You would seem not to have been part of the group, Professor."

"How do you know all that?" Lestrade demanded.

"Thank you for that," Moriarty said. "Don't look so disappointed, Holmes. There *are* other criminals in the world."

Holmes sat on the edge of the sofa and stared at Moriarty with a curious expression on his face. "Then they have the girl," he said. "Tell me what you know about them."

"Still the girl?" Moriarty said. "Then you weren't following me?"

Holmes took a cigarette case from his coat and removed one. He started to return the case to his pocket, then paused and offered it to Moriarty. "Try one," he said. "They're made for me by Drucquer's."

Moriarty took a cigarette and returned the case to Holmes, who shoved it back into his pocket. Barnett noted the gesture and saw that, for these two men, there was no one else in the room at this moment.

Holmes struck a wax vesta and lit the two cigarettes, and the two men stared silently at each other as smoke gradually filled the room. "The Duke of Ipswich received a note," Holmes said.

Moriarty lifted an eyebrow. "Finally," he said.

"I was prepared," Holmes said. "The note was delivered in an ingenious manner, but I managed to follow the deliverer, and a chain of other underlings, until I was led to this house. The trail seemed to end here. I was sure that the answer lay here. That either the girl was here, or I could round up enough of the gang here to break its back and ascertain her whereabouts."

"It's a good thing they got away, then," Moriarty said. "Had you captured those who were here, without the girl, she would surely have been killed."

Holmes nodded. "But you see," he said, "I thought it was you. And you are a fairly reasonable man. Whatever else you are."

"What did the note say?" Moriarty asked. "They didn't want money."

"This is to go no farther than this room," Holmes said.

"I pledge myself and my associates," Moriarty answered.

Holmes looked at Lestrade. "What, *me*?" the little detective said. He took his bowler off. "My solemn word," he said.

"It is common knowledge in certain circles," Holmes said in a low, clear voice, "that the Duke of Ipswich is to become foreign minister when Lord Halder resigns, probably in a few weeks. The note informed the Duke that if he wished to see his daughter alive again, he was to perform certain actions in regard to a certain foreign power."

"He could refuse the appointment," Moriarty said.

"And assure the death of his daughter."

"Of course," Moriarty said. "And, of course, the duke as a loyal British citizen has no intention of following these instructions, even if it means the death of his daughter."

Holmes nodded. "I must find the girl before he takes office," he said. "The first note, on the night she was taken, warned against publicity. The duke has complied with that. And now this."

"What is he going to do," Moriarty asked, "if you don't find his daughter?"

"He is going to accept the portfolio," Holmes said, "and perform his job. On the day that he learns for certain that his daughter is dead, he is going to put a bullet through his brain."

Moriarty nodded. "That clever bastard," he said.

"What?"

"I assure you I'm not referring to the duke," Moriarty said. "Unfortunately I can't give you too much information. Nothing, I'm afraid, that would be of immediate assistance to you. However, I can tell you this: the abductors of Lady Catherine have no intention of returning her alive. She may already be dead, but probably not. They knew the duke would not obey instructions. Indeed, they are counting on it." He stood up. "And I'll tell you something else; one of the benefits they looked for in this abduction, and the reason they waited until now to send these further instructions, was to set you against me. It kept you from looking for *them*, you see."

Holmes thought about that for a moment, and then nodded. "Who are they?" he asked. "Surely you can tell me something about them. You can't have been here by accident. And the nation involved—we have both been there recently."

"I can tell you nothing more at this time," Moriarty said. "It is not my personal secret, you see. In any event, I know nothing that would be of material benefit to you in your search beyond what you already know or can surmise. But I can tell you this, Holmes; in this matter our interests run together. If I discover anything of value to you, I shall convey it to you immediately. At any rate, come around to Russell Square in a day or two."

"I'll do that," Holmes said.

"Wear one of your less elementary disguises," Moriarty suggested, "for both our sakes."

THE HAT TRICK

*You shall seek all day ere you find them,
and, when you have them, they are not
worth the search.*

—SHAKESPEARE

Moriarty spent most of Monday dissecting the cap they had picked up in the Lambeth house and subjecting the pieces to a variety of microscopic, physical, and chemical tests. By the time he went up to dress for dinner, he had filled several notebook pages with the results.

Barnett came in late for dinner, which, by household custom, did not wait for him. Mrs. H set the table, served, and cleared at specified unvarying times. If one didn't make those times, then one didn't eat dinner. Of course, one could always go into the kitchen and have Mrs. Randall fix one a plate and eat it at the kitchen table. But as Mrs. H would say, that wouldn't be dinner, now would it?

Barnett plowed right into his meal, ignoring the soup and slighting the fish to get directly to the roast while it was still on the table. When he had enough on his plate to keep him alive until breakfast, he paused to be sociable. "Evening, all," he said.

Professor Moriarty was glaring at him. "I fail to see the purpose of dressing for dinner," he said coldly, "if one proceeds to behave like an aborigine at the table."

Barnett put his fork down. "Right, Boss," he said. "I'll just wear my breech-clout and feathers next time."

"And don't call me 'Boss,'" Moriarty said. "It is a particularly abominable Americanism."

"Well!" Barnett said. He looked at Tolliver, who was carefully ignoring the whole exchange, and then back at the professor. "I believe I missed something here."

"Eat your dinner," Moriarty said.

"You've been working on that hat all day, right? You didn't get anything from it, right?"

Moriarty sighed. "I shall have to control my petulance," he said. "Not that I mind being disagreeable, but I do object to being obvious. We'll talk about it after dinner."

They had coffee in the professor's study after dinner, and Moriarty produced the hat. "I know a fair amount about it now," he said. "It is made of Egyptian long-fiber cotton, dyed with a vegetable dye not used in this country. It is of fairly recent manufacture, say within the past six months. Its owner is a healthy young man, under thirty-five, with a full head of dark-brown hair. In all probability he is of Eastern European stock, and under five foot six. He is interested in horse racing, or associates with people who are. He is a very neat, clean man. I think that is the best I can do for the time being."

Barnett stared unbelievingly at the Professor. "You got all that by staring at the hat under a microscope?" he asked. "Are you having me on?"

"Not at all," Moriarty said. "I assure you it is all either truth or reasonable assumption. But you see, Barnett, the problem is that it doesn't get us anywhere. I have pulled a collection of interesting but irrelevant facts out of this piece of headgear. I have spent a day at it, and furthered us not one bit."

"Yes, but—" Barnett said. "The things you have pulled out of that hat are still more than I thought could be in it. How do you know what he looks like?"

"He? You mean the owner of the cap? I don't really know what he looks like, just hair color and a reasonable guess as to some other facts."

"Hair color I can understand," Barnett said. "You found one of his hairs in the hat."

"Several."

"What about the other stuff; age, height, Eastern European, even horse racing. Don't tell me there was a horse hair in the lining."

Moriarty smiled. "No," he said, "in the brim. Used for stiffening."

"Then how?"

"As to the age and general good health, that was marked by the condition of the hair—the human hair—I found in the cap. The length of the hairs—none longer than three inches—suggests a man.

The hairs' diameter also affirms that they came from an adult male. The hairs were healthy, as a microscopic examination of the roots confirmed. This suggests that the owner of the cap also was healthy. The relative youth of the wearer I deduce from the lack of gray hairs among the thirty-six samples I found."

"European stock?" Barnett said. "Horse racing?"

Professor Moriarty tossed the cap on the table with a slight spin. "Notice the shape it takes," he said. "That is because it has been blocked by the addition of a folded-up newspaper around the inner liner to make it fit more comfortably. After repeated wearing it has taken up the shape of the wearer's head. Which, you will notice, is long and comparatively slender. The man possesses a typically Slavic skull, from which I deduce that he is probably Eastern European. Professor Alphonse Bertillon, the noted developer of the Bertillon Anthropometric System, would disagree. He marks the long, narrow head as the trait of the congenital criminal. But then, Professor Bertillon is French.

"The size of the man I deduce from the size of the head. I could be quite wrong, of course, that there is an average about these things. The famous bell-shaped distribution curve shows up quite often in human affairs."

"That leaves horse racing," Barnett said.

"The paper folded up inside the crown," Moriarty told him dryly, "is the turf odds page of the *Sporting Times*."

"Ah," Barnett said.

"Quite so," Moriarty agreed.

"Is there nothing further?" Barnett asked. Impressive as the professor's deductive display had been, he was right in saying that it didn't take them anywhere.

"One thing only," Moriarty said. "And it's more in your line than mine." He took a piece of pasteboard from his desk and flipped it over to Barnett. "This was stuck in the hatband."

Barnett examined the fragment carefully. It was roughly square, about two inches on a side, and appeared to have been torn along one edge. There was a slight reddish tinge to it, but whether it was the natural color or the result of having been kept in a hatband, Barnett couldn't tell. One side was blank, and on the other two numbers and an unintelligible word were scrawled. The numbers were printed in the European fashion; in the upper left-hand corner was "1143" and toward the bottom was "2/5/0." The word, which was between the numbers, was completely unreadable to

Barnett and could have been English, French, Russian, or Arabic as far as he could tell. He was fairly sure it wasn't Chinese, but that was about the only possibility he could eliminate. The tear, with the billet held so that the numbers were readable, was along the right-hand side.

"This may be in my line," Barnett said, turning it over and over, "but I haven't the slightest idea what it is."

"There are several possibilities," Moriarty said, "but the most probable is that it is a pawn ticket."

"I see," Barnett said. "I appreciate your compliment as to my experience in this area. However, I would appreciate any facts with which you can supply me."

"The top number," Moriarty said, "would correspond to the number of the item pawned in the pawnbroker's ledger. The bottom number is the amount loaned. The scrawl in the middle is certainly a description of the item, for those who can read it. I, unfortunately, am not among that favored few."

"What pawnshop is it from?" Barnett asked.

"That is the problem," Moriarty said. "Most licensed pawnbrokers have their name and location printed or stamped on their tickets. But there must be thousands of unlicensed brokers in the city—small tradesmen who take a few items in pledge just as a sideline and don't want to pay the yearly licensing fee. The lack of a name on the ticket would indicate a more informal shop, but the high ledger number argues otherwise. The owner would appear to be from the continent, but that is small help."

"It might be a clerk's handwriting," Barnett suggested.

"Ah! You followed that," Moriarty said. "Good, good. No, it is probably the owner, judging by the size of the pledge. Anything over ten shillings is usually only given at the owner's discretion, although there's no hard and fast rule."

"You want me to find the shop?" Barnett asked.

"Yes," Moriarty said. "See what you can discover of the pledger; he may be an acquaintance of the owner, or they may have taken down his name and address—although that's doubtful. Find out what the pledged item is. That may be especially helpful."

"Okay," Barnett said, putting the ticket carefully in his wallet. "I'll start tomorrow morning."

* * *

And so he did. For the next week, Barnett wandered the streets of London, from Chelsea to Greenwich, from Finsbury to Lambeth, seeking out pawnbrokers and moneylenders. He had always thought pawnbrokers to be a secretive lot, but they became quite loquacious, he found, when you talked to them about something other than borrowing money. Unfortunately, none of them could identify the ticket or suggest whence it came. They did verify that the billet was, indeed, a pawn ticket, and an old man in Chelsea even translated the unreadable script. "It's what we calls back-writing," he said. "Don't know why we do it. It's dying out now, but it used to be the custom in this here profession."

"What does it say?" Barnett asked.

"Musical box, it says," the old man told him. "Must be something extraordinary in the way of musical boxes to pull two-pounds-five as a pledge."

Barnett reported the translation to Moriarty that evening, received a grunt in reply, and continued the search the next morning. It was two days later, on Pigott Street in Limehouse, that Barnett succeeded in tracing the ticket to its originator.

Starkey & Sons, Money Lent on Pledge, looked like a small shop from the narrow storefront. But inside it went back for quite a long way. And there were two staircases, one leading upstairs and another down. The establishment was crowded with the most fanciful collection of items Barnett had ever seen. "These are all pledges?" he asked, fingering a stuffed boar's head.

"Not at all, sir," the aged proprietor said. "The goods taken in pledge are all downstairs. We can't sell them in the shop, you see, even after the year-and-a-week. They have to be offered at auction. It's the law. These are all items we've picked up over the years at auctions, or the like, ourselves. My old father sir, bless his heart, had a sense of whimsy." He pointed to a glass-fronted oak case along the wall. "That contraption of leather tubing in the corner is called a serpent, sir. It is a musical instrument used at one time in military bands and the like. It fell out of favor during the reign of George the Fourth, I believe. Next to it is a stuffed and shellacked sand shark. On the shelf below is a collection of crocheted butterflies."

"I take it your father was the original Starkey," Barnett said, "and you are the son?"

"My father," the old man told him, "was the original son. I am merely the original grandson. Feel free to look around, sir. Fascinating incunabula—and a dried lizardskin collection—upstairs. If you see anything you like . . ."

"Actually," Barnett said, "as fascinating as I find this store, I came in to see whether you could identify this pledge." He handed the old man the ticket.

The old man looked up at Barnett suspiciously. "Of course I can identify it," he said. "It's mine, ain't it?"

"I didn't know," Barnett said, cautiously suppressing his feeling of elation. "Are you *sure* it's yours?"

"I should know my own ticket, I suppose," the old man said, adding hostility to suspicion. "You have something to say about it?"

"Why isn't your name on it?" Barnett asked. "I should think that an old, established firm like yours would have printed tickets."

"My old father on his deathbed made me swear. 'Don't print the tickets,' he said. 'Dreadful waste of money,' he said. So what could I do? Anyway, we ain't had any complaints yet—present company excepted."

"Don't misunderstand me, Mr. Starkey," Barnett said. "I'm not complaining. I'm delighted to find you. Could you tell me something about the pledge—a musical box, I believe—and the man that pledged it?"

"You're not claiming it yourself, then?"

"What, the musical box? No."

"Ah!" the old man said, losing his suspicious expression. "For a minute there I thought it was the old higgledy-piggledy. More than one man thinks that pawnshops are fair game for all sorts of diversion. But they don't get away with it in here, I can tell you."

"I'm glad to hear that, Mr., ah, Starkey," Barnett said. "Tell me, might I take a look at the musical box?"

"The box has been claimed," Starkey said. "Taken away."

"Oh," Barnett said unhappily.

"And as the gent didn't have the ticket, I thought that you—as you do have the ticket—were going to try to claim the item. It's an old game, but it's no less than twice a year that some clever gents will rediscover it."

"You mean you thought I was in collusion with the man who reclaimed the musical box?"

"It was not beyond the bounds of possibility," the old man affirmed, striking a large wooden match and applying the lighted tip to the bowl of his ornately carved briar.

"It's nothing like that, I assure you," Barnett told him. "I am merely trying to find out who the man is so that I can return some property to him. There was no identification with the property, save this unlabeled ticket."

The old man stared at Barnett silently for a minute. "It must have taken you some time to locate this shop," he said, speculatively.

"Days," Barnett agreed.

"It must be impressive property for you to go to all this trouble to return it, and you must be an exceptionally honest man."

"Well . . ." Barnett said.

"Never mind," the old man said. "None of my business. Come to think of it, that was certainly an unusual musical box."

"Really?" Barnett said.

"A square box, about eight inches on a side and two high, made of some hard, light wood. Put together with tiny ornamental brass screws and bands. On top of the box was a miniature grand piano some five or six inches wide with a small doll in a full dress-suit sitting before it, turned away from the keys. Exquisite work."

"It sounds impressive," Barnett said.

"Ah!" the old man said. "But when you turn it on and it plays one of its sixteen selections—Bach, Beethoven, Rossini; a bit tinny, but real impressive—the doll turns to face the keys and begins playing. And its hand motions follow the music! Never seen anything like it."

"I've never even heard of anything like it," Barnett said. "Where was it made?"

"France," the old man said. "In the twenties, I think. It is signed on the bottom by Jean Eugène Robert Houdin, who served as court magician to Louis XVIII."

"Court magician?" Barnett asked. "In the eighteen twenties?"

"Oh, yes," the old man said. "Houdin was famous for his clockwork mechanisms. My father told me about them, being something of a connoisseur, as the French put it. He once made a miniature carriage, pulled by four miniature horses. And, sir, it actually worked. But this was the first thing of the sort that I've actually seen with my own eyes."

"What can you tell me about the man who pawned it?"

"Well, for one thing he wasn't French. Polish or Russian, I'd say."

"I see."

"And he was very fond of that musical box."

"But he pawned it."

"That is true. But not for anything like its true value—even in pawn. He told me he did it just to keep it safe for the next few months."

"I see," Barnett said.

"But then he came back the day before yesterday and took it out again. Told me he'd lost the ticket, which I see was the truth. I told him I remembered him, which was so, and that I'd be sorry to lose the box."

"Can you describe him for me?"

The old man considered. "I'm not much on describing the way people look," he said. "I have a picture of him in my mind's eye, don't you see, but I couldn't exactly put words to it."

"Well, was he short or tall?"

"Not too tall, I'd say."

"Young or old?"

"If I had to put a finger on it, I'd say twenty-six or seven."

"Did you happen to hear his name?"

"Hear it!" the old man snorted. "Better than that, sir; I have it written down."

"You do?" Barnett wasn't sure he should believe this stroke of luck.

"Indeed! *And* his address, for that matter."

Barnett felt weak. "You have the man's name and address written down?"

"Naturally. You don't think I'm going to let anyone walk out of here with a pledged item and no ticket unless I get some proof of his identity, do you? I've been in this business for fifty years, and nobody has accused me of being soft in the head."

"But I thought you said you recognized him," Barnett said.

"And so I did. If not, I wouldn't have let him retrieve the object no matter how many papers he signed."

"May I get a look at the paper you had him sign?"

"Gladly. In exchange for the pledge ticket. I hate to have them outstanding, you understand."

"A fair deal," Barnett agreed.

The exchange was made and Barnett copied down the information. Not that he had any real hope that the name and address were genuine, but it was certainly worth checking out. The name and address were block-printed on a buff card. PYOTRE I. AZIMOF: 7 SCRUTTON COURT. A scrawling signature was below.

"Good-bye, sir," Barnett said. "Thank you for your assistance.

You have a fascinating shop here. I will have to come back and really wander through it someday."

"It will be here," the old man assured him. "And, for so long as I have anything to say about it, so shall I."

Barnett pulled his *Greene's Pocket Guide to London Streets & Thoroughfares* from his jacket and discovered that there indeed was a Scrutton Court, and that he was no more than seven or eight blocks from it. He resolved to scout out the building himself, without waiting to check with Moriarty, and try to get a look inside if he could think of a reasonably subtle way.

But first he would pause for a bit of lunch. While eating he would plan an approach that would be the least likely to raise suspicion. He felt it would not be wise, with Trepoff, to raise suspicion.

The Jack Falstaff Tavern on Cable Street had a pleasant grill room, and the proprietor, on hearing Barnett's accent, brought him a plate of lamb chops and grilled tomatoes, which he described for some reason as his "American lunch." It was quite good. Then, in a burst of Anglo-American friendship, the proprietor produced a pot of coffee which had been boiled only briefly and was actually drinkable.

Barnett sat over the coffee and tried to pick an approach. Building inspector? Gas-meter reader? "Excuse me, sir, but I believe my pigeon just flew in your window. Mind if I look?" Professor Moriarty would have seven acceptable schemes for getting inside the house, surely Barnett could come up with one. Barnett debated enlisting the professor's aid instead of proceeding on his own initiative, but then decided it would be more to his credit if he could prove himself an effective sleuth without help from the old master.

Barnett finished his third cup of coffee and got up. He'd check the house out from the outside. Maybe something immensely clever would occur to him as he walked by. Maybe not. Maybe there was no such house; the man had probably given a false name and address anyhow. Better check it out and see where to go from there.

Scrutton Court was a double row of two-story red brick buildings facing a narrow stone-paved street. Someone had built it early in the century as housing for the deserving almost-poor, and so it had stayed for the past sixty or seventy years. Barnett had to walk the length of the street twice before he located the building numbers, which were painted in whitewash on the curb. A row of apathetic women watched him without interest from their porches as he passed, and then went back to hanging their wash from the lines that paralleled the houses.

Dingy white curtains covered the windows at number seven, and there was no sign of life from within. What sort of sign from what sort of life Barnett had expected to see, he had no idea. The house could be deserted, or there could be an army camped within, and the only way to tell was to get inside and look.

Barnett approached the woman on the porch directly across the street from number seven. "Excuse me," he said.

She looked up, her broad face expressionless. "Aye?"

"Could you tell me if there's anyone living across the street? That building there," he pointed.

"Couldn'a say," she said.

"Well, have you seen anyone going in or out, in the past week, say?"

"Couldn'a say."

"I see," Barnett said. "Thank you so much for your help."

He crossed the street and stood in front of number seven. Then it occurred to him. The perfect approach. And it was so obvious that he was ashamed for not having thought of it immediately. Old Mr. Starkey had told him about the musical box, and he wanted to see it with an eye toward making Pyotre Azimof an offer. He knew Pyotre wouldn't sell, but surely he couldn't resist showing the musical box off to an interested collector.

Barnett mounted the stairs and knocked on the door. After some seconds, it was opened, and a burly man in rough nautical garb stared out at him.

"Good afternoon," Barnett said. "Does Mr. Pyotre Azimof live here?"

The man silently stepped aside, and Barnett walked in. "Would you tell him someone would like to see him about his musical box?" he said.

The door slammed and Barnett was grabbed from behind. A rag with sweet-smelling fluid on it was held over his mouth and nose.

"Good afternoon, Mr. Barnett," a soft, guttural voice said from further inside. "It is a shame that your friend, Professor Moriarty, did not accompany you. But you will have to suffice."

The room tilted and spun. Bright lights whirled around in Barnett's head, to be quickly replaced by harsh blackness. He struggled like a man submerged in quicksand, without really knowing what he was doing. Then nothing.

THE BIG BANG

And the night shall be filled with music.
—LONGFELLOW

Barnett woke up slowly. A syncopated pounding thrummed across his temples, and a profound nausea replaced any other sensation. For a long time nothing else mattered. And then he was very sick.

Hands reached for him and held him up. A white basin appeared under his head, and he retched into it for what seemed several lifetimes. Then nothing more came up, and the retching changed to gasping, and the pounding of his racing heart overrode the pounding of his head. Slowly, very slowly, his heart calmed and his breathing slowed.

His eyes began to focus.

Guttural instructions were shouted, and more hands pulled Barnett to his feet. A bucket of cold water was brought and dumped over his head, then another, and a third.

Barnett shook his head and opened his eyes. Slowly the room and the people in it came into focus: the thin man with the crooked nose holding the bucket and grinning; the heavy man who had let him into the house; a man in a black suit sitting in the corner, his face hidden under a black cotton mask; a man with wire-rimmed glasses who looked like a cobbler or tailor talking softly to a man with a small mustache, who looked like a radical student even to the two books under his arm. None of them appeared interested in Barnett, except for the man with the bucket and the man behind the cotton mask.

The man behind the mask barked out a new set of instructions, and the man with the crooked nose put down the bucket and yanked Barnett over to a wooden chair. He pushed Barnett down and tied him quickly and expertly to the chair, his hands behind the back and one leg lashed to each of the chair's front legs. Barnett was too weak and sick even to protest out loud, much less resist the man who bound him.

The man behind the mask came over to glare down at Barnett. His eyes were hard behind the two thin slits. "We meet again," he said.

"Huh?" Barnett said weakly, still not sure what was happening. "What'sat?"

"The last time, I struck you over the head with a brass monkey. One of that English lieutenant's treasured possessions, no doubt. 'Hear no evil,' or some such conceit."

Barnett shook his head to clear his foggy vision and the pounding at his temples. "So *you're* the guy," he said thickly.

"I do apologize for your present condition," the masked man said solicitously. "I assure you you'll be all right in a few minutes. A pad saturated in chloric ether was applied over your nose and mouth to render you unconscious as you entered the house. But instead of collapsing, you fought like a madman, which resulted in your absorbing much more of the vapor than is good for you. It's your own fault, really."

"I fought?" Barnett remembered none of it.

"Those bruises on your arms were not gratuitous," the masked man said. "Nobody kicked you while you were down, Mr. Barnett."

"I don't remember," Barnett said. The fog around his brain was lifting and full awareness of his present position was creeping in to replace it. Barnett was not feeling too pleased with himself.

"It doesn't matter," the masked man said. "No one here holds a grudge against you. We are the ultimately rational men. We do what we must, and we allow ourselves neither remorse nor pleasure at our actions."

"That's very—sensible," Barnett said, twisting at his wrists to test the rope that bound them. There was no give, no slack, and no stretch in the rope. He relaxed.

"I am glad you feel that way," said the man behind the mask. "Then you will understand that what we are about to do is not out of malice but merely political necessity."

"What are you going to do?" Barnett asked. The headache was slowly lifting, but he could feel the pain in his bruised muscles now, and the soggy chill of his clothing, soaked from the buckets of water dumped over his head.

"It will be a glorious event!" the masked man said enthusiastically. "It will make the great sluggish mass of the British people aware of anarchy. It will be a new height. It will kill you, as you Americans so aptly put it."

"You mean that literally, I suppose," Barnett said.

"Oh, quite," the man behind the mask assured him. "We were hoping to get Professor Moriarty himself, but I'm afraid you will have to do. You and the girl."

"This was all a setup," Barnett said.

"When that gentleman over there," the masked man said, indicating the man with the slight mustache, "—let us call him—no, let him remain nameless—when that gentleman over there reported to me that he had lost his cap and that a pledge ticket was in the band, I at first castigated him severely. Then I realized that with proper management the pledge ticket would lead Professor Moriarty, or Sherlock Holmes—I had really hoped for one of the two—into my trap. It has at least produced you. I suppose it is too much to hope that the professor is going to attempt a rescue. I would like the chance to show him that I learn from my misjudgments."

"Any minute now," Barnett said.

The man behind the mask made a sound that was supposed to represent a laugh. "No, no," he said. "You have come here on your own. That is clear." He struck a thoughtful pose. "But you do have information of interest to me. How much Moriarty knows. What his source of information is. What his intentions are. You could tell me this."

It was Barnett's turn to laugh. "In return for what?"

"Your freedom."

Barnett laughed again. "How can you convince me that you will set me free once I've told you what you want to know?"

The man behind the mask thought this over. "My word, I suppose, isn't good enough?"

"Your word!" Barnett felt slightly hysterical. "Why, you've got all these poor fellows believing that you're on their side! You—"

The masked man slapped Barnett across the face, and then again, and again. Slow, deliberate slaps, delivered with all the man's force. "That is enough!" he said sharply. "You will not malign these brave men with your talk. Shortly you will no longer talk at all! You two—

take him to the upper room! We must complete our preparations here."

The two men picked Barnett up, chair and all, one in front and one behind. They carried him up a flight of stairs and deposited him in a rear bedroom. Then they left, closing the door behind them.

"Hello!"

It was a girl's voice, and it came from behind him. Barnett tried to look around, but couldn't turn his head far enough. So he hopped the chair by jerking his body and applying torque to it, until he had turned enough to see. There was a young girl tied, spread-eagled, to the bed behind him.

"My God!" Barnett said.

"If you don't mind my asking," the girl said, "who are you?" Her voice was quite normal, and well-modulated, but there was panic in her eyes.

"My name is Benjamin Barnett. And you must be the Duke of Ipswich's daughter, Lady Catherine."

"Yes," she said. "Were you looking for me? Is anybody looking for me? What are they going to do with us, do you know?"

"Your abduction is not general knowledge," Barnett said, "but there are men—some very good men—out looking for you. What have they done to you? Why are you tied up like that?"

"I haven't been mistreated—beyond having been brought here in the first place, I mean. They've kept me locked up in a small room. They feed me twice a day. Usually bread, cheese, and wine. Once, for two days, they had hot food brought from somewhere. I tried leaving a message under the plate, assuming the service would be returned to whatever restaurant it came from. I heard nothing about it, but the next day I was back on bread, cheese, and wine. Then, a couple of hours ago, they dragged me in here and tied me like this. I have no idea what they intend to do. Do you? I've been imagining all sorts of horrid things."

"I'd rather not try to guess," Barnett said.

"A man with a great black mask over his face came in and stared down at me for a long time. Then he said that I was about to go down in the history of the struggle against bourgeois imperialist oppression, and I should be grateful to him. Then he laughed and stomped out of the room. What was he talking about?"

"I think I'm beginning to get the idea," Barnett said.

"Why are you here?" she asked. "Did they abduct you, too?"

"Sort of. Only I came and knocked on the door and practically invited them to."

The girl twisted on the bed. "These ropes are cutting into my wrists," she said. "I don't think this is very funny. My poor father must be worried to death about me. He gets positively furious if I go anywhere alone, as though I were still quite a baby. You're an American, aren't you?"

"Quite right," Barnett said. "Is it that obvious?"

"I like Americans," she said. "What are they going to do to us? They're not going to let us go, are they? I mean, ever."

"I don't know what their plans are," Barnett said, trying to sound cheerful, "but don't lose hope. We'll get out of here somehow."

"I've been here for weeks. You just arrived. I hope you have something in mind, Mr. Barnett, to get us out of here. Because the Lord knows I've tried everything I could think of. And I wasn't even tied up. But now I'm tied up, and they put you in here. And you're tied up, and I don't even know you, and we can't even move, so how can we possibly ever get out of here?" And she turned her face away and sobbed quietly into the pillow.

"I'm sorry," Barnett called softly. "Really, I'm sorry if I upset you. I was trying to cheer you up."

She turned back. "How can you possibly cheer me up?" she demanded.

Barnett considered. "I can wiggle my ears and imitate a rabbit," he said. "If my hands were untied I could do wonderful shadow pictures."

"Shadow pictures of what?"

"Hands."

"Oh." She sniffed and then giggled. "Can you really do a rabbit?"

Barnett wiggled his ears and twitched his nose and turned his head in little, rabbitty motions.

"That's very nice," the girl said, smiling. "What do you do, Mr. Barnett, when you're not tied up?"

"I am a journalist."

"How did you get here?"

"I knocked on the front door, and here I am."

"Oh, dear," the girl said, twisting her head on the pillow. "My nose itches." She tried to twist around far enough to scratch her nose against the pillowcase, but the ropes holding her arms were too tight. After fighting her bonds futilely for a minute, she gave up and burst into tears.

"Listen," Barnett said, "it's going to be okay."

"No," she said. "No, it isn't. I can't even scratch my own nose. It's horrible. And those people—they're going to kill us! They've kept me here for six weeks, cooped up in that little room. And now they're going to kill me. It isn't fair! And you, too."

Barnett didn't know what to say. He couldn't argue against it without her thinking him feebleminded, and he couldn't agree to it without depressing her even more.

Further speech was rendered pointless when the man behind the mask came into the room. "Greetings," he said.

"What do you want with me?" the girl sobbed.

"Patience, woman," the man said. "In five minutes it will be seven o'clock."

"Thank you," Barnett said sarcastically. "I had been wondering."

The man behind the mask gestured behind him and the man with wire-rim glasses came in carrying the musical box that had lured Barnett to that house. "This is somehow fitting," the man with the mask said. "I hope, Mr. Barnett, that you enjoy classical music, and that you don't mind the rather tinny sound of the musical box."

"Why?" Barnett asked.

"Because it will be the last thing you hear on this earth," the man told him.

The other man placed the musical box on a table and, taking a large brace-and-bit from his belt, drilled a hole in the floor by that table.

"What's happening?" Barnett demanded.

"I think you should know," the man behind the mask told him. "In the room directly below this one there are several hundred pounds of explosive. Much more than we need, actually, but we can't cart it away with us anyway."

The bit went through the flooring and the man with the glasses knelt down and peered through the hole.

"The explosives," the man behind the mask said, warming to his subject, "are tightly packed around a central core in such a fashion as to direct the main force of the explosion up, rather than out. With any luck we shouldn't demolish more than two or three buildings on either side of this one."

The man with the wire-rim glasses said something in a guttural foreign language and left the room. The man behind the mask snapped something at him in the same language as he went, and then pulled out his pocket-watch and shook his head in annoyance.

"A problem there, Trepoff?" Barnett asked.

The man behind the mask looked up at him. "No man may say that name and live," he said. "Which, in your case, is not the most powerful threat I can imagine."

A muffled shout sounded from the room below, and Trepoff walked over to the drilled hole and thumped his cane on the floor by the hole. "They have to drill a hole in the ceiling below to line up with the one in this floor," he told Barnett. "Although why they couldn't have thought of that before . . . This is liable to put us off schedule."

"There are incompetents in every line of work," Barnett told him. "Even in yours."

Trepoff turned to him. "A shame you won't be able to write this up in your best humorous style, Mr. Barnett," he said. "A companion piece to your miraculous escape from the Turkish prison."

"You are going to kill us!" the girl cried, twisting in her bonds to face Trepoff. "Why? What have I ever done to you?"

"You were born," Trepoff said. "Think of it this way, woman: your death is to be useful in a great cause. How many people go through their entire dull, drab lives and die meaningless deaths without ever having been useful to anything beyond themselves? But you, mademoiselle—" There was an impatient rapping from below, and Trepoff broke off to bend down and grasp two wires that had appeared in the newly drilled hole. He pulled the wires up through the hole and attached them to two brass screws that had recently been screwed into the wood of the musical box.

"You are about to participate in a great experiment," Trepoff said. "When I start the musical box, the little pianist on top will turn to his piano and play sixteen tunes, each one precisely three minutes and forty-five seconds long. Thus, in exactly one hour he will be finished, the machine will turn itself off, and the pianist will once again turn away from the piano. In doing so, he will complete an electrical connection between these two wires, and a current will pass from the galvanic batteries in the room below through a voltaic arc apparatus inserted into a tube of compressed guncotton. This will serve to detonate the explosive mass. At that moment the two of you will cease to exist. Have you any last words?"

"It does seem a shame, Mr. Trepoff," Barnett said, "to destroy that beautiful musical box."

"Ah, yes," Trepoff said. "But let us console ourselves with the thought that art must die so that ideals may live." He thumped his cane on the floor three times and received a three-thump reply from below. "It is time to leave you now," he said, turning back to the musical box and releasing a catch on the side. The metallic notes of J. S. Bach's *Well-Tempered Clavier* wove a pattern of sound around him as he left.

"He's gone," Barnett said.

The girl did not reply. Barnett turned to her and saw that she had her face turned away and was crying softly into the pillow.

Bach faded away, to be replaced by Handel, and the girl screamed, putting into that one sound all the fear, frustration, and anguish of six weeks of imprisonment ending in an afternoon of death.

"Here, now!" Barnett cried, hopping his chair closer to the bed by jerking his body forward. "You mustn't—" Suddenly he realized what he had just done. He had moved the chair! If he could do it to go three inches closer to the bed, then, with work, he could do it across eight feet of floor to get to the two wires.

Very slowly he hopped the chair around to face the wires. He had to be extremely careful not to tip over; if he fell on his face he might not be able to get up again.

Slowly he hopped his way across the floor. Handel gave way to Couperin, and he had gone almost two feet. Couperin was replaced by Liszt, and he had gone four feet. His shoulders and pelvis ached from the strain.

There was a banging from below, and the sound of running on the stairs, and Trepoff reappeared in the doorway. "Something was nagging at my mind," he said. "And I see that I was right! Inexcusable carelessness on my part."

He stepped aside and two men entered the room and dragged Barnett back to the bed. Using a length of thick rope, they tied him and his chair securely to the heavy post at the foot of the bed. Then they left.

Trepoff stood in the doorway for a second, surveying the room. He nodded. "Adieu," he said. And then he was gone.

The miniature pianist atop the musical box continued running his doll-fingers over the keys, and composition after composition was rendered in tinny tones. Barnett lost count. The girl was now silent. Perhaps she had fainted. It would be a good thing, Barnett thought, if she had; he would have made no attempt to revive her even if he could. He twisted and struggled until his arms were raw under the jacket, but the ropes held.

Suddenly, as a Rossini overture began either the fourteenth or fifteenth piece, a pounding noise sounded faintly and far-off from below. Someone was at the front door.

Barnett yelled, but to no effect. Nobody outside on the street could hear him from upstairs. Shortly the pounding stopped.

Rossini ended with a click and whirr, and Scarlatti began the fifteenth—or sixteenth—selection.

The pounding at the front door began again. It was too late now. Even if someone did get in, they would never make it upstairs in time if this were the sixteenth selection.

But if it were only the fifteenth, there might be time. "Help!" Barnett yelled. "Help! Upstairs!"

The door flew open and Sherlock Holmes strode into the room, a great revolver in his hand. "Well," he said. "What have we here?"

"Quick, man!" Barnett screamed. "There are two wires affixed to that musical box. Unfasten one of them immediately. And, for the love of God, don't let it touch the other wire!"

Holmes raced over to the box and pulled one of the wires from its screw. As he did so, the Scarlatti drew to a close and, with a whirr and click, the little doll-figure turned away from the piano. Silence.

Barnett looked from the musical box to Holmes and, for once, words failed him. His lips moved but no words came out.

"You have just saved all our lives, Mr. Holmes," Barnett managed to say at last. "I don't know how to thank you."

"If that young lady on the bed is Lady Catherine," Holmes said, "I am sufficiently recompensed."

"She is," Barnett said.

"Is she all right?"

"I believe she has just fainted."

Holmes took a clasp-knife from his pocket and severed their bonds. "Wasn't that Scarlatti?" he asked.

"I believe so," Barnett said. "I was rather preoccupied."

Holmes nodded. "Scarlatti." He eyed the musical box. "An exquisite thing, that."

The banging on the front door began again, and Holmes looked up. "If you'll excuse me for a second," he said, "I will go downstairs and admit my colleague, Dr. Watson. While he revives Lady Catherine, we can talk."

TWENTY

ELEMENTARY

My friend, judge not me,
Thou seest I judge not thee.
— WILLIAM COMDEN

Two days passed before Sherlock Holmes came to Moriarty's front door and demanded entrance. Mr. Maws showed him into the study. "You're to wait," he said. "The professor is expecting you."

Ten minutes later Moriarty entered the study and crossed to his desk. "Good afternoon, Sherlock," he said.

"You expected me?" Holmes demanded, turning from the cabinet he was examining.

Moriarty glanced up at the complex face of the brass chronometer which hung over the door. It was six twenty-nine. "Not quite so soon," he said. "I apologize for leaving you in here alone, and thus putting temptation across your path. The drawers and cabinets, as I'm sure you found, are all locked."

"I had never imagined anything else, my dear Moriarty," Holmes said, moving over to the high-back chair and sitting down. "Still, one can always hope."

Moriarty leaned forward over his desk, his deepset gray eyes contemplating Sherlock Holmes unblinkingly for many seconds. Then he shrugged slightly and leaned back in his black leather chair. "The girl is all right?" he asked.

"The duke had two of Harley Street's most lettered specialists to examine her," Holmes said. "She didn't seem to need them. An amazingly resilient creature."

"You spoke to her?"

"A bit. Not as much as I would have liked. It is clear that you had nothing to do with the abduction."

"Thank you."

177

"You expect me to apologize?"

"I expect nothing."

Holmes struck his right fist into his open left hand. "I am mortified, Professor," he said. "Not for having suspected you; we both know that you are capable of any act." He looked earnestly at Moriarty, who did not change his expression in the slightest, but merely waited patiently. "No, I am mortified at having allowed this suspicion to become an overwhelming obsession. It is true, I admit it. I allowed my emotion to color my rational processes, without which I am nothing. I should have known almost immediately that you were not involved. There was no demand for money."

"The first communication?" Moriarty suggested.

Holmes nodded. "It was indicated in the first note the duke received that money would not be required. I confess that rather than come to the proper deduction, I formulated fifteen different schemes you could have been devising."

"Ah, Holmes. After all this time. Surely you should know me better. I won't pretend, here in this room, that I don't satisfy my incessant need for funds by abetting, or even indulging in, acts you might term criminal. But you must know that I would see a difference between quietly emptying a safe and abducting a seventeen-year-old girl."

"I see no difference," Holmes said stubbornly.

"Surely—"

"An apparent difference in scale, yes," Holmes said. "But you cannot measure the results of either act. And they are both against the law. Who are you to decide which is right and which wrong?"

"And who, pray tell, is the state to decide for me?" Moriarty demanded. "If I steal fifty pounds from a safe, I may go in for seven years' penal servitude. If I steal fifty thousand pounds by selling watered stock, I may make the honors list. If I murder a man on the streets of London and take his watch, I will be hung by the neck until I am dead. If I murder a hundred men on the Gold Coast to take their land, Her Majesty's government will send a gunboat to bring me back in triumph."

"I do not claim that the laws are uniform or just," Holmes said. "But they are what we have. They are better—infinitely better—than the chaos that would result without law."

* * *

Moriarty stood and began to pace behind his desk, his chin sunk onto his chest. Then he stopped and laughed. "We argue law and we argue right and wrong," he said, "yet we are what we are, you and I, for reasons that lie deeper in us than can be reached by writs of the court or by statutes. I think it is good that we are both satisfied with what we are, for I do not think argument will change us. And I must say that this discussion, enjoyable as it is becoming, is drifting off the subject."

"The subject?"

"Trepoff."

"Ah, yes; Trepoff. The masked man."

"Yes," said Moriarty.

"He is planning some major outrage?"

Moriarty nodded. "So I believe."

"He told Lady Catherine something to that effect," Holmes said. "Her abduction was to be prefatory to the main abomination." Holmes shook his head. "The murder of innocents to draw attention to the plight of anarchists."

"So he would have you think," Moriarty said.

Mr. Maws knocked on the study door and then stuck his head in. "Count Gobolski," he announced.

"Ah!" Moriarty said. "Show him in. Count, how good to see you. You have something for me? Allow me to introduce Mr. Sherlock Holmes. Holmes, His Excellency Count Gobolski, the Russian ambassador to St. James."

Gobolski shook Holmes's hand firmly. "The inquiry agent," he said. "I have heard." He turned to Moriarty. "He can listen? No matter, I have nothing to say. I have a paper for you from St. Petersburg. Here. I am no longer being followed. Good day." He thrust his hat back onto his head and stalked out of the room. At the door, he stopped and turned back for a second. "We will play chess again some evening, Professor," he said. "I will be in touch. You owe me a return match." With the merest hint of a bow, he was gone.

Moriarty stared at the slip of paper and then dropped it on his desk. He rang for Mr. Maws. "Barnett should be returning shortly," he told his butler. "Please inform him that I would like to see him when he arrives."

Mr. Maws nodded and left.

The slip of paper held one word, block-printed, and Holmes easily read it where Moriarty had dropped it.

SUBMARINERS.

"What does that signify?" Holmes asked.

Moriarty looked at him. "It concerns Trepoff," he said. "What is your interest?"

"Trepoff must be stopped! I intend to do so."

"I, also," Moriarty said.

"Then I must ask you, in turn," Holmes said, "what is your interest? Surely not pure beneficence."

Moriarty smiled. "Like you, Holmes, I am for hire."

Holmes frowned. "The Duke of Ipswich is naturally not satisfied to let matters rest now that he has his daughter back. He has commissioned me to apprehend her abductor, although I would almost certainly continue the investigation anyway. Who has employed you, and why?"

"I would like nothing better than to discuss it with you," Moriarty said. "But first I must know that we are working together."

Holmes considered this. "Surely a first for you, Professor," he said, "finding yourself on the side of the law."

Moriarty nodded his head ponderously. "Indeed, Holmes. And this is surely a first for you, on the side of your old mathematics professor."

"You are suggesting that we pool our talents?"

Moriarty nodded. "We haven't much time, I'm afraid. If we both arrive at the same solution, from two separate paths, fifteen minutes late, it would be the height of folly."

Sherlock Holmes rose and slowly walked over to the great bookcase that filled one wall of the study and stared absently at the titles. "To work with you—" he said. "You would expect nothing from the duke?"

"Nothing."

"The miscreants are to be turned over to the authorities?"

"Assuredly."

Holmes strode back to the desk and put out his hand. "Done!"

Moriarty and Holmes shook hands solemnly. "I pray that this is indicative of the future, Holmes," Moriarty said.

"I fear that this is unique, Professor," Holmes replied.

Moriarty sighed. "What a shame," he said; "what a waste." He took his pince-nez from his breast pocket and thrust them onto his nose. "Let's get on with it," he said.

* * *

For the next hour Moriarty told Holmes the Trepoff saga in its entirety, omitting no detail, however trivial, in case Holmes might be able to draw some inference from it that had escaped him. Holmes made no notes, but merely stared intently at the professor as he spoke. Twice he interrupted to ask brief questions and nodded in satisfaction at the answers.

During this monologue, Barnett came in, and was silently waved to a corner chair by Moriarty. He listened and was properly amazed at the exchange of confidences by the two antagonists.

When Moriarty had finished, Holmes, in a curiously distracted way, recited what had happened to him since the Duke of Ipswich had sent for him on the night of his daughter's disappearance. It was a tale of false clues, dead-end leads, and provocative accidents. Several of the clues had pointed directly at Professor Moriarty before disappearing in a labyrinth of complications and misdirections. "Of course, the whole occurrence was an elaborately staged misdirection," he said. "I can see it now."

"It is, in a way, a compliment," Moriarty said.

"Excuse me," Barnett said from his corner chair, "but what are you two talking about?"

Holmes swiveled around. "The abduction of Lady Catherine was arranged for our benefit;" he said. "Not the act itself, but the way it was done. Trepoff wanted to keep me busy chasing Moriarty, and the professor busy avoiding me. So he planted clues. And, because they accorded with what I expected to find, I did not examine them too critically. As a result, I wasted a lot of time."

"You sure showed up in the nick of time the other night," Barnett said.

Holmes smiled. "I am not altogether incompetent," he said.

"Those sailors Trepoff sent for were submariners," Moriarty told Barnett. "From where could he acquire a submarine?"

"Not from the Royal Navy," Barnett said, remembering Lieutenant Sefton's story. "They don't use them."

"There is one," Holmes said, "at the Thornycroft yards at Chiswick. It was dredged from the bottom of the Thames after sinking three times in three trials. Not submerging, you understand, sinking. It is not in working order."

"Holmes!" Moriarty said. "You never cease to amaze me. I had no idea you were interested in submersibles."

"I'm not in the least," Holmes said. "My brother, Mycroft, however, is a fount of such information. Among other things, he does some work for the Admiralty. Only last week—no, two weeks ago—he was after me to take on a case involving the theft of some Whitehead torpedoes."

"Ha!" Moriarty said, taking his pince-nez glasses off and polishing them with a small rag. "A case which you were unable to take up because of your involvement with the abduction."

"That's correct," Holmes said.

Moriarty fixed Barnett with his gaze. "If I remember correctly," he said, "you told me that one of the features of the Garrett-Harris submersible was its ability to release Whitehead torpedoes while submerged."

"That's right," Barnett said. "But it blew up. Do you think there's another one?"

Moriarty waved a hand at Holmes. "There's your misdirection," he said. "They didn't want you investigating the theft of those torpedoes."

"An intuitive leap," Holmes sniffed.

"Not at all," Moriarty said. "Barnett, your knowledge of coming events must be copious. What event is coming up in the next week or so involving the sea? Something major."

"The sea?"

"Correct. The launching of a new battleship, perhaps. I don't suppose the Tsar is coming for a state visit by ship? Something of that sort?"

"Nothing," Barnett said. "Of course, I might have missed something. I can go to the office and check the file."

"Nothing nautical?" Moriarty said.

"Not on the scale of battleships," Barnett said. "There's the regatta tomorrow, but they're small private yachts."

"What regatta?" Holmes demanded.

"The Queen's something," Barnett said. "I don't remember. Wait a minute and I'll get the evening paper. I'm sure the *St. James Gazette* is covering the story in full." He left the room and was back in less than a minute, riffling through a newspaper.

"Yes, here it is," he said. He creased the paper back. "The annual regatta for the Queen's Cup is to be sailed Saturday, August first—that's tomorrow—between ships of the Royal Yacht Squadron and ships of the Royal West of England Yacht Club. Her Majesty will give the cups out herself. There are actually several cups, apparently. Let's see; there will be one winner in each class, and a special cup for the club with the highest point average."

"Fascinating," Holmes said.

"Go on," Moriarty said.

"I don't know what else you want," Barnett said. "The Prince of Wales is the Commodore of the Royal Yacht Squadron, and H.R.H. the Duke of Wessex is Commodore of the R. W. of E. Yacht Club. The course, something over fifty miles, is laid in the Solent. It begins at Cowes, goes eastward to the Nab lightship and around, back past Cowes to Lymington, and then back past Cowes again to Portsmouth, finish line lying between the block house and the *Victoria and Albert*, the Queen's own yacht, from which she will be watching the affair."

"That's it!" Moriarty said.

"Could be," Holmes admitted.

"What?" Barnett asked, folding the paper.

"The Garrett-Harris submersible," Moriarty told him, "was *not* destroyed. I should have realized it weeks ago. It is a fatal error to make assumptions based upon facts not in evidence."

"But I saw it blow up!" Barnett said.

"Did you?" Moriarty asked. "What exactly did you see?"

"Well," Barnett thought back, trying to recapture the moment in his memory. "It was going through the water, just submerged, leaving a phosphorescent wake, the slight 'V' of foam from the periscope imposed over that. Then it sighted its prey—a sloop—and began stalking it. The submersible sank beneath the sea until it was totally invisible and moved forward to line itself up for the torpedo launch. As it launched the torpedo, it exploded. A great geyser erupted from the sea, drenching the ship I was on, and the two broken halves of the submersible appeared briefly on the surface before going to their final resting-place in the mud below. It seemed to me that I saw the body of a man in one of the sections. At any rate, neither of the operators was ever found."

"A wonderfully concise description. And it shows that you saw nothing."

"I saw the whole thing!" Barnett protested.

Holmes clapped his hands together. "It has always fascinated me," he said, "how people will swear to have seen something when an analysis of their own description clearly shows that they didn't and couldn't have."

"It's the principle of most sleight-of-hand," Moriarty said.

"What didn't I see?" Barnett demanded.

"You didn't see anything," Moriarty told him, "from the time the submersible disappeared under the sea."

"If you mean I didn't have the craft directly in my sight the whole time," Barnett said, "then you're right; I didn't. But the inference of the following events is certainly valid."

"Is it?" Holmes asked, chuckling.

"I offer you this scenario, Mr. Barnett," Moriarty said, speaking clearly and distinctly as one explaining the obvious to a child. "Let us suppose that Trepoff, for whatever reason, wanted a submersible."

"Okay," Barnett said. "Let's."

"So, hearing that the Turks are testing one, he went to Constantinople. It would be a coup to get one from Russia's traditional enemy, the Ottoman Empire. He went to where the submersible was docked and managed to get access to it."

"How?" Barnett demanded.

"Three or four methods occur: forged papers, bribed guards, stealth, or some combination thereof. We may never know which method he adopted. Once there, he determined that he would need some time to effect the removal of the craft. I assume it had to be hoisted aboard some freighter, disguised as a large piece of machinery.

"What better way to gain time than to make it appear that the craft has been destroyed? Trepoff quickly acquired a large metal structure of the approximate size—I suggest a large boiler of some description. He towed it to the appropriate spot the night before and sank it, along with a powerful bomb. Trepoff is good at bombs. Possibly he planted a body on the boiler."

"What about the two Americans who ran the ship?" Barnett asked.

"One of them was undoubtedly the body that you saw. The other was kept alive. Somebody had to run the craft. That he was subsequently killed is shown by Trepoff's need for the four submersible-trained sailors."

"Possible," Barnett said.

"And then they took it out and ran it for the sea trials that you saw. Up to the point where the craft submerged. At that moment it turned away from the show and headed back toward the freighter, which was to pick it up and take it to England. The explosion a minute later blew the boiler and the murdered American submariner to the surface for one brief appearance, which was enough to convince the onlookers that it was the submersible."

"And Trepoff," Holmes said thoughtfully, "returned to England with the Garrett-Harris submersible, which is capable of releasing Whitehead torpedoes while submerged."

"That is my theory," Moriarty said.

"And a pair of Whitehead torpedoes was stolen from the naval establishment at Devonport a fortnight ago. Each of them, according to Mycroft, possessed of several hundred pounds of the latest explosive."

"And Her Majesty Queen Victoria, whose picture I found gracing the meeting hall of Trepoff's no-name society, is going to spend tomorrow on board her yacht, the *Victoria and Albert*," Moriarty said. "And if I were an anarchist, the queen of the largest empire in the world would certainly be a tempting target."

"They'd never dare!" Barnett exclaimed. "The public revulsion would set their cause back a hundred years."

"Exactly Trepoff's aim," Moriarty said.

"We must get to Portsmouth without delay!" Holmes said.

Moriarty stretched out his hand for his *Bradshaw's*. "Let us see what the British Railways have to say about that. It is fourteen minutes past nine, and the next train to Portsmouth . . ." He riffled through the pages thoughtfully, then put the guide down. "It appears that we cannot get to Portsmouth by any scheduled train any earlier than eleven-oh-four tomorrow morning. Which will never do."

"Intolerable!" Holmes said. "What shall we do?"

"Hire a Special," Moriarty told him. "I'll send out Mr. Maws now to arrange it. If you'd like to go back to Baker Street and pack, Holmes, I'll meet you at Waterloo Station in an hour."

"Very good," Holmes said, getting up. "A Special. If you don't mind, I shall bring my companion, Dr. Watson, along. He is a good man to have at your back."

"By all means," Moriarty said. "Barnett, will you join us?"

"You couldn't keep me away!" Barnett exclaimed.

TWENTY-ONE

VICTORIA AND ALBERT

> *MENE, MENE, TEKEL,*
> *UPHARSIN.*
> —THE BOOK OF DANIEL

It was eleven twenty-six before way clearance was obtained for the trip, and the Special—one ancient engine and two cars—pulled out of Waterloo Station. Sherlock Holmes and his taciturn friend Dr. Watson joined Moriarty and Barnett in the compartment farthest from the engine, where it was quietest, and discussed the situation.

Dr. Watson was a portly, ruddy-faced, handsome man with a well-trimmed mustache. Barnett had met him briefly when he and Holmes had come to Barnett's rescue in the house of the explosive musical box. Now Barnett took the opportunity to study him more closely. He was the epitome of the Victorian Englishman, and the perfect foil for Holmes. Stolid, slow, without Holmes's incisive mind or ready wit, he was nonetheless brave, loyal, and as tenacious as an English pit bulldog. He contributed little to the conversation, but seemed content to sit back and appreciate every word uttered by Sherlock Holmes.

"We must decide upon a course of action," Moriarty told Holmes, modulating his voice to be easily heard over the clacking of the wheels. "We will have precious little time."

"If we are right," Holmes said.

"I admit that the probabilities are only slightly better than half," Moriarty said, "but it is on the strength of that half that we are all aboard this Special, puffing through Guildford at a quarter past midnight."

"I thought you were both convinced that you were right," Barnett said.

"It was not the conviction that we were right, but rather the fear that we *might* be right that has compelled us to this trip," Moriarty said. "And now we must proceed as though we had no doubts."

"We will have to alert the authorities," Holmes said.

"Police or naval?" Moriarty asked. "And tell them what?"

"Nevertheless the attempt will have to be made."

Moriarty shrugged. "As you will," he said. "The most important thing is to locate the submersible. We will, of course, attempt to capture Trepoff as well, but stopping the submersible must have the first priority."

"Consider that the submersible may be already submersed," Holmes said. "Sitting on the bottom, awaiting the proper moment."

Barnett shook his head. "No chance," he said. "There are two problems: air and fuel. When the craft is submerged it runs on electrical storage batteries, which give off noxious fumes when in use. As a result the air must be purged every two hours, which is also when the batteries expire and must be recharged."

"Let us suppose," Holmes said argumentatively, "that the craft merely rests on the bottom and does not call upon the batteries for motive power. How long then?"

Barnett shook his head. "I'm no expert," he said. "I'm just remembering what I was told by Lieutenant Sefton—the man I was supposed to have murdered—before the trials. I believe that the air does foul, but at a slower rate. The oxygen in the air gets used up by the occupants' breathing, in any case."

"Trepoff will need all his submerged time to make good his escape," Moriarty said. "The submersible will remain in its hiding place until Trepoff is ready to strike. Then it will proceed directly to its target, blow up the *Victoria and Albert* with the queen aboard, and leave the harbor. Somewhere in the Solent a ship will be waiting to pick up the submersible—or at least its crew—and remove them from the area."

"What makes you think Trepoff will be so solicitous of the welfare of his agents?" Holmes asked.

"He may well be aboard himself," Moriarty said. "And although certainly a brave and daring man, he tends to be careful of his own welfare. Besides, he couldn't afford to have four Russian sailors, clearly not anarchists, captured. Killed, perhaps; but not captured."

"That brings us to an interesting question," Holmes said, thoughtfully pressing the tips of his fingers together. "How is Trepoff planning to make it clear that this is an anarchist outrage? Surely he isn't going to leave it to be supposed."

"Somehow anarchists are going to be apprehended for this crime," Moriarty agreed. "Probably in such a state that they can't reveal too much."

"Dead," Barnett said.

"Quite probably," Moriarty said.

"Dastardly plot," Doctor Watson said.

As the Special chugged and clanked its way across the quiet English countryside, the four men in the compartment looked silently at each other. This was not the proper setting for such horrors. They should take place in an alien clime, not in damp, stolid, virtuous Victorian England. They did not belong here, and the possibility of their presence was disquieting.

"I don't see that we can accomplish anything useful tonight," Moriarty said. "We won't arrive until about half past two. I suggest we get a few hours sleep and start fresh in the morning."

"I agree," Holmes said. "Creeping around in the dark in a city one is not familiar with would not be overly productive."

"My feeling is that Trepoff will pick the moment of the awarding of the cups as his prime moment to attack," Moriarty said. "It will create maximum effect and confusion. The area will be full of boats going in all directions. That should maximize his chances of escaping."

"What time is that, Professor?" Watson asked. "When is Her Majesty presenting the cups?"

"The newspaper estimated that it will take place around six in the evening," Moriarty said. "If we start looking at six in the morning, that will give us twelve hours to find the submersible before it is employed."

"God grant that it is enough time," Holmes said.

"All the inns in Portsmouth are most probably filled this weekend," Moriarty said. "I have taken the liberty of adding a sleeping car to our special, as, fortunately, one was available."

"I was wondering what the extra car was," Barnett said.

"We shall each have our own compartment," Moriarty said. "Not exactly the ultimate in luxury, but it will serve."

"The expense for the sleeping car must have been considerable," Holmes said. "Surely this was an extravagance."

"I believe the Tsar can afford it," Moriarty said.

* * *

The special pulled into a siding in the Portsmouth yard shortly after two in the morning, and the group separated to get what sleep they could.

Barnett would have been willing to swear that it was no more than a few minutes after he lay his head on the small pillow that a fully dressed Moriarty was poking him awake. Barnett groaned and sat up. "What time is it?" he asked.

"Ten past six," Moriarty told him. "I've let you sleep late."

"I don't know how to thank you," Barnett said.

"Get dressed as quickly as you can," Moriarty instructed him. "Holmes and I have been studying a map of Portsmouth. We've decided to make the Royal Standard public house our base of operations, and it's a two-mile walk."

"Any particular reason why the Royal Standard?" Barnett asked.

"Yes. Two. It's fairly centrally located along the docks, and the guidebook says it sets a fine breakfast table."

"I'll be right with you," Barnett said.

After a brisk walk to the Royal Standard, they consumed a hasty breakfast, selecting from a buffet table that groaned with solid English fare.

"Now we begin," Moriarty said. "Two south toward the Battery and two north toward Whale Island, and we somehow contrive to inspect everything that touches the water or floats on it that is large enough to conceal a Garrett-Harris submersible."

"The Navy may object to our poking around some of their docks," Barnett said.

"Well, we'll have to assume that they object just as strongly to Trepoff concealing his submersible there," Moriarty said.

"We must notify the authorities," Holmes said.

"I doubt if you will be able to convince them of anything," Moriarty said. "But feel free. I shall come with you if you like. It will be interesting to hear you accusing someone other than me of unspeakable misdeeds and evil acts."

Holmes stood up. "Very well, then," he said. "Come along. There is a police station three blocks from here."

Moriarty nodded. "Barnett," he said, "why don't you and Dr. Watson walk south along the harbor and see if you can determine anything of interest. After we speak to the authorities, Holmes and I will proceed north."

"Very good," Barnett said.

"We shall meet back here in, let us say, four hours to compare notes. And by the way, Barnett, do not try to be a hero all by yourself this time. If you find the craft, don't attempt to do anything whatsoever on your own. Come back here for reinforcements. If it makes you feel any better about it, we shall do the same."

"Okay," Barnett said.

Watson looked to Holmes for instructions and Holmes nodded. Watson beamed. "We'll find the little sinker for you if it's there, eh what?" he said, looking very pleased with himself. With that, he clapped his bowler on his head and left with Barnett.

Holmes and Moriarty walked to the police station, and Holmes strode up the stairs and through the oak door. "Good morning, Sergeant," he boomed at the blue-coated man behind the desk. "Who is in charge here today?" Moriarty stood quietly by the door.

"Good morning, sir," the sergeant said. "That would be Inspector Peebles, sir."

"And may I speak with him?"

"May I inquire as to the nature of your business, sir?"

"My name is Sherlock Holmes, Sergeant," Holmes said. He waited a second for a reaction, and when he got none, he continued, "I have some information which will be of interest to Inspector Peebles."

"Yes, sir. Might I inquire as to the nature of that information?"

Holmes sighed. "I really don't want to go through it twice," he said. "Time is limited. It concerns a plot against the life of Her Majesty the Queen!"

"Yes, sir," the sergeant said. "Another plot against the life of the Queen. Very good of you to come in and warn us about it. I can assure you, sir, that proper precautions are being taken."

Holmes rapped his stick against the desk. "This is not a joke, Sergeant!" he said. "I insist upon speaking to the inspector."

The sergeant sighed. "Yes, sir," he said. "If you will excuse me for a second sir, I'll tell him he's wanted." The sergeant left his desk and disappeared into the back.

Holmes looked over to Moriarty and saw that he was silently laughing. "This is not amusing!" he rasped.

"No," Moriarty agreed. "Of course it isn't."

Inspector Peebles, a plump, smiling man, entered the room with the sergeant. "Now, now," he said, chuckling happily, "what's all this?"

"My name is Sherlock Holmes, Inspector," Holmes said, "and I have information regarding an attempt that is going to be made against the life of Queen Victoria."

"Now, that's very serious," the inspector said, still smiling. "Just how is this attempt going to be made?"

"By submersible boat."

"By what, sir? What was that?" A puzzled look replaced the smile.

"By submersible boat. Submarine. We have reason to believe that a foreign agent has smuggled a submersible boat into the harbor and is planning to blow up the *Victoria and Albert*."

"Now, now, that's quite serious, sir," the inspector said ponderously. "Just where is this submersible located now, sir?"

"I don't know," Holmes said.

"I see, sir," the inspector said. He turned to Moriarty. "Is this gentleman with you?"

"That's right, Inspector," Moriarty admitted.

"Well, why don't you and your friend just go out and find this submersible for us. As soon as you have found it, you be sure to come back here and tell us where it is." The inspector's smile returned. "Then we'll take care of it for you."

"Yes, Inspector, we'll certainly do that. Thank you, Inspector. Come along now, Holmes."

They left the station together, Moriarty silent and Holmes fuming. "They didn't believe me," he said, the line of his jaw rigid with fury. "They treated me as though I were mad!"

"Well, it is a rather incredible story," Moriarty said. "I'm sure that if Lestrade were here you could convince him, however. You seem to be able to convince him of anything."

"We've got to find that boat by ourselves," Holmes said.

"Yes," Moriarty agreed. "And I think we'd best be about it."

They proceeded north along the waterfront, poking into and exploring every wharf and jetty they passed. Gradually, Holmes regained his good humor as he became intrigued with the problems of the search. Moriarty stopped in fascination at a clearing by the Naval Barracks where two great balloons were slowly puffing up on the ground. They were being filled with hydrogen gas, generated by a complex self-contained apparatus resting in two wagons by the side of the field. Canvas pipes, treated with gutta-percha, connected the generator with the balloons.

"What's happening here?" Moriarty demanded of a frock-coated man who was directing the operation.

The man turned to him and took off his stiff top hat. "Balloons, sir," he said. "Observation balloons."

"I can see that," Moriarty said. "I have some small knowledge of aerostatics myself. My name is Professor James Moriarty and this is Mr. Sherlock Holmes."

"I am Hyman Miro," the man announced. "Scientist and inventor and developer of the Miro-graphy system of wet-plate photography."

"Ah, yes," Moriarty said. "I am somewhat familiar with the system. It employs a reversal process using a collodion plate and the bromide of silver. The developer, if I remember correctly, is largely pyrogallic acid."

Miro beamed. "That is correct, sir. Pyrogallic acid and ammonium carbonate, with potassium bromide. You have employed my system?"

"Yes, sir," Moriarty said. "The photography of celestial bodies requires rapid, fine emulsions. Yours is quite adequate."

"We, ah, have business, Moriarty," Holmes said, tapping his foot.

"Patience, Holmes," Moriarty said. "Meeting Mr. Miro may prove very useful. You are," he asked Miro, "planning to use these balloons as tethered observation platforms for the purposes of photography?"

"I am," Miro said. "If the weather remains fine, I should be able to expose my plates for no more than the tenth part of a second and still get a complete image. I will be able to stop the motion of the ships on the water, sir. A wonderful thing."

"And you are going to be up in them all day?"

"Up and down, sir. Up and down. The wet plates must be developed within minutes of being exposed or they lose detail. The darkroom will be erected between the two balloons, which will be lowered and raised on command by a powerful winch."

"Very clever, sir," Moriarty said.

"Until six o'clock, sir," Miro said.

"Ah?" Moriarty said.

"Yes. The P.L.R.F.C. is taking over the balloons at six to prepare for their fireworks display. Can you imagine, sir, fireworks from a hydrogen balloon? It's the height of idiocy!"

"The P.L. . . ." Holmes said.

"Yes, sir. The P.L.R.F.C. The Portsmouth Library and Recreation Fund Committee. They are in charge of the evening's festivities. Fireworks!"

"Really, Moriarty," Holmes said.

Moriarty raised his hand. "Mr. Miro," he said. "I am about to entrust you with a grave responsibility."

"Sir?" Miro said.

"We have reason to believe that an attempt is going to be made to blow up the *Victoria and Albert*."

"The Royal Yacht?"

"Correct. A madman who has stolen, and has in his possession, a submersible craft, is going to use it to approach and destroy the Royal Yacht, with Her Majesty on board. We are trying to apprehend him now, but if we fail, then in a matter of hours he will carry out his plan."

"Well, sir," Miro said, "what can I do about it?"

"A submerged craft is much more readily visible from high above than from the side. It is a matter of the angle subtended. The craft has to be within a hundred yards of the Royal Yacht to release its Whitehead torpedo. You'll have a fine view."

Miro's eyes lit up. "What a photograph!" he said. "But you can't mean that you want me to spend the day searching for this undersea craft? I wouldn't be able to get any photographs."

"No, sir," Moriarty said. "What I'd like is to send my assistant up with you. Not this gentleman," Moriarty said quickly, as Miro eyed Holmes, "but another."

"What good will that do?" Miro asked. "We'll be up there, and you'll be down here."

"You said something about fireworks," Moriarty said. "My assistant could take some up with him, and let off a colored rocket if he spots the craft."

Miro thought for a minute. "Sounds crazy to me," he said. "But . . . you say you've used my process for astronomical photography?"

"I'll be delighted to show you my plates," Moriarty said.

Miro clapped his topper back on his head. "Send your man over," he said. "It doesn't matter when: I'll be up and down all day."

"Thank you, sir," Moriarty said. "You're doing a great service for your country—and your queen."

"I'll be in touch with you," Miro said, "about viewing those plates."

Holmes and Moriarty continued their northward quest, examining the Filling Basin and the Rigging Basin of the big naval shipyard, and on to Fountain Lake, the tidepool where the frigates were moored. Whale Island, with its great Gunnery School, thrust out into the commercial harbor beyond. They walked slowly around each pier and mooring, looking for a place where a forty-foot-long submersible could be hidden. There was no such place.

"Well, Professor," Holmes said, as they scrambled back from examining the inside of a closed boathouse through a window overhanging the water, "at least this had the negative virtue of eliminating most of the inner harbor. When we get back to the pub, we'll know hundreds of places where the craft is not."

"Perhaps our companions had better luck," Moriarty suggested. "It's about time to head back now, anyway."

"Right," Holmes said. Then he grabbed Moriarty's arm and pointed. There, in the sky in front of them, the great bulk of a tethered hydrogen balloon slowly filled the sky as the device rose higher and higher at the end of its cable.

"Interesting," Moriarty said. "Note the unusual ratio of the height of the balloon to the chord of the diameter. I would think it would cause a loss of stability, but perhaps not. I'll have to speak to Mr. Miro about that."

"That's the wave of the future, Moriarty," Holmes said, staring up at the balloon with an intent expression on his face.

"If so, it's taking a long time waving," Moriarty said dryly. "The Montgolfier brothers made the first balloon ascent one hundred and two years ago, on June fifth, seventeen eighty-three."

"Someday," Holmes said, "passenger-carrying balloons will be crossing the oceans at unheard-of speeds, linking the peoples of the world into one great hegemony, led by a just and powerful nation that flies a flag quartering the Union Jack with the Stars and Stripes."

"Why, Holmes," Moriarty said, tapping him gently on the back, "that's almost poetic."

"Come," Holmes said, "we'd better get back to the public house."

Twenty minutes later, they arrived back at the Royal Standard to find Barnett and Dr. Watson waiting for them. Over a hasty but excellent lunch, washed down by a fine cider, Barnett told the tale of the unsuccessful search to the south. "No submersibles," he said, "no Russians, no inaccessible areas on the dock; nothing but a lot of people enjoying the spectacle of hundreds of sails crisscrossing the bay."

"We've been going about this wrong," Holmes said.

"How's that?" Moriarty asked.

"We've been on land trying to search the sea. We should be on the sea. We should hire a boat. A steam-launch."

"Excellent, Holmes!" Moriarty said. He thumped on the table. "Landlord! I say, landlord!"

The portly proprietor of the Royal Standard hurried over. "Is something the matter, gentlemen?" he asked, drying his hands on the towel tied around his ample waist.

"Not at all," Moriarty said. "A fine establishment you have here. Excellent food."

"Why, thank you, sir. Food is important to me, so I always assume it's important to my customers, too."

"And right you are," Moriarty assured him. "Now tell me something, sir; I'm sure you know what goes on in these parts better than anyone. Where could we hire a steam-launch at this particular time?"

"That's a hard one, sir," the proprietor said, screwing his face up into an attitude of concentration. "Captain Peterson's rig has been let to a party of journalists. Lowery's is still in repair; busted boiler, it has. The *Blue Carbuncle* is over in Cowes for the day. Hired out to a photographer, I believe. The *Water Witch*—why, that's right! Captain Coster was in here this morning. He's the skipper of the *Water Witch*. Complaining, he was, that his party what chartered the boat for the day had as of yet not shown up. That was some hours ago, but if they've not appeared yet, I'm sure he'd take you out. Are you gentlemen from a newspaper?"

"You might say," Barnett said.

"Could you direct us to this Captain Coster?" Moriarty asked.

"Nothing easier," the landlord said. "To the left as you leave and then to the right at the second crossing. The *Water Witch* is white with black trim and a broad red stripe on the funnel. You can't miss her."

"Thank you, sir," Moriarty said, rising from the table. "Come, gentlemen; this might be just what we need."

As they left the inn, Moriarty gave Barnett his new task. "Miro is expecting you," he said. "Try to make yourself useful to him, but not at the expense of failing to search for the submersible. Take signal rockets up with you, and make sure you have an igniter. If you sight the craft, set off a rocket. Use different colors for different directions. Let us say red, white, blue, and green for north, east, south, and west."

"Yes, sir," Barnett said. "I'll keep a careful lookout. Is the direction to be from the balloon or from the *Water Witch*?"

"What an excellent thought," Moriarty said. "You'll be able to keep us in sight, of course. From the *Water Witch*, then."

"You'd better stay with us," Holmes said, "until we're sure we get the craft."

The *Water Witch* was still at its mooring, and Captain Coster was only too happy to take them out. "Want to go out and watch the regatta, do you?" he asked. "I can get you in a good position for that, although I daren't get too close. They'll have my license for sure if I interfere with the race."

"We just want to stay in the harbor for now," Moriarty told him. "There's a particular boat we're looking for and we want to cruise around and see if we can find her." He swung around to Barnett. "We're settled here. You'd better go off to Miro. We'll be looking for your signal."

"Okay," Barnett said. He trotted off down the wharf.

Captain Coster built up a head of steam in the *Water Witch* and they headed across the harbor toward Gosport Town on the far side. There they gradually made their way around the curve of the shore, pulling alongside every wharf and jetty to peer into boathouses, hulks, sheltered moorings, and anything else that looked like a possible hiding-place for the forty-foot steel cigar.

After two hours' futile searching, they crossed back and resumed the hunt on the Portsmouth side. Dr. Watson kept his eyes on the tethered balloon, as they worked their way toward it and again away from it. Captain Coster pulled the *Water Witch* as close as he could to the various objects they wanted to examine, and Holmes and Moriarty took turns leaping aboard a variety of boats, barges, and assorted flotsam that graced the harbor and could provide shelter, however unlikely, for the Garrett-Harris. What Captain Coster thought of this, he didn't say. He was obviously used to the odd requests of his paying passengers.

It was five o'clock when the *Victoria and Albert* steamed into the harbor and stopped at its spot at one end of the finish line. Several small Navy steam cutters took positions around the Royal Yacht, presumably to fend off overenthusiastic sightseers. On the upper deck, a stout somber woman dressed in black sat alone under a canopy and wrote in her diary.

There was no sign of the submersible.

EARTH, AIR, FIRE, AND WATER

Speed bonnie boat, like a bird on the wing.
—HAROLD EDWIN BOULTON

Disgraceful," Captain Coster said, puffing away on the thin black rope he called a cigar.

"What's that?" Moriarty asked.

"Them barge captains. They have no regard for any of the rest of us. They're so used to being pushed about they can't even take the responsibility of properly mooring their barges. Look at that one now, come adrift. I'll have to notify the port director when we dock, and he'll have to send a tug to pick her up."

"Does it happen often?" Moriarty asked, staring speculatively at the drifting barge.

"All too," Captain Coster said. "Although usually only when the beggars are empty. This one has a full load of coal, I notice. Some colliery is going to be delighted if she smashes up on the Head or beaches herself."

Holmes, who had been considering the barge carefully, came over to Moriarty. "Look closely at that craft," he said. "Does anything strike you?"

"Yes," Moriarty said. "I've been thinking the same thing."

"That's it, then?"

"The probabilities would so indicate."

"What is it, Holmes?" Watson asked, staring at the barge.

"Captain Coster," Holmes said, "please look carefully at the barge. Does it seem to you that it is riding too high on the water? Compare it with those barges at the pier to our left, which are also fully loaded with coal."

"Why, yes," Coster said. "That had been bothering me, but as

I couldn't think of anything to account for it, I decided I must be mistaken."

"Pull alongside that barge, Captain," Moriarty directed. "Carefully, very carefully, if you don't mind."

Slowly the *Water Witch* edged alongside the coal barge. Moriarty took a small self-loading pistol from his pocket and worked the slide to chamber a bullet. Dr. Watson pulled his old service revolver from his belt, and Sherlock Holmes produced a smaller, silver-plated revolver from an inside pocket of his traveling cape.

Captain Coster did his best to look calm and unconcerned at his passengers' odd behavior. "This person you're looking for," he said. "I take it he's not a friend of yours."

"Hush!" Holmes said, putting his finger to his lips. "Keep your ship alongside. We'll be back."

The three of them, Holmes in the lead, leaped across the two feet of water separating the two craft and scrambled up the rough wooden side of the barge. The craft was nothing more than a huge rectangle full of coal from front to rear. At the very stern was a small wooden superstructure resembling a shed with windows cut in it. Black curtains shielded the windows from the inside, and there was no sign of life.

Slowly they worked their way to the stern. "It seems unlikely that we haven't been seen—or perhaps heard," Moriarty whispered. "We had best be ready for a warm welcome."

Holmes smiled grimly. "It occurs to me," he said, "that if we're mistaken, some poor bargee is about to experience the shock of his life."

Holmes and Watson lay prone on a bed of coal, their weapons pointed at the door, while Moriarty snapped it open with a well-placed *baritsu* kick and ducked aside. It swung wildly back and forth with a clatter that echoed off the water. Still nothing moved.

After a cautious moment, Moriarty dropped to the deck and carefully peered around the doorway. Then he stood up and dusted himself off, looking disgusted. "Come here, gentlemen," he said, "Look at this."

Inside the cabin were three men. Two of them were sprawled opposite each other across a small table and the third was crumpled on the floor halfway to the door. The two men at the table each had a hole in his chest, a great, ugly gaping hole of the sort caused by a large-caliber handgun fired from close range. The man on the floor had three such holes in his back. He lay in a clotted pool of his own blood, his face turned up, eyes opened, wearing a surprised expression. On the table was a small mound of anarchist literature, now covered with dried blood.

Stepping gingerly to avoid the blood, Holmes bent down to examine the body on the floor. "Dead for some time, I should say," he said. "What do you think, Watson?"

Watson stooped over and pressed his fingernail into the flesh of the wrist and then opened the dead eye and peered at it. "Four or five hours, as a quick estimate," he said. "Nasty way to go—not that any death is pleasant. Still, the massive trauma of a half-inch piece of lead pushing its way through the human gut must rank as one of the less desirable ends."

"Well," Moriarty said. "Trepoff has his dead anarchists. Now what has he done with the submersible?" He knelt down and began tapping on the deck, to be rewarded almost immediately with a dull thumping. "Down here," he said. "There must be a trap door."

Holmes joined him and, together, they pried and tapped and examined and pushed and prodded at the boards of the cabin floor. It took them five minutes to find the catch, hidden between two floorboards. Moriarty pushed at it, and it dropped a pair of hinged doors to reveal a three-foot-square hole. Holmes went over to the table for a candle which stood between the two dead anarchists and lighted it.

"He's gone, of course," Moriarty said.

"But we'd best check," Holmes said.

"Of course," Moriarty said. He swung himself over the side of the trap and climbed down the ladder affixed to the edge. When his head was level with the floor, Holmes handed him the candle, and then he disappeared below.

A few moments later he was back. "Come down here," he called to Holmes. "This is impressive. You should see it. Bring another candle or, by preference, one of the oil lamps."

Holmes and Watson removed two oil lamps from the gimbals that tied them to the cabin walls, lighted them, and clambered down the ladder to join Moriarty. The whole interior of the barge proved to be a vast, empty chamber. A board and beam load-bearing ceiling roofed it over, and provided support for the one or two feet of coal above, which disguised and concealed the chamber. Along the two sides and the aft section where they stood ran a wooden platform. Water came up to about three feet below the platform, filling the whole center of the chamber.

"Here," Moriarty said, "is where the Garrett-Harris was moored."

"There must be a hole in the bottom of the barge," Holmes said, "just large enough for the submersible to come in and out."

"At the moment," Moriarty added, "it is out. We can investigate this later, but right now we'd best get back to the *Water Witch* and see if we can determine where that blasted steel cigar is lying in wait."

They had no sooner reached the upper cabin than they heard Captain Coster hallooing for them. Moriarty raced out on deck and over to the side. "What?" he yelled.

Captain Coster pointed up. Moriarty turned. There, in the air above them, was the fading light of a blue signal flare. Suddenly a second flare arced up to join the first. This new one burst forth with a brilliant white ball of light.

"Blue, then white," Moriarty said. "Southeast. Very clever of Barnett." He scrambled over the side of the barge and onto the steam-launch, with Holmes and Watson only a few steps behind. "Southeast," he told Captain Coster. "Head southeast. Holmes, get forward and see if you can spot the thing."

"What can we do if we find it, now it's submerged?" Watson asked.

"Ram it!" Moriarty snapped. "It won't be more than four or five feet down. We should be able to split it open like an eggshell."

"Here, now!" Captain Coster said. "What is it you're talking about ramming with the *Water Witch*? Her hull is none too strong, you know. Besides, I can get into an awful mess of trouble if I go about ramming other boats."

"Don't worry about that, Captain," Moriarty said with firm authority. "Just make your course, and quickly! We're on the Queen's business. If any harm comes to your boat, you shall be completely reimbursed for damages."

"The Queen's—"

"Get a move on, Captain," Moriarty said. "There's a submersible out there somewhere stalking the *Victoria and Albert*, and we have to stop it!"

"Yes, sir," Captain Coster said, snapping him a firm salute. "Aye, aye, sir." He grabbed the wheel and headed the *Water Witch* around.

The sea was cluttered with small pleasure-boats—a thousand Sunday skippers all out to cheer their favorites as the great race drew to a close. The first of the big yachts were now coming into sight in the distance, tacking into the bay and lining up on the *Victoria and Albert* and the finish line.

The *Water Witch* cut a line due southeast, passing to the left of the Royal Yacht and heading into the Solent. "We'll pass well to the lee of the yachts," Captain Coster said, "so that's all right. But where is this submersible?"

"Perhaps your associate saw a partly submerged tree trunk," Holmes suggested.

"I say!" Watson called from the bow. "Look!" he pointed to a rocket trail streaking into the sky about them. As they watched, it burst into a shower of green sparks cascading over their heads.

"Green," Moriarty said. "West."

"Perhaps it merely signifies the start of the evening display," Holmes suggested sourly.

"No," Moriarty said. "Barnett is sending the best information he can with but four colors as a language. Captain, turn this craft due west."

"As you say," Captain Coster said, swinging the ship around.

Moriarty climbed up to the top of the cabin and stared about him, examining the positions of the ships in the bay. Then he jumped down. "Of course!" he said, snapping his fingers.

"What?" Holmes demanded.

"The submersible is circling the *Victoria and Albert* from the west," Moriarty said. "Trepoff wants to have nothing between himself and the Solent channel after he makes his shot. Barnett must have estimated that we couldn't catch up with him in direct pursuit, so he sent us around this way." He turned to the captain. "Cut in closer to the *Victoria and Albert*," he directed.

"Those Navy steam cutters surrounding her will stop us," Coster said.

"We'll take that chance."

"We'll be cutting across the finish line in front of the yachts. The commodore won't like it."

"We'll live with that too," Moriarty said. "Cut it close, there. And open up that engine!"

Captain Coster yelled instructions to his one-man crew, who was down below stoking the boiler, and the *Water Witch*, engine racing, moving in to cut across the side of the *Victoria and Albert*. Two

Navy cutters came to life and sprung out to intercept her. The nearer one was alongside in a minute, just as the *Water Witch* came parallel to the side of the Royal Yacht. A skinny young man in a full-dress uniform with the thin, curled stripe of a sub-lieutenant on his sleeve was leaning out from the prow of the cutter, his gold sword flapping against his leg. "Ahoy there!" he yelled, cupping his hands against the wind, "Heave to, you men!" Captain Coster shrugged and started to comply.

"There!" Watson suddenly yelled. "There it is! I can see it. Off to the left there!"

Moriarty peered out and saw the barely visible submersible, a menacing cigar-shaped shadow beneath the waters. Suddenly, a streak of white foam detached from the bow in an upward arc and sped toward the *Victoria and Albert*; a Whitehead torpedo with a two-hundred-pound nitrocellulose warhead creating its destiny, racing to meet the monarch of one-third of the world's people.

"It's now running on the surface!" Moriarty yelled. "Quick, kick that engine in and get off this boat!" He grabbed the wheel and spun it around, as Coster, who had shut down the throttle, slapped it full open again.

"Here, you!" the sub-lieutenant yelled, "where the deuce do you think you're going? Stop or we'll fire!"

"Holmes, Watson, get off this boat!" Moriarty yelled, swinging the *Water Witch* onto a path that would intercept the Whitehead torpedo. "Captain Coster, jump!"

Holmes swung himself over the aft rail. "Leap for it, Watson," he yelled, before cutting the water with a clean dive toward the Navy cutter. Watson spun his bowler toward the horizon and joined Holmes in the water. The ship's one crewman appeared from somewhere below and leaped overboard.

"My boat man!" Captain Coster screamed, trying to grab the wheel from Moriarty. The professor picked him up by the front of his pea jacket. "Victoria will buy you a new one," he said savagely, and with seemingly superhuman strength he lifted Coster high and threw him over the stern rail.

Moriarty made a final adjustment in the course of the boat, lashed the wheel in position, and then raced back to the stern rail. Making one last check on the closing trajectories of the boat and the torpedo, he decided that the *Water Witch* would intersect a full ten yards before the torpedo reached the *Victoria and Albert*. Then he stripped off his jacket and dove, a long, flat dive, into the bay.

He was in the water no more than a few seconds when the Whitehead torpedo punched into the *Water Witch*. It drove through the scantling on the port side, all the way through the boat, and out the starboard side before it exploded. A great geyser shot up, cresting a hundred feet in the air, and fell back across the bow of the *Victoria and Albert*, causing the big yacht to rock ponderously in place. A moment later the concussion wave reached Moriarty, throwing him out of the water and putting a deep trough under him when he fell back down. Then the water closed over him and he had to struggle hard to reach the surface before his lungs gave out.

The *Water Witch* took on water rapidly, settling by the bow. The deck was already awash, and only the small cabin was clear of the sea. Then the stern lifted clear of the water and the bow plunged. It stood frozen in that position for a long moment before sliding, bow first, to the bottom.

A moment later the Navy cutter reached Moriarty, and two seamen pulled him from the water. Holmes, Watson, Captain Coster, and his crewman were already on board. Holmes was deep in discussion with the young sub-lieutenant.

"Oh, my God," Watson suddenly screamed, pointing across the water to the Royal Yacht. There, etched by the rays of the Western sun, the clear wake of a second Whitehead torpedo could be seen cleaving a path toward the bow of the *Victoria and Albert*.

One of the guarding Navy steam cutters, now on the lookout, raced to intercept it. For a moment it seemed as though the cutter would be too late, but then, scant feet from the bow of the Royal Yacht, it crossed the line of the torpedo. The sailors on the cutter scattered, jumping overboard in every direction; but the young officer at its helm stayed motionless behind the wheel, calmly steering the craft into the torpedo.

And then the cutter was gone, and an exploding cloud of white water marked where it had been. A second later the *crump* of the explosion reached them, rocking and shaking their boat. Then the cloud of water fell back, obscuring the *Victoria and Albert* for a moment and drenching its decks. A large concussion wave spread out from where the launch had been, and the Royal Yacht bobbed up and down like a rowboat for a few seconds. Of the cutter and the young officer, there was no sign.

The sub-lieutenant, his face white, turned to Moriarty. "Mr.

Holmes has been telling me what this is all about, Professor Moriarty," he said. "I am Lieutenant Simms. How can I help?"

"Find that damned submersible," Moriarty said.

"Has it any more Whitehead torpedoes?"

"I think that's the lot," Holmes said.

"It can't fire more without surfacing at any rate," Moriarty said. "I'd like to get him before he has a chance to reload."

"You think he's going to try?"

"No. I think he's going to leave as expeditiously as possible. He—look there!"

A red starburst lit the sky above them. "North," Moriarty said. "Barnett is still on the job. Trepoff has decided not to run the Solent."

Another red burst spread its crystal light, followed by a white ball of fire.

"North-northeast," Moriarty said. "Have you a compass?"

"Don't need one," the officer said. "It would be, let's see . . ." He looked around and sighted along his arm. "Just that way."

"Right back toward Miro's tethered aerostats," Moriarty said. "Trepoff may have a land vehicle concealed somewhere about. We must try to beat him to the shore."

Lieutenant Simms leaned over to a brass speaking-tube by the wheel and blew into it. "Engine crew!"

"Aye, sir?" came a thin voice out of it.

"I want you men to shovel coal into that boiler until you redline the gauge. That's an order."

"Aye, aye, sir."

"Kelly," the lieutenant said, turning to the young seaman at the wheel, "make a straight course for that great tethered balloon abaft the fitting station. As straight a course as you can without running us aground or hitting anything."

"That balloon's coming down, sir," the sailor pointed out.

"It's pretty big," the lieutenant said. "I don't think it will descend from sight. But if it does, then make a course for where it was."

"Aye, aye, sir."

In a minute the sturdy cutter was plowing through the water in a mechanical frenzy, the tie rods from the double pistons clanking madly in their housing. In two minutes the escape valve for the boiler was whistling and burbling as it released some of the tremendous pressure that had been built up.

"Is this safe?" Watson asked the young officer, looking nervously at the escaping steam.

"They don't usually blow up," Lieutenant Simms said. "They are supposed to be built for a twenty-five percent overload. Of course, this is an experimental model. We shall see."

"Umph," Watson said, and he made his way to the bow.

Holmes stood on top of the wheelhouse, clutching the small signal mast for support. "There," he said. "Look! It has surfaced."

Moriarty peered over the water in the direction of Holmes's pointing finger, but he couldn't make out anything, so he climbed up to join Holmes. "Where?"

"Over there!"

"Oh, yes," Moriarty said. The thick metal cigar was moving rapidly through the water dead ahead of them, with its small conning tower completely above water. "On the surface, with air for its engine, it can make surprisingly good time." He pulled out his watch and timed the closing distance between the cutter and the submersible against the submersible's approach to the shore. "It will beat us ashore," he said. "But only by a minute or so."

"Ashore or not," Holmes said, "he will not escape me. I will get this man."

"We," Moriarty corrected, "will get this man."

Holmes turned a bleak eye on him. "Did you see the Queen?" he asked.

"What do you mean, Holmes? When?"

"After the *Water Witch* exploded—you were still in the water—I saw Her Majesty come forward on the upper deck of the *Victoria and Albert* to watch what was happening. The wave from the second explosion washed right over her."

"Was her Majesty hurt?"

"I don't believe so. But, dammit, Moriarty, that was the Queen of England! That man was trying to assassinate the crowned head of the English people merely to accomplish a political end in a country two thousand miles away from here."

A sudden gust of wind blew salt spray in Moriarty's face and he took out his handkerchief to wipe it. For a moment he was surprised to find that his handkerchief was soaking wet already. "True," he said.

"She is not perfect, Moriarty," Holmes said, clenching his fist.

"I'll admit that, dammit, she is not perfect. But I've never known England without Victoria, and I have no desire to. She stands for decency and morality and everything that's good in this imperfect world."

"I don't want to argue with a man in the grip of a patriotic passion," Moriarty said, doing his best to wring his handkerchief out. "Besides, you may be right. At any rate, we saved her life. Doesn't that make you feel good?"

"You saved her life," Holmes said. "You and the officer at the wheel of that cutter. What a strange thing fate is that it should twist so: Moriarty saving the life of his queen. Surely one of the great ironies of our time."

They had gained greatly on the submersible in the past minute, and it was now clearly in view. But it was also much closer to the shore by now. Even with the great difference in speeds, the submersible would reach the shore ahead of the cutter. The only question was by how much.

Silently, impotent in the hands of the immutable laws of physics and mechanics, Holmes and Moriarty watched the submersible ground itself on the rocks of a small strip of beach, even as the cutter halved the distance between them. Three men popped out of the forward hatch of the submersible and ran off up the rocks.

"She's beached!" Lieutenant Simms yelled. "The sub is beached. We'll reach her in less than a minute. I'll run the cutter right in alongside her. Probably rip the bottom out." He whistled into the speaking tube. "Stop shoveling! Prepare to run aground!" Then he turned to his wheelman. "Kelly, I'll take the wheel. You stand by that strain valve and be ready to release the pressure on my command. Instantly, you understand, or we'll all be blown into the next life."

"Aye, aye, sir," Kelly said, taking a firm grip on the strain valve rope.

Lieutenant Simms artfully headed the launch into the same small strip of rocky beach that the submersible had found, aiming for a spot immediately to the right of the submersible. Holmes and Moriarty went forward to join Watson, and the three of them braced themselves against the coming shock of running aground.

At the last possible second Simms threw the engine out of gear and yelled: "Now, Kelly!"

The cutter slid smoothly up on the beach in a screaming, billowing cloud of steam that pierced the ear and obscured all vision for fifty yards in every direction. As soon as the cutter jammed to a halt, Moriarty and Holmes leaped off and raced over the stony beach, with Watson close behind them.

Once clear of the billowing steam, they paused to look around. Holmes grabbed Moriarty's arm and pointed. "Look!"

In the clearing ahead of them the two hydrogen balloons had been winched down and had their gondolas resting on the ground. The three men from the submersible had commandeered the near balloon, and were keeping its crew away with large wicked-looking revolvers. Two of the villains had boarded the gondola, and the third was hacking it free of the heavy rope tether with an axe. Miro and his assistants were standing with their hands high over their heads, looking startled and frightened out of their wits.

Holmes and Moriarty raced toward the clearing, but before they arrived the balloon was free. The axe man dropped his axe and clambered aboard, pulled up by the other two, as the great balloon bounded upward, lofting into an English heaven.

"Here! Over here!" someone called as Moriarty and Holmes reached the clearing. "Quickly!" It was Barnett, who raised his head from where he had been hiding—in the gondola of the second balloon—and beckoned to them. "I've almost got it free," he called. "Come on. Climb in and we'll go after them."

Moriarty and Holmes raced across the field to the second gondola and climbed in. Watson puffed up to them a couple of seconds later.

"Don't get in, Doctor," Barnett said sharply. "If we're too heavy—or too light—we won't be able to match velocities with them."

"Notify the Navy, Watson," Holmes said. "We'll be heading out to sea. Get a ship to follow us if you can."

And with that, they were free. "I'll do my best, Holmes," Watson yelled up at them as they pulled away from the field.

"How'd you do that?" Moriarty asked Barnett. "They had to hack that other balloon loose."

"There's a release for the tether in the bottom of the gondola," Barnett said. "In case the balloon begins to drag on something, I suppose. Nobody told Trepoff. I assume that was Trepoff?"

"I certainly hope so," Holmes said.

"You've done very good work," Moriarty told Barnett.

The balloon was already more than a hundred feet above the ground and rising rapidly. Their quarry was a hundred yards ahead of them and several hundred feet higher. "They seem to be pulling away from us," Holmes noted.

"There is a steady wind of about twenty knots at roughly the five-hundred-foot level," Barnett said. "They must be in it already. When we reach it, we'll keep up with them."

"Keeping up isn't enough," Holmes said, fingering his revolver. "We must catch them."

They were heading generally southwest across the bay. Below them the white sails of the regatta yachts were circling the *Victoria and Albert*. Ahead of them, the town of Gosport, a mile or so of land, and then the Solent and the Isle of Wight. "They'll have the steam cutters out to support us," Moriarty said. "If we can force Trepoff down in the Solent, he'll be picked up by the Navy."

"Perhaps we can shoot him down," Holmes suggested, still clutching his silver-plated revolver.

"Too far for pistol shooting," Moriarty said. "Besides, a pistol bullet passing through the fabric of the balloon would merely cause a minor gas leak which would have no discernible effect on the performance of the aerostat."

"We must do something!" Holmes declared.

They passed over Gosport and the mile-wide strip of land, steadily gaining altitude. Trepoff's balloon was now several hundred yards ahead of them and holding that distance. They were over water now, and the ships below looked like precise toys, built for some hobbyist's bathtub lake.

A spark appeared in the gondola of the forward aerostat, which grew into a rapidly approaching arc of flame reaching out for them. It burst into a myriad of sparkling colors somewhere over their balloon. Then a second spark shot toward them, to dissolve into a cascading ribbon of red flame directly before their eyes.

"Trepoff has found the fireworks!" Barnett cried. "They were being loaded when he and his men appeared."

"Dear me," Holmes said. "This is liable to prove embarrassing."

"I don't suppose we have any similar cargo?" Moriarty asked, looking around the surprisingly spacious interior of the wicker gondola.

Barnett pointed to three wooden crates on the floor. "There," he said. "I would like to point out, however, that they are very dangerous. Miro gave me a long lecture about the folly of firing off rockets from the basket of a hydrogen balloon. He was not happy about the signal flares, and they're only half the size of these sky-rockets."

"We must be careful," Moriarty agreed. "Let us get these crates open."

As he spoke a rocket burst over their balloon and released four brightly burning blue flares, which descended on silk parachutes, slowly passing in front of them. One of them hit the side of the balloon, sliding along the fabric for a few moments before bouncing off.

Holmes released his breath. "I have never," he said, "felt quite so helpless. Well, Professor, Barnett—dangerous as it may be, I vote for an answering fireworks barrage from this gondola."

They ripped the crates open. A new assault of colored balls popped toward them from the other aerostat, twisting and glowing madly, falling only a few feet short.

The first crate contained three boxes marked "GERBES," and the illustrations on the box covers showed colored balls popping from a tube. "I think we've just seen those," Holmes said. "Next crate."

The second crate held finned skyrockets, packed in firing tubes. "This, I think, is what we are looking for," Moriarty said. "How many are there?"

"Fourteen," Barnett said.

"Not so deep as a well," Moriarty said, "or so wide as a church door, but that should suffice." Three points of red suddenly appeared in the sky above them and burst into a shower of sparks which cascaded over the balloon and fell on all sides of them. "Indeed," he added, "it had better suffice."

He took one of the skyrocket tubes in his hand and examined it. "How ingenious," he said. "The fins are on tiny springs which push them open after they pass through the tube."

"Perhaps," Holmes suggested, "it would be wiser to examine the contraptions later. For now let us concentrate on shooting down that balloon before its passengers succeed in doing the same for us."

"Take your jacket off," Moriarty told Barnett. "Be prepared to extinguish fires started by flame-back from the skyrockets."

"There's a damp horse-blanket here," Barnett said, producing it from a wicker basket built into the side of the gondola. "Miro had it soaked for the same purpose. I'll use it."

"Excellent," Moriarty said.

Holmes propped one of the skyrocket tubes against the side of the gondola and sighted along the top. "This should put it in the general vicinity," he said. "Here, I'll stand aside and you light the fuse." He stood to one side, holding the skyrocket tube firmly at arm's length, propped against the side of the gondola.

Moriarty ripped a length of fuse from one of the gerbes and lit one end with a waterproof vespa, which he carefully waved out and tossed over the side. "Ready?"

"Ready," Holmes agreed.

Moriarty applied the burning fuse to the short fuse of the skyrocket, which sputtered and smoldered and disappeared into the tube. Eight seconds later a blast of flame came out of the rear of the tube, and the skyrocket shot out the front. It arced across the sky, over Trepoff's balloon, and released a series of colored balls before exploding in a shower of red and green sparks.

An answering salvo from Trepoff put a rocket between the gondola and the balloon, but it passed harmlessly through the shrouds before disintegrating into a crowd of flame-snakes that spiraled to the sea below.

Holmes corrected his aim and Moriarty touched off the next skyrocket. This one fell short and exploded in a puffball of blue light that was quickly extinguished by the sea.

Suddenly a spark appeared in Trepoff's gondola, and a flame curved upward. And then, in a moment that etched itself in the minds of all the onlookers for miles up and down the Solent, a tracery of flame worked over the fabric of Trepoff's balloon, creating fiery designs in the rounded sides. Then it burned off, and for a second seemed to have gone out, when all at once the balloon erupted and a plume of flame spurted out the side and enveloped the whole craft.

Barnett saw a white, frightened face at the side of the gondola before the craft fell from the sky, a fiery comet tail streaming out behind it.

"Miro was right," Moriarty said calmly, as the flaming mass struck the water far below. "This is a dangerous business."

"I only hope they find the bodies," Holmes said, "or we shall never know if that was Trepoff."

Moriarty shook his head. "Only the future will tell us whether Trepoff was in that aerostat," he said. "Remember, we have no idea of what he looks like. Barnett, can you get us down?"

Barnett reached up and untied a rope that valved hydrogen out of the top of the gasbag. "It will be a slow descent," he said.

"Good," Moriarty remarked. "I have just seen a fast descent."

By the time their aerostat reached the water, a cutter was standing by to pick them up. The lieutenant in command saluted them as they came aboard. "Good evening, gentlemen," he said. "I have orders to take you to the *Victoria and Albert*. Her Majesty would like to have you presented. At your convenience, of course."

TWENTY-THREE

THE UNWRITTEN TALE

On earth there is nothing great but man;
In man there is nothing great but mind.
— Sir William Hamilton

You are going out?" Moriarty asked.

"I am having dinner with Miss Perrine," Barnett told him.

"Ah, of course," Moriarty said. " *'Jedem nach seinen Bedürfnis-sen,'* as that strange little fellow at the British Museum put it."

"This is to be a business dinner," Barnett said stiffly.

"Could it be otherwise?" asked Moriarty blandly. "Incidentally, I meant to remark on your ept handling of the Trepoff affair in your article for the popular press."

"Well," Barnett said, "I figured if I didn't write it, then someone else surely would. As it is, I preempted the story and selected the facts to be told."

"Excellent," Moriarty said.

Barnett looked pleased. "Thank you."

"You kept my name out of it," Moriarty said. "And I thank you." He looked at the ship's chronometer above the study door. "You'd best go to dinner," he said. "Business before pleasure, after all."

"We are meeting Mr. Bernard Shaw at Covent Garden after dinner," Barnett said. "Cecily—Miss Perrine—is trying to talk him into doing a series of articles for us."

"Shaw," Moriarty said. "I have read some of his criticism. A great talent. Not a genius, as he thinks, but a genuine talent. A well-developed second-rate talent with a first-rate Irish ego."

"Speaking of Irish egos—" Barnett said.

"Go to dinner!"

Sherlock Holmes and his Boswell, Dr. John H. Watson, were on the steps as Barnett opened the door on his way out. "Good evening," he said. "The professor is expecting you, I believe." Barnett tipped his black silk topper at them, adjusted it carefully on his head, and hurried off toward the British Museum.

Holmes and Watson entered the house and were ushered into the study by Mr. Maws. "I've come to thank you for your assistance, Professor," Holmes said, dropping into the leatherback chair in front of the desk. "I owe you that."

"We work well together, Holmes," Moriarty said, adjusting his pince-nez glasses on the bridge of his nose. "I suspected we would."

"It's quits between us now," Holmes said. "You knew that, also."

"I was afraid you were going to say that," Moriarty said.

"I have been engaged to investigate the robbery of the London and Midlands Bank which occurred some six weeks ago," Holmes said.

"Ah," Moriarty said.

"There are certain signs," Holmes said, "which point in a certain direction . . ."

"Oh," Moriarty said.

"Of course, even if I apprehend the actual thieves," Holmes said, "the mastermind behind the plan will somehow manage to remain free."

"Of course," Moriarty agreed.

"I don't think that is right," Holmes said.

"You wouldn't," Moriarty said.

"I am going to do my best to see that he, also, is awarded penal servitude."

"You would." Moriarty stood up. "This conversation is beginning to take on an awful familiarity. Would you like a drink?"

"No, thank you," said Holmes.

"I think not," said Doctor Watson, looking slightly offended.

"Is there any word from St. Petersburg?" Holmes asked.

"They believe," Moriarty said, "that Trepoff is no more. At least, they have no sign that he is still alive. We may have, as they say, done him in."

"Good," Holmes said. "Then our relationship is officially over as of now."

"Back to the old games, eh, Holmes?"

Sherlock Holmes turned to Dr. Watson. "This man," he said, hooking his thumb toward Professor Moriarty, "is the Napoleon of crime. Two weeks ago he saved the life of his sovereign. A month before that he robbed, or caused to be robbed, the London and Midlands Bank of some two millions in bullion."

"They exaggerate," Moriarty said. "These banks always exaggerate. It's for the insurance. Think about that, Holmes."

"Deucedly inconsistent," Watson said.

"When you write up my little cases," Holmes told Watson, "I want you to avoid all mention of the infamous Professor here. Someday either I shall eliminate him, or he will eliminate me. Until that time, do not speak of him or write of him."

"Of course, Holmes," Watson said. "Whatever you say."

"Dear me," Moriarty said, "such a pity. And I do so love publicity."

Holmes rose from his chair. "Come, Watson," he said. "There are a few little matters which engage our attention now. Good evening, Professor."

"As always," Moriarty said, "it has been my pleasure. Do come back soon and we can continue our little talk."

"We can find our own way out," Holmes said. "Good evening!" And, followed by Watson, he stalked out the front door.

Mrs. H came downstairs from the landing, where she had been listening to this final exchange. She sniffed. "An unforgiving lad," she said.

Moriarty shook his head sadly. "Perhaps some day . . ." he said. "But probably not. Have Mrs. Randall fix me a bite to eat, will you, Mrs. H? I shall be downstairs in the laboratory."

THE
PARADOL
PARADOX

It is a damp, chilly Saturday, the sixteenth of April, 1887, as I sit before the small coal fire in the front room of Professor James Moriarty's Russell Square home making these notes; setting down while they are still fresh in my memory the queer and astounding events surrounding the problem with which Professor Moriarty and I found ourselves involved over the past few days. The case itself, a matter of some delicacy involving some of the highest-born and most important personages in the realm, had, as Moriarty put it, "a few points that were not entirely devoid of interest to the higher faculties." Moriarty's ability to shed light on what the rest of us find dark and mysterious will come as no surprise to anyone who has had any dealings with the professor. But what will keep the events of these past days unique in my mind forever is the glimpse I was afforded into the private life of my friend and mentor, Professor James Moriarty.

Certain aspects of the case will never see print, at least not during the lifetimes of any of those involved; and I certainly cannot write it up in one of my articles for the American press, without revealing what must not be revealed. But the facts should not be lost, so I will at least set them down here, and if this notebook remains locked in the bottom drawer of my desk at my office at the American News Service until after my death, so be it. At least the future will learn what must be concealed from the present.

My name is Benjamin Barnett, and I am an expatriate New Yorker, working here in London as the director and owner of the American News Service; a company that sends news and feature stories from Britain and the continent to newspapers all around the United States over the Atlantic cable. Four years ago I was rescued from an unfortunate circumstance—and being held prisoner in a Turkish fortress is as unfortunate a circumstance as I can imagine that does not involve immediate great pain or disfigurement—by Professor James Moriarty. I was employed by him for two years after that, and found him to be one of the most intelligent, perceptive, capable; in short one of the wisest men I have ever known. Most of those who have had dealings with the professor would, I am sure, agree, with the notable exception of a certain consulting detective, who places Moriarty at the center of every nefarious plot hatched by anyone, anywhere, during this past quarter-century. I have no idea why he persists in this invidious belief. I have seen that the professor sometimes skirts the law to achieve his own ends, but I can also witness that Professor Moriarty has a higher moral standard than many of those who enforce it.

But I digress. It was last Tuesday evening, four days ago, that saw the start of the events I relate. We had just finished dinner and I was still sitting at the dining table, drinking my coffee and reading a back issue of *The Strand Magazine*. Moriarty was staring moodily out the window, his long, aristocratic fingers twitching with boredom. He was waiting, at the time, for a new spectrograph of his own design to be completed so that he could continue his researches into the spectral lines of one of the nearer stars. When he is not engaged in his scientific endeavors, Moriarty likes to solve problems of a more earthly nature, but at the moment there was no such exercise to engage his intellect; and to Professor Moriarty intellect was all.

I finished the article I was reading, closed the magazine, and shook my head in annoyance.

"You're right," Moriarty said without turning from the window. "It is shameful the way the Austrian medical establishment treated Dr. Semmelweis. Pass me a cigar, would you, old chap?"

"Not merely the Austrians," I said, putting the magazine down and reaching for the humidor on the mantel. "The whole medical world. But really, Moriarty, this is too much. Two hundred years ago they would have burned you at the stake as a sorcerer."

Moriarty leaned over and took a cigar from the humidor as I held it toward him. "After all the time we have been in association," he said, "surely you can follow my methods by now."

"It is one thing to watch from the audience as De Kolta vanishes a girl on stage," I told him, "quite another to know how the trick is done."

Moriarty smiled and rolled the cigar between his palms. "My

'tricks' are in one way quite like those of a stage conjurer," he said. "Once you know how they're done, they don't seem quite so miraculous." He paused to clip and pierce the ends of the cigar with his silver cigar cutter. Then he lit a taper from the gas mantle on the wall, and puffed the cigar to life. "But think back. This particular miracle should succumb even to your analysis."

I rose and went over to the sideboard to pour myself another cup of coffee. The serving girl had yet to clear away the dinner dishes, and I absently banged the coffee spoon against a wine glass that had recently held its share of a fine '63 *Chateau de Braquenne* Bordeaux. Some months ago Moriarty had cleared up a particularly delicate problem for Hamish Plummet, partner in Plummet & Rose, Wines and Spirits, Piccadilly. Plummet presented the professor with a case of that rare vintage as a token of his appreciation, and tonight Moriarty had uncorked a bottle and pronounced it excellent. I was pleased to agree.

"You read the article," I suggested.

"Bravo, Barnett," Moriarty said. "A capital start."

"And you saw me reading it. But wait—you were across the room, looking out the window."

"True," Moriarty acknowledged. "I saw you reflected in the window glass."

"Ah!" I said. "But how did you know which article—even if you saw me reading—"

"I did not merely see, I observed. You stared down at your free hand, turning it over and examining it in a contemplative manner."

"Did I?"

"You were reflecting on Semmelweis's campaign to get his fellow physicians to wash their hands before treating patients. You were no doubt thinking of how many poor women had died in childbirth because the doctors scorned him and refused to take his advice."

"That's so, I remember," I told him.

"Thus I knew, by observation, which article you were reading. And then you put down the magazine and shook your head, clearly revealing your sequence of thought, and I said what I said." Moriarty returned his gaze to the window and puffed silently on his cigar.

A few moments later Mr. Maws, Moriarty's butler, knocked at the door and entered, and the serving girl scurried in past him and started clearing the table. "There's a milord come to see you, Professor," he said. "I put him in the front room. Here's his lordship's card." Mr. Maws handed Moriarty the rectangular pasteboard.

Moriarty centered his cigar carefully on the lip of an oversized ashtray and looked at the card, and then looked again. He ran his fingers over the surface, and then reached for a glass of water on the table, using it as a magnifying glass to carefully study the printing on the card. "Fascinating," he said. "What does the milord look like?"

"Young," Mr. Maws pronounced. "His attire is a bit on the messy side."

"Ah!" Moriarty said. "Well, I'll see him in my office. Give us a few seconds to get settled, and then bring him along."

"Very good, Professor," Mr. Maws said, and he bowed slightly and backed out of the room.

"The nobility has a sobering effect on Mr. Maws," Moriarty commented, as we crossed the hall to the office.

"Who is it, Professor?" I asked. "A client?"

Moriarty passed me the card. "Certainly he desires to become one," he said. "Else why would he come calling at this time of night?"

I examined the card to see what had fascinated Moriarty. Printed on the face was: *Lord Everett Tams*, and underneath that: *Earl of Whitton*. There was nothing else. "Then you don't know who he is?"

"No." Moriarty went to the bookshelf by his desk and reached for the copy of *Burke's Peerage*, then took his hand away. "And we don't have time to look him up, either, if those are his footsteps I hear."

I sat down on a chair by the window and awaited events.

A few seconds later a harried-looking man of thirty-five or so in a rumpled dark suit burst through the door and stared at both our faces before deciding which of us he had come to see. "Professor Moriarty," he said, addressing my companion, who had lowered himself into the massive leather chair behind his desk, "I am in the deepest trouble. You must help me!"

"Of course, your lordship. Sit down, compose yourself, and tell me your problem. I think you will find this chair by the desk comfortable."

His lordship dropped into the chair and looked from one to the other of us, his hands clasped tightly in front of him.

"This is Mr. Barnett, my confidant," Moriarty told the distraught lord. "Anything you choose to tell me will be safe with him."

"Yes, of course," Lord Tams said. "It's not that. Only—I'm not sure how to begin."

"Let me see if I can help," Moriarty said, leaning forward and resting his chin on his tented hands. His hawklike eyes looked Lord Tams over closely for a few seconds. "You are unmarried. Your older brother died unexpectedly quite recently, leaving you heir to the title and, presumably, estates of the Earldom of Whitton. Your new obligations make it necessary for you to give up your chosen profession of journalism, a result that is not altogether pleasing to you. You and your brother were not on the best of terms, although nothing irreconcilable had passed between you."

His lordship's hands dropped to his side and he stared at Moriarty. The professor has that effect on some people.

Moriarty sat up. "There are some other indications that are suggestive but not certain," he said. "As to the specific problem that brought you here, I'm afraid you'll have to tell me what it is."

"Who has spoken to you about me?" Lord Tams demanded.

"No one, your lordship, I assure you," Moriarty said. "You carry the indications about for the trained eye to read."

"Really?" Lord Tams rested one hand firmly on the edge of the desk and pointed an accusing finger at Moriarty with the other. "The death of my brother? The fact that I am unmarried—and a journalist? Come now, sir!"

Moriarty leaned forward, his eyes bright. "It is, after all, my profession, my lord," he said. "My ability to see what others cannot is, presumably, what brought you to me. Now, what is your problem?"

Lord Tams took a deep breath, or perhaps it was a sigh. "Your surmises are correct, Professor Moriarty," he said. "I am unmarried. My profession, if such I may call it, has been writing freelance articles on economic subjects for various London newspapers and magazines. When an editor wants a piece on free trade, or Serbian war reparations, he calls on me. I have recently—very recently—come into the title, inheriting it from my elder brother Vincent, who died suddenly. It is his death that has brought me here to seek your assistance."

I leaned forward in my chair. The thrill of being in at the beginning of one of Moriarty's little exercises does not diminish with time. "Your brother was murdered?" I asked.

"My brother's death was, and is, completely unexplainable, Mr. Barnett," Lord Tams replied.

Moriarty clapped his hands together. "Really?" he said. "Come, this is quite—interesting. Tell me everything you know of the affair."

"The circumstances are simple. Vincent had gone to one of his clubs—the Paradol in Montague Street—to stay for a few days. On the morning of the third day a waiter went in to bring Vincent his breakfast, which he had ordered the night before, and found my brother dead in his bed. He was lying on his back, his face and chest unnaturally red, his hands were raised as if to ward off some unseen threat, and a look of terror was fixed on his face. The club doctor, a Dr. Papoli, examined him and said it was apoplexy; but, as the doctor is from somewhere in the Balkans, and lacks a British medical degree, nobody seemed to take him too seriously. The police doctor strongly disagreed, although he could not come up with an alternate diagnosis."

"This was at the Paradol, you say? Did your brother commonly frequent the Paradol Club?"

"He has been a member for years," his lordship said, "going perhaps six or seven times a year. But for the past three months he had been going twice a month, and staying for two or three days each time."

"Are you also a member?"

"I am a permanent guest of my brother's," his lordship said. "I occasionally use the reading room, but as for the club's other—functions—I found that they were not to my taste."

"I don't believe I know the club," I said to Moriarty.

"It is for, ah, specialized interests," Moriarty told me. "It is where rich men go to meet with complaisant women. It is an upper-class rendezvous for what the French call *le demimonde*. The French seem to have a word for everything, have you noticed?"

"It is so," Lord Tams agreed. "The Paradol Club exists for those gentlemen who enjoy the company of women of, let us say, loose morals but impeccable manners. It is not the only establishment of its type in London, but it is one of the most exclusive, expensive, and discreet."

"Did your brother express his taste for these sorts of amusements in any other way?" Moriarty asked.

"His whole life revolved around the pleasures of the senses. It's funny, really; Mama was always pleased that Vincent didn't go in for blood sports. She never guessed the sort of sport in which he did indulge."

Moriarty leaned back in his chair and fixed his gaze on Lord Tams. "When was the last time you saw your brother?" he asked.

"The evening before he died."

"Ah! Under what circumstances?"

"I went to see him at the club to ask a favor of him. I am—I was—getting married. I wanted to advance some money from my allowance."

"Allowance?" Moriarty asked. "Then you had nothing on your own?"

"Upon our father's death the entire estate went to Vincent. The house and lands were, of course, entailed, but Vincent also inherited everything else. It was inadvertent. Vincent was fourteen years older than I, and the will was drawn two years before I was born. My parents did not expect another child, and no provision was made in the will for the unexpected. My father died suddenly shortly before my second birthday, and had not gotten around to revising the will."

"I see," Moriarty said.

"My brother has actually been quite generous," Lord Tams said. "The income of a freelance journalist is precarious at best. Vincent gave me an allowance and added a few odd bob here and there when needed."

"How did you feel about his—indulgences?"

"It was not my place to approve or disapprove. Vincent's penchants were his own business. His habits, as he kept reminding me, hurt no one. His view was that his companions were all willing, and profited from the relationship. I remonstrated with him, pointing out that the path of vice spirals ever downward, and that the further along it one travels, the harder it is to get off."

"He didn't listen?"

"He was amused."

"Yes. And you went to see him because you're getting married?"

"I have been engaged to Miss Margot Whitsome, the poetess, for the past two years. We were to have been married next week."

"Were to have been? Then the ceremony has been called off?"

"Delayed, rather."

"By the poetess?"

"By me. How can I allow any lady of breeding to marry me with this hanging over my head?"

"Ah!" Moriarty said. "You are suspected of murdering your brother?"

Our newly ennobled visitor stood and walked to the window, staring out into the dark evening drizzle. "No one has said anything directly," he said. "But I have been questioned by Scotland Yard twice, each time a bit more sharply. My fellow journalists are beginning to regard me as a potential story rather than a colleague. An inspector named Lestrade has been up to see my editor at the *Evening Standard* to ask if I've ever written anything on tropical poisons."

"How imaginative of him," Moriarty commented.

Our visitor turned sharply. "Professor Moriarty, I have been told that you can solve the unsolvable; that you can see clearly where others find only darkness. I hope this is true, for otherwise I see nothing but darkness ahead of me," he said. "I want you to find out what happened to my brother. If he was murdered, I want you to find out who did it. If he met his death by some natural means, I want you to discover the agency that brought it about. My peace of mind and my future happiness depend upon your success! You can name your fee!"

Moriarty rose and took Lord Tams's hand. "First let me solve your little problem," he said, "then we'll discuss the price."

After some further reassurances, Moriarty sent Lord Tams back out into Russell Square, assuring him that he would have some word for him soon.

"All right, Moriarty," I said when we were again alone. "By what feat of legerdemain did you deduce all that? Did you pick the man's pocket as he entered the room?"

"Deduce what?" Moriarty asked, settling back down in his chair. "Oh, you mean—"

"Yes, I mean," I agreed.

"Nothing extraordinary," Moriarty said. "That he was unmarried I deduced from the state of his clothing. No respectable woman would let her husband go out with his suit unpressed and a tear in the jacket pocket. That also told me that he does not yet employ the services of a valet. That his older brother died quite recently I deduced from his calling card. The lower line of type was of a slightly different font than the upper, also the spacing between the two lines was slightly off. The second line was added, probably by one of those small hand presses that you find around printers' offices. The missing valet and the calling card surely indicate that he became the Earl of Whitton quite recently. And he hasn't come into the estate quite yet, or he surely would have had new cards printed, and probably bought a new suit. The hand press also pointed me in the direction of his profession. The column proof that was stuffed into his right-hand jacket pocket completed that deduction."

"His suit looked fine to me," I commented.

"Yes, it would," Moriarty said. "Anything else?"

"How did you know it was an older brother who died? Why not his father?"

"If it were his father, then he would have expected to inherit at some time, and the conflict between career and station would have been resolved long since. No, it was clearly the unexpected death of an older brother that has created this dilemma for him."

"And the antipathy between him and his brother?"

"A glance at his right sleeve showed me the pinholes where a black armband had been. The band had not been tacked on, and the pinholes had not enlarged with wear. His period of mourning for his brother was brief. Surely that suggests a certain coolness between them?"

"But not irreconcilable?"

"Certainly not. After all, he did wear the armband."

The next morning Moriarty disappeared before breakfast and returned just as I was finishing my coffee. "I have been to Scotland Yard," he said, drawing off his coat and hanging it on a peg by the door. "This exercise is promising indeed. I have sent the Mummer out to procure copies of the last two months' *London Daily Gazette*. The crime news is more complete, if a bit more lurid, in the *Gazette*. Is there more coffee?"

"What did you learn at Scotland Yard?" I asked, pouring him a cup.

"The inquest has been postponed at the request of the medical office, who are still trying to determine the cause of death. The defunct earl may have suffered from apoplexy, as diagnosed by Dr. Papoli, probably on the basis of the red face, but that did not cause his death. There are indications of asphyxiation, but nothing that could have caused it, and two deep puncture marks on his neck. The two pathologists who have been consulted can agree on nothing except their disagreement with Dr. Papoli's findings."

I put down my coffee cup. "Puncture marks—my dear Moriarty!"

Moriarty sipped his coffee. "No, Barnett," he said. "They are not the marks of a vampire, and neither are they the punctures of a viper. They are too wide apart, coming low on the neck and almost under the ear on each side of his head. There are some older puncture marks also, in odd places; on the inner thighs and under the arms. They do not seem to have contributed to his death, but what purpose they served is unknown."

Moriarty drank a second cup of coffee, staring at the fireplace, apparently deep in thought. Then Mummer Tolliver, Moriarty's midget-of-all-work, came in with bundles of newspapers, and Moriarty began slowly going through them. "It is as I remembered," he said finally. "Look here, Barnett: the naked body of a young man was found floating in the Thames last week, with two unexplained puncture marks."

"In his neck?" I asked.

"In his upper arms. And here—three weeks previously the body of a girl, clad only in her shift, was discovered in a field in Lower Norwood. She had what the *Gazette* describes as strange bruises on her legs."

"Is that significant?" I asked.

"Scotland Yard doesn't think so," Moriarty said. After a moment's reflection he put down the paper and jumped to his feet. "Come, Barnett!" he cried.

"Where?" I asked, struggling into my jacket.

"Since we cannot get satisfactory answers as to the manner of Lord Vincent Tams's death, we must inquire into the manner of his life. We are going to Abelard Court."

"I thought the Paradol Club was in Montague Street."

"It is," Moriarty said, clapping his hat on his head and taking up his stick. "But we go to Abelard Court. Come along!"

We waved down a passing hansom cab, Moriarty shouted an address to the driver, and we were off. "I must tell you, Barnett," Moriarty said, turning to face me in the cab. "We are going to visit a lady who is a good friend and is very important to me. Society would forbid us calling her a 'lady,' but society is a fool."

"Important to you how?" I asked.

Moriarty stared at me for a moment. "We have shared events in our lives that have drawn us very close," he said. "I trust her as fully as I trust myself."

The address the hansom cab let us off in front of was a paradigm of middle-class virtue, as was the lady's maid who answered the door, though her costume was a bit too French for the more conservative household.

"Is Mrs. Atterleigh at home?" Moriarty asked. "Would you tell her that Professor Moriarty and a friend are calling?"

The maid curtseyed and showed us to a drawing room that was decorated in pink and light blue, and filled with delicate, finely detailed furniture that bespoke femininity. Any male would feel rough and clumsy and out of place in this room.

After a brief wait, Mrs. Atterleigh entered the drawing room. One of those ageless mortals who, in form and gesture, encompass the mystery that is woman, she might have been nineteen, or forty, I cannot say. And no man would care. Her long brown hair framed a perfect oval face and intelligent brown eyes. She wore a red silk house dress that I cannot describe, not being adept at such things, but I could not but note that it showed more of her than I had ever seen of a woman to whom I was not married. I did not find it offensive.

"Professor!" she said, holding out her arms.

Moriarty stepped forward. "Beatrice!"

She kissed him firmly on the cheek and released him. "It has been too long," she said.

"I have a favor to ask," Moriarty said.

"I, who owe you everything, can refuse you nothing," she replied.

Moriarty turned. "This is my friend and colleague, Mr. Barnett," he said.

Beatrice took my hand and firmly shook it. "Any friend of Professor Moriarty has a call on my affections," she said. "And a man whom Professor Moriarty calls 'colleague' must be worthy indeed."

"Ahem," I said.

She released my hand and turned to again clasp both of Moriarty's hands in hers. "Professor Moriarty rescued me from a man who, under the guise of benevolence, was the incarnation of evil."

I resisted the impulse to pull out my notebook then and there. "Who?" I asked.

"The monster who was my husband, Mr. Gerald Atterleigh," she replied.

"Moriarty, you never—" I began.

"It was before you joined my organization," Moriarty said. "And I didn't discuss it later because there were aspects of the events that are better forgotten."

"Thanks to Professor Moriarty, Gerald Atterleigh will no longer threaten anyone on this earth," Mrs. Atterleigh said. "And I pity the denizens of Hell that must deal with him."

Moriarty let go of Mrs. Atterleigh's hands, looking self-conscious for the first time since I had known him. "It was an interesting problem," he said.

Mrs. Atterleigh went to the sideboard and took a decanter from the tantalus. "It is not too early, I think, for a glass of port," she said, looking questioningly at us.

"Thank you, but we cannot stay," Moriarty said.

"A small glass," she said, pouring the umber liquid into three small stemmed glasses and handing us each one.

Moriarty took a sip, and then another, and then stared down at his glass. "My God!" he said. "This is the aught-nine Languert D'or! I didn't know there was any of this left in the world."

"I have a new gentleman friend," she said. "His cellars, I believe, are unrivaled. Now, what can I do for you, my dear professor?"

"Vincent Tams, the newly defunct Earl of Whitton," Moriarty said. "Do you know of him?"

"He died at the Paradol Club last month," Mrs. Atterleigh said. "I believe he was alone in bed at the time, which was unlike him."

"He was a regular visitor to the *demimonde?*"

"Say rather he dwelled in its precincts," Mrs. Atterleigh said.

Moriarty turned to me. "Mrs. Atterleigh is my gazette to the *fils du joi*—the harlots, strumpets, and courtesans of London," he said. "They all trust her, and bring her their problems. And on occasion, when it violates no confidences, she passes on information to me."

I remained silent and sipped my port.

"Was his lordship keeping a mistress?" Moriarty asked.

"Always," Mrs. Atterleigh replied. "He changed them every three or four months, but he was seldom without."

"Do you know who was the current inamorata at the time of his death?"

"Lenore," she said. "Dark haired, slender, exotic looking, artistic; she is, I believe, from Bath."

"Will she speak with me?" Moriarty asked.

"I'll give you a note," Mrs. Atterleigh said. "I would come with you, but I'm expecting company momentarily."

Moriarty rose to his feet. "Then we will not keep you. If you would be so kind—"

Mrs. Atterleigh went to her writing-desk and composed a brief note, which she handed to Moriarty. "I have written the address on the outside," she said. "Please come back to see me soon, when you don't have to run off."

"I shall," Moriarty said.

She turned to me and stretched out a hand. "Mr. Barnett," she said. "You are welcome here, too. Anytime. Please visit."

"I would be honored," I said.

We left the house and walked down the street to hail a cab. As the vehicle took us back up the street again, I saw a black covered carriage stop in front of the house we had just left. A man in formal attire got out and went up the steps. Just as we passed he turned around to say something to his driver and I got a good look at his face. "Moriarty!" I said. "That was the prime minister!"

"Ah, well," Moriarty said. "He is reputed to have an excellent wine cellar."

The address we went to was in a mews off St. Humbert's Square. A small woman with raven-black hair, bright dark eyes, and a cheerful expression threw the door open at our ring. She was wearing a painter's smock, and by the daubs of color on it I judged that the garment had seen its intended use. "Well?" she demanded.

"Miss Lenore Lestrelle?" Moriarty asked.

She looked us up and down, and didn't seem impressed by what she saw. "I have enough insurance," she said, "I don't read books, and if a distant relative died and left me a vast fortune which you will procure for me for only a few pounds for your out-of-pocket expenses, I'm not interested, thank you very much. Does that cover it?"

Moriarty handed her the note and she read it thoughtfully and then stepped aside. "Come in then."

She led us down a hallway to a long room at the rear which had been fixed up as an artist's studio. A easel holding a large canvas on which paint had begun to be blocked in faced us as we entered the room. On a platform under the skylight a thin red-headed woman, draped in artfully arranged bits of gauze, stood with a Greek urn balanced on her shoulder.

"Take a break, Mollie," Miss Lestrelle said. "These gentlemen want to talk to me."

Mollie jumped off the platform and pulled a housecoat around her shoulders. "I'll be in the kitchen then, getting sommat to eat," she said. "Call me when you need me."

A large wooden table piled high with stacks of books and clothing and assorted household goods stood against one wall, surrounded by similarly burdened straight-back chairs. Miss Lestrelle waved in their general direction. "Take your coats off. Sit if you like," she said. "Just pile the stuff on the floor."

"That's all right, Miss Lestrelle," Moriarty said.

"Suit yourself," she said. "Don't bother with the 'Miss Lestrelle.' Lenore is good enough."

"My name is Professor Moriarty, and this is Mr. Barnett," Moriarty told her.

"So the letter said. And you want to know about Vincent. Why?"

"We are enquiring into his death."

"I can't be much help to you there. I didn't see him for several days before he died."

"I thought he was—ah—"

"Keeping me? That he was. In a nice flat in as fashionable a section of town as is reasonable in the circumstances." She waved a hand at the goods piled up on the table. "Those are my things from there. I've just finished moving out."

"Ah!" Moriarty said. "The brother evicted you?"

"I've not seen the brother. This is where I do my work, and this is where I choose to be. I am an artist by choice and a harlot only by necessity. As there was no longer any reason to remain in that flat, I left."

A fair number of canvases were leaning stacked against the near wall, and Moriarty started flipping them forward and examining them one at a time. "You don't seem overly broken up at his lordship's death," he commented.

Lenore turned, her hands on her hips, and glared at Moriarty. After a moment she shrugged and sat on a high wooden stool by her easel. "It was not a love match," she said. "Most men want their mistresses to provide love and affection, but Vincent wanted only one thing of his women: to be there when he called. He was not particularly faithful to the girl he was keeping at the moment, and he tired of her after a few months. As I'd been with Vincent for over three months, I expected to be replaced within the fortnight. The flat he kept, the girls were transitory."

"You had to be at the flat all day waiting for him?"

"After ten at night," she said. "If he hadn't found another interest by ten or eleven, he wanted to have someone to come home to."

"Did he ever discuss his business affairs with you?"

"Never."

"Ever have any visitors?"

"Once we had another girl in for the evening, but aside from that none."

"How did you feel about that?"

Lenore shrugged. "He was paying the bills," she said.

Moriarty looked up from his study of the paintings. "How would you describe his sexual tastes? You can speak freely. Mr. Barnett is a journalist, and therefore unshockable."

"I have no objection to talking about it if you have no objection to listening. Lord Tams was normal that way. No strange desires or positions or partners. He was just rather insistent. He felt that if he didn't bed a woman every night he would die."

I couldn't help but exclaim, "Every night?"

"So he told me." She looked at me. "You're trying to solve his murder?"

"That's right," I said.

She turned to Moriarty. "And you're Professor Moriarty. I've heard of you. Then I guess it's all right."

Moriarty leaned forward like a hound dog catching a scent. "What's all right?" he asked her.

"Talking about Vincent. A person in my trade shouldn't talk about her clients, it isn't professional. And since I haven't found a patron for my art yet, I can't afford to take my departure from the sporting life."

"Has anyone else asked you to talk about Vincent?" Moriarty asked.

"Oh, no," she said. "Not specifically. But there's always men wanting to hear about other men. I figure there's men who like to do it, men who like to talk about doing it, and men who like to hear about it. They come around and buy a girl dinner and ask all sorts of questions about who does what and what other men like to do and what do girls really like, and that sort of thing. Most of them claim to be writers, but I never heard of them. And where could they publish the stories I tell them?"

"The intimate tastes of men are varied, and stretch from the mundane to the absurd," Moriarty commented.

"I'll say," Lenora agreed. "Why I could tell you—" She smiled. "But I won't. Except about poor Vincent, which is why you're here."

"Indeed," Moriarty agreed. "So Vincent saw his prowess as necessary to his health?"

"That he did. About a month ago, when for a couple of

nights he couldn't—perform—he went into a sulk like you've never seen. I tried cheering him up, told him he was just overtired, or ill, and would be up to snuff in no time."

"How did he take to your cheering words?" Moriarty asked.

"He threw a fit. I thought he had gone crazy. He broke everything in the house that could be lifted, and some that couldn't. He knocked me down, but that was an accident. I got between him and something he was trying to break. When everything was broken, he collapsed on the floor. The next morning when he left he seemed quite normal, as if nothing had happened. That afternoon a team of men from Briggs and Mendel came to repair the damage and replace the furniture and crockery."

"And how was he after that?"

"I only saw him a couple of times after that. Once he came to the flat, and once he sent a carriage for me to join him at the Paradol Club. There's an inconspicuous door around the side for the special friends of the members. He was unusually silent, but he had recovered from his trouble, whatever it was. He proved that."

"Did you notice any peculiar bruises on his body when you saw him?"

"Bruises? Why, yes. On his neck. Two bright red marks, almost opposite each other. I asked him about them, and he laughed and said something about Shelley."

"Shelley?" I asked. "The poet?"

"I suppose. He said something about an homage to Shelley, and then for a long time we didn't speak. And then I left, and that was the last time I saw him."

"I see you're heavily influenced by the French school," Moriarty said.

"Excuse me?"

"Your art." Moriarty gestured toward the paintings. "You're quite good."

"Oh. Thank you."

"Will you sell me one?"

"Will I—you don't have to—"

"I want to. I'll tell you what; there's a gentleman who owns an art gallery in the Strand who owes me a favor. I'll send him down to see you, look at your work."

"That would be very kind."

"Nonsense. After he's seen your stuff he'll owe me two favors. We'll have to make up some tale about your past, London society is not ready for a harlot artist. It's barely ready for a woman artist. You won't make as much money as men who only paint half as well, but it'll be better than you're doing now."

Lenore had the wide-eyed look of a poor little girl at the pastry counter. "I don't know what to say," she said.

"Say nothing until it happens," Moriarty said. "And I'll be back next week to pick out a painting for myself."

"Whichever you want, it's yours," Lenore said.

"We'll let Vincent's brother pay for it," Moriarty said. "It's only fitting." He took her hand. "It's been a pleasure meeting you," he said. "You've been a great help."

We exited to the street, leaving behind a pleased Miss Lestrelle. "Moriarty," I said, putting my collar up against the light drizzle that had begun while we were inside, "you shouldn't do that."

"What?"

"You know perfectly well what. Raising that girl's hopes like that. I got a good look at her paintings and they were nothing but blobs of color splattered on the canvas. Why, from close up you almost couldn't tell what the pictures represented."

Moriarty laughed. "Barnett," he said, "you are a fixed point of light in an otherwise hazy world. Just trust me that Van Delding will not consider himself ill-used to look at those canvases. The world of art has progressed in the last few decades, along with practically everything else. And we are going to have to accustom ourselves to even more rapid changes in the future."

"I hope you're wrong," I told him. "Few of the changes that I've observed over the last quarter-century have been for the better."

"Change is the natural condition of life," Moriarty said. "Stones do not change of themselves." He hailed a passing hansom cab and gave our address to the driver. "Well, Barnett," he said as we started off, "what do you think?"

"I think I've missed my lunch," I said.

"True," he admitted. "I get rather single-minded when I'm concentrating on a problem." He knocked on the roof and shouted to the driver to change our destination to the Savoy.

"I don't see as we're any further along with discovering how Lord Tams met his death," I told him. "We've learned a lot about the character and habits of the deceased earl, but it doesn't seem to have gotten us any closer to the way he died."

Moriarty glanced at me. "Scientists must train themselves to use rational deductive processes in solving whatever problems come their way, whether they involve distant galaxies or sordid crimes in Belgravia," he said. "And the deductive process begins with the collection of data. Only after we have all the facts can we separate the dross from the gold."

"Of course, Moriarty," I said. "And what of this case? You must have some facts that are relevant to the problem at hand on which to set those rational processes to work. Lord Vincent Tams may have been a sexual glutton, but I fail to see how a knowledge of his grosser appetites of the flesh will advance our knowledge of how he died."

"Grosser appetites of the flesh?" Moriarty said. "Very good, Barnett; you outdo yourself. If you reflect on what we have learned these past few hours, you will realize that our time has not entirely been wasted."

"I am not aware that we have learned anything of value," I said.

Moriarty considered for a moment. "We have learned that the defunct earl spoke of Shelley," he said, "and that by itself should tell us all. But we have learned more: We have learned that artistic talent can flower in the most unlikely places."

"Flower!" I said. "Pah!"

Moriarty looked at me. "Who, for example, would suspect that such fine writing talent could emerge from a quondam reporter for the *New York World*?"

"Pah!" I repeated.

I had some errands that occupied me after lunch, and Moriarty was out when I returned to Russell Square. I dined alone, and was catching up on filing some accumulated newspaper clippings when the door to the study was flung open and a tall man with a scraggly beard, a dark, well-patched overcoat, and a blue cap strode in. Convinced that I was being accosted by a dangerous anarchist, I rose, trying to remember where I had put my revolver.

"Ah, Barnett," the anarchist said in the most familiar voice I know, "I hope there is some dinner left. I have been forced to drink more than I should of a variety of vile liquors, and I didn't trust the food."

"Moriarty!" I exclaimed. "I will ring for Mrs. Randall to prepare something at once. Where have you been?"

"Patience," Moriarty said, taking off his long gabardine overcoat. He pulled off the beard and reached into his mouth to remove two gutta-percha pads from his cheeks. Then a few quick swipes over his face with a damp sponge, and he was once again recognizable. "Food first, and perhaps a cup of coffee. Then I'll tell you of my adventures."

I rang and told the girl to have Mrs. Randall prepare a tray for the professor, and she returned with it inside of five minutes. Moriarty ate rapidly, seemingly unaware of what he was eating, his eyes fixed on the far wall. I had seen these symptoms before. He was working out some problem, and I knew better than to interrupt. If it was a difficult one he might spend hours, or even days, with a pencil and notepad in front of him, drinking countless cups of coffee and consuming endless cigars, or quantities of the rough-cut Virginia tobacco he favored in one of his briar pipes, and staring off into space before he again became conscious of his surroundings.

But this time the problem had worked itself out by the time he finished the last of the roast, and he poured himself a small glass of cognac and waved the bottle in my direction. "This was laid in the cask twenty years before we met," he said, "and it has aged well. Let me pour you a dram!"

"Not tonight, Moriarty," I said. "Tell me what you have discovered!"

"Ah!" he said. "There was a fact in the new earl of Whitton's statement to us that begged for examination, and I have spent the afternoon and evening examining it."

"What fact?" I asked.

"How many clubs are you a member of, my friend?"

I thought for a second. "Let's see . . . the Century, the American Service Club, Whites, the Bellona; that's it at present."

"And you have, no doubt, an intimate knowledge of two or three others through guest membership, or visiting friends and the like?"

"I suppose so."

"And of these half-dozen clubs you are well-acquainted with, how many have club doctors?"

"I'm sure they all have physician members," I said.

"Your reasoning is impeccable," Moriarty said. "But how many of them have doctors on staff?"

"Why, none," I said. "Why would a club keep a doctor on staff?"

"My question exactly," Moriarty said. "But Dr. Papoli was described by both Lord Tams and Inspector Lestrade as the club doctor, which implies a professional relationship between the doctor and the club. And a further question: if, for some reason, the directors of a club decided to hire a doctor, would they pick one who, as Lord Tams told us, lacks a British medical degree?"

"Certainly not!" I said.

"Quite so. And so I went to that area of the East End that is teaming with Balkan immigrants and I let it be known that I was in search of a doctor. I hinted at mysterious needs, but I was very vague, since I didn't know just what the needs in question were."

"But Moriarty," I said, "You don't speak the language."

"There are five or six possible languages," Moriarty said. "Whenever someone spoke to me in anything other than English, I told him I was from Ugarte, and didn't understand his dialect."

"Where is Ugarte?" I asked.

"I have no idea," Moriarty said. "I would be very surprised if there is any such place."

"What did you find out?" I asked.

"That Dr. Papoli is looked upon with almost superstitious dread by his countrymen, and that he has recently hired several assistants with strong backs and dubious reputations."

"And what does that tell you?"

"That a visit to the Paradol Club is in order for tomorrow. But for now I will enjoy my cognac, and then get a good night's sleep."

Although it was clear that Moriarty had reached some conclusion, he did not share it with me. That night I dreamed of beautiful women in *dishabille* marching on Parliament and demanding the right to paint. The prime minister and Beatrice were singing a duet from *Pirates of Penzance* to a packed House of Commons, who were about to join in on the chorus, when the chimes on my alarm clock woke me up the next morning.

The Paradol Club was housed in a large building at the corner of Montague and Charles Streets. The brass plaque on the front door was very small and discreet, and the ground floor windows were all barred. Moriarty and I walked around the block twice, Moriarty peering at windows and poking at the pavement and the buildings with his walking stick. There appeared to be two additional entrances; a small, barred door on Charles Street, and an alleyway leading to a rear entry. After the second circuit we mounted the front steps and entered the club.

Considering what we had been told of the Paradol Club, the entrance area was disappointingly mundane. To the right was a cloakroom and porter's room; to the left was the manager's office, with a desk by the door. Past the desk was the door to the front reading room, with a rack holding current newspapers and magazines visible inside. A little birdlike man sitting behind the desk leaned forward and cocked his head to the side as we entered. "Gentlemen," he said. "Welcome to the Paradol Club. Of which of our members are you the guests?"

"Are you the club manager?"

"I am the assistant manager, Torkson by name."

Moriarty nodded. "I am Professor Moriarty," he said. "I am here to investigate the death of one of your members. This is my associate, Mr. Barnett."

Torkson reared back as though he had been stung. "Which one?" he asked.

"How many have there been?" Moriarty asked.

"Three in the past three months," Torkson said. "Old General Quincy, Hapsman the barrister, and Lord Tams."

"It is the death of Vincent Tams that occupies us at the moment," Moriarty said. "Has his room been cleaned out yet, and if not may we see it?"

"Who sent you?" Torkson asked.

"Lord Tams," Moriarty said.

Torkson looked startled. "The Lord Tams that is," explained Moriarty, "has asked me to enquire into the death of the Lord Tams that was."

"Ah!" said Torkson. "That would be Mr. Everett. Well then, I guess it will be all right." Pulling a large ring of keys from a desk drawer, he led the way upstairs. "Lord Tams kept a room here permanently," he said. "Our hostesses were very fond of him, as he was always a perfect gentleman and very generous," he added, pausing on the first floor landing and glancing back at us. Moriarty and I just stared back at him, as though the idea of "hostesses" at a gentleman's club were perfectly normal. Reassured, he took us up to the second floor, and down the hall to Vincent Tams's room. Again I was struck by the very normality of my surroundings. One would expect a club defined by its members' addiction to vice, as others are by their members' military backgrounds or fondness for cricket, to have risqué wall hangings or scantily clad maidens dashing from room to room. But from the dark wood furniture to the paintings of hunting scenes on the wall, it all looked respectable, mundane, and very British.

When we reached the door to Vincent Tams's room the assistant manager paused and turned to us. "Do you suppose the new Lord Tams will wish to keep the room?" he asked.

"He is hoping to get married in the near future," I said.

"Ah!" said Torkson. "Then he will almost certainly wish to keep the room." He unlocked the door and turned to go.

"One moment," Moriarty said. "Is the waiter who found his lordship's body available?"

"Williamson," the assistant manager said. "I believe he is working today."

"Will you please send him up here?"

Torkson nodded and scurried off back downstairs. The room was actually a three-room suite. Moriarty and I entered a sitting room, to the left was the bedroom, and to the right a small dining room. The sitting room was fixed with a writing desk, a couch, and an easy chair. A large bookcase took up one wall. Moriarty whipped out a magnifying glass and tape measure and began a methodical examination of the walls and floor.

"What can I do, Professor?" I asked.

He thought for a second. "Examine the books," he said.

"For what?" I asked.

"Anything that isn't book," he told me.

I went to the bookcase and took down some of the volumes at random. Except for some popular novels and a six-volume work on the Napoleonic Wars, they were all books that could not be displayed in mixed company. Most were what are called "French" novels, and the rest were full of erotic drawings displaying couples coupling, many in positions that I had never dreamed of, and some in positions that I believe are impossible to attain. I began going through them methodically, right to left, top to bottom, for anything that might have been inserted between the pages, but found nothing.

There was a knock at the door and I turned to see a thick-set man in the uniform of a waiter standing in the doorway. "You wished to see me, sir?" he asked, addressing the air somewhere between Moriarty and myself.

"Williamson?" Moriarty asked.

"That's right, sir."

"You found Lord Tams's body the morning he died?"

"I did, and quite a shock it was too." Williamson stepped into the room and closed the door.

"Tell me," Moriarty said.

"Well, sir, I brought the tray up at a quarter to eight, as instructed, and entered the sitting room."

"You had a key?"

"Yes, sir. I got the key from the porter on the way up. My instructions were to set breakfast up in the dining room, and then to knock on the bedroom door at eight o'clock sharp. Which same I did. Only there was no answer."

"One breakfast or two?" Moriarty asked.

"Only one."

"Was that usual?"

"Oh yes, sir. If a hostess spent the night with his lordship, she left when he sat down to breakfast."

"I see," said Moriarty. "And when there was no answer?"

"I waited a moment and then knocked again. Getting no response, I ventured to open the door."

"And?"

"There was his lordship, lying face-up on the bed, staring at the ceiling. His hands were raised in the air over his head, as though he were afraid someone were going to hit him. His face were beet-red. He were dead."

"Were the bedclothes covering him?"

"No, sir. He were lying atop of them."

"What did you do?"

"I chucked."

"You—?"

"I threw up. All over my dickey, too."

"Very understandable. And then?"

"And then I went downstairs and told Mr. Caltro, the manager. And he fetched Dr. Papoli, and I went to the pantry to change my dickey."

Moriarty pulled a shilling out of his pocket and tossed it to the waiter. "Thank you, Williamson," he said. "You've been quite helpful."

"Thank you, sir," Williamson said, pocketing the coin and leaving the room.

A short, dapper man with a spade beard that looked as if it belonged on a larger face knocked on the open door, took two steps into the room, and bowed. The tail of his black frock coat bobbed up as he bent over, giving the impression that one was observing a large, black fowl. "Professor Moriarty?" he asked.

Moriarty swivelled to face the intruder. "That is I."

"Ah! Torkson told me you were here. I am Dr. Papoli. Can I be of any service to you?"

"Perhaps. What can you tell me of Lord Tams's death?"

Dr. Papoli shrugged. "When I was called he had been dead for several hours. Rigor was pronounced. His face was flushed, which suggested to me the apoplexy; but I was overruled by the superior knowledge of your British doctors. If you would know more, you had best ask them."

"I see," Moriarty said. "Thank you, doctor."

Papoli bowed and backed out of the room.

Moriarty crossed to the bedroom and gazed at the rumpled bed-clothes. "Picture it, Barnett," he said. "The dead earl staring up at the ceiling, his face unnaturally red and bearing a horrified expression, his arms raised against an unseen foe. And the strange puncture marks on the body, don't leave those out of your picture." He turned to me. "What does that image convey to you?"

"Something frightful must have happened in this room," I said, "but what the nature of that happening was, I have no idea."

Moriarty shook his head. "Nothing frightful happened in this room," he said. "Understanding that will give you the key to the mystery." He took one last look around the room and then went out into the hall. For the next half hour he walked up and down the hallway on that floor and the ones above and below, peering and measuring. Finally he returned to where I awaited him on the second floor landing. "Come," he said.

"Where?"

"Back to Russell Square."

We left the club and flagged down a hansom. Moriarty was taciturn and seemed distracted on the ride home. When we entered the house, Moriarty put a small blue lantern in the window, the sign to any passing members of the Mendicants' Guild that they were wanted. Moriarty has a long-standing relationship with the Mendicants' Guild and Twist, their leader. They are his eyes all over London, and he supplies them with technical advice of a sort they cannot get from more usual sources. About half an hour later a leering hunchback with a grotesquely flattened nose knocked on the door. "My moniker's Handsome Bob," he told Moriarty when he was brought into the office, "Twist sent me."

"Here's your job," Moriarty told the beggar. "The Paradol Club is at the intersection of Montague and Charles. It has three entrances. Most people use the main entrance on Montague Street. I want a watch kept on the club, and I want the men to give me the best description they can of anyone who enters the club through either of the other two entrances. But without drawing any attention to themselves. Send someone to report to me every half-hour, but keep the place covered at all times."

"Yessir, Professor Moriarty," Handsome Bob said, touching his hand to his cap. "Four of the boys should be enough. We'll get right on it."

Moriarty reached into the apothecary jar on the mantle and took out a handful of coins. "Have them return here by cab if there's anything interesting to report," he said, handing the coins to him. "This is for current expenses. I'll settle with you at the usual rates after."

"Yessir, Professor Moriarty," Handsome Bob repeated, and he turned and sidled out the door.

Moriarty turned to me. "Now we wait," he said.

"What are we waiting for?"

"For the villain to engage in his employment," Moriarty said. He leaned back and settled down to read the latest copy of the quarterly *Journal of the British Geological Society*. I left the room and took a long walk, stopping for sustenance at a local pub, which I find soothes my mind.

I returned at about six in the evening, and stretched out on the sitting room couch to take a nap. It was just after eleven when Moriarty shook me by the shoulder. Standing behind him was an emaciated-looking man on crutches, a crippled beggar I remembered seeing at Twist's headquarters in a Godolphin Street warehouse. "Quick, Barnett," Moriarty cried, "our drama has taken a critical turn. Get your revolver while I hail a cab!" He grabbed his hat, stick, and overcoat and was out the door in an instant.

I ran upstairs to my bedroom and pulled my revolver from its drawer, made sure it was loaded, and then grabbed my overcoat and ran downstairs. Moriarty had stopped two cabs, and was just finishing scribbling a note on the back of an envelope. He handed the note to the beggar. "Give this to Inspector Lestrade, and no one else," he said. "He will be waiting for you."

Moriarty put the cripple in the first cab and looked up at the driver. "Take this man to Scotland Yard, and wait for him," he said. "And hurry!"

We climbed into the second cab together and set off at a good pace for the Paradol Club. Moriarty leaned forward impatiently in his seat. "This is devilish," he said. "I never anticipated this."

"What, Moriarty, for God's sake?"

"Two people of interest have entered the back door of the club in the past hour," he said. "One was a young girl of no particular status who was taken in by two burly men and looked frightened to the watcher. The other was the duke of Claremore."

"Moriarty!" I said. "But he's—"

"Yes," Moriarty agreed. "And we must put an end to this quickly, quietly, and with great care. If it were ever to become known that a royal duke was involved—"

"Put an end to what?" I asked. "Just what is going on in the Paradol Club?"

Moriarty turned to looked at me. "The Greeks called it hubris," he said.

We arrived at the club and jumped from the cab. "Wait around the corner!" Moriarty yelled at the driver as we raced up the front steps. The door was closed but the porter, a thick-set man with the look of a retired sergeant of marines, answered our knock after a few seconds, pulling his jacket on as he opened the door. Moriarty grabbed him by the collar. "Listen, man," he said. "Several detectives from Scotland Yard will arrive here any minute. Stay out front and wait for them. When they arrive, direct them to Dr. Papoli's consulting room on the second floor. Tell them that I said to be very quiet and not to disturb any of the other guests."

"And who are you?" the porter asked.

"Professor James Moriarty." And Moriarty left the porter in the doorway and raced up the stairs, with me close behind.

The second floor corridor was dark, and we moved along it by feel, running our hands along the wall as we went. "Here," Moriarty said. "This should be the doctor's door." He put his ear to the door, and then tried the handle. "Damn—it's locked."

A match flared, and the light steadied, and I saw that Moriarty had lighted a plumber's candle that he took from his pocket. "Hold this for me, will you?" he asked.

Moriarty handed me the candle and took a small, curved implement from his pocket. He inserted it into the lock and, after a few seconds fiddling, the door opened. We entered a large room which was dark and deserted. I held up the candle, and we could see a desk and couch, and a row of cabinets along one wall.

"There should be a staircase in here somewhere," Moriarty said, running his hand along the molding on the far wall.

"A staircase?" I asked.

"Yes. I measured the space when we were here earlier, and an area just below this room has been closed off, with no access from that floor. Also water has recently been laid on in this corner of the building and a drain put in. You can see the pipes hugging the wall from outside. Logic says that—aha!"

There was a soft click and a section of the wall swung open on silent hinges, revealing a narrow stairs going down. A brilliant shaft of light from below illuminated the staircase.

Moriarty, his revolver drawn, crept down the staircase, and I was but a step behind him. The sight that greeted my eyes as the room below came into view was one that will stay with me forever. It was as though I was witness to a scene from one of *Le Grand Guignol*'s dramas of horror, but the chamber below me was not a stage setting, and the people were not actors.

The room was an unrelieved white, from the painted walls to the tile floor, and a pair of calcium lights mounted on the ceiling eliminated all shadow and cast an unnatural brightness over the scene. Two metal tables of the sort used in operating theatres stood several feet apart in the middle of the room. Surrounding them was a madman's latticework of tubing, piping, and glassware, emanating from a machine that squatted between the two tables, the purpose of which I could not even begin to guess.

On the table to my right, partially covered by a sheet, lay an elderly man; on the other table a young girl similarly covered had been tied down by leather straps. Both were unconscious, with ether cones covering their nose and mouth. Between them stood Dr. Papoli, his black frock coat replaced by a white surgical apron, absorbed in his task of inserting a thin cannula into the girl's thigh. His assistant, also in white, was swabbing an area on the man's thigh with something that left a brown stain.

"All right, Doctor," Moriarty said, starting toward the tables. "I think it would be best if you stopped right now!"

Papoli looked up, an expression of annoyance on his face. "You mustn't interrupt!" he said. "You will ruin the experiment."

"Your experiments have already ruined too many people," Moriarty said, raising his revolver. "Get away from the girl! The police will be here any second."

Papoli cursed in some foreign language and, grabbing a brown bottle, threw it violently against the wall. It shattered and, in an instant, a sickly-sweet smell filled the room, a smell I recognized from some dental surgery I'd had the year before.

"Don't shoot, Professor!" I yelled. "It's ether! One shot could blow us all into the billiard room!"

"Quick!" Moriarty said, "we must get the duke and the girl out of here."

Papoli and his assistant were already halfway up the stair. Doing my best to hold my breath, I staggered over to the tables. Moriarty lifted the duke onto his shoulders, and I unstrapped the girl and grabbed her, I'm not sure how, and headed for the stairs.

While we were on the staircase two shots rang out from the room above, and I heard the sound of a scuffle. We entered the room to find Lestrade glaring at the doctor and his assistant, who were being firmly held by two large policemen. "He shot at me, Moriarty, can you believe that?" Lestrade said, sounding thoroughly annoyed. "Now, what have we here?"

We lay our burdens gently on the floor, and I staunched the wound on the girl's thigh with my cravat.

Moriarty indicated the unconscious man on the floor. "This is the duke of Claremore," he said. "It would be best to get him out of here before his presence becomes known. Dr. Papoli can safely be charged with murder, and his accomplice, I suppose, with being an accomplice. We'll see that the girl is cared for. Come to Russell Square tomorrow at noon, and I'll explain all over lunch."

"But Moriarty—"

"Not now, Lestrade. Tomorrow."

"Oh, very well," Lestrade said. He turned to a policeman by the door. "Get a chair to seat his lordship in, and we'll carry him downstairs," he instructed.

We took the waiting cab to Abelard Court, and Beatrice Atterleigh herself opened the door to our knock. She did not seem surprised to find us standing at her door supporting a barely conscious girl at one in the morning.

"Will you take care of this girl for a few days?" Moriarty asked. "She has been mistreated. I have no idea what language she speaks."

"Of course," Mrs. Atterleigh said.

The next morning at quarter to twelve our client arrived at Russell Square in response to a telegram. Lestrade arrived at noon sharp, thereby demonstrating the punctuality of the detective police.

We sat down to duckling a l'orange and an '82 Piesporter, and Moriarty regaled us with a discourse on wines through the main course. It was not until the serving girl put the trifle on the table and Moriarty had poured us each a small glass of the Imperial Tokay—from a case presented to Moriarty by Franz Joseph himself upon the successful conclusion of a problem involving the chief of the *Kundschafts Stelle* and a ballerina—that he was willing to talk about the death of Lord Vincent Tams.

"It was obvious from the start," Moriarty began, "that Lord Tams did not die where he was found. Which raised the questions why was he moved, and from where?"

"Obvious to you, perhaps," Lestrade said.

"Come now," Moriarty said. "His hands were raised and his face was flushed. But corpses do not lie with their hands raised, nor with their faces flushed."

"This one did," Lestrade said. "I saw it."

"You saw it full in the grip of rigor mortis," Moriarty said, "which makes the body rigid in whatever position it has assumed. But how did it assume that position? The face gives it away. The head was lower than the body after death."

"Of course!" I said. "Lividity. I should have known."

"Lividity?" Lord Tams asked.

"After death the blood pools at the body's lowest point," I told him, "which makes the skin in that area appear red. I've seen it many times as a reporter on the New York police beat. I'm just not used to hearing of it on faces."

"Your brother was at the Paradol Club to avail himself of the services of Dr. Papoli," Moriarty said, turning in his chair to face Lord Tams. "The doctor claimed to have a method to rejuvenate a man's lost vitality. He transfused his patients with youthful blood. Thus they regained youthful vigor. It is a not uncommon desire of men, as they get older, to recapture their youth. Papoli was preying on men who could afford to attempt it. Occasionally one of his patients died, because for some reason as yet unknown, some people's blood will cause a fatal reaction when injected into another. Papoli claimed that he had devised a machine that would solve that problem—the strange apparatus that was between the two beds. But he was obviously mistaken."

"How do you know that?" Lestrade asked.

"I went to talk to your prisoner this morning," Moriarty said. "He is extremely indignant that he is in jail. He considers himself a savior of man. He is quite mad."

"So other men died besides my brother?" Lord Tams asked.

"Yes, several. But they were elderly men, and their natural vanity had kept them from telling anyone about the operation, so his secret remained safe. Occasionally one of his donors died, but they came from the poorest classes of the city and they were not missed."

"But my brother was not that old."

"True. It was his obsession with sexual vitality that made him seek the operation. It failed. Papoli and his assistant thought your brother had died on the table. They left him there, not wanting to carry a body through the hallway early in the evening. Later, when they came back to take him to his room, they found that he had briefly regained consciousness and partially removed his restraining straps. The upper half of his body fell off the table in his dying convulsions, and he was left hanging from a strap around his legs. That explains his hands, which had fallen toward the floor. When they lifted him, rigor had set in and his arms looked as though they were raised."

Lord Tams sighed. "Poor Vincent." He stood up. "Well, Professor Moriarty, you have saved my marriage, and possibly my life. I had the impression that Inspector Lestrade was preparing to clap me in irons at any second."

"That's as it may be," Lestrade said. "No hard feelings, I trust?"

"None, Inspector. I invite you—all of you—to my wedding. I must be off now to see Miss Whitsome and tell her the happy news. Professor Moriarty, you will send me a bill, whatever you think is right, and I will pay it promptly, I assure you."

Moriarty nodded, and Lord Tams clapped his bowler on his head and was out the door. A minute later Lestrade followed.

"Moriarty," I said, refilling my coffee cup, "two last questions."

Moriarty held out his own cup for a refill. "What?" he asked.

"Do you think the new Lord Tams will keep his brother's rooms at the Paradol?"

"I never speculate," Moriarty said, "it is bad for the deductive process." He leaned back. "But if I were a betting man, I'd put a tenner on it. What else?"

"Miss Lestrelle told us that Vincent had made some reference to Shelley, and you said that that told all. Were you serious? I looked through my copy of Shelley this morning, and I could find nothing that applies."

Moriarty smiled. "I fancy you were looking up the wrong Shelley," he said.

"The wrong—"

Moriarty reached over to the bookshelf and tossed a book across to me. "Try this one."

I looked down at the book. On the cover, in an ornate Gothic type, was the title: *Frankenstein, or The Modern Prometheus*, by Mary Wollstonecraft Shelley.

Moriarty was out all this morning, and he came back with a painting by Lenore Lestrelle. It is all green and brown and blue blotches and seems to be some sort of pastoral scene. I am afraid that he intends to hang it in the dining room.

DEATH
BY GASLIGHT

Now entertain conjecture of a time
When creeping murmur and the poring dark
Fills the wide vessel of the Universe.
From camp to camp, through the foul womb of night . . .
— WILLIAM SHAKESPEARE

PROLOGUE

When I consider life, 'tis all a cheat.
— JOHN DRYDEN

The tall, thickset man in the gray frock coat walked slowly between the double row of headstones. He looked neither to the left nor the right, but stared at something ahead of him that the older man who walked beside him could not see. They stopped at a newly turned grave, not yet covered with sod, and the tall man crouched and placed his hands flat on the bare earth.

"This is it," he said, turning his vacant eyes on his companion. "This is where she lies."

"I'll take care of it, right enough," the old man said, squinting at the ground to note the number on the painted board that marked the place where the headstone would be. "Like she was my own daughter. My word."

"Flowers?"

"Ivery day. My word."

"She likes flowers." The tall man rose and turned to his companion. "I'll meet you at the gate," he said.

The old man stared at him for a second, and then said "A' course," and walked away.

The frock-coated man turned back to the bare earth. "I am here," he said.

The day was somber and the fog was dense. What light there was gladly fled before the encroaching dusk.

"I have discovered another one for you," he whispered. "Another death for your death. Another throat for the blade. It doesn't help. God knows it doesn't help. God knows—" The man's face contorted. "God!—God!" He fell to his knees, his hands twin tight-fisted balls before his eyes. "Someday I'll stand before the God who

255

made what befell you part of His immortal plan; and then—and then—"

He stood up and slowly willed his fists to open. Semicircles of blood had formed where his nails had dug into his palms. "But until then, the men," he whispered, "the godlike men. One by one they shall fall like reeds before the avenging wind. And I am the wind."

He held out his hand and there was a bouquet of flowers between his fingers, which he placed gently down on the moist earth. Beside the bouquet he laid a small gold amulet with an intricate design. "Here is another," he said. "From the last one. The last murderer. The last to die before the wind. This is the sign by which we know them, you and I. The mark of Cain. The hell-mark of the damned."

Standing again, he brushed off his trousers. "I love you, Annie," he murmured to the bare earth. "I do not do this for you; I know you would not ask it, the killing. I do not do it for me; I have always been a gentle man, and it does not ease me. I do not like the blood, the moment of fear. But it is all I can do. I cannot stop myself. I have become the wind, and they shall all die."

He turned and slowly walked away.

ONE

NIGHT AND FOG

There was a Door to which I found no Key;
There was a Veil past which I could not see.
— EDWARD FITZGERALD

Throughout much of March in the year 1887 the city of London was covered by a thick, almost tangible fog that swept in from the North Sea. It chilled the flesh, dampened the spirit, and oppressed the soul. It all but obscured the sun by day, and by night it occluded the stars, the moon, the streetlamps, and the minds of men. Things were done in that fog, in the night, that were better left undone.

In the early morning hours of Tuesday, the eighth of March, the fog blanketed the city; a moist discomforter that swallowed light and muffled sound. Police Constable William Alberts walked his rounds with a steady, measured stride, insulated from the enveloping fog by his thick blue greatcoat and the Majesty of the Law. The staccato echo of his footsteps sounded sharp and loud in the empty street as he turned off Kensington Gore into Regent's Gate and paced stolidly past the line of stately mansions.

P.C. Alberts paused and cocked his head. Somewhere in the fog ahead of him there was—what?—a sort of gliding, scurrying sound that he could not identify. The sound, perhaps, of someone trying to move silently through the night but betrayed by a loose paving stone.

He waited for the noise to be repeated, turning to face where he thought it had come from and straining his eyes to pierce the black, fog-shrouded night.

There! Farther over now—was that it again? A muted sound; could someone be trying to sneak past him in the dark? A scurrying sound; could it be rats? There were rats even in Regent's Gate. Even the mansions of the nobility had the occasional rats' nest in the cellar. P.C. Alberts shuddered. He was not fond of rats.

But there—another sound! Footsteps this time, good honest British footsteps pattering around the Kensington Gore corner and approaching the spot where Constable Alberts stood.

A portly man appeared out of the fog, his MacFarlane buttoned securely up to his chin and a dark-gray bowler pulled down to his eyes. A hand-knitted gray scarf obscured much of the remainder of his face, leaving visible only wide-set brown eyes and a hint of what was probably a large nose. For a second the man looked startled to see P.C. Alberts standing there, then he nodded as he recognized the uniform. "Evening, Constable."

"Evening, sir." Alberts touched the tip of his forefinger to the brim of his helmet. "A bit late, isn't it, sir?"

"It is that," the man agreed, pausing to peer up at Alberts's face. "I don't recollect you, Constable. New on this beat, are you?"

"I am, sir," Alberts admitted. "P.C. Alberts, sir. Do you live around here, sir?"

"I do, Constable; in point of fact, I do." The man pointed a pudgy finger into the fog. "Yonder lies my master's demesne. I am Lemming, the butler at Walbine House."

"Ah!" Alberts said, feeling that he should reply to this revelation. They walked silently together for a few steps.

"I have family in Islington," Lemming volunteered. "Been visiting for the day. Beastly hour to be getting back."

"It is that, sir," Alberts agreed.

"Missed my bus," Lemming explained. "Had to take a number twenty-seven down Marylebone Road and then walk from just this side of Paddington Station. I tell you, Constable, Hyde Park is not sufficiently lighted at night. Especially in this everlasting fog. I am, I will freely admit, a man of nervous disposition. I nearly jumped out of my skin two or three times while crossing the park; startled by something no more dangerous, I would imagine, than a squirrel."

They reached the entrance to Walbine House: a stout oaken door shielded by a wrought-iron gate. "At any rate I have arrived home before his lordship," Lemming said, producing a keychain from beneath his MacFarlane and applying a stubby, circular key to the incongruously new lock in the ancient gate.

"His lordship?" P.C. Alberts asked.

Lemming swung open the gate. "The Right Honorable the Lord Walbine," he said. He lifted the keychain up to his face and flipped through the keys, trying to locate the front-door key in the dim light of the small gas lamp that hung to the left of the massive oak door.

"I served his father until he died two years ago, and now I serve his lordship."

"Ah!" Alberts said, wondering how the stout butler knew that his new lordship was still absent from Walbine House.

"Goodnight then, Constable," Lemming said, opening the great door as little as possible and pushing himself through the crack.

"Goodnight," Alberts said to the rapidly closing door. He waited until he heard the lock turned from the inside, and then resumed his measured stride along Regent's Gate. It was deathly quiet now; no more scurrying, no fancied noises, only the slight rustle of the wind through the distant trees and the echo of his own footsteps bouncing off the brick facades of the Georgian mansions that faced each other across the wide street.

At Cromwell Road, Constable Alberts paused under the street-lamp for a moment and peered thoughtfully around. He had the unwelcome sensation that he was being watched. By whom he could not tell, but the feeling persisted, an eerie, tingling sensation at the back of his neck. He turned and started back down the dark, fog-shrouded pavement.

From some distance away on Cromwell Road came the clattering noises of an approaching carriage, which grew steadily louder until, some twenty seconds later, a four-wheeler careened around the corner into Regent's Gate. The cab sped along the street, the horse encouraged by an occasional flick of the jarvey's whip. Entirely too fast, Alberts noted critically.

Halfway down Regent's Gate, opposite Walbine House, the jarvey pulled his horse to a stop. From where Alberts stood he could make out the form of a top-hatted man in evening dress emerging from the four-wheeler and tossing a coin up to the jarvey. The Right Honorable the Lord Walbine had obviously just returned home for the night. Lemming, Alberts thought, had been right.

The four-wheeler pulled away and rattled on down the street as his lordship let himself into Walbine House. All was quiet again P.C. Alberts resumed his beat, the tread of his footsteps once more the only sound to be heard along the tree-lined street. He kept to a steady methodical pace as he headed toward Kensington Gore.

It took P.C. Alberts almost ten minutes to make the circuit along Kensington Gore, back up Queen's Gate, and then across Cromwell Road to the Regent's Gate corner. As he turned onto Regent's Gate again, from somewhere ahead of him there came a sudden cacophony of slamming doors and running feet. The faint gleam of a lantern wavered back and forth across the street. It caught Alberts in its dim beam. "Constable!" came an urgent whisper that carried clearly across the length of the street. "Constable Alberts! Come quickly!"

Alberts quickened his stride without quite breaking into a run. "Here I am," he called. "What's the trouble, now?"

The butler, Lemming, was standing in the middle of the street in his shirtsleeves, his eyes wide, breathing like a man who has just been chased by ghosts. An older woman with a coat misbuttoned over a hastily donned housedress peered from behind him.

"Please," Lemming said, "would you come inside with us?"

"If I am needed," Alberts said, taking a firmer grasp of his night-stick. "What seems to be the trouble?"

"It's 'is lordship," the old woman said. " 'E just come in, and now 'e won't answer 'is door."

"His lordship arrived home a short while ago," Lemming explained, "and immediately retired to his room. Mrs. Beddoes was to bring him his nightly glass of toddy, as usual."

" 'E rang for it," Mrs. Beddoes assured Alberts, "as 'e always does."

"But the bedroom door was locked when she arrived on the landing," Lemming said.

"And 'e don't answer 'is knock," Mrs. Beddoes finished, nodding her head back and forth like a pigeon.

"I'm afraid there's been an accident," Lemming said.

"Are you certain his lordship is in his bedroom?" Alberts asked, staring up at the one lighted window on the second story of the great house.

"The door is secured from the inside," Lemming said. "I'd appreciate having you take a look, Constable. Come this way, please."

P.C. Alberts followed Lemming up an ornate marble staircase and down a corridor on the second floor to his lordship's bedroom door. Which was locked. Alberts knocked on the polished dark wood of the door panel and called out. There was no response.

"Has his lordship ever done this before?" Alberts asked.

"His lordship has been known to secure the door on occasion," Lemming answered. "But he has previously always responded to a knock, even if it was only to yell, 'Go away!' "

P.C. Alberts thought for a second. "We'd best break it in," he decided. "Lord Walbine may require assistance."

Lemming sighed, the relief at having someone else make the decision evident in his face. "Very good, Constable. If you say so."

The two men applied their shoulders to the door in a series of blows. On the fourth, the wood around the lock splintered. On the sixth it gave, and the door swung inward.

Alberts entered the room first. It was a large bedroom, dominated by a canopy bed. The Right Honorable the Lord Walbine, twelfth baron of that name, was lying quietly in the center of that bed in a fresh pool of his own blood. Sometime within the past ten minutes his throat had been neatly sliced from clavicle to clavicle.

TWO

THE MORNING

*Art in the blood is liable
to take the strangest forms.*
—SHERLOCK HOLMES

Benjamin Barnett opened his *Morning Herald*, folded it in half, and propped it against the toast rack. "There's been another one," he said, peering down at the closely printed column as he cracked his first soft-boiled egg.

"Eh?" Professor James Moriarty looked up from his breakfast. "Another what?"

"Murder," Barnett said. "Another 'mysterious killing among the gentry,' " he read with evident satisfaction.

"Don't look so pleased," Moriarty said. "It might lead one to suspect that you had done it yourself."

" 'The third outrage in as many weeks,' according to the *Herald*," Barnett said, tapping the headline with his egg spoon. "The police are baffled."

"If we are to believe the newspapers," Moriarty remarked, "the police are always baffled. Except when 'Inspector Gregson expects an early arrest.' Sometimes the police are 'baffled' and 'expect an early arrest' in the same paragraph. I can only wish that you journalists had a wider selection of descriptive phrases to choose from. It would certainly add an element of suspense to newspaper reading that is now grievously lacking."

"There's enough suspense in this story to keep even you happy," Barnett said. "A police constable broke down the victim's bedroom door, which was locked from the inside, to find him lying on his bed in a pool of his own blood, with his throat so deeply cut that the head was almost severed and the blood still flowing from the gaping wound in his neck. How's that for suspense?"

Moriarty sighed and shook his head. Taking off his pince-nez glasses to polish them with his linen napkin, he focused his water-gray eyes myopically on Barnett across the table. "Actually it's quite distressing," he said.

"How's that, Professor?"

Moriarty held up the thick paperbound volume that rested beside his plate. "This came in the first post this morning," he said. "It is the quarterly journal of the British Astro-Physical Society. There is more of mystery and suspense in these twelve-score pages than in ten years' worth of the *Morning Herald*."

"That may be, Professor," Barnett said, "but your average news-paper reader is not interested in what's happening on Mars, but in what's happening in Chelsea. He'd rather have a mysterious murder than a mysterious nebulosity any time."

"You are probably right," Moriarty said, laying the journal aside and replacing his pince-nez glasses on the bridge of his nose. "There is, nonetheless, some small comfort, some slight gleam of hope for the future of the human race that can be derived from current sci-entific theory. I read my journals and they comfort me."

"What sort of comfort, Professor?" Barnett asked, feeling that he had lost the thread of the conversation.

"I find solace in the theories expounded by Professor Herschel, among others, concerning nebulae," Moriarty said, pouring himself a cup of coffee from the large silver samovar which squatted at one end of the table. "They would suggest that the universe is larger by several orders of magnitude than previously imagined."

"This comforts you?"

"Yes. It indicates that mankind, confined as it is to this small planet in a random corner of the universe, is of no real importance or relevance whatsoever."

Barnett put his spoon carefully down on the side of his plate. He knew that Moriarty indulged in these misanthropic diatribes at least partly to annoy him, but at the same time he had never seen any sign that the professor was not totally serious about what he said. "I don't suppose you'd care to do a piece for my news service on that general theme, Professor?" Barnett asked.

"Bah!" Moriarty replied.

"I could probably get a couple of hundred American newspapers to carry the piece."

"The prospect of having my words read eagerly over the jam pot in Chicago is, I must confess, one that holds no particular charm for me," Moriarty said. "Having my phrases mouthed in San Francisco, or my ideas hotly debated in Des Moines, has equally little appeal. No, I'm afraid, my dear Mr. Barnett, that your offer will not entice me into a journalistic career."

"I'm sorry about that, Professor," Barnett said. "The world lost a great essayist when you chose to devote yourself to a life of, ah, science."

Professor Moriarty looked at Barnett suspiciously. "When I plucked you from a Turkish prison almost two years ago," he said, "you were as devoid of sarcasm as you were embedded with grime. I no longer detect any grime."

"*Touché*, Professor." Barnett smiled and poured himself a cup of coffee.

Benjamin Barnett had first met Professor James Moriarty in Constantinople almost two years before, at a moment when the professor was being chased down the Street of the Two Towers by a band of assassins in dirty brown burnooses. Barnett and a friend came to the professor's aid, for which he thanked them profusely, although he regarded the assault as a minor annoyance from which he could have extricated himself quite easily without assistance. Which, Barnett came to admit when he got to know the professor better, was most probably true.

Moriarty had reciprocated by rescuing Barnett from the dank confines of the prison of Mustafa II, where he was being held for the minor offense of murdering his friend and the major indiscretion of spying against the government of that most enlightened despot Sultan Abd-ul Hamid, Shah of Shahs, the second of that name. Both crimes of which he was equally innocent, and for either of which he was equally likely to be garroted at any moment at the whim of the Sublime Porte.

But Moriarty had exacted a price for his rescue. "What I want from you," he had told Barnett, "is two years of your life."

"Why?" Barnett had asked.

"You are good at your profession, and I have use for you."

"And after the two years?"

"After that, your destiny is once again your own."

"I accept!"

It had seemed like a good bargain at the time. And even when

Moriarty had smuggled Barnett across the length of Europe and they stood face to face in the professor's basement laboratory in the house on Russell Square, it continued to seem so. Moriarty claimed to be a consultant and problem-solver, but he was strangely vague about the details. After extracting an oath of silence in regard to his affairs, he had put Barnett to work. Barnett had been a foreign correspondent for the *New York World*, living in Paris, when he had gone to Turkey to report on the sea trials of a new submarine and ended up in an Osmanli prison. It was his skills as a reporter that Moriarty wished to use. With Moriarty's assistance, Barnett opened the American News Service, a cable service to United States newspapers for British and European news. This gave Barnett a cover organization to investigate anything that Moriarty wanted investigated. To the surprise of both men, the service quickly began to make money, and soon took on a life of its own as a legitimate news organization.

Gradually it dawned on Barnett that Moriarty's ideas of law and morality were at variance with those of the rest of Victorian society. Moriarty, to put it bluntly, was a criminal. Sherlock Holmes, the brilliant consulting detective, considered Moriarty one of the most reprehensible villains in London as yet unhanged. This was, perhaps, an exaggeration. Holmes had been trying to catch Moriarty at some nefarious scheme or other for nearly a decade, and had yet to succeed. He had foiled one or two of the professor's plans, and apprehended a henchman or two; but he had never managed to link the crime in question to the quondam professor of mathematics now living in Russell Square. This had undoubtedly led to a certain pique, and a tendency to see Moriarty under every bush and a sinister plot behind every crime.

Professor Moriarty was not a simple criminal any more than he was a simple man. He had his own morality, as strict as or stricter than that of his contemporaries. But it differed in tone as well as in content from that smug complacency with which Victoria's subjects regarded "those lesser breeds without the law" unfortunate enough to be born in Borneo, or Abyssinia, or Whitechapel.

Moriarty had kept Barnett isolated from most of his criminal activities, finding Barnett more useful as an unbiased gatherer of information. As a result, Barnett had only hints of the organization that Moriarty commanded, or the activities that he directed. Barnett did know that whatever money Moriarty made from his activities, beyond that necessary to keep up his household, went into supporting his scientific experiments. Moriarty thought of himself as a scientist, and his other activities, legal and illegal, were merely the means of financing his inquiries into the scientific unknown.

Barnett stared at the tall, hawklike man across the breakfast table from him. Moriarty was an enigma: an avowed criminal, he had the highest intellectual and moral standards Barnett had ever known; an evident misanthrope, he quietly supported several charities in the most miserably poor sections of London; a confirmed realist, he showed an irrepressible inclination toward the romantic. It might not be that he sought out adventure; but however he might hide from it, it unerringly sought him out.

"You've always been interested in puzzles," Barnett said, breaking off his chain of thought as Moriarty noticed his fixed gaze. "Doesn't the image of a man murdered inside a locked room appeal to you?"

Moriarty thought over the question for a moment. "Not especially," he said. "I'd need more information than is given in the *Morning Herald* before I find it puzzling. The way they leave it, there are too many possible answers only because there are too many unasked questions."

"For example?"

"What of the windows, for example?"

"Locked. It says so."

"Of course. But what sort of locks? There are gentlemen, I believe, who can open a locked window from the outside."

"And then leave through the window, locking it after them?"

"In some cases, yes, depending upon the type of lock. Or, for example, the murderer could have concealed himself in a cupboard, or under the bed, and not left until after the body was discovered."

"I hadn't thought of that," Barnett said.

"I can list five other ways in which the supposed 'locked room' could have been circumvented," Moriarty said.

"I take it back," Barnett said, laying the newspaper face down on the table next to the chafing dish. "There is no puzzle. I was mistaken."

"There are, however, several items of interest in the account," Moriarty said.

"What items do you find interesting?"

"Ah!" Moriarty said. "More examples are requested. There is, for example, the question of motive. There are five motives for murder: greed, lust, fear, honor, and insanity. Which was this?"

"Scotland Yard is of the opinion that Lord Walbine was killed by a burglar."

"Greed then," Moriarty said. "But surely we have a most unusual burglar here: one who goes straight to the master bedroom when there are cupboards full of silver in the pantry; one who lays his lordship full length out on his bed and slashes his throat instead of giving him a friendly little tap on the head with a blunt object. And then one who disappears in a locked room."

"You just intimated that you knew several men who could have done it," Barnett said.

"Ah, yes. But again we come to the question of motive. Why would a burglar have gone to the additional trouble of closing the room after him? Why not just go out of the window and down the drainpipe?"

"I don't know," Barnett replied.

"And if it was indeed an interrupted act of burglary, what of the murder of Isadore Stanhope, the barrister, last week? Or the Honorable George Venn before that? All with their throats slit; all in their own bedrooms. One with his wife asleep in the adjoining bedroom, the other with a faithful hound lying undisturbed at the foot of the stairs. And nothing of value missing in any of the crimes. A singular burglar indeed!"

Barnett put down his spoon and stared across the table at his companion. Moriarty had not so much as glanced at the morning newspapers. Further, Barnett was willing to swear he hadn't seen a newspaper in the past three weeks. Moriarty scorned newspapers, and seldom opened them. One of Barnett's jobs was to keep a clipping file of current crime stories and other items that might interest the professor, but the last three weeks' clippings lay in a box, unsorted and unfiled, on Barnett's desk. Yet somehow Moriarty knew the details of the three linked murders, as he seemed always to know all that was happening in London and most of what was happening throughout the world.

"You have another theory, then?" Barnett suggested.

"One should never theorize with insufficient facts," Moriarty said. "It is a practice most destructive of the mental faculties. As I said, there are some obvious questions that should be asked. The answers should give one a clear picture of the murderer and his motive."

"Such as?"

Moriarty shook his head. "I don't understand your fascination with this," he said. "A mundane series of murders with nothing to recommend them to the connoisseur. Reminiscent of Roehm in Düsseldorf a few years back, or the notorious Philadelphia Fox murders in '78. The only mystery in such cases is how the police can be so inefficient."

"As I remember," Barnett said, "they never caught the Philadelphia Fox."

"My point exactly," said Moriarty.

"If the investigation were in your charge," Barnett asked, "what would you do?"

"I resist the answer which springs to my lips," Moriarty said, with a hint of a smile, "as the language involved is rather coarse. However—" The professor removed his pince-nez lenses once again and began polishing them with his napkin. As he did he stared absently across the table at the Vernet which hung above the sideboard, a three-by-five-foot oil entitled *Landscape with Cavalry*.

Barnett watched with interest as the professor polished his lenses and stared unseeingly across the room. He was watching Moriarty think, as impressive an event to Barnett as watching Norman-Néruda play the violin or watching W. S. Gilbert scribble. Something incredible was happening right there in front of you, and if you were very lucky there was always the chance that some of whatever it was would rub off on you.

"The question of motive," Moriarty said, readjusting his pince-nez on his nose, "would seem to be the most promising. Of the five I cited, we can eliminate but one: insanity. I would concentrate on the backgrounds of the three men to establish what they had in common, to try to find a common denominator for our killer."

"I don't know, Professor," Barnett said. "The way those three were killed seems pretty crazy to me. Slitting their throats in their own beds, then sneaking out past locked doors and sleeping dogs."

"Slitting their throats may be an action of insanity," Moriarty said, "but it seems to me that the subsequent innocuous departure was eminently sane."

Mr. Maws, Moriarty's butler, appeared at the dining-room door. "Beg pardon, Professor," he said in his gravelly voice, "but there is a gentleman to see you. An Indian gentleman. I took the liberty of placing him in the drawing room."

Moriarty pulled out his pocket watch and snapped it open. "And nine minutes early, I fancy," Moriarty said. "No card?"

"None, sir. He did mention the lack, sir. Apologized for not having one. Gave his name as Singh."

"I see," Moriarty said. "Tell the gentleman I shall be with him in a few moments."

"Nine minutes early?" Barnett asked, as Mr. Maws withdrew to reassure their visitor.

"It is nine minutes before ten," Moriarty said. "This also came in the first post." He extracted an envelope from his jacket pocket and flipped it across the table to Barnett. "What do you make of it?"

The envelope was a stiff, thick, slightly gray paper that Barnett was unfamiliar with, as was the paper inside. The address on the envelope, *James Moriarty, Ph.D., 64 Russell Square, City*, was done with a broad-nibbed pen in a round, flowing hand. The handwriting on the letter itself was more crabbed and angular, written with an extremely fine-pointed nib.

"Two different hands," Barnett noted. "Let's see what the note says":

> James Moriarty, Sc.D.—
> Will be calling upon you at ten of the a.m. tomorrow morning. Am hopeful to find you at home at that instant. Am hopeful to interest you in impossible but potentially lucrative endeavor. Have been informed by several that you are man most likely to talk to in this regard. With greatest hopes and much potential thanks, I am name of Singh.

"Very interesting stylistically, if not very informative." Barnett held the note up to the light. "I don't recognize this paper. No watermark. No crest. But it is a thick, expensive paper of the sort used for printing invitations, possibly. It's an odd size; almost square."

"What does all of this tell you?"

"Well," Barnett considered. "Nothing really beyond what it says. A gentleman named Singh will call at ten and he has some sort of proposition to put to you."

"A reasonable conclusion," Moriarty said, "confirmed by the fact that the gentleman has indeed shown up a trifle before the hour. Nothing more?"

"No, not really."

"Any suggestion regarding the distinctly different hands on the message and the envelope?"

"No. It is curious, I admit. But no ready explanation for it springs to my mind. What does it tell you?"

"That, and the unusual shape of the paper, do offer a field for speculation," Moriarty said, pushing himself to his feet, "but there is no point in indulging in that pernicious habit when the object of our speculation awaits us in the drawing room."

"You wish me to be present at the interview?"

"If you like."

"Thank you, but I think not. I really should get to the office."

"I thought the admirable Miss Perrine was handling the affairs of the American News Service."

"She is, and very well," Barnett said. "She controls a staff of nine reporters, four secretary-typists, three telegraphists, and assorted porters, page boys, errand boys, and the like with a hand of iron. A very exceptional young lady."

"She enjoys this position of authority?" Moriarty asked.

"Her only regret, or so she has informed me, is that her administrative duties leave her little time for writing."

"Well, you'd better leave, then," Moriarty said, "before the young lady discovers that you are dispensable. I will take care of the potentially lucrative Mr. Singh."

"I am going to put a couple of my reporters to work on those murders," Barnett said. "I am convinced that there's a story there."

"There well may be, Barnett," Moriarty said, smiling down at him, "but are you quite sure it should be told?"

221B BAKER STREET

*Deceit, according to him, was an impossibility in the
case of one trained to observation and analysis. His conclusions were as infallible as so many propositions of Euclid.*
—Dr. John H. Watson

Sherlock Holmes waved his visitor to a seat. "Come, this is most gratifying," he said. "Welcome, my lord. I have sent the page boy down for some tea. In the meantime, what can I do for you?"

The Earl of Arundale looked with distaste around the cluttered sitting room of the world's foremost consulting detective. The basket of unfiled clippings on the desk, the jumble of chemical apparatus atop the deal-topped table to the right of the fireplace, the stack of envelopes affixed to the mantelpiece by a thin-bladed oriental knife; could genius indeed exist amid such disorder? He pulled the tails of his morning coat around him and gingerly sat on the edge of the aged leather sofa. "Gratifying?" he asked. "Surely a man of your repute has had noble clients before."

"I was referring to the problem that brought you, my lord," Holmes said. "It is gratifying to have a case that exercises the intellect. Those which have come my way for the last few months have indicated a sad decline of imagination among the criminal classes. As for my clientele, we entertain all sorts here. The last person to sit where you are sitting was a duke, and the person before that, if I remember correctly, was a woman who had murdered her first three husbands and was plotting the death of her fourth."

"Interesting," Lord Arundale murmured.

"Much more interesting than the duke," Holmes agreed. "The reigning monarch of a European kingdom has sat in the chair to your left, and a dwarf who does water colors has sat in the seat beside you. The king was a boor; the dwarf is quite possibly a genius. How may I serve you, my lord?"

"Well, you would seem to know already," Lord Arundale said, nettled at Holmes's attitude. "You are gratified by the problem that brought me here before I've had a chance to tell you what it is. I was told that you had a sort of clairvoyance that enabled you to detect the actions of criminals in the absence of clues visible to the regular police. I was not, however, informed that you could predict the problem that a client would bring to you before he had the opportunity to elucidate it to you. Frankly, sir, the exercise strikes me as pure hocus!"

"No, no," Holmes said quickly. "I do apologize if I seem a trifle sharp. Put it down to the effects of the medication I am taking, my lord. My medical man, Dr. Watson, has prescribed a little something for my bouts of lethargy, and it sometimes has the effect of making me seem a bit testy."

"Then you don't claim to exercise clairvoyance, or other psychic abilities?"

"Not at all, my lord. Whatever abilities I have are founded firmly in a knowledge of the appropriate sciences, an extensive study of the history of crime, and a sharply honed faculty for deductive reasoning."

"Then," Lord Arundale pressed on, "you don't actually know what brought me here, and were merely making a general assumption that I would offer an interesting, ah, case?"

"On the contrary, my lord. I know exactly why you're here. You've come to consult with me regarding last night's murder in Regent's Gate. Ah, here's Billy with the tea. How do you like yours, my lord?"

Lord Arundale allowed his tea to be poured and milked and sugared while he thought this over. "You are right," he said finally. "And if it's hocus, it's clever hocus indeed. For the life of me, I can't see how you know. You must admit that it smacks rather of clairvoyance, or the cleverer sort of conjuring trick."

"Not at all, my lord," Holmes said. "It is, after all, my profession to deduce hard facts from what would seem to others to be scanty evidence."

Lord Arundale sipped his tea thoughtfully. "What other deductions have you already made?" he asked.

Holmes leaned back in his armchair, his thin, sensitive fingers laced together under his chin. "Only the rather obvious facts that you've come from one or more officials of high government rank, probably cabinet ministers, to request that I take over the investigation; that you've been to Scotland Yard already and received the approval of the Commissioner of Police, although the detective inspector in charge of the case feels that I'll only get in the way."

"Astounding!" Lord Arundale said. "You must have agents in the police."

"I assure your lordship—"

Lord Arundale put his teacup on the tray and shook his head. "No need," he said. "Is there anything else?"

"Only that there is some fact or clue of major importance which has been withheld from the public that you have come to acquaint me with."

"By God, sir!" Lord Arundale said. "You must explain to me how you deduced all of that from the mere presence in your sitting room of a middle-aged peer in a morning coat."

"Every trade must have its secrets, my lord," Holmes said, rubbing his hands together. "I learned from my friend Dr. Watson, who shared these rooms with me before his marriage, not to reveal too easily how I attain these effects. The explanation moves them from the miraculous to the mundane. I would draw your attention, however, to the few additional facts that I noted."

"And they are?"

"First, I happened to notice the carriage in which you arrived; not your own, but one of those at the service of Scotland Yard. Next I observed the distinctive red-brown clay adhering to the instep of your right shoe. Surely acquired earlier today, since it seems unlikely that your valet would not see to it that your shoes are polished every night. There are several places around London where you might have picked it up, but the most likely is the east end of St. James's Park, across from the government offices."

"I begin to see," Lord Arundale said. "But I still think it's deucedly clever. Fancy knowing every bit of mud in London."

"In perpetrating a crime, the astute criminal strives to eliminate or disguise the facts surrounding his act," Holmes said. "Where he is most likely to go astray is in the small details, like the dirt on his shoes or the dust on his clothing. Therefore, my lord, you can see that the professional investigator must make a study of such details."

"Fantastic," Lord Arundale said. He picked up the small leather case that he had brought in with him and extracted an envelope from it. "How much do you know of the murder of Lord Walbine?"

"No more than what was in the morning papers, my lord."

"Here then is a précis of all the relevant facts," Lord Arundale said, handing the envelope to Holmes, "as prepared by the inspector in charge of the police investigation. Also included are accounts of the murders of the Honorable George Venn and of Isadore Stanhope."

"I shall read it immediately, your lordship," said Holmes. "I should also like to examine the rooms in which the three crimes were committed."

"Arrangements have been made," Lord Arundale said. "Inspector Lestrade said you'd want to, as he put it, 'crawl around the rooms on hands and knees with a reading glass.'"

"Ah, so it's Lestrade, is it?" cried Holmes. "That is somewhat helpful."

"You know Inspector Lestrade, then. I was favorably impressed with him. He seems to have a good command of his job. Claimed to be running down several promising leads, although he was rather vague as to what they were. Said that he thought arresting the butlers would produce results."

"What sort of results?" Holmes inquired.

"He didn't say. He did say that he thought that bringing you in on the case was quite unnecessary, although he admitted that you've been of some help to the regular force in the past. 'Special circumstances,' he put it. If it weren't that the P.M. feels that a quite out of the ordinary finesse is required in this instance, the Home Secretary and I would feel quite sanguine in leaving the case in his hands."

"Normally he is quite adequate," Holmes agreed. "But then the usual case is just that—usual. A crime of brute force committed without forethought, requiring neither specialized knowledge nor ratiocination to solve."

"Faint praise indeed," Lord Arundale said. "Don't you think Lestrade is capable?"

"As a bulldog, yes. The man is tenacious, unrelenting, brave, honest, and loyal. But as a bloodhound, I'm afraid the more subtle odors of crime escape his nose."

Lord Arundale held out his teacup to be refilled. "That is basically what the Prime Minister said," he told Holmes. "The Home Secretary is convinced that the Metropolitan Police can, and should, handle the problem, but the P.M. felt that it might be too sensitive for the bulldog approach. And you came highly recommended by, if you will excuse my being vague, a member of the Royal Household."

Holmes nodded. "Please thank her majesty for me," he said. "I gather that it is this 'special circumstance,' of which I am as yet unaware, that makes these crimes sensitive and commends me to the attention of Lord Salisbury, the Prime Minister."

"True," Lord Arundale said. "The Marquess of Salisbury is indeed concerned over these murders. He is concerned, to be more precise, with whether or not he has cause to be concerned."

"I see." Holmes looked thoughtful for a moment. "Am I to understand that the crimes may have some political significance, but it is not known at present whether they actually do or not?"

"Yes," Lord Arundale said. "That, concisely, is it. The crimes may, indeed, be the work of a madman, or someone with a long-festering hatred for the four murdered men because of some secret grievance. But they may also be part of an intricate plot by any of three great European powers against her majesty's government. And we must learn which of these possibilities is the truth. And we must know as soon as we can; every day's delay could be disastrous."

"Four men?" Holmes asked. "I know of but three."

"Lord John Darby was found dead about three weeks ago," Lord Arundale said. He stared down at his teacup for a moment, and then drained it and returned it to the tray. "Lord John was the younger brother of the Earl of Moncreith."

"I remember noting it at the time," Holmes said. "But it was reported as a natural death. Heart attack, I believe the newspaper report said."

"Lord John was found on the dining-room table in his flat in Tattersham Court. His throat had been cut. A silver serving platter had been placed on the floor by the table to catch the blood."

"Come now, that is a fascinating detail!" Holmes said, stretching a lean arm out for the cigarette box on the mantel. "May I offer you a cigarette, my lord? They are of a Virginia tobacco, made for me by K. K. Tamourlane & Sons. The weed is noxious, but I find it sharpens the mental processes."

"No, thank you," Lord Arundale said. "But if you wouldn't object to the smell of a cigar—"

"Not at all." Holmes lit a taper from the gas mantle and applied it to the tip of his cigarette while Lord Arundale took a long dun-colored cigar from a tooled-leather case and went through the ritual of preparing it for the match. "Pray continue with your recitation of the strange death of Lord John Darby," Holmes said, lighting Lord Arundale's cigar before tossing the taper into the fireplace.

Lord Arundale took a deep puff. "I usually reserve these for after meals," he said. "Where was I? Oh, yes. Lord John was lying on the table—a great big thing, could easily seat twelve. French, I believe. Turn-of-the-century piece. His arms were spread out to the sides, but his fists were clenched. Interesting how one remembers all the small details."

"You saw the body, my lord?"

Lord Arundale stood and walked over to the bay window. Pulling the drape aside, he stared down at the traffic below. "I *found* the damn thing!" he told Holmes.

"How long would you say Lord John had been dead when you found him?"

Lord Arundale turned to look at Holmes. "I couldn't really say," he said. "Finding corpses is not really in my line, you see. For what it's worth, my impression was that the incident was fairly recent. The blood seemed to be quite fresh."

"Was anyone else there at the time?"

"Quimby, Lord John's valet. He let me in. This was about seven-thirty in the morning. He'd been there all night. His room is off the front hall."

"Had he seen or heard anything during the night?"

"Nothing. He let Lord John in late the night before. He's not sure of the time, but estimates it at shortly before two. Then he went to bed. He had not yet gone in to awaken Lord John when I arrived the next morning, having received no instructions on the matter."

"No other servants?"

"None present. There are a maid and a cook, but they live two flights up in the servants' quarters. The building of flats is designed with a common servants' quarters on the top floor."

"I see," Holmes said. "What sort of nighttime security is there in the building?"

"There is a hall porter on each floor all night, and a uniformed commissionaire at the front door. There are two other entrances to the building, but both are locked and bolted from the inside at eight o'clock."

Holmes reflected silently for a minute. "I am amazed," he said, "that Lestrade has not already arrested the valet."

"Quimby?" Lord Arundale asked. "You think he could be guilty?"

"Not for an instant," Holmes said. "I am, however, amazed that Lestrade shares my opinion."

"The Metropolitan Police have not, as yet, been informed of the crime," Lord Arundale said.

Holmes leaped to his feet. "What?" he cried. "You have concealed a murder from the authorities? Come now, sir. Even a peer of the realm cannot be allowed such liberty with the Queen's justice."

Lord Arundale held up a hand. "Pray calm yourself," he said. "The Prime Minister has been notified; the Home Secretary, who, as you know, is in charge of the Metropolitan Police, has been notified; the Lord High Chancellor has been notified; and her majesty has been told. I think you will have to admit that the formalities have been observed—perhaps on a higher level than is usual, that is all."

"I see," Holmes said, resuming his seat. "And why was this unusual procedure followed?"

Lord Arundale returned to the sofa. "I shall explain."

"You have my attention, my lord."

"I will have to give you the complete background. I arrived at Lord John's flat that morning to take him to a special emergency meeting of the Continental Policies Committee. This is a group of some twelve men who advise the Prime Minister on matters affecting Britain's relations with the great powers of Europe. Only issues of great and immediate concern are taken up by the committee, which is composed of the leading minds in the government. The very existence of this committee is a closely held secret."

"I was not aware of it," Holmes commented.

"Your brother, Mycroft, is a member," Lord Arundale told Holmes.

"He is very close-mouthed about his work," Holmes replied.

"Just so," Lord Arundale said. "At any rate, Quimby asked me to wait while he awakened his master."

"In the dining room?"

"No, in the drawing room. But as I happened to mention that I had not yet broken my fast that morning, Quimby suggested that he have the cook prepare one of her French omelets for me while I waited. I was agreeable, and so I proceeded into the dining room, where I found Lord John."

"It all seems quite clear," Holmes said. "But why did you not notify the authorities? Surely the fact that the man was a member of the Continental Policies Committee is not, of itself, sufficient reason not to call the police when you find his blood-soaked corpse."

Lord Arundale pondered the question for a second, searching for the precise way to phrase his answer. "Lord John Darby had an older brother," he said finally, picking the words carefully, as one would pick the right gold shirt studs from a drawer full of almost identical gold shirt studs. "Midway in age between Lord John and the Earl of Moncreith. His name is Crecy. Lord Crecy Darby. It is an old family name."

"Yes?" Holmes said encouragingly, as Lord Arundale fell silent again.

"I went to school with Crecy," Lord Arundale said. "Hoxley and then Cambridge. We were determined to go into government service together. Crecy was—is—brilliant. He was going to be the first prime minister appointed before his fortieth birthday. I was to be his foreign secretary. We had the details carefully planned." Lord Arundale sighed and shook his head. "Perhaps it was hubris," he said. "But at any rate, Lord Crecy Darby went completely insane over a period of three years. Every specialist in England and on the Continent was called in, and none of them offered any hope."

"What form did this insanity take?"

"He imagined that intricate plots were being woven about him; that complete strangers on the street had been employed by some invisible agency to follow him about; that everything that happened anywhere in the world was somehow directed against him. He became extremely sly and cunning, and would listen in at doorways and stay concealed behind drapery hoping to overhear someone talking about him.

"His father had him sent away to a sanitarium in Basel that had a new treatment that was thought to offer some small hope."

"What sort of therapy?" Holmes asked.

"I was never too clear on that," Lord Arundale said. "Something to do with hot salt baths and encouraging the patient to run about and scream, I believe. At any rate, he escaped from the sanitarium. Nothing was heard from him for two years. Then, on Crecy's thirty-second birthday, as it happens, the old earl received a communication from an attorney in Munich. Lord Crecy Darby, under the name of Richard Plantagenet, was on trial for the brutal murders of two prostitutes."

Holmes flipped his cigarette into the fireplace. "I remember the case," he said. "Although the true identity of the man who called himself Richard Plantagenet never came out. There was no doubt as to his guilt."

"None at all," Lord Arundale agreed. "He killed two street-walkers by slitting their throats with a razor, and then mutilated their bodies in a horrible fashion. Not, I suppose, that there is a pleasant way to mutilate bodies. The trial cost the old Earl of Moncreith a fortune. He was not trying to have Crecy found innocent, you understand, but merely to see that he was spared the death penalty and that the family name remained concealed."

"And what happened to Lord Crecy?"

"He was found guilty and totally insane. He was placed in the Bavarian State Prison-Hospital for the Criminally Insane at Forchheim for the rest of his life."

"I see," Holmes said. "And so when you saw his brother lying dead with his throat cut, you naturally assumed that Lord Crecy must have escaped and returned to England."

"That is correct."

"And to save the present earl and his family from the grief and disgrace—"

"I did not notify the police but went straight to the Lord Chamberlain."

"Who agreed with you?"

"Of course."

"Bah!" Holmes said. "You are not above the law, my lord—neither as a member of the nobility nor as a member of the government. Acting as you have done can only be destructive of the moral fiber of British justice. Nothing good can come of it."

"I have heard," Lord Arundale said, "that you do not always work within the structure of the law. Was I misinformed?"

Holmes gazed sternly at Lord Arundale. "I have on occasion acted outside the law," he said. "But that and setting oneself above the law are two separate and distinct things. If you act outside the law you are still subject to it through the possibility of apprehension. But if you act above the law—if a burglar, for example, could go and clear his crime with the Lord Chamberlain first—then there is no law for you. And if there is law for some but not for others, then there is no law. For a law that is unequally applied is an unjust law, and will not be obeyed."

"You have strong opinions, sir," Lord Arundale said.

"So I have been informed," said Holmes, "on more than one occasion."

Lord Arundale carefully laid his cigar on the lip of the large brass ashtray on the table before him. "I did not come here for your approbation, Mr. Holmes," he said. "Neither did I come here for your censure. I came for your assistance in apprehending a murderer."

"You telegraphed to Forchheim?"

"I did."

"Lord Crecy, I presume, had not escaped?"

"Indeed he had not. How did you know that?"

"Never mind that at the moment, my lord. So the deaths of Lord John and the others are again a mystery."

"Even so."

"And you suspect a possible political motivation. Were any of the other victims connected with the Continental Policies Committee, or otherwise involved in government activities?"

"Isadore Stanhope, the barrister, was an agent for the Austrian government," Lord Arundale said. "George Venn had no known connections to any government, but he is said to have taken frequent trips to Paris. The purpose of these trips is, as yet, unknown. It is being looked into."

"And what of Lord Walbine?"

"A quiet man of independent means. Seldom left London except to return to his ancestral estate near Stoke on Trent, and that but twice a year. The only thing of interest we've been able to find out about the baron is that he had a rather large collection of, let us say, exotic literature in a concealed set of bookcases in the library."

"What fascinating things one finds out about one's fellow man when one is compelled to search through his belongings," Holmes commented.

"Will you take the case?" Lord Arundale asked.

"I will," Holmes said. "As a problem, it is not altogether without interest. I was sure when I saw you arrive, my lord, that you would have something stimulating to offer. And so you do."

"Have you any ideas?"

"My dear Lord Arundale," Holmes said, chuckling, "I'm afraid that you have been given an exaggerated notion of my abilities. Even I cannot solve a crime before I have assimilated its details."

"Well, I wish you luck," Lord Arundale said. "Any assistance you require will be immediately forthcoming from Scotland Yard."

"That should prove to be a novel experience," Holmes said. "I will have to tell Inspector Lestrade and his people of the circumstances surrounding the death of Lord John Darby, you realize."

Lord Arundale rose to his feet. "I leave that to you," he said. "If you feel you must, then do so. As to your fee—"

"My fees are on a standard schedule," Holmes told him. "I shall send my bill to the Foreign Office."

"That will be satisfactory," Lord Arundale said. "There is one last thing you should know."

"And that is?"

"I have just received a second telegram from Forchheim. After being informed of his brother's death, Lord Crecy killed a guard and escaped from the asylum. That was yesterday. Presumably he is headed back to England, possibly to avenge his brother's death. Unless he is apprehended on the Continent, he should be here within the week."

"That," said Holmes, "should make things very interesting indeed!"

FOUR

MISS CECILY PERRINE

Small is the worth
Of beauty from the light retir'd . . .
— Edmund Waller

In just under two years the offices of the American News Service had grown from one small room on the top floor of 27 Whitefriars Street to a set of chambers that encompassed the whole of the top floor and several rooms on the ground floor. The floor between was the ancestral home of McTeague, Burke, Samsone & Sons, who concocted and purveyed a variety of printing inks to the newspapers around the corner on Fleet Street. Benjamin Barnett had cast an occasional covetous eye on the frosted-glass door of McTeague *et al.* as he climbed the stairs to his overcrowded domain; but he knew that the inky firm would neither change locations nor cease to exist at any time in the foreseeable future. For, as the younger Samsone, a gentleman well into his seventh decade, had told Barnett in a characteristically loquacious moment: "It were a McTeague mixture which inked the pages of the first number of the *Daily Courant* in 1702. Thick, tarry stuff they used in them days. If you was to use it in one of them fine modrun-type rotaries now, it'd smear all abaht the paper. And it were McTeague inks what printed six of the eleven dailies what come out within three miles of this spot this very morning. Yes, young man; I tell you that as long as newsprint must be spread with ink, pressmen will trot up to the door to have it formulated."

And so, for as long as the Fleet Street presses continued to rumble, the copy desk and the dispatch desk of the American News Service would remain separated by untold demijohns of printers' ink. And whenever the little bell on the dispatch-room wall tingled, an errand boy would race up the two flights of narrow wooden stairs to pick up the precious sheets of copy and return them to the dispatch desk to be logged and turned over to the telegraphers.

Barnett noticed, as he climbed the stairs on this Tuesday afternoon, that no light was diffusing through the frosted glass on the ink merchants' door. They were closed for the day. McTeague *et al.* was a model of a modern Socialist employer, giving the whole day Saturday off and closing the shop for all sorts of obscure midweek holidays. The employees' delight in the abbreviated work week was perhaps mitigated by the McTeague custom of inviting Socialist speakers in to lecture during the lunch half hour.

At the top of the stairs, the door to his own offices was, as usual, wide open. Barnett dodged a descending errand boy and threaded his way toward the inner offices past the small, cluttered desks of those dedicated to creative journalism. The four secretaries—three gentlemen of varying ages and a young lady of severe demeanor—looked up and issued a variety of polite greetings as he passed. The reporters—two young, intense-looking gentlemen and an elderly lady named Burnside who was an authority on the Royal Family—all affected an air of being much too busy or too deeply sunken into the creative process to notice his passing.

Miss Cecily Perrine was at her desk in the inner office, staring intently at the half-page of copy in her Remington Standard typewriter. Miss Perrine had come to work for him the very day the American News Service had opened for business almost two years before. Her burning desire since early adolescence, for one of those inexplicable reasons that shape our lives beyond our control, was to become a journalist. Now, in the Merrie Land of England when Victoria was queen, and things were just about the best that things had ever been, a lady did not work for a newspaper. Oh, perhaps the society page would have a lady correspondent, but she would certainly never set foot in the actual offices of the paper. Even the secretaries and typists were traditionally male, and against tradition there is no argument.

So the American News Service, as far as it was from being a real newspaper, was as close to journalism as Miss Cecily Perrine could approach. At the beginning they wrote almost none of their own material; instead they bought stories that had already appeared in the London dailies, doing some minor rewriting to make them understandable to American readers. Then, once a day, one of them would walk over to the Main Post Office on Newgate Street to have the stories telegraphed to New York.

Cecily Perrine proved to be innately brilliant at handling all the organizational details in running a business, a fact that surprised her as much as it pleased Barnett. She was calm and even-tempered, and much better at handling people than Barnett. And she was also lovely to look at.

Barnett observed her silently for a moment as she studied the page of copy in her typewriter, noting how the single shaft of sunlight, twisted by some prismatic effect of the ancient glass panes in the small window, highlighted the light-brown curls piled in artful disarray atop Cecily's attractive oval face. She was beauty in repose, a model of graceful elegance, even with her face screwed up in the awful concentration of creativity. Or so Barnett thought as he looked at her.

"Good morning, Miss Perrine," he said as she became aware of his presence behind her. "Busy little beehive we have out there."

"Good afternoon, Mr. Barnett," Cecily Perrine said pointedly, her clear blue eyes meeting his. "As you are the owner of this establishment, I shall not attempt to regulate your comings and goings, but I am bound to point out that when the employer arrives at the office at one-thirty in the afternoon, it is not conducive to creating a good work attitude among the employees."

"Ah, Miss Perrine," Barnett said, "let the staff believe that you are a hard-hearted harridan, capable of vilifying even your employer for an imagined tardiness. But to me, in private with the door closed"—he closed the door—"admit that you're tired of supervising others while they write the stories and get the acclaim and the by-lines. Tell me that you desire to get out into the great city yourself and have doors slammed in your face, and suffer insults that a lady should never hear and epithets that a lady should not even understand."

"Why, Mr. Barnett," Cecily said, "you make it sound so attractive that I blush to admit that such might indeed be the case, for fear that people will think me nothing more than a dilettante!"

"Never, Cecily. You are too fine a woman for that!" Barnett said, going over to his desk and settling into his chair. "I may call you Cecily, may I not?"

"You may," Cecily said. "And I shall call you Benjamin, for that is your given name, is it not?"

"It is, and I should be proud to hear it from your lips," Barnett told her with a grandiloquent gesture that swept half of his morning mail from the desk to the floor.

Benjamin Barnett had an inordinate fondness for the theater. In his youth, in New York City, he had acted in many an amateur theatrical production of *The Drunkard*, or *His American Cousin*. Cecily Perrine had grown up in the theater. Her mother, Laura Croft, had been one of the great leading ladies of the melodramatic '60s. Her father had been a noted villain until, some ten years before, her mother had died and her father had quit the stage, devoting himself to his linguistic studies.

Barnett and Cecily frequently went to the theater together, usually chaperoned by Elton Perrine, Cecily's father. For their own amusement, they occasionally assumed the attitudes of the melodramatic stage in private conversation.

Barnett found the pastime satisfying for another reason. For roughly the past year he had been deeply in love with his office manager, the intelligent, perceptive, beautiful, talented, altogether wonderful Cecily Perrine. Not that love was a new emotion for him; indeed, he had been in love many times before. But his past loves had been light-hearted and evanescent, never deep, or serious, or meaningful, full of pleasant emotion and devoid of either thought or pain.

But this time it was real, and intense, and serious, and damnedly, irritatingly painful. And daily it grew worse and more intense instead of better. Barnett was in the unbearable position of being unable to declare his love to Cecily Perrine, and the need to do so was becoming overwhelming. Love is not normally a silent emotion. And the closest he could come to stating his feelings out loud was in the melodramatic banter that they exchanged. It gave him slight solace, but it was better than complete silence.

Barnett's reticence to speak to Cecily of his feelings lay in his contract with Professor Moriarty. As long as he was obliged to do the professor's bidding, and might at any time be required to perform a criminal act, how could he ask any girl, much less one as fine as Cecily Perrine, to marry him and share his life?

And so, except for the occasional histrionic outburst artfully disguised as melodrama, he kept his silence. He had never explained to Miss Perrine the exact nature of his relationship with Professor Moriarty, or the professor's strange attitude toward the law. How much of it she had deduced or assumed from the circumstances and events of the past two years he did not know. It was a subject that, by tacit agreement, they did not discuss. Nor did he know what Miss Perrine made of his strange ambivalent attitude toward her, and, being but a man, could not begin to guess.

"I've had a hard morning, but useful," Barnett told Cecily, leaning over to pick up his scattered mail. "And you, at least, should be pleased by the results."

"I am all ears, Benjamin; and my heart is aflutter with excitement!"

"John Pummery has been fired from the *Express*."

"The managing editor? When?"

"This morning. It was brewing for some time, he tells me. A political dispute with the new management. So, as of this afternoon, he is working for us!"

"Really?" Cecily said, her voice strangely flat. "That *is* nice."

Barnett caught the tone in her voice. "You are displeased," he said. "I thought the news would please you. Now tell me what the trouble is. Do you dislike the man? Are you peeved because I didn't consult you first? I felt that I had to act quickly, or I might lose the chance, and thus the man."

"I am not, as you put it, *peeved*!" Cecily said, tossing her head. "I am rather hurt. I thought I was doing a good job here."

"But you *are*, Cecily. An excellent job."

"If I am doing such a good job, why am I being replaced? Surely that is what Mr. Pummery will be doing here—my job!"

Barnett sighed. Why was it that he no longer seemed able to say the right thing to Cecily? She seemed to find some source of hurt or anger in everything he said and everything he did for the past few months. He didn't understand what had changed. He knew that he was so blinded by the strength of his feelings toward Cecily that he couldn't be sure whether it was his behavior or her attitude that was now different. But whatever it was, it created, not exactly friction, but more a sense of confusion in his dealings with her.

"I am sorry, Cecily," Barnett said. "I thought you understood. For the past year you have been berating me for keeping you behind a desk. This, you have observed, is not journalism. In hiring Mr. Pummery I was only attempting to free you from what you now do as office manager so that you can become one of the principal correspondents of the American News Service. You will be doing the same job I am myself—covering those stories that are most important to us, or that require a special understanding of the American market."

Cecily looked at him skeptically. "I am not, I trust, expected to devote myself to such 'important' stories as the charity bazaar of the Duchess of Malfi, or the favorite dinners of Our Dear Queen. Or am I?"

"Not at all," Barnett assured her. "Miss Burnside does those stories very well, and would feel quite put out if you were to take them over. 'From each according to her ability,' as Professor Moriarty is so fond of repeating."

"What is that supposed to mean?" Cecily asked.

"This fellow who used to spend the better part of each day in the British Museum said it all the time," Barnett told her. "Something to do with an outrageous economic theory he was developing. Professor Moriarty had many long arguments with the man in the Reading Room before he went back to Germany or someplace."

"And what is my ability?" Cecily asked. "What sort of events am I to cover?"

"I have a subject in mind for you now that I believe you will find of interest," Barnett told her.

Cecily drew her legs up under her in the chair, tucking in the folds of her skirt, and gazed intently at Barnett. Some emotion that Barnett could not fathom sparkled in her eyes. "Elucidate," she said.

"Murder," Barnett stated, staring back into the sparkling pools of clear blue that were Cecily's eyes.

"Fascinating," she agreed. "And whom am I to kill?"

"You," Barnett told her, "are to report. Someone else has been doing the killing."

Cecily turned her head to the side and gazed thoughtfully through the glass window in the office wall. "Why?" she asked. "I appreciate the compliment, of course. But I can foresee many problems arising if I attempt to report on murder stories. I'm sure you must already have realized that."

"There will be difficulties," Barnett agreed. "Having a woman journalist following the course of a murder investigation and reporting on it will be an original idea to the authorities, and I'm sure they will react in an original manner. But I think you will do an excellent job with the story, if the gentlemen of the CID don't put too many obstructions in the way of your journalistic endeavors. I think it's worth giving it a shot, if you're willing."

"A shot?" Cecily smiled. "One of your American expressions? How apt in this instance. I am certainly willing to 'give it a shot,' if you think any good can come of it. But tell me, why do you suppose the readers of two hundred newspapers in the United States are going to be interested in a British murder?"

"The interest that the public—British or American—has for the sensational should not be underrated," Barnett told her. "And I, for one, am perfectly happy trying to fill that interest."

"Very good, Mr. Barnett," Cecily said. "Repellent as the idea is to us, we shall explore the sensational and examine the outré for the sake of our readers. I shall write a series of closely reasoned articles that fascinate by the compelling logic of their conclusions and the immense understanding of human nature so displayed. And I shall sign them C. Perrine, so that none of our readers will be shocked by the knowledge that a member of the fair sex has been delving into the sordid, seamy side of life in the world's greatest metropolis."

"I thought the idea would interest you, Miss Perrine," Barnett said. "But first, of course, we are going to have to go out into the world and catch our man."

"And what man, may I ask, are we looking for?"

"There have been three murders in London within the past month," Barnett told her, "that were, apparently, all done by the same man. The victims were all upper-class, and all three murders were committed in circumstances that were, if not impossible, at least highly improbable."

Cecily Perrine nodded. "Lord Walbine," she said, "and the Honorable George Venn, and Isadore Stanhope. Very interesting cases."

"That's them," Barnett agreed. "I've noticed that you have formed the practice of rewriting all the murder stories yourself, which is why I decided you would be interested in this assignment."

"I consider myself a competent writer, Mr. Barnett, as you know," Cecily said. "But I would not altogether affirm my competence to interview a Scotland Yard inspector in such a manner as to command his respect, and otherwise conduct the necessary investigation. This is my only hesitation."

"I'll assist you the first few times you conduct such interviews, until you get over your tentative feelings and the gentlemen at the CID get accustomed to your presence."

"I would appreciate such assistance," Cecily said.

"It will be my pleasure," Barnett told her. "I, also, am fascinated by mysterious murders."

"A fascination that I trust the rest of your countrymen share," Cecily said. "With both of us working on it, the stories are going to have to be carried by over three-quarters of our total subscription to pay for our time."

"We'll have over ninety percent," Barnett assured her. "This story has the one element that a purely American murder can never have: nobility. Two out of three of the victims were possessed of noble blood. You'll have to remember to play that up."

"Yes, indeed," Cecily agreed sweetly. "I shall research the lineage of Mr. Stanhope, the deceased barrister. Perhaps somewhere this side of the Domesday Book we can find the taint of noble blood running, in ever so diluted quantities, through his veins also."

"Not a bad idea," Barnett told her enthusiastically. "Put someone on that."

"Dear me," Cecily said. "I thought I was being humorous."

"Americans take British nobility very seriously," Barnett told her, "being deprived, as they are, of one of their own."

"It is of their own doing," Cecily said. "Had they remained loyal British subjects a hundred years ago, they could have their own nobility living among them now, and be as lucky as the Irish in that regard."

Their conversation was interrupted by a small person in a loudly checked suit with a spotless gray bowler tucked firmly under his left arm, who trotted between the desks in the outer office and rapped importantly on the inner office door.

Barnett pulled the door open. "Well," he exclaimed, "if it isn't the Mummer!"

" 'Course it is," the little man replied. "Who says it ain't?" "Mummer" Tolliver was a fellow resident of 64 Russell Square, occupying a low-ceilinged room under the eaves and serving the professor as a general factotum and midget-of-all-work.

"Hello, Mummer," Cecily said. "My, you're looking natty today."

"Afternoon, Miss Perrine," the Mummer said, holding his bowler stiffly in front of his chest and giving his head two precise nods in her direction. "You're a rare vision of dainty loveliness yourself, Miss Perrine. S'welp me if you ain't!"

"Why, thank you, Mummer," Cecily said.

"I have a communication for Mr. Barnett from the professor," Mummer said. " 'Into his hand,' the professor told me."

"Why, then, here is my hand," Barnett said, extending his hand.

Tolliver examined the appendage carefully. "Seems to be," he admitted, pulling a buff envelope from a hidden recess between two buttons of his checked jacket and passing it over to Barnett. "There. Now my duty is discharged, and I must be trotting along. Afternoon, Miss Perrine. Afternoon, all." Adjusting his bowler carefully on his slicked-down black hair, he did a neat shuffle-off to the front door and exited.

"What a charming little man," Cecily said.

"He is that," Barnett agreed, as the world's shortest confidence man and pickpocket disappeared around the door.

Barnett slit open the envelope and removed the sheet of foolscap within. *Railways*, the note said in Moriarty's precise hand, *with particular emphasis on the London and South-Western. M.*

"A task for us," Barnett said, slipping the note into his pocket. "Assign someone to research the London and South-Western Railway line. Bill it to the special account."

"What sort of research?" Cecily asked, looking curiously at him.

Barnett shrugged. "General," he said. "Whatever they're up to these days. I don't know. Tell them it's for a comparison of British and American railroads."

"Fine," Cecily said. "What *is* it for?"

"I don't know," Barnett said. "The ways of Professor Moriarty are mysterious. As you know, he is a consultant. Perhaps he has a commission from the railway, or perhaps from a rival railway. He is very close-mouthed."

"Hummm," Cecily said.

"Well," said Barnett, "let us go along to Scotland Yard and see whom we can speak to about these murders."

FIVE

SCOTLAND YARD

Mere theory is not encouraged at the Yard.
—Arthur H. Beavan

The hansom cab passed under the arch and rattled along the ancient, well-worn paving stones of Scotland Yard. Swerving to miss a flock of off-duty constables heading across the road for a "quick 'un" at the Clarence before they went home for the night, it pulled to a stop in front of the dirty yellow brick building that housed the Metropolitan Police office.

"Here we are," Barnett said, helping Cecily Perrine down from the cab and tossing a coin up to the cabby. "The Criminal Investigation Department is in the building to the left here."

The constable guarding the narrow entrance to the CID nodded at Barnett's question. "That would be Inspector Lestrade." He checked a little pegboard on the wall by his side. "As it happens, the inspector is in at the moment. Room 109. You must wait here until I can get a uniformed officer to escort you upstairs."

"Why, Constable!" Cecily smiled sweetly. "We do not look dangerous, do we?"

" 'Taint me, miss," the constable said. "It's the regulations. Ever since that bombing in the Yard three years ago by them anarchists, when all them policemen and civilians were blown about, with three of them dying, some constable stands here day and night, in this unheated doorway, and sees that all visitors are properly escorted upstairs. Them as are in authority were supposed to put a booth here for the constable's use, but it's been three years now and they ain't done it. Now as there's talk of a new building, I suppose they won't ever."

"I thought the bombing was outside," Barnett said.

"Yes, sir," the constable agreed. "Around to the right, there. By the public house. You can still see the damage to the bricks."

"But there's no constable on duty over there," Cecily said.

"No, miss."

"Then somebody could still chuck a dynamite bomb right where the last one was."

"Yes, miss."

"I don't understand."

"No, miss. Ah, here is someone now. Constable Hawkins, will you please escort these two people up to Room 109. Inspector Lestrade."

Room 109 was small, with one tiny soot-covered window, extremely cluttered, and, when they entered, apparently devoid of human life. Constable Hawkins, a small, taciturn man whose uniform looked as though it had been constructed for someone squatter and considerably more massive, obviously felt that he should not leave them alone in the room. So he stood fidgeting silently and uncomfortably, resisting all attempts to be drawn into conversation and turning very red in the face when Cecily spoke to him.

It was about ten minutes before Inspector Lestrade returned to the room, scurrying along the corridor with a sheaf of documents in a leather folder under his arm. "Ha! I know you," he said to Barnett, shaking his hand firmly. "Barnett's your name."

"You have a good memory, Inspector," Barnett said. "It's been almost two years since we met in that house on Little George Street."

"A den of anarchists it was, too," Lestrade said. "You gentlemen were lucky to get out of there alive." He looked around, rather puzzled. "There was someone here when I left."

"No one here when we arrived, Inspector," Constable Hawkins assured Lestrade, standing at full brace like a little figure from a box of tin soldiers.

"Thank you, Hawkins," Lestrade said. "You can go." He turned back to Barnett. "And who is your charming companion?"

"Miss Cecily Perrine, may I present Detective Inspector Giles Lestrade of the CID. Inspector Lestrade, Miss Perrine is a valued associate of mine at the American News Service."

"A pleasure, Miss Perrine," Lestrade said, looking for all the world, as Cecily said later, like an eager bear as he took her hand and pressed it politely. "A sincere pleasure, I assure you."

"Charmed, Inspector," Cecily said. "Are all Scotland Yard inspectors so gallant?"

"You catch more flies with honey, miss," Lestrade said. "It always pays to be polite, and it costs you nothing. Or so I tell my men."

"And here I thought it was me," Cecily said, pouting, "and I find, instead, that it's regulation."

"Well, um, miss," Lestrade said, caught in the realization that his tact was not up to his manners, "I can assure you that in your case it is a pleasure to follow the regulations."

"Neat recovery, Inspector," Barnett said, smiling.

"Um," Lestrade said. "And what can I do for you? No problems, I hope?"

"Nothing for the police, Inspector," Barnett said. "No, we've come here on business, but it's our business rather than yours."

"Ah! And how is that?"

"We are planning an article, or a series of articles, on the murders you've been having here in London," Cecily said.

"Now that covers a lot of territory, miss," Lestrade said. "There've been a great many murders here in London during the twenty-six years I've been on the force."

"We had the recent ones in mind," Barnett said. "Lord Walbine—"

"Him!" Lestrade said. "Come, sit down. Just push the papers off that chair, Mr. Barnett. I'll have someone come along and file them. Should have done it weeks ago. The department is nothing but a maze of paperwork. It's a wonder that any of us ever get any work done, what with all the papers we have to fill out every time we take a step."

Cecily perched daintily on the edge of the old wooden chair that Lestrade thrust toward her. Barnett dropped into an ancient chair with a bentwood back, after taking Lestrade's advice and pushing the papers onto the floor. The chair creaked alarmingly, but it held.

"Now then," Lestrade said. "What do you want to know about Lord Walbine's murder? It *is* a puzzler, that I'll admit."

"And George Venn," Cecily said, "and Isadore Stanhope, the barrister."

"Well now," Lestrade said, "interestingly enough we think we have just solved the Venn and Stanhope murders."

"Is that right?" Barnett asked.

"It is," Lestrade said, looking exceedingly smug. "And, as it happens, arrests are expected momentarily in those cases."

"Congratulations are in order then, are they, Inspector?" Barnett asked. "You have solved a difficult case and brought a dangerous killer to justice. Who was the killer, then, and what was his motive?"

"Well," Lestrade said, glancing at the door, "this is confidential for the moment. The orders have gone out to arrest the culprits, but until I am sure they have been apprehended I would not want the news to appear in the press."

"You have our word, Inspector," Barnett said.

"Did you say *culprits*?" Cecily asked. "There was more than one person involved in the murders?"

"That there was," Lestrade agreed. "Each of the two murdered gentlemen was done in by his own butler!"

"The butler did it?" Barnett asked.

"Incredible, isn't it? But there's no telling to what lengths greed or fear will drive some people."

"What *was* their motive?" Cecily asked. "It was greed, wasn't it? They were each systematically stealing from their respective employer, and were about to be caught red-handed."

"Well, miss, we haven't found any indication—"

"Fear, then! They were both members of a secret society of anarchists, and their evil captain had ordered them to kill their masters under pain of some horrible mutilation or death."

"We have given that theory some thought, miss," Lestrade said seriously.

"You have?" Barnett sounded surprised.

"Yes, sir. You see, there was a mysterious bit of newspaper in Lord Walbine's waistcoat pocket when he was killed."

"How fascinating!" Barnett said. "Was it a clipping from a London paper?"

"It was, we believe, from the *Morning Chronicle* classified section. What they call the agony column. But it wasn't exactly a clipping—more of a ripping," Lestrade said.

"What did it say?" Cecily asked.

"It was ripped from the middle of the classified pages. One column wide by about half an inch high. On one side it said, 'Thank you St. Simon for remembering the knights.' On the other side it said, 'Fourteen point four by six point thirteen: three-four-seven.' Written out, you know; not just the numbers."

"Two separate advertisements?"

"That is right, miss. One on each side of the paper, as you might expect. As far as we know, unconnected. Which one had relevance to poor Lord Walbine, I have no idea. But you must admit they are both odd. Put one in mind of some sort of secret society."

"How does this affect the two butlers?" Cecily asked.

"Well, you see, miss, they are both members of the same club."

"Club?" Barnett asked. "I didn't know there were clubs for butlers."

"There is a club for butlers and valets," Lestrade told him. "It is known as the Gentlemen's Gentlemen, and it is located off Oxford Street in Soho. Margery, who was the butler to the deceased Honorable George Venn, and Lizzard, who was the personal valet to the late Mr. Stanhope, are both members of the said Gentlemen's Gentlemen in good standing."

"Come now, Inspector," Barnett said, "you can't seriously believe that these two men murdered their employers simply because they are members of the same club?"

"That was merely the starting point for what I would like to refer to as a fine example of the value of good methodical police work. With that fact to work on, my men went out and knocked on doors and asked questions. No fancy staring at footsteps under a microscope or examining the dirt under the victim's fingernails or any of that nonsense. Very quickly we discovered that Margery spends his afternoons off at the racetrack, and that Lizzard has a lady friend in Wembley."

"Surely even valets are allowed to have lady friends," Cecily said. "I would have thought that having a lady friend was one of the indelible rights of man."

Lestrade smiled tolerantly. "Yes, but the lengths that a man will go to keep a woman have, on occasion, been known to approach the criminal."

"Oh, was he keeping her then?" Cecily asked.

"I meant that figuratively, miss," Lestrade said. "He was most assuredly trying to keep her interest. At any rate, he was spending far beyond what one would assume his means to be, as was Margery."

"So you think they killed their employers for money?"

"We don't think that they did it themselves," Lestrade said. "Not at all. The similarity of methods used in the two murders would seem to indicate that one man had done both. Our theory is that Margery and Lizzard each, either with the other's knowledge or without, hired the same man to do the killing. After we've picked them up, we should be able to frighten one of them into revealing who the actual killer was. And, when we have him, we may well have the killer of Lord Walbine."

"So you *do* think it was the same man," Cecily asked.

"Yes, miss. But not, if you take my meaning, part of the same conspiracy. We haven't been able to get anything on Lord Walbine's butler, one Lemming by name; and at the time of the murder his lordship was quite without a valet, the last one having left for Chicago to open a haberdashery with his brother-in-law two weeks before."

"Well, I'm glad to see that Scotland Yard is so efficient." Barnett said. "Miss Perrine or I will keep in touch with you as the case progresses. That is, if you don't mind having your name in print in two hundred American newspapers."

"Well, now," Lestrade said, "the Yard discourages personal publicity; but if it's to be in American newspapers, I don't see how there could by any problem. I will, naturally, be delighted to keep you and Miss Perrine fully informed as to the progress of the investigation."

"I thank you, Inspector," Barnett said. "Our American readers will be fascinated to read all the little details as to how a Scotland Yard investigation is carried out."

"I think I can give them a pretty fair example," Lestrade said, trying not to look too self-important. "It is not a matter of brilliance—I don't claim to be brilliant—but a matter of following established procedure and taking care that all the detail work gets done. That's what captures your murderers."

"Well, thank you very much, Inspector," Barnett said. "We shall be going along now. One or the other of us will be visiting you daily to hear the latest details."

"I shall be happy to oblige."

"Thank you. If it's all right with you, I think we shall go now to visit the scenes of the crimes, so that we can better describe them to our readers."

"Certainly," Lestrade said. "The Yard always tries to help out journalists, when it can. You won't let on now about the arrests?"

"My word, Inspector. Not a mention of either of their names until we hear that they are safely behind bars."

"It has been delightful meeting you, Inspector Lestrade," Cecily said. "It is comforting to know that our safety lies in such capable hands."

"We do our best, miss," Lestrade said, escorting them to the door and beaming at them as they left.

"You *are* an ass, Lestrade," a voice behind the inspector said as he gazed down the hall. He turned to find Sherlock Holmes sitting in the chair he had just vacated.

"Holmes! Where did you come from? I thought you had left."

"I got bored sitting there waiting for you to return," Holmes said, "so I started going through your files. When I saw your company approaching, I concealed myself between the filing cabinet and the wall, over there."

"I see," Lestrade said. "And why did you do a thing like that?"

"That young man, Barnett, is in the employ of Professor Moriarty, as you well know. It occurred to me that it might be a good idea to hear what he had to say when he thought himself unobserved."

"So? And what did he say?"

"Nothing. That imbecile of a constable never left them alone. What a shame—it might have been quite instructive."

"You still have that bee in your bonnet about the professor, eh, Holmes?" Lestrade chuckled. "Well, I don't fancy that he's your killer this time. I can't quite see him as an habitué of the Gentlemen's Gentlemen."

"Lestrade, you are incorrigible," Holmes said. "You really believe those poor butlers had something to do with the crimes?"

"I believe it well enough so that I'm having them held on suspicion," Lestrade said. "I don't take such action as a joke."

"Well, do that if it pleases you," Holmes told him. "But there is another action that I want you to take. You are obliged to follow my instructions, I believe?"

"We are," Lestrade said. "Orders is orders, whatever I think of them, and I have been so ordered. What do you want me to do?"

"I think those two came to pump you for information," Holmes said. "And, if that's so, then Moriarty is up to his neck in this in some way, and I intend to find out how. I want you to detail ten of your best plainclothesmen to follow Moriarty wherever he goes from now on, and report to you on his every move."

"If you say so, Mr. Holmes," Lestrade said. "Ten of my best it is. He won't make a move without our knowing of it."

"Nonsense," Holmes said. "Of course he will. I'm just hoping that this will annoy him sufficiently that he'll make a mistake. A small mistake, that's all I ask."

"Um," Lestrade said.

THE FOX

Was it a friend or foe that spread these lies?
Nay, who but infants question in such wise,
'Twas one of my most intimate enemies.
— DANTE GABRIEL ROSSETTI

Old Potts had been with Moriarty from the beginning, and there were few around who knew how far back that went. Slowly, and with great love, over the course of many years, he had converted the upper cellar in the house at 64 Russell Square into a huge, well-equipped basement laboratory and workshop.

The old man had his bed in a corner of the workshop. He seldom came upstairs, and almost never left the house, except for occasional visits to the professor's observatory on Crimpton Moor. And he was happy thus. Professor Moriarty spent much time in the basement with old Potts. It was here that he designed the delicate apparatus with which he studied the cosmos and tested his physical and astronomical theories.

Within the past year, old Potts had helped Moriarty fabricate a mechanism which could determine the speed of light to better than three parts per thousand. Together they had experimented with a series of evacuated glass valves with sealed electrodes of various rare materials, and observed fascinating and as yet inexplicable results when an electric current was passed through. It may be that they also had constructed a device which would enable one to bypass an electrical alarm system without setting off the alarm, and an instrument which would allow one to hear the tumblers falling in the latest model wall safe. If so, it is perhaps reprehensible that such mundane practical engineering projects were necessary to support the professor's flights of pure science. But that is the way of the world.

When Barnett came down into the workshop a few days after

his visit to Scotland Yard, he found Moriarty and old Potts working together on a new design of light-frame astronomical telescope, specially constructed to be carried high above the earth in a giant hydrogen balloon. The telescope was strapped into a great jig on the central table while Professor Moriarty, with his shirtsleeves rolled up, made final adjustments in a series of setscrews around the telescope's rim. Old Potts, with his lab smock wrapped around him, followed behind the professor and put little dabs of cement on each screw to lock it permanently in place.

"Well, it looks as if you've got it just about finished, Professor," Barnett commented, strolling over to inspect the intricate, spidery mechanism that held the highly polished mirror.

"It had better be," Moriarty said. "It lofts next week, if the weather on the moor stays clear."

"You are going off to Crimpton Moor, then?" Barnett asked.

Moriarty nodded. The estate he maintained on Crimpton Moor included a residence, a workshop, and an observatory housing his precious twelve-inch reflector. This was the site of most of his astronomical observations. "Prince Tseng Li-Chang is already in residence, preparing the balloon," he said. "His son claims to have perfected a new emulsion for the photographic plates that will more than double their sensitivity. If it performs as promised, we should get some fascinating pictures."

"What do you expect to learn from these balloon experiments, Professor?" Barnett asked. "And please don't just fob me off with your usual reply that you're furthering human knowledge. I'm sure you are. But as an answer, you will have to admit it is rather vague."

Moriarty snorted. "You, a journalist, are concerned about an answer being 'rather vague'? Truly the millennium has arrived."

"I ask purely out of my own interest, Professor," Barnett assured him. "The great newspaper-reading public will not concern itself with staring at Mars unless it feels that something up there is staring back."

Professor Moriarty made the final adjustment on the aluminum-bronze telescope mounting and put the tiny screwdriver back in its small case. He turned and regarded Barnett with interest. "Now that," he said, "is a truly fascinating notion!"

"How's that?"

"Ah, Benjamin, you know not what you say," Moriarty replied. "For some time I have been pondering ways to interest the common man in the abstruse sciences. You may have just given me a valuable suggestion: 'Something is staring back.' I like the sound of that! And, indeed, there is a good chance that something *is* staring back."

"I assume that you are not speaking religiously, Professor," Barnett said.

"Religiously? Indeed, no. Neither religiously nor metaphorically nor psychically nor figuratively. Somewhere out there, Mr. Barnett, there are intelligences greater than our own. How could it be else? And these beings might, even now, be watching us with the same diligence that a hymenopterologist studies a colony of ants. And for purposes as far beyond our understanding as the hymenopterologist's purposes are beyond the understanding of the ant."

"You really believe this?"

"I am forced to this conclusion by the inescapable logic of the universe," Moriarty said.

"But intelligences superior to our own?"

Moriarty smiled. "I am very afraid," he said, "that any intelligences we find—or who find us—will be superior to our own."

"You speak as a confirmed atheist," Barnett said as he sat on the wooden bench running along the great worktable.

Moriarty shrugged. "It is not that I disbelieve in God," he said, "it is merely that I see no need to drag some immortal being into the equation in order to explain the universe."

Moriarty's housekeeper, Mrs. H, appeared on the landing leading down to the basement. "I trust you are ready with your drayage, Professor," she said, folding her arms across the severe bosom of her stiffly starched black dress. "The dray awaits."

"Splendid," Mrs. H," Moriarty said, rolling his sleeves down and shrugging his arms back into his gray frock coat. "The instrument is ready, and the packing is prepared. It only remains to lower the telescope into the crate and nail it shut."

Mrs. H sniffed. "I shall inform the drayman that you will be within the hour," she said.

"I trust my instructions were followed?" Moriarty asked.

"Implicitly, Professor," Mrs. H told him. "The dray is around the corner on Montague Street, by the hotel. Mr. Maws awaited its arrival."

"Excellent!" Moriarty said. "Then this large crate, which will almost immediately contain the telescope, and these other five crates which are already nailed down, are to be taken out through the accommodation exit and loaded into the dray. Great care is to be taken; this is delicate apparatus."

"I shall see to it, Professor."

"I know you will, Mrs. H. You are a paragon of getting-it-done-properly. You run this household with an efficiency which amazes even me. It is a constant delight to be associated with you. Please send the Mummer down to me now."

"Very well, Professor." Mrs. H nodded and withdrew.

What Moriarty called the "accommodation exit" was a back way that led, through a twisting maze of alleys and two subtly concealed doors in separating walls, to the side entrance to the hotel on Montague Street. "Why are you going out that way, Professor?" Barnett asked. "Are you sneaking this equipment out?"

"I never sneak," Moriarty said firmly. "Since my business is nobody else's affair, I fail to see how my effort to avoid prying eyes can be considered 'sneaking.' "

"I take it back, Professor," Barnett said. "I wasn't aware that we had any prying eyes about. Whose eyes are they, and what are they trying to find out?"

"A good question," Moriarty said, "and one deserving of a factual answer. At the moment I have only conjecture, but I expect—Ah! Perhaps we can find out now; here is the Mummer."

"I didn't want to disturb you while you was at work down here, Professor," the little man said, bounding down the wooden staircase.

"Thoughtful of you, Mummer," Moriarty said. "Did you succeed?"

" 'Course I did, what do you think?" the Mummer said, looking offended.

"With what result?"

"I buzzed the tall gent what's been mucking about outside keeping the admiral company, and found a rozzer in his poke."

"You see," Moriarty said, turning to Barnett. "It is as I suspected."

"What is?" Barnett asked.

"This house has been being watched for the past two days. Three men at least, at all times. Now Tolliver has picked the pocket of the tall gentleman who was loitering across the street by the statue of Lord Hornblower, and found a police badge in his wallet."

" 'At's right," Tolliver agreed. " 'Oo says I didn't?"

"This sudden interest in our doings corresponds with your visit to the CID," Moriarty told Barnett. "There may be some connection between that correspondence and the fact that Mr. Sherlock Holmes has been retained to assist the police in the matter of those murders that so fascinate you."

"How do you know that?" Barnett asked. "Sherlock Holmes certainly didn't tell you. He doesn't seem to have a very high opinion of you."

"Every time a purse is snatched anywhere in the greater London area, Holmes is certain that I am behind it," Moriarty said. "It gets tiresome."

"How do you know that he is helping Scotland Yard solve the murders?"

Moriarty chuckled. "I spoke to his landlady."

"His landlady?"

"Yes. Mrs. Hudson, by name. Charming lady. A bit deaf. I dressed myself as a nonconformist clergyman and went to Baker Street at a time I knew Holmes would be out. I told Mrs. Hudson that I needed the great man's services immediately. I was very put out that he wasn't at home. I told her I needed Holmes in relation to a case involving a politician, a lighthouse, and a trained cormorant. She told me that it was just the sort of thing that Mr. Holmes would be happy to take up, but that at the moment he was working with the police on the baffling murders of those aristocrats."

"I see," Barnett said.

"I told the charming lady how sorry I was to have missed Mr. Holmes, and that I was unable to wait. She begged me to stay, saying she was sure Holmes would want to talk with me. I said something to the effect that I thought so myself, but I really couldn't stay."

Barnett shook his head. "There is a certain justice in all of this, you will have to admit," he said. "While you are out with a false beard questioning Sherlock Holmes's landlady, he is having your house watched by Scotland Yard."

"There is indeed an elegant symmetry," Moriarty admitted. "But I assure you there was no false beard. Ecclesiastical muttonchops was as far as I went."

The Mummer hopped down from the bench, where he had been examining the telescope. "Quite a pickle you've got there, Professor," he said. "Is there anything else you need of me?"

Moriarty thought this over for a minute. "Yes," he said. "Go to that cupboard in the corner and open it up. Mr. Potts, please give the Mummer your key."

Tolliver took the key from old Potts and skipped over to the corner. He opened the cabinet, and for a second Barnett felt his heart rap against his chest and he caught his breath. There, inside the cabinet, was Professor Moriarty!

Barnett half turned to make sure that the professor was still, in reality, standing alongside of him, and then he approached the cabinet to figure out what he had just seen. It still, even from four feet away, appeared to be Moriarty closeted within the narrow confines of the small cabinet. He bent down to examine the apparition. "A dummy!" he exclaimed.

"Indeed," Moriarty said. "It was made at my direction some time ago. Amberly, the forger, did the face of *papier-mâché*, with the coloring accomplished with stage makeup dissolved in wax. Do you think it is good? You are a better judge than I, as my face is seldom visible to me except reversed in a glass."

"Good?" Barnett cried. "It is excellent! Remarkable!"

"I am glad to hear that," Moriarty said. "Because for the next two weeks, that dummy will be me." He turned to old Potts. "Do you think you can make a frame for it that the Mummer can wear on his shoulders?"

Old Potts looked reflectively at Tolliver and at the dummy. "Take a couple of hours," he said.

"Excellent," Moriarty said. "Then I leave with my telescope. Mummer, you will be me while I am gone. Follow Barnett's suggestions in that regard. That should keep the hounds away from Crimpton Moor while I complete these observations."

"I'll do my best, Professor," the Mummer said.

Moriarty turned to Barnett. "I leave you in charge of such of my activities as come within your purview in my absence," he said. "Do not get overenthusiastic. I shall see you in a fortnight."

"Goodbye, Professor," Barnett said. "Good luck!"

"Indeed?" Moriarty said. "Let us hope that luck plays small part in either of our endeavors for the next two weeks. For if you invoke the good, you may have to settle for the other. Goodbye, Mr. Barnett."

SEVEN

INTERLUDE: THE WIND

Thou wilt not with predestined evil round
Enmesh, and then impute my fall to sin!
— EDWARD FITZGERALD

By ten-thirty in the evening he was done with his day's work, which had been his life's work; the daily repetition that had been his life, and was now but a senseless blur that marked the passing time. At ten-thirty he would be able to come to life; the new life that spread its endless days before him: days of seeking, days of hunting, days of revenge, days full of the infinite jest that had become his life, the jest that was death. At ten-thirty, with the sun safely down, the creature of the night that he had become could once more roam the streets of London and stalk its prey.

But he had to hunt out the right streets, for his prey was subtle; stalk silently through the ever-changing streets, for his prey was wily. And his prey was clever, for they went about disguised as gentlemen; but he knew them for secret devils by the mark of Cain, the hidden mark of Cain they wore.

He walked west on Long Acre, with a quick, gliding step, his great cape gathered about his stocky form, and considered where to go; where best to hunt for the hated men, the evil men, the doomed men.

It was the hunt that kept him alive. He did not want to live. His wish, his dream, his desire was but to die; to join his beloved Annie. But first there was this work to do. He was the wind.

This was Wednesday, the last Wednesday in March, and that was good. The fog, the all-enveloping fog, had returned tonight, and that was also good. Wednesday they were out, the men he sought. Wednesday they gamed, they drank, they did unspeakable things to innocent children. This Wednesday, with the help of a nameless god, another of them would die.

Frequently they changed the place at which they met, the building which housed them in their pleasures. Their horrible pleasures. They must have some means of communicating with each other, some devil's post office by which they could know when to change and where then to go. But although he had searched for some clue to what it was in the chambers of those he had already killed, and though he was skilled at reading such clues, he had not found it yet.

But he had his Judas goats, those he knew who would unknowingly be spared so that they could lead him to those he sought.

He quickened his step. It would not do to reach the Allegro after the evening performance had let out. The Allegro always ran a trifle late, trying to cram in fourteen turns where most houses were satisfied with twelve. But it served him well these nights. This Judas goat liked pretty girls, and the Allegro had a line of pretty girls. This Judas goat had a box at the Allegro, the closest box to the stage.

He stopped across the street from the Allegro, out of the actinic glare that curved around the theater entrance from the bright gaslights embedded in the ornate marquee overhead. From this shadowed position he could see all who left the theater through the lobby, without himself being seen. If necessary he could reach the cab stand in a few strides, if he had to give chase.

Five minutes passed, and then ten, as he stood in his dark corner, muffled by the creeping fog. And then the lobby of the Allegro began to fill, and the patrons of such of the arts as were represented by the evening's entertainments prepared to go home. Or elsewhere.

There he was—there! The dried-up little man with the German mustache, the latest baron of an ancient line, the evil man who joined with other men to practice pain, the Judas goat. The little man made no move toward the line of cabs; perhaps tonight he had come in his own carriage. And, indeed, there he was now, pushing his way through the throng, coming out to the curb and looking off down the street, stamping his feet with impatience because his carriage was not already there waiting for him.

And here came the private carriages, turning the corner in a line, fresh from some coop in the next block where the drivers waited until a page boy from the theater raced over to tell them the show was letting out.

The third one, the dull-black brougham with the red tracery, belonged to the little baron with the German mustache. The man who had become the wind stepped off the curb and approached the brougham from the far side, keeping out of sight of the driver, and straining his ears to hear what the Judas goat said.

"Wait here, Hackamore," the Judas goat told his driver. "I will have a charming young companion joining me in a few moments, then we will be going on to Brennen's for a late supper."

The listener who had become the wind slapped his fist into his open palm. So! The baron had an assignation with one of the show girls; there could be no other explanation. Another poor innocent was about to be drawn into his web. And if the baron was going on to a late supper at Brennen's, he would not be visiting his other friends this evening, and so he would be of little use as a Judas goat.

The baron's plans would have to be disarranged.

He went down the narrow alley to the stage entrance of the Allegro, where a pride of young gallants in evening dress were trying to talk their way past the stage doorman. "Evening, Tinker," he said, pushing past the young men to the gate.

"Ev'nin, Perfessor," the stage doorman said, releasing the catch for him. "Good to see yer again. You comin' back to us?"

"It could happen," he said. "You can never tell what's going to happen in this life. But for now, just a little visit."

He went up the circular iron staircase to the dressing rooms and knocked on the door to the girls' chorus. "One of you ladies supposed to meet a skinny gent with a walrus mustache out front?" he called.

The door opened and an attractive slender girl in a rose dressing robe came out. She had long brown hair which curled about her oval face in tight ringlets. "I am," she said. "Tell him I'll only be a couple of minutes more, please."

She must be fairly new to the chorus at the Allegro, he thought. He had never seen her before. He would have remembered. Annie had had hair like that. "I'm not from the baron, dear," he told her. "I've come to give you a warning."

"What?" The girl put her hands on her hips and glared up at him. "Listen, mister. I don't know who you are, and I don't care. But I want to tell you something. What I do is my own business, and I don't need no lessons in propriety, or any of the other social graces! So you can just get your bluenose out of here!"

"No, no, you misunderstand," he said, blocking her attempt to close the door. "Believe me, I have no interest in your actions, young lady, proper or improper. Do as you like with whom you like for all of me. It is your health and your career that concern me."

She stopped trying to close the door and looked up into his face. "That's what the baron told me," she said. "He's interested in my career. What's *your* interest?"

"I don't want to see you get into serious trouble," he said.

"What sort of trouble?"

"The wrong sort," he told her, improvising carefully. "The baron's wife has detectives following him."

"Detectives!"

"That's right. And she is determined to make trouble for him. She won't care about what happens to you in the process. If they catch you with him, it would ruin your career before it's rightly begun."

"Say, what's your interest in this?"

"Nothing," he told her. "I don't want to see you hurt. You remind me of my own daughter."

"Oh," she said. "Listen, I didn't know he was married, mister. Honest, I didn't."

"Of course not," he said. "*He* certainly wouldn't have told you."

"What should I do?"

"Don't go with him. Not tonight or ever, if you want to be safe."

"I won't," she said, looking sad. Perhaps it was the thought of all the fine dinners she would miss.

"You should warn the other girls," he said.

"I will."

"Write him a note. He's waiting out front."

"What should I say?"

"Tell him one of your chums is sick and you have to stay and take care of her. Have the page boy deliver it to him outside."

"All right, mister. Listen, I don't know who you are, but I suppose I should thank you."

"It is my pleasure, I assure you, miss," he told her. "Write that note now!"

"I will."

He tipped his hat and left her, whistling softly to himself. Once back outside he went around to the front, where the Judas goat was waiting by his carriage, impatiently tapping his feet and glaring at his pocket watch.

He crossed the street and stood by the small rank of hansom cabs that were left after most of the throng had already departed.

Here came the page boy now, looking about him for the man the chorus girl had described. He stared at the little baron for a moment, doubtfully, and then decided that it must be he.

He approached the baron and offered the note. The baron took it, and then glared at the boy, who was still standing alongside him waiting for a tip. The boy touched his cap and ran off.

Sweet little Judas goat, thought the man who had become the wind.

The little baron peered at the note, holding it close to his face. Then he stepped under the marquee to try to find enough light to read it. He stared at it intently for a minute, then, with a savage curse, he crumpled the paper into a little ball and threw it into the gutter.

The man watched his Judas goat stamp over to the black brougham, obviously quivering with rage to the roots of his mustache. The baron cursed out his driver and climbed up into the carriage, viciously slamming the door behind him.

The man who had become the wind approached the first hansom in line. "You see that brougham?" he asked the cabby. "I want you to follow it."

"What for, mate?" the cabby demanded, as the man climbed aboard.

"For an extra crown over your fare. A half-sovereign if you don't lose it!"

"A half-sovereign?" the cabby exclaimed. "Right on, mate, you've got it!"

The driver of the brougham flicked his reins, and the Judas goat started off down the dark street. Close behind him followed an avenging wind.

THE HOUNDS

> If once a man indulges himself in murder,
> very soon he comes to think little of
> robbing; and from robbing he next comes
> to drinking and Sabbath-breaking, and
> from that to incivility and procrastination.
> —THOMAS DE QUINCEY

The itinerant street artist, a shabby, crumpled man with a hodge-podge of broken colored chalks, chalk rubble, and chalk dust in an ancient cap by his side, knelt to his work on the pavement at the Russell Square corner of the British Museum, a short distance away from where the guidebook hawkers were plying their dubious wares before the museum's great marble facade. Quickly, and with a deft, sure hand, the street artist sketched a row of pictures on the pavement squares in front of him. His subjects were taken from the great city that surrounded him and was his life. The Crystal Palace appeared in the first square, set in the trees and with a line of carriages along the drive in the foreground. The Houses of Parliament as seen from over Westminster Bridge were the next subject, with one lone tugboat passing on the Thames. Then the West Front of Westminster Abbey appeared, and a parade of well-dressed gentlemen and ladies were quickly chalked in, marching in a stately fashion, two by two, toward the great doors.

A stocky man in a well-worn bowler hat who was lounging by the Russell Square corner came over to stare down appreciatively at the colorful chalkings. "Quite nice, that," he said. "Quite nice, indeed. Here you are!" And he tossed a twopenny bit into the artist's cap.

"Thank 'ee, gov'nor; thank 'ee indeed. Very good of your worship to say so," the artist said, sitting back on his heels. He tossed his chalks back in the cap and stared down at his work. "Is the professor in or out?" he demanded in an undertone.

"What?" The man started backward in surprise, seeming to almost choke for a second.

"Don't be so obvious, my man," the artist said. "Keep looking down at the pavement and answer my question, if you can."

"I don't know what you're talking about," the stocky man said indignantly.

"Don't be ridiculous," the artist said. "You are a CID detective named Gordon. I am Sherlock Holmes."

"Well, I'll be a—" Detective Gordon said, staring down at the grimy artist.

"Quite! Now, is the professor in or out?"

"He went out in his carriage about an hour ago. Macy and Stevens followed behind."

"First time out today?"

"Yes, sir."

"And last night?"

"In at four in the afternoon, and not out again until an hour ago."

"I expected no less."

"How's that, sir?"

Holmes stood up and stretched, stamping some of the stiffness out of his legs. "The body of Sir Geoffrey Cruikstaff, the Minister of Colonial Affairs for her majesty's government, was found this morning," he told the detective. "He was murdered in his study at some time between two and four in the morning, as closely as the autopsy surgeon can tell. It would be too much to expect that Moriarty was abroad and without an alibi to cover the time. And this time, damn him, the police are his alibi."

"Sir Geoffrey Cruikstaff?" Detective Gordon asked. "Why, sir, that is incredible!"

"I agree," Holmes said dryly.

"Why, Sir Geoffrey was under a twenty-four-hour guard. He claimed to have received death threats from some oriental secret society."

"That is correct," said Holmes. "At least his residence was under guard. Sir Geoffrey reserved the right to move about unwatched and unguarded outside his house. Which was, perhaps, foolish. He exercised that right last night, coming home no less than two hours before his death. Nevertheless, it was at home and not outside that he was killed. At the time of his death there were four constables outside the house and two CID plainclothesmen inside the house. And still he was found lying across his desk with his throat cut."

Gordon shook his head. "I had that duty myself a fortnight ago," he said. "Spent the night in his front hall for almost two weeks. And to tell you the truth, sir, I never took them death threats seriously. None of us did. Inspector Gregson just had us there because of Sir Geoffrey's position, you know."

"I know."

"Done in by an oriental secret society. What do you know?"

"It wasn't any oriental secret society," Holmes snapped. "It was the same hand that killed Lord Walbine, and Venn, and Darby, and Stanhope. It was an occidental hand. And, unless I miss my guess, whoever supplied the hand, it was Professor James Moriarty who supplied the brain."

"I can't speak to that, sir," Gordon said, "but I can speak to his location. The professor was in his house all night, and didn't go back out until an hour ago."

"That is when you saw him go out, at any rate," Holmes remarked. "Moriarty is a downy bird, and if he didn't want you to see him going out, why then he would go out without your seeing him."

"Begging your pardon, sir," Detective Gordon said with the apologetic air of one who has interrupted his superiors once too often with information they didn't wish to hear. "It ain't just that we didn't see him go out. We actually, so to speak, saw him at home."

"You *saw* him at home?"

"Yessir. At least, until about one in the morning when the interior lights was turned off in the house."

"I see," Holmes said. "That's good to know."

"Clears him of suspicion, does it, sir?"

"On the contrary," Holmes said. "It makes me more suspicious than ever. Far more suspicious. Exactly what do you mean when you say you *saw* him?"

"We did, sir. Just that. At his window."

"I see. Which window was that?"

"Ground floor, Mr. Holmes. Facing Russell Square. To the right of the door."

"The study window?"

"If you say so, Mr. Holmes. Never having been inside the house,

I couldn't rightly say. What we could see from outside looked like it might be a study."

"What, exactly, did you see? His shadow on the blinds?"

"No, sir. The blinds were drawn aside. We could see right into the room."

"Strange," Holmes said. "And tell me, just what did you observe in the room?"

"We saw the professor. He was sitting behind a desk, or some such. I wouldn't swear it was desk because of the angle, you know."

"And what was he doing?"

"He seemed to be looking at something. We couldn't see what."

"Looking at something? Something on his desk?"

"Not exactly, Mr. Holmes. Something off to one side. There was a part of the room that was not visible from the window, and he was looking over in that direction. Something on the wall, perhaps. Or something in the air."

"In the air?"

"Well, you know, sir. Held up by somebody."

"There was someone else in there with him?"

"Not that we could see, sir. Mr. Barnett came into the room several times, but he didn't stay."

"But there might have been someone else?"

"Yes, sir."

"And Professor Moriarty was looking at something that might have been on the wall or been held up by this possible person whom you could not see. He was staring at this object, whatever it was, the whole time?"

"Well, it may not have been the same thing the whole time," Detective Gordon said. "He would shift his gaze from time to time, as though he were looking at one thing, you know, and then at another."

Holmes stuffed his chalk-filled cap into one of the side pockets of his bulky jacket. "There is something unnatural-sounding in your description," he said. "I wish I had been present to see for myself."

"How do you mean, Mr. Holmes?"

"I'm not sure. Moriarty was sitting at his desk, looking at first on thing and then another."

"That's right."

"For a long time?"

"From nine in the evening until about one or so."

"He didn't leave the study at all in this time?"

"I wouldn't swear to that, sir. But if he did, then it weren't for more than a few minutes. Say ten at most."

"What a strange image," Holmes said. "Moriarty was in his study with the drapes open, sitting behind his desk and looking at something on the wall or in the air in front of him. And he did this for four hours."

"When you put it that way, Mr. Holmes, it does sound strange. But at the time it looked perfectly natural."

"I am sure it did," Holmes said.

"Well," Detective Gordon said, "here he comes now, so if you have any questions, you can ask him yourself."

Holmes dropped to his knees instantly as Moriarty's carriage came into sight down Montague Place. "I prefer to watch without being watched," he told Gordon, pulling the chalk-filled cap out of his pocket and starting on another picture.

Detective Gordon drifted away to lounge on the museum steps, and Holmes began an enthusiastic rendition of St. Paul's Cathedral in pink chalk as Moriarty's four-wheeler passed in front of the British Museum and pulled to a stop at 64 Russell Square. A hansom cab loaded down by two large men in black bowlers who were doing their best to look invisible pulled off into Montague Street right before Moriarty's carriage stopped.

The carriage door opened, and the hulking figure of the professor emerged, his black greatcoat buttoned up to the neck. Holmes stared at the familiar figure. It was Moriarty, all right; there was no mistaking the massive forehead under that top hat, the slightly bulging eyes, the beak of a nose. But there was something wrong; something Holmes couldn't put a name to. Moriarty moved up the steps to his front door with a rapid walk, taking curiously short steps. The door opened as he reached it, and he disappeared inside.

What was wrong? Holmes went over in his mind what he had just seen. Something—

Holmes fell backward to a sitting position on the pavement and threw the piece of chalk in the air. "Perfect!" he yelled. "Oh, perfect!" He burst out laughing.

Detective Gordon came up behind Holmes, trying to look casual. "What is it, Mr. Holmes?" he asked out of the side of his mouth, staring earnestly down at the pink dome of St. Paul's.

"You saw it, didn't you?" Holmes gasped. "You saw Moriarty go into the house."

"I did," Gordon said, sounding puzzled.

"You did!" Holmes broke out laughing again. "Oh, that is rich. I have to give him credit for this one."

Detectives Macy and Stevens, the two bulky gentlemen who had been in the hansom following Moriarty's carriage, came trotting down the street, ready to take up their observation posts. "Those must be your friends coming," Holmes said. "Call them over here, Detective Gordon. Call them over here."

"But Mr. Holmes," Gordon said, "Professor Moriarty might see us together. It is very bad for an observation team to allow the subject to see them all bunched together."

Gordon looked puzzled when this statement also caused Holmes to laugh. He shrugged and signaled Macy and Stevens to join them, and explained to them who the ragged-looking street artist was while Holmes stood up and dusted himself off.

"Gentlemen," Holmes said after shaking hands with the two policemen, "no need to worry about Professor Moriarty seeing us together. No need to keep watching his house, for that matter. The professor has made fools of the three of you. He has almost made a fool of me."

"What's that? What do you mean, Mr. Holmes?" Detective Gordon asked.

"Why, man, you saw it. You just don't know what you saw."

"Saw what, Mr. Holmes?" Detective Stevens asked.

"The gentleman who just left that carriage, Mr. Stevens. The gentleman whom you have been following about for the past few days. It isn't Professor Moriarty at all!"

"What?" Stevens asked.

"But," Gordon protested, "how could you mistake that face? He is a very distinctive-looking man, the professor."

"Indeed he is," Holmes agreed. "And that has been your downfall. You have been so preoccupied with his face that you never noticed his feet!"

"His feet?" Gordon asked.

"And his arms. You really should have noticed his arms. I should say that the motions of his arms were quite worthy of notice."

"But, Mr. Holmes," Gordon protested, "as I remember, his arms didn't move."

"True. They did not. And was that not quite remarkable?"

"I'm afraid I don't understand, Mr. Holmes," Gordon said. Stevens and Macy looked uncomfortably away, as though wishing to disassociate themselves from this madman that the Commissioner of Police had temporarily placed over them.

Holmes looked from one to the other of them, and then burst out laughing again. "Why, men, don't you see? It wasn't Moriarty at all. It was a wax dummy. That's what you saw last night, and that's what we just saw emerging from the carriage."

"A wax dummy, sir? Walking?" Gordon asked.

"Judging by the stride, I should say it was being carried on the shoulders of a midget," Holmes said.

Gordon looked stricken. "A midget!" he exclaimed. "Mummer Tolliver!"

"Exactly!" Holmes said. "Why, man, didn't you see that short stride? It shouldn't have fooled us for a second."

"Well, sir, what do we do now?" Gordon asked.

"We call for some more men to surround the house," Holmes said. "Subtly, very subtly. And then, acting on information received, we get an order from the Home Secretary and proceed to search the house from top to bottom."

"Information received? From whom, sir?"

"From me, Detective Gordon, from me!" Holmes said firmly.

NINE

THE CHASE

As I was going up the stair
I met a man who wasn't there.
He wasn't there again to-day.
I wish, I wish he'd stay away.
—HUGHES MEARNS

A mass of burly policemen in ill-fitting civilian clothes burst through the front door of 64 Russell Square when Mr. Maws answered the bell. Five of them grabbed the powerful butler and were struggling to subdue him and clap handcuffs on him when Barnett, in a mouse-gray dressing gown, armed with a large revolver, ran out of the dining room to see what the commotion was about. "What's this?" he yelled. "Unhand him, you men, and put your hands up! Mrs. H, run outside and whistle for a policeman."

"Come, come, now, Mr. Barnett," Sherlock Holmes said, appearing in the front doorway. "You know quite well that these men are policemen. Now put down that horse pistol and behave like a gentleman."

"Mr. Holmes!" Barnett exclaimed. "Is this your idea? Will you please tell me what it is that's happening? If you are responsible for the hoard of burly savages in this hallway, will you make some attempt to get them to behave in a civilized fashion. Have you a warrant for Mr. Maws arrest? If so, on what charge?"

"Nobody is attempting to arrest your butler," Holmes said. "It merely seemed to us that the element of surprise might be useful. We do have a warrant to search this house. And we intend to do so, immediately."

"That's fine," Barnett said. "Show me the warrant and, if it is in order, go ahead and search the house. There is no call to manhandle the butler."

"Where is your master?" Holmes asked, signaling the policemen to release Mr. Maws.

"I have no master," Barnett said. "I am an American. George the Third was the last man to consider himself our master, and he's been dead these past sixty-seven years."

Mr. Maws dusted off his jacket and trousers. "If any one of you gentleman would like to step outside," he said, his voice a study in exaggerated politeness, "I would be delighted to give him a lesson in proper manners. Or any three of you?"

"I do apologize, Mr. Maws," Holmes said lightly. "These gentlemen were merely overeager, having heard of your reputation as a pugilist, I'm sure. No harm done."

"Lucky thing, that," Mr. Maws said. "Busting in here like that. Grabbing a man and tussling about with him. Where do you think you are, France?"

"The police would like to ask some questions of Professor James Moriarty," Holmes said. "Where is he?"

"Not at home at the moment," Barnett said. "Had you sent word that you were coming, I'm sure he would have stayed around to greet you."

"Where has he gone?" Holmes asked. "And when did he leave?"

"Why?" Barnett asked.

"What do you mean, why?" Holmes demanded, eyeing Barnett closely. "Exactly which of the words did you fail to understand?"

"I mean, why do you want to know?" Barnett said, glaring back at Holmes, his arms crossed across his chest and his voice even. "What right have you to burst in here, attack a resident of the house, and demand to know anything at all about Professor Moriarty? Why did you bring fifteen policemen? On what basis did you get a warrant to search this house? Mr. Holmes, I think perhaps you have gone too far."

"I think not, Mr. Barnett," Holmes said, brandishing a folded-up document at him. "Here is the warrant. On information received, the police are to search the premises at 64 Russell Square, and any surrounding adjacent area. They are to look for any items, objects, personal possessions, dunnage, household furnishings, weapons, or other articles not specified herein, which would serve to connect Professor James Moriarty or other persons as yet unspecified in this instrument with the murder of Sir Geoffrey Cruikstaff, or with other crimes relating to or growing out of the specified murder."

"Murder?" Mr. Maws sniffed. "So now it's murder you are accusing us of!"

"Dunnage?" Barnett asked. "Dunnage? Why not flotsam and jetsam?"

"You may laugh," Holmes said, "but you will also stand aside while we search the house. And where is Professor Moriarty? We would very much like to speak to him in regard to this murder."

Barnett unfolded the paper and glanced at it. "So this is what a warrant looks like," he said. "I suppose it is in order, I've never seen one before. It certainly looks official, with a red seal in one corner and a blue seal in the other. Done at her majesty's order, eh? Why, I'll bet that if I were to ask her majesty right now, she wouldn't know anything about it. What exactly is this squiggle down here, this ink blot?"

"That is the magistrate's signature," Holmes told him. "I assure you it is quite in order. And stalling us will get you nowhere. The house is completely surrounded and nobody is going to get in or out until we have completed our search."

"Go ahead," Barnett said. "I've already told you to go ahead. But this paper had better be legit. I intend to send it to Professor Moriarty's solicitor, and if he informs me that this thing is a phony, or that you have in any way exceeded your authority under it, we shall certainly see what sort of legal trouble we can cause you and your friends of the police." He turned. "Mrs. H!" he called.

The housekeeper appeared in the dining-room door, her fingers laced together at her waist. "Yes, Mr. Barnett?"

"Would you please show Mr. Holmes and his friends whatever they would like to see in the house," Barnett told her. "Discourage them from making more of a mess than is absolutely necessary."

"Very well, Mr. Barnett," Mrs. H said, her face expressionless.

"Have Lucille clean up the breakfast things," Barnett added. "I shall go up and dress now."

Mrs. H nodded, and then turned and focused her gaze on Sherlock Holmes. "Mr. Holmes," she said.

"Mrs. H," Holmes said.

"One cannot expect gratitude in this life," she told the detective, "but one has a right to expect civility. I consider this sort of behavior most ungracious and uncivil."

"I owe you no gratitude, Mrs. H," Holmes said, "nor any more civility than is common between the sexes in this day and age."

"I was not speaking of any debt to myself, Mr. Sherlock Holmes," Mrs. H said, "but to the debt of gratitude that it might be thought you owe to your old friend and mentor, Professor James Moriarty— the man who took you in and treated you like a son. The man whose house you are now so rudely invading and ravaging."

"Ravaging, Mrs. H? Hardly ravaging, I daresay."

"No? What else do you call knocking poor Mr. Maws about? And look at all those men with their muddy boots grinding the dirt into the carpeting."

"Well, call it what you will, Mrs. H," Holmes said. "Anything that happens to this house, or to Professor Moriarty, for that matter, he has brought on himself. In his pursuit of crime to further his own secret desires, in his delight in evil, he has placed himself and his associates outside the human pale. And any ill results that he suffers, he brought on his own head with his own hand."

"What are you talking about, Sherlock Holmes?" Mrs. H asked. "Never in fifteen years has Professor Moriarty so much as lifted a finger to harm you, and yet you continue this senseless vendetta past all reason. And now you bring in the police on some kind of trumped-up warrant! I rather think that is going too far, and I'm sure that the professor will think so also."

"What Professor James Moriarty thinks is of no concern to me," Holmes said. "Not now, and not ever again. Will you show us around, Mrs. H, or shall we find our own way?"

Mrs. H sniffed. "This way," she said. "Mind your boots on the rug."

The search began on the top floor, where Mummer Tolliver slept under the eaves, and slowly worked its way downstairs. Large policemen were stationed at each landing of both the front and rear staircases to make sure nothing was removed in one direction while the searchers looked in the other.

Nothing of interest was found on the top floor.

On the second floor Mrs. H protested loudly when Holmes's minions stamped their big feet into Professor Moriarty's bedroom. Barnett merely watched with interest as the search proceeded. He thought that Moriarty would be more enraged at the coming invasion of his laboratory than at the search of his bedroom.

Sherlock Holmes directed the endeavor, and kept himself busy tapping on walls and measuring the space between closets in search of hidden passageways or secret panels. The search seemed thorough and complete, but Barnett became more and more convinced, watching Holmes, that the detective's heart was not in it. Holmes went through the gestures with the regard for minutia that was his hallmark, having every drawer pulled out and looked under, peering under rugs, thumping at cracks in the flooring, sending someone down the dumbwaiter to see what might be concealed in the shaft. But somehow Barnett sensed that he knew he was beaten before he began; that the professor was not lurking about the house and that there was nothing in the dunnage to connect Moriarty with any crime.

The search of the house took most of the day. Holmes himself spent two hours in the basement laboratory, poking into retorts, peering into dusty jars and canisters, looking through stacks of photographic plates, and otherwise searching for clues.

The Mummer insisted upon following two of the policemen about, telling them that they were getting warmer or colder at random until they finally tried to chase him away. At which he indignantly reminded them that it was his house, after all, not theirs, and he would go where he liked. Mr. Maws settled down to ostentatiously count the silver service in the pantry after the policemen had finished searching in there. Mrs. H stayed ahead of the group, pointing out things they should examine and sniffing with disdain when they did. She kept warning them to mind their feet, and not brush things with their shoulders, until she made one constable so nervous that he knocked over a four-foot Tseng vase while trying to avoid an armoire.

There was a flurry of excitement when one of the policemen discovered the bust of Moriarty in the study. Holmes went over and examined with interest the arrangement of straps that enabled Mummer Tolliver to wear the device on his shoulders. Then he called Barnett over. "What, exactly, is this doing here?" Holmes asked, pointing an accusatory finger at the offending object.

"It doesn't appear to be doing much of anything," Barnett replied.

"That may be," Holmes said, "but we both know what it has been doing for the past few hours. It and Tolliver. Exactly how long has he been parading about with that device on his shoulders?"

"Ask him," Barnett said.

The Mummer was called for, and the question was put to him. "Blimey!" he said. "Ye've discovered me secret. I goes about in me professor disguise all the time."

"And for how long?" Holmes demanded.

"Oh, years and years."

"I see," Holmes said. "To give Moriarty an alibi while he is off committing some deviltry, no doubt."

"None of that!" Tolliver said. " 'Ow dares you talk about the professor that way!"

"Then why do you wear the dummy?"

"It gives me stature," Tolliver explained. " 'Ow would you like to go about being barely four feet high all the time?"

"Bah!" Holmes said.

"Exactly the way I feels about it," the Mummer agreed.

Three hours later, Holmes, having found nothing of official interest, gathered his minions about him in the front hall and prepared to leave.

"I hope you are quite satisfied," Mrs. H said, her voice frigid.

"Not entirely," Holmes told her. "But then, we are not yet done with the investigation."

"What now?" Barnett asked. "Are you going to tear the house down brick by brick?"

"Not at all," Holmes said. "We are done with this house. But I have a second warrant, which I am now going to execute. I was, as you see, prepared for this!"

"What are you talking about?" Barnett asked. "What second warrant?"

Holmes pulled another piece of official-looking paper from inside his jacket and flourished it. "To search the premises and outbuildings of Moriarty's holdings on Crimpton Moor!" he exclaimed, a note of triumph in his voice. "Didn't think I knew about that, did you?"

"In truth," Barnett said, "the question had not occurred to me."

"There is a special train awaiting us at Paddington to take us to Crimpton," Holmes said. "We should be there at dusk. And if we have to spend the whole night and all of tomorrow searching, why then we shall do so." He turned and stalked out the door, followed closely by the Baker Street regulars.

Barnett turned to Mrs. H as the door closed behind the last burly man. "The professor is not going to be pleased," he said.

TEN
DRAWING THE COVER

*On approaching a cover, one whip should go on
in advance and station himself on the lee side of it,
where he may often see a fox steal away as soon
as the hounds are thrown in.*

—E. D. BRICKWOOD

Sherlock Holmes studied the map of Devon which lay open across his knees as the special police train sped west. In the orange-yellow beam of a bull's-eye lantern borrowed from one of the constables to counter the approaching dusk, he peered through his four-inch glass at the web of black lines and crosshatches on the stiff paper. Inspector Lestrade, who had joined Holmes at Paddington, contented himself with sitting silently in the opposite corner of the carriage.

"Bah!" Holmes said finally, casting the map aside. "This is useless."

Inspector Lestrade stirred himself and eyed Holmes. "Useless?" he asked. "I could have told you that before you opened the map. What do we need a map for? We know where we're going."

"As you say," Holmes said. "But you have your ways and I have mine. I would give five pounds right now for a large-scale ordnance map of the area."

Lestrade viewed Holmes tolerantly. "Professor Moriarty's holdings are at Crimpton-on-the-Moor," he explained patiently, as one would to a bright eight-year-old. "For which we detrain at Mossback Station. The only possible confusion is with Grimpon, a hamlet on the other side of the moor, which one gets access to through Coryton Station. The house is called Sigerson Manor locally, apparently after the family which build the house and occupied it for some two hundred years. The last Sigerson passed on some fifteen years ago, and the property stood deserted until Professor Moriarty took it over."

He smiled a smile of quiet satisfaction, and added, "We research these things at the Yard."

"I know all that," Holmes said.

"You know?" Lestrade leaned forward and tapped Holmes on the knee. "Your obsession with Professor Moriarty is quite impressive," he said. "You must spend all your spare time and money following him around. I tell you, Mr. Holmes, I only hope you're right this time. You have made us look foolish before, acting on your accusations."

"I have known of Sigerson Manor all my life," Holmes told Lestrade. "The Sigersons were distant relations of mine. I knew of Moriarty's purchase of the property when it happened five years ago. And as for what you call my 'obsession' with Moriarty"—he paused to blow out the lantern—"the fact that that man is not breaking stone at Dartmoor right now instead of living in luxury in a townhouse in Russell Square and a country estate at Crimpton-on-the-Moor is testimony to his genius, not his honesty. Moriarty is everything foul, Lestrade; inside that vulturelike head is the mind of a fiend incarnate. And I am his nemesis."

"That's all very well, Mr. Holmes," Lestrade said. "But you can't prove a word of it. We found someone murdered in an empty house, and you muttered, 'Moriarty!' But it wasn't. A girl was kidnapped, and you would have had us clap the professor in irons. But it was some Russian did it, not the professor at all. Now, the professor may be everything you say he is and more, but I, for one, am getting extremely tired of apologizing to him. If you can't get him convicted of a crime, Mr. Holmes, if you can't even get him held on suspicion, then don't it make good sense to just leave him be?"

Holmes folded up the map and moved over to the window seat, where he stared out at the bleak Devonshire countryside. "I cannot," he said. "As I am his nemesis, so he is my passion, the focus of my energies. Without Moriarty, Sherlock Holmes is merely a detective." He raised his right hand and balled it into a fist. "But mark this: without Sherlock Holmes to dog his steps, to intercept his secret communications, to apprehend his henchmen, to deduce his intentions and thus to foil his plans, Professor James Moriarty would by now control the largest criminal empire the world has ever seen. He would make the infamous Jonathan Wild look like a bumbling amateur!"

"So you say, Mr. Holmes. So you have been saying for the past seven years. And yet the fact is that if you were to say the same aloud in any public place, Professor Moriarty would have an action of slander against you. And if your friend Dr. Watson were to write one word defamatory of Professor Moriarty in any of the accounts of your cases that he has been writing for the magazines, he could be held for libel."

"No fear of that, Lestrade," Holmes said. "I have requested the good doctor not to so much as mention Moriarty in any of his little cautionary tales during my lifetime, unless it is to record his immediate sojourn, at her majesty's pleasure, in some penal institution."

"Well, let us hope that this is the time," Lestrade said. "When you were acting on your own, so to speak, as an unofficial detective, running about dogging the professor's footprints was your affair. But now you are acting with official sanction, and that brings Scotland Yard into it. The Home Secretary is not going to be pleased if a distinguished scientist brings an action against the Yard for false arrest or harassment."

"It was the Home Secretary who brought me into the case," Holmes reminded Lestrade. "He cannot hold the Yard culpable for my actions."

"Home Secretaries have very selective memories," Lestrade said. "If you succeed in apprehending the killer, he will be very pleased with himself for having appointed you. And the press and the House will hear, in detail, how clever he was. If you fail, he will certainly vocally reprimand the commissioners for their laxness in this important matter."

"A policeman's lot," Holmes quoted, "is not an 'appy one."

"That is so, Mr. Holmes," Lestrade agreed. "And it ain't the felons which make it so, but the sanctimonious bloody politicians."

"Very insightful, Inspector," Holmes said.

"Thank you, Mr. Holmes," Lestrade replied. "You learn a few things in twelve years on the force."

The sun was still above the horizon when the special pulled into Mossback Station. The local constable, who had been alerted by telegraph, had managed to assemble three open wagons to transport Holmes, Lestrade, and the fifteen plainclothes constables from the Yard. The wagons, ancient vehicles that had certainly conformed to some standard pattern of design at one time, had, over decades of hard use and random repair, taken on unique characters. They sat on the road outside the station like a trio of rustic old drunks, clearly willing to do whatever was required of them, but doubtful as to whether they could negotiate the first bump under any sort of load.

The three horses were obviously great-grandmothers, and any member of the R.S.P.C.A. who had happened by and seen them hitched up to wagons would certainly have called the nearest policeman.

The nearest policeman, a thickset village constable named Wiggs, stood proudly next to the drooping head of the forward horse. " 'Taint often we gets a call to cooperate with Scotland Yard out here," he told Lestrade, "but we're right pleased to do our bit."

"What is this?" Holmes asked, encompassing horses and wagons with a wave of his hand.

"Wot does yer mean, sir?" Wiggs asked, pulling his shoulders back and glaring at Holmes. "Transportation fer fifteen ter twenty officers, that's wot we was asked ter pervide, and that's wot we has pervided. 'Taint easy roundin' up transportation fer twenty officers at a moment's notice, like that."

"That's all right," Lestrade said. "You have done very well. I'm sure Mr. Holmes meant no offense."

"Mr. Holmes?" Wiggs asked. "Mr. *Sherlock* Holmes?"

Holmes acknowledged the fact.

"Well, I am truly proud ter make yer acquaintance, Mr. Holmes. I have read yer monograph on identifying cigarette ash."

For the first time in Lestrade's memory, Holmes looked astonished. "You have?"

Constable Wiggs nodded. " 'Twas in the circulatin' library of the Southern Counties Constabulary. Not many people smoke cigars er cigarettes out here; mostly they smoke a pipe er chew. But if a criminous offense is ever committed hereabouts by a geezer wot is puffin' on a Trichinopoly cigar, why, I'll have him cold."

Holmes glared suspiciously at Wiggs, but the constable did not seem to notice. He shifted his glare to Lestrade for a moment, and then turned back to Wiggs. "I am sure you will, Constable," he said. "We had best mount these, ah, wagons, and proceed. The sun is about to dip behind the western hills."

"How far to Sigerson Manor?" Lestrade asked Wiggs.

"No more 'n three miles," Wiggs told him. "Off that way. Is that where yer headed?"

"That's right," Lestrade replied. "Anything of interest happening out there to your knowledge?"

"Aye. Strange and wonderful things indeed. They is constructin' an aerostat, the professor and them people wot lives out there with him."

"A what?"

"An aerostat. Like a balloon. These modrun times wot we live in are truly times of progress and invention. They been fillin' it with hydrogen all day wot they makes themselves."

"A balloon!" Holmes exclaimed. "Come, Lestrade, load your men aboard these wagons. We must get out there quickly."

"Very well, Mr. Holmes," Lestrade said. He turned and, with a crisp series of commands, divided his men among the three wagons.

Holmes clambered up into the forward wagon next to Constable Wiggs, who gathered the reins and prodded the ancient mare into motion. "Where is this aerostat?" Holmes asked. "In the lower field, I suppose. Or the east lawn, past the formal part, where it slopes away to the drive in front of the house? I understand that Moriarty has built an observatory. Where is that? I would have placed it on the old stone foundation for the granary."

"Yer must be right familiar with ther property, Mr. Holmes," Wiggs said. "Have yer been out this way before?"

"Not for many years," Holmes said.

"Well," Wiggs told him, "ther observatory is where ther ruined granary was, like yer said. And ther aerostat is bein' filled on ther lawn in front of ther manor house. A great many of ther young people from ther area have gone over ter watch ther event."

"Do you hear that, Lestrade?" Holmes demanded, bending over to speak to the inspector, who was sitting in the wagon with his back to the driver's seat. "What nerve, what consummate nerve that man has."

"I fear that I don't follow that," Lestrade said.

"Why, man, he's making his getaway!"

"By balloon? I can't see it, Mr. Holmes. Where would he go?"

"France. He must know we have men on the lookout for him at the channel ports, so the clever devil is going to float right over their heads! Once he reaches Dieppe, the whole of the Continent is open to him."

"I still don't see it, Mr. Holmes," Lestrade said. "The French coast must be five hundred miles from here."

"What is that to someone being wafted along by the currents of the upper atmosphere?" Holmes asked. "I tell you, Lestrade, Moriarty is escaping us!"

"But why?" Lestrade persisted. "We have nothing against him."

"Ah, but he doesn't know that," Holmes said. "The guilty flee when no man pursueth.' "

"That'd be ther wicked," Constable Wiggs said over his shoulder. "Ther wicked flee when no man pursueth: but ther righteous are bold as a lion.' Proverbs."

Holmes turned to glare at the imperturbable Wiggs. "Thank you, Constable," he said.

The upper tip of the sun disappeared behind a low-lying hill to the southwest. "It will be pitch-dark in twenty minutes," Lestrade said. "How is this balloon going to navigate in the dark?"

"It will be in the hands of the man who penned *The Dynamics of an Asteroid.* Do you really think that determining in which direction the French coast lies will be too much for him?"

"I suppose not," Lestrade said.

"Can't we go any faster?" Holmes demanded. "It will be dark before we get there!"

"Yer said transportation fer fifteen," Constable Wiggs said. "Yer didn't say nothin' about racin'."

"Confound it, man, I could run faster than this," Holmes said.

"That yer could," Wiggs agreed.

"Then I shall!" Holmes cried, and he leaped off the side of the wagon and rapidly disappeared down the road ahead.

Over the next twenty minutes the last of the daylight gradually dimmed and vanished. The horses, undeterred by the dark, continued stoically plodding along down the center of the dirt road.

About ten minutes after the last of the twilight had disappeared they came upon Holmes standing in the middle of the road waiting for them. "Thank God you're in time," he said. "Moriarty and his men are right over that hill. The whole lawn is lit up bright as midday with electrical lighting. There is a great black balloon tied down in the center of the lawn, and Professor Moriarty is just about ready to ascend, as far as I can tell. A crowd of locals with picnic baskets have gathered at the far end of the lawn, where the road curves about, and they are sitting there, gnawing on chicken bones and watching the spectacle. I tell you, Lestrade, that man has more gall than the Prince of Wales, assembling a crowd to watch his getaway. We must hurry!"

Lestrade climbed down from the wagon and gathered his men about him. "We are at your orders, Mr. Holmes," he said.

"There is no time for finesse," Holmes said. "We will go straight over the hill and apprehend Moriarty and all of his henchmen. He must not get away in that balloon. And unless I miss my guess, the evidence of his crimes will be in the balloon with him. Are you armed?"

"As you instructed," Lestrade said, "we checked out five hand-guns before we left. I have given them to the five men who can account themselves best with them."

"That should be sufficient," Holmes said. "I expect that we have a large enough force so that there will be little resistance. Come now, we must arrive before the balloon goes up."

Lestrade and his men struggled up the hill in an irregular line behind Holmes. As they worked their way up they could see the glow of yellowish light that spilled over from the far side. At the top of the hill, beside an irregular jumble of massive stones that were the remains of some Neolithic temple, Holmes gathered his troop. A few hundred yards ahead of them, down a shallow, brush-covered slope, lay the wide expanse of flat, well-rolled land that was the east lawn. Beyond that, almost invisible past the illuminating circle of electrical lights, sat the massive east wing of the manor house. Built over two hundred years before of large blocks of the native stone, this was the original house, which had been added to over the centuries by gen-erations of Sigersons until it represented less than a third of the pres-ent structure.

At the back of the lawn, toward the house, two low sheds had been erected. One housed the electrical generating plant, to judge by the cluster of wires coming out of the top and leading to the ar-ray of electrical lights strung on the surrounding trees and poles. The other held some sort of machinery. A pair of long hoses ema-nating from the second shed curled across the lawn to the center, where, held to the earth by several thick cables, floated the giant aerostat. The device consisted of three great gas bags separated by a large metal ring, in which was suspended a fabric-covered gon-dola. The whole was painted black, and it rose perhaps ten stories in the air. The top disappeared into the dark sky above the electri-cal lights, and was visible only as an inky presence, blotting out the stars.

Even as they watched, the hoses from the shed were being dis-connected from the couplings to the gas bags. Suddenly two flares, like great skyrockets, shot up into the night, leaving a stream of white light behind them as they climbed.

"Look at that!" Lestrade exclaimed. "It must be some sort of signal."

"Quickly!" Holmes cried. "There's no time to lose!" Leaping up, he led his little force scurrying and sliding down the hill to the lawn below. As they reached the edge of the lawn two of the tethering cables fell away and the balloon flew skyward, trailing a third cable below it like an umbilical cord.

"There he goes!" Holmes yelled, running forward like a demented man to reach the gondola before it was too high. "We must stop him!" He leaped for the bottom of the gondola and managed to grab it with his fingers, but there was nothing to cling to and he fell away.

"Stop! Stop!" the constabulary yelled, racing across the lawn. One of them drew his pistol and fired at the ascending balloon.

"Come back down here!" another one yelled, stopping to take aim at the rapidly rising gondola, "Come back in the name of the law!"

Once the shooting had started it was contagious, and within seconds a fusillade of small-arms fire was directed at the great black object, which was rapidly disappearing into the great star-filled bowl of the night sky. Two of the policemen reached the one cable which, rising from layers of coils on the ground, was still attached to the ascending gondola. One of them leaped for it and was fifteen feet in the air before, realizing the folly of what he was doing, he let go and fell to the ground.

Moriarty's men dived for cover under whatever was available as this strange armed band appeared in their midst and began shooting at their precious aerostat. The locals, who were mostly sitting together on the side of the lawn nearest the road, began shrieking and howling. Most of them ran off into the night, but a few sat stolidly watching, perhaps suspecting that this was all part of the entertainment.

Gradually the shooting and yelling died away, until, within two minutes, the small group of Scotland Yard men were clustered silently in the middle of the lawn together, staring at the sky.

"What is the meaning of all this?" a firm, didactic voice suddenly asked from close behind them. "Inspector Lestrade, have you taken leave of your senses?"

Lestrade jerked around like a man on a string and gaped at the tall, dark-clad figure. "Professor Moriarty!" he gasped.

"I refuse to believe that you didn't expect to find me here," Moriarty said. "Now, what exactly is the meaning of this charade?"

"I—we—thought you were in that balloon."

"I see," Moriarty said. "Anytime you see an aerostat ascending into the sky, you naturally assume that I am aboard. And this, of course, explains why you were shooting at it."

"Ah, well, not precisely—"

Sherlock Holmes came striding toward them across the lawn. "Moriarty!" he yelled.

"Holmes!" Moriarty said, turning and shaking his fist at him. "Now I understand. This moronic escapade was your doing."

"I have a warrant, Moriarty," Holmes shouted, brandishing the document over his head, "to search this property, house and grounds."

"And fire upon any aerostat that you happen to find ascending when you arrive?" Moriarty demanded. "Really, Holmes—"

"There was a murder in London last night." Holmes said, "and I have reason to believe that you were involved."

"There are about three murders in London every week, if the statistical abstracts are to be believed," Moriarty said. "And you believe that I am involved in each and every one of them. Is that any reason to go about shooting revolvers at perfectly innocent teen-age boys?"

"What boys?"

"There are two teen-age boys in the aerostat to work the equipment," Moriarty told him. "And if either of them is hurt, you will answer for it!"

"We thought you were on the balloon, Professor," Lestrade said in what he hoped was a conciliatory tone. "Mr. Holmes said you were escaping."

"Escaping? From what? The aerostat is tethered, as you can see for yourselves if you'd bother to look." Moriarty indicated the one cable which was still uncoiling from the ground and following the balloon into the heavens.

A Chinese gentleman in dark robes and a close-fitting cap came scurrying across the lawn from the house. "They are unhurt," he called to Moriarty. "My son wishes to be informed as to what is going on down here, but neither of them was injured by the cannonade. What is going on down here?"

"Gentlemen," Moriarty said, "May I introduce my friend and colleague, Prince Tseng Li-Chang, fourteenth in line for the throne of Imperial China. His son, Low, at whom you were shooting in the aerostat, is fifteenth in line. They are here in exile, under the personal protection of her majesty, Queen Victoria. Prince Tseng, let me present Inspector Giles Lestrade of Scotland Yard, and Mr. Sherlock Holmes."

"You were shooting at my son?" Tseng demanded, glaring alternately at Lestrade and then at Holmes. "Why were you doing this? Are you agents of the Empress Dowager?"

Lestrade sighed. "I am afraid we have made a mistake," he said. "Please accept my apologies, and the apologies of the Yard."

"Mistake!" Moriarty snorted. "You'll be back in uniform tomorrow, Lestrade, if Prince Tseng complains to her majesty. You'll be lucky not to lose your pension."

"In my country," Prince Tseng interjected, "they would suffer the death of a thousand knives for shooting at a royal heir."

"Let me try to explain, Professor," Lestrade said.

"I can't imagine any possible explanation for what just went on here," Moriarty said, "but it will be fascinating to hear you try. Unfortunately I have no time now. We have a lot of work ahead of us, Prince Tseng and I and the two lads, and we cannot take the time right now. We are commencing a night of astronomical observations by a specially constructed aerostat-carried telescope."

"So you say," Holmes said, "but then what are you doing down here?"

Moriarty turned to glare at him. "The lads are up there to expose photographic plates. They send them down on small parachutes attached to the tethering cable, which also contains a telegraphic wire. We stay down here to develop the plates. Now please leave us alone for the remainder of the night. You have a warrant—go and search the house. Try to refrain from shooting up the furniture."

"Assassins!" Prince Tseng exclaimed.

"I think we'd better go," Lestrade said. "We don't have to search the house. We'll just go back to the city now. Can we talk about this sometime, Professor? I mean, without bringing her majesty into the discussion?"

"Monday," Moriarty said. "Come by and see me at Russell Square on Monday. I'll speak to the prince."

"I have a warrant," Holmes said. "I intend to search the house."

Lestrade looked from Holmes to Moriarty to Prince Tseng, who was glowering at them with unconcealed hostility. "Come along, Mr. Holmes," he said. "We'll go now."

ELEVEN

THE GENTLEMEN'S GENTLEMEN

*Thus in the beginning the world was
so made that certain signs come before
certain events.*

—Marcus Tullius Cicero

Upper Sedgewick Lane ran for two blocks south of Oxford Street, terminating abruptly at the high brick wall to the rear of Good Sisters' Hospital. Despite the best efforts of the residents and shopkeepers, the lane degenerated into shabby disrepute as one traveled the two-hundred-yard length of that final block.

The blame, if any, could be laid at the door of Good Sisters' Hospital. A massive rear door sheathed in heavy iron plate, studded with spikes and crusted with layers of muddy green paint, it was the only acknowledgment that Good Sisters gave to Upper Sedgwick Lane. And it was never used.

The front door of the hospital was on Beverton Street, a three-and-a-half-block semicircle from the lane. It was there that the carriages came and went, and there that the attentive doctors smiled and nodded at their respectable patients.

This sealed door was the subject of much speculation in Upper Sedgwick Lane. Rumor had it that in the darkest hours of the blackest nights, the green door opened.

In the dark of the moon, so the whisper went, mysterious carts, their wheels muffled with rags, would thump slowly over the ancient cobblestones and back up to the green door. Then the door would be opened by unseen hands and corpses, wrapped in white linen, would be whisked inside. Why the carts were said to be delivering bodies to the hospital instead of taking them away was never discussed. That is what happened, everyone knew it. They hadn't seen it themselves, but they could name two or three who had, if they hadn't promised to keep their mouths shut.

Then there was the matter of the epigraph circumscribed around the hospital wall, which was always referred to by the lane's residents as "them words." The full and proper name of Good Sisters' Hospital was "The Hospice and Sanitarium in Holy Charity of the Good Sisters of the Miraculous Scars of the Bloody Body of Our Lord and Savior Jesus Christ." The architect and builder of the hospital, one Matthew Creighton, had wrapped a frieze around the upper story of the structure with this title deeply chiseled thereon, intended to last until the final trumpet should make hospices redundant. And the portion of this full and proper name that happened, by some malicious chance, to come around on the Upper Sedgewick Lane side, two feet high and five stories up, in deep relief, was: ARS OF THE BLOODY BODY.

Upper Sedgwick Lane had never recovered from this indignity.

"It is by such fortuitous happenings," Mr. Nathaniel Palmar told Barnett, "that the destinies of men and nations are determined. Were it not for Matthew Creighton's infantile sense of humor—for there can be little doubt that the placement of the lettering on that infamous frieze was deliberate—then Upper Sedgwick Lane might not have slowly degenerated over the past hundred years. Had that not happened, then this fine old mansion, once the home of Admiral Sir George Tallbouys, would never have been available at such a remarkably reasonable price. And had it not, then the Gentlemen's Gentlemen, through lack of a proper home, could never have come into being."

"That would have been a shame," Barnett said, running his hand over the dark mahogany woodwork of the entrance hall, with its patina of a hundred years' polishing and waxing.

"It would," Mr. Palmar agreed, "it would indeed." He led the way into the guests' parlor; a large room with a scattering of armchairs toward the front balanced by an ancient, well-used billiard table at the rear. "Yes, we owe a lot to Matthew Creighton. 'For his work continueth,' as the poet says, 'far beyond his knowing.' Were it not for the whimsical builder and the inadvertent benefactor, we would not be here."

"The inadvertent benefactor?"

Mr. Palmar indicated a large oil portrait on the wall behind them. Done in the whimsically realistic style of the '40s, it showed a portly gentleman with a choleric expression, wearing hunting tweeds and carrying a shotgun in the crook of his right arm and a brace of dead birds in his left hand.

Barnett peered at the brass plate under the portrait. " 'Sir Hector Billysgait,' " he read. "He was your benefactor?"

"It is a complex story involving an unexpected predeceasing, a residual legatee, and a gentleman whose taste for practical jokes extended even to the grave," Mr. Palmar said.

"Fascinating!" Barnett said sincerely. He took out the small notebook that was his reporter's disguise. "If you don't mind telling me about it . . ."

"In brief," Mr. Palmar said, "Sir Hector, though knighted for a service to the Crown, was merely the impoverished younger son of a baronet. Impoverished only in terms of his family and class, you understand. It was a constant struggle for him to maintain his flat in the city and his various shooting boxes and fishing rights and the like. He hardly ever killed as many creatures in a year as he would like to have done. And his income ceased upon his death, the principal reverting to the entailed estate which progressed from eldest son to eldest son."

"I see," Barnett said. "The man had no money."

"None to call his own," Mr. Palmar agreed, "beyond the value of those possessions which he had acquired over a lifetime—rifles, shotguns, fishing tackle, framed oils of men killing animals in a variety of ways, and a remarkable variety of clothing for tramping through the woods and shooting at things or wading in mountain streams with a fishing rod."

"So," Barnett said.

"Over the long years of their relationship," Mr. Palmar continued, "Sir Hector grew more and more in debt to his valet, Fellows. It was a gradual process—a couple of pounds borrowed here, a quarter's wages unpaid there—but eventually the total grew to in excess of two hundred pounds. Which, although a comparatively small sum to someone of Sir Hector's class, was a fortune to Fellows.

"Now Sir Hector was something of a practical joker. He promised Fellows, who was his junior by some twenty years, that he would leave him everything in his will. 'Every penny I have,' as he put it."

"But," Barnett interjected, "I thought he had no money of his own."

"True," Mr. Palmar agreed. "And when he died his income would cease. But his possessions remained part of his estate—those things he had bought over the years. And several of the firearms were of themselves worth well into the hundreds of pounds. Sir Hector did not stint himself."

"I see," Barnett said. "It still doesn't sound like enough to purchase a building and endow a private club."

"Ah," Mr. Palmar said, "but here is where the hand of fate takes over, and a strange chain of events turns a practical joke into a legacy. May I offer you a glass of sherry?"

Barnett accepted the sherry, which proved to be a particularly fine Garrett d'Austine '67. He sipped it, savored it, commented on its quality.

"Butlers and valets," Mr. Palmar said, "are particularly well-placed to develop a fine palate for wines, especially fortified wines." He sipped from his own glass and continued with the story he never tired of telling.

"Sir Hector died quite suddenly one morning in September, 1878. And he proved to be as good as his word. Exactly as good, and no better. Fellows was made residual legatee, meaning he was to have whatever was left over after all the specific bequests had been fulfilled. What quickly became apparent as the will was read was that the specific bequests would consume all of Sir Hector's real and personal property. The only thing left for Fellows was the bit of actual money that Sir Hector had on his person and in his flat at the moment of his decease. It amounted, if I remember aright, to a trifle over thirteen pounds. Fellows was rather disappointed."

"I can understand that."

"But then it transpired that Sir Hector's youngest brother, Sydney, who had been shooting in Bengal, had met with an untimely and very fatal accident. He was staking out a goat to attract a tiger when the goat, sensing perhaps that what was about to happen was not to his best interest, butted Sir Sydney in the stomach. Ruptured his spleen. It took a while for news of this to reach England. It actually happened several months before Sir Hector died."

"I see," Barnett said. "And Sir Hector was Sydney's heir?"

"Sydney was still youthful enough to be unaffected by intimations of mortality. He never made a will. But they both had an elderly aunt named Agatha, who passed on about a week before Sir Hector. And thus, you see, a month or so after Sydney, although nobody realized it at the time."

"Yes?"

"Dame Agatha had left her considerable private fortune to Sydney, long her favorite, to sustain himself with and to use for whatever good works he deemed appropriate. But as Sydney predeceased Dame Agatha, her estate went to Sir Hector. He died without ever knowing that he was a millionaire."

"And the valet?"

"As residual legatee, Fellows suddenly found himself a man of considerable wealth. Since his unwitting benefactress, Dame Agatha, had wished part of her fortune to be used for good works, Fellows endowed the Gentlemen's Gentlemen as a club for butlers and valets in service in London, along with a generous fund to take care of former or retired men of these professions who have fallen on hard times."

"A fine gesture," Barnett said, looking up from his notebook. "Is Fellows in residence here himself?"

"No longer," Mr. Palmar said.

"I see," Barnett said. "Has he, ah, passed on?"

"In a sense. He has moved to Paris. Having reverted to a family name which I am not at liberty to tell you, he has taken up painting in oils. Now, is there any other way in which I can be of service to you?"

"I think so," Barnett said. "What brought me here in the first place, Mr. Palmar, was a Scotland Yard report that the two gentlemen's gentlemen who were arrested on suspicion of murdering their employers this past week are both members of this club."

"Ah!" Mr. Palmar said. "Lizzard and Margery. Yes, they are indeed. Let me point out, purely in the interest of accuracy, that they are both butlers. In current usage, the phrase 'gentleman's gentleman' properly applies only to a valet."

"I understand," Barnett said. "Thank you for making that distinction. In my profession we strive for verbal accuracy, of course. But we need all the help we can get. Do you know Lizzard and Margery? Can you tell me anything about them?"

"I actually don't know either of them too well," Palmar said. "As club steward, of course, I am acquainted with all of our members, but both Lizzard and Margery were noticeably reserved with their confidences. Which is not unusual, you must understand; their vocations tend to encourage habitual reticence. I believe, however, that I can introduce you to someone who knows them both quite well."

"I would appreciate that," Barnett said.

"I shall go and see if he's here." Mr. Palmer excused himself and went off down the dark wood-paneled hallway. Barnett sipped his sherry and considered multiple murder. He composed his thoughts and began to construct the lead paragraph for the article he would write for the American News Service. A bit of philosophy to lead off. It would make the reader feel as though he were exploring the human condition instead of merely indulging a morbid curiosity.

As ripples in a pond, Barnett scribbled in his notebook, *radiate from every stone, no matter how casually flung, so do unforeseeable consequences emanate from every human action, no matter how seemingly minor.*

Barnett paused to chew on his pencil and stare down at the page. It read fairly well, he decided. After all, as an unforeseen result of this series of murders, Professor Moriarty, who was completely unconnected with the crimes, had been seriously inconvenienced by the unwarranted attentions of Sherlock Holmes and Scotland Yard. But surely any of the victims would rather have been seriously inconvenienced than have had his throat cut.

Barnett decided to work on the text of his article later, make a few notes first, and try to produce something that was actually worth saying. *NOTE:* he wrote large on the rest of the page, *Murder is the worst crime of all. Why? Because it is the only one which cannot be taken back and cannot be apologized for.*

Not a bad thought, Barnett decided, folding his notebook and sticking it back in his pocket. With a little work he should be able to get five hundred to a thousand words out of it.

Palmar came back down the hall. With him was a slender, stoop-shouldered man, whose intelligent brown eyes peered out of a face that was habitually set in a serious mien. "Mr. Barnett," he said, "permit me to introduce Mr. Quimby. Mr. Quimby was, until recently, the valet for Lord John Darby. He has been staying with us since his lordship's unfortunate demise, and has had occasion to become reasonably well acquainted with both Lizzard and Margery."

"A pleasure," Barnett said. "Please, sit here. You don't mind if I ask you a few questions? I trust Mr. Palmar has explained what I'm here for."

"A journalist," Quimby said, continuing to stand.

Barnett sensed hostility. "That's right," he said, trying to look as open and honest as possible. "I'd like to talk to you about your friends Lizzard and Margery."

"Why?"

"I am trying to gather information on the events surrounding the murders of their employers."

"They were not responsible."

"I am convinced of that also," Barnett said.

"Scotland Yard does not seem to be. They have been placed under arrest."

"I know. I believe that Inspector Lestrade was acting hastily."

"That's so," Quimby agreed. "And it was the newspapers that made him do it. Long stories about how nobody was safe, not even the nobility. Not even in their own homes, or in their own beds. The people were becoming agitated, and the Home Secretary had to do something. Scotland Yard had to arrest somebody, and right quick, too, just to show they was doing their jobs."

"There may be something in what you say," Barnett admitted. "And if journalistic outcry caused your friends to be incarcerated, then perhaps a renewed outcry can get them released again."

"The authorities will have to let them go soon anyway," Quimby said, nodding with satisfaction. "Five killings all committed the same way, and the last while they were already locked up. It stands to reason."

"Five?" Barnett asked, surprised. "I know of only four."

"Five," Quimby said. "And I'm the one who should know."

"Let's see," Barnett said, counting on his fingers. "There's Venn and Stanhope and Lord Walbine and Sir Geoffrey Cruikstaff—"

"And my late master," Quimby said. "Lord John Darby."

"He was murdered?" Barnett asked. "I don't remember hearing of it. When did it happen?"

"His body was found early in the morning of Tuesday, the fifteenth of February."

"By you?"

"No, sir. By the Earl of Arundale."

"In his bedroom?"

"No, sir. In the dining room."

"I see." Barnett leaned back in his chair, which creaked alarmingly. He shifted forward again. "What makes you think that your master's death is related to the others?"

"His throat was cut. And there was no way for anyone to have got in or out. An impossible crime, Mr. Barnett. The only one who could have committed it was me."

Barnett nodded. "I take it you didn't kill Lord John," he said.

"No, sir," Quimby said. "He wasn't a particularly easy man to work for, but I had no reason to wish to do myself out of a position. Besides, I can't stand the sight of blood."

"I see," Barnett said. "If, then, for some reason you *had* wanted to do his lordship in, you would have used poison."

Quimby shook his head. "I couldn't do that to good food," he said. "No, sir; if I ever decide to do anybody in, I fancy I shall use a very large, very blunt instrument."

Barnett pulled out his notebook. "May I ask a few questions regarding your late employer and your two friends Lizzard and Margery?" he said.

"I will assist you," Quimby said, "because I live in fear that Inspector Lestrade will decide to add a third manservant to the two he already has in quod."

"That is one of my questions," Barnett said. "Why hasn't he? That is, why haven't I read anything about the death of Lord John Darby?"

Quimby poured himself a glass of sherry from the decanter and then seated himself gingerly on one of the hardback chairs beside the upholstered armchair Barnett had settled into. "That I cannot tell you, Mr. Barnett," he said. "Lord Arundale is a powerful enough man to have the news of the murder quenched, and he has done so. But what his motivation is, I do not know."

"Do the police know of the murder?"

"I am not sure. I would think not. There is a private inquiry agent working with the police—a Mr. Holmes—who does know about it. He has questioned me extensively. He also thinks Lizzard and Margery are innocent; he told me so."

"What did he ask you about?"

"Everything you can think of. He asked me how long I had been employed by his lordship, whether his lordship had any enemies that I knew of, what sort of books his lordship liked to read."

"Books?"

"Yes, sir. That's what he asked."

"And what did you reply? What sort of books *did* Lord John like to read?"

"I can't recall ever seeing his lordship with a book in his hands, unless it was Bradshaw."

"He restricted his reading to the railway timetables, eh?"

"His lordship did take a newspaper, sir. The *Daily Gazette*."

"I see. Can you remark on anything else of note, either in Mr. Holmes's questions or in your responses?"

"It's hard for me to tell, sir. Being interrogated is a novel experience for me."

"Well then, did Mr. Holmes seem particularly pleased or distressed at any of your responses?"

"No, sir. He did compliment me on my powers of observation at one point."

"When was that?"

"He asked me if anything was missing from the house or from his lordship's person. I replied in the negative, with the possible exception of a thin gold chain that his lordship wore on occasion around his neck. I said I couldn't be sure it was taken, as his lordship didn't always wear it."

"Did you check where it was kept when Lord John wasn't wearing it?"

"Mr. Holmes asked me that, also. I told him that I couldn't say, because I have no idea where his lordship kept it. His other personal jewelry was kept in a box on the dressing table, but I never saw the chain in there. It was when I mentioned that to him that Mr. Holmes complimented me."

"Was the chain found among his lordship's effects?"

"I don't believe so. I was present at a preliminary inventory, conducted by the family solicitor, and it was not found at that time."

"Did Lord John have anything suspended from this chain?"

"Yes, but I cannot tell you what. He always kept it beneath his shirt, next to his skin."

"I see," Barnett said. "An interesting idiosyncrasy, although probably bearing no relationship to the crime. The object cannot have been very large, and if it had been of great value, I'm sure its existence would have been known of by some other member of the family."

"That is probably so," Quimby agreed.

"What I find most interesting is the secrecy," Barnett said. "I can see why the murderer wouldn't wish to advertise, but why the Earl of Arundale would want to suppress knowledge of a murder I don't know. But I will do my best to find out. I suppose there is no chance that this earl did your boss in?"

"Did him in? No, sir. The homicide assuredly occurred before the arrival of the earl."

"Pity," said Barnett, with the heartlessness of a true newspaperman. "Now, about Lizzard and Margery. How well do you know them?"

"Fairly well," Quimby said. "As well as one can get to know somebody in a short time. We are all in the same boat, so to speak, and it gave us a strong community of interest. We were possessed of a great desire to discover who committed the murders, and how they were accomplished, even before we discovered that we ourselves might be blamed for them."

"Did you come to any conclusions?" Barnett asked.

"No, sir, unfortunately not. Of course, it is not a field that we are particularly competent in. That is why I was so pleased to discover that Mr. Holmes is taking an interest in the problem. He is highly thought of."

"In your own mind there is no chance that either of your friends might actually have had a hand in the, ah, crimes?"

"No chance, sir. Neither of them had a motive. On the contrary, they both lost good positions upon the deaths of their employers."

"Scotland Yard contends that they were paid off by some third person to either commit the deeds themselves or allow someone else access to the bedrooms."

"I cannot believe that, Mr. Barnett. Neither of them is the sort of man who would murder his employer. Also, neither of them was in a position where a desire for immediate financial gain would outweigh the need for security of employment."

"I understood that Margery was an inveterate racecourse-goer."

"Yes, sir. He has what I believe is called a 'system,' sir. Has put away quite a little nest egg with it."

"You mean he wins?"

"Not invariably, but certainly more than he loses."

"And what about Lizzard? Word is that he has a lady friend in Wembley."

"Mr. Lizzard is seeing a lady who lives in Wembley, sir. That's true enough."

"Was his butler's salary sufficient for his, ah, needs in this regard?"

Quimby pondered this for a moment. "Actually, sir," he said, "the size of Mr. Lizzard's salary is not relevant in this case, the lady in question being the sole owner and proprietress of a public house. She has asked Mr. Lizzard to come into the business as her partner, feeling, as she says, that the presence of a man about the establishment is desirable."

"It sounds like a subtle proposal of marriage," Barnett commented.

"I have no doubt that matrimony is in the lady's mind," Quimby said, "but the offer is a straightforward business offer. I would assume that she's waiting for Mr. Lizzard to do the proposing."

"An enviable position for the gentleman to be in," Barnett said, "if he is fond of the lady. And it would certainly seem from that as though Lizzard was not in any desperate need of funds."

"I would say that was so," Quimby said.

"Thank you for your assistance in this," Barnett said. "Is there anything else that has come to your attention during these past weeks that I have neglected to ask about that you think might have any bearing, however slight, on the question of the murders of your employers?"

"Well, sir," Quimby said, "as I declared before, the field of criminal investigation is out of my provenance; I really can't say what would be of interest to the trained investigator." He paused. "There is one thing, however, which I find interesting."

"And that is?"

"Well, sir, it's possibly only indirectly related to the murders themselves, but it is curious just the same. There has been another gentleman here asking questions. And despite the lack of publicity given to the subject, he seemed to know the details of the killing of my master, Lord John Darby."

"That is curious," Barnett agreed.

"Not only that, sir, but there's something even more curious about it."

"Yes?" Barnett urged.

"Well, sir, he called himself Mr. Plantagenet, but he was the spitting image of Lord John. Could have been his brother."

TWELVE

INTERLUDE: NOT TO BE

> *The fever called "Living"*
> *Is conquered at last.*
> —EDGAR ALLAN POE

The night had been long and physically exhausting; but his sport was the game of life, the game of truth, the devil's game, the only game worth the playing. And this night the game had been piquant and especially fine. Desmond Chauvelin had been loath to leave the squalid building wherein lay concealed his very private club.

Two girls this time, the older a hardened street-wise moll, course and foul-mouthed. But the younger—no more than sixteen, slender, with pale, unblemished skin and a fair, frightened face. A delicate flower to find among the street weeds with whom they usually practiced their arts. Where did the Master Incarnate find such a girl? Better, he realized, not to wonder. And, in truth, Chauvelin was really not interested in the girl's antecedents. It was her slender, unmarked body, her youth, her innocence, and her capacity for terror that he found so supernaturally exciting. There is a special quality in tortured innocence—a pain-heightened wide-eyed terror: fear mingled with disbelief, and the constant hope of surcease—that is highly valued by the connoisseur.

The rose-trimmed ebony brougham coursed through the deserted streets of the West End of London, its steel-shod wheels pounding an allegro along the pavement. Chauvelin stretched his plump body across the wide cushioned seat and idly watched the gaslights pass in orderly procession outside the coach window, which was rolled up against the predawn chill. For all that life was tedious and dull, he mused, there were brief moments that blazed out with a hellish fire.

He sometimes thought that at a certain point in the intricate, prolonged ceremonies of this game of games, the slaves became truly aware. He could see it in their eyes: he could watch the comprehension grow with the careful repetition of pain, the measured torment, until it surpassed the fear, and transcended the weak flesh. So it had been with this girl; knowledge had grown under the screams. The knowledge that was greater than wisdom: that all was hopeless and that there was no escape; that life had no more meaning than death, and that pain—physical pain—endless pain—sensual overwhelming pain—was the closest one could come to reality. They all said they were grateful, of course; he made them say it. It was one of the rules. Humble appreciation for the pain that gave them meaning and assured them that they were still alive.

The brougham turned off Old London Road onto Bentham Way, and the coachman slowed up as they approached the gate to Infant Court, the small, private circle on which fronted three residences: that of a duke, another of an exiled queen, and his own.

Chauvelin was roused sufficiently from his reverie by the brougham's slowing and stopping before the gate to watch as two guards—in the comic-opera uniforms of the deposed queen's household troops—opened the gate and waved the coach through. He chuckled as they closed the gate behind him. Guarded like royalty, he was. Buttoning his waistcoat and the top button of his jacket, he allowed the coachman to swing down and open the brougham's door for him and then stepped gingerly out and waddled across to his own front door. The coachman, wise in the ways of his master, clambered back up to the driver's seat and swung the brougham away without pausing for further instructions. Chauvelin expected his servants to behave like automata, without prompting, without recognition, without gratitude. When he stretched his hand out for his evening snifter of brandy, it had best be there. How it arrived there was not his concern.

The butler was neither required nor expected to man the front door after midnight; Chauvelin trusted no man's discretion save his own. He let himself in with his own two keys, lit a taper with a wooden safety match, and thumped his way up the broad staircase to his bedroom.

His bedroom was a rectangular room, much longer than it was wide. The ancestral four-post canopied bed crouched at the far end, away from the windows. Across from the door were three matched chiffoniers and a specially built triple-size wardrobe closet. Desmond

Chauvelin did not believe in being far from his extensive collection of costumes and accouterments. Whatever one does, one must be correctly garbed for the occasion; and one might be called upon to do the strangest things on the shortest notice.

To the left of the door, by the large casement windows, stood his dressing table; and it was to this that he repaired, casting his garments to the right and left as he entered the bedroom. He paused only to light the gas mantle on the wall and the two beeswax candles in simple porcelain holders on the dressing table. The plum velvet jacket he hung on a drawer handle, the gold brocade waistcoat he draped over the back of a chair, the cravat he suspended from a brass hook on the gas fixture. The night's exertions had left Chauvelin happy. When he was depressed he was excessively neat.

He investigated his face in the large looking glass on the dressing table. He had heard it said that the health of the body and the soundness of the spirit could be determined by examining the eyes. Opening his eyelids wide, he stared through the glass at himself. The pupils seemed to have an unnatural luster, he thought, suggestive more of putrefaction than of health. He shook his head as if to clear it of the unnatural thought. It must be an effect of the candlelight; or the lateness of the hour. He examined his cheeks. They seemed red and puffy to him, and he could make out the tiny blue threads of broken veins beneath the skin. He pushed away from the mirror. *I lead an unhealthy life*, he thought. The idea seemed to amuse him.

What was that? A motion in the mirror? Something behind him, some great black object, flickered across his field of view in the shadowy light of the gas lamp.

There was someone in the room with him. He had not heard the door open or close, but nonetheless—

Chauvelin did not believe in ghosts, but it was with an almost supernatural dread that he leaped to his feet and turned to face the unknown intruder. He clutched at the hardbacked chair he had been sitting in and raised it chest-high, thrusting the chair legs aggressively out in front of him, examining the room through the cane bottom.

At first he thought he had been mistaken, so hard was the man to see, but after a few seconds the man's actions made him visible. It was not one of his servants, Chauvelin realized, but a tall, bulking man, he had never seen before, dressed in what seemed to be evening clothes covered by a full black cape that swirled in a full circle around him, his face shrouded beneath a wide-brimmed hat of a strange design. The man appeared to be going through the pockets of Chauvelin's discarded jacket. It was incredible! Right here in Chauvelin's own bedroom, with Chauvelin fifteen feet away waving a heavy chair at him!

"Who are you?" Chauvelin demanded, noting with some pride the calmness of his voice. "How did you get in here? And what in the name of all that's holy do you think you are doing?"

The man cast the jacket aside with a grunt of annoyance, and began deftly going through the pockets of the waistcoat. The presence of Desmond Chauvelin, who was advancing slowly toward him with the wooden chair held waist-high, did not seem to deter him in the slightest.

It was certainly a lunatic, Chauvelin decided, escaped from some local asylum. Any burglar would have run at his presence, and anyone with designs on his person would not pause to rifle his jacket pockets. Chauvelin debated calling for assistance. It seemed a good plan, except for the fact that almost certainly nobody would hear him. If he could get past the man to his bed, he could use the bellpull. There was nobody presently in the butler's pantry to hear the *ting* of the bell, but in four and a half hours, when the butler came downstairs to start his day he would see the little telltale flag on the call board and come to investigate.

The man dropped the waistcoat and for the first time turned to Chauvelin. "Where is it?" he asked, in the measured, reasonable tone of one who sees nothing unusual about his question. It might have been "What is the time?" or "Unreasonably chilly, isn't it?" from an acquaintance at the track. But it wasn't. It was a cloaked stranger, in his bedroom at four o'clock in the morning.

"Where is it?" the man repeated.

"What?" Chauvelin asked. "Look, my man." He took two steps forward and prodded at the apparition with his chair. "I don't know how you got in here, or what it is you think you're doing, but I am not amused. Come to think of it, how did you get in here, anyway?"

The man knocked the chair aside as a thing of no consequence and grabbed Chauvelin by the shirtfront with his left hand. "The bauble," he said, forcing Chauvelin to his knees. "Where do you keep it?"

Chauvelin's bowels knotted with fear. He felt a great desire to be calm, to be reasonable, to keep the conversation with his uninvited guest on a friendly level. "Bauble?" he asked. "What's mine is yours, I assure you. You have but to ask. What bauble? I don't go in for baubles. I have an extensive collection of cravats—"

"The bauble," the man repeated. "The device, the signet, the devil's sign."

"Devil's—" A strange look crossed the face of Desmond Chauvelin; a look of comprehension, and of fear. Of its own volition his right hand reached down and touched the fob pocket sewn into the top of his trouser waistband.

"So!" the man said. Slapping Chauvelin's hand aside, he reached into the small pocket and pulled out a circular gold locket designed like a miniature pocket watch. He flipped open the lid and looked inside, and the devil, arms akimbo, stared back at him. Spaced evenly around the outside of the engraving, circling and confining the devil, were the capital letters D C L X V I.

"Oh, that bauble," Chauvelin said.

The man picked Chauvelin up and threw him across the room. Chauvelin hit the floor and slid and tumbled, coming up hard against the high oaken sides of the four-poster bed. He felt something wrench and snap inside of him, and an intense pain centered itself on the left side of his chest. He did not lose consciousness, but the bubble of reason popped inside his brain and he began to whimper like a frightened baby.

There was, deep inside Chauvelin, a point of awareness, an observer that remained detached, and quizzical, and faintly amused, while his body retched with fear and curled into a tight little ball on the floor. That was interesting; he had always surmised that it would be so.

"I am going to kill you," the dark man said, striding across the room. "Don't vomit; none of the others have vomited."

Chauvelin raised his right arm defensively before his face.

From somewhere the tall dark man produced a cane. He looked down at Chauvelin almost compassionately. "I must do this, you understand," he said. "I am the wind."

Chauvelin gagged and puked all over his white shirtfront.

The tall man twisted the cane and pulled out a slim knife with a razor-sharp nine-inch blade. "The wind," he said. He bent over Chauvelin.

THIRTEEN

THE PROBLEM

Laws were made to be broken.
—CHRISTOPHER NORTH

For the past five days, since the evening of his return from the observatory, Professory Moriarty had remained in his room. Surrounded by a great pile of books, mostly on loan from one of the libraries of the British Museum, he spent each day wrapped in his blue dressing gown, stretched out on his bed reading, or pacing back and forth across the small rectangle of floor between the bed and the dressing table, drinking tea, and smoking a particularly acrid brand of Turkish cigarettes.

"It is the cigarettes I object to mostly," Mrs. H told Barnett over breakfast the next Friday. "It will take months to get the smell out of the drapes and bed curtains. And when he is not smoking the wretched things himself, he cannot abide the smell."

"I find these periodic retreats of the professor's to be very trying," Barnett said. "This is the fifth time in the two years I've been here that he has disappeared into his bedroom for an extended period, and it always happens at the most awkward times. Everything has to grind to a halt around here while Moriarty takes to his bed and reads about aardvarks."

"You misunderstand," Mrs. H said, leaning forward and waving a buttered muffin in Barnett's face. "He is not retreating, no indeed! The professor is working this time. I've been with him for a good many years, and I can tell. It's his smoking those cigarettes that makes the difference. When it's lethargy or lassitude, Mr. Barnett, he smokes a pipe. When it's work, it's those vile cigarettes. And then he's asking for specific books to be brought to him. When he's in one of his sulks and in seclusion from the world, he merely works his way alphabetically through the collections in the Grenville Library or the King's Library of the British Museum."

"So the professor's hard at work up there, pacing back and forth," Barnett said.

" 'At's right enough," Mummer Tolliver said from his perch in the large armchair at the head of the dining table, where he was gorging himself from the platter of fresh, hot muffins and the stoneware jug of marmalade. "And it's a fine thing to see. Not that you can see the process—the wheels turning, so to speak—it's the results! Professor Moriarty is in his room, thinking; and the world had better watch its step!"

Barnett poured some fresh cream into his coffee and stirred it with one of the delicate lace-pattern Queen Anne spoons from what Mrs. H insisted upon referring to as "the old service." "What do you suppose he spends his time thinking about while he's pacing back and forth and puffing Turkish smoke?" he asked.

"Once it was about gravity," Mrs. H said. "About how it keeps all the stars and planets circling in their proper places. He was watching this asteroid through his telescope, what he calls a 'bit of rock flinging itself around the sun,' and it was just the slightest bit late in getting to where it was supposed to be. Well, the professor went up to his room and stayed there for weeks, pacing up and down and thinking about it. Other scientists might have just decided that their observations had been faulty, but not the professor! He wrote a paper on it when he came down that tells how all the parts of the universe relate to each other. Just from watching this tiny ball of rock out in space."

"*The Dynamics of an Asteroid*," Barnett said. "I've seen it."

"Another time he designed a safety gas mantle that would shut off the gas supply if the flame blew out. And then once he composed an epic poem in classical Greek in honor of a German archaeologist named Schliemann."

"Was it any good?" Barnett asked.

Mrs. H smiled. She carefully chewed and swallowed a bite of buttered muffin before replying, "It was Greek to me."

Tolliver chortled. Barnett frowned.

"It's when 'e 'as a real problem that the professor, 'e goes off like this," Tolliver offered. "Why, I remember one time when 'e figured out 'ow to make a whole building disappear without a trace."

"Why would he want to do that?" Barnett asked.

"It were a bank," Tolliver explained.

"Ah!" Barnett said. "I wonder what sort of problem it is this time—a heavenly equation or an earthly conundrum."

"I think it's something what might be considered in the line of business," the Mummer offered. "That Indian gent, says 'is name is Singh, has been to see the professor two afternoons this week. He's the only bloke what the professor *will* see."

"Oh, yes," Barnett said. "The author of that strange note. What sort of fellow is he? Do you think he has a commission for Professor Moriarty?"

Mrs. H rose from her seat, sniffed, murmured, "I must get about my work now," and left the room.

"*She* doesn't like to hear about that sort of thing," Tolliver commented, pointing a silver spoon at Mrs. H's retreating back. "*She* likes to suppose as 'ow we is all living off wealth what we 'as inherited from deceased uncles. The fact that we occasionally break the law in pursuit of our 'ard-earned nickers is a consideration upon which Mrs. H don't like to dwell. A right proper lady, she is."

"There are those of us who don't like to be constantly reminded of our iniquities, Mummer," Barnett said. "No matter how righteous we may feel about our particular morality, and no matter how strong a logical case we can build up for our actions, if that morality or those actions differ too strongly from those in which we were reared to believe, the struggle to convince ourselves fully will never be completely won."

Tolliver looked up at Barnett with his head cocked to one side and his mouth opened, a pose that he firmly believed connoted awe. To Barnett it looked more as though the little man had just swallowed something that had unexpectedly turned out to be alive. "You talk pretty sometimes," the Mummer said. "Like the professor."

"Your speech has a certain fascination also, Mummer," Barnett said. "You have the strangest mixture of dialects and street cant that I've ever heard."

"That's 'cause of where I were brought up," the Mummer said. "Which were everywhere. My folks was traveling people, they was. Longest we ever stayed in one place, that I can remember, were about three months. And that were when my dad broke 'is arm. We missed the whole steeplechase circuit in the north of England that season."

"Your father wasn't a jockey, was he?" Barnett asked.

"Naow, course not. 'E worked the crowds, same as my mum. Real elegant-looking 'e were, too, when 'e were working. 'E were the best dip I ever saw. Didn't work with nobody, neither. Cleaned out the mark all by 'imself 'Lightfingered Harry Tolliver,' they called 'im."

"I see," Barnett said. "Then you were just carrying on the family tradition when you became a pickpocket."

"My dad taught me everything I know. 'E were better than what I ever been. 'Course 'e 'ad a natural advantage over me, being somewhat taller in stature."

"I should think being short would be more desirable. You can sort of melt into the crowd and disappear while the hue and cry is being raised."

"It don't work that way," Tolliver said. "Consider the respective sizes of the fox and the fox hunter."

"At first glance," Barnett said doubtfully, "that appears to make sense."

"Course it were great while I looked like a little innocent," Tolliver said. "Being pushed about in my pram, dipping into hip pockets as we passed the toffs. I mean, even if anyone had caught a glimpse o' the action, who would have believed it? I can hear it now: Lord Cecil turns to his neighbor and 'e says, 'I say, Colonel, did you see that?'

" 'What?' asked the colonel.

" 'Sir Henry just 'ad 'is pocket picked!'

" 'By Jove!' says the colonel. 'What a rum show! And where's the blighter what did it?'

" 'There's the blighter, there,' says Lord Cecil, pointing into the pram.

" 'What, the little bloke with the sunbonnet what can't be more than three years old?' asks the colonel. And pretty soon, you see, the subject is changed by mutual agreement."

"You must have been a charming baby," Barnett said.

"I was," Tolliver agreed. "For years and years."

Barnett finished his coffee and then went upstairs to see Professor Moriarty before leaving the house. He was meeting Miss Cecily Perrine for luncheon at Hempelmayer's. He had a question to ask her that could make this one of the most important occasions of his life, but there were some details to be taken care of first.

Moriarty was up and dressed for the day, to Barnett's surprise. His tweed suit suggested a venture into the outside world, and probably in a direction away from the city. Moriarty described clothing as "mere costume," but nonetheless he was usually correctly attired. "One should always be in the right disguise," he had said. And since gentlemen did not wear tweeds to town, the professor was probably headed toward the country.

"I was just coming down," he told Barnett. "There is a lot of work to be done in a short time. I have spent many years assembling, from among London's criminal classes, a talented and able crew of assistants. What Sherlock Holmes calls my 'henchmen.' These are men and women who, had they been better born or been given any sort of chance in life, would be serving England proudly now as statesmen, soldiers, or artisans. But they have had no such chance, so instead they serve me. And here is the job that is going to require all the talents, all the skills, all the brains that I have so painstakingly assembled."

"I gather there's a job on," Barnett said.

"*A* job!" Moriarty rubbed his hands together and looked satisfied. "My dear Barnett, we are going to commit the crime of the century, you and I."

"I see, Professor," Barnett said. "Just the two of us?"

"I fancy we will need a little assistance," Moriarty said. "Twenty-five or thirty people should suffice. And the artifices of all my skilled artisans. I have a task for Benlevi that should appeal to him; and old Roos the chemist, and Gilchester, the Mummers' gaff. And I need to find someone who makes uniforms."

"It sounds extensive," Barnett said.

Moriarty gathered together some drawings on sheets of foolscap that were loose on his bed and put them, together with some drafting and surveying instruments, in a small portfolio. "I venture to say that no other organization but mine could attempt this," he said. "And certainly no other brain than mine could have conceived the plan necessary to penetrate the interwoven nest of formidable defenses guarding our prize."

"Which is?"

Moriarty picked up the *Morning Herald* and tossed it to Barnett. "Examine page one," he said.

"I thought you never read the newspapers," Barnett said.

"Only in the way of business," Moriarty told him. "Never for pleasure."

Barnett unfolded the *Herald* and looked over the stories on the front page. " 'Police Baffled at Latest Slasher Outrage,' " he read.

"No doubt," Moriarty commented.

Barnett looked at him, and then back at the paper. "That's not it, then." He studied the headlines. " 'French Official Detained by Germans in Alsace—Boulanger Protests.' "

Moriarty strapped the portfolio closed without looking up.

" 'Home Rule Bill Will Face Parliament Again.' "

Moriarty chuckled.

" 'Lord East Arrives on *Drakonia*.' "

"Ah!" Moriarty said. "You might further peruse that article. It has certain points of interest."

Barnett read: " 'Lord East, Viceroy of India until relieved February last by Sir Harry Wittington, arrived in Liverpool yesterday afternoon aboard the Anglo-Indian Line steam packet *Drakonia*. His lordship will proceed directly to London to make arrangements for the reception and transportation of the justly famous Lord East collection of Indian artifacts.

" 'The collection, a vast assemblage of archaeological material, artwork, and precious metals and gems from all over the Indian subcontinent, has been placed by Lord East on indefinite loan to the Crown for display at selected locations throughout London on the occasion of her majesty's impending Golden Jubilee.

" 'The Lord East Collection is due to arrive at Plymouth aboard Her Majesty's Battleship *Hornblower* for transport by rail to the five museums in London which have been designated custodians for the duration of the Golden Jubilee, after which a permanent exhibition site will be picked and proper housing for the collection constructed.

" 'The special train which is planned for carrying Lord East's priceless treasure is to consist of twenty cars—ten goods wagons for the collection, and ten special troop cars for the military escort. Unusual precautions are being taken to safeguard the treasure, which our correspondent is given to believe has been threatened by an Indian secret society dedicated to the overthrow of the British raj.

" 'Lord East has held the title of Viceroy for the past six years, and is generally considered to have been most effective in spreading British rule throughout the subcontinent and bringing the civilizing influence of British law and custom to every corner of this vast land.' "

"He has also," Moriarty said, interrupting Barnett's reading, "succeeded in looting a five-thousand-year-old civilization of such items as were gaudy or valuable enough to catch his fancy, and in the process has damaged, defaced, or utterly destroyed everything he touched that he didn't covet or understand. The man is a vandal."

Barnett put the paper aside. "I have an intimation of what the problem is that you have been pondering for the past few days," he said. "Considering this article, paired with the fact that a gentleman of Indian background has been visiting you of late."

"Ah, Barnett, there is something of the investigator in you after all. Which is to the good, as that is what I've been principally employing you for during these past two years." Moriarty left the room and preceded Barnett down to his study. "I assume you wish to speak to me," he said, settling into the leather chair behind his massive desk.

"A few words, Professor," Barnett said. "I have to leave the house shortly, but I thought I'd better apprise you of a decision I've made."

Moriarty silently studied Barnett for a few seconds. "You have my approval and my blessings, for what they're worth," he said. "The state of matrimony is not for me. By its nature it cannot be an equal relationship, and I would take neither part of an unequal relationship. But I think you, if I may use a metaphor, are the sort of ship that needs a rudder."

Barnett's face turned bright pink. "Come now, Professor," he said, staring down at Moriarty, "how can you possibly know what I intend to ask you before I have done so?"

"An elementary problem, my dear Barnett. Our agreement terminates in a little over a month, I believe?"

"That is so."

"Yes. And it has been preying on your mind. You have made several oblique references to the fact over the past weeks. Usually during dinner. So, after two years of harmonious association, you wish to go your own way."

"How do you know I don't wish to extend the contract for another year or two?" Barnett asked.

"It seems clear that in that case it wouldn't occupy your thoughts. You know that I find our association satisfactory, so you can't be concerned as to whether I am preparing to throw you out. It must be that you are preparing to sever the connection. But by the same token, if you had already definitely decided to leave, you would certainly have informed me shortly after making the decision. You would, as you might say, get it off your chest."

"Probably," Barnett admitted.

"So, when my observations and deductions had taken me that far, I was faced with the following question: here is my trusted associate planning to leave my service. But his plans aren't definite, or he would certainly have informed me. Therefore, his leavetaking is predicated upon some future event that might not happen as anticipated. At first, I will admit, I contemplated the possibility that you had received an offer from some other organization; something perhaps entirely inside the law, something offering more remuneration or more interesting and varied assignments."

"Professor—"

Moriarty held up his hand. "But upon reflection," he said, "I realized that that could not be. You are not unhappy here. You are one of those who finds a necessary vitality in the practice of our endeavors. Quick thinking, fast response, the ever-present scent of danger; these things serve as anodyne and stimulant to you."

"I admit to feeling more alert, even more vital, when I'm risking my life and liberty in your employ," Barnett said. "But I am not altogether sure that it is the most sensible way to achieve that result."

"So far my logic took me," Moriarty said. "Some further reflection made it evident that you were preparing to propose marriage to Miss Cecily Perrine. If she accepts, you will wish to leave my employ, it being unchivalrous to ask her to wed someone who might conceivably be convicted of a felony."

"That is so," Barnett said.

"Therefore I offered you my approval and blessings."

"It is pointless to try to keep a secret from you, Professor," Barnett said. "I am meeting Miss Perrine for luncheon, and I expect to broach the subject to her at that time."

"I doubt whether you will surprise the young lady, either," Moriarty commented. "In my experience, although the man does the proposing, he is often the last to know."

"I'm afraid that I shall have to give up my services to you, except for those which come through the American News Service," Barnett said. "This Indian venture will probably be the last effort in which I am directly involved."

"Are you sure you desire to take part in this one?" Moriarty asked. "After all, with only a month left, and a marriage impending—"

"The lady hasn't accepted me yet," Barnett said. "I certainly hope she will, but if not I will surely need something to keep my mind off her refusal. And if she does accept, well, I'm sure the marriage will be several months off. And, after reading the newspaper description—" He paused. "Well, let me put it this way. If you are planning to remove a treasure shipment from either the *Hornblower* or a troop train, that's something I wouldn't miss for the world!"

FOURTEEN

THE ART OF DETECTION

And lo, between the sundown and the sun,
His day's work and his night's work are undone;
And lo, between the nightfall and the light,
He is not, and none knoweth of such an one.
— ALGERNON CHARLES SWINBURNE

If you are not satisfied with my reports, or with the progress I've made in the investigation," Sherlock Holmes said, rising from his caneback chair and fixing his sharp, piercing gaze on the man across the desk, "then by all means get another investigator. I shall consider myself off the case from this moment, and I shall submit no bill. Please call your clerk and ask him to retrieve my overcoat."

"No, no, Mr. Holmes, you misunderstand," the Earl of Arundale said, leaping to his feet and placing a placating hand on Holmes's arm. "We are all distressed that this murderer has not been apprehended, but I am satisfied that no man could have done more than you in the attempt. Your reports are, indeed, full of detail that was overlooked or unseen by the regular police."

Holmes dropped back onto the brocade-covered seat of his chair and stared glumly across the desk. "I apologize for taking offense so easily, my lord," he said. "But this is a vexatious problem with which you have presented me. With each subsequent murder our killer manages to make himself more obscure. This is contrary to my experience. There is something—some essential fact—which connects these killings, which I am failing to grasp. I'm certain that it is there, in those documents, staring me in the face. I have gone over them for countless hours, both the police reports and my own notes. I sense that the answer is there, sometimes I feel that I almost have it, and yet it eludes me."

"You have given us a description of the murderer," Lord Arundale pointed out. "Something that the regular police have been unable to do. And that without anyone's having seen the man."

"Bah! A description that would fit thousands of men walking about London at this moment." Holmes hit his fist against the side of the desk. "I tell you, my lord, it is maddening!"

Lord Arundale's butler, an ancient retainer in red velvet knee breeches and a swallowtail jacket, knocked on the study door and pulled it open. "The Count d'Hiver has arrived, my lord," he announced, pronouncing the name "Deever."

"Show him in, Threshampton," Lord Arundale said. He turned to Holmes. "The name is pronounced 'd'Hiver,' he explained, giving it the full value of its French ancestry. "The count is interested in this affair. He has what we would call in legal terms a 'watching brief' from the Lord Privy Seal. Her majesty herself is quite concerned. She does not, for obvious reasons, wish this concern to become known. D'Hiver regularly travels abroad for the Home Office, I am given to understand, on assignments of a confidential nature. He is considered quite perceptive and quite able. Some people find him rather abrasive—I give you warning."

"I understand, my lord," Holmes said, sounding thoughtful, "but surely—"

"What is it?"

"Nothing—nothing important. But tell me—the Count d'Hiver? Certainly that is not a British title, neither in style nor name."

"The title is French," Lord Arundale said, "but the d'Hivers are English for the last hundred years. The present count's greatgrandfather, or some such, came over one jump ahead of Robespierre. Got out of revolutionary France by a neck, if you see what I mean."

The count was a slight, delicate-looking man with a precisely trimmed beard that made his face look angular. His family's hundred years in England did not show in his taste in clothing; his doublebreasted blue foulard suit jacket covered a white flowered waistcoat with just a touch of lace along the collar. The effect was so unBritish, so Parisian, as to skirt the bounds of taste for a proper London gentleman. But Count d'Hiver bore it well. His every move reflected an air of panache and a manner of self-assurance that made it clear that he valued no man's opinion save his own. He strode into the room and stopped in the middle of the carpet, his gaze darting about like that of a predatory animal in search of its lunch.

The Earl of Arundale rose and performed the necessary introductions. "Mr. Holmes was just about to discuss with me some of the conclusions he has reached," he said.

"I have read your reports," d'Hiver said, looking down his aquiline nose at Holmes, "and those of the police. The police are bunglers. You show a little imagination, Mr. Holmes. But still, we don't seem to be any closer to apprehending our killer."

"That is, unfortunately, the truth," Holmes admitted. "There has been very little to work on so far. The first four killings took place before I was called in. Thus I was unable to examine the scenes of the crimes until well after the most suggestive evidence had been handled and tramped over by a dozen other people. Three of the murder rooms had been cleaned before I got to see them. Nonetheless several facts of interest have been uncovered. I have initiated several lines of inquiry, but so far they have all proved fruitless."

"In your last report there is a description of the man you claim is the killer," d'Hiver said. "How much of it is guesswork?"

"I never guess," Holmes said. "And if I were prone to guesswork, I certainly wouldn't do it in my reports. What I have given you is my considered opinion, based upon investigation and deduction. It may prove to be wrong in one or two particulars, but on the whole it is accurate."

Count d'Hiver perched himself on one of the caneback chairs, his body rigidly erect and tilted slightly forward, his hands crossed over the massive gold knob on his ebony cane. "Accurate it may be," he snapped, "useful it is not! Your description is as vague as the fortune-teller's fabled 'tall, dark man.' "

"Sketchy, perhaps, Count d'Hiver," Holmes said, "but hardly vague. The man is between five feet ten and six feet tall, weighs about twelve stone, is neither adolescent nor aged—I estimate his age at forty to forty-five, but there I could be off. He has light-brown hair of medium length, dresses like a gentleman, is not obviously disfigured, and is probably Eastern European. If so, he speaks English fluently."

"Really?" D'Hiver said, his voice showing aristocratic doubt. "And this description of a man who has not been seen is pieced together from your examination of rooms where the experts of Scotland Yard can find no clues. Tell me, is there anything else that has eluded the professionals?"

"A few items," Holmes said, apparently oblivious to d'Hiver's sarcastic tone. "The man is in good physical condition, athletic and robust. He picks his victims carefully, not at random. All of the murdered men have—for the killer—something in common."

D'Hiver leaned forward in his chair, his eyes like dark gimlets peering at Holmes. "And that is?"

Holmes shook his head. "That I cannot tell you. That is the point which has succeeded in eluding me."

"Then this is not the work of a lunatic?" Lord Arundale asked.

"On the contrary, my lord," Holmes said. "This is clearly the work of a lunatic. But the killings are not random. This lunatic has a pattern, a goal, a fixed purpose. And he knows something that we do not."

"What do you mean?" Lord Arundale asked.

"Look at it this way, my lord. Let us say that the killer hates the color red, and is killing everyone he sees dressed in red. Well then, the pattern should be obvious, but we don't see it. We are colorblind. We cannot solve this hypothetical case until someone who is not colorblind happens to mention that all of the victims have been clad in red."

"You believe these victims are tied together in some fashion?" Count d'Hiver asked.

"Yes, I would say so. Something definite and precise, beyond the obvious similarities of sex and class."

"Why? What evidence have you of this?"

"Evidence? I have nothing so strong as to be called 'evidence.' I have, rather, hints, suggestions; nothing better. However, I also have my knowledge and experience, and upon that I base my conclusion."

"You have found nothing that would support my fears of a foreign connection?" Lord Arundale asked.

"None," Holmes said. "It was in following that possibility that I got led astray some days ago and ended up at the country estate of my old friend Professor James Moriarty."

"I read of that," Lord Arundale said. "The police report of the raid did not go into much detail. I had the feeling much was left out."

"It doesn't matter, my lord. It was a mistake. Sometimes specialized knowledge can lead one astray. The knowledge that there is one great villain yet unhanged can temporarily blind one to the fact that other villainy can coexist. I am not yet totally convinced that Moriarty is not involved, but I must admit that the preponderance of evidences would so indicate."

"These 'hints' of a common tie between the victims." Count d'Hiver said. "Upon what sort of facts, of clues, are they based?"

Holmes turned to face the count. "I would rather wait until I have had a chance to assemble a few more facts," he said. "I dislike presenting my conclusions piecemeal in this fashion. I agreed to keep you informed as to my progress only because of the unusual circumstances, and because her majesty is interested. This is not my usual way of proceeding, and I don't like it."

"My dear Mr. Sherlock Holmes," Count d'Hiver said, "we don't have time for you to assemble. There are decisions that must be made now, and to make them intelligently we must have all the available information. I'm sure you understand." He smiled. His teeth were even and white, and gave the impression of being sharp.

"Let *us* tell *you* what is happening, Mr. Holmes," Lord Arundale said. "There have been six men murdered in London in the past six weeks. All gentlemen of the upper classes. All apparently murdered by the same hand while they were in their own home—in some cases in their own bedrooms. The police have been powerless to stop these attacks."

"It is difficult to stop what you are unable to anticipate," Holmes commented.

"Mr. Holmes," Lord Arundale said, "the people are getting restless."

"The people," Holmes said, "only know of five of the six killings."

"And a good thing, too," Count d'Hiver said.

"Considering how selective our murderer is," Holmes commented, "it is clear that the great majority of the citizens of London would be better off worrying about being run down by a horse tram. Unless one is a male, over thirty-five, has an income in excess of twenty thousand pounds a year, and has some pretensions to aristocracy, one is almost certain not to find himself on our killer's little list."

"The point is," Lord Arundale said, "that if a mysterious killer can take these six lives without our being able to stop him, then nobody in London is safe. And the people, even the common people who are admittedly not targets, are beginning to sense that. There is a certain nervous tension building in the city."

"I concede that," Holmes said.

"The last major riots in London were over twenty years ago,"

Lord Arundale said, "but this could provoke the sort of feeling that leads to riots."

Holmes tapped his finger on the desk. "The feeling that leads to riots," he said, "is more easily provoked by the sort of behavior the police are currently indulging in. At, I believe, the instigation of the Home Office."

"We must keep them busy," Count d'Hiver said. "Let them feel that they are accomplishing something. It is necessary for their morale."

"Rounding up everyone who has ever been arrested for a crime in the past fifteen years?" Holmes asked. "Scotland Yard doesn't have the manpower for that sort of job. As a result the people they are rounding up are bullied and harassed merely because the police do not have the time to do the job right. You are making the criminal classes apprehensive, which is not a good way to maintain law and order."

"Doubtless," Count d'Hiver said. "But expediency is not the best basis for a standard of law enforcement. Tell me, what evidence have you found that indicates to you that the victims of these murders share some specific connection?"

"Aside from the dramatic evidence of their common *fate*?" Holmes leaned back and laced his fingers together. "I'll tell you," he said, "but I warn you that you won't be as impressed by it as I am. It is a delicate skein, only seen by the experienced observer. And right now these clues are tentative, since I don't know where they lead. I need more time. I must have additional evidence."

"You think a few more murders will provide you with the evidence you need?" Lord Arundale asked.

"Most certainly, my lord. And since there is no indication that the killer is planning to stop, I imagine the necessary clues will soon be forthcoming."

D'Hiver frowned. "A heartless viewpoint."

"If I could catch the killer now," Holmes said, "I would. On the other hand, if he were to stop the killing now without having the grace to identify himself, I should consider that preferable to his committing the one last murder that traps him. I am not heartless, merely rational."

Lord Arundale sighed. "I am glad this doesn't seem to be a political crime," he said. "I would not like to be charged with deciding which of the great European powers is killing off the English aristocracy. I would enjoy even less having to take some action against such a power or accuse it in some public forum of such a vile act."

"Accuse?" Count d'Hiver snorted. "Talking never got anyone anything but hoarse. Retaliation, that's the key to international affairs. An eye for an eye." He tapped his cane impatiently on the hardwood floor. "Come now," he said to Holmes, "tell us your theory about the connecting link between the murders."

Holmes considered. "Certain similarities point in the direction of a common cause," he said. "For example, either the room or the body of each of the victims was searched by the murderer."

"That sounds perfectly normal," Lord Arundale said. "Not that I have any great knowledge of what is normal for a murderer; but I should think that if one is going to go to the trouble of killing someone, one would want to gain something out of it."

"Robbery was not the motive for any of these killings." Holmes said.

"Quite so," Count d'Hiver said. "That much is clear from the reports. Not the primary motive, certainly. But a quick search for some extremely portable wealth? I mean, a man who commits a murder is quite probably willing to steal."

"Lord Walbine had a pocket watch on his person," Holmes said, "crafted by Pronzini and Wilcox. The cloisonné inlay work on the case alone should have made it a national treasure. I can't think of anything more portable. Even the meanest fence would feel guilty at offering less than five hundred pounds for it."

"The villain, whoever he is, might have missed it," Lord Arundale said.

"Isadore Stanhope had a ruby stickpin the size of a robin's egg," Holmes said. "George Venn had fifty pounds in Bank of England notes on the table by his bed. Sir Geoffrey Cruikstaff had a solid gold cigarette case in his pocket and an extensive coin collection in the top drawer of his secretary. None of these was disturbed."

"Then nothing was taken?" d'Hiver asked.

"I believe," Holmes said carefully, "that *something* was taken. The murderer searched for and found some small object at the scene of each of his killings. That object is what he took away with him."

"What object?" Lord Arundale asked.

"That I don't know," Holmes said. "Inferential evidence suggests that it was small, unremarkable, easily concealed on the person, and of little intrinsic value."

"You say the killer took something from *each* of his victims?

What sort of thing do you suppose it could be?" Count d'Hiver asked.

"A key, perhaps," Holmes said. "Or a medallion or signet of some sort."

"Key to what?" Lord Arundale asked.

Holmes smiled. "I would welcome ideas as to that, my lord. The only thing I would suggest is that whatever the object is, it was an identical object for each of the victims."

Count d'Hiver stared silently at Holmes, his thoughts clearly somewhere else. Lord Arundale tapped his fingernails on the polished surface of his desk thoughtfully. "Some small object," he said, "taken from each of the victims, and identical in each case. Why do you feel that it's the same object in each case?"

"The murderer was certainly looking for some specific object," Holmes said. "Such insistence would indicate that the object, whatever it was, must be in some way part of the motive for the crime. Surely it would be stretching the bounds of credulity to suggest that it was a different object in each case."

"I don't know about that," Count d'Hiver said. "Perhaps our killer is some sort of fetishist. Perhaps he merely wants some small memento from each of his victims. Something to wear on his watch chain."

"Perhaps." Holmes stood up. "Is there any further way in which I can assist or enlighten either of you gentlemen at the moment? No? Then I shall get back to my investigations. It may be that with luck I can prevent another killing. But I am not sanguine, my lords. I am afraid that there will be more blood shed before we reach the bottom of this."

"Keep us informed," Lord Arundale said.

"I shall, my lord," Holmes assured him.

FIFTEEN

A MODEST PROPOSAL

When Chloris to the temple comes,
  Adoring crowds before her fall:
She can restore the dead from tombs,
  And every life but mine recall.
I only am by love designed
To be the victim for mankind.
— JOHN DRYDEN

When one is in the grip of a powerful emotion, small events can hold magnified significance. Benjamin Barnett paused at a flower stall on his way to lunch with Cecily Perrine and purchased a bunch of violets. Then, as he walked the last few blocks to the restaurant, he found himself staring at the flowers and thinking what a paltry, inappropriate gift they were for the woman one intended to marry. This thought grew into a conviction, and so he paused at a confectioner's and selected a pound of mixed chocolates, which were wrapped in fancy paper and tied with a bow. But then, after he had paid for the chocolates, the indecision returned, and he found himself unable to choose between the flowers and the chocolates.

The problem, Barnett realized, was not with the gifts. He would have liked to have given her something major, something important—a ring, a pendant, a brooch speckled with precious gems—but he couldn't very well do that. It would be in *very* bad taste until after he had asked her father formally for her hand. But under the circumstances, limited to a token gift, flowers were nice. Chocolates were acceptable. It was the imminent proposal itself that was making his hands go clammy and his heart beat triple-time against his chest. He certainly wanted to ask her—more than anything in the world he wanted Cecily Perrine to be his wife. He fully intended to ask her.

But he wasn't sure that he actually could. He felt his heartbeat increase in speed and pressure as he just walked along with a bunch of flowers under one arm, a pound of chocolates under the other elbow, and *thought* about proposing to Cecily.

What if she turns me down? he thought. *What if she smiles at me gently and says, "Benjamin, you know that I do love you—but it is like a brother. I've never thought of you the other way!"* After all, it could happen. He knew she was fond of him, but he had no assurance that it went beyond that. What if she *laughed* at him?

On the whole, Barnett decided, women had it much better in this society than men did. Men had to do the asking. Everything from "May I have this dance?" to "Will you marry me?" If a woman was rejected it was indirect, by not being asked; and if no one knew that she expected to be asked, then it remained a private, personal grief. Romantic traces of such past opportunity lost could be seen as a secret anguish in love-haunted eyes. A man was rejected as a public act, a direct holding up of one's innermost desires and most private feelings to the jeers of the crowd, a humiliation that could be felt as a physical wrenching, like a knife in the pit of the stomach.

When Barnett reached the front door of Hempelmayer's, he still had to choose between the chocolates and the flowers. Walking in with both, he was convinced, would make him look ridiculous. And if there's anything a man in love cannot stand, it is to look ridiculous. Especially since he realizes that in word and deed, he is already sufficiently ridiculous with no external aid. Or so Mr. Wilde, the American News Service's favorite epigrammatist, would maintain. But then, Mr. Wilde didn't seem to like women very much.

Barnett looked at his two purchases and realized that he would have to make an arbitrary decision.

"Are you married?" he asked the elderly doorman who pulled open the ornate brass-on-glass door for him.

"For these past twenty-eight years, sir," the doorman told him. "Nine little ones. Some of 'em nary so little anymore."

"Well then, here," Barnett said, handing the man the elaborately wrapped box of chocolates. "A present for your wife."

"Thank ye, sir." The doorman touched the brim of his uniform cap with his knuckle. "Thank ye very much."

Cecily was perched like a princess on an overstuffed plush couch in the anteroom, waiting for Barnett. "About time you arrived," she said. "You are a quarter of an hour late."

"I'm sorry," Barnett said. "I didn't realize the time. My watch must be slow. I stopped to get you some flowers. Violets. Here." He thrust the bunch at her.

"Well, that's very nice," Cecily said in an insincere voice. "Quite thoughtful of you." She rose and took the tissue-paper-wrapped bunch, holding them at arm's length, as though they had a bad odor. "I'll just leave them in the cloakroom until after our meal."

"I'll do it," Barnett said, retrieving the vegetation. "I have to hang up my topcoat anyhow." He disposed of his coat and the flowers in the cloakroom and returned. A short, fussy man with a prim mustache showed them to their table, presented them with their menus, and pranced off. Barnett looked across the table at Cecily. "Would you have preferred chocolates?" he asked. "It will just take me a second to switch with the doorman."

Cecily looked up from the menu. "What's that?" she asked. "Switch what?"

"The violets. I didn't know you disliked violets. Very few people have a natural antipathy to them. It's just my misfortune that you are one of them. Well, live and learn, I always say. Now that I've learned, I shall never offend your delicate nostrils with the scent of violets again."

"Benjamin, my dear, I like violets," Cicely said, looking over her menu at him. "I assure you I am very pleased that you have brought me violets. I shall put them in water as soon as I can, and carry the vase about with me everywhere until the poor things wilt and the petals fall off. I *love* violets."

"The way you treated the poor things when I handed them to you, I had formed quite a contrary opinion," Barnett told her.

"I am sorry," Cecily said. "I was distracted. I was angry. I still am, if it comes to that. But I do apologize for taking it out on you."

"Angry?" Barnett asked. "Why are you angry? Listen, Cecily, if someone has offended you, tell me about it and let me be angry too."

"Circumstances conspire to offend me, Benjamin," Cecily said. "This most recent circumstance has, I fear, provoked a reaction quite out of relation to its cause. The fault, I believe, lies in the fact that I was raised by my father. And my father is a man most intolerant of the stifling stupidity of convention and the rigid imbecility of custom."

"I see," said Barnett, who didn't at all. "Some custom has angered you? What sort of custom?"

"Have you ever stopped to realize how unequal is the relationship between men and women in our society?" Cecily asked, staring intently across the table at Barnett. "Have you ever considered how much freedom men have in everyday discourse and commerce, and how stifling it is to be a woman?"

"I am not sure what you mean," Barnett said, taken slightly aback by the intensity with which his loved one was speaking on a subject to which he had never given much thought.

"I arrived at this restaurant fifteen minutes before you did," Cecily said.

"I told you I'm sorry—"

Cecily raised a hand to stop him. "Not you," she said. "I asked to be seated when I arrived. The manager informed me that unescorted women are not seated in his establishment. The way he said 'unescorted' was, of itself, an insult. I told him my escort would be along shortly. He replied that when my escort arrived he would be pleased to seat us both."

Barnett thought about this for a moment, and then his face turned red, and he started to rise, but Cecily reached across and put her hand on his shoulder. "Please don't make a scene," she said. "That would accomplish nothing except to make me feel worse."

"Someone should teach a boor like that to have proper respect for a lady!" Barnett exclaimed.

"Perhaps," Cecily said, "but an altercation in a public place will not accomplish that end. If I thought it would, I would have started one myself."

Barnett relaxed on his seat. "Yes," he said, "I guess you would have."

"This is merely a symptom of the condition of women in our society today," Cecily said. "*That's* what makes me angry!"

"Now, I don't think that's fair," Barnett said. "This boob, this scoundrel, is obviously *non compos mentis*. Anyone who is capable of confusing a lady like you with a, ah, woman should not be in a position where he has to make such fine discernments."

"That is not my point," Cecily insisted. "It's the inequality of the situation that frustrates and angers me. If a man wants to eat in here alone, and is reasonably well dressed, the manager doesn't ask to see proof of his gentle birth. If a woman, no matter how well dressed, wishes to eat lunch but is not currently in possession of an escort, the manager feels free to assume that she's 'no better than she ought to be.' In the first place, what authority has he to assume any such thing? In the second place, even if it were so, is that any reason to deprive her of the right to eat lunch?"

"Now, Cecily," Barnett said. "Women in this society are protected, guarded; all in all, they are treated far better than men."

"Protected from whom?" Cecily demanded. "Guarded from what?"

"You are an intensely independent person, Cecily, quite determined to have your own way in everything. And I admire you for it," Barnett said. "But most ladies enjoy the protection of their special status."

"You think so?" Cecily asked. "Try asking some of them. You might be surprised."

Barnett realized that now was not a propitious time to propose marriage. He should probably postpone the question until another day. But he had spent all morning building up the courage and it would probably be even harder another time. He decided to wait until dessert.

They spoke of many things during the course of the meal. One of the hallmarks of a good journalist is a wide and searching curiosity. The conversation ranged from the possibility of a new war in Europe to the claims of a Scottish inventor that he was perfecting a machine that could fly. The question of the rights and indignities of women gradually faded into the past, although Barnett was sure that it was not forgotten. He would have to give it some thought.

Toward the end of the entrée they reached the subject of the series of murders. Cecily was quite wrapped up in the articles she was doing about the murders. "There must be something that connects these crimes," she insisted to Barnett. "The poor man is obviously in the grip of some overpowering compulsion that causes him to seek out these particular victims."

"By 'the poor man,' I assume you are referring to the mysterious individual who has been slitting the throats of perfectly innocuous middle-aged men in their own bedrooms," Barnett said.

Cecily poked thoughtfully at the remains of a poached whitefish on her plate. "A man who commits a heinous crime," she said, "has put himself outside the bounds of common human intercourse. This is not an easy thing to do, not an easy decision to make. To choose to be isolated from the rest of humanity, there must be a compelling need. One can feel a revulsion at the deed, and at the same time pity the man who felt compelled to commit it."

"I'd rather save my pity for the victims," Barnett said. "The frightening thing about a murderer like this one is that he *isn't* isolated from society. We could breathe easier if he were. He is embedded in our midst, and hidden by the camouflage of assumed innocence. There is nothing about his appearance or manner to proclaim him as a secret slitter of throats. He probably discusses each murder with his friends, and shakes his head in wonder that anyone could commit such a horrible deed."

"A man like this has no friends," Cecily said. "That is one of the signs of the type of abnormality that causes a man to feel impelled to commit this sort of crime."

"How can you be so sure about that?" Barnett asked. "He may be the most popular man in his club. He may have to employ two social secretaries to respond to all his invitations."

Cecily put down her fork and pushed her plate aside. "I don't think so," she said. "I've been doing some reading, you might say research, on the background and antecedents of the killer type, and I would say that almost certainly he is a very lonely man."

One waiter returned to hand them dessert menus, while another sneaked in behind the first and removed the fishy remains from in front of Cecily.

"Now," Barnett said, after the waiter went off to have vanilla soufflés constructed for their desserts, "what have you found in your research that indicates our murderer is such a lonely man? You think he is driven to commit these crimes out of simple boredom?"

"No," Cecily told him. "You have it wrong way around. I believe this man is so driven by his need to commit these crimes that he has no time for normal human desires like companionship, or love, or recreation."

"What about eating?" Barnett asked.

"I would say he eats as an animal eats," Cecily said. "He ingests food to give him the necessary energy to keep going. I doubt if he cares what he eats, or is even aware what the dish in front of him contains."

"And upon what do you base this stark image of a man driven by forces stronger than himself?"

"On my study of similar crimes committed in the recent past," Cecily said. "The Düsseldorf Slasher of fifteen years ago was a man named Roehm. When the police apprehended him he was living in a bare, unfurnished room with only a couple of blankets on the floor to sleep on. The only clothing he possessed was several changes of

undergarments and one extra shirt. And this was a formerly respectable, middle-class man."

"Who was he killing," Barnett asked, "and why?"

"He killed three magistrates, two clerks of the court, two bailiffs,
and a man that drove the prison wagon before he was captured."

"He must have had it in for the courts."

"His wife was arrested and convicted of a homicide and sentenced to the mines. Three years later it was discovered that she was
innocent, and she was released. It was too late; the hard labor and
terrible conditions at the mines had weakened her until she was beyond medical help. The state gave her thirty gold marks for recompense. She died six months later. A year after that the murders
began."

"I'd say the man had a just grievance," Barnett commented.
"Imagine what emotions must have been bottled up inside of him.
It's not surprising that they came out as a series of slashings."

"He was certainly acting under the influence of a powerful compulsion," Cecily agreed. "As was the Mad Bomber of Paris in 1878,
who went around leaving infernal devices in the left-luggage rooms
of railway stations. As was Mr. Pinkley of Chicago, who made it his
practice to give bonbons laced with arsenic to ladies of the street."

The soufflés were delivered at this moment, and Barnett stared
down at his. It was very attractive, rising a full three inches off the
top of the dish. "Arsenic, eh?" he said.

Cecily laughed. "Don't worry," she told him. "I've heard of its
being sprinkled into omelets, but never a soufflé."

Barnett looked up and grinned at her. "You can't be too careful," he said.

"So I've been led to believe," Cecily said.

They ate their desserts in contemplative silence. The time, Barnett
realized, had come. He took a deep breath. "Cecily," he said, "there
is something I'd like to ask you."

"Yes, Benjamin?"

He took another deep breath. "I, ah, would like to ask your
father for your hand in marriage."

Cecily put her fork down carefully on the side of the plate and
nudged it with her finger until it was in the perfect position. The
silence stretched on.

"Say something, Cecily," Barnett finally blurted out.

For another long moment there was no response. Cecily's eyes
darted around as though she felt trapped at the table and was looking

desperately for a way out. Then she turned to Barnett and pointed a finger at him. "I'm certain you don't realize this," she said, "but that proves my point, what you just said. It's so typical. And you're not even aware of what you did."

"What do you mean, 'not aware'?" Barnett demanded, his voice cracking slightly with the effort to suppress both his anger and his bewilderment at this reaction. "I just proposed marriage to you, that's what happened."

"No, it isn't," she said. "You just informed me that you were going to ask my father. Is it my father that you wish to marry? If not, then why are you going to ask him?"

This, Barnett decided, was not his day. Perhaps there was something to astrology after all. "It is the custom," he said. "What I'm actually doing is asking you, you know that. But your father has to give you away."

"Why?" she asked. "Supposing Father says no?"

"I, ah, hadn't thought of that," Barnett said. "Frankly, if you say yes, I don't give a damn what your father says."

"That is courageous of you," she said.

Barnett dropped his fork onto his plate with a little silver clatter. "All right!" he said. "I'm not asking your father, I'm asking you. Cecily, will you marry me?"

"I don't know," she said.

"What?"

Cecily leaned forward and took his hand. "I would like to marry you," she told him. "But I'm not sure you'd really like to be married to the sort of wife I'd be."

"Cecily, I love you," Barnett said. "This table's too wide for me to hold you properly, but I love you more than anything and I want you to be my wife. I know that's trite, but there it is. I have loved you for some time. Since the day you first knocked on the door of the American News Service, as a matter of fact."

"It took you long enough to get around to declaring it," she said.

"I had commitments," Barnett said. "There were reasons."

"No, never mind that," she said. "That was unfair of me. I've been aware for some time of how you feel about me. And I'm honored."

"Honored," Barnett said. "Which means that you don't love me."

"No, it doesn't," Cecily said. "Benjamin, dearest, I do love you. I even wish to marry you, I just don't think you *really* want to marry me."

"With all my heart," Barnett said.

"You want me to be your wife."

"Yes."

"You want to set up a home for me."

"*With* you."

"You want me to quit work."

"Of course."

"Well, I want to marry you, Benjamin, but I have no desire to give up my career. I want to be a reporter. I don't want to just sit home and tend the babies—if we have any babies."

"Why not?" Benjamin asked. "What's wrong with tending babies?"

"I'll tell you what," Cecily said. "I'll keep my job and *you* stay home and tend the babies."

"Cecily!" Benjamin said, sounding positively shocked.

"Those are my terms," Cecily said. "Have you a counter offer?"

"Don't be ridiculous," Barnett said.

"You think it's ridiculous, do you?" Cecily demanded. "All my life I've wanted to be a reporter. And now, when I've just begun to make it, when I'm doing a series that's picked up by our whole list, when I've been offered a job in the city room of the *Chronicle*, you think I should give it up just because you happen to love me and I happen to love you. Well, I tell you, Mr. Barnett, it won't wash. It just won't wash!"

"You love me?" Barnett said.

"Of course I love you," Cecily replied. "What do you think I've been telling you?"

"Oh," he said. "But—now let me see if I understand this correctly—you don't want to marry me because then you'd have to stay at home and tend the babies, if we had any babies, rather than being free to pursue your career as a journalist."

"That's right," Cecily said. "Although you make it sound horrible. What is so wrong with a woman's wanting to do something with her life?"

"I, ah, don't know," Barnett confessed. "I've never given it much thought. I mean, basically I see nothing wrong with it at all. I think women should certainly be as free as men to do—most things. But when I think of my wife, I must confess that I picture her at home running the household while I battle the outside world."

"I agree it is a lovely image," Cecily said. "And there are undoubtedly many women who would dearly love to occupy the position you imagine. Which is why I think that although I might love you, we should not marry. It would be stifling to me and dreadfully unfair to you. I must be free, Benjamin, to take advantage of whatever life has to offer!"

"Well," Benjamin said, "if you must . . ." He stared into his coffee. "I will admit that I have not given much actual thought to what I want or need from a wife. What I have is mostly half-formed images involving you and me sitting around a fire and holding each other in various, ah, postures."

"I am sorry, Benjamin," Cecily said.

Slowly Barnett raised his eyes to meet hers. "The *Chronicle*?" he asked.

"I meant to tell you about that," she said.

THE GAME

In a contemplative fashion
And a tranquil frame of mind,
Free from every kind of passion
Some solution let us find.
— W. S. GILBERT

It is commonly believed that work is anodyne of sorrow: Benjamin Barnett reminded himself of this as he focused his energies on the work at hand. First there was the necessary rearranging of the staff of the American News Service in the absence of Cecily Perrine. Then there was the detail work for Professor Moriarty, as he perfected his plans for the impossible crime. But the sorrow remained. There seemed to be nothing he could do that did not, in some tortuous way, remind him of Cecily. She had left the American News Service office to take a feature reporter's position with the *Morning Chronicle*. He did not begrudge her that. It was the sort of experience she could not get at the Service. And she was very sincere in wanting the experience. She had taken a cut in salary on accepting the new position.

The American News Service had not actually lost Miss Perrine as a writer, since they were free to buy her stories from the *Chronicle* for the American wire. But the office was certainly empty without her. Through a conversation with the *Chronicle*'s general manager, who was simultaneously resentful and apologetic about acquiring Cecily Perrine, Barnett found out how and why the job offer was made. The *Morning Chronicle* suddenly realized that it was in great and immediate need of a female reporter. This discovery was the direct result of Lord Hogbine's having left the sixty-year-old newspaper to his wife in his will. And Lady Hogbine, who had already used much of the unentailed Hogbine fortune to endow an undergraduate ladies' college at Oxford, a home for unwed mothers in Stepney, and a trade school for female typewriter operators in Bethnal Green, was shocked to discover that there were no ladies on the reporting staff of the *Morning Chronicle*. Cecily Perrine was one of the few experienced reporters who also happened to be a lady.

"She does love me, you understand," he told Moriarty in a confidential conversation in the privacy of the professor's study. "It is the prospect of matrimony that she finds unacceptable. She is not willing to give up her freedom to become any man's wife."

"A sensible girl," Moriarty said. "Wife is the only position of involuntary servitude left in the civilized world since Mr. Lincoln's Emancipation Proclamation."

Barnett snorted and left the room. He had felt the need to confide in someone, but this was not what he wanted to hear.

Moriarty sent Barnett to Plymouth to meet the *Hornblower* when she docked. "My plans are nearly complete," he said. "But there is certain information that is sketchy or absent. You are a reporter. You have unquestioned access to the various officials and a historical right to ask stupid questions. Find out everything you can about the transportation of the treasure."

"What, exactly, do you want to know?" Barnett asked.

"Details," Moriarty told him. "I want all the picayune, unimportant little details. Everything, no matter how small or seemingly insignificant, is of interest to me."

"Supposing they don't want to tell me anything?" Barnett said. "After all, they will be transporting a priceless treasure. The police and the army may be smart enough to want to keep their exact plans a secret."

"Don't go to the military or police authorities," Moriarty said. "Interview Lord East. He is the sort of busybody who will insist upon knowing every facet of the plan. Actually, he probably formulated the plan himself. He fancies himself awfully clever."

And so Barnett arrived in Plymouth the day before the battleship *Hornblower* was scheduled to tie up to the military dock. That evening, in his hotel, Lord East allowed himself to be interviewed by the gentlemen of the press. He and his entourage occupied an entire floor, and they seemed to have brought along enough furnishings and paraphernalia to outfit an expedition to Tibet. Lord East was a short, fat man whose once-fair complexion had turned beet-red from years of exposure to the Indian sun. He dressed in the best Savile Row approximation of an oriental potentate, and carried a swagger cane of dark-brown wood, traced with a delicate ivory inlay.

"Always glad to talk to you newspaper wallahs," Lord East told the score of fidgeting reporters who had gathered in his receiving room. He climbed up onto a rattan footstool, which one of his Hindu servants placed carefully in front of his feet. "The average Briton doesn't know nearly enough about the empire we've been carving out for him for the past hundred years. The Indian subcontinent is a vast and fascinating region, more than ten times the size of these little islands. And we have made it ours; sent forth the best we breed, our sons and brothers, and made it ours. We have unified some two hundred petty kingdoms under the British raj. I am proud of my small part in this great achievement."

A stocky man with a great walrus mustache who stood in the left-hand lobe of the flock of reporters raised his hand. "Tell us, your lordship," he called out, "would you say it has been as rewarding for the natives as it has been for the British?"

Lord East looked down at him in annoyance. "What was that?" he asked.

"This conquest," the man said with a slight, undefinable mid-European accent. "These unifications—would you say they have been on the whole good for the native peoples in question? Educational, perhaps?"

"Who are you, sir?" Lord East demanded.

"Heinrich von Hertzog, your lordship. *Berliner Tagenblatt.*"

Lord East struck a pose on his footstool that would have been the envy of many a piece of heroic statuary. "Welcome to England, Mr. Hertzog," he said, his voice carrying a burden of frigid disapproval that is only achieved at the better public schools. "It is certainly a pleasure to have you among us. To answer your question, what's good for Britain is good for the empire. That should be self-evident."

The *Berliner Tagenblatt* correspondent noted down the answer, and seemed satisfied with it. Even pleased. Perhaps he was picturing how it would sound to his two million Anglophobic German readers. "Thank you, your lordship," he called.

Lord East looked around. "Anything, ah, else?" he asked.

"The treasure, your lordship," called a beefy gentleman in a broadly checked jacket that would have looked more at home on a racecourse tout than a reporter.

Lord East peered down at him. "I didn't know the 'pink 'un' was represented here," he ventured, and smiled broadly when he got the laugh he had been trying for.

"Jameson, your lordship. *Daily Telegraph*," the beefy reporter said, joining in the general chuckle. "Excuse the inappropriate attire, but I was called here from a rather different assignment."

"Indeed?" Lord East remarked. "I trust you backed a winner." Satisfied that his reputation as a wit was secure, his lordship now struck another pose. "The Lord East Collection," he said, "how can I describe it to you?"

There was a rustling from the crowd, as reporters pulled out their notebooks and licked the points on their pencils.

"India is a land of unbelievable contrasts," his lordship began. "The grandeur of past ages surrounds one in India hidden under the filth and squalor of the present. When I first arrived in Calcutta twelve years ago, as resident director of the Northeastern and Southern Indian Railway, I determined to make it my job to rescue as much of the rapidly disappearing storehouse of irreplaceable knowledge and archaeological beauty as possible. My concern was for the instruction and pleasure of all the people of the empire, and especially the people of India itself, so that they could know their own past before it was eradicated brick by brick. I also strove for the future, so that those who come after us can have some knowledge of those who came before. I have not stinted of my own time or fortune in making these acquisitions, and the result, twenty tons of unique and irreplaceable archaeological treasure, is arriving tomorrow aboard Her Majesty's Battleship *Hornblower*."

As Lord East paused for breath, the man standing to Barnett's right, a gentleman named Higgins who was a correspondent for the *Pall Mall Gazette*, leaned toward Barnett and whispered, "He stole it all, you know."

"Stole it?" Barnett whispered.

"Exactly. Oh, there are other words. One item was 'sequestered,' another was 'confiscated,' columns and friezes were 'salvaged' from where they'd stood for twenty centuries. The Indian treasure was not purchased with Lord East's personal fortune, the Indian treasure *is* Lord East's personal fortune. He's not giving it to the Crown, you know, only loaning it."

Barnett nodded. "I'm not surprised," he whispered. "They say history is written on the backs of the losers."

Higgins stared at him. "I don't think that's *exactly* what they say," he said, "but I suppose it's close enough for a wire service."

"It must make you nervous, Lord East," one of the reporters suggested.

"Very little makes me nervous, young man," Lord East said. "To what were you referring?"

"Safeguarding all that treasure," the reporter said. "Seeing it safely back to England. Taking it overland to London."

Lord East leaned back with his arms on his hips, and managed to look exceedingly smug. "One of the guiding principles of my vice-royship, and before that of my tenure as resident director of the Northeastern and Southern Indian Railway, was that a well-armed militia is more than a match for any group of brigands. Another is that rigorous planning and preparation before the battle pay for themselves many times over when the battle begins. No, young man, I am not nervous. I am confident."

"Beg your pardon, my lord, but isn't there some native Indian secret organization that has threatened to recover the Lord East treasure and return it to the Indian people?" Higgins called out.

"I have received threats from such a group," Lord East admitted. "But I do not take them seriously. Hàtshikha nà Tivviha, they call themselves. It means 'the Seven Without Faces.' "

"Romantic," one of the reporters commented.

"Barbaric," Lord East said.

"Have they made any attempts on the treasure yet?" Higgins asked.

Lord East snorted. "They wouldn't dare *do* anything," he said. "Talk is cheap. Letters pinned to my pillow in an attempt to frighten me do not achieve their desired effect. But I doubt whether they have actually gone any further than that."

"Then I take it that you are not worried about this Indian group, your lordship," Barnett said.

"Not at all. I am more concerned about common thieves. The Lord East Collection would make a tempting target."

"But Lord East," Higgins said, "how far could a thief, or even a group of thieves, get with a ten-foot statue, or a twenty-five-foot column?"

"Quite true," Lord East agreed. "But the smaller pieces are vulnerable. The Rod of Pataliputra, twenty-two inches long, crusted with diamonds and rubies, said to be the symbol of authority given by Alexander the Great to Chandra Gupta, known to the Greeks as

Sandrocottus, King of the Prasii. The Káthiáwár Buddha, carved out of one single piece of red carnelian, fifteen and one-quarter inches high. The dagger of Allad-ud-din Khalji, a gift to him from Malik Kafúr, who is believed to have had a precious stone set into its hilt or sheath for every Hindu priest he murdered. It contains over six hundred gems. I have over two thousand such items, small, highly portable, of great historical interest, and valuable out of all relation to their size."

"Can you describe the safeguards you have taken, your lordship?" Higgins called.

Barnett nodded agreement. "Yes, please do. That is the sort of detail that will fascinate our American readers."

"Unless you are afraid that a published description of your security measures will attract the very brigands you seek to avoid," von Hertzog suggested, tamping the tobacco down in an oversized pipe he had produced from an inner pocket.

Lord East glared at the German. "My security measures are designed to discourage any attempt at theft," he said. "And such criminals as are not discouraged will either be thwarted or apprehended."

"Very wise, your lordship," Higgins said.

"You will remember that I have some experience with railways and railway equipage," Lord East said. "Let me describe my plan.

"When the *Hornblower* docks tomorrow, I shall go aboard to inventory the collection. This will take three days, as I intend personally to inspect each item and check it against my list. In the meantime a special train is going to be assembled and prepared."

"Will you describe the train for us, your lordship?" Barnett asked.

"A Drummond engine pulling twenty-one cars," Lord East said. "Ten specially prepared goods wagons for the collections; seven troop-carrying cars for two companies of Her Majesty's Bengalese Foot; three drop-side wagons for the one platoon of the Twenty-third Light Horse, who will ride with their mounts; and one guards van bringing up the rear, which will hold a few selected crack marksmen along with the usual railway guards."

Lord East paused for breath, and to wait for the hastily scribbling reporters to catch up with him. "The ten goods wagons will be fitted in as a unit between the Bengalese Foot," he continued, "and all of the wagons from the coal tender to the guards van will be wired together with a special electrical wire designed to set off a loud alarm if it is broken anywhere along its length. This will prevent any attempt to shunt one or more wagons to a side track while going around a curve and then reconnect the remaining cars. A method that was actually attempted some years ago in the Punjab, let me say.

"The goods wagons themselves are being prepared now to receive the treasure. This preparation is in two parts. The first is an inspection of the wheels, axles, coupling mechanisms, and the entire exterior body, sides, bottom, and top. The second is lining the interior of each car with a layer of seamless white muslin."

Featherby-Ffolks of the *Manchester Register* raised his pencil from his notebook page and looked up, his finely trimmed mustache twitching suspiciously. "White muslin?" he asked. "You are having the sides covered with fabric?" Ever since he had scooped the London papers with the story of the successful cross-Channel flight of the Quigsly Ornithopter, only to discover that it was all an elaborate hoax, he twisted each new coin between his teeth, examined all notes under a reading glass, and twitched his mustache at the slightest unusual or unexpected detail in any story.

"Yes, that's correct," Lord East said. "One can have trapdoors or secret panels in wooden walls or metal framing, but it is difficult to conceal a panel or a door in seamless white muslin."

Featherby-Ffolks considered this for a moment, and then nodded. "I see, your lordship," he said.

"Each goods wagon will have three triangular frames constructed of metal pipes placed equidistant down the center line of the wagon floor. Large objects, such as marble columns and stone statuary, will be placed on special supporting harnesses atop these frames. The treasure trunks will, likewise, be placed on metal rods running almost the length of the wagons, which will be fitted onto the triangular frames, leaving just enough room to get around them."

"Your lordship," Barnett-interrupted, "excuse me, but what exactly is the advantage of this arrangement?"

"It prevents the use of a whole bag of tricks of the sort common to brigands and thieves. This is the way the treasure was safeguarded as it was moved about India, and if it foiled the brigands of India, my good fellow, rest assured it will succeed here.

"The triangular frames serve to support the treasure three feet from the floor of the wagon, and at least two feet from either side. There is no place of concealment, as all is visible. What is more, from the time the treasure is placed upon these supports until the time it is removed, it will be impossible for any man to achieve entrance to any of the wagons."

"Ingenious," Barnett said.

"Indeed so," Lord East agreed. "You have to get up very early in the morning to pull the wool over my eyes!"

THE CANDLE

Oh, East is East, and West is West, and never the twain shall meet,
Till Earth and Sky stand presently at God's great judgment seat;
But there is neither East nor West, Border, nor Breed, nor Birth,
When two strong men stand face to face, though they come from the
ends of the earth!

— RUDYARD KIPLING

Benjamin Barnett arose and packed his kit-bag at five o'clock the next morning. The earliest train to London left Plymouth at 6:08, and he had the whole first-class compartment to himself. He stretched out across the seat and caught an additional two hours' sleep, and then used the next three hours to go over his notes and write them up into a comprehensive account and analysis of Lord East's philosophy of acquiring and guarding Indian treasure. By the time the train arrived at Waterloo Station, he had two versions of the Lord East treasure story prepared, one for the American News Service, and one for Professor James Moriarty.

"Hm," Moriarty said, reading Barnett's account of the interview, "it is as I assumed. Lord East does not venture into the unknown. He continues to use the same rituals to safeguard his hoard that he practiced while he was acquiring the loot in India."

"I imagine one comes to trust those techniques that have worked for one in the past," Barnett commented.

"Easily understandable and very human," Moriarty admitted. "I certainly cannot fault him for that. Furthermore, it does simplify my task."

"If you say so," Barnett said. "Although I can't see how you intend to get near the train. It's never going to stop from the time it leaves Plymouth until it reaches London, not once. And if you some-how do manage to halt it, a regiment of very large guardsmen with loaded rifles will have the train surrounded in seconds, and a troop of light horse will be leaping off of their wagons to chase anyone who appears in their way."

"The military escort will not affect my plan one way or the other," Moriarty said. "It makes no difference whether there is a company of men or a field army guarding the treasure, it shall be removed."

"Are you saying that the treasure will leave Plymouth, but it won't make it to London?" Barnett asked.

Moriarty smiled. "To paraphrase a former Lord of the Admiralty," he said, "I don't say the treasure will not arrive in London, I merely say it won't arrive in that train."

Mr. Maws opened the study door. "Beg pardon," he said. "There is a delegation to see you, Professor. Six gentlemen. They have no cards."

Moriarty looked up. "Gentlemen, you say, Mr. Maws?"

"In a manner of speaking, Professor. Gentlemen of the night, gentlemen of the mask, gentlemen of the Hidden Ways. I believe all these appellations have been applied to our guests, Professor."

Barnett smiled at the butler. "Well, Mr. Maws, you astound me," he said. "You have hidden depths."

"Yeah? 'Oo says?" Mr. Maws demanded, his face remaining expressionless.

"Do we know any of these gentlemen, Mr. Maws?" asked Professor Moriarty.

"Yes, sir," Mr. Maws replied. "There's the Snoozer, and Twist, and Upper McHennory, and the Twopenny Yob, and Colonel Moran, and Percy the Painter."

"Well, well," Professor Moriarty said, rubbing the side of his nose, "an impressive gallery of rogues. What could have brought them all together; and what on earth could have brought them here to see me?" He adjusted his pince-nez glasses. "Well, the best way to find out is to bring them in here and let them tell me. Mr. Maws, if you would."

"Would you like me to leave?" Barnett asked, as Mr. Maws silently closed the door behind him.

"Not at all," Moriarty said. "You already know one or two of these gentlemen, I believe. You would be doing me a favor if you sat quietly in the corner and, ah, observed."

"My pleasure, Professor," Barnett said, and he was speaking no less than the truth. It sounded like a fascinating meeting from any point of view. "Let's see—Twist I've met, of course; head of the Mendicants' Guild. I'm an honorary member, I believe."

"That's so," Moriarty said. "And the Snoozer's a sneak thief. Got his name from his favorite method of operating, which is to pretend to be asleep in railway terminals or hotel lobbies and then wake up and calmly walk off with a few pieces of luggage. Upper McHennory you met briefly two years ago; he gave you a couple of lessons in opening the simpler sort of tumbler locks."

Barnett nodded. "Tall, sandy-haired fellow," he said.

"Quite right," Moriarty said. "Expert at his craft. Specializes in the smaller wall safes, of the sort found in private houses or small businesses."

"And the Twopenny Yob?" Barnett asked.

" 'Yob' is reverse slang," Moriarty said. "The Twopenny Yob, now a man in his fifties, dresses and looks like the younger son of an earl. His precarious but quite remunerative occupation is crashing parties in the West End or other haunts of the rich and going through the pockets of all the coats in the cloakroom."

"You can really make a living doing that?" Barnett asked.

"One can," Moriarty said, "if one happens to have the appearance of an earl's son and the morals of a guttersnipe. He also makes friends with chambermaids to get into houses while the owners are away." Moriarty removed his pince-nez and thoughtfully polished the lenses. Barnett could tell that the usually unperturbable professor was as curious as he was about the purpose of the impending delegation.

"Colonel Sebastian Moran," Moriarty continued, "is probably the most dangerous man in London. I have used him for a couple of assignments, and he has performed well. The colonel is intelligent, diligent, and obeys orders, but he is as unstable as a bottle of nitroglycerine. Someday someone is going to jar him the wrong way, and he's going to do something unfortunate. He has the cool courage of a man who singlehandedly hunted man-eating Bengal tigers in India, but he was cashiered out of the Indian Army for an incident involving a young native girl and his very violent temper.

"Percy the Painter, now, is a meek, gentle man who runs a small, very exclusive gallery for *objets d'art* and antiques. He dislikes associating with riffraff, but is known to pay good prices for the odd bits of gold or lapis lazuli one may happen upon in the course of one's earnest endeavors."

"A fascinating group," Barnett commented. "It sounds as if

we're going to be entertaining the cast of characters of a medieval morality play. 'Enter Malice and Cupidity; exit Avarice and Lust. Jealousy speaks to Everyman.' "

Moriarty looked as though he were about to comment on this, but Mr. Maws's triple knock on the study door interrupted him. "This way, gentlemen," the butler said, opening the door and stepping aside to allow the strange assortment of guests to file into the room.

Twist, in the lead, scurried across the carpet and hopped up into a red leather chair to one side of Moriarty's large oaken desk. "Morning, Professor," he said, his eyes shifting about the room. "Morning, there, Araby Ben. Been a while, it has."

"Araby Ben?" Moriarty asked, with an amused look at Barnett.

"My, ah, nickname in Mr. Twist's guild," Barnett said, trying not to look embarrassed.

"It's 'is moniker in the Maund Book," Twist said. "Which I signed 'im in personal-like these two years ago. 'Cause 'e took such an interest, you see. Gives 'im the right to beg on any streetcorner in London what ain't otherwise occupied."

"A singular distinction, Mr. Barnett," Moriarty said. "And one that might, in some strange circumstance, come in useful. One never knows where the vagaries of life will lead."

Twist, a misshapen little man with a patch over his right eye, grinned up at Moriarty. "There's many as do worse," he said.

Barnett examined the others as they entered, and found that he had no trouble telling them apart. Upper McHennory he remembered: a tall, serious-looking man, dressed like a superior artisan, which he was. Snoozer had the appearance of a soft-goods drummer from Manchester, who had somehow misplaced his sample bag. The Twopenny Yob, a tall, pale man with almost no chin, had a sort of insubstantial, vague, aristocratic look, as though he had wandered into the room by mistake, and was hoping his valet would appear and tell him where he was supposed to be. Colonel Moran was the image of the hale, bluff colonial officer in mufti. With his wide shoulders and solidly planted feet, he had a look of carefully controlled power. His bushy mustache could not disguise the hint of sadistic cruelty that showed in the twisted corners of his thin-lipped mouth. Percy the Painter was a small, fleshy man with altogether too many gold rings on his chubby fingers and an air of determined petulance.

The six distributed themselves about the study, each according to his preference. Barnett noted that they all kept instinctively clear of the front windows. Moriarty rose to greet them. "Good day, gentlemen," he said. "This is my colleague, Benjamin Barnett. To what do I owe the honor of this visit?"

"It's on the way of being a consultation, Professor," Upper McHennory said.

"We is here to ask you to help us, Professor," the Snoozer said.

"To put it concisely," said Colonel Sebastian Moran, shouldering his malacca walking stick and giving an automatic twist to the corners of his precise mustache, "we are a delegation, sent here by our comrades-in-crime, to solicit your aid."

"You never were one to mince words, Colonel," Percy the Painter said approvingly. " 'Comrades-in-crime.' Yes; within the confines of this lovely room—I particularly admire that Berkman oil to the left of the door—I admit to the justice of that description. Lovely."

"Beg pardon," the Twopenny Yob said, "but I believe we are creating sound without facilitating the exchange of information." He turned to Moriarty. "Professor, we have come to see you on behalf of the Amateur Mendicant Society. We are a specially formed committee of that society empowered to represent the entire membership in our discussions with you."

Moriarty sat back down in his chair and leaned forward, peering with his intense gaze at each of his visitors. "The Amateur Mendicant Society," he said finally. "I don't believe I am acquainted with it."

"It's a brand-new organization, Professor," Upper McHennory said. "A group of us from the different corners of the snide decided we had to get together and discuss subjects of mutual benefit—"

"Such as what it is what we is going to be telling you about." Twist interrupted.

"There are things happening in London," said the Twopenny Yob, "that are against the common interests of us artisans of the underworld. So we decided to get together and discuss these things. But you can see the problems an attempt on the part of our collective brethren to assemble would cause. The authorities would not encourage such a gathering. Particularly at the present time, they would frown upon it. They would do their best to discourage it."

"The present time?" Moriarty asked.

"You bloody well said it there, Professor," Twist said. "The present times is different from other times, 'cause of some bloody bastard what is going about knocking off the toffery."

"Ah! The murders," Moriarty said.

"Indeed," the Twopenny Yob agreed. "And so we formed a club. It was Percy the Painter's notion—"

Percy shrugged modestly. "It comes of employing a competent solicitor," he said. "Expensive, but well worth it in times of need. My solicitor pointed out that gentlemen's clubs were quite legal, quite common in London, could have anyone they wished as members, and could exclude nonmembers from attendance if they wished. So we formed a club. The Amateur Mendicant Society. We rented the ground floor and vault of a furniture warehouse, and fixed it up quite nicely."

"Vault?"

"For private discussions," Snoozer explained.

"Ah!" Moriarty said. Barnett, who had come to know his moods quite well over two years, could tell that he was doing his best not to look amused. Since the average person couldn't tell when the professor *was* amused, his attempt at concealment worked quite well. "So now there is a club—no doubt with billiard tables and a reading room—for gentlemen purse snatchers, pickpockets, panderers—"

"Sir!" Colonel Moran said sharply, his face flushing. "We may indulge in occasional activities which are technically on the wrong side of the laws of this effete country, but we are none of us lacking in respect for the ladies. There are no panderers welcome in our group!"

"Accept my apologies, Colonel," Moriarty said. "I was carried away by the lure of alliteration. So, at any rate, you have discovered that it is possible to make a den of thieves respectable by giving it the facade of a gentlemen's club."

"Well," Upper McHennory said, smiling, "it has worked so far."

"Can we get back to the purpose of this visit?" Colonel Moran said, impatiently slapping his walking stick against the side of his shoe.

"Very well," the Twopenny Yob said. "Professor Moriarty, in the name of the collective membership of the Amateur Mendicant Society, we request your assistance. We must see to it that this vile murderer who has been haunting the West End is apprehended."

"I see," Moriarty said. "And why this interest? A sense of civic duty, perhaps?"

"Pah!" Twist exclaimed, scrunching forward in his chair. "The rozzers 'as been 'arassing us sumfing awful. Knocking my boys off the street corners, chasing blind and lame beggars up the street. I tells you, it ain't good."

"I believe you," Moriarty said. "Seeing a lame beggar outrun a bobby must stretch your customers' credulity."

"You wouldn't think it humorous," Percy the Painter commented, "if it was your men being harassed and arrested by the police anytime they enter a swank neighborhood. And keeping them out of swank neighborhoods is not sensible. Stealing from the poor goes against ancient English tradition; it's in bad taste and it's unremunerative."

Moriarty raised an eyebrow. "What about the great and growing body of the middle class?" he asked. "Surely you can still steal from shopkeepers, factory owners, salesmen, innkeepers, bank clerks, and assorted merchants, tradesmen, and professionals?"

"You doesn't grasp the magnanimousness of the situation," Twist said. "Strangely, when the rich are struck at, it is the middling classes what feel most threatened."

"It's the truth," the Twopenny Yob said. "Now, with this madman going around and murdering the aristocracy, you could clearly see where it would make my profession difficult. The swells are just naturally going to be more cautious as to who they let into their mansions. Even during the wildest soirées, they are not going to suffer the chance of having their throats cut merely for the privilege of having their pockets picked."

Very nicely put, Barnett thought, and made a note to use it in a future article.

"But the odd thing about it," the Yob continued, "is the reaction of your bourgeois shopkeeper. He feels personally threatened, and writes letters to the *Times* about it. The public uproar causes the police to cancel all leaves and bring in auxiliary men, and get a visible patrol on every street. Calms down the masses, don't y'see."

"And, just for the raw fun of it, " 'cause they ain't got nothing else to do," Snoozer added, "the rozzers arrest everybody in sight for 'suspicious loitering.' Now I tell you, Professor, it's a sad day when a chap can't do a bit of suspicious loitering without getting thrown in quod for his troubles!"

Moriarty leaned back in his chair and pursed his lips. "An interesting scene you are painting, gentlemen," he said. "And a sad tale it is, indeed, that this one unknown murderer is putting the entire criminal class of London out of business. What, exactly, is it that you want me to do about it? Help you compose a letter to the *Times*? Get the police off your collective backs? What?"

"They're on your back too, you know," Percy the Painter said, and then put his hand to his mouth, as if frightened by his own audacity.

Moriarty turned his head slightly and inspected Percy speculatively for a moment. "Pray tell me, Percy, whatever are you talking about?"

"One of my customers, you know," Percy said. "Collector of Georgian china. Which I can't imagine why, for the life of me. Ugly, hideous, gross chamber pots they are, too. But he likes them. Lestrade is his name."

Professor Moriarty laughed. "Giles Lestrade, a collector of Georgian chamber pots! The man has untold depths."

"You know him then? Scotland Yard inspector. Always makes me a bit nervous when he visits the shop, if the truth be told. Well, last time he came in, about three days ago, it was, he had one of his Scotland Yard buddies with him, and they were having a conversation, which I couldn't help overhearing, while they looked at the china."

"And what did they say?" Moriarty asked.

"Inspector Lestrade said that Sherlock Holmes—he's—"

"I know who he is," Moriarty growled. "Go on."

"Well, Inspector Lestrade said that Sherlock Holmes was still convinced that you, Professor Moriarty, are responsible for these murders. The chap with him—named Gregson—said it was Holmes's *idée fixe*, and there wasn't anything to be done about it. And he hoped they wouldn't have to keep too many men away from their other duties for too long, while Holmes has them following you about. It seems that Mr. Holmes is in some position of authority over at Scotland Yard, at least insofar as this investigation is concerned."

Moriarty nodded, and allowed his gaze to rest briefly on each of his guests. They were silent while he prepared to speak. "You're telling me that my interests coincide with yours on this matter," he said. "I will not dispute that; it is partly so. But not wholly. When the murderer is finally apprehended, and the level of police activity once more falls to normal, you gentlemen are free to resume or continue your nefarious activity. But it will not free me of the attentions of the master sleuth. Sherlock Holmes will inevitably suspect me of whatever heinous crime comes to light next."

"He will certainly lose his official status when this case is solved," Percy the Painter said.

"That's so," Moriarty admitted. "Which will once more lower

his nuisance value to a more tolerable level. Is this what you wish me to do—solve the crime? Apprehend the murderer?"

The six of them shifted uncomfortably, all looking vaguely unhappy, except for Colonel Moran, who looked pugnacious. Barnett was briefly puzzled by this, but he suddenly realized: to these men, asking Professor Moriarty to solve a crime was like asking the Archbishop of Canterbury to commit one. It was the antithesis of the ordinary.

"Not *necessarily*, Professor," Snoozer said.

"What we want is that you should get the rozzers off our backs," Twist said. "Catching the gent what's committing these outrages seems the easiest way, but if you come up with another, that'd be jonnick with us."

Professor Moriarty stood up and removed the pince-nez from the bridge of his nose. "It is an interesting situation, and an interesting problem," he said, polishing the lenses with his pocket handkerchief. "If I agree, and I apprehend this killer, what would you have me do with him?"

"Whatever you think best. If you want to turn 'im over to the rozzers, that's jonnick," Twist said. The others all nodded agreement, looking even more uncomfortable.

Moriarty looked up sharply. "Even if he's one of yours?" he asked.

"He isn't," Upper McHennory said firmly.

"But if be is?"

"The agreement holds as stated," Percy the Painter said. "Do whatever you want with the bloke, as long as you get the forces of law and order to direct their attentions elsewhere."

"I see. No complaints from you gentlemen, or your colleagues, no matter who the killer turns out to be?"

"None!" said Colonel Moran, with unnecessary force. The others nodded.

"And what," Moriarty asked, "is to be my remuneration for removing this obstacle from the paths of the unrighteous?"

"What do you want?" Upper McHennory asked.

Moriarty thought about it for a moment. "I want from you—from the Amateur Mendicants—just what Sherlock Holmes is getting from the government."

"That don't sound too unreasonable," Twist said. " 'Er majesty's paymasters, from what I understand, is not known for their largess."

"How much, precisely, would it be?" Percy the Painter asked. "Just for the record, you know."

"I'll have to find out what Mr. Holmes's monetary arrangement is," Moriarty said, "but as Twist says, it's certainly not excessive. Be aware, however, that there's another half to that. I want the sort of support from your people that Holmes is getting from the Yard."

"Support?"

"That's correct. You will be my eyes and ears. You will assemble information for me, interview people, follow people, lurk in doorways, pounce upon clues and bring them here for my perusal. I will tell you what I require done as the tasks come up. How you divide the labor is up to you, except that I shall expect you to be very careful to select the right men for the job."

"The London Maund is yours for the calling," Twist said. "Every stook-buzzer, thin-wire, prop-nailer, thimble-screwer, sneaksman, till-frisker, bluey-hunter, and tosher in the book."

"Fine," Moriarty said. "I expected no less. What about the rest of you? And what of the various and assorted Amateur Mendicants?"

Colonel Sebastian Moran stood up and tucked his walking stick firmly under his arm. "They'll go along, Professor," he said. "I shall see to that! And if you should happen to need my services, it happens that I find myself at liberty at the moment. A liberty, let me say, that will end when you apprehend this contemptible maniac and get the rozzers off our backs."

"Ask and you shall receive," Moriarty said. "Such assistance as I do require will be paid for at my usual rates, so the requests should not seem too onerous. These expenses will be passed on to your membership along with my bill."

Percy the Painter clasped his palms together. "We shall, of course, expect you to use judicious restraint in the matter of expenses," he said. "Some of the members will be dunned at a higher rate than the others."

"I'll keep that in mind," Moriarty promised.

"We thank you," the Twopenny Yob said, rising and buttoning his Chesterfield overcoat. "On behalf of the membership, we thank you for what we are about to receive, as the bishop said to the lady of the chorus. As one of those whose livelihood is most directly affected by the overly ambitious attempts of Scotland Yard, I, personally, thank you. When will you begin?"

"I have something on right now that will keep me fully occupied for the next few days," Moriarty said. "But if Colonel Moran wouldn't mind waiting in the library for, let us say, two hours, I will prepare a list of the various reports and investigations that I will require you to undertake immediately, so that the information will be awaiting me when I return."

"I shall run across the street to the British Museum," Colonel Moran said. "I should have no trouble keeping myself amused for a few hours in the Mausoleum Room."

"Very good," Moriarty agreed, ringing for Mr. Maws. The six Amateur Mendicants solemnly shook hands with the professor, and then allowed themselves to be escorted from the room.

"A fascinating gathering, Professor," Barnett said when the room was clear. "It's hard to believe that those people are professional criminals. They're very well mannered and polite."

"You saw them on their best behavior," Moriarty said. "A circus lion may seem quite tame as it jumps from place to place with no more than a gentle urge from the trainer. Had you met these men in their native environment, they might well have behaved more like the wild animals they are. Snoozer would have stolen your suitcase, Percy the Painter would have removed your gold cufflinks, the Two-penny Yob would have picked your pocket, and Colonel Moran would have cut your throat."

Barnett considered. "That may be so, Professor," he said. "But nonetheless it was quite a meeting, and I'm glad to have sat in on it."

"So," Moriarty said, turning his gaze toward the corner where Barnett was just rising from his chair. "And what was your impression of the event?"

"Well, Professor," Barnett said, "I think they have you suckered in right good, as we'd say at home. Scotland Yard's been after this bird for a month, and they haven't come anywhere near him. He doesn't seem to leave any clues behind—just corpses. Even Sherlock Holmes has gotten nowhere with his investigation. And you're coming to a very cold trail, which has already been stomped over by every detective, amateur sleuth, and journalist in London. I don't see how you're going to get a handle on it. Tell me, Professor, are you really going to try solving this thing, or did you just agree to look at it to keep your friends happy?"

"I doubt whether these people would stay happy if I failed to get results," Moriarty said. "But it is not quite as hopeless as your analysis would indicate."

"You mean you have some clue as to who the murderer is?" Barnett asked.

"Not at all," Moriarty said. "But I discern seven separate and distinct approaches to the problem. However, that must all be put aside for now. We have an appointment with a baggage car."

RICHARD PLANTAGENET

Don Desperado
Walked on the Prado,
And there he met his enemy.
— CHARLES KINGSLEY

Qunicy Hope was dead. His body, throat gashed open from ear to ear, lay supine on the floor in his consultation room, arms stretched out cruciform, feet, curiously, raised neatly up onto the seat of the leather couch. He was still in his evening dress, just as he had been when he arrived home a half hour before he was found, missing only his hat and shoes.

"I haven't touched a thing, sir, I assure you. Not a thing. I couldn't," Gammidge, the valet, told Mr. Sherlock Holmes. A tall, skinny, stoop-shouldered man whose garb appeared too large for his frame, Gammidge stood right inside the room, hovering by the door, and seemed on the verge of tears. "Everything was exactly like this when I found the master, and no one has entered the room since that moment. I only left long enough to go outside and whistle for a policeman. What a dreadful thing, sir."

"You did right, Gammidge," Holmes said soothingly. "What sort of room is this?" It was a long, rectangular room on the ground floor, to the right of the main entrance of Quincy Hope's large, luxurious house. Across from its paneled door was the comfortable leather couch upon which rested the legs of the corpse, from the black-trousered knees to the black silk-stockinged toes. To the left, a low table and some chairs were by the front windows; to the right, a massive flat desk and chair, flanked by a tall glass-front cabinet and a wooden examination table.

"It's Hope's consultation room, Mr. Holmes," Inspector Lestrade said. "Mr. Hope would appear to have been some sort of medical man."

"What sort?" Holmes inquired.

"Why, he was—I don't really know," Lestrade said. "Gammidge?"

"I couldn't say, gentlemen," Gammidge told them. "I served only as Mr. Hope's valet. There were several persons who came in during the daytime and aided the master with his medical practice. I really know nothing about it."

"What about the other servants?" Lestrade asked.

"Well, sir, Frazier, the butler, may know more about the master's affairs."

"Right enough. Bring him down here, then. Tell him Scotland Yard wants to talk to him."

Gammidge shrank back slightly. "I'm sorry, sir," he said, with the air of one who knows that whatever happens, it's all his fault, "but Frazier isn't here this evening. He and the other servants have the night off. They have all, I believe, gone home to various relatives."

"All gone, eh?" Lestrade asked, sticking his head forward pugnaciously.

"I believe so, sir," Gammidge said, twisting his hands together nervously as he talked. His eyes darted about the room like a caged bird who thinks that an invisible carnivore has somehow entered his cage. "I'll go and check, if you like."

"What's the matter with you, Gammidge?" Lestrade asked suspiciously. "Something on your mind?"

"No, sir; only . . ."

"Yes, yes; only what, Gammidge?"

"Only, Inspector, I'd like to leave this room, if I may. It's making me quite faint, really it is; being in here with the master's body and all. It's not the sort of thing I'm used to, you see, and I've always had a weak constitution."

Lestrade stuck his nose square in front of the poor valet's face, making him inadvertently leap backward. "Are you *sure* that's all, Gammidge? Are you *sure* you don't know something more about this? You'd better speak up now, you know; it will save you a lot of trouble later."

Gammidge turned white. "I don't feel so good," he said, and fainted dead away on the floor.

"Very clever, Lestrade," Holmes said sharply. "You've managed to render unconscious the only man who was here while the crime was committed; the only one who might be able to tell us anything of what happened here."

"So you say, Mr. Holmes," Lestrade said, looking down unsympathetically at Gammidge, who lay crumpled on the rug. "*I* say he's faking; and *I* say he could probably tell us a good deal of what happened here; and *I* say it's a most peculiar circumstance that the rest of the servants have the night off, but this here one remains."

"Let us be honest, Lestrade," Holmes said. "You like finding the servants guilty of crimes because you still suffer from an inborn reverence for the upper classes. Every time you hear someone speaking who clips his vowels, you instinctively want to tug your forelock. If the criminal classes would take elocution lessons, Scotland Yard's arrest rate would be cut in half."

"Now, Mr. Holmes, that isn't hardly fair," Lestrade protested, following after the consulting detective as he dropped to his hands and knees and began examining the floor in the murder room with his magnifying lens. "We usually end up arresting the lower orders because most crime comes from the lower orders. Which only makes sense, after all. No call for a duke with an income of a hundred thousand clear every year to cosh someone for his wallet."

"I'll grant you that, Lestrade, but murder knows no social boundaries. Would you turn up those gas mantles on the wall? I need more light."

"Um," Lestrade said, doing as he was bidden. "I don't know what you expect to find, crawling about on the rug."

"Truthfully, Lestrade, I don't know what I expect to find, either. That's why I look."

The valet sat up, looked around for a second, a puzzled expression on his face, and then pushed himself to his feet. "Is there anything further I can do for you gentlemen?" he asked weakly, holding onto the doorframe for support.

Lestrade turned around and advanced on the valet, raising a hectoring finger.

"Why, yes, Gammidge," Sherlock Holmes said, looking up from the rug and cutting Lestrade off as he was about to speak, "I'd appreciate it if you would go up to your master's bedroom and have a look about. See if anything has been disturbed, and especially see if anything seems to be missing."

"Very good, sir," Gammidge said, and he fled up the stairs.

"Bah!" Lestrade said. "You expect something to be missing? What?"

"I expect nothing," Holmes said. "But I would like to know."

"But Holmes, how do you expect to learn anything from what *isn't* here?"

"What *is* here," Holmes said, carefully extracting a bit of brown matter from the green rug and inserting it into a small envelope, "is suggestive, but what *isn't* here is even more suggestive, and I expect, with any luck, to learn a great deal from it."

"What *isn't* here?" Lestrade looked around, baffled. "What on earth are you talking about, Holmes? What isn't here?"

"The victim's shoes, Lestrade. They are missing. Along with his top hat. I have great hopes for the victim's shoes, although, frankly, I don't expect as much from the hat."

"You think the missing shoes are important?"

"Very!"

Lestrade shrugged. "If you say so, Mr. Holmes. But we'll probably find them under the couch, or in the bedroom."

"I've looked under the couch, Lestrade. And he never got up to the bedroom."

"Then why send that valet up there?"

"The murderer may have got to the bedroom."

"Oh." Lestrade thought that over. "Nonsense!" he said. "Missing shoes. Missing hat. I'd say that all that shows is that he had a new pair of shoes. The murderer probably took them for himself."

"Could be, Lestrade," Holmes said. "That's good thinking. Only . . ."

"Only what, Holmes?" Lestrade asked, looking pleased at the compliment. "Just you ask me. I'll be glad to give you the benefit of my years of professional experience. What's troubling you about this case?"

"Only, Lestrade, if he took Hope's shoes, then what did he do with his own?"

"Well—carried them off with him, I suppose."

"Come now, Lestrade. You think our murderer has developed an acquisitive instinct for his seventh killing? What about all the fine jackets and waistcoats and cravats and assorted men's furnishings at each of the previous victim's abodes?"

"It's just possible the fellow needed a pair of shoes," Lestrade insisted. "Perhaps he suddenly developed a hole in one of his own, or the uppers separated from the lowers. And he didn't leave his own behind because he was afraid of our finding some identifying mark on them."

"So he took them off with him to discard unobtrusively?"

"Right, Mr. Holmes. Like that."

"I don't think so, Lestrade. I think he took the victim's shoes because he wanted the victim's shoes; but not to wear. I think he wanted the shoes themselves, or something concealed in them. But with any luck we may soon find out whether you're right or I'm right. Lestrade, have your men scour the area for ten blocks in every direction. Have them carefully examine gutter drains and dustbins, and any other place of concealment. Instruct them to bring back any article of clothing they find, most especially shoes or parts of shoes."

"Certainly. Mr. Holmes. Whatever shoes they turn out to be, I agree that it will be useful to find them. I'll send to the division station for some large bull's-eye lanterns and put some men right on it."

"Very good. Where is that medical examiner? We've been here half an hour already."

"Dr. Pilschard doesn't like coming out after midnight, Mr. Holmes. We'll have some of our men bring the body in to St. Luke's in a death wagon, and he'll examine it in the morning."

"Is that his standard practice? Well, send somebody after Dr. Pilschard and inform him that I want the body examined *in situ*, and I want it examined soon. The man gets a two-guinea fee for every body he cuts up; let him do something to earn it!"

Lestrade shook his head. He didn't see what difference a few hours would make, but the commissioners, in their infinite wisdom, had seen fit to put Sherlock Holmes in charge of this investigation, and orders is orders. He left the room and whistled up a pair of his plainclothesmen, and sent them on their way. When he returned to the room, Holmes had reached the victim's head in his crawl across the carpet, and was concentrating his attention on it. It was not an attractive sight, jaws gaping open, eyes staring, lying in a pool of half-clotted blood.

"Help me move the couch, Lestrade," Holmes said, carefully placing the corpse's feet on the floor. "I didn't want to touch the body until the medical examiner had seen it, but time passes and the killer gets farther away. I'll disturb it as little as possible. Let's just take the couch over to the left, along the wall. That's the way. Careful where you step!"

They put the couch down, and Holmes examined the great pool of blood that was now revealed. "As I thought," he said, kneeling and peering through his glass. "The poor man was certainly killed right at this spot. The paucity of blood under and around the head had me worried, considering the depth of the wound. But a slight slope of the floor explains that. It all ran under the couch."

"It certainly did," Lestrade agreed.

There was a disturbance at the front door, and one of the constables stationed outside came in and stopped smartly in front of Inspector Lestrade. "Beg pardon, sir," he said, "but there's a gentleman outside, just pulled up in a carriage, who demands access."

"Ah!" Lestrade said. "Friend of the victim?"

"No, sir," the constable said. "Says he's a friend of the commissioner, sir."

"Is that right?" Lestrade said. "How curious; at one in the morning. Fellow must have a powerful interest. What's his name?"

"He says he's the Count d'Hiver, sir."

Sherlock Holmes looked up from the corpse. "D'Hiver?" he asked. "Show his lordship in, Constable!"

"And just who is 'his lordship'?" Lestrade demanded, as the constable retreated to the front door.

"As it was described to me," Holmes said, "he has a watching brief from the Privy Seal. I'm not sure what that actually signifies, but I assume it covers visiting the scene of the crime."

"He may have a 'watching brief,'" Lestrade said, "but how did he know there was anything to watch? How did he find out about the crime so quickly, and at such an unlikely hour?"

"We shall ask him," Holmes said, getting to his feet. "I myself am curious as to how—and why."

The Count d'Hiver burst through the door with that excess of energy that seems to possess many people who are of less than normal stature. "What's happening here?" he demanded of the empty hall. "Who's in charge? I want to see—Oh, there you are, Holmes. My God! He certainly is dead, whoever he is. Who would have known the human body had so much blood in it?"

"I assume the question is rhetorical, my lord," Holmes said. "Let me introduce Inspector Lestrade, who is in charge of the investigation for Scotland Yard."

"Lestrade," d'Hiver said, nodding slightly. "I have heard the name. You are well thought of."

"Thank you—"

"Which, frankly, I consider astounding: seven corpses and no arrests, barring the idiotic detention of a brace of servants."

"We do our best, my lord, We can't all be Sherlock Holmes," Lestrade said, his face suffusing with the red tint of suppressed anger.

"It seemingly wouldn't be of any great help if you were," d'Hiver commented coldly, fixing his gaze on Holmes. "Well, have you made any progress, Mr. Holmes? Have you found any clues?"

"I have been here only for some thirty minutes, my lord," Holmes said calmly. "The hunt for information—for clues, if you will—is painstaking and time-consuming. Perhaps, if you wish to converse, we had best go out into the entrance hall. It is better to disturb the area immediately around the body as little as possible, for fear of destroying possible evidence."

"Destroying evidence?" D'Hiver sniffed. "How can my mere presence in the room destroy any evidence?"

"A hair can be evidence, my lord," Holmes said, rising and stalking into the entrance hall himself, so that d'Hiver was forced to follow. "Or a bit of fluff, or a speck of dirt lying on the carpet. Just by walking over such a minuscule object, you may remove it; or you might inadvertently leave behind a hair or a few grains of dust yourself, thus confusing the real evidence."

D'Hiver stared at Holmes, trying to decide whether the famous consulting detective was serious. "Preposterous," he said uncertainly.

"Not at all, my lord," Holmes assured him. "The smallest trifle can be of the utmost importance, to one trained to observe and practiced in making logical deductions from what he observes. I once cleared up an obscure murder by winding a watch; and another time I descerned a dreadful secret because I noticed the depth to which the parsley had sunk into the butter on a hot day. Then again, I once cleared a man named Estermann of the charge of murdering his wife because of noting something as fragile as a cobweb."

D'Hiver pursed his lips thoughtfully, continuing to glare up at the hawk-nosed consulting detective. "If you can make so much of so little," he said, "why don't you have more on this case? Seven murders so far, Mr. Holmes."

"I am aware of the body count, my lord," Holmes said. "This is only the second opportunity that I have had to arrive in time to try to rescue some of this small detail before it is ground into the dust by hordes of police inspectors, Home Office officials, reporters, curiosity seekers, and cleaning women. I have hopes of developing something from what we find here." Noting Lestrade's frantic signaling from behind. Count d'Hiver's head, Holmes continued, "May I ask how it happens that you are here, my lord?"

"Come now, Holmes, you know of my position and my interest."

"Indeed, my lord," Holmes said. "It is your information that I question. How did you know to come here?"

"Ah!" d'Hiver said. "Now I comprehend. You wonder how I popped up so mysteriously at the opportune moment at the—what do you call it?—scene of the crime. Is that it?"

"Yes, my lord."

"It is not so strange. The commissioner notified the Earl of Arundale when word came in, and Arundale notified me. And here I am. I confess I rather fancied the chance to view the actual site of one of these senseless killings so soon after it happened; but I was not prepared for the appearance of that corpse. It makes death look very unappealing. One would just as soon not see such a thing soon after a meal."

The soft footsteps of Gammidge, the valet, coming down the stairs, interrupted the conversation. He looked startled as three pair of eyes turned to watch him descend. "I could find nothing amiss, Mr. Holmes," he said. "As far as I can tell, no one has been in the master's bedroom since he left it this evening."

"And the hat and shoes?" Holmes asked.

"Not in evidence, Mr. Holmes."

"Come now," Count d'Hiver said, "this sounds interesting. Hat and shoes?"

"Missing, my lord," Lestrade said. "I have sent some men out looking for them."

"The victim's?"

"Yes, my lord," Holmes said. "Evening dress: a black silk hat and black patent-leather shoes."

"Taken by the killer? How very fascinating. Whatever for?"

"Mr. Holmes knows," Lestrade said, "but he's not saying."

"I have a theory, that's all," Holmes said. "The recovery of the shoes will tell whether I am right."

"And if they're not recovered," Lestrade said, "it will show that *I'm* right: they were taken to replace the killer's own shoes."

"It does seem an odd thing to do," Count d'Hiver said, "taking the victim's shoes and top hat."

The door of the library, down the hall from where they were

standing, opened, and a team of two plainclothesmen emerged. "We have checked all around the ground floor, Inspector," the taller of the two told Lestrade. "As far as we can tell, there is no way that the murderer could have entered or left the premises. All windows are securely fastened; the rear egress is double-bolted from the inside; the stairs to the cellar, which emerge in the butler's pantry, have a door which is closed and bolted at the upper end. It is a flimsy bolt, but nonetheless it has not been violated."

Lestrade nodded. "What we expected," he said. "Just on the off chance, MacDonald, check around upstairs, also."

"Yes sir!" MacDonald said, making a perfunctory gesture that somewhat resembled a salute, and the two plainclothesmen turned and headed up the broad stairway.

"If you don't mind, my lord, I would like to go back to my examination of the victim and the murder room," Holmes said.

"If you don't mind, Mr. Holmes," Count d'Hiver replied, "I'd like to watch." He held up a hand to cut off Holmes's retort. "I'll stand in the doorway," he promised, "and I will not disturb you, except, perhaps, with a very occasional question. I know you think me overly critical, but it may be because I do not grasp the complexities of your task. I begin to see that this is so from the conversation we have just had. Perhaps if I am permitted to observe, it will instill in me a proper appreciation for the difficulties of your profession."

"Perhaps, my lord," Holmes said dryly. "At any rate, if you wish to observe, silently, from the doorway, you are welcome to do so."

One of the constables guarding the portals came into the hall. "Beg pardon, sir," he said to Lestrade, "but there's a reporter outside who wants to speak with someone in charge."

"A reporter?" Lestrade swiveled around.

"*Morning Chronicle*, sir."

"Tell the *Morning Chronicle* to return in the morning," Holmes said. "We can't be bothered with that now. Tell him we'll have a complete report of the crime available to the press in the morning. Say seven-thirty."

"Beg pardon. Mr. Holmes, but it's a young lady."

Holmes looked irritated. "*What's* a young lady?"

"The reporter, sir."

"A young lady?" Lestrade was clearly scandalized. "The reporter for the *Morning Chronicle*?"

"Yes, sir. There is a gentleman with her, a sketch artist. They would like to see the, ah, room, Inspector. Where the victim is, you know. And she says that she is put to bed at three, so she would really like the information now."

"She is put to bed at three?" Count d'Hiver asked, looking vaguely amused. "By whom?"

"No, no," a musically feminine voice said from the front door, and the reporter for the *Morning Chronicle*, Miss Cecily Perrine, entered the hall. Behind her trailed a small man with a brown bowler hat, a wide walrus mustache, and a sketchpad. "It is the newspaper that is put to bed at three," Cecily Perrine explained, unfastening her wide brown sealskin cape and folding it over her arm. "Which is why I would like some details of the crime now, so that my readers will have the opportunity of learning all about it over their morning kippers."

"Miss Cecily Perrine, isn't it?" Sherlock Holmes said. "I thought you were a valued employee of the American News Service."

"Life is change, Mr. Holmes," Cecily said. "Good morning, Inspector Lestrade. I see you're wondering what I'm doing here. My editor sent a boy with a carriage around for me and my colleague here when he received word of the murder. He would not allow the late hour, nor the fog, nor the chilling weather to interfere with his reporters' getting a good story."

"And just how, if you don't mind my asking, did he get word of the murder?" Lestrade asked.

"I have no idea," Cecily Perrine said. "I imagine he has a friend at the Yard. You'll have to ask him."

The Count d'Hiver stepped forward and took Cecily's hand. "Allow me to introduce myself," he said, bending forward at the waist with what was almost a parody of a Continental bow. "The Count d'Hiver at your service."

"Charmed," she said. "Miss Cecily Perrine, crime reporter for the *Morning Chronicle*. And this is Mr. William Doyle, sketch artist for the same paper."

At this moment the outer door slammed, and one of Lestrade's plainclothesmen rushed into the room, past Miss Perrine and Mr. Doyle, and stopped, panting, in front of the inspector. "We've got it, sir!" he declared, brandishing a bundle wrapped in oilcloth. "And a fortunate thing it was, too, us spotting it in this fog. It was all wound up in this piece of scrap oilcloth, just like it is now, and tossed down one of these stairwells that leads to a cellar door around the side of a manor house on Pettigrew Court in the next block."

"Very pleasing work, Thompson," Lestrade said, taking the bundle. "Now we'll see." He turned to Holmes. "Well, Mr. Holmes, would you care to attempt a description of the contents of this oil-cloth before I open it?"

"Certainly, Lestrade," Holmes said. "One black silk top hat; one pair of black patent-leather shoes."

"Is that all?"

"I think you'll find that one or both of the shoes have been cut or ripped apart. And you'll certainly find bloodstains on both shoes."

"Bloodstains!" Lestrade ripped open the bundle. "Here's the hat. The shoes—yes, they're inside." He gave the hat a cursory glance, and then put it aside and held the shoes up to the light. "Yes, they do seem to be splattered with some sort of stain. Blood! I believe it is blood. Amazing, Holmes; how ever did you deduce that? But they would seem to be whole." He held the pair of shoes out to Holmes. "No ripping or slicing appears to have been done on either shoe."

Holmes took the shoes and examined them, one at a time. He sniffed, he peered, he pried, he took his magnifying glass to them. "Ah!" he said. "Lestrade, look here! There was no need for the killer to destroy the shoes. The matter is self-evident!" He took the left shoe and, with Lestrade peering over his arm, and the rest of his audience gathered closely behind, sharply twisted the heel. It rotated a half turn, revealing a meticulously cut-out compartment in the leather. "This is what the killer was after," Holmes said. "The contents of this compartment. Which, I note, he now has."

"You expected to find that?" Lestrade asked.

"Something like it," Holmes said. "The killer was searching for something, as he was in each of the other murders, and somehow he discovered that it was concealed in one of the shoes. Probably the victim told him, hoping to be spared a few moments longer. This business is grotesque,"

"Then why did he take the top hat?" Lestrade demanded. "Was there something concealed in it also?"

"Yes, Inspector, there was."

"What?"

"The bloody shoes. The killer didn't want to wait in the victim's house to discover the secret of the shoes. Perhaps he heard the valet descending from upstairs. He also didn't want to be seen on the street carrying a pair of bloody shoes. So he concealed his own hat under his outer garment—probably a collapsible topper—and borrowed the victim's."

"Why not conceal the shoes under his own hat, or his top-coat or cloak or whatever?"

"All that blood, Lestrade. Remember, the blood was a lot fresher when he departed with the shoes."

"That's so," Lestrade admitted.

"Fascinating!" Cecily Perrine said softly, making obscure scratches with her pencil in her small notebook.

"Indeed a remarkable bit of deduction," the Count d'Hiver agreed.

"Elementary," Holmes commented. "The real question is, what was the object which was once concealed in this shallow space?"

Lestrade took the shoe and stared into the hollow heel. "Precious gems?" he suggested.

"That is a possibility," Holmes said. He took out a slender ivory rule and carefully measured the cavity, making a sketch of it in his pocket notebook and jotting down the measurements.

"Well," the Count d'Hiver said, "this has all been very interesting. I thank you for your patience, Mr. Holmes. And you, Inspector. I will not stand in your way any longer. I only hope that the unfortunate demise of Mr., ah, Hope brings us to a solution of these damnable—excuse me, Miss Perrine—murders. I will await with interest your report on this affair." And with that, he nodded abruptly to each of them, carefully adjusted his top hat on his head, and strode through the door.

"*Au revoir*, Count," Sherlock Holmes murmured, staring after the departing nobleman with a bemused expression on his face.

Once outside, the Count d'Hiver buttoned his topcoat, nodded to the two constables at the door, and hurried down the steps to the sidewalk. He stared up and down the street for his carriage. The fog had settled in, and it was hard to see more than a few feet in any direction. The brougham was not in evidence, but it could have been no more than four of five yards down the block and, still been completely invisible. He could have asked one of the constables where his driver had settled in to wait, but it seemed somehow demeaning not to know where one's own brougham had gone.

He headed off to the left, the direction the vehicle had been heading when they stopped. It would, he realized with a wry internal chuckle, serve him right if his driver had taken the brougham around the block and pulled up a few feet before the Hope mansion. Then the two constables would see him backtracking, the very image of a man who didn't know where his own carriage was. He could always go back into the house for a moment, as though he had forgotten something; then, perhaps, they wouldn't notice. The Count d'Hiver was a man who couldn't stand to be embarrassed, and he found the potential for embarrassment in every trivial act.

There was a carriage ahead. Was it his, or the young lady journalist's? A few more steps and—

An arm, a muscular right arm, appeared from nowhere and hooked around his throat, forcing the chin up, cutting off the windpipe, stifling any attempt to cry out, to breathe. "Greetings, gov'nor," a soft, deep, curiously familiar voice said behind his ear. "Let's go over this way, shall we?" And he was dragged, effortlessly, his heels clattering along the pavement, into a small alley beside the Hope mansion.

"What?—who?—why?—" He forced the words out as the pressure around his windpipe was ever so slightly relaxed.

"Well," the deep voice said, "quite a little journalist we're becoming, isn't it, Count? Who, what, why, when, where; all questions that will shortly cease to concern you."

"My wallet is in the breast pocket of my suit jacket," the Count d'Hiver gasped. "Take it. There are forty or fifty pounds in it. Only for God's sake let me breathe!"

"Your wallet, d'Hiver?" the voice persisted. "Now what would I want with your wallet? Fifty pounds is of no interest to me. It's you I want."

"Me?" The count struggled to turn around in the iron grasp, suddenly realizing the import of his attacker's use of his name. This was not a random street crime; he was not an accidental victim. "Who are you? What do you want with me? What do you think you're doing?"

"You may call me Richard Plantagenet," the voice said. "And I want vengeance." Somehow the mild, soft insistence of that voice was more frightening than a thousand screaming fanatics would have been.

"Vengeance? Vengeance upon whom?" d'Hiver rasped the question out with the little air permitted him. "And what has it to do with me? You cannot get my assistance by choking me to death!"

"Vengeance on you, d'Hiver," the voice said, mildly, calmly, rationally. "And you can't help. You could, however, assuage my curiosity by explaining just why you are killing these gentlemen off, before I cut your heart out."

"I?" The Count d'Hiver could feel his heart pounding against his rib cage as though it were trying to break through. "I have done nothing! I have killed no one! You are making a horrible mistake! Do not do this thing! Let us reason this out. Plantagenet? I know no one called Plantagenet." And yet he had a horrible feeling that, from somewhere, he knew that voice.

"That is so," the voice admitted, a hot, horrible breath in his ear. "You do not know me by this name. But I know you! I know you by all your various names: the Count d'Hiver; Clubmaster; Hellhound; Master Incarnate of the Ancient and Evil Order of Hellfire. I know you!"

D'Hiver felt a momentary shock almost greater than the physical pain. He had not expected that. He twisted his arm around and thrust his heel backward in a swift kick, making a sudden desperate attempt to break free. He felt the heel connect hard against his captor's leg. But despite his twisting and kicking, and the grunt the kick drew from Plantagenet, the arm never loosened from around his neck.

"You're making some sort of mistake," he insisted, giving up the struggle. "I have no idea what you're talking about!"

"No?" the soft voice of Richard Plantagenet breathed. "Pity. Then you'll die for nothing. For whether or not you tell me why you are killing the others, I shall still certainly kill you. And within the next few minutes, too. I will lift my arm"—he applied just a little upward pressure, and a great knot of pain thrust itself through the back of d'Hiver's neck and up into his brain—"and you will be quite uncomfortable. And then you will be dead."

"Wait, wait; listen," d'Hiver croaked. "Let me talk."

"Talk."

D'Hiver took a few deep breaths, to try to calm himself. There was always a way to turn any situation to your own advantage, if you were smart enough. Even this one.

The pressure increased on his throat. "Waiting for someone to come by and save you? Won't happen; you have my word it won't. Talk."

"I am who you say I am," d'Hiver gasped, squeezing the words through his compressed windpipe.

"I know you are," the other said reasonably. "Did you think I was guessing? Is that what you have to tell me?" The pressure increased again.

"Wait! Wait! Think! If you know who I am, if you know who the men who died were—then how can you think that *I* killed them?

409

I was their master; I was their guide. I was not their enemy. Whoever is committing these murders must surely be after me, too. You can see that, whoever you are."

"We are brothers, as are all men," the whisper sounded in his ear. "I am your brother, and you are my brother; you have killed my brother, and I must kill you. Simple, isn't it?"

"Not so simple," d'Hiver insisted. "I did not kill your brother."

"Who did," the soft voice asked, "and why?"

"I am trying to find out who is behind these killings," d'Hiver said. "You think I am not? Who is your brother?"

"Was," the voice corrected. "My brother was Lord John Darby; now he is dust."

"*Crecy!*"

The arm tightened around his throat. "You may call me Richard Plantagenet," the man who had once been Lord Crecy Darby said.

"Of course, of course! I'm sorry. Plantagenet it is. Where have you been, Cr—Plantagenet?"

"Away. I have been performing experiments. Remember how we used to experiment, d'Hiver? I have done more—much more. But someone murdered my brother, and so I have come back. To speak with you; perhaps to kill you."

"Not me, Plantagenet. Help me catch the man who is really doing this. I need your help."

"If I am to believe you."

"Listen, you know who I am. You know where I live. You know how to find the club. If I'm lying to you, you can kill me later."

"That is so." The grip around his throat lessened, but did not release. "I want to find the murderer of my brother. This is distracting me from other work."

"I will help you," d'Hiver insisted. "It is to our interest to find the killer, and to eliminate him before Scotland Yard gets to him."

"So?"

"His motive must intimately concern us, since everyone so far identified murdered by this maniac has been one of us."

"Someone within the group?"

"I do not think so. Come home with me; my carriage is over there. We will discuss the possibilities."

"Fair enough." The hold around his throat was released.

Together, they moved out of the shadows.

There was the clicking sound of high heels on the pavement, and a cloaked figure rapidly headed back up the street.

"How long was she standing there?" d'Hiver demanded.

"I don't know. I didn't hear her. Who is she?"

"A girl reporter. She must have heard too much. Grab her—silently. I'll pull my carriage up."

The large figure disengaged from d'Hiver and raced silently up the street. There was a strange sound that could have been the beginnings of a girl's scream, suddenly choked off. The two constables outside the front door heard it and ran down the street, flashing their lanterns about.

The Count d'Hiver descended from his carriage and helped them look about. They found nothing. Nobody thought to look in the Count d'Hiver's carriage.

NINETEEN

THE GREAT TRAIN ROBBERY

> *Beyond (51½ M.)* Beer *(or* Bere*) Ferrers we cross
> the* Tavy *and skirt the E. Bank of the* Tamar *(p. 151).*
> *55¾ M.* St. Budeaux *(for* Saltash, *p. 151); 57 M.* Ford;
> *58 M.* Devonport & Storehouse *(see pp. 150, 151). We
> then pass the suburban stations of* North Road *and*
> Mutley *and enter the* Friary Terminus *at (62½ M.)*
> Plymouth.
>
> —BAEDEKER'S *Great Britain*

It took Barnett and Professor Moriarty the better part of two days to reach Plymouth. Moriarty left the train repeatedly, to confer with an odd assortment of agents who were awaiting him in such places as Weston-super-Mare, Taunton, Newton Abbot, Totnes, Dawlish, Teignmouth, Paignton, Okehampton, Tavistock, and nine other, even smaller, towns. It seemed to Barnett, who tagged along, that the professor was pleased with the results of these conferences.

Barnett listened to the usually brief conversations, but they told him very little, and Moriarty volunteered no additional information. "Are the pit reinforcements holding?" Moriarty asked the short Welshman who had rented a house in Dawlish for himself and his crew. "With nary a shiver," the Welshman told him. "Are the false cross-ties completed?" he asked the skinny Cockney who had opened a workshop in Teignmouth. "Work like a dream," he was informed. "How is Toby's nose?" he asked the slender man in the well-worn tweeds who awaited them at the Totnes Station. "His nose, his lungs, his voice, and his fightin' heart are all waitin' on your needs," the tweedy man told him. At each stop Moriarty passed an envelope to the person awaiting him. "Here are your instructions from this moment; take every care," he told each.

At Plymouth, Lord East's preparations were well in hand for the loading of the treasure train, which was scheduled to take place the next morning. The two companies of Her Majesty's Bengalese Foot, which had been encamped in a park by the west wall of the Citadel, had moved to the railway assembly yard and were busily patrolling the area between the H.M.S. *Hornblower* and the line of railway goods wagons, which had been meticulously prepared to receive the treasure. The Twenty-third Light Horse were occupying themselves by cantering about Plymouth, giving the citizenry an exhibition of precision horsemanship.

Barnett and Moriarty took rooms at the Duke of Clarence, an ancient and venerable inn some blocks from the scene of the Lord East activity. When they arrived, Barnett went to his room and collapsed for several hours, exhausted by the inactivity of train travel. Then he gave himself a quick sponge bath and put on, among other things, a fresh collar. Moriarty awaited him in the gentlemen's reading room on the first floor, a long, narrow room with a low beam ceiling, which went across the front of the hotel, overlooking the street. It had been completely outfitted, according to a plaque on the wall, with furniture and fittings from the admiral's cabin, the captain's cabin, and the wardroom of the 96-gun ship of the line H.M.S. *Indefatigable*, which had carried Admiral Pellew to Egypt in 1803, salvaged when she was turned into a hulk in 1836.

"Damned fine history," Moriarty said, when Barnett insisted upon reading him the plaque, "damned uncomfortable furniture."

"Which is probably why the admiral left it behind," Barnett said, going over to the window and staring down at the street below. "What time is it, Professor?"

"Ten past seven," Moriarty said, snapping open his pocket watch, consulting it, and then snapping it shut again. "Have you an engagement?"

"No," Barnett said. "However, the thought of food has crossed my mind. I was just wondering why there are so many people on the street at this hour. But now that I take a good look at those passing below, it seems to me that about one out of four is a policeman."

Moriarty came over, polished his pince-nez, and glanced out the window. "I believe you're right," he said. "There's no mistaking the peculiarly heavy regulation shoe leather, and the special flatness to which a plainclothes policeman chooses to adjust his bowler."

"You don't suppose that our presence here has anything to do with their presence here, do you?" Barnett asked. "I should have thought that Lord East would regard the various military units as sufficient guard for his treasure."

"I'm sure he does," Moriarty said. "The police are here to protect tomorrow's crowds of onlookers from having their pockets picked. Every gang of dips in England is probably here tonight."

"Ah," Barnett said, continuing to stare thoughtfully out the window. "So you don't think the presence of these flatfooted gentlemen with the bowler hats will interfere with your plans?"

"No," Moriarty said. "Is this a subtle interrogation? You realize that there are some things that it would not do to print, even in an American newspaper."

"No, no," Barnett said hastily. "I was just wondering."

"Nothing could interfere with my plans now," Moriarty told him, "except a major flood. Which I do not anticipate. Shall we dine here at the hotel, or have you a better suggestion? Perhaps some establishment where your compatriots of the press will gather."

"Well," Barnett considered. "The Railway Arms commercial hotel is probably where most of the London reporters will be staying. But I doubt if the restaurant is very good; reporters' expense accounts are not up to first-class bills of fare."

"Nevertheless," Moriarty said, "it might behoove us to dine in that establishment, if they serve so late."

"I believe the dining room is open quite late," Barnett said. "They cater to the traveler."

"Well then, let us travel!"

The Railway Arms served a buffet dinner until ten, and was, as Barnett had anticipated, full of reporters come to witness the next morning's activities. Much to Barnett's surprise, the usually antisocial Professor Moriarty was quite pleased to meet Barnett's associates and seemed fascinated by the stories they had to tell. Barnett's surprise lessened when he realized that the professor was artfully turning each of the stories to extract the last bit of information about Lord East, the treasure, and the train ride. Which, since that is why they were all there—in one way or another—was not hard to do.

"I say, Barnett," said Harry Inglestone, a *Morning Chronicle* staff reporter who had just come straight down from London, pausing at their table, "Caterby-Cahors is rather perturbed at your young lady."

Barnett stifled the remarks that sprang to his lips at Inglestone's innocent use of the phrase "your young lady." A forced smile creased his face. "What is your editor concerned about?" he asked. "If you are referring to Miss Perrine, formerly of the American News Service staff, she is one of the most competent reporters I have ever known, aside from possessing sufficient organizational skills to run an office single-handedly."

"Which is what makes it so puzzling," Inglestone commented, sitting himself down at their table and happily accepting Moriarty's offer of a glass of something. "A nice after-dinner claret," he told the waiter.

"What?" Barnett asked.

"I beg your pardon?" Inglestone said, looking totally confused.

"What is so puzzling?"

Inglestone thought over the recent conversation, trying to pick up the missing thread. "Oh, yes; Miss Perrine's disappearance. Thought I mentioned it, old man."

"What do you mean, her 'disappearance'?" Barnett demanded. "When did she disappear? What are you talking about?"

"Sorry again, old man. I should have realized that you'd be concerned. Ex-employer, and all that. Should have occurred to me that you didn't know. Well, I tell you, just between us, if she doesn't turn up quickly, she's going to lose her job, Lady Hogbine or no Lady Hogbine. Ah! The claret; thank you, Binns. It is Binns, isn't it? I shall mention you in the dispatches. Binns of the Railway Arms. A lifesaver."

"Disappearance," Barnett prompted.

"Oh, yes. Well, it's this way, old man. The lady went out on an assignment last night. No, it would be night before last, now. Doyle went with her. Artist fellow. Fine work. Well, Doyle left to take the carriage back to the Warren." He turned to Professor Moriarty. "That's what we call the lovely common room maintained for the reporters, 'the Warren.' "

"How clever of you," Moriarty murmured politely.

"Yes, well, Miss Perrine never showed up at the carriage. Doyle finally decided that she was chasing up some information or other, and returned to the Warren by himself. And, well, to make a long story short, she never did come back."

"Never got back? To the office, you mean?"

"Yes. Caterby-Cahors sent someone around to her house, and her pater was quite concerned at her absence. Claimed that she hadn't been there, either. And it certainly wasn't her custom to stay out all night. But if a lady is going to choose to be a reporter—well, you know, exigencies of the job, and all that. At any rate, Caterby-

Cahors was furious. He can't even stand tardiness, so you can imagine how he feels about unexcused absence. He was ready to fire her outright until the note came."

"The note?"

"Miss Perrine was considerate enough to send a note. She said she was after a very hot lead, and not to wait the story for her, but to write it as it stood. She might be a few days, she said. Well, Caterby-Cahors was fit to be tied. Had to get the information on the murder she was covering from Doyle. Nice fellow, Doyle; good sketch artist, but no reporter. Caterby-Cahors has given Miss Perrine three days to turn up with story in hand, and it had better be a dilly. That was Caterby-Cahors's term, 'a dilly.' "

Barnett turned to Moriarty. "Something's happened to her," he said.

Moriarty considered. "I believe you are right," he said. "She has been covering that series of murders?"

"Yes." Barnett felt the blood drain from his face. "My God! You don't think—"

Moriarty put out a restraining hand. "No, I don't," he said. "Stay calm."

Inglestone looked from one to the other of them. "I say!" he said. "You don't suppose something has happened to Miss Perrine?"

"Something has definitely happened to Miss Perrine," Moriarty said. "Even my rather sketchy acquaintance with her over the past two years tells me that she didn't run off. And she certainly isn't skulking about on some London street, following a suspect. If she were, she would have found a better way to communicate than a brief note. And she certainly would have informed her father."

"But—"

"On the other hand, Mr. Barnett, the pattern of this murderer we're dealing with shows that he doesn't attack women; that he doesn't make the sort of mistake that would have enabled Miss Perrine to walk in on him; and that he doesn't conceal bodies. So, as no body has been found, we must conclude that whatever happened to Miss Perrine, it was not the doing of our multiple killer."

"That's very reassuring," Barnett said. "She may be lying bleeding on some street, sliced up by some maniac, but at least it's a *different* maniac! I've got to get back to London!"

"What for?" Moriarty asked.

"What do you mean, what for? To find Cecily. Nobody else seems even to be looking."

"I shall remedy that," Moriarty said. "I'll put a telegram in at the desk, and there will be five hundred people out looking for her in an hour."

"I say, you chaps really do seem to be taking this thing seriously," Inglestone said. "You don't actually suppose that anything nasty has happened to the young lady, do you?" He chuckled. "Well, if it has, it would serve old Caterby-Cahors right, I'll tell you."

Barnett stared incredulously at Inglestone for a second, not sure he had heard right. How callous it was possible to be about someone one didn't know very well. And Inglestone didn't seem to think he had said anything at all strange.

"I'd better pass the telegram in now," Moriarty said, rising and heading for the door. "Meet you in the lobby, Barnett."

Barnett also rose. "Very good chatting with you, Inglestone," he said. "We must do it again sometime. You don't mind paying, do you? There's a good chap!" And with that, he slapped Inglestone on the back and hurried after Moriarty.

"I say!" Inglestone exclaimed.

"I really think I should go back to London," Barnett told Moriarty, catching up to him in the lobby.

"I have given a telegram to the porter," Moriarty said. "It will be clacking its ways over the wires in ten minutes and will be delivered to 64 Russell Square within the hour. It is now ten o'clock. Before midnight, five hundred people will be searching for the young lady. By tomorrow morning the first report on the search will be awaiting me at the desk of this hotel. If there is any definite word on her whereabouts earlier, I will be immediately notified. Believe me, Barnett, I know how you feel; but no more could be done if you were present, and I need you here."

"I appreciate that," Barnett said. "I certainly don't want to desert you. But we both know that any of fifty men could do what you would have me do tomorrow. I am not in any way essential to your plan. I should get on the next train to London."

Moriarty put his hand on Barnett's shoulder and peered at him intently. "Understand me," he said. "I am not an unfeeling man. If there were anything that you could do in London that would further the search for Cecily Perrine, I would hire a special for you and put you on it. If there were any way in which my presence would help, I would join you."

"Thank you, Professor," Barnett said. "I'm sure you're right; and I appreciate what you say more than I can tell you. It's just that—"

"Furthermore," Moriarty said, "whatever your opinion of yourself, the fact is that I *do* need you here. You are not irreplaceable, but you are intelligent, competent, and resourceful, and the man with whom I would have to replace you might lack one or more of those virtues.

"I pledge you this, Barnett: if any word comes of Miss Perrine—at all—and it seems desirable for you to go to London, I'll have that special put on for you immediately. In any case, we shall both be on the next regular train for London. I shall leave it midway, but you will go on through."

"The next train?" Barnett asked.

"Yes. There are no more trains scheduled tonight, and the first train out tomorrow morning is the, let's see"—he pulled out his schedule—"the six-oh-eight doesn't run on Saturdays, so we shall be on the seven-forty-two. Will that suffice?"

"I suppose," Barnett said unhappily, "that it will have to."

He slept fitfully that night. If asked, he would have sworn that he slept not at all. Complex images kept springing into his mind, unbidden. Images of the myriad ways in which Cecily, by chance or by design, could have discovered the mysterious murderer. And then the image would unfold and become horrible, as the murderer, in turn, found Cecily. Barnett's mind rebelled from the worst possibilities, but even the ones his mind would accept did not bear dwelling upon.

The loading of the treasure was set to begin an hour before sunrise, which, according to *Whitaker's Almanack*, would occur at 5:42. And so at a little after four in the damp, chilly morning of the first Saturday in April, Barnett found himself dressing by candlelight so that he could go to watch large, heavily guarded boxes being loaded onto goods wagons in the predawn blackness for transport to London. And do his small part in seeing that they did not arrive.

The reporters, sketch artists, and such of the idly curious as could drag themselves out of bed at such an hour were to be assembled on a three-tiered grandstand specially erected in the goods yard for the event. This would give them a splendid view of the proceedings and yet keep them out of the way. The real crowds would gather later in the morning, when the military guard was added and the treasure train prepared to leave.

Barnett had wondered how they were going to move treasure from the ship to the goods wagons in the dark; even with the route marked with a line of lanterns, it would not seem a prudent procedure from the standpoint of security. And indeed, when he and Professor Moriarty arrived and took their seats in the front row of the grandstand, the brightest object around was the conductor's lantern, which was carried by the railway guard. There was no line of lanterns, and no apparent motion from what Barnett believed to be the direction of H.M.S. *Hornblower*, a quarter mile away at Stonehouse Basin. "Are we early?" he whispered to the guard, looking around at the ten or fifteen other people already in the stands.

"No sir, you'm jest a'time," the guard told him in a broad north-counties accent. And as if merely waiting for his word, the entire goods yard was suddenly bathed in an intense white light.

Barnett blinked, squinted, and shielded his eyes from the intense glare. "What on earth is that?" he asked no one in particular.

"They appear to have four Drummond apparatuses mounted in towers," Moriarty said. "We are now bathed in a light as bright as the sun, if rather more limited in scope."

"Drummond?" Barnett peered out from between his fingers. His eyes were starting to adjust now, and he could see slightly between his fingers as he shut off most of the light with his hands. The professor was right; except for the bizarre shadows cast by the four light sources, it could have been daylight within the limited area of the goods yard.

"The light is generated by application of a flame of hydrogen gas burned in a stream of oxygen to a core of calcium oxide. You should be intimately familiar with the principle, fond as you are of attending the music halls."

"Music halls?" Barnett asked.

"Calcium oxide is perhaps better known as lime," Moriarty explained.

"Limelight!"

"Correct. The same light that illuminates your favorite singers, jugglers, and acrobats, done on a much larger scale. This sort of Drummond apparatus is usually found in lighthouses, where the beam can be seen from twenty miles away. The only difference is the shape of the mirrored reflector; parabolic in lighthouses, and, I would assume, conical here. It covers a much wider field, you see."

"I see," Barnett said. And he was beginning to. He took his hands away from his face and looked around. "It's quite a shock, going from pitch-black to daylight in an instant. I'm not sure that the human eye was built to take that sort of transition."

The grandstand was now filling up rapidly with the gentlemen of the press. The area before them, a loading platform with one of the specially prepared goods wagons pulled up before it, was curiously devoid of life and motion. It reminded Barnett of a stage setting in the moments before the curtain went up on the first act. Which, he realized, was probably a fair assessment. Lord East had arranged this show for the press, and he was going to see that they got their money's worth. For whatever motive, Lord East craved the public eye, and he had spent thirty years learning how to stay in it.

A line of red-coated soldiers marched into the limelight from the left, the direction of the *Hornblower*, and the Lord East treasure. Leading them, astride three spirited chargers, were a colonel, a brigadier, and Lord East. It was, as it had been contrived to be, an inspiring sight.

As the reporters fell silent at Lord East's approach, Moriarty leaned over to Barnett and whispered, "Ready?"

"Yes," Barnett replied, feeling his heart beat faster.

Moriarty nodded. "We have one thing to thank that mysterious murderer for," he commented.

"We do? What's that?"

"Were it not for him, Sherlock Holmes would even now be sitting behind us disguised as an itinerant colorman, breathing down our necks."

"He did have three Scotland Yard men following you about," Barnett reminded Moriarty.

"Yes, but we were able to divert them with little trouble. Holmes would have been much more difficult to get rid of. Even now he must be spending whatever time he can spare in wondering where I've got to. It is these small things that make life worth living."

"You are a vindictive man, Professor," Barnett said.

"Nonsense!" Moriarty whispered. "I would gladly be willing to relinquish the childish pleasure I get in thwarting him if he would give up following me about and spying on me. I think East is about to speak."

"Welcome!" Lord East bellowed to the assemblage on the grandstand, maneuvering his horse in close to the railing. "I apologize for getting you all up at such a ridiculous hour to witness the loading, but we want to have a clear run to London during the daylight hours. I'm sure you can understand." As he spoke, his horse began walking around in a small circle. His lordship, trying to ignore this, gradually twisted around in his saddle until he was speaking over the animal's rump. Then, in a sudden fit of anger, he put his spurs to the animal to make it obey the reins. The horse responded by kicking up sharply with its hind feet, causing his lordship to lose his stirrups and almost fly head over rump to the earth below. He caught himself, barely, by grabbing onto the saddle with both hands, pulled himself up, and savagely yanked the horse around to face the group. "Military mount," he said in an annoyed undertone that carried across the field. "Always give the best of everything to the military!"

The soldiers had now formed a double line leading from somewhere to the left of the limelit area to the loading platform. The shifting of the Lord East Collection from the battleship to the railway train was about to commence. "It should take a bit over two hours to transfer the entire collection into the ten goods wagons," Lord East explained, having regained control of his mouth. "But you must understand that this is, metaphorically speaking, only the tip of a vast iceberg. Hundreds and hundreds of man-hours have already gone into the preparations. Wafting the collection ashore and loading it onto the baggage carts which will bring it here was a process which began yesterday evening and was not completed until but a short time ago."

" 'E don't want us to think it was easy," someone behind Barnett muttered.

"Where is the official photographer?" Lord East fretted. "I wanted the whole process captured on glass plates. History is being made here!"

The first baggage cart appeared, pushed between the twin rows of soldiers and onto the loading platform by an octet of workmen who, judging by their appearance and dress, must have been brought back from India by Lord East. It held twelve large statues of different ancient gods and goddesses of various Indian religions, deities that would have been very surprised to have ended up on the same small cart. The workmen rapidly and efficiently prised the statuary off the cart and into the goods wagon, tying the pieces into place with a complex of ropes and scaffolding.

There was a pause in the loading now, and a certain amount of backtracking, while the official photographer bustled up and set up his apparatus to the side of the grandstand. Lord East and his entourage assumed a variety of poses that were supposed to suggest the earlier stages of the operation before continuing with the job.

The next cart held what looked like a load of bricks. Lord

East's audience broke into a subdued chattering at the sight of it, as the reporters tried to guess the history and purpose of the load. Some of the suggestions as to the uses to which the bricks could be put were rather imaginative. "Sun-baked bricks," Lord East explained, "forming a lovely frieze that went around the wall of a four-thousand-year-old temple. Quite beautiful. A pair of hunters accosting a lion, I believe. The bricks were all numbered with Chinese chalk when we took it apart, but many of the numbers seem to have rubbed off during the journey. Or perhaps during the five years in storage. I hope we can reassemble it, nonetheless; it really was quite striking."

Barnett's brief but essential part in Professor Moriarty's master plan for the acquisition of the Lord East Collection was to be enacted as the third treasure chest was being loaded. What he was to do was clear, and not overly difficult, given the known habits of his brother reporters. Why he was to do it was another matter. Moriarty was not communicative with his plans. It was enough for one to execute his part; one was not called upon to understand what he was doing, or why. Barnett gave a mental shrug as he prepared to move.

The third wagon was loaded now, and sealed; the fourth was about to be rolled into its place before the platform. Lord East rode over to the loading platform to supervise as his most precious cargo was installed in its place.

Barnett unostentatiously moved up one row in the grandstand and over toward the middle. His colleague Inglestone was sitting a few seats over from where Barnett now found himself, doing his best to ignore Barnett's existence. He must be still smarting from having to pay the bill the night before, Barnett decided. He would serve well as Barnett's unwitting ally.

Barnett slid over along the bench and slapped Inglestone on the back. "How are you, friend?" he asked solicitously. "Sleep well?"

"As well as could be expected, old man," Inglestone said frostily. "You owe me fourteen bob."

"Do I?" Barnett leaned back, his elbows on the seat behind. He pitched his voice just loud enough so that the reporters in the seats surrounding could overhear. "Well then, I'll tell you what: I'll give you a chance to get even."

"How's that?" Inglestone asked, sounding annoyed. "It wasn't a question of a wager, old man; this was cold, hard cash."

"Ah, yes," Barnett said. "But there's wagers and there's wagers." He indicated the first treasure chest, now being loaded into the wagon. "I'll bet you five quid on the nose that there's nothing in that there box."

Inglestone turned to stare at him. "What do you mean?" he asked. "The treasure chest?"

"You've got it," Barnett said. "Five quid says that the so-called treasure chest is empty."

"What are you saying, Barnett?" the columnist for the *Evening Standard* demanded, his mustache twitching.

The first chest was now in place in the goods wagon, and the second was being brought up. "I say they're empty," Barnett said.

"That's ridiculous!" the *Morning Intelligencer-Whig* declared. "Do you know what you're saying?"

"Have *you* seen inside any of those chests?" Barnett demanded. "I'm saying there's a reason. I say they're empty!"

Heinrich von Hertzog, British correspondent for the *Berliner Tagenblatt*, nodded his head sagely. "It could be," he said. "It makes sense."

Barnett was glad to hear that, because the one thing that had worried him was that his accusation made no sense whatsoever, as far as he could tell. "Of course it does," he agreed.

"What sort of sense?" Jameson of the *Daily Telegraph* demanded.

"Lord East creates all this excitement, all this preparation, all this display, to draw attention to the treasure train," von Hertzog explained. "But the real treasure is sent otherwise. A clever man, Lord East."

Barnett nodded. "I'll up it to ten quid," he said. "Any takers? Ten quid says those boxes are as empty as an editor's heart."

"That's nonsense!" Inglestone said. "It certainly doesn't make any sense that I can see. Do you know what you're talking about, Barnett?"

The second chest was now in place. "Ten quid says I do," Barnett said.

"Come on, Barnett," Jameson said. "Don't try to make money on your friends. If you know something, spill it. Don't just sit there looking smug."

The cart with the third chest on it was being pushed up onto the loading platform. "Easy enough to check," Barnett said. "Any takers? Ten quid; easy money."

"How would you establish the contents of the chests?" von Hertzog asked.

"Open one," Barnett said.

"You're on!" Inglestone said, coming to a decision. "Ten pounds says that you're mistaken; that those chests are, indeed, full of the pieces in the Lord East Collection. But understand that this wager has nothing to do with the fourteen bob you owe me."

"Fair enough," Barnett said. "You can deduct it from my winnings. Well, shall we go find out? His lordship can't object to a reasonable request to open one of the chests. We'll all promise not to touch; won't we, boys?"

Now that the suggestion had been advanced, the reporters were unable to leave it alone. It became imperative to them to discover whether a possibility that none of them had even considered five minutes ago, that was unlikely in the extreme, that was actually none of their business, was true. In a body they left the grandstand and advanced toward the loading dock, the treasure chest, the goods wagon, and Lord East.

The four plainclothes policemen who were guarding the grandstand moved to stop the cluster of them as they advanced. "Gentlemen, gentlemen, please!" one of them cried, opening his arms wide, as if to encircle the group himself. " 'Ere now, what's this?" a second barked, running around to the front of the group. The other two also raced around to the front to place themselves uncertainly between the reporters and the platform.

Lord East heard the disturbance and turned to see the cluster of correspondents advancing on him. For a second he looked nonplussed, but then he gathered himself and guided his horse over to the group, placing himself and his horse between the reporters and the platform. "You gentlemen were requested to remain on the grandstand," he said sternly. "You must realize that we cannot compromise our security arrangements, even to oblige the press. Please return immediately whence you came."

The third chest was now inside the goods wagon, placed carefully on its supporting frame, and the Indian carters were emerging from the wagon as the fourth chest was pulled up in its cart. "If you don't mind, my lord," Barnett called up to him, "we'd like to see inside that box."

"Box?" Lord East looked uncertain for a moment. "You mean the treasure chest, sir?"

"Yes, my lord," Higgins, of the *Pall Mall Gazette*, called. "There seems to be some doubt as to whether the treasure is actually in the chests, or whether this is merely a ruse."

"A ruse, gentlemen?" Lord East looked shocked. He had just been accused of doing something un-British.

"The suggestion is, my lord," Inglestone said, "ridiculous as it sounds, that you have spirited the treasure away by some alternate means, while encouraging us to believe that it is still in those chests. Thus supposedly foiling possible criminal attempts upon the collection."

Lord East considered for a second. "And just why should I do that?" he asked. "The treasure is quite safe where it is. Certainly safer than any other place I could put it. I do not like these devious methods you speak of, nor do I resort to them. They are unnecessary."

"Then, my lord, the treasure is, indeed, in the chests?" Inglestone asked, looking inordinately pleased. "You affirm that?"

"There is my seal," Lord East said, pointing with his riding crop to the lid of the fourth chest, now being inserted into the goods wagon. He indicated the strip of ribbon that went across the lid's opening, sealed above and below. "It has not been broken."

"You will permit us to check?" von Hertzog asked.

"I most certainly will not!" Lord East said sharply. He waved the chest on into the wagon. "Gentlemen, this is outrageous! How dare you question me! The chest will be opened at the Royal Albert Museum, in the presence of a representative of her imperial majesty, and not a jot before. Please return to your seats."

The reporters, muttering uncertainly, returned to the grandstand. Barnett watched as Lord East checked the inside of the goods wagon and then ordered it closed and sealed from the outside.

Barnett's part of the job, whatever it had accomplished, was done. Now there was nothing to do but wait for the train that would take Moriarty to Hampermire Station and himself through to London. How the little act he had just put on would further the cause, he didn't know, and at the moment he didn't care. Somewhere in London, Cecily Perrine had disappeared; somewhere in London she was at this very moment. In what state she was, Barnett did not care to speculate. How he would find her, he had no idea. But if she was still alive, find her he would.

The sun was coming up, and the area outside the limelight was just beginning to be visible. Moriarty and Barnett left the grandstand and returned to the hotel. There was a telegram waiting for Moriarty when they arrived. He opened it and read it in a second. "Nothing," he said. "Sorry, Barnett. No trace of the lady yet."

"I'll find her," Barnett said.

"Of course you will," Moriarty told him.

TWENTY

ALWAYS DARKEST

I had a dream, which was not all a dream.
The bright sun was extinguished, and the stars
Did wander darkling in the eternal space,
Rayless, and pathless, and the icy Earth
Swung blind and blackening in the moonless air;
Morn came and went—and came, and brought no day. . . .
—GEORGE GORDON, LORD BYRON

Cecily Perrine awoke. Slowly, dimly, her awareness returned, and she was amazed to realize that she had been asleep. She had no idea how long she had slept; there was no way to mark the passage of time in her pitch-black surroundings. She rose from the ticking full of dank straw that was her mattress on the cold stone floor, and felt her way around the smooth stone walls. She did not know what she hoped to find, and in any case her groping fingers encountered nothing but damp stone. The cell she was in was approximately six feet square, and higher than her fingers could reach with her arms fully extended. It contained the straw-filled ticking, a chamber pot, and Cecily. The door in the corner of one wall was no more than a foot wide and four feet high, and held neither a peephole nor a doorknob.

She was not sure how, or why, she had arrived where she was. She remembered leaving the Hope mansion and walking toward her carriage. She had passed an alley where the Count d'Hiver was engaged in earnest conversation with some tall man. She remembered wondering who the man was, and where he had sprung from at such an hour. Then, on an idle whim, she had turned to hurry back to the mansion; she had thought of an unimportant question she wanted to put to Mr. Holmes. It would wait, but after all, she was there now. Rapid footsteps had sounded behind her, and a large, powerful man had grabbed her from behind. She had instinctively started to cry out, but her assailant had instantly clamped one great hand over her mouth, cutting her scream to no more than a loud gasp. He had then carried her a short distance, where some other person draped a sweet-smelling rag across her face. It must have been dosed with chloroform or some similar substance, for the next thing Cecily knew she was in this chamber.

It *must* have been Count d'Hiver and the man he was talking to who had done this thing to her; so she decided once again, as she had a dozen times before. But it made no sense. Why would the count, the representative of the Privy Seal and thus of the Queen, abduct Cecily Perrine? Why would he abduct anyone, for that matter? What did he want with her? Why had no one come to her cell—except the man in black—since she had been there?

The man in black! Four times since she had awakened from her drugged sleep to find herself in this featureless stone cell, the man in black had entered. He had given no warning; suddenly she had heard the bolts being thrown back and the door had opened. The cell had been bathed in a bright light—how bright she could not tell, since in her darkness a candle would have seemed the sun—and a man dressed all in tight-fitting black garments, even to a black hood and black mask, had stepped in.

She had, at first, tried speaking to him, reasoning with him, pleading with him, screaming at him; but to no avail. Four times he had put down bowls of rancid-smelling gruel and cups of water. Three times he had turned and left, wordlessly, gesturelessly. The fourth time he had reached out a hand and touched her on the arm; briefly, probingly, experimentally. And this had been the most horrible thing of all. He had not touched her as a man touches a woman, not even the gloating, possessive touch of a captor for his captive. This was immeasurably worse. There had not been even the humanity of lust in that touch. He had touched her as a farmer might probe a prize pig, to test the firmness of its skin, to feel its muscles, and how well fatted it was.

She could not tell how long she had been held a prisoner. She had been fed four times, but at what intervals? She had eaten but little of the gruel, and was still not hungry; but this was no indication. She felt wretched and afraid and alone, and such feelings would keep her from hunger for weeks, not merely days.

Cecily shrank back into the corner: there was that sound now, the *snick-snick-snick* of three bolts being thrown. The narrow wooden door was pulled open, and light flooded into the tiny cell. The tall man in black had once again come to visit. This time he brought no gruel. This time he took her by the arm and propelled her, as though she were a rag doll, out into the narrow stone corridor beyond the door. She resisted an impulse to cry out, feeling obscurely that it would give him satisfaction, and maintained a passive silence as he pushed her ahead of him down the corridor. He did not appear to notice her silence, any more than he had heeded her crying and pleading on his previous visits.

Cecily tried to prepare herself for whatever might happen. Her mind was in a turmoil, and she realized that she had no idea what to prepare herself for. This was so far outside her experience as to be a succession of unbelievable happenings, one long nightmare from which she was unable to wake.

The light, which had seemed so blinding from within the black cell, proved to come from a row of gas-mantle fixtures set high in the corridor wall. From the way that the pipe ran along the outside of the wall, right below the ceiling, it was evident that the stone corridor and its row of cells had been constructed long before the coming of gaslight. She was captive in the ancient cellar of some great house, the house of a man important enough to plan on keeping captives in his own basement, back in the days when influential noblemen might expect to have a few captives of their own. And now the present owner of the house was using his inherited cellar for purposes that nineteenth-century authorities would frown on, if only they knew. That was a fact to be filed away. Probably useless, but a fact nonetheless. Collecting and sorting facts kept her mind busy and active, and that in itself was helpful.

The man in black paused at the end of the corridor to unlock a thick wooden door, and then to lock it behind him. Just habit? Or were there other prisoners in that hellish black dungeon?

After three more locked doors and a twisting iron staircase, they came at last to a room, a well-appointed study, the floor deeply carpeted and the walls lined with bookcases filled with leather-bound books. For all its fine appointments, there was something strange about the room, and it took Cecily a minute to figure out what it was: there were no windows.

Behind an ancient, ornately carved oak table in the middle of the room, perched on a chair that would have served as a throne in many lesser kingdoms, was a small man clad in a black velvet lounging suit, his face concealed behind a great harlequin mask. Cecily thought it looked suspiciously like the Count d'Hiver—the size and build were about right—but she couldn't be sure.

The man in black brought Cecily to the front of the table, facing the harlequin, and released her. The harlequin stared intently at her, his blue eyes peering through the mask's eye slits, and said nothing.

Cecily felt a mixture of strong emotions all trying to surface at once; fear, astonishment, hatred, and rage boiled inside of her, causing her heart to thump loudly in her chest, her face to flush, her hands to feel alternately hot and cold. She wanted to cry, to scream, to beg, to hit out with all of her might at the man in black, to throw herself across the desk and throttle the smug harlequin. And so she did nothing. She felt that the harlequin was waiting for her to speak, perhaps to beg, to entreat, to demand; and so, mustering all the self-control she had available in her weary, frightened body, she remained mute.

"Welcome!" the harlequin said at last, in a deep voice. (Artificially deep? The voice of d'Hiver, lowered for effect or disguise? She couldn't be sure.) "Do you know why you are here?"

"What?" The single syllable was drawn out of Cecily involuntarily, so shocked was she by the question. "Listen, you," she said, putting her hands flat on the table in front of her and leaning aggressively forward toward the masked man. "I've been kidnapped, drugged, locked up in a black, dank cell, fed some kind of repulsive gruel, ministered to by this ape behind me, and you want to know if I know why I'm here! I'm here against my will, obviously at your behest, and you shall suffer for this. You can't expect to get away with a thing like this in the middle of London in 1887, as though you were some sort of feudal lord. My friends are looking for me, and you will live to regret this. Don't think they won't find me!"

The man in black grabbed her by the hair and lifted her straight up and back away from the table, actually raising her off the floor with one hand. The suddenness of the act, the shock and surprise, and the almost unbearable pain made her scream and brought tears to her eyes. She grabbed for his hand just as he released her hair, causing her to fall heavily to the floor. "Stand!" he commanded— the first word he had spoken in her presence.

Cecily struggled to her feet, tears stinging her eyes. "You bastards!" she screamed across the desk. "If Benjamin were here—"

"You are here as an acolyte, a supplicant, a slave," the harlequin said, precisely as though nothing had just happened, as though she had remained respectfully silent. "There was some discussion at first about what you might know, or not know; but it was realized that it does not matter. What will grow in you, what will become of paramount importance, is your own knowledge of your condition. And that will change from day to day, from moment to moment."

She gaped at him. "What are you talking about?" she demanded. "Do you know what you're doing—what you've done? You must be insane!"

"I am the Master Incarnate," the harlequin continued, ignoring her outburst. "In the course of time, you will come to know other masters. You are to be removed from here, and taken to the place of your service. You will learn what it means to be a slave."

"Listen!" Cecily yelled, anger at this man, so smug behind his silly mask, outweighing her fear. "You—"

The harlequin turned to the man in black. "Is it time, Plantagenet?" he asked.

The man in black nodded.

The harlequin smiled. It was not a pleasant smile. "Take her!" he commanded.

"Now, look—" Cecily said.

The man called Plantagenet wrapped his right arm around her body, pinning her arms to her side. She tried to fight, but was unable to move in his iron grip. His left hand came up to her face, and there was a sweet-smelling rag in it.

"No!" she cried . . .

INSIDE OUT

In the still air the music lies unheard;
In the rough marble beauty lies unseen;
To wake the music and the beauty needs
The master's touch, the sculptor's chisel keen.
—HORATIUS BONAR

After an uneventful journey through some of England's most beautiful countryside, Lord East's treasure train arrived in London shortly after four o'clock, Saturday afternoon, and came to rest at a specially designated siding in Hampton Court. It remained there, sealed and surrounded with its military escort, until two o'clock next afternoon, Sunday, when her imperial majesty's personal representative, the stern and splendidly choleric Duke of Denver, eighty years old and ramrod-stiff in the saddle, trotted officially over to accept delivery of the Lord East Collection, as an indefinite loan, in her majesty's name.

The seals on each of the special goods wagons were now broken, and the great doors rolled aside, one at a time. The contents of the first three wagons—statuary, pillars, walls, friezes, and great stone urns—had passed the trip in fine condition. The fourth wagon, holding the five great treasure chests, appeared to be as it was when it was sealed. With a flourish, Lord East himself opened the first chest—

—which was empty.

In a haste approaching frenzy, the lids of the other four chests were pried off, revealing the impossible: each chest contained nothing but air, and dust, and one small seed pearl which was found wedged in a crack on the bottom of the third chest.

All the color drained out of Lord East's face, and, were it not for the instant aid of his two faithful Indian companions, he would have fainted dead away on the wagon floor. "It's impossible!" he screamed to the Duke of Denver, as his aides helped him over the side of the wagon and down to the ground. "I tell you, the thing's manifestly impossible! They *can't* be gone!"

The Duke of Denver wheeled in his saddle and turned to his escort, the Captain Commander of the Household Guard. "Get me Sherlock Holmes!" he ordered.

Benjamin Barnett did not return to the Russell Square house until late Sunday night, having spent every moment since he arrived back in London on Saturday afternoon doing his best to find out what had happened to Cecily Perrine. As far as he could discover, she had left the Hope mansion slightly after two o'clock the morning of Thursday, the thirty-first of March, and then disappeared off the face of the earth. He could seem to get no further.

When he entered the house, Professor Moriarty was in his study, reading a late-edition *Evening Standard*. "Ah!" Moriarty said, waving him into the room. "The wanderer returns. You look exhausted. Have you eaten? Take a glass of sherry."

"No, thank you," Barnett said, dropping onto the leather couch and pulling off his shoes. "I haven't sat down in, it must be, twenty-four hours. I confess, I don't have much energy left."

"Not surprising," Moriarty said. "You have been quite busy, although it has been the purposeless busy-ness of a headless chicken. You scurry here, you scurry there, you accomplish nothing."

"You've been having me followed!" Barnett accused.

"Nonsense!" Moriarty responded. "But most of the places you've been, most of the people you've spoken to, are being covered by my agents, who are just about ubiquitous at the moment. I told you I'd have five hundred people on the street. In addition to the minions usually in my employ in such cases, every member of Twist's Beggar's Guild is now keeping his eyes open for Miss Cecily Perrine. I have offered a hundred pounds reward for any word. More would be counterproductive."

"That's very nice of you," Barnett said. "But what good will it do? How would they know her if they see her?"

"Mr. Doyle, the sketch artist, was kind enough to do a portrait from memory, which I have had reproduced on a small letterpress."

Moriarty lifted a piece of paper from his desk and, with a flip of his wrist, skimmed it across the room to Barnett. "A good likeness, I think."

Barnett stared at the picture on the four-by-five-inch card. "Amazingly good," he agreed, trying to ignore the lump that rose in his throat. "They should certainly recognize her if they see her, with the aid of this. But supposing they don't?"

"Always possible," Moriarty said. "I have taken certain other steps which might lead to Miss Perrine. I don't want to raise false hopes—"

"What are they?" Barnett demanded. "Please tell me what you're doing."

Moriarty shook his head. "They may lead to nothing," he said. "But then, if so I will think of something else. Perhaps some slender shred of information, some slight indication, will come in; that's all I need, a slender thread. I have been known to accomplish wonders with a slender thread."

Barnett stared morosely at Moriarty, and then shook his head. "I know you're trying to cheer me up," he said. "And don't think I'm not grateful. I am. I've never known you to go to such trouble before over someone else's problem; and I know you probably consider it weak of me to be so emotional about it—"

"Not to have emotions is to be less than human, Mr. Barnett," Moriarty said. "The trick we British learn is not to display them. Perhaps I have learned that trick better than most. But you are not British. And your emotions are entirely understandable. You should not, however, allow them to cloud your reason, which will be of much greater use in actually recovering Miss Perrine."

"She may already be dead," Barnett said, speaking aloud for the first time what had been preying on his mind for the past day and a half.

"I doubt it," Moriarty said. "If whoever abducted her wished her dead, he would have merely killed her. It is, after all, so much less trouble."

"Perhaps—" Barnett paused. "A fate worse than death . . ."

"Don't torture yourself, Mr. Barnett," Moriarty said. "Besides, despite the Romantic writers, there is no fate worse than death. Any pain, indignation, or horror that Miss Perrine may experience at the hands of her abductors will fade away with time—and love. Death, Mr. Barnett, will not fade away."

Barnett sat up. "I suppose you're right, Professor," he said. "It's doing nothing—at least, nothing useful—that's driving me crazy. If there were only something I could do!"

"Get a good night's sleep," Moriarty said. "Get your mind off this thing, at least as much as possible. I promise you that tomorrow you will start useful activity."

Barnett stood up and stretched. "Your word's good with me, Professor," he said. "I guess it has to be. I'll do my best. Tonight I sleep. Tomorrow I follow your instructions. If the blisters on my feet allow me to walk at all."

"Have Mrs. H give you a basin in which to soak your feet," Moriarty said. "She has some sort of concoction that works wonders on abused feet."

"I'll do that," Barnett said. He pointed to the *Evening Standard* that Moriarty was holding. "I read about the great mystery," he added. "Two tons of precious jewelry disappears from a locked goods wagon. The mystery sensation of the age. I was part of it, Professor, and I confess that I have no idea of how you managed it."

"Let us hope that the authorities remain as puzzled as you are," Moriarty said. He reached to the side of his desk and picked up a small bronze statuette that Barnett had never noticed before. "May the luck of Uma stay with us."

"Uma?" Barnett asked.

"A Hindu goddess," Moriarty told him. "Consort of Shiva. A fascinating, complex religion, that."

"That's not part of the, ah, loot, is it?" Barnett asked, looking alarmed.

"Never mind," Moriarty said. "It's not important. Go to bed."

"Tell me how you did it," Barnett said.

"Did what?"

"The robbery. Tell me how you removed two tons of jewelry from a locked wagon while it was surrounded by armed guards."

Moriarty considered. "Briefly," he said.

Barnett nodded.

"Like most things that seem impossible," Moriarty said, "it was actually quite simple. I'm afraid that telling you will ruin the effect."

"Please, Professor," Barnett said. "After all, I was part of it."

"True," Moriarty admitted. "And a very important part, although you knew not what you did."

"What did I do?"

"The problem was," Moriarty said, "to get someone into that sealed wagon."

Barnett nodded. "That was indeed the problem," he agreed.

"And you did it," Moriarty said.

"*I* did?"

"With a brilliant bit of misdirection. You see, I already had an agent in place: one of the Indian porters was my man. He arranged to be among the crew who carried the third treasure chest into the wagon."

"And then?"

"And then, while you drew the momentary attention of everyone with your clever little wager, he merely stayed behind in the wagon while the others left."

"But that's impossible," Barnett said. "Lord East inspected the wagon after it was loaded, and there was no place for anyone to hide. The walls were even covered with fabric."

"Indeed," Moriarty said. "And an interesting quality of any such solid-color material is that from more than two feet or so distant, you cannot tell how far away you are from any piece of identical fabric without an external referent."

"What does that mean?" Barnett asked. "I confess that you've lost me."

"Picture a table, placed, let us say, five feet in front of a fabric curtain," Moriarty said. "You are staring at the table with the curtain behind it. Wherever you look you see the curtain—above the table, to the right of the table, to the left of the table, between the legs of the table. Correct?"

"I guess so."

"I know, it sounds too obvious to be worth stating. But now, supposing I take a piece of fabric that is identical to the curtain and fasten it between the back legs of the table, from the rim of the table to the floor. When you look at it, you'll think you see the back curtain, but in reality you'll be staring at a piece of fabric that is five feet closer to you."

"I see," Barnett said.

"And between that fabric and the actual curtain," Moriarty said, "I could hide a man, a donkey, a small cannon, or anything else that would fit, and you'd be willing to swear that you could see the whole area clearly, and there was nothing there."

Barnett thought this over. "So that's how you did it," he said.

"That's how *you* did it," Moriarty replied. "You distracted the crowd for long enough for my agent to drop a fabric curtain that he had rolled around one of the carrying bars for the chest. There he was, crouched down, in the supposedly empty area between the chest and the wall. Lord East thought he could see the far wall, but he couldn't."

"So the wagon was sealed with the man inside."

"Just so."

"But how did the man get the treasure out?"

"One piece at a time."

"And the guards?"

"It was invisible to the guards."

"You mesmerized them?"

Moriarty chuckled. "Listen, and I shall describe the rest of the operation," he said. "The agent in the goods wagon waited until the train was in motion. Then he pried up a one-foot-square section of the sheet-metal floor with a device that I had fabricated, which looks a great deal like an oversized tin opener. After which he took a small keyhole saw and leisurely cut out the underlying boards. For this task he was allowed two hours.

"The next step was to stop the train at a precisely predetermined point."

"A snap," Barnett commented.

"Indeed it was," Moriarty agreed, "if I correctly interpret that barbaric expression. Especially a 'snap' if you consider that the engine driver was almost certainly not going to overrun a danger signal on the semaphore repeater. And if you consider that the railways use a 'positive' system of signaling, which assures that the normal condition of the signal arm will be 'danger.' This means that if any natural misfortune occurs to the semaphore apparatus, it assumes the 'danger' position rather than the 'safety' or 'caution' positions."

"A natural misfortune?"

"Correct. In this case, a severely corroded cable accidentally snapped. The maintenance division must be sternly spoken to. A 'snap,' as you say. There are substances known to chemists which can incredibly speed up the corrosion of any metal object."

"And the signal swung to 'danger'?"

"Just so. And the engine driver of Lord East's caravan stopped the train. What else was he to do?"

"And then?"

"A hatch opened between the metals—what you would call the

rails—in the track bed. Carefully disguised as two wooden sleepers and the space between, the hatch covered a specially constructed chamber buried in the embankment. The hatch was so placed as to be directly beneath the hole in the floor of the wagon when the train halted at the signal."

"That simple?" Barnett marveled. "And the treasure was just handed out?"

"No, no, the stop would not be nearly long enough for that," Moriarty said. "I estimated three minutes. As it happened, they took seven, but even that would not have been nearly long enough for the transfer of that bulk of boodle. No, Mr. Barnett, what happened at this carefully prearranged pause was that certain materials were handed up into the wagon. And then a second man joined the one who was already there.

"This second man was an expert in the ancient craft of reproducing seals. And he brought with him the needed equipment—to wit, a spoon, a candle, and a loaf of bread."

Barnett sat back down on the couch. Moriarty had obviously succeeded in his attempt to distract his assistant from his troubles, at least for the moment. "A loaf of bread?" Barnett asked.

"The best way to duplicate a wax seal in anything like a reasonable length of time," Moriarty said, "is to take an impression of it with moist bread which you have kneaded between your palms. Done by an expert, it's as effective as any other method. What the expert does in this case is to use a hot wire to separate the seal from the treasure chest, first making a bread impression of it in case it breaks while being removed."

"Yes, but why bother?" Barnett asked. "Why not just break open the chests?"

"It adds an extra element of confusion," Moriarty said. "It is my experience that a crime should be either so simple that there is no place to look for a solution, or so confusing that there are too many places to look. In this case, I chose the latter."

"How do you mean, Professor?"

Moriarty thought for a second. "In a simple crime," he explained, "you know all the elements, but they take you nowhere. A man is hit on the head, and his purse is taken. When he comes to, there is nobody around. You know everything that happened, but unless he recognized his assailant, it is virtually hopeless to try to recover the purse.

"In a complex crime, there are so many factors to trace down that much time is lost before you find out which are pertinent. The seals are broken on the chests, and they are found to be empty. But you don't know when the treasure was removed. Before the chests were loaded on the train? After the train left Plymouth? After it arrived at Hampton Court? Each of these must be investigated. It confuses things, you see."

"What did happen?" Barnett asked.

"After the train started up again, my agents opened the treasure chests, removed all the baubles, and closed and very carefully resealed the chests. Then, immediately after the train passed through Hampermire Station, they spread newspaper on the floor, and carefully immersed each article in a basin containing an oily solution, with just a hint of creosote, which dyed the item a dingy brown. Then they tossed it through the hole. The jewelry was spread over six miles of track, and quite invisible unless you were looking for it. Even then it would be easy to miss."

"You were at Hampermire," Barnett said.

"True. And Toby was waiting for me."

"Toby?"

"A hound I borrowed from a friend. Quite a nose, Toby has. I believe he could follow the scent of creosote through a windstorm in a peppermill."

"Ah!" Barnett said.

"The rest is obvious," Moriarty said. "The two in the wagon cleaned up, leaving no trace of themselves, and tossed the detritus onto the track, where other agents immediately removed it. Then they themselves went into a carefully prepared hole when the train was forced to stop for a herd of cows which had unaccountably broken through their fence and wandered onto the track. They pulled a specially prepared metal patch over the hole in the floor and, by igniting a thin strip of magnesium which came out the bottom, caused it to solder itself into place."

Barnett thought this over for a while. "Very neat," he said. "They'll never catch on to it. It will be one of the mysteries of the century."

"I doubt that," Moriarty said. "The authorities will, sooner or later, discover how it was done. Especially if, as I suspect, they call in Sherlock Holmes. But by the time they figure it out, the back-trail will be so cold that all their leads will peter out into dead ends. Your little bit of misdirection, I believe, will elude even Mr. Holmes."

"I sincerely hope so," Barnett said. "I have developed a distinct aversion to prison food." He got up and, taking his shoes in his hand, hobbled out of the study and started up the stairs.

TWENTY-TWO

TETE-A-TETE

> *"He knows that I know, and I'm sure he knows that*
> *I know he knows. But for all of that, can I assume*
> *that he knows I know he knows I know he knows?"*
> *"I don't follow that," the baroness replied. "And*
> *I wish you'd stop; you're giving me quite a headache!"*
> —D'ARCY ST. MICHEL

At ten o'clock the next morning, Sherlock Holmes was at the front door of 64 Russell Square, yanking on the bellpull. "Tell your master I wish to see him," he announced when the butler opened the door.

"Yes, sir," Mr. Maws replied, bowing and stepping aside in a parody of butlerian stiffness. "Alone today, are you, sir? Please follow me into the study. The professor is expecting you. I shall inform him that you're here, and he will be down directly."

"Expecting me, is he?" Holmes asked, stalking into the study and glaring around at the furnishings.

"Yes, sir," Mr. Maws said. "So he told me, sir."

Ten minutes later, when Moriarty came downstairs and entered the study, he found Holmes crouching in front of the desk, unabashedly going through the third drawer down. "Looking for something?" Moriarty demanded, reaching around his desk and slamming the drawer.

Holmes jerked his hand aside. "Always, Professor," he said. "And someday I'll find it." He retreated to the black leather armchair on the other side of the desk. "I have this insatiable curiosity about you, Professor Moriarty. Every little thing you do is of interest to me. Every little scrap of paper in this room helps, in some small way, round out my picture of you and your activities."

"Would you care to go through the bottom drawer?" Moriarty asked. "I assume you've already been through the upper two."

"Very kind of you," Holmes said. "Some other time, perhaps."

Moriarty settled into the chair behind his desk and regarded Holmes unblinkingly. "You have lost all shame, Holmes," he said. "It was but a few weeks ago that you and a squad of cloddish policemen went through this house from attic to sub-basement, examining the contents of every drawer, scratching furniture, bending lampshades, ripping curtains, breaking porcelain, and no doubt stealing the silver. After that farce it will be a long time before you get any judge to issue you another warrant against any of my property. And yet here you are again, going through my desk."

"Your butler had me wait in here," Holmes said mildly. "I was merely amusing myself while I waited."

"I admit I should have locked the drawers and cabinets before you arrived," Moriarty said. "But I keep forgetting, Holmes, that you are capable of such appalling manners."

Holmes chuckled. "Perhaps you are right," he admitted. "But only in my dealings with you, Moriarty. I assure you that when it comes to the rest of humanity, I am considered urbane and civil, and my manners are irreproachable. There is something about our relationship that brings out my worst qualities. I think it is, perhaps, the fact that every time I see you sitting there in your sack coat and your striped trousers and your impeccably knotted cravat, with a painting worth ten thousand pounds hanging on your wall and library filled with rare books and a winecellar filled with rare vintages, I cannot help reflecting that were there any justice in this world, you would be wearing gray cloth and occupying your time by walking the treadmill at Dartmoor."

"Justice, Holmes? Were there any justice, you would be forced by the state, whose rules you admire so greatly, to spend your time in some profession more fitting to your talents, such as giving diverting lectures in music halls, and identifying the occupations of ten random ticket holders. Instead you spend your days following me about and annoying me at every opportunity."

"Your butler said you expected me," Holmes said.

"And so I did," Moriarty replied.

"Why? I had no appointment with you."

"There was a major crime yesterday, was there not?" Moriarty inquired. "An 'impossible' crime, one of the newspapers called it. Surely it was not a wide leap of logic to assume that you would be called in. And even more surely, you would immediately scurry around to see me. Hoping, no doubt, to find a great pile of stolen artifacts on the rug."

"Indeed," Holmes agreed complacently. "Almost startled not to. You don't object, I suppose, if I look *under* the rug?"

Moriarty sighed. "Understand, Holmes, that I am somewhat honored that you suspect me of committing every crime in London that you can't solve. However, it does get to be wearing after a time."

"Not the crimes I can't solve, Professor," Holmes said, smiling tightly. "In several instances I have solved them to my satisfaction, I have just been unable to provide enough proof to bring the case before a jury. That is where you have shown yourself so infernally clever, my dear Professor Moriarty. *I* know you for the rogue you are, but I can't prove it. However, you and I know that I shall not stop trying; and one of these times, I shall succeed. And then you will exchange your black sack coat for prison gray. But enough of this cheery conversation; I wish to speak to you of trains and treasures."

"Curiously enough, Holmes, I also wish to speak to you, although on another subject. Shall we discuss the fate of the Lord East Collection first, and then get on to more consequential matters?"

There was a knock at the door. "That would be Mr. Barnett," Moriarty said. "I have asked him to sit in on our little *tête-à-tête*, if you don't mind?" Then, without waiting for Holmes's response, he called for Barnett to come in.

"Good morning, Professor," Barnett said, coming through the door with a cup of coffee in his hand. He looked tested. "Good morning, Mr. Holmes." He sat down on the leather couch and sipped his coffee.

"It has all the markings of a Moriarty crime," Holmes said, ignoring Barnett. "I can sense your hand in this undertaking just as an art connoisseur can recognize a work of Goya or of Vernet, whether or not the canvas is signed. And then when I learned that you were actually present at the loading of the goods wagons, how could I doubt further? Moriarty was present; a fortune was stolen: *Quid hoc sibi vult?*"

"I was there," Moriarty said. "I make no apologies for my presence. It was mere vulgar curiosity. And as a matter of fact, it was not gratified. We did not get to see the treasure, as I'm sure you know."

"That's true," Barnett commented. "I mentioned it at the time.

Loudly. How were we to know it was even in those boxes? Why wouldn't Lord East open them? What was he hiding? It is my duty as a journalist to ask these questions."

Holmes turned and favored Barnett with a scowl, then he returned his gaze to Moriarty. "I have indications of the method already," he said. "I believe the floor of the goods wagon has been tampered with. I have discovered that the train stopped twice on the way to London—both times briefly, both times accidentally. It is, perhaps, a flaw in my nature that I distrust such accidents."

"So?" Moriarty demanded. "Would you like to drag me off to prison now, or wait until you get some sort of proof that I was actually involved?"

"Don't ask me what I'd like to do, Professor," Holmes said, his long fingers tapping restlessly on the arm of his chair. "You know very well what I'd like to do."

"Pshaw!" Moriarty said. "Let us turn from the fanciful to the pertinent, Mr. Holmes." He reached down and, opening the bottom drawer of his desk, pulled out a thick handful of file folders. "I would like to discuss with you the seven murders which have taken place since the twenty-second of February."

Holmes stood up and pointed at the folders. "Those," he said, with a slight quaver in his voice, "are the official files!"

"Not quite," Moriarty said. "They are merely accurate transcripts of the official files. Certified duplicates of all the material contained in the files."

"Where did you obtain them?" Holmes demanded.

"From Giles Lestrade," Moriarty said. "There's no secret about it. I am, after all, working on the case."

"You're what?"

"I have offered my services to Scotland Yard, and have been accepted. Without a fee, of course. I have a private client, but there is no conflict of interest since my client's only concern is to have the murderer apprehended."

Holmes stared at Moriarty with fascination. "I don't believe it," he murmured.

"Why not?" Moriarty asked. "I am, after all, a consultant."

"Let us not discuss what you are, for the moment," Holmes said. "What I'm trying to figure out is what you'll be getting out of this."

"Paid," Moriarty said. "I will be collecting a fee from my private client."

"There is that, of course," Holmes said. "Frankly, Professor, I had just about concluded that you were not involved in the killings when I heard about the robbery. Then I was sure. Since you are so clearly involved in the robbery, you wouldn't really have had time to take part in the slaughter of the upper class."

Moriarty tapped the pile of folders in front of him. "I've been reading these reports, Holmes," he said. "And I would like to see how your conclusions compare with mine."

Holmes leaned back in his chair and laced his fingers together. He stared thoughtfully at Moriarty over his cupped hands for a minute. "Go ahead," he said.

"We'll start with basics," Moriarty said. "One murderer."

"Agreed."

"Male."

"Agreed."

"Early forties."

"Most likely."

"Average to slightly above in height."

"That's all in my report!" Holmes said. "All you're doing is reading my own report back to me."

"What report?" Moriarty asked. "There is no such report in these files."

"Ah!" Holmes said. "I gave that report directly to Lord Arundale. I suppose he never bothered returning it to the Scotland Yard files."

"I have noticed this regrettable tendency myself," Moriarty said. "It would seem that the aristocracy has little regard for record keeping. Except tables of genealogy, of course. Tell me, what other observations about the murderer have you detailed on this absent report?"

Barnett, watching this exchange with interest, could see how speaking civilly to Moriarty, how volunteering information to this friend and mentor that he had turned into an enemy, caused the muscles in Holmes's jaw to tighten, forming his lips into an involuntary grimace. But Holmes, with an effort of will, conquered his feelings. "I believe he is a foreigner," the detective said. "Probably Eastern European."

"A logical interpretation," Moriarty agreed. "But if so, he almost certainly speaks English like a native."

"I truly dislike interrupting, and I wouldn't doubt either of you for the world, but from where are you two getting these notions?" Barnett asked. "I've been following these killings, as you know, and you lost me a while back, right after you decided it was a man. For me, even that would still be conjecture."

"Oh come now, Mr. Barnett," Holmes said, swiveling around to look at him. "These crimes all take place late at night, for one thing. A woman skulking around at such an hour would certainly be noted."

"A woman in man's clothing?" Barnett suggested, just to keep up his side of the argument.

"Then there is the matter of simple physical strength," Moriarty said, tapping his fingers on the desk. "Each of the victims would seem to have been easily overpowered by his assailant."

"Drugs," Barnett suggested.

"There is no sign that any of them ate or drank anything prior to their demise," Holmes said. "With several of them, it is certain that they didn't."

"All right," Barnett said, giving up on that point, "but what about the rest of it?"

"We presume a single murderer because the killings are idiosyncratic, each like the others down to fine detail," Moriarty said. "More than one person would surely have more than one opinion as to how to properly knife a man, at least in some small detail. And then, you note how easily our killer assumes a cloak of invisibility? Hard as it is for one man to vanish as easily as our killer has, it is at least twice as hard for two."

"The age is more of a probability," Holmes said. "Not an old man, because of the required physical strength in the murders and physical dexterity in the disappearances—however they are contrived. And yet not a young man because of the care taken in the crime, and the economy of savagery in what are clearly murders of passion."

"Passion?"

"Probably revenge," Moriarty said. "Which is why we put it to a foreigner."

"Englishmen, I take it, are incapable of acts of revenge?" Barnett inquired.

"Not at all," Moriarty said. "But they would usually use their fists, or some handy weapon, and do it immediately and in public. Englishmen do not believe, as do the Italians, that revenge is a dish best eaten cold."

"And your hot-blooded Latin races would probably not commit such a surgical murder as each of these has been," Holmes said.

"This, of course, is not conclusive, it merely indicates a direction for investigation."

"I'm not convinced," Barnett said.

"Luckily, that is not essential," Moriarty said.

"What about Miss Perrine's kidnapping?" Barnett asked. "How do you fit that in?"

Holmes pursed his lips. "That is a problem," he said. "It certainly doesn't coincide with the murderer's pattern, and yet it would be stretching the bounds of credulity to suggest that it could be unrelated." He chuckled. "Lestrade thinks it was the murderer returning to the scene of his crime. It makes one believe in competitive examinations for the rank of detective inspector."

"Have you any information that is not on these reports, Holmes?" Moriarty asked.

"On the killings or the disappearance?"

"Either," Moriarty said. "We are interested in both."

"Only the possibly relevant fact that, for the past few days, someone has had me followed about by a gang of street ruffians. However, I strongly suspect that the someone is you."

Moriarty nodded. "I admit it," he said.

"An unpardonable liberty," Holmes stated.

Moriarty chuckled. "Not at all," he replied. "Indeed, it is strange to hear you say that, considering that you have a substantial portion of the plainclothes police force following me about on every occasion when they are not otherwise occupied. Turnabout, Holmes."

Holmes smiled grimly. "Revenge, Professor?"

"On the contrary, Holmes. It occurred to me that whoever removed Miss Perrine from the public eye might not be satisfied with this one triumph, but might go after bigger game. If so, I wanted to have my agents at hand when he did. Unfortunately, the idea seems not to have occurred to him. I take it no murderous attacks have been made on your person in the past few days that I do not know of?"

"You think someone might be after me?" Holmes asked, clearly astounded at the notion.

"I think it possible," Moriarty said. "I don't think it probable, but I decided it would be worthwhile to keep an eye on you."

"Well!" Holmes said. "You suspect that Miss Perrine might have been kidnapped because of something she knew? But she knew nothing that wasn't published the next day in ten morning newspapers."

"Perhaps the kidnapper was not aware of that," Moriarty said. "Or perhaps she discovered something of which we are unaware."

"Really, Moriarty," Holmes said. "I profess, I dislike this role reversal, whatever your excuse. Let us keep things in their proper perspective: you are the criminal and I am the detective."

"One of the first things you must realize about categories, Holmes," Moriarty said, lecturing the detective in the dry, didactic tone he was so fond of, "is that they are not immutable."

"Come now, Professor," Holmes said. "As a scientist, you surely cannot maintain that the truth is not a fixed quantity."

"No, sir, but I can and do maintain that our perception of the truth is ever changing. What was regarded as 'truth' in science but a generation ago is laughable now. And human affairs, Mr. Holmes, change even more rapidly. Also human beings are far more complex than you give them credit for. It is not enough to read the calluses on a man's fingers and know that he is a cork-cutter. To understand him, you must also be able to read his soul: to know his fears, his needs, his ambitions, his desires, and his secret shames."

"All of which you, undoubtedly, perceive at an instant, eh, Professor?" Holmes said smugly.

"I do not claim to be a detective, Holmes. The hearts of stars are, to me, far more transparent than the hearts of men."

"Are you going to persist in having me followed?" Holmes demanded.

"Not if it bothers you," Moriarty said. "I wouldn't dream of it. Are you going to persist in having me followed, Holmes?"

"Of course," Holmes said. He stood up. "If you can name this mad killer, or locate Miss Perrine, I shall be the first to applaud. But I still intend to establish your complicity in the treasure-train robbery."

"You'll understand if I don't wish you luck," Moriarty said dryly.

"Is there any other action which you have taken in regard to these killings that you have failed to mention?" Holmes asked.

"One obvious measure," Moriarty said, "in an effort to precipitate some sort of reaction." He handed a folded copy of the *Morning Telegraph* to Holmes. "I placed a small boxed advertisement in several dailies. Here is its first appearance."

Barnett stood up and read over Holmes's shoulder.

**LOST—several small medallions. Identical designs.
Apply 64 Russell Square. REWARD.**

"Interesting idea," Holmes said. "If it is, indeed, a medallion that the murderer has been taking from his victims."

"That's the most likely word to describe whatever the objects are," Moriarty said.

"You don't think the killer is going to answer your advertisement?" Barnett asked. "I mean, he's going to a lot of trouble to collect these things, whatever they are. He's not likely to band them over to you."

"That's so," Moriarty agreed. "But strange things happen in this world, especially if one encourages them. He may have an avaricious landlady who wonders why he is collecting so many identical artifacts. Or he may just leave them somewhere after using them for whatever he does use them for. Or a sneak thief may by some great chance filch them from his bureau drawer, where he has them secreted. One can never tell, can one, Holmes?"

Holmes put down the newspaper. "I must go," he said. He reached out for the small bronze statuette of Uma that stood on a corner of Moriarty's desk. "I shall borrow this for a while if you don't mind, Professor."

"You'll *what?*" Moriarty demanded, leaping to his feet. "Now look here, Holmes—"

"I hold in my hand," Holmes said, raising the object to eye level, "a small bronze statuette inlaid with precious and semiprecious stones, obviously of Indian origin. It was not here the last time I visited. Indeed, I can safely say that it was nowhere in the house. And now, shortly after a vast Indian treasure has been stolen, I find it here on your desk. Surely, knowing of my suspicions, you want me to take this statuette away with me and compare it against all the items on Lord East's list, don't you, Professor? You want to show me up, prove that my suspicions were for naught, have the last laugh—don't you, Professor James Moriarty?"

Moriarty glared at his thin, intense antagonist. "I am tempted to say no," he said. "The impulse to annoy you as strongly as you annoy me is almost irresistible. You know you have no right to remove that bronze without my permission unless you get a warrant, showing probable cause. Which would be stretching the truth, something you would not consider in other circumstances. I am strongly tempted to make you step outside and whistle up a policeman, and force the poor fellow to scurry off in search of some complaint magistrate who is unaware of your vendetta against me and might possibly issue such a warrant. But then I'd have to put up with your sitting here glaring at me for half the day, clutching the bronze to your breast, wondering whether the warrant had been issued or not.

"And so I won't. I haven't the time for such fancies. Take the thing, Holmes. Give me a receipt for it. And when you're forced to return it, I shall frame the receipt and hang it next to the ten-thousand-pound Vernet you object to so much."

Holmes brought out his small notebook and scribbled a receipt on a page, which he ripped out and handed to Moriarty. "I shall be back within two days, Professor," he said. "Either to return the bronze, or to take you away. Which do you suppose it will be?"

"I expect an apology," Moriarty told Holmes, "when you return the bronze."

"I expect a confession," Holmes replied, "when I take you to prison. Do you suppose either of us will be satisfied with what we actually get? But enough! Much as I am enjoying our little chat, I really must be off."

"If you must—" Moriarty said.

Holmes turned to Barnett. "Dealing with Professor Moriarty creates in me an attitude that is destructive of my manners and my sentiments," he said. "I want you to know that I am aware of your attachment to Miss Perrine, and I fully sympathize with the sense of loss that you must be feeling now."

Barnett nodded his thanks. "It is more a sense of futility," he replied. "There is little I can do that is useful. I can keep busy, which keeps my mind off the problem but brings me no closer to finding Miss Perrine."

"I and my temporary associates of Scotland Yard are doing everything we can to locate and rescue the girl. I pray we will be successful," Holmes nodded to Moriarty. "Don't bother showing me out."

With a final glance around the room, Holmes stepped purposefully to the front door and threw it open. "*Au revoir*, Professor," he called, striding through the door and slamming it behind him.

"A unique man," Barnett commented.

"True," Moriarty agreed. "For which I am profoundly grateful. More than one Sherlock Holmes on this planet at the same time is an idea that I do not wish to contemplate."

"Tell me, Professor," Barnett said, "*is* that statuette from the robbery?"

"Yes," Moriarty said.

"Can Holmes prove it?" asked Barnett.

"That remains to be seen," Morjarty replied.

A loud clattering sound came from the street outside the house, followed almost immediately by a great crash. Moriarty and Barnett jumped to their feet. Before the sound of the crash had died away, the voices of several people yelling and the shrill sound of a woman screaming joined the cacophony.

Barnett rushed to the front door and ran outside, with Moriarty right behind him. There on the pavement in front of the house a large poultry cart had overturned; its wheels were still spinning in the air. The horse had apparently broken free, and was racing off in a maddened frenzy down the road. Right behind it raced a small covered chaise, its driver whipping its horse to even greater effort.

" 'Megawd!" an elderly woman screamed, pulling her shawl about her as bystanders started to gather around the scene. "I ain't never seen nothing like it. " 'E done it on purpose, 'e did. Rode right up on the pavement, right at the poor man. 'E never 'ad a chance! It were murder!"

"Calm down, woman!" Moriarty ordered. "Who murdered whom?"

"The Johnny what were atop of the cart," the old lady sobbed. "The Johnny what leaped into that other gig and ran off after 'e'd started the cart toward the pavement. 'E deliberately aimed the cart right for that poor gentleman there!" She pointed. On the ground, almost buried under crates of terrified geese, lay the unconscious body of Sherlock Holmes.

THE POSSIBLE

*Truth, like a torch, the more it's
shook it shines.*
— SIR WILLIAM HAMILTON

With the assistance of the curator of the Egyptian Collection of the British Museum and a retired sergeant of marines, both of whom were passing at the moment of the accident, Moriarty and Barnett carried Sherlock Holmes up to the front bedroom and placed him gently on the bed. Holmes's face was bloody, but his breathing was regular and even. Moriarty checked his pulse and pulled an eyelid back to examine the eye.

"How is he?" Barnett asked.

"Alive," Moriarty replied. "Unconscious—perhaps suffering from concussion. No broken bones that I can tell. My expertise in medical matters goes no further." He pulled out his handkerchief and dabbed tentatively at Holmes's bloody face. "Thank you gentlemen for your assistance," he said to the sergeant and the curator. "You'd best leave your names, as the police may wish to question you about the incident."

The two men both protested that they had not actually observed what happened, but allowed Barnett to write down their names before bustling off downstairs.

Mrs. H appeared in the bedroom doorway with a basin of warm water and a sponge, and shooed Moriarty and Barnett aside. "I'll take care of him," she said. "I have sent Mr. Maws off to Cavendish Square to fetch Dr. Breckstone."

"I don't know what I'd do without you, Mrs. H," Moriarty said.

She sniffed. "I don't either, professor, and that's the truth!"

"A wonderful woman," Moriarty told Barnett as they headed downstairs to the study. "She is both secure and humble in her certain knowledge of her proper place, which is most assuredly on God's right hand." He took the bronze statuette, which he had retrieved from where it had fallen alongside of Holmes, and replaced it on the corner of his desk. "Very curious," he said. "Very curious, indeed."

"Mrs. H?" Barnett asked.

"No, no; the, ah, incident."

"It certainly is," Barnett agreed. "Who could have done a thing like that? I don't imagine that there is any doubt that it was deliberate?"

"I wouldn't think so," Moriarty said dryly. "One doesn't usually prepare a getaway from an accident. The question is, why was Holmes assaulted, and why at this peculiar place and time?"

"I'm sure the man has many enemies," Barnett said.

"I am amazed that he has any friends," Moriarty commented. "There is always his faithful hound, Dr. Watson, of course; but you'll notice that Holmes has never married."

"Neither have you, Professor," Barnett said.

Moriarty glared at Barnett for a minute, then he nodded. "Touché!" he said. "But, nonetheless—" He broke off and stared, musingly, at the windows for a minute.

"What is it?" Barnett asked.

"It occurs to me that we have probably just had the first response to our advertisement," Moriarty said slowly.

"We have?"

"Indeed. It came in the form of an attack on Sherlock Holmes."

"You think that was the killer out there?"

"No," Moriarty said. "That's what had me puzzled at first. It's not his method. Curiously enough, I believe we have taken a tree with more than one apple. Someone else was frightened by the advertisement, frightened enough to feel the need for direct and drastic measures. He must have come along to see if the advertisement meant what he feared it meant. Perhaps he meant to come inside, but that proved unnecessary. He found out what he needed to know from the outside, and he was prepared to take instant action."

"But why against Holmes?" Barnett asked.

"That was his clue," Moriarty said. "The presence of Holmes must have signified something to him—clearly something that it does not signify to us. He recognized the detective as a part of the menace."

"Farfetched," Barnett said. Moriarty merely smiled.

The front door slammed, and Mummer Tolliver came limping into the room. " 'E got away," he announced.

"Too bad," Moriarty said. "Who?"

"The bloke what I was following. The bloke what drove that cart against poor Mr. Holmes."

"You were following him?" Barnett asked, surprised.

"Well, I were out there to follow Mr. Holmes. But when that cart 'it 'im, I didn't think as 'ow 'e were going anywhere for a while. And I thought the professor might be interested in the bloke what did it. So I 'opped aboard the trunk rack on the rear of the chaise what 'e jumped into. I tell you, Mr. Barnett, that were a ride!"

"I'll bet it was, Mummer," Barnett said, picturing the little man clinging to the trunk rack, inches off the roadway. As the chaise careened down the road behind a galloping horse. The experience had deprived the usually nonchalant Tolliver of his painfully acquired aitches.

"How did you lose him?" Moriarty asked.

"I fell off," the Mummer said belligerently. "But it weren't my fault. 'E went around a corner like no carriage has any right going around a corner, and then bumped against the curb in the process. But it ain't no big deal, on account of I got 'is name."

"You have his name?" Moriarty patted the little man on the back. "Very good, Mummer. Indeed, excellent work. I am proud of you. What is it?"

"I 'eard 'is driver call 'im 'Deever,' " Tolliver said.

"Deever?" Barnett repeated doubtfully.

"D'Hiver," Moriarty said. "The Count d'Hiver. How very odd. You're sure, Tolliver? You heard him say d'Hiver?"

"Right as a puffin. Deever it were."

"Not *Count* d'Hiver?"

"No."

"Curious. But it must be he; coincidence can only stretch so far. That is very valuable information, Tolliver, you have done well. Now I have another job for you. Notify the Amateur Mendicants that I wish the Count d'Hiver to be followed from this moment on, wherever he goes; and I want his residence and any other place he frequents to be put under constant surveillance. Tell Colonel Moran that he is in command, and that I will hold him responsible for any slipups." Moriarty scribbled on a slip of paper. "Here is the count's address. Tell Moran that those who follow the count are not to be seen. I want him to send me reports every three hours, or more often if the situation warrants."

"I got it, Professor," Tolliver said. "I'm on my way. I won't even stop upstairs to change my suit, which 'as suffered somewhat in the past 'alf 'our—I'll be off!"

Moriarty shook the little man's hand, and Tolliver limped rapidly from the room.

"The Count d'Hiver?" Barnett asked: "The man who was at the Hope mansion the night Cecily disappeared?"

"That is my assumption," Moriarty told him.

Barnett stood up. "Do you suppose—"

"I try never to suppose," Moriarty said. "We shall find out."

"I must help," Barnett said. "What can I do?"

"As it happens," Moriarty told him, "I have another task for you. One more particularly suited to your talents and abilities."

"Please, Professor, don't try to fob off some meaningless job on me just to keep me busy," Barnett said.

"I wouldn't think of it," Moriarty said.

And so Barnett found himself in a hansom cab, commencing an afternoon of investigation. His objective: the lower end of the Strand, with its appendage streets and lanes, and the theatrical agents and managers whose offices were clustered about the area.

"What, exactly, am I supposed to be looking for?" he had asked Moriarty before the professor hustled him toward the door.

"You are seeking truth," Moriarty explained. "You are trying to identify a murderer."

"In a theatrical agent's office?"

"There are very few possibilities," Moriarty said. "Very few facades beneath which our killer could be lurking. I have had most of them investigated already: locksmiths, burglars—"

"You said some time ago that it wasn't a burglar," Barnett interrupted.

"I said some time ago that it was not someone intent on burglary," Moriarty replied. "We are not now looking for motive, but training and ability. There are few people as knowledgeable and competent in the field of surreptitious entry as our killer has shown himself to be. This is an acquired skill, not an innate ability. Most of those who are known to have acquired such a skill have already been investigated, either by my own men or by Holmes's official minions, without turning up a possibility."

"And so?" Barnett asked.

"When you have eliminated the impossible," Moriarty told him, "it is time to take a hard look about and see what's left."

The first offices Barnett visited were those of Simes & McNaughten, Theatrical Agents, Specialty Acts, Bookings for London and the Provinces. He spoke to Mr. Simes, a man who looked as though he could have been the model for the puppet Punch.

"Magicians, you say?" Simes asked. He went to a cabinet and pulled open a dusty lower drawer. "I'd say we've handled a fair number over the years. None recently. They used to be very popular as a music-hall turn. Drew top money, top billing. Kind of died out now, though. Some really big names there were, back in the sixties and seventies. Manders, the Modern Merlin, was a top draw for, maybe, twenty years. Retired to Sussex. Still around, I believe. Keeps bees."

"Have you handled any in the past few years?" Barnett asked.

"I specialize in animal acts now," Simes said, waving his arm to indicate the posters on the surrounding walls. "Seals, dogs, bears, doves. No magicians. They're too temperamental. Most of them these days are foreigners. Italians and such."

"Thanks for your time," Barnett said.

He visited three more theatrical agencies with similar results. But then he arrived at the offices of Ditmar Forbis, Theatrical Representative—All Major Cities.

Ditmar Forbis was a tall, thin man with deeply set, searching eyes, who was dressed immaculately and tastefully in a hand-tailored black sack suit. Barnett's impression was that the man was miscast as a theatrical agent. He was much too somber and far too elegant. Barnett decided that by appearance and inclination, Forbis should be an undertaker to royalty. "You say this is for a newspaper article, Mr. Barnett?" Forbis asked.

"That's correct," Barnett told him. "Probably turn into a series of pieces on music halls and vaudeville."

"Vaudeville, Mr. Barnett, is an American phenomenon."

"I write for an American news agency," Barnett told him.

"I see," Forbis said. "Magicians, you say. As it happens, I handle most of the magical gentlemen working London today."

"Well," Barnett said, relieved that he had finally come to the right place, "is that so?"

"Yes, it is. They are mostly foreign gentlemen, you know. Largely Italians or Frenchmen. Even when they're not Italians or Frenchmen, they tend to take French or Italian names. Signor Gespardo, the Court Card King, for example; he is really a Swede."

"The Court Card King?"

"Yes. He does tricks with playing cards, but he only uses the king, queen, or jack—the court cards."

"Strange," Barnett commented.

"They are that—all of them." Forbis reached for a wooden box on his desk. "I've got cards on all the magicians who are currently active. Must be twenty or thirty of them. I don't imagine you want to see them all. How shall we sort them for you?"

"I'd like to concentrate on escape artists," Barnett said, taking out his notebook and flipping it open to a blank page. "People who are expert at picking locks and the like."

"That's not what they do, you know," Forbis said. "Or, at least, that's not what they admit they do. It's supposed to be some sort of miraculous power they have; nothing so mundane as a lockpick."

"What sort of things do they do?" Barnett asked. "Can you give me an example?"

Forbis shrugged. "Anything you can think of. And if you think of something they haven't done, why one of them will try it." He groped behind him and came up with a handful of handbills. "I'll show you a few examples of the sort of stuff they advertise. Here— here's one." He waved it across the desk.

The four-color illustration on the handbill portrayed a man in evening dress with his arms stretched out in front of him, hands clasped. He was shackled by every variety of handcuff and chain imaginable, but there was a confident glare in his clear blue eyes. Across the top of the print was the semicircular legend KRIS KOLONI THE HANDKUFF KING.

"He does challenge escapes," Forbes said. "You name it and he'll get out of it. Last year he escaped from a patented strait-waistcoat used at the Beaverstream Lunacy Asylum."

"That's the sort of chap I'm interested in," Barnett said enthusiastically, writing the name on the top line of his notebook. "Can I get in touch with him?"

"I'm afraid he is in Paris at the moment. In jail, as it happens."

"Jail?" Barnett was now definitely interested. "For how long and for what crime, do you know?"

"For the past four or five months, I believe. Refuses to pay alimony to his ex-wife."

"Ah," Barnett said, drawing a line through the name. "I assume you're reasonably sure of your facts—that is, that the fellow is still in jail?"

"I received a letter from him just last week," Forbis said. "Pleading for money, as it happens. Performers are just like children—totally incapable of handling their own affairs, most of them. Here's another chap." Forbis pulled a handbill free of the pile. "Moritz the Wonderful Wizard, he calls himself. His specialty is escaping from locked steamer trunks. Actually a very boring act. For twenty minutes the audience has nothing to look at save this trunk in the center of the stage. Then all at once Moritz pops out, waving his arms about as though he's done something clever. You understand that if you were a theater manager from the Midlands, that isn't how I would describe the turn. But just between us, that's the effect."

"Doesn't sound precisely like what I had in mind," Barnett said.

"Don't blame you," Forbis said. "Let's see, what else have I?" He riffled through the card box. "There's Professor Chardino—the Invisible Man. That's the way he bills himself. Works with his daughter; has a very interesting stage presentation. It's a sort of challenge to the audience. Gets them involved. He escapes from things people bring with them to the theater. Trunks, boxes, canvas bags, leg irons, handcuffs, animal cages, anything you can think of. It may sound superficially like Moritz the Wonderful's act, but I can assure you that the effect is entirely different. The man has a wonderful grasp of stage presence and stage personality. He makes the audience *care* what happens to him."

"How so?" Barnett asked.

Forbis frowned in concentration, his right hand grasping the air for the right word. "Let me describe it," he said. "Chardino is locked into the restraint—whatever it happens to be—usually by a committee of spectators. Through his conversation with the committee and the audience he has established the difficulty of what he is about to attempt and won the sympathy of his audience. Then his daughter covers him, and whatever he may be locked into, with a large drop cloth. There is now a period of waiting. The daughter, after standing expectantly for a minute, commences to pace nervously, obviously worried. There is a muted conversation about 'air supply' or something else possibly relevant. The audience are on the edge of their seats. Then it happens! Sometimes he appears from under the cloth; sometimes she whisks the cloth aside and he has disappeared completely. Sometimes she raises the cloth up to cover herself also, and then it drops and Chardino has taken his daughter's place, and it is she now locked inside the restraint. Once a society of undertakers in some provincial town brought along a coffin, and they took him to a local plot of land and buried him in it. After a while, when nothing happened, they dug the coffin up and opened it to find him gone. He beat them back to the theater."

"Why does he call himself the Invisible Man?" Barnett asked.

"Chardino specializes in getting in and out of impossible places—often without being seen."

Barnett made another entry in his notebook. "What sort of places?"

"Well, let me see." Forbis referred to his card. "He was locked in the tower room of Waldbeck Castle and escaped while two companies of guardsmen were surrounding the building. They saw nothing. Another time he was locked in the vault of Bombeck Fréres, in Paris, and was found to be gone the next morning when the time lock permitted the manager to open the door. The man is a great showman."

Barnett nodded slowly. "I would very much like to meet Professor Chardino," he said. "He sounds like just the sort of person I have been looking for."

"Fascinating to talk to," Forbis agreed. He flipped over a few more cards. "Then there's the Amazing Doctor Prist—the World's Leading Escapist. It sort of rhymes, you see."

"He escapes from places also?"

"Oh, yes. Not as good as Chardino perhaps, but very showy, with a great many flourishes. He's been trying to arrange an escape from the Tower of London for the past five years, but the authorities won't let him. Naturally he plays that for all it's worth. By now he's gotten almost as much publicity out of the fact that the authorities refuse to allow the escape as he would have from successfully accomplishing it."

Barnett wrote the name Prist down in his notebook. "Any others?" he asked.

"Well, if it's escapes you're particularly interested in, there's Walla and Bisby," Forbis said, pulling out another card. "You can see them at the Orion right now, as it happens. Their specialty is walking through a brick wall, which is constructed right on stage in full view of the audience."

Barnett sighed. "I can see that I'll need more detail about all of these people, if I'm to do my job right," he said. "I hate to impose on you like this. Have you some free time? Perhaps we could discuss this over a drink at the Croyden?"

Forbis grabbed for his hat. "Delighted," he said.

TWENTY-FOUR

INTERLUDE: THE EVENING

> *A Londoner can always be summed up*
> *by his clubs.*
> —ARTHUR WILLIAM á BECKETT

The purifying rain fell steadily, gently, caressingly, the drumming sound it made on the wet paving stones drowning out the casual noises of the surrounding city. He stood on the pavement on the corner of Montague Street and Upper Keating Place, awaiting his prey, his great cape wrapped around him against the rain. Not that he minded the rain; the cleansing rain, the obscuring rain, the protecting rain, the rain that washed away blood, that cleansed the hands, if not the mind. The rain that renewed everything in its wake, but could not bring forgetfulness. Memory was pain, but nepenthe would bring death, for he had nothing to keep him alive but memory. His actions now were the continuing result of the memories that went beyond pain and the mission that went beyond life. He was the wind.

He had been content for all the days since—since—the thoughts whirled as his conscious mind rejected the thought thrown up by his unconscious. That frightful image must, at any cost, be suppressed. That thing had not happened. Could not have happened. A red haze of grief and pain passed before his eyes, and then all was clear once more. He had been content, for all the timeless days that had passed since he had become the wind, to follow the same mindless progression. The details had fully occupied his conscious mind, had mercifully filled his thoughts, as he accomplished the deaths, one by one, of Those Who Must Die. He had always been very careful about details, even in his other life that had once been so important and was now so meaningless. Except that it had given him the skills he needed for his new tasks.

Like a man caught on the rim of a great wheel, fated to follow the same endless ellipse turn after turn, with only the scenery changing, he had traced, followed, located, entered, searched, killed, and silently departed.

This work, for a while, had so filled his conscious mind that further thought was unnecessary, and the attempt difficult. This cycle had served temporarily to suppress the pain, briefly dull the gnawing anguish that filled the well of his soul. But of late it had not been enough. The process was becoming too automatic, too easy; although he still took scrupulous care with each event, it no longer filled the whole of his conscious mind. Now the pain remained. The anguish grew.

Now the nameless gods that drove him demanded that he go further. He must risk himself, and yet win out. They must all die. He must track them to their lair and destroy them all. He must enter hell itself, in the guise of the devil, and terminate this corruption and all its foul, flagitious spawn.

A four-wheeler clattered and splashed down Montague Street and pulled to a stop in front of the house he watched. The jarvey jumped down from his seat and knocked on the front door. In a few seconds it opened a crack, and then closed again, and the jarvey resumed his soggy seat. Two minutes later a well-bundled-up gentleman left the house and secreted himself inside the cab, which promptly pulled away.

Lovely, lovely, thought the man who had become the wind. *The horse won't be in any hurry tonight. And the jarvey won't be peering about and getting rain in his face.* He retrieved a rubber-tired bicycle from the fence paling and set off through the rain in leisurely pursuit of the gentleman in the four-wheeler.

For the first twenty minutes the growler traveled vaguely northward through the empty streets, with the bicycle pedaling discreetly behind. Past Regent's Park and Marylebone to Camden Town the four-wheeler rumbled; and then it turned east and passed the Cattle Market and Pentonville Prison. In a few minutes it had entered an area of London with which the bicyclist was entirely unfamiliar. He looked about him as he pedaled with the simple pleasure of a child surveying a new playground. Ten minutes later, on a quiet residential street with well-separated houses, the four-wheeler clopped to a halt. The bicyclist stopped a respectable distance behind and pulled his machine out of sight behind a convenient hedge.

The passenger pushed open the carriage door and, after peering out and sourly observing the still-falling rain, gingerly climbed down, pulling up his collar and wrapping his overcoat closely around him for protection. He looked about him uncertainly, as though not quite sure what to do next. Then, signaling the jarvey to remain where he was, the man walked slowly down the street, peering at the houses on both sides as though trying to make out details of their gaslit interiors through the rain-fogged windows. Halfway down the block he found the one he wanted. By what sign he identified it, the watcher was too far away to determine. The man turned and waved the four-wheeler away, and then scurried down the short path to the doorway.

The watcher hurried up the street until he was close behind, and then he silently leaped over the low wall which bordered the path leading up to the house and concealed himself by crouching behind it. He watched as his quarry yanked the bellpull and impatiently shifted from foot to foot awaiting a response.

A panel in the woodwork to the left of the door slid open, exposing a four-inch-square gap at about waist level. The man removed what appeared to be a small gold coin or medallion from his pocket and, holding it between his thumb and forefinger, inserted it in the open panel for long enough for whoever was on the other side to get a good look at it. Then, as nothing happened immediately, he put the object back in his pocket and resumed his fidgeting.

A few moments later an arm extended from inside the panel, holding in its outstretched hand a piece of black cloth, which the waiting gentleman promptly snatched away. The arm was instantly withdrawn, and the panel closed. The man quickly removed his hat and pulled the black fabric over his head. It proved to be a face mask that covered the whole face down to the nose, leaving only the mouth and chin exposed.

When he had properly adjusted the mask, the man knocked a triplet on the door, and it swung open. He was surveyed and then promptly admitted to the house by a man dressed all in tight-fitting black, and wearing a similar mask. No sooner had the man disappeared inside and the door shut behind him than another man came up the path to the door, and the admittance process started anew. There must be a protocol, the watcher realized, discouraging one man from approaching the door before the man ahead was admitted.

The watcher remained crouched where he was while four more

gentlemen donned masks and entered the house. It must, he decided, be the small medallion, the devil's mark, that was being displayed through the open panel. He took a leather wallet from a special pocket in his cape and carefully felt around inside one of the compartments. There it was, the gold medallion he had removed from the shoe of his last victim. He had not had occasion to dispose of it yet. Now he was glad. It would be his passport. It was now time for him to imitate the ones he had just watched, to don the devil mask and enter this hell.

The house was large and richly furnished, and had many rooms. The man who was the wind, having gained admittance, wandered from room to room, cloaked behind the ubiquitous mask. He was now as one with the servants of the devil, observing the operation of this special subdivision of hell. The men, even the servants, were all masked. The women, scantily clad hussies who wandered from room to room and made themselves available to any masked man who beckoned, were bawdyhouse women. They made the best of the hand fate had dealt them, selling the only skills they had.

He was familiar with these girls; the pattern of his life had brought him into contact with many such, and he had always been impressed by their stoic good cheer. But in this house, the gaiety seemed forced; beneath the pouting lips, deep in the flirting eyes, there lurked the shadow of fear.

The rooms were dedicated to various pleasures. In one a roulette wheel spun, surrounded by masked men and by women in dishabille; in another chemin-de-fer and vingt-et-un tables were kept busy separating masked men from their coins. All transactions were conducted in cash in this house, since credit could not easily be extended to masked men who made a point of not recognizing one another.

These childish games, where men hiding behind masks felt a special illicit thrill, were not the activities the watcher had been drawn here to see. The premise of this gentlemen's club, where the gentlemen hid behind masks and the devil peered out through the eye slits, must be that in the confines of this house, the minor vices were but a prelude to the most consummate evil.

Somewhere in this building that darker evil must exist. And he must find it. He went deeper into the building, up a flight of stairs, past several closed doors, and there he found what he had expected to find. And despite his foreknowledge, despite his own activities of the past six weeks, this once-gentle man who had become the wind was horrified.

To believe, even on the best evidence, that human beings can behave like imps from hell is an intellectual exercise; to be confronted with such behavior is a gut-wrenching truth. When the Executioner of Lille, a dedicated man, separated the head of Gilles de Rais from its slender body he was acting under orders of the court, and knew of the seigneur's crimes only secondhand. Perhaps if he had seen the twisted, tortured bodies of more than a hundred small children, victims of the mad baron, laid out before him, his hand might have trembled, the ax might have slipped, and the job would not have been so neat.

The man who had become the wind hardened his heart, and determined to keep his work professional, regardless of what he saw. He saw rooms dedicated to strange and terrible variants of the sexual appetites of man. He saw rooms equipped for bondage, and for torture. He saw instruments of pain of such delicate design and exquisite manufacture that it was clear that the artisans who made them regarded them as works of art. And he saw these rooms and these instruments in use.

A servant came down the halls, whispering, "An auction, an auction," to all whom he encountered. The man who was the wind drifted behind the others and followed them into the auction room. He had seen enough. He knew what he must do. He would pause in this room, surrounded by Those Who Must Die, long enough to see what they did here. Then he would leave and prepare. Then he would return.

The childish masks these imps of Satan hid behind to practice their perversions made it all too easy for this spy in their midst. But a spy would have to have the device—the gold medallion—to enter this house of the damned; this was their positive protection from the outside world. The medallions, in the hands of their owners, were carefully protected. The watcher smiled grimly at this thought. So was life itself carefully protected—and he took the one as easily as the other.

A short man climbed up on the low table in the center of the room, stepping up from a small stool that had been placed by one end for that purpose. He was garbed entirely in black like most of the others, and masked; but his cuffs were edged with crimson cord and his mask was crimson silk.

"Quiet!" a pudgy man standing near the watcher whispered to a companion. "It's the Master Incarnate!"

The watcher grimaced and his hands tightened involuntarily into fists. This then was the man! Here was the chief of the devilish clan. He must learn to recognize this man. Perhaps the so-called "Master" did not always wear the crimson; in pure black, surrounded by his vermin, he would be harder to single out. The watcher moved closer so that he could study the ears, and memorize the shape of the lobe. By this would he know the Devil Incarnate when next they met, no matter how he might be attired.

"Welcome," the Master Incarnate said, in a deep, commanding voice. "There are three items today." He gestured, and three servants, each a giant man, entered the room. Each of them carried a woman over his broad shoulders. The three women were bound and gagged with silken cords, and each wore a white shift and, as far as the watcher could tell, nothing else. Two of the women were passive, and the third was twisting and kicking vigorously, but completely ineffectually, in the arms of the giant who carried her.

After an "examination" of the women that was as degrading as it was offensive, the auction began. There was an atmosphere of obscene gaiety in the room as the bidding on each of the handsome, terrified women in bondage progressed. The bidding remained spirited in this carnival of depravity, and the offers quickly ran up into hundreds of pounds for each of the women. The dearest was the spirited one, who kept up the fight, even while wrapped in the massive arms of the impassive servant. Bidding for her closed out at six hundred and twenty-five pounds. *And so*, the watcher thought, *my Annie must have been sold to one of these swine, in a room very much like this one.* And then he decided not to think about that anymore.

The three winners of this unholy auction did not carry a large enough purse with them to redeem their prizes. The understanding was that they were to return the next evening with the required cash. In order to identify the right masked gentleman, and ensure that he got the girl he had bought, each of them ripped a pound note in half and gave one half to the Master Incarnate to match up the next evening.

"Tomorrow," the Master Incarnate said, indicating the three terrified women with a wave of his hands.

Tomorrow, and tomorrow, and tomorrow, the watcher thought.

"Tomorrow you three fortunate men will claim your rewards!"
The Master Incarnate clapped his hands, and the three trophies were
carried off. "Tomorrow evening," he said. "You have much to look
forward to."

And all our yesterdays have lighted fools the way to dusty death,
the watcher said to himself as he took his leave. He had a day now
to think, and to plan. Dusty death.

TWENTY-FIVE

AGONY

How then was the Devil dressed?
O, he was in his Sunday's best;
His coat was red, and his breeches were blue,
And there was a hole where his tail came through.
— ROBERT SOUTHEY

Sherlock Holmes was not grateful. He awoke from his encounter with the poultry cart with a severe headache, a bruised hip and left leg, and a foul temper.

"How do you feel?" asked the portly man who was bending over him as he opened his eyes.

Holmes took a minute to focus on the man's face. "Rotten," he said. "Who the devil are you?"

"I am Dr. Breckstone," the man told him, enunciating carefully. "Professor Moriarty sent for me. You've been in a most serious accident. Do you remember anything about what happened?"

Holmes looked blurrily about, gathering his thoughts and his energy. Then he focused back on Breckstone. "Thank you, Doctor, for whatever you've done for me. I do remember what happened. I am fine now. I must be on my way."

"My dear man!" Dr. Breckstone said. "You must remain where you are for some hours at least. I'm not altogether sure yet that you've escaped serious internal injuries. And the head, my good man, is not the preferential site for internal injuries! You're lucky to be alive, and no more gravely injured than you appear to be. But I must really insist that you remain lying down here for a few more hours at least. Perhaps overnight."

"Nonsense," said Holmes, sitting up and swinging his spindly legs over the side of the bed. "Where are my clothes? And, incidentally, who undressed me?"

"I wouldn't know," the doctor said. "But your clothes are there, on that chair. Now at least sit still for a minute and let me take a look at you." He peered into Holmes's right eye, and then the left. "Look to each side," he said. "Very good. Pupils seem normal. Coordination is fine. Tell me, do you know where you are?"

"My dear doctor," Holmes said, pushing himself to his feet, "I am not suffering from mental confusion, or aphasia, or amnesia, or anything else save a severe headache and a powerful need to be on my way." He weaved back and forth, and almost fell forward, but was saved by Dr. Breckstone, who grabbed his arm and helped him sit back down on the bed. "Well, perhaps I *am* a bit wobbly," Holmes admitted. "But I'll be fine in a few minutes. Again, I thank you very much for your efforts. You may send me a bill, of course."

"There'll be no bill. Professor Moriarty is taking care of that," Breckstone said. "If you are determined to leave, then please dress yourself and walk about the house for fifteen or twenty minutes before you go. That will give a subdural hematoma, or whatever else may be lurking inside your skull, a chance to make itself known while I'm still here to do something about it."

Holmes rubbed his head above the left ear. "As you say, Doctor," he agreed grudgingly. "I need some time to think in any case. I'll find a room in which to pace back and forth for the next twenty minutes and smoke a pipeful of shag. I always do my best thinking when I'm pacing back and forth."

"I shall go tell Professor Moriarty that you're conscious," Breckstone said. "If you feel the slightest touch of vertigo or nausea, let me know immediately."

Half an hour later Holmes appeared in the doorway to Moriarty's study. "I apologize for any inconvenience, Professor," he said. "And I thank you for providing medical attention."

"Someone tried to kill you, Holmes," Moriarty said, peering down from the high shelf where he was sorting through a collection of large astronomical atlases. He selected one and climbed down from the stepladder with it under his arm.

"I am aware of that," Holmes said. "I must confess, Professor, that for a moment I was surprised to wake up in this house."

Moriarty regarded Holmes thoughtfully as he went over to his desk and set down the massive atlas. "Surprised that I took you in, or surprised that I allowed you to wake up?" He smiled. "A bit of both, I expect."

Holmes glared at him and walked stiffly over to the desk. "I am

surprised that you didn't take the opportunity to dispose of this statuette," he said. "And now I'm afraid that both I and it must be on
our way." He snatched the bronze statuette from the corner of the
desk and stalked from the room.

"Take care, Holmes!" Moriarty called to the detective's retreating back. "There seems to be something about you that brings out
murderous impulses in total strangers; so you can imagine how your
friends feel." He chuckled at the sound of the front door slamming,
and then went into the hall to make sure that Holmes had really left.
Returning to his desk, Moriarty immersed himself in the dusty pleasures of the well-worn astronomical atlas, determined to get a few
hours' research done before Barnett or one of Colonel Moran's minions returned with a report that would bring him back to this world.

While studying the columns of figures that interested him in the
astronomical atlas, Moriarty was suddenly put in mind of another
set of figures, and he pulled the Scotland Yard file from his desk and
searched through it intently for the copy of the newspaper fragment
that had been found on Lord Walbine's person when he was killed.
Then he went over to a locked cabinet and removed a variety of
maps, charts, and atlases of the London area and spread them open
on his desk.

After performing cabalistic rituals over each of the maps with
a ruler and a piece of string, Moriarty rang for Mr. Maws and had
him go to the basement and retrieve the stack of daily papers for
the last three months. Then he closed the door to the study and left
word that he didn't want to be disturbed for anything but the most
urgent news.

It was Barnett who disturbed him. At two o'clock in the morning
Barnett burst through the front door, slammed into the study, and
almost did a jig to Moriarty's desk. "I have your killer!" he announced, grinning broadly and waving an olive-colored envelope in
front of him.

Moriarty looked up from the vast mound of books, charts, note
pads, newspapers, and assorted drawing and measuring materials
that now covered his desk top. "Where?" he asked.

"Well, I don't know *where* he is, yet, Professor; but I know *who*
he is. And I have a pretty good idea of why he's doing it." The elated
expression suddenly left Barnett's face, and he wearily shook his
head. "Which is wonderful, I suppose, after all this time—a hell of
a scoop, and all that. The only thing is, Cecily is still missing, and I
don't see how this gets me any closer to finding her."

"I believe they are related problems," Moriarty said. He tapped the pile of charts and newspapers with a pencil. "And I believe I can find the young lady."

"You're jesting!" Barnett exclaimed.

"I assure you, I would never jest about a thing like that," Moriarty said. "I am quite serious. But first tell me about the murderer."

"He'll keep," Barnett said. "I mean—I'm sorry, Professor, but if you know where Cecily is—"

Moriarty laced his hands together and leaned back in his chair. "It is only a supposition at the moment," he said. "It remains to be confirmed."

"Well, if you think you know even where Cecily might be, if there's a one-in-ten chance, or a one-in-a-hundred chance, give me the address," Barnett said, leaning over the desk and speaking with an unaccustomed intensity. "I'll confirm it in very short order, believe me!"

Moriarty shook his head. "I'm sorry, Barnett. I didn't mean to raise your expectations to quite the fever pitch. It will take a bit more research and investigation before we can establish the present whereabouts of the young lady; and that depends upon my being right about who has taken her and where. But the logic is consistent, and I'm confident that we will find her, and before this newborn day is out. I have the key, but I'm not yet sure that I have the right lock."

Barnett sat back down in the chair facing the desk. "I don't follow that," he said.

"I shall explain," Moriarty assured him. "But first, tell me what you have found out about the murderer. Who is he, and why is he doing this? I assume by your attitude that you are fairly sure of your facts."

"I would say so," Barnett agreed. "You were right, Professor, which I'm sure doesn't surprise you. The man is a professional magician—an escape artist. Calls himself Professor Chardino—the Invisible Man."

"Very apt, considering what we know of his abilities," Moriarty commented. "What makes you pick out this one magician from the scores of performers that must be active on the stage today?"

Barnett tossed the olive envelope he was holding onto the large chart of greater London covering one side of Moriarty's desk. "I won't bother telling you what attracted me to him in the first place," he said. "Let me just put it that his name quickly led to all the rest. And when I looked for confirmation, all the pieces fell into place as if they were waiting for me to stumble across them. First of all, he has disappeared from view, moved from his usual theatrical rooming house, and refused any offers of work for the past four months, even though he is in great demand. His daughter—"

"Ah!" Moriarty interrupted. "That's interesting. He has a daughter!"

"He *had* a daughter. Annie. About eighteen years old. She died on the seventh of January in mysterious circumstances."

"Fascinating!" Moriarty said. "Go on—in what way were these circumstances mysterious?"

"The death is officially listed as the result of 'injuries received in a street accident.' Supposedly, she was thrown from a carriage. But from the description of the attending physician, whom I happened to find on duty in the emergency room of St. Luke's, it appears the girl was probably tortured. And over a period of several days. The physician didn't want to come right out and say it, since he had no way to prove it, and he could get into considerable trouble if he was wrong. But that's clearly what he meant."

"You have indeed been busy, Barnett," Moriarty said. "Anything else?"

"On some obscure impulse, I went to the graveyard where the daughter is buried. I think the idea at the back of my mind was to see if I could get an address for the professor from the sexton—that's what the fellow who keeps the graves is called, isn't it?"

"Usually," Moriarty agreed. "It's also the name of a beetle of the genus *Necrophorus*. Go on."

"Yes, well, I was assuming that Professor Chardino might visit his daughter's grave occasionally."

"And leave his card?"

Barnett shrugged. "He might leave something. Perhaps flowers, which could then be traced back to the florist by someone with the deductive genius of a Professor James Moriarty."

"Did he?"

"As it happens, he did. Unfortunately, by the evidence of the sexton, who, come to think of it, did look a little like a beetle, they were always purchased from a florist right down the street. A little outdoor stand."

"Pity," Moriarty said. "And no card with the sexton?"

"No," Barnett said. "But"—he waved his hand at the olive envelope—"he did leave something else!"

Moriarty reached for the envelope and tore it open. "Well," he said, sliding the contents onto the one clear spot on the desk. "What's this?" He picked up the two small objects that had been in the envelope and examined them closely, comparing one with the other. "Identical medallions, except for such differences as one would expect from wear and handling, and for a tiny hole drilled at the top of one. Presumably for the link of a gold chain, as the medallions themselves would seem to be gold."

"That's it, Professor," Barnett said, smiling. "I think those are what you've been looking for."

"What Holmes had been looking for," Moriarty said. "I have no doubt. Exactly where did you find them?"

"At the gravesite, buried in the dirt."

"Ah. And what prompted you to look in the dirt?"

"The sexton. He told me that Chardino used to sit by the grave for long periods of time, talking to his daughter. And he thought that Chardino occasionally left things there besides the flowers. 'Trinkets,' he called them. So I looked, and I found two."

"You did indeed. Curious things, these." Moriarty hefted the two medallions in his hand. "They tell the whole story—and a horrible story it is."

"What do you mean?"

"This sigil has an interesting history," Moriarty said. "Oh, not these particular baubles, of course; but the design, the pattern, the notion behind it. It explains all to one who understands such things."

"And you do?"

"Indeed," Moriarty said. "As you know, I have always been interested in the obscure, the bizarre, the esoteric—the darker recesses of the human mind. I have seen you, on occasion, perusing my collection of books on these subjects."

"What has this to do with that?" Barnett asked.

"I will explain," Moriarty said. "Let us examine these medallions. On the obverse: a satanic figure, legs wide, arms akimbo, staring out at the observer. Around the figure, evenly spaced, the letters D C L X V I On the reverse"—Moriarty flipped over the medallion—"a floral design twined about the tracery letters H C. Do you agree?"

Barnett, who had picked up the other medallion, examined it closely and nodded. "That's what it looks like to me," he said.

"Let us take it from front to back," said Moriarty, holding his medallion up to the light of the desk lamp and examining it through a small lens. "The pleasant-looking figure glaring out at you is a chap named Azazel, leader of the Sleepless Ones."

"The Sleepless Ones?"

"That's right. The symbolism is very interesting. The story is in Genesis, in an abbreviated form." Moriarty stretched his hand behind him for an old black leather-bound Bible, and opened it. "Here it is: Genesis Six: 'And it came to pass, when men began to multiply on the face of the earth, and daughters were born unto them, That the sons of God saw the daughters of men that they were fair; and they took them wives of all which they chose.

" 'And the Lord said, My spirit shall not always strive with man, for that he also is flesh: yet his days shall be an hundred and twenty years.

" 'There were giants in the earth in those days; and also after that, when the sons of God came in unto the daughters of men, and they bare children to them, the same became mighty men which were of old, men of renown.

" 'And God saw that the wickedness of man was great in the earth, and that the whole imagination of the thoughts of his heart was only evil continually.' "

Moriarty closed the book. "Right after that God asks Noah to build himself an ark."

"I'm sorry, Professor, but I don't follow any of that," Barnett said. "I never really paid much attention in Sunday school."

"Let me expand on it for you," Moriarty said. "And I assure you, that they did not teach you this in Sunday school. The old myths sometimes tell us a surprising amount about the human unconscious. The 'sons of God' were angels; specifically in this tale a group of angels known as the Sleepless Ones, whose particular job it was to watch over men."

"Headed by this fellow," Barnett said, tapping the medallion. "Azazel."

"Correct. Now, these Sleepless Ones observed the 'daughters of men,' and they liked what they saw. They lusted after these beautiful human women, and so eventually they came down and married them."

"Naturally."

"Angels, I would imagine, can be very persuasive. But since they were angels, their children were not human children, but the Nephilim, or giants. And these giants were unruly children. Wait a second." Moriarty went over to a bookcase and ran his fingers along the spines of the books. "Here's the one. The whole story is in the Book of Enoch. A different, and longer, version of the story from that in Genesis. 'And it came to pass when the children of men had multiplied that in those days were born unto them beautiful and comely daughters. And the angels, the children of heaven, saw and lusted after them, and said to one another: Come, let us choose wives from among the children of men and beget us children.' "

Moriarty ran his finger down the page. "Here's more; now we get to the giants: 'And when men could no longer sustain them, the giants turned against them and devoured mankind, and they began to sin against birds and beasts and reptiles and fish, and to devour one another's flesh and to drink the blood.' " Moriarty closed the book. "This, according to one legend, was the origin of evil on the earth."

Barnett thought this over. "That's interesting," he said, "even fascinating, but what relevance does an ancient legend have on what is happening today?"

"Think of it this way, Barnett. What sort of people would chose to use Azazel, the progenitor of evil, as their symbol? What do they say about themselves? They are either fools, or knaves, or—*they* are evil!"

"Evil." Barnett stared down at the medallion he held. "It is a term that doesn't seem to have direct relevance anymore, not to this day and age; but you make it seem to come alive."

"*They* make it come alive, not I. Any man who does not believe in the existence of evil—pure, deliberate, virgin evil—or who believes it to be a thing of the past is not truly aware of the world in which he lives. But the evil, my friend, is within us. We need no Azazel to bring it to life."

"What of these letters around the rim of the medallion?" Barnett asked.

"There is, indeed, the other half of the story," Moriarty said. "Think of the letters as Roman numbers: D C L X V I. Six hundred and sixty-six."

Barnett looked blank. "So?"

"The answer to that is, once again, in the Bible—this time in the Book of Revelation." Moriarty flipped through the last few pages of his Bible. "Here it is—Chapter Thirteen:

" 'And I stood upon the sand of the sea, and saw a beast rise up out of the sea, having seven heads and ten horns, and upon his horns ten crowns, and upon his heads the name of blasphemy.'

"And then, at the end of the chapter, after describing how evil the beast is: 'Here is wisdom. Let him that hath understanding count the number of the beast:—for it is the number of a man; and his number is six hundred threescore and six.' "

"What does it mean?" Barnett asked.

"Nobody is sure," Moriarty said. "The Book of Revelation is by far the most obscure book of the Bible. The most usual belief is that it somehow represents the anti-Christ through some cabalistic numbering code."

Barnett leaned back and stared at his medallion, considering the sort of people who would favor this particular symbolism on their watch fobs. He found that he was weary from his day's exertions but still eager to go on. "What's on the back?" he asked.

Moriarty flipped over the medallion he was holding. "The flowers traced around the letters are *Veratrum*, commonly called hellebore. In ancient times it was believed to cure madness, and the soothsayer and physician Melampus is supposed to have used it to cure the mad daughters of Praetus, King of Argos."

"You seem to know an awful lot about these medallions, Professor," Barnett said. "I am aware that you have a most impressive store of esoteric knowledge. Many's the time you've told me that there is no bit of information that is not worth knowing. But this approaches prescience. Have you ever seen one of these trinkets before?"

"You suspect me of clairvoyance?" Moriarty asked. "No, I've never seen one exactly like these, but I've been expecting to run across something similar at any time over the past fifteen years. It seemed to me inevitable that someday I'd be staring at a sigil very much like this."

"It's new to me," Barnett commented. "I assume it has some specific meaning to you. What does it signify?"

"The letters HC on the reverse tell all," Moriarty said. "It is an example of the extreme conceit of those we're dealing with that they left the initials."

"HC?"

"Hellfire Club," Moriarty said. "A new incarnation of a three-hundred-year-old disgrace."

"The Hellfire Club?" Barnett looked thoughtful. "It rings a faint bell," he said. "Sometime in the past I have come across the name before, but for the life of me I can't recollect specifically where or when."

"There's usually a line or two in the history books," Moriarty said. "An amusing sidelight to the time of the Restoration. When Charles the Second returned to England, ten years after his father lost his head, and wondered why he'd been away so long. As a reaction to ten long years of rule by the stuffy old Puritans, a bunch of the young sprigs of the nobility went around raising hell. After all, they hadn't been allowed to so much as dance while the dour old Cromwells made the rules. So they called themselves the Hellfire Club. They drank, and they gambled, and they wenched, and they rode all over other people's fields, and they thoroughly enjoyed themselves."

"Boys will be boys," Barnett murmured.

Moriarty nodded. "And it seems that some boys will be boys at forty if they haven't been allowed to at twenty. But at forty, some of them have developed very advanced ideas of raising hell.

"Gradually the Hellfire Club became something other than it had been at the beginning. I imagine it happened as the 'boys' who just wanted a chance to run around a bit and sow an occasional wild oat had their fill of the missed excitement of youth and dropped out of the club to take up more serious pursuits. Those who remained were, let us say, more seriously dedicated to the single-minded pursuit of pleasure. And the pleasures they pursued gradually became more and more selfish, illegal, and sadistic. They went in for abduction, rape, torture, and murder."

"A lovely-sounding lot. Whatever happened to them?" Barnett asked.

"They were suppressed at the direct order of King Charles himself, who was never one to confuse freedom with license. They were suppressed again by a royal commission appointed by King William. It is believed that at this time they saw the wisdom of becoming a thoroughly secret society."

"That's it, then?" Barnett asked, when Moriarty paused.

"The club surfaced again briefly about sixty-five years ago, during the reign of George the Fourth. It was not identified by name at that time. A house in Cheswickshire burned to the ground, purely by accident as far as was known. In the burned rubble of the house, which was believed to be unoccupied, were found an exemplary collection of apparatus designed to restrain and torture human beings, along with the burned bodies of three young women. Subsequent investigation turned up the fact that several men, described as looking like gentlemen, were seen running away from the building at the time of the fire. One of the items rescued from the fire was an amulet with a strange design on it—a design much like that which you now hold in your hand."

"So that's what you meant when you said you've been expecting this?" Barnett asked.

"Indeed," Moriarty answered. "Ever since I learned of the events concerning the house in Cheswickshire, and realized the connection with the supposedly extinct Hellfire Club, I have expected someday to come across this medallion. There are some malignancies that do not die of their own accord, but have to be excised time and time again. I'm convinced that this is one such."

Barnett stared at the gold sigil he held, flipping it from back to front and peering closely at it as though he expected to read some great secret from its depths. What a catalog of horrors was represented by this small device. The devil on the front—Azazel, according to Moriarty—seemed to Barnett to be smirking at him in the gaslight. "It would seem," Barnett said, "that Chardino has been doing an efficient job of excising all by himself."

Moriarty nodded. "He has been going through the membership of the Hellfire Club like a scythe through wheat," he said. "In a way, it will seem a pity to stop him; in fact, I'm not altogether sure that there isn't a better solution."

"What would that be?" Barnett asked.

"I don't know yet," Moriarty admitted. "It is true that on humanist grounds our friend the magician should be discouraged from indiscriminate killing; but is his killing really that indiscriminate? And is it not equally true that the gentlemen-members of the club in question should be discouraged from—whatever it is they are doing?"

"You think that the Hellfire Club is responsible for the death of Chardino's daughter?" Barnett asked.

"Don't you?" Moriarty replied.

"How do you suppose he knows who the members are and where to find them?"

Moriarty shook his head. "It is pointless to suppose," he said. "We must discover!"

Barnett nodded. "And just how are we going to do that?" he asked. "It doesn't seem to me that we're really much further forward.

We know who the killer is, and who he's killing, and we can surmise why; but we don't know *where* he is, or where his victims can be found before they become his victims. I suppose we could always put an advertisement in the paper for members of the Hellfire Club to come forward and be saved, or put a twenty-four-hour watch on the churchyard, in hopes that Chardino will visit his daughter again before he kills too many more of these charming people."

"It's not really as bad as all that," Moriarty said. "I believe I can locate the Hellfire Club."

"You can?"

"Yes. I think so. The club's location is almost certainly transient, but I believe I have the key to their travels."

"The key—*that's* what you said about Cecily's location. My God! You don't mean you think they have her?"

"I'm sorry, I thought you had already guessed that," Moriarty said. "It is the only logical answer. Of course, I didn't know until you walked in that these people we are after are the newest incarnation of the Hellfire Club."

Barnett took a deep breath. "I didn't want to think about it," he said. "I mean, I knew *somebody* had to have her, as it's clear that she was abducted. If anything else had happened the authorities would have found her—or her body—by now. But I didn't want to think about by whom—or why—she was taken away. What do you suppose is happening to her?"

"It is just as pointless to suppose that as to suppose anything else," Moriarty said. "We will find her and take her away from her abductors. With any luck, we'll do it before the day is out. Now, since morning approaches rapidly, I am going to get some sleep."

"How do you know where Cecily is?" Barnett asked.

"I don't—not yet. But I shall. Join me in here after breakfast, say at nine-thirty."

"What about eight-thirty?" Barnett suggested.

"The most useful thing we could do with that extra hour," Moriarty told him, "is sleep. And I, for one, intend to do so."

Barnett had to be content with that, but he did not sleep well. Along about morning he finally did fall into a deep sleep, and then he had to drag himself out of bed a few hours later when Mrs. H pounded on his door and told him that breakfast was ready.

Moriarty was not at breakfast. Barnett could feel the tension rising in him while he ate, the tension he had become so familiar with in the past few days. Compounded of all the emotions that cramp the muscles and hit at the pit of the stomach: frustration, guilt, rage, fear, anxiety, and an increasing sense of helplessness. The feeling had by now become a permanent knot of pain, twisting away deep inside of him. Thoughts that he was not allowing himself to think were expressing themselves as sharp knives digging into his belly. He did not eat well.

As he was finishing, Moriarty entered the room. To Barnett's surprise, he could see that the professor had already been out of the house, and was evidently just returning. "A quick cup of coffee," Moriarty said. "We have work to do!"

Barnett rose. "What sort of work?"

"Sit down," Moriarty insisted. "I need my coffee." He dropped into his chair. "I have broken the code," he said. "I was just out checking my results and now I am sure."

"What code?" Barnett asked, fearful that Moriarty had gone off on some entirely new tack and had lost interest in the Hellfire Club and the missing Cecily. The professor's interest in any subject outside of mathematics and astronomy was all too likely to prove evanescent.

"Think back," Moriarty said. "Do you remember that among the effects of the late Lord Walbine there was a scrap of newsprint?"

"Vaguely," Barnett said.

"It was from the agony column of the *Morning Chronicle*," Moriarty reminded him, pouring himself a cup of coffee from the large silver urn in front of him. "On one side it said, 'Thank you St. Simon for remembering the knights.' On the other: 'Fourteen point four by six point thirteen, colon, three-four-seven.' "

"Something like that," Barnett agreed.

"I assure you, it was that, exactly," Moriarty said. "Now, on reading the report on the death of Quincy Hope—whose mysterious profession, by the way, turns out to have been quack doctor—"

"Quack?"

"Indeed. He cured people of any disease by placing bar magnets on various parts of their anatomy and taping them in place. At any rate, on reading the report of his death I noted that one of the items found in his room at the time of his death—some sort of anteroom or waiting room, I believe—was a morning newspaper. I procured a copy of that paper from our basement file and perused the agony column. I found no mention of St. Simon, or any of the knights, but

I did find this: 'Nine point eleven by five point two, colon, red light.'"

Barnett nodded. "You think that's a code?"

"It is."

"How is the Count d'Hiver involved in this?" Barnett asked. "If he's the one who attacked Sherlock Holmes, he must know something."

"I have had people watching his house since yesterday," Moriarty said. "He has not yet returned home."

"Do you think he's one of them?" Barnett asked. "Is he a member of the Hellfire Club?"

Moriarty pursed his lips thoughtfully. "I believe he is," he said. "Moreover, I believe d'Hiver, himself, is the Master Incarnate."

"The what?"

"The Master Incarnate, which is what the leader of this devilish organization calls himself. You may wonder why I believe this of d'Hiver on so little apparent evidence. The inductive chain is a strong one, and the links are sound. The members—if I may call them that—of the Hellfire Club must wear masks when physically present at the club, and thus do not know one another's identities. It is one of the strictest of this despicable organization's rules. The only person who knows the name of a member, except for the one who proposed him, is their chief, the Master Incarnate."

"And so?" Barnett asked, feeling that he had lost one of the links of Moriarty's chain.

"And so, Mr. Barnett, the only person who could have known, by their names, that the victims of our mad magician were all members of the Hellfire Club is the Master Incarnate. Since none of the victims seems to have taken unusual precautions for his safety before he was killed, I think we can assume that the Master Incarnate did not pass on to his disciples the fact of their mortal danger. But he himself must have been at least intensely curious as to who was killing off his membership.

"If we assume the Master Incarnate to be d'Hiver, it would explain his passionate interest in the progress of Holmes's murder investigation, and his clandestine presence outside this house in response to my advertisement. From which he must have assumed greater knowledge on our part than we actually possessed. It would, therefore, explain his attack on poor Holmes. He must have panicked when he saw Holmes leave this house. Had he time for reflection, I am sure he would not have done so. Although he does seem to have come prepared to attack someone."

"Wasn't he afraid of being recognized, sitting out there?" Barnett asked.

"I would assume he was in disguise," Moriarty said. "Remember, the Mummer identified him by an overheard name, not by his appearance."

Barnett rose and refilled his own coffee cup. Then he resumed his seat and sipped quietly while he thought over Moriarty's notions. "What about this code?" he asked.

"Ah, yes," Moriarty said, removing a bulky object from his outside jacket pocket and passing it across the table to Barnett. "I wondered when you would ask. Please examine this; on it I base my case."

Barnett took the bulky object and found that it was the "Jarvis & Braff Compleat Map of the Great Metropolis of London & Its Environs, *Showing All Omnibus, Tramway, and Underground Lines As Well As Points of Interest*," closed with its special "Patented Fold."

"What is this?" Barnett asked, after staring at it for a minute and extracting no meaning beyond that declaimed on the cover.

Moriarty sighed. "It is a map," he said. "It is also what we codebreakers call a 'key.' "

Barnett unfolded the map, which was closed with a sort of zigzag accordion pleat. It appeared to be no more than what it advertised: a map of London. "Is this the 'key' you were talking about last night?"

The professor nodded. "It is."

"That's wonderful," Barnett said, spreading the map out on the table. "Just what does it say?"

"It gives us the current location of the Hellfire Club," Moriarty explained. "They don't stay in any one place very long. They wouldn't want to take any chances on the neighbors' getting too friendly. But then they have the problem of informing their membership of the new location of the, for want of a better term, clubhouse."

"This map," Barnett said, gesturing at the large five-color rectangle on the table before him, "gives the location of every place in London. But it isn't specific, that I can see."

"No," Moriarty agreed. "But the code message in the agony column pins it down."

"How does it work?"

"It is ingeniously simple." Moriarty rose and left the dining room for a second, returning with an eighteen-inch steel rule from his study. "I'll let you work it out for yourself." He tossed the rule to Barnett. "Let us start with the message found on the late Lord Walbine. 'Fourteen point four by six point thirteen.' What do you make of that?"

Barnett took out his pencil and jotted the numbers down on the margin of the map. "Measurements," he said.

"That's it," Moriarty agreed.

"Well, it wasn't very hard to figure that out after you handed me a ruler," Barnett said. "But just what do I measure?"

"There are several possibilities." Moriarty said. "Top, bottom, either side; or, for that matter, from some arbitrary point on the map—say the tip of the Tower, or the gate of the Middle Temple. Luckily for us, they were not that subtle. Measuring in from the left side and then down from the top will accomplish our purpose."

Barnett held the ruler uncertainly, staring down at the map. "I'm not sure—" he said.

"It's the lack of scientific training," Moriarty said. "Scientists are never at a loss as to how to mark up someone else's papers. I suggest you start by marking the first measurement along both the top and bottom margins of the map. Notice that the ruler is marked off in inches and sixteenths. I assumed those were the proper fractions, as it is the common marking for such rules, and I was proved to be right. So your first measurement is fourteen and four-sixteenth inches from the left-hand border."

Barnett marked this distance carefully along the top edge, and then again along the bottom, as Moriarty instructed. Then he laid the rule carefully between the two marks, and measured six and thirteen-sixteenths inches down from the top, marking the place with a small pencil dot. "I see you've been here ahead of me," he said, noting a second small dot almost directly under his.

"Babbington Gardens," Moriarty said. "Northwest corner."

"That's what I get," Barnett affirmed.

"Well, that was my first stop this morning," Moriarty said. "My assumption was that the final number—three-four-seven—was the identification of the proper building, and, therefore, almost certainly the house number. Two houses in from the corner, along the east side of the street, I found it. It is, at present, untenanted. Certainly strongly suggestive, if not proof positive."

"Didn't you break into the house to look around?" Barnett asked.

"Certainly not!" Moriarty said, looking faintly amused. "That would be illegal. But I did speak to the tenants in the houses to either side."

"You did?"

"In the guise of a water-meter inspector. It never ceases to amaze me what information people will gladly give to a water-meter inspector. I learned that the house was occupied until mid-March, that it would seem to have been used as some sort of club, that gentlemen came in carriages at all hours of the evening and through the night, and that on occasion strange noises were heard to emanate from somewhere inside. I also learned that neighbors who attempted neighborly visits were rudely rebuffed at the door."

"That sounds as if it must be the right place," Barnett said.

Moriarty nodded agreement. "It would be stretching the bounds of credulity to assume it to be a coincidence," he said. "But just to be sure, I then went to the location derived from the Hope Newspaper."

Barnett roughly measured off the distances indicated, and found Moriarty's pencil mark on the map. "Gage Street," he said. "How accurate is this system, Professor?"

"If you are careful in your measurements, it is sufficiently accurate for the needed purpose."

"Well, if that is so," Barnett asked, "then how secure is the code? If you found it this fast, why haven't others?"

"They have to know what to look for," Moriarty said. "Even if someone should guess that it is a map coordinate code he would have to know what map to use."

"You did," Barnett said.

"*I* had a list of the effects of the murdered men," Moriarty said. "Two of them had Jarvis & Braff maps close enough to their persons when killed to have them mentioned on the inventories."

"And the others didn't?"

"Presumably," Moriarty said, "the others had their copies of the map in an unremarkable place—the library, perhaps, or the hall table. That being so, the existence of the map was not remarked. Really, Barnett, I should have thought that was obvious."

"What is obvious to you, Professor, is not necessarily obvious to others. If that were not so, you might be in my employ instead of I in yours."

Moriarty began to frown, and then chose to smile instead. "A touch, Barnett, a distinct touch," he admitted.

Barnett retrieved his coffee cup from under the map. "What did you find on Gage Street?" he asked. "And, incidentally, why didn't you ask me to accompany you?"

"This was for reconnoitering purposes only," Moriarty said. "I knew the club was no longer there. The present whereabouts is indicated in the agony column of this past Wednesday's *Morning Chronicle*. And you needed your sleep." He laced his fingers together and stretched his arms out before him, palms forward. "I found the house almost immediately, despite the absence of the specified red light, because it, also, was still vacant. A lovely old manor house, set back on its own bit of land, surrounded by the ever-advancing squads of identical row houses. It was perfect for their purposes. Since the neighbors, in this case, could tell me nothing, I investigated the interior."

"You broke in?" Barnett asked. "For shame, Professor. That's against the law."

"I broke nothing," Moriarty insisted. "The front door was ajar, and so I walked in."

"There was, I assume, no one there," Barnett said.

"You assume correctly. The house was devoid of both inhabitants and furnishings. The only things I found to verify my theory were a pattern of screw and bolt holes in the floors, walls, and ceilings of certain of the rooms, suggestive of the apparatus that must have been fastened there. And this." Moriarty reached in his pocket and removed a small bit of knotted leather, which he held in the palm of his hand. "I found this—this artifact—by chance, in a crack in the baseboard in one of the rooms."

Barnett took it and examined it closely. To his eye it was nothing but a short, stiff, discolored strand of leather, tied in a knot. "What does it do?" he asked.

Moriarty took the object from Barnett's hand. "I remember once reading a description by Admiral Sturdy of life in the old sailing navy," he said, tossing the bit of leather from hand to hand like a magician about to do a conjuring trick. "He was a midshipman about the time of Nelson, and one of his clearest memories of that period was of the floggings he was forced to watch. The lash was tied with a little knot at the end to keep it from splitting. After each use—after some poor sailor had had his back laid open for some minor infraction—the ends of the lash were soaked in salt water to remove the blood. For if they allowed the blood to dry on, you see, the leather would get stiff; and the next time the lash was used, the tip, knot and all, might break off."

Barnett looked with sudden horror at the small leather knot. "You mean—"

"Whoever used this," said Moriarty, holding the tiny thing between thumb and forefinger, "didn't know about the salt water."

TWENTY-SIX

INTERLUDE: ECSTASY

Did ye not hear it?— No; 'twas but the wind.
— George Gordon, Lord Byron

He would get but one chance, and he must perform flawlessly to succeed, to live. But so it had been all his life, each escape more difficult, more critical than the last, each allowing no margin for error.

The notion had come to him the night before, while wearing the devil's mask and spying on the devil's entertainments. The satisfying pattern that he had been following—the stalking, the confrontations, the deaths of these devil's imps one by one—would no longer serve. It had filled his need, this singular obliteration, it had satisfied his soul. But ripping off the leaves would not kill the tree; he must strike deeper, and harder, and crush the root so that it could not spring to life again.

The plan he evolved was simple, but the details required much thought and preparation. All through the night he had thought, and all morning he had prepared. Shortly after noon he was ready to proceed.

It was almost one o'clock when he pulled up before the devil's house in his rented wagon. He climbed down from the driver's seat and carefully dusted off his green-and-brown-checked suit and meticulously adjusted his brown bowler before strutting up to the front door. With a conscious skill acquired over a lifetime of deluding people, both at stage distance and face to face, he had become the part he was playing. His face, indeed his entire character, wore an air of smugness that was proof against all casual inquiry.

The door opened at his insistent pounding, revealing a tall, hawk-nosed man garbed as a butler, wearing the noncommittal, disinterested air of the well-trained household servant.

This place has no need for such as a butler. It is clear that we are, the both of us, liars, he thought, glancing up cordially at the hawk-nosed man. *But I am the better.* "Afternoon," he said, touching the brim of his bowler. "I take it this is 204 Upper Pondbury Crescent?"

The hawk-nosed man thought the question over carefully before committing himself. "What if it is?" he asked finally.

"Delivery." He jerked his thumb over his shoulder, indicating the wagon. The man in the butler suit peered in that direction, reading the big, freshly painted sign hanging on the vehicle's side. GAITSKILL & SON, it said, WINE MERCHANTS.

"Brought 'em myself." Taking off the bowler, he wiped his forehead with a large almost-white handkerchief. "I'm Gaitskill. Needed in a hurry, they told me, so I brought 'em right along. Regular carter off this week. Mother quite ill. Streapham, or some such place. Damned inconvenient time. Bertie's on the Continent on a buying trip. That's the son. So here I am. Where do you want 'em?"

"What?" asked the hawk-nosed pseudo-butler.

The pseudo-Gaitskill pulled out a sheaf of consignment orders and shuffled through them. "Here it is," he said. "Twelve firkins of best claret. Where do you want 'em? My lad will help you take 'em in." He indicated the gangly youth sitting with his legs dangling over the back gate of the wagon. "Hired lad. Not too bright, but willing. A cool spot is best."

"How's that?" asked Hawk-nose. "Best for what?" A touch of confusion shaded his supercilious expression.

"The claret," Gaitskill explained impatiently. "Best in a cool spot. Keep for years that way. Decades. Best not moved around too much. Give each firkin a quarter turn every five years or so."

The hawk-nosed man stared at the two-foot-long casks neatly stacked in the rear of the wagon. "I don't know," he said.

"Wine cellar is best," said the merchant. "As you might imagine from the name. Wine."

"I haven't been informed about this," the hawk-nosed man said.

The man who was the wind shrugged a merchant's shrug. "Someone forgot to tell you," he said. "Makes no difference to me. *I've* been paid. I'll take 'em away with me, or leave 'em here on the street, as you please. But I haven't all day, you know. Suppose me and the lad just stack the firkins neatly like on the pavement? Then you and yours can do as you like with 'em—at your leisure."

"No—well—" He paused to consider, to weigh the possibilities for error against each other. Obviously his master was not there to consult. "The cellar, you say?"

"Best place." The wind nodded.

"Well, come around back, then. There's an entrance to the cellar around back. No need to go through the house."

"No need indeed," the man who was the wind agreed, signaling to the lad he had hired to bring the first firkin around with him as they sought out the cellar door.

In half an hour they were unloaded, and the small casks were neatly stacked on an old shelf in the stone cellar. "This should keep 'em cool," the wine merchant told the butler. "I think your master will find that the vintage exceeds his expectations. Just let 'em settle for a day or so before you broach the first one."

"It's good quality, then?" the butler asked.

"Heavenly," the merchant assured him. "Ta, now. I must be on my way."

TWENTY-SEVEN

RESCUE

Here lovely boys; what death forbids my life,
That let your lives command in spite of death.
— CHRISTOPHER MARLOWE

The rain began again in late afternoon, a cold rain falling through the gusts of a chill spring wind. By sunset it had fallen steadily for several hours, and promised to continue indefinitely. The overhanging clouds shut out what remained of the twilight, prematurely darkening the sky. The bay cob, for whom the rain was but one more indignity, plodded stolidly through the puddled streets, and the four-wheeler bounced and lurched behind. Barnett hunched forward in his damp leather-covered seat and stared through the mist-covered window at the shifting murky shadows of the passing scene: buildings, pavement, lamp poles, pillar boxes, occasional people scurrying to get out of the rain. It all had an unreal quality, as though it possessed no separate existence, but had been placed there, as a stage set might be, at the whim of some godlike director.

Barnett felt himself caught up in this world of unreality; for some reason he could not understand, he felt curiously divorced from himself, from where he was and what he was doing. He shook his head sharply to try to drive away the mental fog and turned to Professor Moriarty. "How much longer?" he asked.

Moriarty glanced outside for a moment, getting his bearings. "Ten more minutes should see us there," he said. "A bit early for our needs, I'm afraid. We may have to skulk in some doorway for a bit."

"I don't know if I can tolerate waiting once we're in sight of the house," Barnett said. "I feel as though I've already been waiting for centuries. Besides, I don't like to think of what might be happening inside that house while we are outside waiting."

"Practice patience," Moriarty instructed. "It is the one virtue that will stand you in good stead in almost any circumstance. In this case, it is essential. If we burst in before the time is ready, we will most assuredly do more harm than good. God only knows what these good citizens and accomplished clubmen we are planning to visit might do in a panic."

"I thought you were an atheist," Barnett commented.

"I am also a pragmatist," Moriarty said. "Therefore, what we must do is insinuate ourselves amongst them, and, at the propitious moment, effect a rescue of Miss Perrine."

"If she's there," Barnett said. He suddenly found that he was biting his lower lip, and consciously restrained himself.

"If she is not there," said Moriarty grimly, "we shall cause one of the gentlemen who is there to desire very strongly to tell us just where she is! You have my word, Barnett, before this night is out we shall have located and repatriated your lady."

"I pray that is so," Barnett said. "This is the fourth day she's been in their hands. It is not pleasant to contemplate what might have happened to her by now."

Moriarty looked at him. "That is self-defeating," he said. "Whatever has happened to Miss Perrine has already happened; there is nothing you can do to change it. And whatever it is, you must not blame her or yourself for it. You must accept it and go on."

"Are you saying one should do nothing about what is past?" Barnett asked.

"One can learn from the past," Moriarty said. Then, after a pause, he added softly, "Vengeance, occasionally, is acceptable."

A few minutes later the four-wheeler pulled to a stop, and the jarvey opened the tiny communicating hatch on the roof, cascading a small puddle of water onto the seat next to Barnett. "We're 'ere, Professor, just like you said," he yelled down. "Right around the corner from the 'ouse in question."

"Very good, Dermot," the professor replied. "Are any of our people in evidence?"

The jarvey put his ear to the small hole in order to hear the professor's question over the wind. "There's a couple of individuals what are loitering in doorways on the next block," he replied. "But as to 'oo they are, I can't rightly say from this distance, what with the inclement weather and all."

"Well, let's go see what we can see," Moriarty said, nodding to

Barnett. "Wait here, Dermot. You might as well get inside the carriage and keep warm and dry until you are needed."

"Too late," Dermot yelled down, and he slid the hatch closed.

Barnett followed Moriarty across the street in front of them, which he noted from the corner sign was Upper Pondbury Crescent. The street, bordered by orderly rows of well-spaced houses, set comfortably back from the pavement, went off in either direction with only the slightest hint of a curve. "What do you suppose," Barnett asked the professor, "makes this a crescent?"

Moriarty glanced at his associate. "The vagaries of Lord Pondbury's business manager," he suggested. "A fondness for the term 'crescent' when he turned his lordship's private game preserve into sixty-five unattached town houses."

Mummer Tolliver appeared from behind a hedge and came trotting over. "Morning, chum," he said, nodding at Barnett. "Morning, Professor. That's the house over there." He pointed across the street at a house about halfway up the block. "The one with the chest-high stone wall running along the walk to the front door."

"Chest-high?" Barnett asked, peering through the gloom at the house Tolliver indicated.

The Mummer glared at him. "My chest," he explained. "Your arse."

Barnett looked down at the little man. "Don't be coarse," he said. "And what do you mean, 'morning'? It happens to be eight in the evening. Ten after, as a matter of fact."

"I 'ere tell as 'ow it's morning somewhere," the Mummer said coldly, dropping his aitches for emphasis. "Don't you know no science whatsoever?"

"Save your horological repartee for another time, Mummer," Moriarty said, staring suspiciously at the house across the street. "Are you certain that's the right place?"

"That is the place, Professor, no mistake," the Mummer said.

"Did you find a green cross?" Moriarty demanded. "That is the identification in this month's advertisement—a green cross," he explained to Barnett.

"There's a Maltese cross done in green glass set into the front window to the right of the door," the Mummer said. "You know, like them windows in a church."

"Stained glass?" Barnett suggested.

"You've got it," the Mummer agreed. "It shows up real good when you're right in front of it, 'cause of the light behind it; but you can't hardly see it from either side 'cause the window's inset quite a bit."

"Very good," Moriarty said. "This must, indeed, be the right place. Has there been much traffic while you've been watching?"

"Very little in-and-out," Tolliver said. "A cluster of gents went in shortly after I set myself and the other lads up here—that would be about six o'clock. Shortly after it started raining. Six in since then, and two out. They left together in a trap. And, o'course, one strange event."

"What's that?"

Tolliver led Moriarty and Barnett a few houses down from where they were standing and pointed out a bicycle which had been well concealed in the shrubbery to the side of the house. "A gent came pedaling up on this contraption and discarded it here, carefully out-of-sight like. Then he went over to the house what we're watching and immediately snuck off around the corner of the house. I can't say whether he went inside or not, but he didn't use the front door. That were about ten or fifteen minutes ago."

"Come now, that's fascinating!" Moriarty exclaimed.

"I would have merely assumed it was a servant, perhaps being a bit secretive on account of being late for work, feeling the necessity of using the back door," the Mummer said, "were it not for the peculiar circumstance of this here bicycle."

"That is, indeed, a peculiar circumstance," Moriarty agreed. "What do you make of it, Barnett?"

"You've got me," Barnett said. "Someone else watching the house?"

"Perhaps," Moriarty said. "But he must be myopic, indeed, to need to watch it from so intimate a distance. How many more of our people have we here, Mummer?"

"Fourteen, at present," Tolliver said. "Scattered up and down the street in places of concealment."

"Good, good," Moriarty said. "That should suffice. Now let us settle ourselves down and try to remain comparatively dry. The, ah, membership should start arriving any time now. Mummer, do you think you can insinuate yourself close enough to that door to enable you to get a good view? I want to know what the entrance procedure is."

"One of the few advantages of being small," Tolliver said. "I can hide in half the space it would take a person of standard stature. I'll give 'er a try."

"Good lad, Mummer," Moriarty said, patting him on the back. "Remember, discretion is the watchword. It is more important for you not to be seen than for you to see every detail."

"Don't worry, Professor," the Mummer said cheerfully. "I may be seen, but I won't be caught. And they won't nary suspect nothing, either. Here, watch this!" Tolliver shrugged his coat off and twisted his jacket around. Then, taking the dripping-wet bowler hat off his head, he removed a cloth cap from its inner recesses. He put the cap on and pulled it tightly down around his ears. Slouching and throwing his shoulders forward, he tilted his head a bit to the side, and allowed an innocent expression to wipe the usual sly grin off his face.

Barnett blinked. Before his eyes a miraculous transformation had taken place: the dapper little man had become a street urchin. Fifteen years had been wiped off his appearance, and no one seeing him now would believe he could possibly have anything more on his mind than retrieving a stray ball.

The Mummer wiped his nose with his sleeve and stared up at Moriarty. "Wat'cher think, gov?" he demanded in the nasal whine of the slum child. "Do yer 'pose I'll do?"

"Mummer, you're an artist!" Moriarty exclaimed.

"It's nuffink, Professor," the Mummer said. "Now, if you'll 'scuse me, I'll go practice me art." And with a skip and a slosh, he ran off down the street.

The man who was the wind was in the cellar of the devil's house. He had stealthily unlocked a small window over a long-disused storage bin when he had delivered the casks of wine. And now he was among the casks. He could hear footsteps, faintly, overhead, as the devil's imps arrived upstairs one by one. It was good. He took off his coat and rolled up his sleeves. There was plenty of time. Smiling a horrible smile, he reached for the nearest cask.

The Sons of Azazel began arriving at their clubhouse shortly after Moriarty and Barnett settled down to watch. One after another, at short intervals, the clatter of horses' hooves would sound over the rain, and a carriage would pull up somewhere along that block of Upper Pondbury Crescent. Two broughams, three hansoms, a quartet of four-wheelers, and an elegant barouche with a black canvas panel covering what must have been a crest on the ebony door—all arrived within the first half hour. From each vehicle one heavily cloaked man emerged and proceeded toward the front door of the Hellfire house. When one of these gentlemen arrived close on the heels of another, he would wait on the pavement, stamping his feet impatiently, while the first was received at the door.

Tolliver dashed back across the street as the latest hansom was disappearing around the corner. "I got a fix on 'er now, Professor," he said. "They goes up to the door and gives a pull on the bellpull. Then this little hole what is beside the door—over on the left—is opened from the inside. The gent what's outside sticks something in the hole for the gent what's inside to take a dekky at. I couldn't get a good look at the item, but I think it's one of them medals like you got. Then the gent what's inside hands the gent what's outside a mask, which he promptly sticks over his face. Then the door finally opens, and the gent what's outside goes inside. You got me, Professor?"

"I got you, Mummer." Moriarty turned to Barnett. "That explains one thing," he said. "I have been wondering why there have been no masks found in conjunction with any of the bodies, since they maintain the habit of going masked. A nice little solution to the problem. It means, also, that we won't have any trouble in entering the house."

"How are we going to do this, Professor?" Barnett asked. "I'm ready for whatever has to be done."

"It looks as though you and I will be the only ones entering directly," Moriarty said. "We each have a medallion, and we are, each, disguised as a gentleman. That should be enough to get us inside."

"Okay," Barnett said, raising the collar on his coat and adjusting his hat. "Let's go!"

"One at a time, remember," Moriarty cautioned him. "I shall go first, and await you in the inner corridor. If, for some reason, that should prove too conspicuous, I shall be in the first accessible room. Try not to speak."

"Excuse me, Professor, before you go," Tolliver said, "but when will you want me and the other lads to join in the festivities?"

"Keep close watch outside," Moriarty told him. "Here, take this; it's a police whistle. If I need you, I will signal by throwing something through one of the front windows. Then you blow the whistle to assemble our men and head right in through the front door. Otherwise, just be prepared to give support if we have to exit quickly."

"Right enough, Professor," Tolliver said. "I'll pass the word along to the lads to keep out of sight, but be ready to act if they hears the whistle."

"Who are these 'lads'?" Barnett asked.

"Colonel Moran," Tolliver told him, "and some of his pals from the Amateur Mendicant Society. The colonel 'as a look on him like he wants to hit something: and I'm sure squatting under a porch in the rain ain't doing his disposition no good, neither."

"Tell him how things stand," Moriarty said. "Tell him the answer to his problem is inside, and I shall bring it out. I'm depending on you, Mummer. Come along, Barnett, be right behind me now."

Barnett stood on the pavement in front of the house, fingering the small medallion and watching as Moriarty was admitted through the front door. Then it was his turn. His heart pounding loudly, he advanced to the door and pulled the wooden bell knob.

His preparations were just about complete now. One final check—couldn't have anything going wrong—and he would find his way upstairs and join the festivities. Festivities? He smiled. Eat, drink, and be merry, he thought, for it is almost tomorrow.

Moriarty waited for Barnett in a small room to the left of the entranceway, just out of earshot of the greeter at the door. Barnett looked around. "How prosaic," he whispered to the professor. "A cloakroom."

"The prosaic is ever intermingled with the bizarre and the frightful," Moriarty commented. "The Executioner of Nuremberg wears a dress suit and white gloves, and uses a double-bladed ax. The Mongol hordes invented the game of polo, but they used a human head in place of a ball. The castle of Vlad the Impaler was noted for its fine view of the Carpathian Mountains. I'll wager this place also has a washroom, and quite probably a kitchen."

Barnett shook his head slightly. "Has anything ever surprised you, Professor?" he asked.

"Everything constantly surprises me," Moriarty replied. "I think this is the direction we want to go."

They went down the hallway, peering into each room as they passed it. Barnett tried to look nonchalant under his mask, but he kept having the feeling that every pair of eyes that turned his way would immediately see right through his disguise, and that any second one of the well-dressed masked men strutting about the hall was going to point a dramatic finger in the direction of his nose and exclaim, "That man in the wrinkled suit is obviously not one of us! Apprehend him!"

But the other masked men in the halls and rooms of this hellish club saw no difference between Moriarty, or Barnett, and themselves. And, Barnett was surprised to note, without seeing their faces he could detect no difference between them and other men. He wasn't sure what sort of difference he expected to see, but once he got used to seeing a mask instead of a face, these Hellfire men bore no stigmata visible to Barnett. In their dress and bearing they would not have looked out of place strutting down the halls of the Bagatelle, the Carlton, or the Diogenes. Perhaps on other evenings they did just that.

The rooms off the short entrance hall were dedicated to games of chance. There were three small rooms, fitted out for baccarat, whist, and vingt-et-un; and a large room with two roulette wheels and a piquet table. The action was spirited at these tables, and the stakes were high. The games were supervised by a pair of stewards in severe black garments, wearing identical *papier-mâché* masks modeled to look like smiling faces, painted porcelain white, with black eyebrows and a pencil-thin black mustache. The dealers and croupiers were all attractive women in their twenties; their colorful dress and easy manner placed them as belonging to that segment of society which the French called the *demimonde*, the English having no polite term for it.

It was a bizarre scene that Barnett found himself wandering through; masked men and scarlet women playing at card games with a savage intensity under the actinic glare of the multiple gas fixtures that were scattered about the walls like perverted gargoyles. There was another game going on too, a subtler game played with nudges and winks and nods and indirect conversation, and blushes and giggles from the *demimondaines*. This was also being played with a fierce intensity, although Barnett could not, from what he overheard, clearly discern the rules, rewards, or penalties. The game, superficially sexual in content, had the flavor of evil and decay. Barnett noted a cynical hardness around the eyes of the women, and he thought he detected in some of their eyes the glitter of fear.

"What do you think?" he whispered to Moriarty, as the two of them stood in an isolated corner of the large room near the piquet table.

Moriarty looked at him for a long moment, as though debating which of the many ways to answer that question he would choose. "I think we are on the periphery of evil," he said. "We must proceed inward, toward the center. Prepare yourself for scenes that will not please you, and try not to give yourself away by reacting prematurely to whatever you see. Blend in with your surroundings, as distasteful as that may be."

Barnett looked around. "If I have to play, I'll play," he said. "I have had practice. Which way, do you suppose, is the center?"

"I have been watching," Moriarty said, "and as far as I can determine, the door in the opposite corner of this room would seem to be the portal to the netherworld of infinite and infernal delights. It leads to a corridor, and the corridor leads to—what, I wonder? I have seen several of the masked gentlemen go through it, but none of the, ah, ladies. Are you ready?"

"I hope so," Barnett whispered.

"Stiff upper lip!" Moriarty said. "Or, at least, *act* as though your upper lip is as stiff as an Englishman is supposed to keep his upper lip. You are going now into the *sanctum sanctorum* of this blessed club, the delights of which are the reason you pay the Master Incarnate his twenty guineas a month."

"I suspect I shall get more than my money's worth," Barnett murmured. "Lead on, Professor."

He was among them now. They smiled and laughed and played at their devilish games; and he smiled and laughed under his mask, and played well his own game. He took out his watch, a gift from the Burgermeister of Fürth after a successful escape from the ancient dungeons beneath the Rathaus: it was now quarter past ten. In one hundred and five minutes all games would cease. Midnight, the witching hour. He laughed again, aloud, but nobody noticed.

The house was divided into four sections, which like the levels of heil in Dante's *Inferno*, were separated according to the sins favored by the inhabitants. Each level of greater sin was accessible at only one place, through the level of lesser sin. Moriarty and Barnett progressed from Level One, Gambling and Lechery; then to Level Two, Various Exotic Perversions with Willing—or Persuadable—Women. The room they entered, large, effusively ornate, and yet subtly tawdry, resembled nothing so much as the parlor in an expensive brothel. Which was certainly deliberate, and was in no way inaccurate.

Barnett ran his gaze over the flocked red plush wallpaper; the deeply cushioned chairs and couches, done in matching fabric; the elaborate and tasteless candelabrum, decorated with flowers and cherubim and remarkably voluptuous female angels; and the equally voluptuous ladies lounging on the couches, garbed in imaginative dishabille. "Aside from these idiotic masks," Barnett whispered, "this could be any one of fifty clubs in London, all catering to the same 'sporting' population."

"*Nemo repente fuit turpissimus,*" Moriarty murmured. "I find Juvenal quotable at the most unusual times."

"How's that?" Barnett asked quietly.

Moriarty shook his head slightly in mock annoyance. "Your American schools just don't believe in a classical education," he commented. "No wonder your English prose is so flat and unmellifluous; you are all innocent of Latin."

"Discuss my educational deficiencies some other time, Professor," Barnett requested firmly. "What did you say?"

"Roughly, 'No one ever mastered the heights of vice at the first try.' These chaps have to start somewhere, after all."

Suddenly a scream sounded from one of the nearby rooms—a high-pitched cry of unendurable agony. Barnett jerked his head around, seeking the source of the sound, but none of the others in the parlor reacted at all, except for a few of the women, who twitched nervously.

Barnett clutched at Moriarty's sleeve. "What was that?" he demanded.

"Casual, Mr. Barnett," Moriarty whispered intently. "Remain casual. This sort of thing must happen all the time. Remember the part you are playing. You are well used to such sounds. Indeed, it is why you are here."

Barnett stiffened his back and lifted his head into a parody of nonchalance. "What is it exactly that happens all the time," he asked, "which causes girls to scream in distant rooms?"

Moriarty leaned casually against a patch of flocked wallpaper. "You really don't want to know," he said. "Suffice it to say that other people's ideas of sexual pleasure may be far removed from your own."

"You mean—but why would they put up with it? The women, I mean?"

"These ladies are all imported from elsewhere for service in this house. This is a practice that is common in London houses of this sort, although these people take more advantage of it than others might. They serve for about two months, which is probably the length of time that the house stays in any one location, and then are sent back whence they came with a sum of money in hand. If necessary, as it frequently is, their, ah, wounds are first tended to in a hospital far from here, where the causes behind their injuries are overlooked by mutual agreement."

"Horrible!" Barnett said. "Much worse than any stories I've heard about the brothels in France."

"Your studies in depravity did not descend deep enough," Moriarty commented. "There are many similar places in Paris, as indeed in Berlin, Vienna, Prague, Warsaw, and every other European capital. With the possible exception of Rome—the Italians don't seem to be as prone to institutionalize their violence. As to what happens in such houses in the Osmanli Empire and the Arab world, they make our friends here look like dilettantes."

Barnett looked around him. "You make this place sound like a garden party," he commented.

"You are mistaken," Moriarty replied. "I said it was horrible, not unique. Besides, this is merely the, let us say, middle level of experience. The upper levels, for which they kidnap women off the street and throw dead bodies back onto the street, probably more nearly meet your requirements."

Barnett clutched convulsively at Moriarty's sleeve again, and then forced himself to let go. "If you can believe it, I had forgotten for an instant," he said. "Let us go on!"

"We must locate the door through which the initiates go to practice vices few others even know exist," Moriarty said.

"You expect to find Cecily at this next level?" Barnett demanded. "And yet you think she is still all right?"

"They must have cells," Moriarty said, "where women are held for, ah, future use. I expect to find the lady in one of these cells, and I expect to find the cells deep in the heart of the beast."

"Cells?"

"Yes. There were signs in the now-deserted houses that certain of their rooms had been used as cells."

"Well then—" Barnett began.

"Grab that man!" a harsh, commanding voice suddenly rang out from somewhere behind Barnett. "Don't let him escape! He is not one of us, he is a spy! Be sharp, now!"

Barnett started at the words, twisting around, and expecting to feel a heavy hand on his shoulders. To his amazement and relief, the short, imperious man who had barked out the commands was not pointing his accusing finger at Barnett, but at a slender man who had been quietly sitting by the piano.

"Here, now," the accused said, rising to his feet. "What's the meaning of this? Who are you, sir, and what do you mean by such an accusation?" He seemed amused, rather than alarmed. "Is this your idea of fun, little man?"

Several men who were dressed as servitors of the club appeared from different doorways, as though they had been awaiting the command, and moved closer to surround the tall, slender man.

"*I* am the Master Incarnate," the little man announced. "And you are a spy!"

"Whatever makes you think that?" the slender man asked, ignoring the surrounding servitors with a splendid nonchalance. "Are you absolutely sure you're right? Remember, Master, unveiling a member would be a very bad precedent to set, especially for you. Are you sure you wish to risk it, in front of all these fellow members?" With a wave of his hand, the slender man indicated the cluster of masked men, who had all stopped whatever they were doing and turned to watch the scene.

"I am sure," the Master Incarnate barked. "Especially as I can name you where you stand, and then prove it by unmasking you . . . Mr. Sherlock Holmes!" He reached for the mask and yanked it off, exposing the sharp features of the consulting detective.

"I must hand it to you, Count," Holmes said, edging toward the wall. "You have cleverly revealed my identity. But, after all, are you quite certain that I'm not a member?" He took a firm grasp on his stick and flicked it in the general direction of one of the servitors, who was approaching him from behind. The man jumped back with alacrity.

"Thought you could fool us this afternoon," the Master Incarnate said, grimacing his satisfaction, "grubbing about in the cellar."

"The cellar?" Holmes repeated, sounding surprised. "Whatever are you talking about, Count d'Hiver?"

The count ignored Holmes's use of his name. "I heard about it as soon as I returned this afternoon," he said, "and watched through a concealed peephole to see who would attempt to gain entrance this evening that shouldn't. And it was you, Mr. Holmes—it was *you*. I had a feeling during the course of this investigation that you were going to prove too clever for us."

"I suppose there would be no point in advising you that this house is surrounded?" Holmes inquired, backing the rest of the way to the nearest wall. The way to the entrance door was now blocked by two brutish-looking servitors of the house.

"There would be no point at all," the Master Incarnate declared savagely. "It isn't, and it wouldn't change things for you if it were. Take him!"

Five of the burly servitors leaped for Holmes, who lifted his walking stick and whirled it about him, fairly making it sing as he beat them off. In an instant two of them were down, and the remaining three were circling respectfully out of range of the lean detective and his three feet of ash.

Barnett gathered himself to rush to Holmes's aid, but he felt Moriarty's restraining hand on his shoulder. "To the other door!" Moriarty whispered urgently. "That door over there. I shall bring Holmes. Prepare to open it for us as we arrive, and close it firmly and promptly once we are through. Go now!"

Barnett sidled over to the door Moriarty had indicated and put his hand on the knob. Assuring himself that it opened easily, he nodded his readiness to the professor.

With a broad gesture, Professor Moriarty whipped his mask off and blew two sharp blasts on a police whistle. Everyone in the room froze in position for a second, forming a bizarre tableau that would remain forever etched on Barnett's memory.

"Over here, Mr. Holmes," Moriarty called. "I must ask the rest of you to remain where you are. You are all under arrest! Constables, take charge of these men!"

Without waiting to find out where these constables were, or where they might have come from, the masked Hellfires in the room made a dash, as one, for the far door. Count d'Hiver screamed at them to stop, yelling that Moriarty was a fraud, that it wasn't so; but they did not pause to listen. In a few seconds there was a plug of human bodies squeezing ever harder into the entrance door. Two men had already lost their footing, and were down under the pack, with little hope of getting up. As Barnett watched, another man was lifted bodily from the doorway by several others and hurried over many heads to the ground at the rear.

Holmes broke free and leaped across to where Moriarty stood, imposingly, belligerently firm, next to a couch. "This way," Moriarty said, and the two of them stalked across the room to the door Barnett was guarding for them. In a second they were through it, and Moriarty threw the two heavy bolts on the far side.

"This should hold them for a few minutes," the professor said. "Time enough for us to do what we have to, if we get to it."

"Glad to see you, Moriarty," Holmes gasped, leaning against the wall to catch his breath. "Never thought I'd hear myself saying that. You do show up in the oddest places, though."

"I didn't expect to find you here, either, Holmes," Moriarty commented. "And what on earth have you been doing in the cellar?"

"But I wasn't in the cellar, old man," Holmes replied. "I have no idea what that was about."

"Curious," the professor said, "very curious. But come now, there's work to be done. We can compare notes some other time."

"You realize there's almost certainly no way out of this unusual establishment from this side of this door?" Holmes asked. "We have managed to place ourselves one step deeper into the web. As soon as Count d'Hiver and his cohorts are over their momentary confusion, admirably contrived though it was, they will surely assault this door with a convincing show of strength."

"True," Moriarty admitted. "But what we have come here for is certainly up these stairs. I would not leave before accomplishing my goal, and I'm quite sure that Mr. Barnett would not allow it were I to attempt to do so."

Holmes glanced at the still-masked Barnett. "So that's who you are," he said. "Should have known. Glad you're here. And now, just what is it that we are after? Ah! Of course! Miss Perrine; I should have guessed."

They made their way cautiously up the narrow staircase, Moriarty in the lead, and found themselves about a third of the way along a hallway that ran down the middle of the upper floor. There were rooms off each side, and each of the rooms had been fitted with a heavy, solid door, with a strong bolt affixed to the outside.

Moriarty threw open the door to the nearest room, and found it empty; but there were a pair of posts fastened to the floor in the center of the room, with leather thongs running through eyebolts in the posts. Barnett did not like to contemplate what such an apparatus might be used for.

In the next room they tried there was a girl, clad only in a white shift, who shrank away from them in horror as they opened the door. The shift was in tatters, and they could see the strips across her back and thighs where she had been beaten. It was not Cecily Perrine.

"It's all right, miss," Sherlock Holmes said, advancing into the room. "We've come to get you out of here. It's all right, really it is. We won't hurt you." He continued talking to the girl and walking slowly toward her, as she, eyes wide, speechless with fear, retreated into the farthest corner of the room.

"See here, Holmes, there's no time for this," Moriarty said. He turned to the girl. "Any minute now there's going to be an awful row. Those people who have done this to you are going to try to stop us from freeing you and the others. You'd best come with us now, and help with the other girls as we release them. We'll see if we can find a room where *you* can bolt the door from the inside. When it's all over, I shall see that you and any other ladies up here are removed from this place and taken care of. Properly. Do you understand?"

"Yes, sir," the girl said, but her voice was heavy with doubt and fear.

Moriarty reached around inside his jacket, behind his back, and, after fumbling for a second, pulled out a long, flat leather truncheon. "Come here, girl," he said. "Take this. If anyone approaches you while we are otherwise occupied, hit them in the face with it. Aim for the nose. That will discourage them."

The girl came forward hesitantly and took the proffered instrument. "I shall," she said, slapping it tentatively against the palm of her hand. She winced, finding the device surprisingly painful. "I shall," she repeated, staring directly into Moriarty's eyes. Her voice gained strength. "I shall! Oh, indeed, I shall."

"Very good," Moriarty said. "Now, stay close behind us."

They returned to the hallway. "I doubt if we have much time," Moriarty said. "Each of you take a room. Dispose of any resident masked men in it as you see fit—as rapidly as you can. I suggest we open all these doors immediately, and release any more captive young ladies."

"I—think—so," Holmes said, staring back at the strange, dreadful equipment in the room they had just left. "How horrible. It is difficult to believe that these men are Englishmen."

"I occasionally find it difficult to believe that our Parliamentary representatives are Englishmen," Moriarty remarked dryly. "Let us proceed; I think I hear pounding from below. If either of you happen to notice a window facing the front of the house—which would be that side, there—kindly heave some article of furniture through it."

Holmes looked speculatively at Moriarty. "Some of your minions downstairs?" he asked. "Well, I shall be glad to see them. I fancy all the windows are boarded up; there seems to be a false wall across that side of all the rooms."

In the third room that Barnett entered he found himself staring at a scene that he would never forget. The floor was bare and covered with sawdust, and at its center was a six-foot oaken X which dominated the room. Cecily Perrine, clad only in a long white shift, had just been unchained from an eyelet bolted to the wall and, her hands bound with thick cord, was being dragged across the floor by a short, thickset, hooded man.

The man giggled inanely as he pulled Cecily toward the oaken torture device. He brandished a short, many-stranded whip which he flicked occasionally into the empty air as though to get in practice for the delights that would follow.

"My God!" Barnett screamed.

Cecily turned and stared impassively at this second hooded man who now stood in the doorway.

The man with the whip pushed Cecily aside and whirled around. "What are *you* doing in here?" he demanded petulantly. "Get out! Get out! This is my room. Mine! She is mine! Get out! You know better than this!" He bounced up and down with excitement and anger, and waved his whip at Barnett. "Leave!"

Barnett snatched at the whip, pulling it out of the man's grasp. "You bastard!" he yelled, scarcely aware of what he was saying. "You slime! What are you doing with this woman?"

"She's mine," the thickset man insisted in a shrill voice. "I paid for her, didn't I? Now you just get out of here, or I'll report you to the Master Incarnate. Get your own female!"

Barnett could feel the blood rising to his face, and the mantle of reason lifted itself from the primitive emotions beneath. Like a distant observer, cool and detached, he watched himself lift the short whip and bring its weighted handle down again and again on the head of the thickset man. The man fell to the floor, and Barnett stopped—not through compassion, but because the target of his rage was now out of reach.

Slowly the haze cleared from before his eyes and he looked at

Cecily. Then he quickly looked away. He did not want to see her like this, he did not want ever to think of her like this, bound and helpless, and subject to the whims of evil men.

He crossed to where she lay and quickly, tenderly, untied her hands. "Cecily," he said, "what have they done to you?" To his surprise, he found that he was crying.

"Benjamin?" she whispered. "Is it you?"

He took his mask off—he had forgotten it was still on—and held her to him for a long moment. There was a robe in the corner which he used to cover her. "Can you walk?" he asked. "We must hurry."

"Yes," she said. "Get me away from here."

There were a total of seven women in the various rooms of this upper floor, and, at that moment, five men. Moriarty immobilized the men by tying their thumbs together behind their backs with short pieces of wire, which he produced from one of his innumerable pockets. By this time they could hear a steady pounding noise coming up from the door below.

"There is no other way out," Holmes said. "I have tried all the doors. Presumably we could find our way to the roof, but what then? It's a long way to the ground."

"I suggest we remove the false wall from one of the rooms facing the front of the house," Moriarty said. "If I can get to a window, I can get assistance."

"What good could your men do us now?" Holmes demanded. "They're down there and we're up here."

"A group of determined men assaulting the front door." Moriarty pointed out, "would at least provide a much-needed diversion. It would most probably complete the job of panicking the rank and file."

"Perhaps I can be of some assistance," a deep, well-modulated voice said from behind them.

They all turned. A tall man in elegant evening dress bowed to them politely before removing the mask that covered his face. "Allow me to introduce myself," he said, with just the slightest hint of a Middle European accent coloring his flawless English. "My name is Adolphus Chardino."

"Ah!" Moriarty said.

"Who are you?" Holmes demanded, shielding the seven young ladies behind him.

"That is of no moment at the present," Chardino said.

What is meaningful is that I can assist you in your efforts to leave." He removed a large pocket watch from his vest and glanced at it. "And I would earnestly suggest that you hurry; it would be wise to be gone within the next fourteen minutes."

"Why?" asked Holmes suspiciously.

"Well, you see, in fourteen minutes it will be midnight," Chardino told him earnestly. "And tomorrow—is another day."

"How do we get out?" Moriarty demanded.

"Follow me," Chardino said. He led them down the hallway to a small door.

They paused. "That," Holmes said, pointing to the door, "is a closet. I believe this man is in need of the services of an alienist."

"When these houses were built," Chardino said, opening the closet door, "some eighty years ago, the builders of the day separated the ceiling of one level from the floor of the next with a dead-air space to minimize the transmission of sound from one story to the next—a practice the architects of today would do well to emulate. In this building the space is two feet deep."

"How do you know about that?" Holmes asked.

"It is my profession to know such things," Chardino said. "It is such knowledge that enables me to perform miracles." He knelt down and searched with his fingers in a corner of the closet. "There is an access panel," he said. "Here!" He pulled up and the floor of the closet lifted out.

"How do you like that!" Barnett exclaimed.

"What sort of miracles?" asked Holmes.

"The usual sort," Chardino said. "Appearing, disappearing, escaping; what you might expect from a stage magician."

"Oh," Holmes said.

The sounds from the stairs increased. Now a chopping, cracking sound was added.

"They have found an ax," Moriarty said. "If we are going to leave, we should do so expeditiously."

"If one of you gentlemen would care to lead the way," Chardino said, "I would suggest that the ladies follow, and then the other two gentlemen. You will have to go single file."

"To where?" Barnett asked.

"There is no light," Chardino said. "I have placed a cord. Keep it to your left hand. It terminates at an access port leading to another closet on the floor below."

"Won't they see us coming out of the closet?" Barnett asked.

"It is in a seldom-used room," Chardino said. "And I shall do my best to distract them. Trust me. The art of misdirection is one I understand well. Now, hurry!"

Holmes looked doubtful, but he took the lead. It was a tight fit, but he managed to squeeze his lanky body into the small hole. "Here is the cord," came his voice from the black depths. "I shall proceed." A moment later he had disappeared into the narrow, pitch-black world under the floor.

Three of the rescued girls dropped into the space without comment, and crawled out of sight after Holmes; but the fourth balked.

"I can't!" she cried. "I just can't!"

"It's the only way out," Barnett said. "Come on, now, buck up."

"I have always been afraid of dark places," she said, backing away from the hole and shaking her head, her eyes wild. "Go without me if you must. I simply cannot crawl down there."

Chardino took her face in his hands and stared into her eyes. "You must go," he said clearly and simply. "You can do it; this one time you can. You will think of nothing. You will clear your mind of all thought. You will close your eyes and picture a bright meadow, as you crawl on your hands and knees, following the cord. There will be no other thoughts in your mind while you do this, and you will hear only the sound of my voice. I will be telling you that you *can* do it—you *can* do it. It is not hard, for you. Not this once. Not with my voice to guide you through the bright meadow which would be there if your eyes were opened. But they will stay closed. Do you hear me, girl?"

"Yes," she said, staring back into his eyes. "Yes, I hear you."

"Do you understand?"

"Yes, I understand."

"Then go! Remember, I am with you. You will hear my voice, as now, comforting you. For the sake of my daughter, go!"

The girl turned and lowered herself into the hole. In a second she was gone from sight.

Cecily Perrine was next. She dropped easily into the hole and crawled away.

The other two girls followed. As Barnett was about to go after them, he heard a splintering crash. "That's from the stairs; they must have chopped through!" he exclaimed.

"Go!" Moriarty commanded. "I wish to have a brief word with Professor Chardino, but I will follow right behind."

Barnett turned and lowered himself into the hole. He found the cord, a thin, very rough twine, and followed it into the dark. Ahead of him he could hear the sliding, thumping sound of the girl who had preceded him. Behind him, nothing.

It was not easy going; he found himself crossing over joists every few feet and ducking under beams the alternate feet. Once he got into the pattern of crawling, however, he found he could move steadily. But where was Moriarty? He should have been close behind him.

There was a sudden rattle from overhead, a stamping of feet, a banging of doors. If Moriarty wasn't on his way now, he would never make it. If the hatch in the closet wasn't closed, they would probably none of them make it. The Count d'Hiver would, assuredly, allow none of them to live.

There, ahead of him, was a glimmer of light from below. It rapidly grew clearer as he crawled, and then he found himself staring down into the illumination of one candle in an otherwise empty closet. He lowered himself down, carefully avoiding the candle. The door was open, and the others awaited him in the room beyond.

It seemed like an hour, although it could not have been more than a minute, before Moriarty's feet appeared at the trap, and the professor dropped into the closet. "Everyone made it safely?" he asked, looking around. "According to our friend, the front door is around to the left. We have no time to spare. Don't stop for anything! The masked men will have gone upstairs in response to d'Hiver's yells. They will be occupied for a time seeking us. We should have little interference down here. Stay close together."

"What of Chardino?" Barnett asked.

"He is keeping our opposition busy by flitting from room to room and drawing them deeper into the house," Moriarty told him. "Come!" He led the way from the little room and down a short corridor to the left, which terminated at a closed door. They met no one. Holmes, taking the lead, opened the door cautiously, peered through, and then closed it.

"As you thought, it is the entrance hall," Holmes whispered. "Front door to the right, gambling rooms to the left. There are six of them, that I could see, standing by the door and doing their best to look vicious. D'Hiver must have alerted them."

"Six?" Moriarty thought for a second. "No matter; we shall have to rush them." He grabbed a chair. "Keep the ladies back here. Put your masks on—it might gain us a second."

Barnett took a deep breath and prepared to follow Moriarty. He was, he decided, becoming a fatalist.

"Now!" Moriarty whispered, and the three of them plunged

through the door, Holmes in the center, Barnett hugging the wall on the left, and Moriarty—his chair held chest-high—on the right. The six by the door froze for a moment, staring at the oncoming trio. Perhaps it was the chair that puzzled them. But then, with an assortment of oaths that would have been out of place in any respectable men's club, they rushed to the defense. In a second Barnett found himself assaulted by several men larger than himself.

The area was too small for any effective punching, kicking, or gouging on either side, and there was no room for the use of sticks or canes. Barnett was finding it all he could do to remain where he was, while Holmes, with a flurry of brilliant boxing, was holding three men off and actually making a little progress.

Moriarty, parrying one gigantic doorguard off with his chair, made a dash for the small cloakroom door to the right of the hall. Once inside, he heaved his chair through the small window facing the street, and then ran back to the hall in time to pull a guard off Barnett.

About twenty seconds after the chair went through the window, they heard battering sounds from outside the front door. A minute later Colonel Moran burst through, brass knuckles on each fist, at the head of a flying squad of Moriarty's minions. Colonel Moran scattered the resistance before him like a child scattering marbles, and in seconds the way was clear.

"Good!" Moriarty called. "Now out, quickly, all of you!"

"Let us clean the place out," Colonel Moran insisted.

"Trust me, Colonel," Moriarty told him. "It shall be done. But you get the boys out of here and away—now!"

The habits of a military lifetime were too ingrained to permit argument. Moran barely resisted saluting. "Yes, sir," he said, and gathered his troop before him on his way back out the door.

"Let us get the ladies, Barnett," Moriarty called. "Quickly now!" He went to the door behind which they waited and shooed them into the hall like a mother hen.

Barnett paused at the cloakroom door and grabbed an armful of capes and overcoats, wrapping one around the shoulders of each girl as she passed out into the rain. Moriarty, after seeing them start safely out, darted back to the door of the large gambling room. "Quick!" he called to the house girls who were lounging about awaiting the return of the masked men. "Out into the street! No time to explain! The police are coming! Move—move!"

The urgency in his voice must have communicated itself to the women, because they boiled out of the room and joined him in a mad dash through the outer door.

Barnett stopped on the pavement about one hundred feet from the house to gather the young ladies in his charge. "Around the corner," he told them. "There's a carriage. We won't all fit—"

"I have a four-wheeler on the next block," Holmes volunteered. "It's a rotten shame, isn't it?"

"What?" Barnett asked.

"Whistling for a policeman would accomplish nothing. One or two bobbies could not prevent that assemblage from dispersing all over London. We'll be lucky to apprehend more than a couple of them. There's no way I can get a raiding party here from Scotland Yard in time to do any good at all."

"I wouldn't worry about it," Moriarty said, coming up behind them. He had his watch out, and was staring at the face.

"Why?" Holmes demanded.

"There is no time," Moriarty said, closing the watch and putting it away. "Get down!" he ordered. "All of us. *Now!* I just hope we're far enough away." He dropped flat to the pavement, and the others followed. Barnett did his best to shield Cecily from whatever was to happen.

The Mummer came running over. "What's happening, Professor?" he demanded, staring down at the group.

Moriarty's hand came up, grabbed Tolliver by the lapel, and pulled him down to the pavement. A second later the earth lifted and heaved, and a sound that was beyond sound filled the air. It seemed to go on and on, and then, abruptly, it stopped. For a few seconds longer there was a new sound, coming from all about them—the splattering, smacking noises of large objects hitting other large objects, or hitting the ground. And then that too died out.

Barnett lifted his head. Where the house had been there were now several fires. But—and this his mind did not grasp for a moment—there was no longer a house.

"Midnight," Moriarty said. "The start of a new day, and the end of the old. Let us go home."

THE GIFT

> *So she went into the garden to cut a cabbage
> leaf to make an apple pie; and at the same time a
> great she-bear, coming up the street, pops its
> head into the shop. "What! no soap?" So he
> died, and she very imprudently married the
> barber; and there were present the Picninnies,
> and the Joblillies, and the Garyulies, and the
> Grand Panjandrum himself, with the little
> round button at top, and they all fell to play-
> ing the game of catch as catch can, till the
> gunpowder ran out at the heels of their boots.*
> —SAMUEL FOOTE

Barnett spent the better part of a day composing the letter. It was as short as possible, considering all he had to put into it. He rewrote it fourteen times, and each time was convinced that he sounded just as much like a stuff-shirted prig as the last time. Whenever he tried to lighten the tone, it sounded frivolous to him; and he would not sound frivolous.

Marry me, Cecily, the letter said. And then it went on to tell why. It spoke of love and understanding and mutual aid and trust. It touched on a woman's right to have a career, and how he understood, and was willing to honor that. (*Prig!*) It skirted the issue of complete independence for women by pointing out that although he *most* assuredly believed in it himself, that would change neither the laws nor the customs of Great Britain.

It was six pages long in his small script.

In the late afternoon he went over to Cecily Perrine's house. It was a week since the clubhouse had exploded, and Cecily had been confined to her bed for that time, tended by her father. The first three days of bed rest were for her health and recuperation. The last four were more for her father. The old man seemed to feel that her ordeal was somehow his fault, so Cecily stayed in for a few extra days to allow him to fuss over her.

Barnett came over every day, clutching some small idiotic present to his chest as he entered her room. This day he brought a potted plant, which he placed on the window ledge. Then he chatted politely with Cecily for two hours—afterward, he could not remember what they had talked about. As he got up to leave, he handed her the envelope.

"Read this at your leisure," he told her, "after I leave. It tells you how I feel. Somehow I'm afraid that if I try to do it in person, we will get sidetracked and have an argument, which is the last thing I want. Answer me when you are ready."

Then he shook her hand and left. The words that he had intended to add remained stillborn on his lips. He had practiced them, but he could not say them. He had planned to say that he, with this letter, was once more proposing marriage to her, and that if she turned him down this time he would have to stop coming by. Seeing her would become too painful.

That was what he had intended to tell her. But at the last moment he had lost his courage. Supposing she said no—she would probably say no—she had said no once before. Would he actually have the courage to walk away and no longer see the woman he loved? It was probably the wisest thing, but it sounded so final. Perhaps if he stayed around, someday he would ask her a third time, and that time she would say yes.

He shook his head as he walked away from the house. Never would he have believed that he could behave this way. Love, he thought, is an unstable, unkind, thoroughly demoralizing emotion.

Back at Russell Square, Moriarty was entertaining a guest. Barnett recognized the visitor as the Indian gentleman who had called himself Singh. "This house," the guest was saying as Barnett entered the study, "the explosion demolished it completely?"

"Utterly," Moriarty said. "My calculations indicate that there must have been at least two hundred pounds of gunpowder packed into the cellar. There was one fireplace standing complete from cellar to chimneypot, like an angry brick finger pointing at the sky, but all else was gone. Bits and pieces of the Hellfire Club were found a quarter mile away."

"How many bodies? The newspaper accounts varied."

"Twenty-six that they could be sure of."

Singh nodded. "Professor. Chardino believed in a vengeful God. A fascinating case, indeed."

Barnett looked curiously at the slender, dapper Indian gentleman, who turned and extended his hand to him as Moriarty introduced them. "Mr. Singh," Moriarty explained, "has come to arrange for the transportation of the treasure. It is being returned to those from whom it was stolen—spiritually, if not actually."

"Ah, Mr. Barnett," Singh said, taking his hand and shaking it briskly, "it is a pleasure to meet you. Allow me to commend you on how well you perform under stress."

"Thank you," Barnett said. "I am grateful for any compliment, but to what occasion are you referring?"

"The incident of the loading of the treasure train," Singh explained. "Your little bit of misdirection was masterfully done!"

"Well, thank you again," Barnett said, smiling. "Were you there?"

"Ah, yes," Singh said. "You would not recognize me, of course, clad, as I was, in a *dhoti* and busily loading treasure chests. I was but scenery—a donkey laborer."

Barnett pointed a finger at him. "You—"

"Indeed," the Indian agreed. "Such is life."

Mr. Maws appeared at the study door. "Mr. Sherlock Holmes is here, and would speak with you," he informed the professor.

"Ah, yes, Holmes. He is expected," Moriarty said. "Send him in."

Holmes stalked through the door and up to Moriarty's desk without acknowledging the presence of anyone else in the room. "I have you now, Professor Moriarty!" he exclaimed. "Professor of thieves!"

Moriarty smiled. "Mr. Holmes," he said. "Allow me to introduce—"

"Your friends?" Holmes chuckled. "I shall shortly introduce *you* to a judge—and a good British jury. You have gone too far!"

"Of what do we speak?" Moriarty inquired mildly. "Have you a purpose behind this tirade, or is it merely something you've eaten that disagrees with you?"

"That statuette," Holmes said. "That bauble. A bronze statuette of the goddess Uma, one of Shiva's consorts. Worth thousands, according to Lord East. It is one of two identical pieces, over a thousand years old." Holmes consulted a scrap of paper he carried. "One belonged to Lord East, and the other to the Maharaja of Rajasthan." He looked up and glared at Moriarty. "And just how did one of these priceless pieces come into your hands?" He smiled and folded his arms across his chest.

"Allow me to introduce you," Moriarty said, indicating Singh, "to the Maharaja of Rajasthan. Your Highness, Mr. Sherlock Holmes. A bit impolite, but a good solid investigator. When his reach does not exceed his grasp."

The Indian extended his hand. "My pleasure, Mr. Holmes," he said. "I have, of course, heard of you."

Holmes glared at the Maharaja, and then back at Moriarty. He sighed, and a look of resignation crossed his face. "You have, I'm sure, some means of identifying yourself?" he asked the Maharaja.

"But of course," the Maharaja agreed, pulling out a passport. "If there is any doubt, I am known to Lord Pindhurst, her majesty's Minister of Imperial Affairs, as well as to her majesty, Queen Victoria. Indeed, I had lunch with her today."

"I am sure you did," Holmes said, handing the document back to the Maharaja. "And I am sure that you gave the statuette to Professor Moriarty. I won't even ask you what service the professor performed in return, your highness. It is a pleasure to meet you, despite the, ah, circumstances." He turned back to Moriarty. "There is a certain inevitability about this moment, Professor. I should have expected it, but I am ever the optimist."

"I am sorry to disappoint you," Moriarty murmured.

"I have not had a chance to properly thank you for coming to my assistance in that hellhouse," Holmes said. "It was very sporting of you."

"Think nothing of it," Moriarty said. "Whatever were you doing there, Holmes? It was an unexpected pleasure."

"You don't suppose you're the only one who reads the agony columns, do you?" Holmes asked. "I—borrowed—one of those pretty medals from someone who would not need it for a while, left him lying peacefully in a bush, and entered. By the by, Professor—that fellow Chardino; he was the killer, was he not?"

"He was," Moriarty agreed.

"I see." Holmes looked thoughtful for a moment. "One cannot justify murder under any circumstances, but there are some that come closer than others. Is there anything we should do—about his demise, I mean?"

"I am having a headstone erected for him next to his daughter's grave," Moriarty said. "You may contribute."

"What will it say?" Holmes asked.

"I think, 'A Loving Father,' " Moriarty answered.

"I will subscribe," Holmes said. "He certainly was that."

"A bit of news that you might want to pass on to your friends at the Yard," Moriarty said. "One of those Hellfire devils escaped the blast."

"Oh?" Holmes said.

"Yes. Colonel Moran saw him picking his way out of the rubble and recognized him, but he escaped in the confusion."

"Who was it?"

"Lord Crecy Darby. Colonel Moran knew him years ago in India."

"Plantagenet!" Holmes said.

"That's the chap," Moriarty agreed. "Colonel Moran calls him the most dangerous man he's ever known. Likes to cut up prostitutes. I would suggest you make an effort to find him, or we'll be hearing from him in a way we won't like."

"I shall pass the word on," Holmes said. "Well, *adieu*, gentlemen." He clapped his hat on his head and turned to leave.

"Do come back and entertain us again sometime," Moriarty said. "*Au revoir*, Holmes."

"Beg pardon, sir," Mr. Maws said, as Holmes stalked by him. "A district messenger has just come with this." He held up an envelope. "It is addressed to Mr. Barnett."

Barnett grabbed it out of Mr. Maws's hand. It looked like—it was certain'y Cecily's handwriting. He ripped it open.

One word only on the stiff paper inside: *Yes.*

"Catch him, someone!" Moriarty called. "Help him to a chair. Mr. Maws, bring the brandy. I think the poor man needs a drink!"

ABOUT THE AUTHOR

A plump, middle-aged man with graying hair and mild, hazel eyes looking out from behind wire-rim glasses, Michael Kurland has the perpetually nervous look of a rabbit invited to lunch at the Lions' Club. He has been a teacher of obscure subjects to disinterested children, the editor of a magazine even more idiosyncratic than himself, a seeker of absent persons, an explainer of the obscure to the befuddled, and guest lecturer at numerous unrelated institutions and events. But he has never wandered far from his chosen profession of scrivener for very long, since he finds the fawning idolatry of his fans a useful counterbalance to the disinterest of landlords and the disapproval of bank managers.

In Kurland's numerous nonfiction works he has thoroughly explored his fascination with the miscellaneous. He has written on topics as diverse as forensic science, criminal law, memory, espionage, amateur radio, and the history of crime in America, and his books have been selections of the Military Book Club, the Readers' Digest Book Club and the Writers' Digest Book Club, among others. Cur-

rently in print are How to Solve a Murder: the Forensic Handbook and How to Try a Murder: the Handbook for Armchair Lawyers.

His series of novels starring Professor Moriarty (the chief villian of the Sherlock Holmes stories), began with The Infernal Device, which was nominated for both a Mystery Writers of America "Edgar" award and an American Book award, and Death by Gaslight, and will shortly be joined by The Great Game, which will be published by St. Martin's Press in August 2001.

Two other books of Kurland's published by St. Martin's Press are Too Soon Dead and The Girls in the High-Heeled Shoes, both set in the 1930s and chronicling the mystery-solving talents of Alexander Brass, a columnist for the New York World.